MARTYN CROFT

The Omnibus Edition

Anywhere and Nowhere

The Haunting of Eddie Compton

Heaven on Earth

ISBN: 978-0-9559872-3-6

This omnibus edition published 2009 by arrangement with

www.Lulu.com

14th June –14th November 2008

CONTENTS

ANYWHERE AND NOWHERE

For Hayley and Shell

'Sure, the next train has gone ten minutes ago'

(Punch vol. lx, p. 206, 1871)

CONTENTS

1
Eddie's Train Set

The August school holidays had been hot and dry, unusually so for Fenton-on-Sea. Best friends, Eddie and Len had spent the first two weeks swimming in the sea and playing beach cricket on the sands near to the pier, whence they repaired occasionally to buy ice-creams and drinks or just to play the one-penny slot machines.

Eddie had scarcely thought about the magical journey which he and Len had experienced that May half-term. No one in the small East Anglian seaside town knew anything about what had happened to the two boys. Even Eddie and Len themselves had begun to doubt whether the journey had really taken place. They certainly hadn't discussed it openly; perhaps just the odd knowing wink when the loss of Eddie's billiard table – in the sea off Fenton beach – was mentioned by their parents. As time had gone on, they reassured each other less and less that the extraordinary events had actually taken place. In the end, by the start of the summer holidays, there was a tacit agreement between the two twelve-year-olds that the fantastic journey would not be talked about. Each, in their own way, knew that the events *had* taken place, but since no one else knew and because they could never prove it to anyone, they put it to the back of their minds, along with all the other deeply imagined fantasies that boys of their age were prone to invent. They realised that a momentous thing had happened and they knew that they had been used as pawns in a plan instigated by God, or some greater power. Neither boy was particularly religious but both knew that something otherworldly existed, whether they were prepared to admit it to each other or not.

If they hadn't talked about their journey much, they'd talked even less about the mysterious Mr Canter – George, as they had come to know him. Eddie's purchase of the mysterious object from George's junk shop in Mill Road had, after all, sparked the fantastic journey in the first place anyway. The gifts they'd received by way of a 'thank you' for their part in restoring the treasure to the new synagogue in the Polish city of Bialystok, lay unopened in their respective bedrooms. George Canter had wanted to repay the two boys for helping him overcome his guilt and provide him with the impetus to start a new life in his home city. Canter's junk shop was now no longer the mysterious place that attracted customers to buy things, whether they wanted to or not. In fact, it was now Watson's Electrical, the second shop of that name in Mill Road, almost opposite Watson's the ironmongers and both owned by Mr Paul Watson and sons Jed and Paul junior.

Len's brand new football, signed by the entire 1962/63 Tottenham Hotspur football team, was still in its plastic wrapper and Eddie's electric train set was boxed and taped as it had been that Wednesday at the end of May when the two gifts had arrived by post, courtesy of Mr George Canter. Neither boy had opened their surprise gifts for one or two reasons. Firstly, the warm weather that summer had not been conducive to playing indoor games or, as Len would say,

"You don't play 'footie' on the 'rec' in the summer; it isn't cricket!"

Len always giggled at his clever double meaning, while his friend would just groan. In any case, there were too many games of cricket played on the 'rec' – their local recreation ground – to be able to kick a ball about. The second reason, however, was stronger. Neither Eddie nor Len wanted to be reminded of their previous adventure, in case it sparked off something else equally amazing and, perhaps, more frightening. Not that they'd been scared before, but what had happened had opened their minds to all kinds of fantastic possibilities. Indeed, they would never, any longer, accept fantasy as an impossible concept or reality as certainty.

Saturday, August the 17th was the first day of the summer holidays that either boy could remember not being sunny and hot. In fact, by nine o'clock – the regular time that Eddie would call on Len at number 7 Lime Tree Avenue – it was cool, damp and a sea mist was cloaking the promenade and beach. After Len had opened his front door to Eddie's impatient knocking, he frowned at his friend.

"Whatcha Eddie, mate. What *are* we going to do today?"

"Dunno, looks like rain – autumn's in the air. What about a kick-about on the 'rec'?"

"Haven't got a ball, Eddie. The one I bought from Canter's junk shop has at last given up the ghost."

Eddie looked oddly at his friend.

"Yes, you have. What have you done with the one George sent you?"

"Don't really want to use it, mate – might damage the signatures. They've got to be worth a bob or two," replied Len, nervously.

Eddie smiled and, almost before he spoke, Len knew what his friend was going to say.

"Don't you think it will be protected, just like the billiard table was protected in all the incredible games we played with it? Got to be worth a try and anyway you said that the signatures looked like they were written in indelible ink."

Len was not convinced. His reply surprised Eddie.

"I suppose that it's not really that I'm bothered about. I kind of just said it as an excuse. Anyway, I've got most of the present team's autographs in my book, thanks to Uncle Joe who lives in Edmonton and my dad's friend, Bill, who lived next door to us when we lived in Whitechapel. I send them my book every so often when they're going to White Hart Lane."

"So, what is it, then?" said a curious Eddie.

"Well, what if playing with it starts some magic, like before with the billiard table you bought from Mr Canter."

"That was different," responded Eddie. "Mr Canter *gave* you the football, and me the train set, as gifts for helping him in his quest. I *bought* the billiard table from his junk shop," he continued, even though he'd had the same thoughts about his own present, the electric train set.

"He *made* you buy it, if you remember, Eddie. Or, that's what you thought at the time, mate. Who's to say that he sent the gifts because he knew, like before, that they would do magical things," said Len.

"Oh, that's nonsense and you know it, Len. Mr Canter got us home from Bialystok safe and sound – he's our friend now."

Len looked a little sheepish at having suggested George Canter would put them into unnecessary trouble and began to relent.

"I suppose you're right, Eddie. It's not like we can sit on a football and fly off into the sunset. I mean, how ridiculous would that be?"

Both boys grinned at Len's words. After all it had happened with the billiard table, hadn't it!? That thought, however, was far from their minds as they left number 7 and headed purposefully for the 'rec'.

By the time the two boys had reached the end of Lime Tree Avenue, the decision, however cleverly engineered by Eddie, seemed pointless anyway, as the light drizzle had turned to quite heavy rain, thus curtailing any visit to the 'rec' and experimenting with Len's football. Len looked a little relieved, despite his acceptance of Eddie's argument. They had reached a point equidistant from both their houses, prompting Len to remark,

"Might as well go to your house, mate, and play with your train set – can't do anything else today; it's pouring down."

Eddie, like his friend earlier, looked a little nervous at the suggestion, but knew he shouldn't show it. His train set was only a model and he'd been keen for Len to play with his gift as well.

"Suppose you're right, Len. Do you want to take your ball back first?"

"No, not bothered, it's just as quick to go to your house. C'mon let's run – won't get as wet that way."

Eddie smiled, almost disdainfully. He knew his friend wasn't clever enough to understand the Physics and Mathematics of the choice of running quickly or walking slowly as the best method of getting the least wet. He himself hoped, with his love and interest in Science, and Maths in particular, that one day he would be able to decide.

Eddie's mum was the only one in when the boys arrived, breathless and sweating from their 100 yard dash to 38 Fir Tree Close. Fred Compton, Eddie's dad, was at Fenton railway station where he worked as the senior clerk in the booking office and Jennifer, his sister, was serving in Sam Arleson's bakery, a job she'd held since leaving school the previous summer. Jenny was seventeen and excited by the prospect of the rest of the family going on holiday to Ludmouth, in Devon, for a week starting in two day's time. Excited, because she wasn't going; the first time she had been allowed to miss a family holiday. Ann Compton thought her daughter old enough to be left on her own for a week – she'd be at work for six of the seven days anyway. Fred had his doubts, especially as he wasn't too enamoured of her latest boyfriend, Gary Jones, unemployed as he was.

"Hello you two – thought you'd be back as soon as the rain came," said Eddie's mum, as they burst through the front door. "Here, get yourselves dry with this towel," she continued. "Going to play some card games are you?"

"No, Mum. We thought we'd set my electric train set up – the one Mr Canter sent me," replied Eddie.

Ann Compton smiled. She'd had a soft spot for George Canter ever since he'd taken an interest in her son. She had been delighted with Eddie's surprise present which he'd sent after he'd left to go back to Poland, selling his junk shop in the process. Ann Compton knew that the electric train set didn't come from the shop, as her son had tried once or twice to buy one there, only to end up with the billiard table, which, as far as she and her husband knew, had been washed far out to sea when Eddie and Len had tried to float it as a raft back in late May. She hadn't really understood why her son hadn't wanted to open the box at the time and had put it down to him having grown out of such things, studious as he was. She was thus as curious as the boys to see what was in the box under Eddie's bed. She had wondered if the set was Polish, or foreign, at least. As far as Ann Compton was aware, Eddie and Len's presents had been a way of repaying the boys for things George Canter had sold them earlier in the year; a football that had disintegrated after one kick-about and a billiard table that had been lost at sea.

A few minutes later and the box was on the Compton's dining room table. Eddie and his mum had seen the box when it had first arrived, but Len had not and only the brown wrapping paper had been removed. The events of that last Saturday in May had somehow warned Eddie that all might not be what it seemed. He had needed time, like Len, to build up the courage to open the box, in case it had power like the billiard table. His encouragement of Len to use his football had really been to 'test the waters' as a precursor to the time when he knew he had to open his own gift. He was more relaxed now that nothing had happened when Len had produced his football minus its clear plastic wrapper. It hadn't taken to the air or worse!

There was nothing on the front of the white box apart from some gold lettering to indicate what Eddie's gift was, and, indeed, there had been times since it had arrived when Eddie had thought that the box might be something else. The bold lettering read:

ELECTRIC TRAIN SET

HANDLE WITH CARE

Eddie turned the box over to slit the tapes and for the first time spotted the word *Harrods* in tiny gold lettering; so tiny were the letters they almost seemed like an apology. Len, however, recognised the name at once.

"You lucky sod!" he exclaimed. "Most expensive shop in London, if not the world, mate."

Lifting up the lid of this outer box revealed another one inside and Eddie recognised what the inner box would contain.

"It's a *Hornby* set – *The Flying Scotsman!*"

So there it was – emblazoned on the front of the box – the most famous steam locomotive of all time, gleaming in the famous original LNER 'Apple Green' livery, with 4472 painted in gold on the coal tender. It looked as though it had come straight out of the golden age of those pre-war years when steam ruled the rails. Indeed, the box seemed to fit strangely with that era, which went unnoticed by the boys. Eddie could hardly contain himself and said excitedly,

"Wait till my dad sees it. He'll want to play with it! He's actually been on it when he was a guard, years ago, before I was born."

"Well, open the box, then, Eddie," said his mum.

Eddie again looked nervous. What if…? But removing the lid brought about no alarms, just a moderate gasp of awe from the two boys as they saw the beauty of the craftsmanship. There inside, in the neat compartments lay the engine, tender and three gold/brown carriages plus a sizeable amount of track with the necessary equipment to run it off the mains. Just then the phone rang and Eddie's mum went out into the hall, almost reluctantly, to answer it.

Eddie had discarded the lid of the box as he gazed at his gift, but Len had been studying the picture on the front of the box, and turning it over, he suddenly whispered (not wanting Eddie's mum to hear),

"There's something stuck on the inside here, mate."

"What's there?" asked Eddie, with a slight tremor in his voice.

Len pulled a folded piece of paper from its place, taped to the inside of the box lid and handed it to his friend.

"Looks like a letter – I can see some writing through it. You'd better read it. It's your box."

Eddie unfolded the single piece of paper and began to read.

Dear Eddie and Len,

I guess if you're reading this, then you must have opened your gifts. I've put this letter in your present, Eddie, as it was easier to conceal it in the box. I suspect, also, that it has been a while since you received your presents. I bet you still had a bit of fear that I might have sent you both something that could cause you problems, like before, eh? Well relax, my boys; the presents are to say thank you for helping me and all the Polish Jews of Bialystok. By the time you are reading this I hope to be settled in my home city and starting to help with the revival of the work of the new synagogue.

I have spent a few days shopping for you here in London, as you can see, and I hope your presents are to your liking. I got you what you wanted in the end, boys. The football won't rot and disintegrate this time, Len, and, Eddie, you came to my shop for the first time to buy a second-hand electric train set, and, even though you eventually were persuaded to buy something else, you've now got the best that money can buy.

Well, take good care of your gifts, boys. Have fun with them and share them. Though I cannot guarantee they will not misbehave (who can, except God?), trust me that nothing bad will ever happen to you two lads. God and the Jewish people of Bialystok owe you so much for your unknowing involvement in the fantastic adventure in that week (?) in early summer.

Look after yourselves and remember me to your parents, who love you dearly. You never know, we might meet again some day.

Your friend,
George Canter.

Eddie's mum was still nattering on the phone to Martha Wilby, Len's mum, when Eddie had finished reading the letter out loud and neither boy spoke for what seemed an eternity. Len, trying not to show any emotion, as usual, broke the eerie silence.

"It's always *Eddie and Len*, not *Len and Eddie*," he said, "and the letter was in your box, mate."

"Shh! Don't let my mum hear us, Len. How on earth would we explain what George has written?" whispered Eddie, sternly. "Anyway he's explained why the letter was in my box, and besides, your football is unique with the Spurs' signatures. I think he chose gifts that we each wanted. I'm not that keen on football and you got an electric train set last Christmas."

"Broken now, though," said Len.

Silence suddenly emanated from the hall and Ann Compton reappeared just as Len had finished speaking. The boys thought that she couldn't have heard any of the letter's contents and that they were only arguing mildly about something. However, Eddie's mum then responded to what she thought the argument was about and it sounded rather ominous.

"I think Mr Canter would want you to share the presents."

She paused with a questioning look on her face. Eddie and Len looked nervously at each other. Had Eddie's mum heard more than she was supposed to?

"What's that you've got, Eddie?" asked his mum, pointing to the piece of paper, now folded, that Eddie was still clutching. Len pretended not to notice and Eddie thought quickly.

"Oh that? That's the instructions, Mum," he said, hoping she wouldn't see the glossy booklet which Len had also pulled from the box. However, Len, wise to the situation had, in the meantime, managed to cover said booklet with the box lid and smiled sweetly at his friend's mum. From her reaction, the boys knew that Eddie's little white lie had been believed.

"Good. Well I'm off shopping down town. Use the socket in the corner, Eddie. Put the set together on the floor. You should have enough room, if you go under the table as well. Have fun and by the way, Len, your mum says she might have some good news for you when you get home," she said rather cryptically and with that Ann Compton went to get ready. Eddie smiled and winked at his friend almost as if he was party to the good news that was awaiting Len when he returned home later that morning, but Len just remarked casually,

"I bet they've rung to say that my new football kit is in at Gough's in Hamsden. I expect we'll have to go and collect it this afternoon on the bus."

Hamsden was a sizeable town situated about twelve miles inland and had a much wider and better range of shops than the boys' quiet seaside town.

Hardly a word was spoken while Eddie's mum got ready to go out. Both boys unpacked the train set and, while Len put the track together, Eddie perused the real instruction booklet, studying how to use the transformer and the controls. The minute they heard the front door close, Len exclaimed,

"Whew, that was a close one, mate!"

"Do you think my mum heard anything?" queried Eddie.

"Don't think so – too busy chatting to my mum."

Eddie looked relieved, but still had some lingering worries which he shared with his friend. He suspected that Len had had the same thoughts over the previous two or three months.

"Do you think our parents suspect anything about that last Saturday in May, Len?"

"No way, mate. How could they? I mean we were back from the beach well before one o'clock. Mr Canter is the only other person who knows what really happened. Apart from the people we met on the journey, that is, and they're not likely ever to come to Fenton, are they, if they ever existed anyway?"

"Suppose you're right, Len, but…."

"But what, mate?"

"What if we were seen at Heath Row, when we flew back with Mr Canter or on the train back here, or…?"

"Or what?"

"Or on the platform at Fenton station, dressed in our futuristic anoraks? How would we explain that?"

"If anyone had seen us, surely something would have been said by now," replied Len finally, and then for the first time since the extraordinary events in May, the two boys began to share their thoughts, which had, each in their own way, plagued their sleeping and waking moments. The unwritten agreement not to talk about their journey was broken at last and both boys felt a weight had been lifted from their shoulders, prompting Eddie to conclude,

"It did happen, Len, and we are privileged to have experienced it. It wasn't a dream. I mean, how could two, no, three people with George, be party to the same dream?"

Len mumbled his agreement but hoped that his and Eddie's parents would never visit the Polish city of Bialystok and be told there that their sons had helped put the synagogue's most treasured item back in its rightful position! As had happened in the past, all worrying thoughts soon disappeared from our two friend's minds and they settled down to play with Eddie's train set.

Len had made the track into an oval about five feet by three with part of it encircling a table leg, and on the opposite side he'd managed to balance some books as a makeshift tunnel. When he'd finished, he said,

"My dad made me a proper tunnel out of wood, moulded and painted, Eddie. Do you want me to ask him to do the same for you? We could help him tidy up his woodshed like we did before."

Len's dad, Cyril Wilby, was Head of Woodwork and Metalwork at Fenton Secondary Modern School – Len and Eddie had just finished their first year at Fenton Grammar, the neighbouring selective school.

"Good idea, mate; if he would," replied Eddie, as he carefully placed the engine and carriages on the track and issued his instructions.

"You watch the tunnel, Len and I'll operate the control."

"Roger, Mr Driver!"

"Off we go," said Eddie.

Eddie pulled the switch over and *Flying Scotsman* moved smoothly away, with almost realistic sounds coming from the rails.

"She goes well, Eddie; better than mine did," said Len.

"Yeah, but you took yours to pieces before we played with it. What did you expect? They're pieces of precision engineering."

Neither boy seemed worried that, like the billiard table, the train might do something out of the ordinary, though Len did remark,

"Well at least we haven't flown off on the back of the train, have we Eddie?"

Eddie laughed a little nervously. Everything so far had gone too smoothly, he thought and just at that moment the tunnel collapsed knocking two carriages off the rails.

"Whoops, Mr Signalman, you're supposed be in charge of the tunnel," said Eddie.

"Sorry, sir," and Len tried to replace the books, but however he tried this time, they would not balance properly to allow the train to pass without brushing them.

"Don't bother, Len."

"My turn, I think, Eddie please."

The two boys swapped positions on the carpet and Len took up the control as his friend reconnected the set. Len pushed over the switch as far as it would go.

"Steady, Len, don't break it."

"It's alright, mate; let's see if we can really make this thing shift."

"Wow!" said Eddie. "What did you do? It's going faster."

"You didn't have the lever over all the way."

"I'm sure I did, Len, and anyway she'll crash. You're going too fast."

But crash it didn't as all at once it seemed to slow to a comfortable pace. Len's thumb still seemed glued to the switch, with no apparent relaxation. Len looked nervously at his hand but said nothing.

"That's better," said Eddie. "My turn now."

The train slowed to a halt and again Len said nothing, even though he had the distinct impression that not only had the train started to slow before he'd released any pressure from the switch, but also that it had stopped before he had taken his thumb completely off it. He decided that his imagination was wandering and the set was probably made that way to detect even the smallest change in pressure on the switch.

Eddie took over and for the rest of the morning nothing untoward occurred until Len took his last turn at the control. This time, he thought, the train seemed to start even before he'd applied any pressure to the switch. Eddie noticed nothing.

"Got to go, Eddie," said Len after a few minutes – he'd not noticed anything else unusual. "Want to try my new kit on," and, looking outside at the slightly improving weather, he continued,

"Fancy football on the 'rec' after lunch? I could wear my new kit."

"Can't, mate – Mum says we've got to get ready for our holiday to Devon. We set off early Monday morning by train, and I've got to go to church, as usual, tomorrow. She doesn't want me to get my clothes dirty."

"Alright, chief. See you when you get back. Hope you get awful weather," joked Len.

The two boys packed the train set away carefully and Len left to walk the short distance back to his house, Eddie leaving him with,

"Hope it rains all week in Fenton as well!"

On his way home Len pondered briefly the morning's events. He was pretty certain nothing had really happened. The switch had worked normally and it was only his fervent imagination that had almost wanted something extraordinary to happen. By the time he burst in through his front door he had forgotten anyway; his mind was now excited and focused on his new football kit.

2

Fossils and Cream Teas

It was clear from the look in his parents' eyes that the surprise was going to be more important that just a new football kit. His dad stood in the kitchen with a cheeky grin on his face, similar to the one he always presented when, at every Christmas, he gave Len his main present. His mum looked excited too.

"Well, son, had a good time at Eddie's?"

"Not bad, Dad. Eddie's train is brilliant. Mr Canter sent him the Hornby *Flying Scotsman*. It's better than mine – must have cost a fortune."

"Like your football, I should think," said his mum, but his dad continued,

"Expect you'd like to play with it all next week. It's your last but one full week of the holidays. We all go back to school on the 2nd."

"Yep, if the weather's not good enough to play outside. Otherwise we'll start playing football again – got to get in practice for the new season. I'm in the Under-13's this year, you know, Dad. Haven't used my new football yet.

"I know you haven't. I wondered when and if you would ever use it. You've got all the autographs and they shouldn't come off anyway."

Martha Wilby couldn't seem to hold back any longer and said,

"Go on, Cyril, tell him."

"Tell me what, Dad – have you got tickets for Spurs' first home game? Have you?" asked Eddie, excitedly.

"No, son, I haven't. But…."

"But what, Dad?"

"But you don't want to just watch or play football or be indoors with Eddie's train set all week, do you? How would you like to go to Devon for the week?"

Len thought he'd misheard his dad and replied,

"Devon? But Eddie's going to Devon. Are we going as well? Will we be anywhere near them?"

"*We're* not going, Len," said his mum.

"But, Dad said…."

"*You* are going, son, *and* you're going with the Wilbys. You'll be with Len all week in Ludmouth right by the sea. They have booked a bed and breakfast overlooking the promenade, fifty yards from the beach," said Cyril Wilby.

Len almost leapt up and down on the spot, but managed a relatively calm response.

"Oh excellent," said Len. "Do you really mean it? Where will I sleep? Who's gonna pay? What….?"

"Slow down, Len," his dad continued. "It's all taken care of. It's our little gift to you for surviving a year at Fenton Grammar and doing so well at football, rugby and cricket."

Len's mum had all the answers.

"Your return train ticket is in your bedroom and Eddie's mum and dad had already booked a room with two bunk beds for you two boys. They did it at the start of the holidays. We just kept it from you and Eddie, so you wouldn't get too excited too early. Mrs Compton is telling Eddie right about now. I phoned her earlier this morning to finalise the arrangements. We've paid for your ticket and your share of the accommodation, even though Eddie's mum said there was no need. All you need is some pocket money for the week and I'm sure your dad has put an envelope in your room alongside the rail ticket. I've given Ann Compton some money for any food and other essentials."

'So that was what the phone call had been about', thought Len and this time he did a jig around the kitchen and hugged his mum and dad, to Cyril Wilby's embarrassment.

"Steady on, old boy, no need for that. Just promise me that you and Eddie will behave and not get into any scrapes and you, Len, do everything that Mr and Mrs Compton tell you to – they're in charge of you for the week."

"Yes, Dad. Absolutely, Dad! When are we going?"

"First thing Monday morning and I mean first thing. You all catch the 6.19 train from Fenton station. Mr Compton has all the details. He knows the route you are going and I think he got a substantial discount because of his job. No one better at booking a rail journey, eh, son? Mr Beeching's cuts haven't started to take place yet and you can still get mostly anywhere by train in the country, even somewhere as small as Ludmouth. Only one thing though; you are all one family, otherwise you wouldn't have got a reduction."

"No problem, Dad – we're like brothers anyway."

Len was immediately reminded of another time when he and Eddie had had to pretend to be siblings and he grinned at his dad. 'If only he knew', he thought.

After the surprise had sunk in Len ran upstairs and found his ticket and the envelope which he ripped open to find FIVE crisp pound notes; several month's pocket money!

Meanwhile, back at 38 Fir Tree Close, Eddie had had his suspicions confirmed. He'd guessed that his mum and dad had been planning all along to take Len with them on the holiday to Devon. Little hints had been carelessly or, indeed, carefully dropped ever since he had said he wouldn't have anyone to play with when in Ludmouth. In previous years he'd always had his sister, Jenny, and while she hadn't wanted to do the things he liked, she had, at least, been company and they could always occupy time just arguing!

It continued to rain on and off for the rest of the day and Eddie and Len spent the time organising what they were going to take with them on holiday. Len wanted to take his cricket bat, ball, stumps *and* his new football, but when his dad told him he would have to carry them himself as well as his own suitcase, he gave up the idea, settling on a tennis ball and his football in a carrier bag. Eddie had less to worry about – he knew it would be impractical to take his new train set, which he'd already packed away carefully and placed at the back of his wardrobe. He'd hidden it there behind his science fiction magazines, not only for tidiness, but also because his sister hadn't seen it and he didn't wanted her 'messing' with it as she usually did when he'd appeared to get something extra to her. He would pick his time to show his dad his train set, probably when his sister was out, so she couldn't comment.

Eddie's dad and Jenny arrived home from work within ten minutes of each other at just before six. Jenny always worked Saturdays at Arleson's the bakers and having done all six days that week she felt she'd earned the right to spend Saturday evening out with Gary, her boyfriend. Gary was nineteen and had a car, so the world was her playground, or at least, any pub within reasonable driving distance; seventeen or not, Jenny looked older. While Fred Compton strolled round his prize back garden for a quiet smoke Jenny and Eddie sat down for tea and began their usual sibling banter.

"Mum says you've opened your train set at last," said Jenny, a little sarcastically. "What were you frightened about? Did you think it would explode or something?"

"No, I just wanted to save my surprise and, anyway, you're only jealous."

Jenny sneered and retorted,

"Don't be stupid, brother dear, what would I want with a train set – it's for kids. Are you still a kid, Eddie?"

"Mum, tell her. I bet my dad plays with it. Are you calling Dad a child, Jenny?"

Just at that moment Fred Compton came in for his tea.

"What's that, Eddie – who's a child?"

"He is," said Jennifer.

"That's enough from you too. I want my tea without the usual squabbling, thank you. It's been a long day with so many people travelling for their holidays."

Quiet descended on the Compton household for a few minutes, until Eddie couldn't resist telling his dad his news.

"Opened my train set today, Dad. It's brilliant and, Dad, it's the *Flying Scotsman*!"

"Really, son – we'll have to set it up after tea. It will bring back memories of the one time I went on it from London, before I started in the office – why didn't you open it before? There were a couple of times when I nearly went and opened it for you. Didn't have things like that when we were kids."

Eddie made his 'I told you so grin' at his sister. Everyone seemed to eat their meal more quickly than usual. Eddie and his dad wanted to play with the train set, Jenny was anxious to be her best painted self for when

Gary called at seven and Ann Compton had more packing to do. Just before Jenny was going to repair to her bedroom, her mum said,

"Off to the Blue Iris tonight Jen, love?"

"Expect so, Mum. Can't go far – Gary hasn't got much money to put petrol in his car," she lied.

"He should get a job, then, shouldn't he?" interjected her dad.

Her parents would probably be horrified if they knew that the Fisherman's Rest at Canford, and not the Blue Iris coffee bar, beckoned and that Gary often filled his car up courtesy of some of Jenny's wages from the bakers.

Eddie and his dad spent an hour or so playing with the *Flying Scotsman*, with Fred Compton telling Eddie about all the extras he should buy to make the track more realistic. It seemed to Eddie that with the possibility of Len's dad making a tunnel, the adults wanted to get as much enjoyment out of the set as he and Len.

Sunday passed slowly for both Eddie and Len. The Comptons, minus Jennifer, went to St Andrews near the seafront for morning service, while Len sorted through his holiday things for the third or fourth time. Jenny was quiet for most of the day after being told off for not getting in till well after eleven the previous night, with explanations demanded because the Blue Iris closed at ten-thirty. Eddie spent a few minutes window shopping at Watson's Electrical, in Mill Road – they had recently started stocking models and Eddie had spotted some of the 'extras' his dad had mentioned. Maybe he could persuade him to buy something. After all, his dad would get the enjoyment too!

Neither boy slept much that Sunday night, excited as they both were. Len was ready, suitcase and bag in hand, by five-thirty and his mum escorted him to Eddie's house for quarter to six. With a slightly tearful goodbye, she left her only son in the capable hands of the Comptons, repeating all the usual instructions and warnings that had been drummed into him the day before. The Comptons and their 'adopted' son walked the few hundred yards to Fenton railway station, both boys complaining about carrying their heavy suitcases, until Eddie's dad remarked,

"You filled the cases, boys, and besides, wait till we get to Ludmouth – it's over a mile from the station to our guest house."

"We're not going to have to walk it, are we, Dad?"

"Only if you boys keep complaining and don't behave on the journey. We've three trains and the underground to catch. I could have made it more and saved us ten shillings, but I went for the most direct route in the end: Hamsden, Liverpool Street, Waterloo and then the Atlantic Coast Express."

'That sounds exotic', thought Len. 'The Atlantic' conjured up the idea of faraway places in his mind and he wasn't sure where Ludmouth was anyway.

"Where is Ludmouth, Mr Compton?" he asked politely.

"South Devon coast and we'd better be called mum and dad by you, Len; at least until we get there. Then I think we'd prefer Aunty Ann and Uncle Fred, if you don't mind."

"Yes, Dad!" replied Len, cheekily and he continued, "Is Ludmouth on the Atlantic, then?"

"No, son – it's called the Atlantic Coast Express because it goes right down to Cornwall and that's where it meets the Atlantic."

They had reached the station by then and they headed for Platform One. Eddie and Len exchanged knowing winks, remembering that Saturday lunchtime in May when, accompanied by Mr Canter, they had arrived on Platform Two after the fantastic journey of a lifetime.

A mundane diesel rail-car transported them to Hamsden in twenty-eight minutes precisely (as Fred Compton pointed out on arrival) and by five past seven they were sitting patiently in the London train which was due to leave at ten past. Eddie's mum had packed more than enough food for the journey. Egg sandwiches and hot tea from one of two flasks quickly satisfied Len's and Eddie's hunger, after their meagre rations of porridge and cornflakes, respectively, which they'd eaten hurriedly about two hours earlier. Much to the boys' disappointment their engine was of the modern diesel type and not steam like Eddie's new train. However, there was something interesting about it, as Fred Compton pointed out.

"This is the same type of diesel engine which pulled the mail train that was looted in The Great Train Robbery, boys."

Eddie and Len looked at each other nervously.

"Don't worry, lads, there's nothing much of value on this train – it's only for passengers," said Eddie's dad reassuringly. The biggest ever robbery Britain had ever known had only just taken place about ten days earlier and it was still filling the newspapers every day.

They reached Liverpool Street just before nine and, with a hot and sweaty negotiation of London's confusing underground system, they arrived at Waterloo station by ten-fifteen, well in time for the Atlantic Coast Express (ACE), which was due to leave on the hour at eleven. This time to the boys' and Fred Compton's great joy, the ACE was pulled by a steam locomotive – not *The Flying Scotsman* as Eddie hoped, but by the *East Asiatic Company* which, nevertheless, sounded more exciting anyway. They left exactly on time and they had to negotiate a couple of separations of some carriages at Salisbury and Ludmouth Junction, which fascinated the boys as they had to move carriages quickly, but never actually got off the train and as they left Salisbury, Eddie's dad remarked,

"No longer on the ACE. We're on a different train."

"Can't be," said Len. "We haven't moved trains."

"We may be in the same carriages, but we're being pulled by a different engine – diesel by the sound of it."

Len still found it difficult to understand how the change had happened and it got worse when it happened again at Ludmouth Junction. Whatever had occurred they arrived at Ludmouth proper at two-fifteen and when they disembarked, hot and tired, Len looked back at the train and exclaimed in horror,

"We've lost most of the train, Mr – I mean, Dad. There are only two carriages left! We started with at least eight; I counted them in London before we left."

"Now do you see what happened, Len?" said Eddie's dad, but it still seemed a mystery to Len and he would be teased mercilessly by Eddie for the whole holiday with comments like:

"Found those missing carriages yet, Len," and "Did you hear the couplings break?"

Once outside the one-platform station both boys groaned at the prospect of the long walk to their accommodation in the hot afternoon sun. For such a small place as Ludmouth, a mile was clearly a long way as there seemed to be little evidence of any habitation near by.

"Here's our transport," said Eddie's dad.

Eddie breathed a sigh of relief.

"Are we going by taxi, Dad?"

"Not a taxi as such – that must be Mr Brewin over there; he and his wife own *Summer Breeze* where we're staying," said Fred Compton, pointing to a rather large and rotund gentleman standing by a battered Vauxhall Cresta.

"Hello there," shouted Mr Brewin, as he had spotted the only possible family that had arrived. Coming closer, he continued, "You must be the Comptons, I guess. I'm Bob Brewin; BB for short. Everyone calls me that. Wanted to call the guest house BB's B and B, but the wife thought it a stupid pretentious name, so we settled on *Summer Breeze*; almost like Summer B's, eh?"

He paused while he waited for everyone to laugh at his awful pun and when no one did he turned to the two boys and said,

"And you're Eddie and Len, lads? Nice to meet you all. Let's get your luggage in the boot and get you all to our bumble, I mean, humble guest house!"

The boys could tell that BB must have used the line time and time again, but they managed the obligatory groan of laughter, which seemed to please their host. Once in the car, Len asked,

"Do you run a taxi as well, Mr Brewin?"

"No, most of the guest houses and hotels have to pick up their residents from the station – it's just too far to walk, especially with luggage. All part of the service and call me BB."

"Why was the station built so far from the town?" asked Ann Compton.

"To keep the day trippers away – Ludmouth has always been a rather gentile resort, perfect for families with children who stay for a week or more. It has very safe bathing and there's lots to do, even though it has deliberately kept its quiet nature."

Eddie and Len didn't look too sure. What did BB mean by 'quiet'? Was it going to be boring? More boring than Fenton-on-Sea was sometimes? Impossible!

They were on the seafront by then and BB pulled the Cresta to a stop outside *Summer Breeze*, a three story white Edwardian terrace, which looked beautifully kept and, with the *No Vacancies* sign in the window, obviously well-liked. Eddie and Len had immediately noticed that they were the width of the road and the promenade away from the sandy beach.

"Excellent, mate," said Eddie as they piled out of the car.

However, apart from the beach and some awesome looking cliffs away to their left, there didn't seem to be much else that could be described as entertaining for two twelve-year-old boys. No pier. No one-armed bandits that they could see. Maybe behind the Edwardian façade of the seafront there were more interesting things to explore. Time would tell.

After they had all checked in and signed the residents' book, BB helped them carry their luggage and showed them to their rooms on the second floor; one for Eddie's mum and dad and one for the boys. As BB left the 'family' to wash and change, he said,

"When you're ready, come down and meet the wife, Patricia, Pat. She's preparing the cream teas we serve at four, free to all our guests. Will you be eating dinner with us?"

"No, BB," said Eddie's dad. "We're going to take the boys for a walk later and have a buzz round town to sample the local fish and chips, but cream teas sound excellent. We'll be down at four."

"Dad, stop it!" whispered Eddie, as he grimaced at his dad's dreadful joke. Fortunately, BB didn't seem to have heard the reference to his nickname and quickly made his way downstairs.

The dining room at *Summer Breeze* was small and intimate, but apart from the Comptons and Len there was only a retired couple in one corner when they went down for their cream teas at four. The other guests, said Eddie's dad, were probably out for the day, hot and sunny as it was.

There were tables enough for about fifteen people giving an indication of the size of their accommodation.

"Let's get the tables by the window," said Eddie.

There were three tables; each set for two in the large bay window overlooking The Esplanade and the boys took the one on the left while Eddie's mum and dad took the one on the right, leaving the one in the middle empty. It meant that Eddie and Len could talk independently of Mr and Mrs Compton and vice-versa.

"Wow! What a view," said Len. "Look at those sands; they go for miles."

"Must be low tide. Better sand then Fenton by the looks of it. Bet football will be great on it," replied Len.

"Full cream tea?" asked a rather plump lady, who was obviously Pat, BB's wife. "I'm Pat, by the way. Nice to meet you all. Hope you have a lovely stay. Don't hesitate to ask me or BB if you need anything. Now what will you have?"

"Full cream teas, hey boys?" said Fred Compton.

"Absolutely," said the boys in unison.

The cream teas, when they came, were delicious: scones filled with Devon cream and topped with strawberry jam and very, very filling as Len pointed out.

"I'm stuffed, mate."

"Fish and chips later," Eddie reminded him.

"Heaven, chief – absolute heaven. We'll be as fat as pigs by the end of the week."

"You're getting that way already, Len! Have to lose a few pounds before the football season starts, old mate."

Len pulled a face and then asked,

"What shall we do tomorrow, I mean, apart from just playing football?"

"You should go fossil hunting," said a voice that seemed to come out of nowhere.

Neither boy had noticed the old man that had sat down at the table between them and Eddie's parents. He looked at least ninety, but possessed a younger smile, much younger, thought Eddie as he turned to face the voice's owner.

"Fossils, sir?"

"Yes, boys. You are on the Jurassic Coast – it's famous for them and dinosaur bones."

"Where, sir?" asked Len.

"Did you see the big red cliffs when you arrived, away to the east?"

"Yes, sir," replied Eddie.

"Well, if you go at low tide, you can often find them at the foot of the cliffs. Dinosaur bones are sometimes washed up in the rock pools a bit further on and it's Jake by the way; Jake Manders."

"Thank you, Jake," said Eddie. "We'll definitely try it."

"Good, but only go at low tide. People have been trapped by the rising sea in the past so please be careful."

"We will, sir – Jake."

"Something to take home to Fenton to show your friends, eh?"

The boys looked at each other and then Eddie turned back to face the stranger.

"How did you know we…?"

He didn't finish because the old man was already on his way out of the dining room. Eddie looked puzzled; Len less so as he tucked into his last scone.

"How could he know we're from Fenton, Len? I mean, I'm sure we didn't mention it and, anyway, no one's ever heard of it."

"Dunno, mate. Maybe he asked BB or Pat where we're from, or checked the visitors' book. Perhaps he heard your mum and dad talking."

Eddie didn't look too convinced, but concluded that the old man had probably checked out the new 'family' because he was wary of children.

"Suppose so. Maybe he spoke to Mum and Dad when they checked in. He was old though, wasn't he, Len. Did you notice his skin? It was like leather and so thin. I thought I could see his bones through it!"

"A real dinosaur, eh, mate?"

"A proper fossil!" replied Eddie, but in the back of his mind he was still bothered by the fossil's knowledge of where they lived. 'People that old didn't normally take that much interest in their fellow guests', he thought.

Eddie's mum and dad didn't seem to have heard the boys' conversation with Mr Manders, having been occupied with their own thoughts and plans for the week. They had finished their teas and time had gone quite quickly as Fred Compton said,

"Come on, lads, it's gone five and we want to have a quick nap before we go out. You two can play cards in your bedroom till about seven."

"But, Dad, can't we go and explore?" said Eddie. "It's such a beautiful afternoon."

"No, son – not until your mum and I have looked round the town this evening. Then you can go off on your own and, when you're on the beach, you don't go beyond the end of the cliffs you saw when we arrived and only as far as the small headland in the other direction. Understood?"

"Yes, Dad," said Eddie, reluctantly

"C'mon, mate, let's go and play *Cheat*. We'll keep score for the week," said Len, remembering his own dad's instructions to do everything his temporary parents told him.

The Compton's 'buzz' round Ludmouth town didn't reveal much to excite the two boys; mostly gift shops, tearooms and estate agents whose market was obviously the retired and reasonably well heeled. Returning to the seafront in the late evening sun, Len did spot a couple of shops selling buckets and spades together with all the other paraphernalia for a beach holiday.

"Could get a cricket bat and stumps from there."

"And a bucket and spade," said Eddie.

"Oh, come on, mate. We ain't building sand castles!"

"I meant for digging and collecting fossils."

"Fossils?" said Eddie's mum, now interested in the boys' conversation. She knew that her son's love for all things scientific should be encouraged. "How do you know you can find fossils here?" she continued.

"Mr Manders told us at tea time," replied Eddie.

"Who's Mr Manders," interjected his dad.

"He sat next to us in the dining room."

Fred Compton briefly stopped walking along the promenade and looked thoughtful.

"Didn't see anyone sit next to you."

Len pulled Eddie's shirt sleeve and gave him a knowing look.

"Oh, you were deep in conversation with mum and he only stayed a few minutes anyway," replied Eddie quickly.

"What did he look like, Eddie," asked his mum, also curious.

"He was really old, Mum."

Len interrupted the conversation trying to steer it off the subject. He had worries that he would have to discuss with his friend later.

"There's a fish and chip shop and it looks busy," he said hurriedly.

But Eddie's dad wasn't happy.

"You're making this up, son – just so your mum and I will buy you a bucket and spade, eh?"

"No honestly, Dad, he wa…."

Len knew he had to take control of the situation and pushed Eddie playfully onto the sand, where they both fell in a heap.

"Here, watch it, mate," said an embarrassed Eddie.

"Pretend you made it up, Eddie," whispered Len as they rolled in the sand. "Just pretend."

"Come on, you two, that's enough of that," said Ann Compton, "and stop telling fibs, Eddie. There was no one at the table between us, was there?"

"No, Mum – only joking! I read about the fossils on a brochure back at the guest house. This part of Devon is called the Jurassic Coast."

Len pulled Eddie back onto the promenade and they both brushed as much of the sand off as they could. Eddie's dad had his April the 1st grin on his face.

"Knew it, son – I thought I was losing my marbles! How on earth did you come up with the name Manders in your little joke?

Eddie thought quickly.

"Well, he was a *man*, Dad. Get it?"

Fred Compton got it, but Len and Eddie didn't. As they crossed over The Esplanade each boy was wrapped in his own thoughts, both knowing that there *had* been a Mr Manders, and this was the frightening part: their parents hadn't seen him, even though he was just feet away at the time!

The fish and chips out of a local newspaper and eaten on a promenade bench were quickly devoured by all and they were back at *Summer Breeze* at just before ten. Mr and Mrs Compton repaired to the small bar for a nightcap allowing the boys to take a couple of drinks back to their room. It wasn't until the boys were laid in bed with the light off that the inevitable conversation began.

"Oh no, Len – is it happening again, mate? My mum and dad were convinced there was no one at the table. But there was, wasn't there, Len? Please say there was," pleaded Eddie.

"Of course Mr Manders spoke to us," replied Len. "As I see it there are two possibilities: one – your mum and dad were tired and too engrossed in their own conversation and missed seeing him or two – Jake was invisible to everyone except you and me. I prefer to accept the first option. We may be letting our minds wander because of what happened before, when we became invisible at times."

"I suppose you're right, Len, but next time, if he reappears I'm going to introduce him to my parents. Then we'll see for certain, one way or the other."

"Forget about it, Eddie and let's enjoy our holiday. Fossil hunting tomorrow, and I mean the inanimate kind, mate!"

Tuesday was not as warm as the day before and while Fred and Ann Compton hired some bowls from a club just off The Esplanade, intending also to do some shopping later, the boys bought a bucket and spade and headed for the red cliffs. The tide was going out and they had at least until early afternoon before it would become difficult to get back along the beach. BB had given them a tide table for the week and Pat had made them packed lunches. Eddie's parents were going to sample some of the local seafood.

Not many holidaymakers were about on the beach as they strolled east jumping over breakwaters and they soon noticed how different the sand was from that at Fenton-on-Sea.

"Some of this sand is almost black," said Eddie.

"It's got bits in it," replied Len as he bent down to pick up a handful. "Makes it easy to walk on."

"Probably tiny pieces of shells of prehistoric sea creatures – read it in a leaflet back at the guest house."

Fortunately for Eddie he had found a brochure on the Jurassic Coast, like he'd told his mother the previous night, just in case she checked.

"This must be the place, Eddie," said Len pointing to what looked like the highest part of the red cliffs that towered over the two boys. They made their way to the bottom of the cliffs and started their search. Len, for one, was not sure what he was really looking for until Eddie remarked,

"The brochure said you could find two types of fossils: *Ammonites* and *Belemnites* and they're either shaped like a coil or a pencil; forget which way round."

"Got one, I think," shouted Len from his position behind a huge rock.

Eddie trotted over and, after a careful study of the piece of rock, he soon agreed that Len had his first fossil, a beautifully preserved coil-like specimen about three inches across.

"Well done, mate," he said, a little jealously.

They spent the rest of the morning searching for more, but it wasn't for at least another hour that Eddie managed to find one too – another *Ammonite*; smaller and not as well preserved as Len's example. They also played with Len's tennis ball for a time, paddled in the surprisingly warm sea and tried in vain to scale the cliffs, falling back onto the sand every time they got more than a couple of feet off it. By one o'clock Eddie was anxious to start the walk back to The Esplanade, which seemed a relief to

Len, who had had enough of scientific discovery for one day. They didn't see much else of interest on the way except for some large pieces of wood at the foot of the cliffs, which Eddie seemed to be able to identify.

"They look like railway sleepers, Len. Dad's got a couple in the garden."

"Railway sleepers?"

"Yep. Probably washed ashore years ago – they're well worn though. Must have come from some foreign country by ship."

Len didn't look too convinced, particularly as he thought that it was strange that the four or five pieces were gathered together in one place, all within a radius of a few yards. The tide was coming in quickly by then and the boys had to run the last few hundred yards back to the promenade where they ate their packed lunches.

A significant change in the weather took place that evening as Len and the Comptons returned from their obligatory fish and chips. They'd opted out of the cream teas to make a visit to Ludmouth's small zoo where they had compared and identified their fossils – and *Ammonites* they indeed were. Black clouds had curtailed the normally light evening; it being almost dark by seven-thirty. Rumbles of thunder could be heard in the distance and there was a stillness that was very eerie in the failing light.

"Storm approaching," said Eddie's dad as they walked up the steps into *Summer Breeze*.

The next few hours brought one of the worst storms to hit that part of Devon for several years. A tired and windswept looking BB told all at breakfast the next day, Wednesday, August the 21st,

"Must have had over an inch of rain, boys and what a gale. Blew my sign of its hinges and we've lost a few tiles from the roof. Did it keep you awake? Did you hear the thunder and see that lightning?"

"Yes," said a bleary-eyed Len. He and Eddie had spent most of the night either buried under the bed covers or – when brave enough – peering out to sea from behind the curtains and clinging on to each other in unashamed fear. The thunder had been deafening and what lightning they had dared to look at had lit up the night sky like daylight. However, Eddie was very quiet when BB was talking, being clearly preoccupied with something else. He'd had bad dreams of vanishing old men and curious sea creatures that started as *Ammonite* coils and then unravelled into incredibly and impossibly long snakes. He was not happy and he also kept looking round nervously to see if Mr Manders would appear for breakfast. He made up his mind to check the visitors' book that morning when no one was looking. His mum disturbed his thoughts.

"What's the matter, Eddie? Didn't you get any sleep? You look very pale, dear."

"Not much, Mum – must have had some nightmares as well."

"What about?"

"Can't remember."

"You shouted something on a couple of occasions," said Len.

Eddie remembered that bit. A black and green snake had started to wrap itself around him and was squeezing tighter and tighter. He then suddenly felt sick, but fortunately his dad lightened the conversation by announcing the plans for the day.

"Cheer up, son. We're going to the pictures this afternoon and you and Len can play football or cricket on the beach this morning now that the weather's improved."

Eddie glanced out of the bay window and his spirits were immediately lifted by the brightness of the day. He was suddenly excited by the day's prospects. He was on holiday and all at once he made a conscious effort to present a happy smile which seemed to lift the colour in his freckled face and his ginger hair shone in the sunlight.

After breakfast the boys headed for the beach with Len's football while Eddie's parents went off to play bowls again, hoping that the club had not closed the greens owing to the amount of rain they'd taken. On the way out, and with nobody about or in attendance at the counter, Eddie stopped to look at the visitors' book and his suspicion was confirmed when, try as he might, he couldn't find the name Manders anywhere in the previous few months. Len had gone out into the sunshine before he realised that his friend hadn't joined him and turning back he met Eddie at the door and said,

"What'ya doing, mate?"

"Nothing, Len. Just though I'd check to see if there was a Mr Manders in the book at reception."

"And?"

"And there wasn't one that I could see."

"So what? Plenty of non-residents must come in for the cream teas. It's advertised in the window and on a sign near the road and, anyway, I think you're getting paranoid about him. We did talk to him, Eddie. Now let's forget it and go and get you some exercise and wipe that frown from your face – it's too nice a day to think about phantoms and whatever horrible things you dreamt about. Come on, race you to the beach!"

3

The Rock Tunnel

Eddie cheered up quickly as the two friends played football on
Ludmouth's sandy beach. As usual, Eddie spent most of the time in goal
– he enjoyed diving onto the pebble free sand. He was not, unlike Len,
particularly proficient at football and certainly had never been considered
for the school team; Len, indeed, being captain for the next season at
Fenton Grammar. But, for whatever reason, Eddie seemed to be able to
stop most of Len's shots with ease, also seemingly able to anticipate
which way Len was going to send his penalties nine times out of ten. Len
was getting frustrated with this. Eddie had never really bothered to try to
save his penalties before. Why now?

"You're getting good as a goalkeeper," said Len eventually.

"Yes, I know. It's easier on this sand and I seem to be able to guess
which way you're going to send the ball," replied Eddie. "I don't mind
staying in goal all the time, mate."

"You'll have to try for the school team. Our present goalie, Andrew
Walsh is rubbish."

"I'm not that good and besides, I don't like playing on grass – it's
not as soft as sand."

They continued to play as they were for another half an hour; Len
getting more and more frustrated with Eddie's almost impossible and
freak anticipation until he had had enough and, pausing to take breath, he
posed the question that had began to form in his mind.

"What's going on, mate? There's no way you could save all those
penalties. Sometimes even I don't know which way the ball is going to go.
Do you think it's got something to do with the ball itself? Has Mr Canter
sent me a magic ball?"

"Maybe, Len. We won't know unless we try another ball when we get back home to Fenton. I'm just diving randomly each time, I think. I'm hardly looking at the ball."

That convinced Len that something *was* going on and to make certain he made Eddie take the penalties to see if it worked for him too, but Eddie missed nearly every one, either kicking sand or ballooning the ball wide of the makeshift goal. Eddie did eventually get the ball on target, three times in all and, unlike his friend, Len only stopped one of the shots.

"I must have been lucky, I guess," said an exhausted Eddie finally.

"Guess so," replied Len, but he still wasn't that convinced. His normal practical self didn't want to admit that the greater power might have started working again after nearly three months. Indeed, the feeling he'd got about his ball reminded him of the same sense of anticipation that he himself had experienced when playing with Eddie's new train set only a few days previously. Were both Mr Canter's presents magic in some way?

The ball didn't 'misbehave' again that morning and, apart from the fact that it didn't seem to be scuffed or marked in anyway at the end of their session, nothing else untoward occurred. As they turned to make for the promenade Eddie glanced at the red cliffs away to his right.

"Looks different over there somehow today, Len. I think there's been a rockfall from the cliffs."

"Bet last night's storm caused it," said Len observing a huge pile of rocks at about the same position as they had found the wooden railway sleepers.

Ludmouth Playhouse was even smaller than the Regal Cinema in Fenton-on-Sea. The awful storm of the previous night had made many holidaymakers abandon other plans in case the bad weather continued,

48

although as the boys had found out that morning, it had actually been very pleasant; fresher and a little cooler. For whatever reason, including the film being offered, the Playhouse was packed and uncomfortably warm. *Summer Holiday*, with the popular Cliff Richard in the starring role, had been retained for a second week in Ludmouth. It was a perfect family film for the majority of the cinema's clientele; families and holidaymakers as they were. After the film had finished the boys let Eddie's mum and dad wander back to *Summer Breeze* ahead of them as they dawdled, looking in the gift shops in the town. They seemed to have enjoyed the film probably more than most boys of their age group, because as Len observed as they left the cinema,

"Did we go where the bus went, Eddie? It looked familiar, didn't it?"

"Yes, I thought so too and Mr Canter might have looked like Cliff when he was his age, with his shiny black hair swept back like Elvis."

"Yeah, but he can't sing like Cliff," joked Len.

"I wonder what he's doing now?" asked Eddie.

"Who – Cliff? Probably on a tropical beach somewhere."

"No, you idiot, I mean George."

"Dunno, mate. Expect he's got another junk shop. Hope he's not ripping people off in Poland."

"No way," said Eddie. "If you remember, he paid everyone back as well as us with our gifts. He didn't need to do that did he?"

"Do you often think of him, then, Eddie?"

"Sometimes I do. Sometimes I think he's watching over us like we were looked after when we went on our fantastic journey. I mean, we could have, no, should have been killed lots of times, but we survived."

Len looked thoughtful for a moment.

"Yeah, I suppose so. I still wonder, you know, whether it really happened. Could all three of us have dreamt it?"

"No, I've told you before the chances would be astronomical," said Eddie.

"Yeah, but what if we had different dreams, mate?"

"Oh, come on, Len, you're going into the realm of fantasy. We're back in reality now. As I keep telling you: what happened – happened and there's nothing you or I can do about it. Let's just remember it as a game. That's how we accepted it when it happened. You think too much, Len."

Eddie seemed to have calmed his friend's imaginings and they made their way back to their guest house chatting about plans for the rest of the week. They all took dinner in the dining room that evening and while Eddie's mum and dad wrote some postcards and had one or two drinks in the bar, the boys found a putting green near by which, together with a little TV in *Summer Breeze*'s lounge, occupied them till bedtime.

Thursday was non-eventful and the boys spent it mainly on the beach and the newly found putting green. Everyone seemed tired that evening and, after a brief walk and some more fish and chips, they went to bed early and caught up on some missed sleep. The boys decided, as they lay in bed, that next day they would go to the red cliffs again and investigate the rockfall they had spied on Wednesday.

Owing to the slight alteration in the tides, Eddie and Len didn't set off until just after lunch on the Friday. When they had got to within fifty yards or so of the rockfall it was clear to them both that the fall had been very substantial. The storm had washed down a large amount of debris from the cliffs and the resulting pile was bungalow height. Reaching the bottom of the pile of freshly disturbed rocks Eddie looked behind it at the cliff face and exclaimed excitedly,

"There's a cave or something over there!"

There was certainly a large gaping hole in the cliff face only a few feet above ground level. As they got closer they could see that it was easily tall enough for people to enter in an upright position.

"It looks man made," said Len, who had reached the cave entrance. "Wait a minute, Eddie, it's not a cave – it's a tunnel, I think."

"Wow, Len!" said Eddie. He had caught his friend up and they stood side by side in the entrance. "Do you think the storm made it, Len?"

"Don't think so, mate. I think it was already here; just covered by rocks and stuff which the rocks from above have dislodged."

"How far does it go? Can you see?" asked Eddie.

"It's too dark to see anything, but it must go somewhere. Maybe it's a smugglers tunnel."

"Smugglers?"

"Yeah, I think this coast was notorious for smuggling in years gone by, maybe even today."

"Can't have been used for ages. It was blocked when we came the other day," said Eddie and he paused as he looked to the left of the tunnel entrance and also behind him near the pile of rocks. "You know what I think, Len?"

"What?"

"I think it's an old railway tunnel; those railway sleepers are only over there. I bet they didn't float in from the sea, but have been washed out of the tunnel by the waves and, perhaps, other storms over the years."

"Could be, mate. It would make sense. But why build a tunnel here?"

Eddie thought for a moment.

"Not sure, Len, but Fenton used to have a beach station so that trains could take trippers there directly."

"But this is a good half a mile from the seafront," responded Len.

"Maybe the line ran along the beach under the cliffs."

Len wasn't convinced.

"Doubt it – there's no evidence of any track."

"Probably been washed away over time," said Eddie finally.

Whatever its use and whether it had been for a railway track or not, both boys knew they would explore it, despite any possible dangers, which, unlike adults presented with the same opportunity, they did not recognise anyway.

"In we go, Len," said Eddie at last.

"You first, I'll follow."

Fortunately for their safety, for which they'd had no apparent concern, the tunnel came to a halt within ten or fifteen yards, blocked by another smaller pile of rocks which reached right to the tunnel's ceiling. With their eyes now adjusted to the light they could see that the excavation was definitely made by man as the regularity of the tunnel's sides displayed.

"More sleepers here," said Eddie as he peered into the furthest corner away from the entrance. "Definitely a railway."

"What's that noise, Eddie?" said Len who was still much nearer the entrance than his friend.

"That's the sea, mate," replied Eddie. "Like when you hold a shell to your ear."

"No, not that. Listen."

Eddie listened and he could suddenly hear the different type of sound that Len was referring to. A low rumble reverberated in the air and all at once the tunnel seemed to vibrate. It got louder and louder and it had a regular beat.

"Oh God!" said Eddie. "The tunnel's going to collapse! Get out, Len!"

Len didn't move, but seemed to be transfixed as if he was in a dream.

"Run, Len!" shouted Eddie. "For God's sake, run!"

But Len had placed the palms of both of his hands against the side wall and said calmly,

"There's no vibration, Eddie. It's just a noise."

The noise was very loud now and it reached a crescendo without either boy moving. Suddenly the noise abated and slowly reduced to silence over a few seconds. The whole event had taken less than half a minute. When they had both stopped shaking, Len managed to break the silence. He knew what he'd heard and so had his friend – it was unmistakeable.

"You know what that sounded like, don't you, mate?"

"Yes, Len. It was a train and an old one at that – sounded like a steam engine."

"It was as if the train was in the tunnel with us, Eddie."

"I know. Did you notice the Doppler Effect when the noise suddenly decreased? Just like when a train goes past."

"Yes. What's happening, Eddie?"

"Don't know, but let's get out of here. I'm frightened."

Len didn't need a second invitation and he made for the tunnel entrance. Just as he was about to emerge into the welcoming sunlight his eye was caught by something on the tunnel wall.

"What's this?"

Eddie, in his haste, ran into Len's back and the two boys ended up with their faces almost touching the object Len had spotted.

"It's a rusty metal plaque," said Eddie as his eyes focused properly. He read out loud its fading words written in another century.

To the memory of Jacob Denham Manders
who was tragically killed on this spot
August 19th 1863
You can go anywhere by rail
R.I.P.
1815 – 1863

"Now it leads nowhere," said Eddie with irony well beyond his years.

Questions as to whether he had died excavating the tunnel, or he was the architect, as seemed likely from the motto, or both, were irrelevant to the two boys as they stood in silence taking in the personal significance of the words and especially the date.

4

Football Practice

Few words were exchanged about their discovery; both on the way back
to the guest house that Friday afternoon, and indeed, on the remaining
two full days of the holiday. They both knew what they had read and
heard. Mr Manders was a ghost from the past and that final acceptance
pigeonholed the experience into something which they could handle, as if
by so doing the idea became commonplace. Should they tell Eddie's
parents, or BB, or the police? Would they be believed? Did they
themselves believe what they'd seen? All these questions plagued the two
friends and, just as in the past, there emerged an almost silent agreement
that they would say nothing. They didn't return to the tunnel and,
unbeknown to them, it became unstable in a few days and fell in on itself;
its secret once again hidden and maybe this time forever.

Saturday and Sunday were spent on the more mundane and
traditional seaside pastimes. Eddie and Len confined themselves to the
short stretch of beach in sight of *Summer Breeze*, ignoring several
suggestions from the adults to venture further. Time seemed to go quickly
in those last hours with each boy wanting to get back to the perceived
safety and reality of their homes in Fenton-on-Sea. The return train
journey was as equally tiring as the outward one, not helped by several
delays and the reduced Bank Holiday service. Eddie's dad tried his best
to tell the boys about the various engines they saw, but eventually put
their obvious disinterest down to tiredness and the heat of the day. The
boys, for their part, had had enough of trains and railways for the time
being!

Remarkably, when they arrived home that Monday evening at just after nine, Jenny was in at 38 Fir Tree Close. She had made some sandwiches and had the kettle on to make a pot of tea. Though her mum had telephoned the day before to apprise her of their arrival time, they were, in fact, over three hours late and Jenny looked relieved to see her family. Her reaction when Eddie and her parents came through the front door said more about the real Jenny than the one she liked people to see. She had missed her mum and dad all week, demonstrating that, at seventeen, she was far from being ready to cope in the world on her own.

"Where on earth have you been? I've been worried sick," she said, hugging her mum and sounding like *she* was the adult talking to her children.

"Connection problems, Jenny love," said her dad. "What's all this? You've made supper. Jenny you're an angel."

His daughter blushed. Her dad never paid compliments to her; just moaned about her coming in late and her choice of boyfriends. Even Eddie gave his sister a brief and unemotional hug.

"Get off, Eddie."

'Back to normal', thought Ann Compton, but she said,

"Now then, you two, don't start. Eddie and Len have been good all week. In fact, I complimented Len to Mr and Mrs Wilby when we took him back ten minutes ago."

"He tries to suffocate me, Mum. He does it on purpose."

"No I don't," said Eddie, and he was nearly going to say that he'd missed her, but restrained himself. By ten-thirty the Compton household had fallen silent. They were tired from the long journey or, in Jenny's case, from anxiety.

Len's mum and dad had also been worried when Len hadn't arrived by six o'clock, almost as worried as they might have been, it seemed to Len, when he and Eddie had gone missing on that Saturday in May. He was their only son and had never been away from home for even a night before. After something to eat and some garbled tales of fossils and the likeable host, BB, Len climbed the stairs to bed, tired but happy. He placed his prize *Ammonite* on his windowsill, hoping it wouldn't continually remind him of the other 'fossil' to make him have bad dreams like his friend had had.

Next morning at breakfast, Eddie had a question for his dad that he'd wanted to ask ever since the visit to the rock tunnel. Just before Fred Compton got up from the table to return to work in the booking office at Fenton station, Eddie said,

"Dad?"

"Yes, son."

"Dad, can you go anywhere in England by rail?"

"More or less, Eddie. Why do you ask?"

"Oh, it's just that on the way back from Ludmouth even the smallest villages had a station and we seemed to stop at every one," he hastily concocted. His dad went on,

"We did, but mind you, by the time good old Mr Beeching has finished, you won't be able to get to even some quite important places – Ludmouth for example, let alone many small hamlets. I think the line between Ludmouth Junction and the town is scheduled for closure next year."

"Oh, Dad – does that mean that we won't be able to go back there? Len and I had a fantastic time."

"We'll see, son. The line may still be open this time next year and who knows? If you're good...."

"I'll be good, Dad! I liked BB and Pat."

"Yeah, they were nice people – pity about BB's jokes!"

Eddie thought he and Len needed to know more about Mr Manders and the mysterious rock tunnel.

The two boys saw little of each of each other over the last week of the school holidays, though they did play with Eddie's train set on the Friday when Len's parents were both in school at Fenton Secondary Modern for the day. Cyril Wilby as Head of Woodwork and Martha as the new chief cook both had much preparation to do before the autumn term began on the Monday. Len spent most of the day inside at Eddie's house as the weather was appalling – torrential rain and strong winds. Len had been nervous, at first, when using the controller but nothing untoward seemed to happen. They tried to build a variety of tunnels out of cardboard, but none of their attempts seemed to be sturdy enough to last very long. Len again promised that he would get his dad to make a proper tunnel out of wood and Eddie said he was going to save his pocket money that term to buy some other additions to the set – a station with platforms, a signal box and even some extra track and points if he could find where to get them from.

They both returned to Fenton Grammar on Monday the 2nd of September as proud second years and at the first football practice of the term after school on the Thursday, Len told his P.E. teacher, Mr Smithson, that Eddie deserved a trial in goal, despite Eddie's protests earlier in the day that he wasn't really any good. 'Smithers' told Len to bring his protégé along the next Thursday and at four o'clock sharp Eddie presented himself reluctantly on the lower field in his football kit, hastily purchased from Gough's in Hamsden the previous weekend. Mr Smithson marched over to Eddie as soon as he arrived, shouting,

"Right then, young Compton – I hear you're the next Gordon Banks! You can be in goal for the first twenty minutes and then Walsh can take over."

"Yes, sir," replied Eddie nervously.

But Eddie didn't last twenty minutes because in less than half the time allotted he let in five goals including two which came from back passes from his own players! 'Smithers' had seen enough and stopped the seven-a-side game exclaiming,

"Right, I've seen enough, Gordon. Swap with Walsh and you go on the wing where you might do less damage."

Poor old Eddie slouched out to the left wing and passed his friend Len on the way who said,

"What's up, mate? Did you let them in on purpose so you wouldn't be picked for the team?

"No, I just kept guessing wrong I suppose."

Eddie managed to touch the ball on only two occasions, or at least the ball touched him, as both times it just ricocheted off him into touch as he tried in vain to control it. After the practice and on their way home down South Road Len put his arm round his friend and said,

"Don't worry, mate. It was probably just nerves."

"No it wasn't, Len. I'm just no good at football.

"You were good in Ludmouth."

"That was different."

Eddie paused and slowed to a halt. He looked oddly at Len who seemed to have forgotten what had happened on the sand on holiday.

"You know what I think, Len?"

"What?"

"I think I was good on the sand in Devon because we used your ball – Mr Canter's ball. I said then I needed to try out a different ball to see if I could save it every time."

Len was doing his best to prevent his own 'worries' surfacing and he still tried to ignore his friend's argument and his own memories from Ludmouth.

"What do you mean? What difference does a ball make? I mean, if anything, I should be the one it should help, not you. It's my ball and George wanted me to have it. Anyway you were just lucky in Ludmouth; you said so."

Despite his down-to-earth reaction, inside Len knew that his friend was probably right – he remembered he'd been convinced before in Ludmouth that something magical had been starting again. Eddie broke his train of thought and continued.

"It's just a feeling, Len. I can't explain it, but I bet if I came next time and the squad used your ball, then I'd save everything."

"You won't get the chance, old son. 'Smithers' told me off afterwards for wasting his time."

Eddie didn't indeed get another chance to test out his 'magic' ball theory and as term got into full swing he became fully occupied with his academic studies anyway. Simultaneous equations and his introduction to the mysteries of electricity were far more to his liking than sport on a cold autumn football pitch. His dad helped him to improve his train set with various items procured from some of Fenton station's employees, many of whom were keen model railway enthusiasts themselves; better than spending money. Fred Compton was a careful man with regard to finance. Eddie soon had quite a good layout, including a hardboard base which was simply an old advertising hoarding pinched from Fenton station when it had undergone a refit. Eddie and his dad played with it most weekends; Fred Compton seemed to enjoy the time more than his son. Len and Eddie didn't see much of each other that autumn term at weekends, apart from the inevitable visit to Woolworth's on Saturday mornings to spend their pocket money; Len's afternoon was often tied up with school football matches. Eddie always went to church with his mum and dad on a Sunday morning and the rest of the weekend was spent on his homework which was getting harder and longer. This was greatly to Eddie's satisfaction because he had found much of the first year work fairly easy except, perhaps, for English where he still had difficulty expressing himself on paper. English was always left to last thing on a Sunday evening!

The October half-term turned out to be very wet for most of the week and the boys did, at last, spend more time inside playing together. Eddie's train set came out and was set up most days at the Compton's house – the dining room table being used, suitably covered with a tablecloth. The actual process of setting up and arranging the set often took up as much time as playing with it. Both boys had their own ideas as to how it should be done and with a signal box, station, plastic trees and passengers as well as various buildings all given free to Eddie's dad by his colleagues, there was almost an infinity of ways the process could be done. Eddie had managed to save for some extra track – bought from a model and toy shop in Hamsden – so that they had sidings, buffers and an engine shed into which they sent *Flying Scotsman* at some speed. Fortunately for Len, he experienced nothing strange when he was in charge of the controls – it didn't seem to anticipate his actions and he, along with his friend, had no more thoughts of fantasies for the time being. Even the spectre of Mr Manders had receded from their minds, waking or sleeping, and certainly from their conversations. Neither boy would want to be the first to introduce the subject. As time went on memories of magic footballs or their Ludmouth holiday became hazier. The greater power was lying dormant.

5

From the Jaws of Death

Gary Steven Jones had had several jobs since leaving school at fifteen, four years previously. He'd tried his hand at labouring for a local builder but gave it up when he found out they worked in all weathers, including on cold days in winter. He had also helped out Bill Stevens fetching and carrying at the Red Lion in the High Street and latterly, when he'd turned nineteen, he'd served occasionally behind the bar. He was, however, soon sacked when Bill realised that he was giving the wrong change more often than not, simply because his basic arithmetic had hardly improved from his primary school days while he had been at Fenton Secondary Modern! His last job had been unloading and stacking shelves in Fenton's only supermarket, Downsway, near the station. Again, in May, he'd been asked to leave when the manager had found a whole shelf of canned vegetables stocked with packs of butter which should have been in the refrigerated section! Poor old Gary may have had the brain of one of his cousins from some species of primate, but he did have two redeeming qualities as far as the members of the opposite sex were concerned. He was handsome and always immaculately dressed in the latest fashion *and*, more importantly, he owned a car, given to him by his dad who owned a garage in Hamsden. His parents had threatened on many occasions to throw him out of the family home, but the embarrassment that that would have caused to a respectable local businessman had always prevented them carrying out the threat. Gary had been unemployed for over five months, but Jennifer Compton still swooned over him, ever since they'd first gone out together over eight months previously.

The last Saturday of the October half-term would bring about a change in Gary and his outlook on life. It was the first day for nearly a week when the weather looked set fair for the day and Gary called for Jenny at ten. She had the Saturday off from Arleson's as she always she always did at the end of each month.

"Fancy a coffee in Hamsden, Jenny?" said her boyfriend as they sat in Gary's turquoise blue Austin A40 outside 38 Fir Tree Close. "Then we could meet up with Mick and Bev and go to the game at Freeman Street. Town are playing Borchester.

Borchester United like Hamsden Town were in the Third Division and were also Town's local rivals, situated as they were just thirty miles further north.

"If you like, Gary, but I must be back by six. Mum wants me to stay with Eddie as she and Dad are going to the Regal cinema for the evening."

"No problem; the game finishes at quarter to five and even given the football traffic we should be back in Fenton by quarter to six."

"Can we do some shopping as well, Gary? I got paid yesterday."

"Course you can, as long as you pay for the match and give me ten bob for petrol."

Jenny was about to say no, but just as she was about to open her mouth, Gary focused his deep blue eyes on her and she changed her mind as she always did.

"O.K., Gary, but you give me the petrol money back next time."

"Sure, honey."

Gary gunned the A40 and they sped away from Fir Tree Close in a cloud of exhaust fumes with the odd curtain being pulled back to see what noise was disturbing the otherwise quiet cul-de-sac. Gary drove too fast and erratically.

Eddie and Len met down town at eleven and spent some time in
'Woolies' as well as on the pier's amusements – it was the last day it
would be open until the following Easter. Eddie was going to watch
Grandstand with his dad on the television that afternoon and as the two
boys parted for lunch Len said,

"Fancy a quick kick-about on the 'rec' at five, mate?"

"Have to be quick; Mum and Dad are going out this evening."

"Just till six, then."

"O.K., I'll see you up there later, Len."

Jenny managed to buy a new pair of shoes in Hamsden and she and Gary
were therefore both in good moods after the match, since Town had
thrashed United 5 – 1, with Ray Baker scoring a second half hat-trick, his
third of the season. After saying goodbye to Mick and Bev they returned
to the car and Gary weaved his way through the back streets of Hamsden
trying to avoid the congestion caused after the match. They were on the
outskirts of the town by twenty past five and had time to stop for some
petrol at the last garage before the dual carriageway that led back to
Fenton-on-Sea. Gary's euphoria brought about by Town's victory
exhibited itself in his driving. He reached speeds well in excess of sixty
and approached the A40's claimed maximum of seventy-two. Once or
twice it seemed that he was going to lose control and Jenny shouted,

"For God's sake, slow down, Gary!"

But the only thing that made her boyfriend ease his foot of the
accelerator was the thirty mile per hour sign as they entered Fenton *and*
the fact that they would pass directly past the police station on South
Road. However, as soon as they had left said establishment behind, Gary
put his right foot hard down again and they almost reached fifty before
the turning into Fir Tree Close. Then disaster struck. Gary slammed his

foot onto the brake but, alas, had left it too late to negotiate the ninety degree left turn. The A40 slewed across the road, hit the kerb and Gary was thrown clear out of his door which had flown open in the impact. He seemed to 'fly' for a second and, clearing a low brick wall, landed with a sickening thud on the front lawn of number 4. He screamed in pain at impact clutching his left arm which had borne the brunt of the crash and then he went silent. Meanwhile, the A40 had rolled onto its right side and slid for another fifty yards with Jenny trapped inside. Petrol leaked from the ruptured tank and Fir Tree Close then descended into an eerie silence.

Eddie and Len had duly met up for some football as arranged at five o'clock. Both boys were a little nervous in case Len's ball displayed any of its strange powers as before. Eddie went into goal between the permanent posts, muttering,

"Five – one, mate."

He then kept telling Len that he wouldn't put one past him let alone five! But Len did put one past his friend and many more as Eddie, this time, seemed to dive completely the wrong way each time. He was as hopelessly wrong this time as he had been incredibly correct when they had been on holiday. Whatever happened, it made both boys feel, perhaps, that there was now no longer any strange power at work with Len's football. Suddenly Eddie looked at his watch and shouted to his friend,

"Got to go it's five to."

The two boys trotted most of the way back and Len left Eddie at the entrance to Fir Tree Close at six o'clock precisely. Len had walked about fifty yards towards Lime Tree Avenue when he suddenly heard the frightening sound of the screech of brakes from a car which he glimpsed, as he turned round, to be heading directly for his friend, Eddie who had walked a similar distance into Fir Tree Close. Eddie had heard the powerful noise too and looking over his right shoulder he saw a turquoise blue Austin A40 crash and roll over. The car slid many yards along the road to come to a halt feet from where he was standing on the pavement. He could smell petrol fumes and spotted a passenger still trapped. Eddie would not really be able to describe what he did next. With almost super human strength and effort he leapt onto the side of the car and wrenched open the passenger door which was now pointing vertically upward and some feet off the ground. Without a moment's thought for his own safety or the condition of the obviously injured passenger, he grabbed the person roughly by the shoulders and bundled the body onto the road. Jumping down Eddie dragged the girl, as girl the passenger obviously was, managing to get her onto the pavement on the opposite side of the road. A split second later and EFY 504 exploded into flames which engulfed the whole car choking Eddie as he lay protecting the injured girl.

Len had reached the corner of Fir Tree Close just as the car had burst into flame and he hesitated before going further, fearing the worst for his friend who had seemed from his angle to be directly in the way of the sliding car. But then he saw Eddie crouching over an injured passenger and he ran the few yards to his friend.

"Are you alright, mate?"

Eddie didn't move. He was in floods of tears and shaking uncontrollably.

"It's Jenny, Len! It's Jenny!"

"Oh my God!" was all Len could manage. He could see that Eddie's sister was badly hurt. She moaned and tried to move. By now several people had gathered, including Dr Entwhistle from number 5 who took over the supervision of Eddie's sister, shouting,

"Get back, give me room! Someone phone for an ambulance! Get the fire brigade!"

The next few moments were the worst in Eddie's short life as he fell into his mum's arms. Fred and Ann Compton had heard the noise of the crash even from their fairly distant position right up the cul-de-sac at number 38.

"Oh Mum, is she dead?"

His mum didn't answer – she was in too much shock to do anything but cling deliriously to her son almost as though she needed evidence that she still had children. Meanwhile, Mrs Dunn from number 4 was tending to Gary who seemed to have fared rather better than his girlfriend. He was at least sitting up on Joan Dunn's lawn clutching what appeared to be just a broken arm. Just a broken arm seemed to be trivial when compared to his girlfriend's likely injuries or, indeed, her condition if Eddie had not pulled her clear before the car burst into flames. Mr Dunn had also called an ambulance and within ten minutes both teenagers were stretchered and on their way to Fenton Cottage Hospital near the top of East Hill.

Ann Compton went with her daughter in the ambulance while Eddie's dad looked after his son. Sergeant Owen Hughes from Fenton police station had arrived and he and his constable were busy organising the necessary arrangements in the aftermath of the crash. Fenton's only fire engine had also arrived and Gary's car was now a drenched and blackened wreck. Len stayed with Eddie and his dad until Martha and Cyril Wilby arrived to collect him. Eddie and to lesser extent, Len, were important witnesses, though Eddie didn't seem to be in a fit condition to answer any questions from Sergeant Hughes or anyone else. He just kept asking,

"Is she dead? Is Jenny dead?"

Jenny wasn't dead nor was she as seriously injured as it had first seemed from her low moans and then her silence. Doctor Entwhistle, who apart from being a neighbour of the Comptons, was also their GP and he went in the ambulance with Jenny and her mum. He'd told Ann Compton on the way that Jenny's pulse was strong and that all her vital signs were good. She was in extreme shock, he said, and they wouldn't know the full extent of her injuries until the hospital had examined her.

Dr Entwhistle went with Jenny into the Casualty unit while her mum stayed in a waiting room. After various X-rays had been taken and about half an hour of nervous waiting, he reappeared from his discussion with the Casualty consultants and sat down beside Jenny's mum.

"Broken ankle, a dislocated shoulder and some nasty bruising that won't improve her looks temporarily."

Ann Compton breathed a sigh of relief.

"Is she going to be alright?"

"Yes, Ann, but she does have some concussion too which needs to be monitored for a day or too. They're going to put the shoulder back and see to her ankle under anaesthetic in the next hour. You can stay if you like and see her onto the ward. She's going to be fine."

Jenny's mum knew that the concussion might be serious as her daughter apparently hadn't once asked as to Gary's injuries. Ann Compton burst in to tears. But Dr Entwhistle had more information.

"Dr Carter says she probably didn't get the dislocation to her shoulder in the crash, but afterwards, since it would require a different type of trauma to cause it.
Did anyone move her after the crash?"

"I don't know. When I got there her brother, Eddie, was trying to comfort her on the pavement. Maybe he moved her. He hasn't been able to speak about the crash yet. Sergeant Hughes is interviewing him now, I think."

"How old is Eddie now?"

"Twelve."

Dr Entwhistle looked pensive.

"Couldn't have been him, then. It would take considerable pulling force to dislocate a shoulder – an eighteen stone weightlifting rugby player might be able to do it. I expect Dr Carter has got it wrong. It must have happened in the crash."

There would be a reminder of the accident for the residents of Fir Tree Close which would remain for some time to come. The tarmac outside number 4 was discoloured and pockmarked and it would not be repaired until the following spring. It would take much longer for other scars to heal and some would always be there.

Jenny stayed in hospital for ten days. Though her ankle and shoulder had been relatively straightforward to see to, Dr Carter needed to make sure that there were no side effects to her concussion. Of the two main injuries Jenny's shoulder was the most painful after her operation and she didn't sleep well while in hospital. The rest of the Comptons visited her every day as well as many of Jenny's friends, but though Gary was released within three days with his simple single wrist fracture he did not come to see her. He was both mortified and embarrassed. His parents had thought he should go and visit Jenny, but after discussions with Sergeant Hughes they agreed to Owen's instruction that the two teenagers should be kept apart so that they could not discuss the accident. He wanted to interview them both separately in order to get as full and as accurate a picture of the crash as possible. Jenny did eventually ask about Gary and seemed relieved when told that he only had a broken wrist which should mend quickly.

At first, when Owen Hughes interviewed Gary at his parents' home, he admitted to losing control of the A40, but not to excessive speed. The burly Welsh policeman was not satisfied as he had witnesses who had seen a blue A40 doing 'at least 40' on South Road at about the time of the accident.

"Now come on, Gary, it's better to tell the truth. I'll ask you again: What speed were you doing as you turned into Fir Tree Close?"

"Well, like I said, it must have been about thirty. I must have braked too late, Sergeant. It was an honest mistake."

Though the results of tyre marks on the road weren't back from Hamsden, Owen said,

"The tyre tracks show unequivocally that you must have been doing in excess of forty before you hit the brakes."

"What's 'uniquiv,,,ly', Sergeant?"

"Now don't get cocky, son. Were you speeding? This is a very serious matter. You could have killed Jennifer Compton or yourself. You're lucky that neither of you were seriously hurt. I don't know yet whether the Comptons are going to prosecute you for dangerous driving."

Gary's face dropped at the word 'prosecute'.

I suppose I must have been over the speed limit, but I never looked at the speedometer – it's dodgy anyway. I'm really sorry, you know. Jenny's my girlfriend. I never meant any harm."

Gary burst into tears and from his experience Owen could tell that the tears were genuine as all the emotion of the previous few days began to surface.

"Alright, son, that's all I needed to hear."

"What happens now, Sergeant?"

"Well, that largely depends on the Comptons. As far as were concerned you've admitted to dangerous or, at least, inconsiderate driving and the courts will probably ban you from driving for quite a long time and maybe impose a fine."

"Will I go to prison?"

"No, probably not, first offence and all and particularly if you show genuine remorse and honesty to the judge. Don't try to be clever. But…"

"There's a 'but'?"

"Yes. As I said before, it will depend on what Mr and Mrs Compton decide. That's why it's probably not a good idea to go and see their daughter just yet. Perhaps a letter to her parents would be a start."

"Yes, Sergeant."

A few days earlier Eddie seemed to have little or no recollection of the accident. He was sitting with his dad in the Compton's kitchen immediately after the crash. When asked by Sergeant Hughes as to what he could remember he just said,

"Heard a loud screech of brakes and turned round to see the car sliding down the road. Next thing I knew I was holding Jenny on the pavement."

"How did she get there, Eddie? Take your time."

"Don't know. She was just there on the path and she was moaning and I thought she…."

Eddie broke down and Fred Compton got up and put his arm round him and said,

"Don't you think that's enough, Owen? He's in no fit state to answer your questions. He's still in shock."

"Sorry, Fred, but I just have one more."

Eddie seemed to recover his composure.

"It's O.K., Dad; I'll try and answer as best as I can, but I don't really remember anything."

Owen Hughes leant forward and asked quietly,

"Did you pull your sister out of the car, Eddie?"

"No, Sergeant."

Owen Hughes smiled and patted Eddie on the arm. The sergeant didn't know what to think. In his mind he thought that the chances of both occupants being thrown clear and in totally opposite directions to be slim, if not impossible. He had to accept that Eddie was still in shock. Maybe later, if he talked to him again, he might remember more. For now he just thanked him and went on his way to check with the only other likely witness, Leonard Wilby.

"What did you see, Len?" asked Owen Hughes when he eventually got to 7 Lime Tree Avenue.

"Just this bluish car trying to turn into Eddie's road. It was going fast."

"How fast?"

"I don't know, but faster than they normally do."

"What happened next?"

"Well, the car seemed to hit the kerb and roll on its side and I thought it was going to hit Eddie, but it must have been the angle I was looking from. When it stopped I couldn't see Eddie as the car was in front of him. He was hidden. I ran as quickly as I could and when I got there Eddie was on the pavement with his sister. That's all I saw, Sergeant."

"Are you sure? You didn't see Eddie go to the car?"

"No. It all happened too quickly and I must have been nearly a hundred yards away."

The sergeant thanked Len and made for the scene of the accident which he'd left solely in the hands of his constable.

Guy Fawke's Night, November the 5th had an extra significance that year for the Comptons – Jenny had been released from hospital in the afternoon. She looked a sight; left ankle in plaster balanced by her right arm in a sling. Her facial cuts and bruises had largely healed and she wouldn't be scarred for life, which had been her main concern.

Though tired she still enjoyed the extra special celebrations in the Compton's back garden with the four of them reunited again. It would be well into December before she would be out of plaster and able to walk unaided. Her shoulder would need constant and longer physiotherapy to restore it to full use.

The Comptons did not, in the end, press charges; Jenny eventually persuaded her dad not to. Despite what had happened she didn't blame Gary and deep down she idolised him even more. 'Love is blind' was certainly true for Jenny! As for Gary and for one reason or another, he didn't make contact with Jenny – he had never been as smitten with her as she had been with him. The Comptons did receive an almost illegible letter from Gary which seemed to express his sincere apologies for the accident and also another from his parents offering compensation, which Fred Compton refused. Gary was banned from driving for a year and fined £50. The whole experience changed him for the better. He immediately got a job working for Steve Paton at his garage just outside Fenton and without personal transport he was not such an attraction to the opposite sex despite his good looks. Word spread quickly among Jenny's friends that he wasn't the catch that they'd all previously thought. Jenny seemed to get over the fact that her relationship with Gary was over, but somewhere inside her she hoped that it might be rekindled one day.

6

Eddie Saves the Day

Jenny was out of plaster and off her crutches by Wednesday the 11th of December and, unusually, Eddie was at home when she returned that morning from Fenton Cottage Hospital. Fenton-on-Sea's schools had been hit by a 'flu epidemic since the previous Friday. So many children had been affected that both secondary schools were closed on the Tuesday and Wednesday. Eddie was, so far, one of the few in his year that had escaped the virus, whereas Len had been in bed with it for four days.

Head of PE, Dave Smithson, was very worried. The U13 football team had reached the final of the County Cup and the game was on the following Saturday at Hamsden's Northgate School. On the Monday he'd counted just six fit players from the squad. He didn't know how many more might go down while the school was closed for two days. The other finalists, Midhouse School from the small town of Bellsby twenty miles away, seemed to be unaffected by the virus. Discussions with Midhouse's Head of PE revealed that the final *had* to be played that term as neither school played football in the spring term and finding a venue might prove difficult anyway. Short of moving the fixture to the middle of the last week of term which finished on the 17th there didn't seem to be a solution to Mr Smithson's problem. It was with this in mind that Eddie's mum received a strange phone call at just before five that Wednesday.

"Mrs Compton? It's Mr Smithson from school. Is Eddie there?"

Eddie hadn't mentioned Mr Smithson's name to his mum and dad, since he didn't teach an academic subject and Ann Compton hadn't met him at any of the parents' evenings.

"Yes," she said hesitantly. "What's it about?"

'Was he in trouble', she thought.

"I wondered if he was free on Saturday to play football for the school."

"Football? I don't think he's any good at football, Mr Smithson."

"Well, he wouldn't be my first choice, but we're so short of players that it would really help us out if he could. It would look good on his record. I'm sure the Head would be extremely grateful to him."

That comment tipped the balance for Ann Compton and she called to Eddie,

"Eddie! Mr Smithson is on the phone for you."

Eddie came through into the hall and looked anxious. 'What have I done', he thought as he took the phone from his mum.

"Hello, Mr Smithson."

"Eddie, are you available to play football on Saturday? I'm desperate for players. Please can you help us?"

"But I'm no good, sir."

"I'd only want you to play in goal. The other side aren't very good – we beat them 6 – 0, last time we played them. You'd probably have nothing to do, son. What do you say? I'm sure you'd do better than at the practice."

"Go on, Eddie," whispered his mum in the background. "Say yes. Dad'll take you wherever it is."

"There'll be a coach, Mum," whispered Eddie as an aside and then to Mr Smithers,

"Alright, sir. Will Len Wilby be playing?"

"Yes, if he's better. At least he was one of the first to go down with it. We've got another three days to get a team together. In fact, Eddie, you may not be needed if the others recover as well, but I've only got seven at the moment even with you and some of them might still get it."

After the phone call Eddie rang Mrs Wilby to check on his friend's condition. He'd feel much better if Len was able to play. She had reasonably good news as Len was out of bed and had had some lunch earlier. He was about to eat his evening meal and Martha Wilby put him on the phone.

"How're you doing, mate," said Eddie.

"Much better – I'm coming back to school tomorrow. It is open, isn't it?"

"Yep, but I bet we're in half classes and Len...?"

"What, Eddie?"

"Len, 'Smithers' has asked me to be in goal on Saturday for the final. You must be really desperate."

"Oh, well done, mate. You'll be alright; just think of Ludmouth!"

"Didn't work last time at the practice, did it?" Eddie paused and continued. "And Len, can you bring your football with you when we go on Saturday?"

"Why, Eddie? There'll be a match ball. We won't be able to use it."

"I know, but I'd just feel better if it was there. I could put it in the back of my goal as a lucky mascot. Please, Len."

"Alright, mate, no problem."

Regular goalkeeper, Andrew Walsh, did not return to school that week so at Friday lunchtime Mr Smithson finally told Eddie he would definitely be playing in the big match. Enough boys had returned for 'Smithers' to have exactly eleven players but without reserves. Most of the team's families, a few second year girls and some teachers were going to be the U13s travelling supporters' club. Headmaster, Mr D.J. Hempsall hoped to attend for the second half – he had once been Deputy Head at the

Northgate School in Hamsden where the match was being played on neutral ground.

Eddie joined Len for a short team talk and practice after school on that Friday and to Mr Smithson's relief he made one or two reasonable saves or, at least, the ball was deflected by Eddie's body and bounced to safety! 'Edward Compton would have to do', thought Dave Smithson.

Eddie didn't know when or indeed, if he would put his plan into operation at the big game on the Saturday afternoon. By school standards, there was quite a large crowd lined up on the touchline at the start of the match between Fenton Grammar and the Midhouse School and he realised that he would have to choose his moment for his little subterfuge. Midhouse won the toss and kicked off. It was soon clear, even to Eddie that their minor public school rivals were not very good and Fenton quickly established a two goal lead, Len providing the final pass for the second strike. However, Midhouse's first two real attacks quickly saw them equalise owing largely to fumbles by Eddie.

"Keep your eye on the ball, lad," shouted one irate Fenton parent after a third Midhouse goal, the ball going straight between Eddie's legs. Things got even worse when the opposition converted a penalty, hopelessly missed by Eddie who dived completely the wrong way amid unkind laughter from some Midhouse parents.

Midhouse led 4 – 2 at half-time and Mr Smithson was not best pleased, though Eddie did not take the brunt of his anger. That was reserved for the forwards who had missed countless chances. Dave Smithson just smiled at Eddie and said,

"Keep going, Compton, just get something in the way."

Len also gave some words of encouragement.

"Don't worry, mate, us forwards will get a hatful second half."

But hatful they didn't get and with five minutes left Fenton still trailed 5 – 4, but then, at last, the equaliser came. Len had tried all afternoon to set up his centre forward and he'd missed almost all his chances. This time Len was selfish. He got the ball on the halfway line and performed a mazy dribble which ended with an unstoppable shot from twenty yards that soared high in to the opposition net. Three minutes were left and Eddie joined the rest of his team in mobbing Len, their hero. When they all reached the centre circle Eddie performed his swap. He had carried Len's football with him to the celebration and no one had noticed in the excitement. Turning quickly round he carried the match ball back to his goal covered in the towel he'd had wrapped round Len's ball. Apart from the now fading signatures the balls were indistinguishable. Midhouse kicked off and still no one spotted the changed ball. Then disaster struck. A long through ball reached Midhouse's centre forward who bore down on Fenton's goal. He sidestepped Eddie but just as he was about to put the ball into the empty net Eddie dived and managed to put out a hand for the ball. Unfortunately his hand caught the boy's trailing leg and the striker fell in a heap. The ball rolled harmlessly past the post.

"Penalty! Penalty!"

The verdict was unanimous from the opposition team and supporters and the neutral referee agreed, pointing immediately to the spot. Mr Smithson ran behind Eddie's goal and whispered to his keeper out of earshot of the referee.

"Go left, Compton! Dive left!"

Whether Eddie heard Mr Smithson or not was going to be irrelevant. The ball was placed on the spot and Midhouse's top scorer strode back several yards. The referee told Eddie to stay on his line and not to move until the penalty was taken. The opposition player ran menacingly towards the ball and hit his shot perfectly at the top left hand corner. Eddie 'flew' high to his right and with both hands plucked the ball out of the air inches before it could cross the line. There were seconds left and Fenton's celebration were cut short by Mr Smithson bellowing,

"Get it downfield, Compton! Kick it as hard as you can!"

Eddie got to his feet and ran a few yards through various players of both sides, who were idling for one reason or another and launched an enormous kick high into the air. Eddie knew he'd never kicked a ball that far before as soon as it left his boot. It soared over halfway and landed almost on the edge of the opposition penalty area. Only one defender had remained behind when the penalty had been taken and he just headed it straight up in the air. Len, who had been the most alert of his team mates controlled it instantly it came to earth and then unleashed a scorching drive into the roof of Midhouse's net. There was barely time for a restart and seconds later the game was over and Fenton Grammar School were County U13 cup winners beating Midhouse School 6 – 5.

Eddie thought he would have difficulty in swapping the balls back, but the referee awarded him the match ball and no one was any the wiser when he walked off the pitch until, that was, Len went to retrieve his ball from Eddie's goal. He chased after his friend and whispered,

"I knew you were up to something when you asked me to bring my ball. I just knew it – now let me have my ball back and you can have the real match ball."

The two boys engineered the swap before they got on the coach back to Fenton so none of his team mates would be aware of anything amiss.

Eddie's name was mentioned in final assembly on the following Tuesday and he was awarded his colours. Dave Smithers spent the last two days of term mumbling to his colleagues,

"He's a b....y genius. Best penalty save I've ever seen and what a kick!"

Fortunately for Eddie, with the rugby term approaching after Christmas, he would not have the opportunity to demonstrate his supposed prowess for at least another nine months, by which time he hoped his freak show would be forgotten!

7

The Magic Tunnel

Wednesday, December the 18th was the start of the Christmas holidays and was also the first real opportunity that Len and Eddie had had to talk undisturbed about Eddie's amazing save and subsequent punt downfield in the cup final. They hadn't seen each other on the Sunday; it had been Len's thirteenth birthday and the last two days of term had been hectic with Len involved in just about every House football competition and Eddie with the Junior House Larkfield Cup for Technology innovation. Len called round to Fir Tree Close at ten and was greeted with the usual,

"What ho, comrade Len!"

Eddie had started using the appendage to Len's name when they had done a project on Lenin in History.

"Whatcha, sport!" came Len's reply. "Or should that be, Gordon?"

"Stop it, Len! By the way you never said what you got for your birthday."

"Nothing special – just some money and a few clothes. Oh, and thanks for the card by the way, which arrived today; only three days late, mate."

Eddie smiled guiltily at his friend as he emerged from his front door. It was a cold and clear day in Fenton-on-Sea and the boys headed for the High Street with some Christmas shopping in mind. Eddie had his sights set on a nice present for his sister who had had such an awful time for the previous six weeks. He also wanted to look in Watson's Electrical to see what additions he could make to his train set, now that the holidays had arrived and he would have more time to assess his layout. The two boys avoided looking at the scarred road surface as they came out of Fir Tree

Close and it wasn't until they'd crossed over South Road that Len broached the subject of the U13 cup final.

"Do *you* know what happened when you used my ball, Eddie? Did you feel anything? Did you sense which way to go?"

Len's questions seemed endless and Eddie stopped walking and replied,

"Of course I didn't feel anything. I just knew I would save it. That's why I swapped the balls. I felt like I was in Ludmouth again. Old 'Smithers' told me to dive left and I was going to, but right at the last moment I just knew where the ball would go. Don't ask me how I knew, I just did."

"But what about the kick, Eddie? I've only seen professional goalkeepers kick it that far."

"I don't know, Len, what I did. I remember thinking where I wanted the ball to land and just looked there and it worked."

"Was it like it was before with the table? Did you just will it there?"

"Maybe, but I did kick it didn't I?"

"Oh yeah, you kicked it alright!"

"Do you think it's happening again, Len – the magic, I mean?"

"I thought that in Ludmouth, now I'm certain."

Eddie then had a more difficult question.

"If we think what happened on Saturday was magic or out of this world, why haven't people commented on it?"

"Mr Smithson did – I heard him in the corridor," replied Len.

"Yeah, but if what I did was so fantastic, then surely it would be headline news, wouldn't it?"

"Suppose so. Maybe people didn't quite see what we saw. Maybe they weren't allowed to see!"

Eddie guessed what his friend meant. Maybe, like before, some greater power was controlling the 'magic' and they had been chosen again to experience it. They had reached the High Street and their thoughts turned to other things with Len's final comment.

"Rugby next term anyway, mate."

Eddie's search for a nice present for his sister was fruitless and even Watson's Electrical didn't have anything that took his fancy. Coming out of the shop Len suddenly remembered something.

"Forgot to tell you, Eddie; Dad's nearly finished the tunnel for you. I've seen it and it looks brilliant. He's made it special because of what you have been through with your sister. He was finishing it this morning. Shall I come over this afternoon with it?"

"Oh yes, excellent!"

Len wasn't as excited as his friend but tried not to show it. He still had vague memories of the time he had first used the controller and, though nothing really outrageous had happened then, he still had a slight feeling it might in the future. It had with his football! Eddie, for his part, had experienced nothing extraordinary and neither had his dad.

Coming back up out of Mill Road and into the High Street once more they paid their statutory visit to Woolworth's, but didn't stay long or spend any money – it was packed with Christmas shoppers and the queues were yards long. Eddie left his friend at the entrance to Lime Tree Avenue and made his way home for lunch. Len would come round between two and three with the newly made tunnel.

Jenny had been out of plaster for just a week when she went back to work at Arleson's the bakers that Wednesday morning. She had wanted to go back at the start of the week, but her shoulder had still been in a sling and serving and taking money would have been so slow for her that Sam

Arleson would have lost money and customers. Remarkably, her ankle had healed much quicker than Dr Carter had suggested at the end of October and she was able to walk the three quarters of a mile to work in relative comfort, albeit, slowly. Sam Arleson insisted that she sat on a stool for most of the day and served customers as and when she could. He also paid for a taxi to take her home at the end of the day.

That Wednesday was one of the three days each week when Danny Arleson helped his dad by tending to the ovens at the back of the shop. On Monday and Tuesdays Danny helped Steve Paton in his garage, Paton's Autos, two miles out of Fenton on South Road. Ever since she had returned to work that morning, Jenny had been plucking up the courage to ask Danny how Gary was getting on in his new job which he had held for over seven weeks. Just before lunchtime, when the morning rush was over, Jenny went out back to the bakery on the pretext of collecting the afternoon's batch of bread. She had to be careful as far as talking to Danny was concerned because of an incident that had occurred back in early January when, only sixteen, she had tried to flirt with him and then accused him of trying to kiss her. Soft and slightly naïve Danny, despite his thirty-eight years, had forgiven Jenny for her 'game' and was probably flattered by the whole experience anyway. Danny looked a little nervous when Jenny approached him with obviously more to say than just: 'Where's the bread, Danny'?

"Danny?"

"Yes, Jennifer?"

"How's Gary getting on with Mr Paton?"

"Alright, but he's not much use as a mechanic yet. Tyre changing and washing and polishing are about his limit. I think Steve Paton finds his dad's contacts in the trade to be useful though – often gets him good second-hand cars to sell."

"Does he seem happy, Danny?"

"I don't know what you mean by happy. He does what Steve asks of him and he's polite to the customers. I'm only there three days a week and for one of those Gary is at college in Hamsden doing car mechanics."

"Does he have a girl friend?"

"No idea. How would I know that, Jenny?"

"Does he talk about anyone, then?"

"He doesn't talk much at all. The accident seems to have quietened him down. I think he spends a lot of his spare time at home listening to his records. At weekends he helps his dad in his car showroom in Hamsden. He may follow his dad into the business of buying and selling cars."

'He *has* changed', thought Jenny as she remembered all the times that Gary had sworn blind that he would never follow his dad into the family business. She thanked Danny politely and just managed to get back to the front of the shop before Danny's dad appeared to see where she'd gone to.

"Come on, Jen, there are customers waiting to be served. The afternoon bread won't be ready yet."

"Yes, Mr Arleson."

Jenny had a warm feeling inside her for the rest of that Wednesday afternoon. Gary appeared unattached and a reformed character. Time would tell whether she would still swoon over the new slightly boring Gary Jones. She made up her mind that she would try to find out by engineering a visit to Steve Paton's Autos or to Richard Jones' Cars in Hamsden.

Cyril Wilby came with his son to bring the newly made tunnel to Eddie's house. He wanted to see if it fitted the track layout. Len had given him all the measurements including the height and width of *Flying Scotsman*. Wrapped in newspaper, it wasn't unveiled until everyone, including Eddie's mum, was in the Compton's dining room. Eddie gasped with delight.

"Oh wow! It's brilliant!"

"Glad you like it, Eddie," said Len's dad. I know you must have had a terrible time these last few weeks – just wanted to brighten your life up."

"Thanks, Mr Wilby. What's it made of and how did you know it would match all the other bits?"

"I had a spy, Eddie!"

Len grinned. The tunnel itself was bigger than Eddie had imagined it to be – at least two feet long – long enough to 'swallow' the engine and nearly two of the three carriages. Cyril Wilby continued.

"It's mainly made from wood and I used a special resin to make the moulded shape, both inside and out. Let's put it in position. I hope you got the measurements right, Len."

Mr Wilby needn't have worried because it fitted perfectly, enclosing either of the long side pieces of the track with enough room on entry and exit for the train to negotiate the curves at either end. Eddie had added track piece by piece and the layout now completely covered the hoarding base which itself overlapped the extended table by a few inches all round. The tunnel also fitted snugly over the siding which extended the oval at one end.

Ann Compton made Cyril a cup of tea before he went back home. Len and Eddie spent some time arranging and rearranging the layout. Len seemed quieter than usual and Eddie eventually asked,

"What's up, mate? You seem preoccupied with something – not getting the 'flu at last, eh?"

"No, I'm fine. I was just thinking of the other tunnel and our ghost, Mr Manders."

"You haven't seen him in Fenton, have you?" said Eddie sarcastically.

"Yeah, Dad and I saw him on the way over here. He had a pick and shovel in his hands!"

"Don't joke, Len, you might start something."

Eddie took the control first while Len did the timing of each circuit with the second hand of his watch, but after a few minutes they both thought that the tunnel's position needed adjusting as the train seemed to be brushing against its inside. Eddie managed to get the train to stop with most of it in the tunnel while his friend peered inside to see if he could spot any places where the train was touching the sides or roof.

"All clear, driver, plenty of room!"

Eddie slowly eased Flying Scotsman out of the tunnel and Len checked that it remained clear when the train followed the curve of the track.

"Alright now, Len."

"Yep, but have you got some tape that we can use to hold the tunnel in place? It might be the train's vibration that makes the tunnel wander away from its position."

"Good thinking, guard!"

Eddie found some sticky tape in a kitchen draw and by folding pieces over he managed to fix the tunnel reasonably securely in place. The two boys swapped positions and roles. Len pushed the lever over and the train responded precisely and without anticipation, – so far so good, he thought. Eddie timed four circuits but still seemed unhappy.

"It doesn't go as fast with the tunnel."

"How do you know?"

"Just a feeling. I know – take the tunnel away and we'll do a control test without it."

Len pulled the tunnel from its position and Eddie said,

"We'll do three circuits and you just time the whole journey, then we'll divide the total time by three."

"You mean, you'll divide the total time by three," replied Len.

"Ready, Len? Time the circuits using the front of the engine. Three-two-one, go!"

After a short while Len announced,

"Forty-one seconds, chief."

Immediately Eddie said,

"Thirteen point six recurring."

"Alright, Einstein, now what?"

"Now we do the same with the tunnel in place."

The tunnel was returned to its taped position and they went through the whole procedure again. This time at the end Len said,

"Fifty-two seconds."

"Seventeen point three recurring," said Eddie. "That's nearly four seconds a lap slower."

"So what?"

Len was getting bored with his friend's scientific experiments and his mental calculations and said,

"I've had enough, Eddie. It doesn't prove anything. You might not have had your thumb hard on the lever all the time."

"I did, Len. I know I did."

"Well there might have been a drop in power. There are all sorts of reasons."

So Eddie insisted on repeating the experiment and this time with Len at the control. He smiled knowingly when the same results were more or less achieved.

"Three point five seconds slower."

Len didn't seem to hear his friend, but was still staring at the tunnel. He came out of his trance and said quietly,

"I noticed something else this time, mate."

"What?"

"When the train was in the tunnel, the engine didn't come out until all the carriages were in!"

"That's impossible, Len, look I'll show you!"

Eddie engineered the train into the tunnel and positioned it with the front of the engine just poking out. One and half carriages were still outside the tunnel at the rear.

They tried another circuit without timing it and with Len operating the control. Both boys stared intently at the tunnel focusing on the whole train. They couldn't believe how they'd missed it before. For a split second NONE of the train was visible outside the tunnel. When both boys had done the timing before they had been too busy concentrating on *Flying Scotsman's* front end that they'd never even glanced at its rear!

"Oh no, Len!" said Eddie. "My train's like your football – magic."

"Not your train, mate, it's my dad's tunnel doing it."

"Yeah, but the tunnel didn't disappear like my train. Where did it go?"

Ever practical Len didn't have an answer this time and simply said,

"It was like the train concertinaed and occupied less space than it needed."

Thoughts of Einstein's Theory of Relativity surfaced in Eddie's mind and even some of the tales from his science fiction comics where spaceships experienced time warps and instant movement through space. Len quickly broke his daydream.

"I wonder if Mr Canter knew his presents were magic."

"How could he know? I mean the train set came from Harrod's."

"It was *in* a Harrod's box."

"What d'you mean, Len?"

"I mean he could have got the train set elsewhere and just put it in a Harrod's box and besides, there are no manufacturer's markings on the inner box, so who's to say where he got it from."

It was true, thought Eddie, that the inner box just had a print or painting of the *Flying Scotsman* and a fairly old one at that, maybe from the thirties when the train had been in its heyday. The engine and carriages, however, had all the hallmarks of sixties technology. Len interrupted his thoughts again.

"Eddie, you take the control and I'm going to look into the tunnel and try and see what happens."

Len knelt down and, putting his head to one side on the table, positioned himself in such a way that he could see right through the tunnel from one end to the other. Eddie nervously pushed the switch over.

"She's coming, Len."

"Hurry up! I've got neck ache."

Eddie watched from the outside as again the train momentarily disappeared. Len took a sharp intake of breath.

"Oh God, Eddie!" was all he could muster.

"What, mate?" asked Eddie nervously.

"Do it again. Quick, do it again!"

Eddie did it again and this time Len seemed to be so mesmerised that he forgot to lift his head out of the way and his gaping mouth nearly formed a second tunnel for the *Flying Scotsman*! Eddie was so excited he nearly pushed his friend out of the way to see if he could catch a last glimpse.

"What did you see, Len? What?"

Len stood up and he was shaking while he tried to express in words what he'd seen.

"It was real, Eddie. It was real, mate!"

"Real?"

"It was like I was in a film. I could see the driver and there was a passenger with their head out of the window and…." Len sat down on a chair and went on, "and the train had its lights on and there was smoke filling the tunnel and…."

"Slow down, Len, and keep your voice down. Mum's still in the house somewhere."

As if on cue, Eddie's mum poked her head round the door and asked,

"Some orange squash, boys?" and seeing Len, she continued, "Are you alright, Len?"

"Oh, oh, yes, Mrs Compton. We're having a great time."

Eddie's mum disappeared into the kitchen to make the drinks and Eddie whispered,

"You'd got to your fourth or fifth 'and', mate. What else did you see?"

Len went pale and looked sick.

"When you sent it in the second time the passenger with their head out of the window was still there and they…, they didn't see something sticking out of the tunnel wall and…."

Len didn't need to finish his description of the ghastly scene as Eddie said,

"Alright, Len, it wasn't real, mate."

"You have a look, Eddie. Please, you have a look."

Eddie's mum returned with their drinks and said,

"Have a look at what, Len?"

"Oh nothing, Mum. Len was just asking me to have a look at the controller as it didn't seem to be working properly," Eddie lied.

"Are you alright, Len? You look pale. Not coming down with the 'flu, are you?"

"No, Mrs Compton, I'm fine."

Ann Compton made her way back out of the room and as she did so, Eddie asked,

"Where are you going now, Mum?"

His mum looked somewhat oddly at her son.

"Just to do some more reading in the garden, if you need to know," and with that surprised remark she was gone. The boys gave Eddie's mum a few minutes to reach the isolation of the back garden and Len repeated his plea.

"You've got to have a look, Eddie."

"Alright, but if you're making this all up to scare me the train set goes straight away and you won't play with it again. O.K?"

Len mumbled his agreement and Eddie took up the required position with his head on the table. Len pulled the switch and waited in trepidation for his friend to get the fright of his life, whether the same or a different scene took place.

"Here she comes!"

The train moved smoothly into the tunnel disappearing fully as had become almost normal. Eddie kept his head down until the last moment and then stood up.

No sharp intake of breath. Len was shaking with anticipation.

"Well, what did you see?"

"Nothing."

"Nothing?"

"Well nothing out of the ordinary, Len. I saw the engine come in – just the toy engine and although it seemed to take longer than it should, I didn't see anything else. It didn't even look as if it became compressed, but you wouldn't be able to tell that from head on anyway."

"No people?"

"Afraid not, Len. All I could see was the front of the engine and it was *my* engine."

Len paced up and down the Compton's dining room. Eddie couldn't work out whether he was still in shock from the ghastly sight he'd seen or he was simply distraught because his friend hadn't seen a thing. In the end Eddie tried to placate his friend with,

"You know, we shouldn't be that surprised if only one of us sees something or experiences something. Take your ball for example. It only worked its magic for me. Maybe my train is only going to perform its full repertoire of tricks for you. We know well by now that fantasy and so-called magic only happen to a chosen few. You can't have forgotten that only I could control the table on our fantastic journey."

Len began to calm down and sat at the table, somewhat exhausted. Again the greater power had used Eddie to settle his friend's imaginings.

"I know you're right, Eddie, but it was horrible, just horrible."

Eddie was about to say: 'I know, Len', but stopped himself because he didn't know. He didn't know or want to know what his friend had actually seen, though he could guess. Instead he said,

"I hope you can soon forget it, mate. We both know what you saw wasn't real."

Even as he said the words Eddie knew they sounded hollow and pointless as there was a fine line between nightmares and reality. Some of Eddie's dreams in the past had probably been as real as Len's experience but therein lies the problem, he thought, 'Could nightmares become reality or, indeed, reality turn into nightmares'?

Within another few minutes Len began to cheer up, almost despite Eddie's feeble attempt to bring reality to the situation. It appeared to Eddie that some other force or thought had worked its power on Len and within no time he was his jovial and ebullient self, but he had had enough of playing with Eddie's train set.

"Probably just imagined it, mate and anyway, I'm bored with it now."

However, Eddie guessed that his friend *hadn't* imagined it and Len himself, deep down, actually knew he hadn't too.

8

A Birthday Present and a Reunion

When Len eventually went home that afternoon, and despite the apparent lightening of his mood, he still seemed a little troubled by his experience with Eddie's train set. He left his friend standing in the doorway to number 38 and was about halfway down the Compton's front path when he suddenly turned round and said in a quiet voice, so that no one else should hear,

"It *was* real, Eddie. What do you think it means?"

"Nothing, mate; just try to forget it and remember, it's *my* train set and it's still at *my* house."

But Len had another question and he walked back up the path to confront Eddie.

"Do you think it has got anything to do with that tunnel we discovered in Ludmouth? I mean, that was a railway tunnel, wasn't it?"

For once, Eddie had not been thinking of the same possible link and was genuinely surprised by his friend's thought.

"How could it be? There's no way that the *Flying Scotsman* was ever on that small branch line from Ludmouth Junction let alone in a tunnel that was either never used or if it was, then only up to a hundred years ago"

But Len had more to say.

"You never heard it, Eddie. I would swear that both trains sounded the same – the same rhythm from the wheels on the rails."

"Most trains sound the same, Len," said Eddie. "It's to do with the rails not necessarily the particular train."

"Suppose you're right; it just seems a strange coincidence."

"Len, it's four months since we were in Ludmouth. How could you remember the noise correctly anyway? Your mind is just playing tricks on you. I'm not dismissing the idea – I just think your mind is bound to make a connection between the two totally unrelated events, considering the state it was in an hour ago. If I'd seen what you hinted at then I would probably make the same link. Doesn't mean there *is* a link, though."

Len seemed about to say something important but merely nodded and finished with,

"Yes, I guess so. Just a coincidence, as you say. Anyway, got to go. See you tomorrow. Fancy going to Hamsden on the bus to do some Christmas shopping –better than Fenton?"

"I'll see what my mum says. Come round anyway between nine and ten. Alright?"

"O.K., Eddie."

After Len had gone, Eddie did eventually pack his train set away but not before he had tried it out several times more. He shut the dining room door and with the controller in one hand he peered into the tunnel, but nothing untoward happened. Even watching from a normal position the train didn't 'disappear' in the tunnel; no compression or any concertina effect. However, he knew that his friend was still bothered by what had happened. They never went by bus to Hamsden – always by train.

Len came round to Eddie's house by nine-thirty the following morning, clutching what looked like a thick old book under his arm. He was clearly much brighter in spirit when Eddie opened his front door.

"Whatcha, sport!" he announced.

"What ho, comrade!"

"Got another present today, in the post, Eddie."

Len looked excited, as though he was about to say: 'I told you so'!

"What?"

"This!" and Len produced his surprise from under his arm. "It's a railway timetable. It's got over a thousand pages."

Eddie read the cover of the massive volume.

Bradshaw's General Railway, Steam Navigation And Hotel Guide For Great Britain And Ireland 1935

"Wow! Even my dad hasn't got one of these, Len," said a spellbound Eddie. Can he have a look at it later?"

"Of course he can; that's why I brought it round. I bet it might be worth a lot of money, since it's in such good condition."

'Good condition' was indeed an understatement for the book which Eddie held in his hands. Though clearly old, as the date on the cover confirmed, it was in as pristine a condition as the day it had been printed; still in its original buff dust jacket with the white pages inside looking as if they had never felt human fingers or thumbs before.

"It looks brand new, Len."

"Yep, and it's got Ludmouth in it and the ACE still left Waterloo in 1935 as it did when we went on it last summer."

Len had been so excited with his present that Eddie had not had a chance to ask the obvious question.

"Who gave it to you, Len?"

Len paused and, looking behind his friend, he whispered,

"Let's go inside and I'll tell you."

They were still standing at Eddie's front door and Eddie's mum was approaching in the hall. Len held the timetable behind his back.

"Hello, Len, I hear you and Eddie are off to Hamsden."

"Yes, Mrs Compton."

"When are you going?"

"Catching the ten past ten bus, Mum," interrupted Eddie.

"Bus?"

"Yes, Mum. We thought it would make a change and, besides, it's cheaper."

"Alright, what are you going to do until then?"

"Len's brought a new game that he got for his birthday," lied Eddie. "Can we use the dining room?"

Yes, as long as you leave it in the state you find it. I'll be in the kitchen; just let me know when you're going. Happy birthday by the way, Len – a teenager at last!"

"Yes, Mrs Compton."

The boys disappeared into the Compton's dining room, conveniently situated at the opposite end of the hall from the kitchen. Once inside, and with the door shut as was usual when they played card or board games, Len was first to speak.

"Why on earth did you say I'd brought a game, Eddie? What if your mum had asked to see it?"

"Well, she didn't, did she?"

Len placed the book on the table and said,

"Have a look inside the front cover, mate. Go on."

Eddie looked nervous, but bent over and turned the front cover over.

"Read what it says," said Len.

Eddie's eyes could barely focus on the copperplate writing, because immediately on opening the book they had been distracted by a familiar name. However, he read out loud,

"To Len for your thirteenth birthday,
from your friend Jake Manders."

Eddie went silent. Underneath, and in slightly different writing though still clearly by the same hand, was written:

Sorry if this arrives late, JDM.

Eddie closed the book as if by doing so he could pretend that he hadn't read what he'd read. After what seemed an age he managed to think in practical terms.

"What did you tell your mum and dad? Didn't they want to know who Jake is or was? What did you say, Len?"

"Dad was out when the post came and my mum only had a brief look when I showed her. She didn't look inside and I just told her we'd met a Mr Manders when we were on holiday and he'd sent it. I said we'd met him at the guest house and that he'd told us about the fossils."

"Didn't she seem surprised that you received a present from a complete stranger?"

"Not when I told her it was only an old train timetable. I also made up that I'd told him I was keen on trains after our journey from Fenton to Ludmouth."

Eddie thought for a moment. Several other questions had formed in his mind, but he had an immediate worry.

"I can't show it to my dad, Len. We made Mr Manders up, remember?"

"I've thought of that – you can say that my Uncle Reg sent it from Chester."

Eddie thought his friend to be pretty dense and said,

"Don't be stupid, Len. He won't believe that. The book is too new; like it was printed only yesterday. He knows too much about railway timetables. This one seems to me to be all part of the same 'magic' surrounding my train set. You just can't find forty-year-old books in this condition, not unless they had been vacuum sealed and stored in darkness for all that time and Len...."

"And what?"

"And is your Uncle Reg's other name Jake Manders, then?! All things considered," Eddie continued, sarcastically, "I don't think I'll show it to Dad, Len."

"Oh, alright, then. I suppose you're right, Eddie, but why did he send it to me?"

"I don't know, mate, but aren't you forgetting something?"

"What?"

"You are joking, aren't you? Mr Manders is a ghost, Len!"

Len laughed and realised the funny side of the situation, but Eddie had more questions for his friend.

"Didn't your mum want to know how our 'ghost' knew where you lived *and* when your birthday was? Because, Len, old son, if she didn't want to know then there's someone else not sitting a million miles away from you, that does!"

"Who?"

Eddie couldn't believe his friend's idiotic question.

"Me, you fool!"

Len grinned.

"Well, *old son*, you too are forgetting that Mr Manders is a ghost, so surely, anything is possible."

"Agreed as far as we're concerned, but your mum doesn't know he's a ghost, you twit! She must have been surprised, if not staggered, that he knew your address and birthday. Didn't she ask you?" asked Eddie again.

"Yes, and I simply told her he must have got them from the visitors' book. If you remember we had to write our names and addresses there. I put mine separately from your mum and dad's."

"Yeah, but what about the date of your birthday?"

"I told her that I'd mentioned to the man that I was going to be thirteen, ten days before Christmas. He'd asked me how old I was, I told her. She seemed satisfied. That helped explain the bit about the present possibly being late."

Eddie seemed satisfied that Mrs Wilby had believed her son's story to explain the arrival of the present, but had one more concern.

"What if your mum mentions to my mum about the present and that a Mr Manders sent it to you? We or, at least I, made him up!"

Len had clearly not thought of the possibility. He shrugged his shoulders.

"Mum hasn't seen much of your mum since our holiday – they hardly meet up in the winter."

"But they phone each other," Eddie continued. Len was quiet until he said,

"I've got an idea to cover that possibility, Eddie."

"So you agree it's a possibility, then."

"Yes, but there may be a way round the problem. My mum doesn't know I was going to bring the timetable over here to show you; she'd already gone down town shopping before I left to come here."

"So?"

"So I'll simply say that I don't want you to know about it as I didn't think Mr Manders got the date of your birthday. I was the only one who had talked about our ages and I'll tell her you would be jealous if I was to get a birthday present and not you. That way, when and if my mum talks to your mum, she won't mention the book."

"We'll have to hope you're right, mate," said Eddie finally. "Best if you hide the timetable away in your room somewhere and hope that your dad doesn't want to see it. He may not accept your story of how you got it."

"He won't see it. He's not interested in trains; not like your dad, anyway. If he asks I'll just say it's an old railway timetable; probably from a jumble sale – as I say, my mum didn't get much of a look at it."

Eddie seemed satisfied that adult investigations might not take place and looking at his watch he said,

"It's ten to, Len; you'll have to take the timetable home before we catch the bus, so we need to go now. Have you got a key to get in?"

"Yes, I just hope my dad's not back. He was going into school to tidy up the workshop."

Eddie shouted a quick goodbye to his mum and the two boys left 38 Fir Tree Close and ran to Lime Tree Avenue where Len dashed to his house while Eddie waited on the corner. Len soon rejoined his friend and from his demeanour all seemed well.

"Dad's not back and I stashed it at the back of my wardrobe behind loads of other books I never read. Mum never goes there."

It was five past ten and the two boys sprinted the 200 yards or so to the bus stop on South Road almost knocking someone over in the process.

"Leonard, slow down!" shouted Cyril Wilby as he grabbed his son by the arms.

"Whoops, sorry, Dad; we're late for the bus," and wriggling free, he continued, "got to go, see you later."

Mr Wilby was left slightly dazed and bewildered, but was none the wiser to where his son had just been.

The bus was nearly five minutes late in arriving and in that time Eddie made an observation on his friend's apparent well-being after the previous day's ghastly event.

"You seem happier today, mate."

"Yes, I am; now I'm convinced there is a connection between all the events, whether real or not and whether imagined or not. I'm sure Mr Manders is at the heart of it."

Eddie found it hard to disagree as he had apparently the previous day and, deciding not to raise the question of where his friend's football fitted in, he said simply,

"I agree, Len."

Almost as Eddie had finished speaking, a bright red Eastern Shires double-decker bus appeared from the High Street and turned into South Road. The boys caught the number 201 and alighted at Hamsden bus station at five to eleven.

Eddie eventually managed to buy his sister a nice, and rather expensive, boxed soap and perfume set in her favourite fragrance – a sneaky visit to Jenny's bedroom had given him the brand name. Len bought some small gifts for his mum and dad and the two boys just managed to catch the quarter to one bus for the return journey home. Sitting at the front on the top deck they returned to their earlier conversation.

"Do you think George and Mr Manders are connected in some way," said Len.

"How could they be? They were born in different centuries and different countries," and Eddie paused. "I don't think there has to be a reason this time for what's happening, you know, Len."

"What do you mean?"

"Well, I've been thinking about George's letter. He said we were to have fun and to share the presents and, although it hasn't been much fun for you yet, we do seem to be in some sort of game and he also said that we wouldn't come to any harm. I just think that he wants us to have fun like we did before, but not, this time, with necessarily any goal in mind. It's just his way of repaying us for the help we gave him. The ball he sent you helped the school win the cup and that was fun for me. My train set seems to give you visions and not me, so that we're kind of sharing the presents as well, just as George said."

Len seemed cheered by his friend's assessment and said,

"So that means all kinds of things might happen to us, both good and bad."

"Maybe, Len. I think it makes it easier to think of it like that. Though what you saw was as real as anything else you see, it should make us both relax, if we assume we can never come to any harm. The fun bit is not knowing what's going to happen next."

"Maybe we'll go somewhere like we did before," said Len.

Jenny had the last Saturday before Christmas off from the bakery; she had agreed to work until four Christmas Eve. She hadn't ventured out of Fenton since that awful day at the end of October. Her mum was not too happy when she announced at breakfast that she was going to go on the train to Hamsden.

"Oh Jenny, love, are you sure you're ready to walk round Hamsden? It will be very busy today."

"Yes, Mum. I'm sure. Mr Arleson let me stay on my feet all yesterday morning in the shop and I must have walked miles back and forth," she exaggerated.

"Why don't you come with us in the car – we're going shopping there this morning. In fact, I insist, dear."

Jenny's plan to go and see Gary was beginning to go awry as her mum looked adamant. She relented slightly thinking that if she was dropped on the east side of town she'd be close to the garage in any case.

"Oh alright, Mum; as long as dad drops me near the library. I want to get a book to read."

Ann Compton had a wry look on her face and said,

"A book, Jenny? You're going to read a book, love?"

"Yes, Mum," and she paused. "No one to go out with now so I might as well occupy my time some other way," she lied, as her dad looked up from his paper with an odd look on his face. Fred Compton knew his daughter too well to believe that she'd suddenly become interested in reading books. He didn't know, of course, that Hamsden public library was situated less than fifty yards from Richard Jones' Cars. Fortunately, also for Jenny, Eddie had already gone back up to his bedroom before meeting up with Len to go down town to 'Woolies'. If he had heard that his sister was going to get a book to read he would likely have fallen off his chair in disbelief, let alone the merciless taunting she would have got.

"And, Mum…?" Jenny continued.

"What, dear?"

"If I come with you and Dad, I'm not coming round the shops with you –alright?"

"O.K., but at least you won't have that long walk to and from the station. We'll meet up with you for a coffee in Pritchard's later."

"Good, I'd like that," said Jenny finally, thinking at the same time that it would be a small price to pay.

Len called round for Eddie just as Jenny and her parents were climbing into Fred Compton's Morris Minor. The morning was sunny but cold and the weather looked set fair for the day, prompting Ann Compton to call out after her son,

"Don't be later than half past one, Eddie."

"O.K., Mum," shouted Eddie as the two boys made their way out of the front gate.

Thirty-five minutes later Fred Compton dropped his daughter as near as he could to the library in Hamsden. As she was about to get out of the car Jenny's mum said,

"Have you still got your library ticket, love?"

"Yes, Mum," lied Jenny.

"You may have to get a new one, love. Yours was only valid till you were sixteen."

"I know, Mum," replied Jenny and with that she stepped onto the pavement and was quickly lost among the Christmas shoppers.

Jenny decided to just look in the window of the showroom, hoping she could catch Gary's eye. She wandered up and down in front of the glass and double-fronted building, ignoring the occasional strange look from passers-by. Jenny pretended to be studying the cars in the window which, as far as the male shoppers of Hamsden were concerned, was not how an attractive seventeen-year-old girl should spend her Saturday morning. As a result, she had to endure one or two stereotypical comments. Jenny didn't at first spot Gary – only Mr Jones was visible in the showroom attending to a potential customer. Peering over one of the second-hand cars she managed to just glimpse his fair hair in the office at the rear of the showroom and tried to attract his attention without his dad noticing. She soon realised that it was almost impossible to accomplish such a task and even thought that Richard Jones had seen her. Jenny didn't know what to do. She was still attracting odd looks; one or two shoppers were even peering over her shoulder to see what she was staring at. After another five minutes had gone by, Jenny decided to go to the library and, at least, carry out the pretence for coming to Hamsden. She would try to come back later, she thought.

Gary Jones *had* seen Jenny peering through the showroom window and it had disturbed him. He didn't know what to think. Was she looking for him and if so, why? He didn't really want to see her – he still felt too embarrassed and he had never actually said sorry to her face. He'd tried several times to build up the courage to go and see her, particularly latterly when she had still been in hospital. It was eleven o'clock and he couldn't concentrate on his job. He wandered into the showroom not sure what to do next. His dad left the customer he was dealing with and marched over to him. He immediately suspected something was wrong when he had to repeat his question three times.

"Get the file on the Wolseley, Gary."

"What, Dad?" replied Gary eventually.

"The Wolseley. Get the log book and service history. I've got a customer waiting."

"Yes, Dad."

"What *is* the matter, son? You look like you've seen a ghost."

"Nothing, Dad – I'll get the file from the back office."

The simple task that his dad had set him seemed to take Gary ages and his dad had to come looking for him.

"It's under W, Gary!" he barked in his son's ear.

"Sorry, Dad, I've got it now," said Gary and he handed the file to his dad.

"You're useless. Go and take a break – have a walk in town and get yourself a coffee or something."

Gary didn't need a second invitation and quickly made his way out of the showroom. 'Maybe I can find Jenny', he thought.

They met entirely by accident. Jenny had spent some time in the library renegotiating her borrower's card; the young assistant being initially unwilling to issue a new one without seeing the old one, but eventually a more senior colleague came to Jenny's rescue. She then had gone straight to the romantic fiction section and selected the first book she saw: *A Chance to Dream* by a Barbara Waverton. She thought the title very apt as that was precisely what she had been doing over the previous few weeks. Now all she needed was *A Chance Meeting*.

She spent the next half an hour wandering aimlessly around the shopping area of Hamsden desperately trying to avoid bumping in to her parents. In the end she disappeared into the anonymity of Osborne's, the biggest department store in the town. She decided to browse the ladies' fashion department on the top floor which happened to also house the store's coffee shop. Jenny had looked at several winter jumpers and was just going to try one on when a familiar voice called to her from the coffee area.

"Jenny!"

Jenny turned round and, seeing no one, thought initially that the voice was just in her head.

"Jenny, it's me, Gary," said the voice now right beside her. There stood Gary Jones, smiling nervously and with his head tilted to one side. Jenny thought she was going to faint and wanted to throw her arms round the subject of her dreams, but Gary pre-empted her and planted a light kiss on her forehead. He seemed reluctant to hug her because he was still unaware of her physical condition. He held her right hand gently and said,

"Jenny, I'm so sorry. I was a fool. I don't expect you to forgive me, but I just want you to know that I am deeply and truly sorry for what I did."

Jenny was in shock. She had never heard Gary talk so honestly and she could see from his face that his guilt was genuine. This was not the old Gary and she actually felt that he had probably been through more pain and torture in his mind than she had with her physical injuries. She could see real tears welling up in his eyes and she knew that it had taken a lot for him to say what he had just said.

"Don't, Gary. Don't feel guilty and I *do* forgive you. I know you were only showing off to me and you've taken your punishment."

"But, Jenny, I could have killed you."

"Or both of us," said Jenny. "But you didn't and anyway, you didn't set out deliberately to cause the accident – you just drove too fast and you've learnt your lesson, I hope."

"I'm not sure I want to drive again and can't for another year anyway."

They had been standing for several minutes facing each other and Gary had not released his surprisingly gentle grip on Jenny's hand and he now led her to where he had been sitting having his coffee. As they sat down Jenny seemed reluctant to let go of his hand, almost as if she thought she might lose him. Gary was first to speak.

"What have you been doing, Jenny?"

"Nothing much, you idiot! I've only been out of plaster for just over a week."

Gary blushed deeply.

"What about you?" continued Jenny nervously – she was fearful of what he might say.

"Same as you – nothing."

"You're not going out with…?"

"No, Jenny, I'm not. Maybe *we* could…"

Then Jenny's eyes went watery and a single tear rolled down her cheek. She felt safe and happy again.

The two reunited teenagers chatted together for another twenty minutes, until Jenny suddenly realised that she should have been at Pritchard's Coffee House ten minutes earlier to meet her parents. Gary wanted to escort her there but Jenny told him that it was best if she went on her own as her parents would probably not be happy to see him. She left him quickly, planting a kiss firmly on his lips and with a whispered:

"See you soon. I'll phone you."

Jenny was relieved to find that her parents had only just arrived at the coffee shop when she got there. After they were all seated at a table Jenny's mum said,

"You look happy, Jenny. What's cheered you up?"

"Oh nothing, Mum, just met some old friends who I hadn't seen for ages."

"Who, dear?"

"You wouldn't know them – just some girls from school."

Jenny's mum seemed satisfied. She was certainly pleased that her daughter was getting back out and about again. Fred Compton wasn't so sure and suspected that the excited and flushed face of his daughter could mean something else.

9

Nowhere

Len and Eddie didn't see much of each other again until the Saturday immediately following Boxing Day. Both boys had actually been quite keen to play with the 'magic' train set again given that they believed they were now in some sort of 'friendly' game. Circumstances, however, had only allowed them their morning visit to 'Woolies' on the Saturday when Eddie's sister had been reunited with Gary Jones. Mr and Mrs Wilby did invite Eddie round for tea on the day before Christmas Eve when the boys tried to make *Len's* train set work, but without much success. Otherwise both friends were tied up with all the usual preparations for Christmas and the various visits of relations. Eddie, for one, was beginning to grow out of the traditional magic of Christmas and also the inevitable hugs and kisses from Aunties he saw once a year. He had other magic he wanted to experience.

It was pouring with rain when Len called round to Eddie's house on Saturday, December the 27th and they quickly ruled out going down town, despite the start of the after Christmas sales. Both boys had money to spend but didn't want to go with Eddie's mum and dad who were off to Hamsden for the morning. Jenny had already gone to work and, unbeknown to her parents, she had arranged to meet Gary at lunchtime. He was not back at work until the following Monday and he was now full-time with his dad in the showroom.

Eddie and Len, therefore, had the house to themselves and there was only one thing on their minds. The layout was put together in record time; each of them expected something strange to happen at any moment. Eddie wanted a slight change to the track.

"Put the tunnel on the opposite side of the track, Len."

"Why?"

"Just to see what happens and, besides, the light shines into it better there."

Len looked nervous until Eddie continued,

"It's only a game, mate."

"You hope."

Len took the controller and starting the train from the opposite side to the tunnel he pushed the lever. He didn't feel any anticipation this time and *Flying Scotsman* moved smoothly away. Eddie was already in position peering into the tunnel while Len watched for any 'compression'. The train came out and Len eased his thumb off the switch bringing the train to a halt more or less where it had started.

"Well?" asked Len.

"Nothing that I could see, mate, but...."

"I knew there'd be a 'but'," said Len.

"It sounded very loud; the noise from the rails, I mean," said Eddie.

"I didn't hear anything unusual from here. Sure you weren't imagining it?"

"Not sure. What about you – did the train concertina, like before?"

"Yes, definitely."

The boys swapped positions and roles. Len was very nervous – he'd been the one for which the train had misbehaved. Consequently he didn't look inside the tunnel but just put his ear to the track.

They repeated the process but as soon as the train entered the tunnel Len jumped up and screamed,

"Stop it! It's deafening!"

Len stood up completely and moved away from the table.

"I could hear the engine and the whistle. It was real and just like I was right inside the tunnel; it was that loud, Eddie. You must have heard it."

Eddie shook his head.

"Sounded normal to me. Did you hear anything else," said Eddie half expecting his friend to say, 'Just someone screaming', but he replied,

"Don't think so; just the whistle and the steam from the engine. It was unbelievably loud."

They tried it again with Eddie looking and listening at the tunnel's exit but this time he couldn't decide if the train noise was louder than normal or not.

"Not as loud as last time and anyway maybe it sounds louder because I was so close."

Again they repeated the experiment and this time neither of them listened at the tunnel's exit but watched from the opposite side of the table. The concertina effect was much more marked as the whole train seemed to completely disappear for a second or two, but there was no change in the noise level.

"I hope it doesn't disappear and not come out again," said Len.

"Let's take the tunnel away and see if anything happens," replied Eddie.

Len seemed to notice something on the second circuit without the tunnel.

"I'm sure it still seemed to disappear, Eddie, or at least, it looked fainter as though I was looking at it through a misty window. Did you notice it?"

Eddie shook his head.

"Did it shrink as well?"

"No, I don't think so."

They tried it several times more, still without the tunnel in place, but nothing untoward happened – no shrinking or disappearance, faint or otherwise. Finally, Len knew what his friend was going to suggest – to place the tunnel back on the side of the track where it had been when he had had his horrible experience.

"I'm not watching, though," he said.

"Neither of us will," replied Eddie. "Give me the controller."

Len stood as far from the track as the walls of the dining room would allow and waited while Eddie pushed the switch. The train entered the tunnel and immediately it did so the room was plunged into blackness, absolute and all-encompassing. The room shook with the reverberation of engine and track noise. Eddie dropped the control and fell backwards against the dining room wall and screamed,

"What the....?"

After what seemed an age both boys slid down the opposite walls of the dining room and sat down in silence and utter darkness. The noise of the train had stopped, but not the shaking. Eddie felt around himself and whispered to his friend,

"I'm sitting on a chair, Len."

"So am I."

Eddie, for one, knew that the dining table chairs had been pushed snugly under the table before the blackness had descended. But the two boys were not sitting on chairs as Len remarked,

"I'm on a bench of some kind, mate."

"Me too," replied Eddie as he felt to both sides.

"Eddie? You still there?" whispered Len with obvious fear in his voice.

"Yes, and Len, I think were in a railway carriage."

They could feel the rumble and rhythmic beat of the wheels on the rails. Suddenly, the darkness lifted slightly and the boys focused their eyes on their surroundings. They were sitting on opposite sides of a fairly ancient carriage, furnished with green leather bench style seats. Len looked to his right through the side windows and out into the corridor.

"We're still in your dining room, I think, Eddie."

Eddie glanced to his left and saw alternate images of his parents' dining room mirror and the water colour of Fenton promenade go flashing by. Suddenly they were plunged into darkness again and the train noise seemed to echo all round them.

"We're in a tunnel, Len," said Eddie.

"We're in *your* tunnel, mate," replied Len and then it dawned on the two boys almost simultaneously what was happening. Eddie spoke for them both.

"We're in *my* train, Len! We're in the *Flying Scotsman*!"

Round and round they went with questions flying through their minds: How will we stop? Where's the controller? What if somebody comes back from shopping?

Suddenly both boys glanced at the corridor and a nightmare stood before them and he was sliding open the carriage door.

"Tickets please, boys."

Eddie grinned at Len, as if to say, 'It's only a game', but Len wasn't smiling.

"We haven't got any," said Eddie with an innocent look on his face.

"Then you'll have to get off the train at the next stop, I'm afraid."

"Where's that, sir?" said Len.

"Fliston," said the ticket collector. "Where are your parents?"

"In the next carriage," said Eddie.

The man gave both boys an odd look, staring in particular at their clothes as if they were from another age. After he had gone to check on their fictitious parents Len said,

"We've gone back in time."

Eddie didn't reply as he had noticed something else.

"We're taking longer and longer to go round the room."

As soon as he had finished speaking the train entered the tunnel again and the carriage was pitched into total darkness. Though seeming to still be going at the same speed the train did not emerge and several minutes went by.

Meanwhile, Fred and Ann Compton had had enough of shopping in Hamsden and left early to go back home. Eddie's dad pulled his Morris Minor onto the drive of number 38 Fir Tree Close just as *Flying Scotsman* entered the tunnel with the ticket collector looking for Eddie's other parents.

"Very quiet here," said Fred Compton as he walked into the hall. "Have they gone out, do you think, Ann?"

"Doubt it in this weather," replied his wife as she followed him in. "Try the dining room."

Eddie's dad approached the door and gently pushed it open. He looked into the room and saw the train layout all in position, but no sign of the boys or the train.

"Not in there," said Fred Compton.

"I'll try upstairs – they're probably in Eddie's bedroom," said Eddie's mum as she climbed the stairs.

Eddie's dad went into the kitchen to make a cup of tea and then heard his wife call out,

"Not up here!"

"Must have gone out, love – maybe to Len's," shouted Fred Compton.

The train took ages to move through the tunnel with no apparent loss of speed and the boys had just begun to think it never would when Len said,

"I can see light, mate."

They emerged into the normal light of the dining room and were immediately blinded by a sudden extra flash of pure white light. It took a few seconds for their eyes to focus on their surroundings and simultaneously they discovered that they were no longer in the railway carriage but sitting on the floor of the dining room. They heard voices coming from the hall. The train was stationary having just come out of the tunnel.

"Well they shouldn't have. I told Eddie to stay here until we got back and we're early."

The door opened and Eddie's mum came into the room.

"And where have you been?"

"Nowhere, Mum."

Both boys had managed to rise to their feet when they had seen the door opening and Eddie's dad would swear blind that he'd looked carefully into the room, but Eddie would say in reply that he and Len had been hiding behind the door. Fred Compton had to admit to himself and his wife that he probably didn't push the door right back as it always caught the sideboard.

"You're getting senile, dear," were Ann Compton's final words.

10

A Once-in-a-Lifetime Trip

Len helped Eddie to pack the train set away; both almost numb with excitement so that occasionally pieces ended up on the floor. It was difficult to talk freely with Eddie's parents in the house and liable to come into the dining room with lunch imminent.

"Did we leave the room, Eddie?" said Len at last.

"Of course not."

"So what year do you think we were in?"

"Pre-war, I think," said Eddie after some thought. "I wouldn't be surprised if it was 1935, you know," he continued.

"Why 1935?"

"Because, your railway timetable had 1935 on the front cover. What was it called? Brad something?"

"Bradshaw's."

"Thought the conductor looked like Mr Manders," said Eddie.

"Don't be stupid," said Len. "Mr Manders was at least ninety!"

"I meant he looked like how Mr Manders might have looked when he was younger."

Len dropped another piece of track and, hearing Eddie's mum in the hall, pulled his friend down to the floor. He had another question to ask.

"Here, watch it, Len!"

"Shh – your mum's coming."

"Are you two alright? What are you doing on the floor?"

"Just picking up some bits and pieces, Mum," said Eddie. "Nearly finished."

"Good. Lunch is in ten minutes and you ought to be going home, Len."

"Yes, Mrs Compton."

Eddie's mum returned to the kitchen and Len asked his question.

"Eddie, where's Fliston?"

"Fliston?"

"Yeah, the conductor said the next stop was Fliston."

"He didn't tell us that, Len."

Len stopped putting some track away and said,

"Yes, he did; right after he said we have to get off at the next stop."

Eddie now stopped what he was doing as well.

"All I heard him ask was where our parents were."

"Didn't you hear me ask where the next stop was before that?"

"I heard that, but I didn't hear a reply. He just went straight on to ask where our parents were."

In the end the two boys had to agree to disagree on what they'd heard. Both were adamant as to what the conductor had said or not, as the case had been. On his way home Len remained puzzled as to why his friend hadn't heard the name of the unknown place. He decided, finally, that either Eddie genuinely hadn't heard the name or he himself had been the only one *allowed* to hear it. After all, he reminded himself, Eddie hadn't seen the head poking out of the carriage window and…. Len did, however, make up his mind to look up the name Fliston in his school atlas and, if he could find it, in the mysterious railway timetable.

After lunch Len repaired to his bedroom under the pretext of doing some reading and located his atlas buried under other underused school books. Unfortunately, his school atlas didn't seem to be detailed enough to list all the small villages in England – if indeed Fliston was a small village – and the place was not to be found. He pulled the huge railway timetable from the back of his wardrobe but again without success. Unless he knew which line or route it was on he had little chance of finding it. He needed a more detailed gazetteer of England. Perhaps Eddie would have one, or at least his dad might, since he drove a car. He resolved to ask his friend the next time they met which would probably not be until the Monday. That was, of course, if Eddie could be bothered since he'd claimed not to have heard the name Fliston mentioned by the ticket collector.

Len went round to see Eddie fairly early on the Monday morning, having smuggled the Bradshaw's timetable out of his house in some old newspaper. Once in the dining room Eddie was curious as to why his friend had brought the railway timetable.

"Did you tell your mum that I wasn't supposed to know about the timetable?"

"Yes, that's why I had to smuggle it out. She didn't see me leave."

"So why have you brought it, if I'm not supposed to know about it?"

"I want to find Fliston and thought you might have a better atlas than mine, or your dad might. Then we could find it in the timetable."

"Dad's gone back to work after Christmas. It's a normal timetable today," said Eddie. "Besides, I bet the place doesn't exist, and there's another thing."

"What's that?"

"The *Flying Scotsman* only ran between London and Edinburgh in the thirties. I asked my dad."

"So?"

"So, he said it only stopped at big cities like York and Newcastle. He never mentioned Fliston."

"Did you ask, then?"

"No, of course not. Remember, I didn't hear the name, Len."

"Has your dad got a road map or book of England and could I look at it?"

"Don't know, Len. He might have one in the car."

"Could you get it?"

Eddie was getting a bit frustrated with Len's insistence on finding his phantom place and said,

"Car's probably locked and, anyway, Mum's still in."

Len wouldn't give up.

"Is she going out?"

"Probably, later."

"Please can you look if she does go out, Eddie – it's bothering me?"

"You can say that again, but yes, I'll see if I can get in the car later."

Len looked relieved and then he and Eddie began to set up the train set, seemingly forgetting what had happened two days previously until Eddie said,

"Ought we to be doing this, Len?"

Neither boy had given it a moment's thought as if they were being led by a power beyond their control or imagining. Deep inside they were both desperate to try the train set out again; they had been excited in the short intervening time since their last mini-adventure.

"Why not? You said we should treat it just as a game," said Len.

"But my mum's still here and I'm not sure that Jenny has left for Arleson's yet."

"So?"

"So? Oh, Len, you're so thick. What if we disappear and they really can't find us this time? How would we explain that, old son? Just say we've been nowhere when we eventually get back? And, what if we don't get back?"

"If it's a game we're bound to get back."

Despite Len's persistence Eddie managed to curb his friend's enthusiasm for the unknown and they put the train set to one side and played cards instead. They heard Eddie's sister leave within about ten minutes but had to wait a full hour before Eddie's mum popped her head round the door.

"I'm off down town, Eddie. Are you two going out – it's a lovely day?"

Eddie smiled as he thought that he and Len might very well be going out and a long way from Fenton-on-Sea too, but said,

"Probably not, Mum. How long will you be?"

Ann Compton looked at her watch.

"Well, it's ten now – I should be back by twelve at the very latest. O.K?"

"Yes, Mum."

After his mum had gone Eddie and Len went to explore the garage. They pulled back one of the double doors just far enough for them to squeeze by one at a time. Fred Compton rarely used the pale green Morris Minor 1000 to go to work; only when the weather was too bad to walk. Today was a beautiful sunny winter's day.

"Is it open, Eddie?" asked Len.

"Hang on. I'll try the driver's door."

Fortunately, for Len at least, the door popped open easily and Eddie climbed in and sat in the driver's seat. He found what Len wanted almost immediately. A yellow AA Member's handbook for 1959-60 was poking out of the passenger glove box.

"Here it is, Len."

Eddie passed the slim book to his friend and with much more effort than was needed to open it, they closed the garage door and made their way back to the Compton's dining room. Len had already been flicking through the list of place names in the handbook.

"Got it!" said Len excitedly. "There is a place called Fliston. It's got one hotel and one garage listed."

"Where is it?" asked Eddie, realising finally that the chances that his friend had made the name up were slim indeed.

"Map number 24."

Len found the right page and, studying the map reference, said,

"It's not far from Oxford; just outside a place called Didcot."

"Is there a railway line running through it?"

"Dunno," said Len. "It's only a road map, Eddie."

"Look in your timetable," said Eddie.

Len opened the huge volume and said,

"What route shall I look for?"

"Oxford's a big city. Try all routes out of Oxford."

It didn't take Len long to find the correct page. Fliston was on the mainline between Oxford and Birmingham; the fourth of six stops between Oxford and Didcot. Len was very excited.

"It's here! We must have been between Gallisford and Fliston when the conductor asked us to get off or, no, wait a minute; between Penton and Fliston if we were coming from Didcot."

"That's a lot of 'ifs', mate," said Eddie.

"Proves I did hear him correctly, though."

"Maybe."

Len thought for a moment.

"Where's Oxford or Didcot?"

"Midlands, I think," replied Eddie. "Birmingham is the second largest city in England – that I do know and Oxford has a posh university.

Mum keeps saying I ought to go to Oxford or Cambridge when I'm older."

"Is it near Ludmouth?"

"No, Len. How could it be? Even you should know that Ludmouth is on the South Devon coast and that could hardly be called the Midlands, could it?"

Eddie looked at his watch.

"Mum's going to be back in just over an hour and a half. Shall we try the train set out?"

"Why not? I'm game, if you are," said Len.

Within ten minutes the two boys were standing on opposite sides of the dining room table and Len had the controller in his left hand ready to push the switch. Eddie waited nervously in anticipation. The tunnel was in the same position as the last time.

"Ready?" said Len.

"All systems go!" replied Eddie, pretending to blow an imaginary whistle.

Len hardly noticed that *Flying Scotsman* started moving a split second before his thumb had touched the switch.

"She's off!" shouted Len.

A few seconds later and Eddie exclaimed,

"It's gone! She's totally disappeared!"

The train had entered the tunnel and was completely hidden from view. Eddie tried to count down the time in seconds.

"Eight-nine-ten-...."

The train emerged and neither boy noticed it at first until Eddie shouted,

"We've lost a carriage! There are only two now!"

125

They couldn't believe their eyes. Len's thumb was still glued to the switch and Eddie continued,

"Stop the train, Len! Stop it before it goes back into the tunnel."

Len managed to pull the train up just as the engine was about to enter the mysterious tunnel.

The boys looked at each other for several seconds before the ever practical Len grabbed the tunnel and pulled it from its position taped to the hardboard base. The carriage was not under the tunnel.

"What does this mean, Eddie?" asked Len eventually.

"Not sure, mate," replied Eddie. "Maybe we've got to go and find it and it's all part of the game."

"So what do we do, then?"

"How should I know, Len?"

Len was studying the two remaining carriages and suddenly asked,

"Which carriage is missing, Eddie – can you tell?"

"Not sure, mate. But I'd guess it's the rear one."

"Are we going to start it up again?" said Len.

Eddie again looked at his watch.

"We've an hour – should be long enough," but immediately he had said it he realised that time probably wasn't going to matter. He picked up the control from where Len had dropped it.

"Get ready, Len. Three-two-one, go!"

The train entered the tunnel and disappeared as before; neither boy knew what to expect. Would they lose another carriage? Would the missing one return or would the train disappear completely? Eddie started counting and this time he reached twenty before the engine emerged from the tunnel.

"Still two," said Len. "Keep it going, Eddie."

Two more circuits and the same disappearance occurred which seemed to get longer each time until on the third occasion the room was plunged into darkness. Eddie tried to cling onto the controller but it was whisked out of his hand and landed on the table with a loud clatter. Both boys braced themselves against their respective walls and waited. The noise of the train reached a crescendo and, as before, they slid to the ground clutching hands to their ears. Seconds later and the blackness lifted allowing them to refocus their eyes on their surroundings. They were sitting opposite each other with no one else in the carriage.

"It's like the carriage before, Eddie," said Len.

"Not quite, mate," said Eddie. "Some of the fittings look much newer and more modern and there's…."

Eddie didn't finish as he had seen a label fixed to the outside window of the carriage and he couldn't believe what it said. Even though it was stuck to the window so that it faced outwards he reversed the words in his head and read out loud,

'Flying Scotsman'
Solihull to Didcot and Oxford Special
Octber 30th 2005
First Class

Neither boy spoke for a few seconds until Len stated the obvious.

"We're over forty years in the future, Eddie!"

"You sound surprised, Len. It's happened before – remember Calais?"

A second nightmare appeared at the door to the corridor but this time it didn't appear to be a ticket collector even though he seemed to be wearing a similar uniform to the previous apparition. He opened the sliding door and asked simply,

"Everything alright, lads?"

"Oh yes, sir," replied Eddie quickly.

"Are you enjoying the trip? I bet your mums had to ask for you to be excused school or are you on half-term this week? I can never tell these days."

Again Eddie was quick with his reply.

"On half-term, sir. Are we going to stop soon?"

The guard laughed.

"Thought you would have had enough stops by now. Next one is Fliston and that's the thirteenth since leaving Solihull. Another three after Fliston before we reach Oxford. What do you think of the old girl – scrubs up well, doesn't she?"

It took Eddie a little longer to answer this time but he eventually worked out that the 'she' was the *Flying Scotsman*.

"Yes, sir. Is this a special trip?"

The guard laughed again and had an odd look on his face.

"Well, didn't your parents tell you? Of course it's a special trip. The old girl hasn't been in regular service since 1963. She's been specially refurbished for this once-only journey and she'll probably go to the museum in York afterwards."

The year registered with both boys and they said nothing. The guard had one more question.

"Are you staying on for the return journey from Oxford?"

"No, we're getting off, sir," replied Eddie hoping it was the correct answer to give. With that the guard seemed to be satisfied that the two boys' parents' were elsewhere and he left them with,

"Enjoy the rest of the trip, lads."

The train began to slow down and Eddie made a quick decision.

"I think we should get off and see if there are three carriages."

"Why?"

"Because if there are, we should sit in the rear one and just hope and pray."

The train was still slowing and Len had a comment of his own, having listened in silence to Eddie's conversation with the guard.

"1963, Eddie. He said that the last regular service was 1963 and that this was a special once-only trip."

"So?"

"So, what if we can't get back to our time – 1963?"

There was no time for Eddie to answer Len's impossible question as the train lurched to a halt and the two boys moved quickly to the door which was kindly opened by another guard on the platform at Fliston station.

"Can't get off here, boys."

"We're not. We're just going to see our parents – they're in the last carriage."

"Well, be quick. The train leaves in two minutes."

Len and Eddie dashed to the rear of the train, both relieved that there were exactly three carriages. They failed to notice the many odd looks from passengers both already on the train and those waiting to board. Their forty-year-old clothes were the cause of the stares. Fortunately it appeared that there would be an Indian summer in 2005 and the boys' indoor clothes were eminently suitable for the warm weather. As soon as they climbed back aboard they noticed that the third carriage was obviously second class and consequently every seat was taken.

Len had an idea.

"Let's hide in the toilet until the conductor has finished checking in the new passengers and then…."

"And then?" asked Eddie as they stood conspicuously in the corridor, but Len didn't have time to continue as the boys had to dash for the toilet to avoid the new passengers and the guard. Once they were safely (?) locked inside the train pulled out from the station.

"Well, what next?" said Eddie as he looked at his watch and horror was etched on his face. "It's five to twelve! Mum's due back in five minutes."

Len had visions of his friend's train set still going round in circles, until he remembered that the controller was still on the table.

"It'll be O.K., mate."

An age seemed to pass by. Eddie called out the time again.

"One minute to."

Suddenly the lights came on in the compartment and the train went into a tunnel which was dark and seemingly long.

"Thank God," said Eddie, but nothing happened for a few seconds until the train noise became deafening and all the lights went out instantly. Blackness followed by a strange silence descended on the boys' world broken suddenly by,

"Eddie, I'm home!" to be followed by, "What *are* you two doing?"

Bright light lit up the boys' world of fantasy. Eddie's mum stood in the doorway to the dining room staring at her son sitting on a chair with his best friend standing beside him and gripping him tightly by the shoulders. Len responded quickly.

"Oh, just showing Eddie a wrestling move, Mrs Compton."

"Well, I think you should do that outside before you wreck my dining room –alright, Len?"

"Yes, Mrs Compton. Sorry."

"Anyway, Eddie, lunch will be ready soon. I suggest that you two get some air this afternoon."

"Yes, Mum."

After his mother had gone Eddie breathed a sigh of relief.

"Whew! That was close, Len, and you can let go of me now."

What with readjusting their eyes to the light and answering Eddie's mum's instant questions, neither boy had had time to study the table and both were suddenly very apprehensive. Both turned simultaneously towards the table but all seemed well. The tunnel was still in place and the familiar green engine and half the first carriage were visible poking out of the tunnel, but…. Eddie reached over and lifted the tunnel.

"It's back, Eddie!"

Both boys looked relieved. They had played the game and won. They had made the correct decision to move to the rear carriage and the greater power had responded. Eddie smiled at his friend – they could go down town after lunch safe in the knowledge and excited by the prospect that nothing could go wrong when they played with Eddie's train set.

11

A Falling-Out

The two friends had a spring in their step that afternoon as they made their way down town with no particular purpose in mind. It remained a beautifully sunny day, crisp and cold. They reached the top of the footbridge over the railway line at Fenton station and paused, as they often did, to gaze at the view out to sea. The horizon was bare of any shipping, large or small, except for the permanent fixture of the Eastway Lightship in the distance, prompting Len to remark,

"Don't stare too long at the lightship, Eddie."

Eddie seemed to be in a world of his own as he continued to concentrate on the horizon.

"Just thinking of our journey, Len. It all started here, didn't it?"

"Yes, mate, but I don't want you sending us both out to sea with your mind. We haven't got our magic table to sit on and protect us!"

"I know, but after this morning I've been thinking that we might go on another fantastic journey via my train set. That would be fun, wouldn't it?"

"Just so long as it's only a game, Eddie. I'm opting out if we're given another mission like before."

"I don't think we will be this time. George said in his letter we were to have fun."

Len turned to face his friend and said quite seriously,

"Yes, but I hope if anything does happen again that there is a little bit of danger just to spice it up. I've told you before that it becomes boring eventually if we always know we're going to get out of trouble."

"What kind of danger did you have in mind; not physical, I hope."

"No, mate," and Len paused as his cheeky grin appeared on his face. "But like this morning when your mum found us in a somewhat embarrassing position or, even worse, she hadn't found us at all when she got back and…."

"And what?"

"And the train had been missing as well!"

"You call that fun?"

"Well, it would be different," said Len finally.

The two boys continued on their walk over the footbridge, and fantastic thoughts were soon forgotten as they concentrated on the reality of the sales and visiting Woolworth's in the High Street.

When they got there the famous shop was packed with children most of whom seemed to be younger than Len and Eddie. After ten minutes of jostling with big and tiny tots alike, Len for one had had enough.

"Let's get out of here, mate."

"I'm with you, chief," replied Eddie.

Both boys were awakening to the sad or not so sad fact that they were slowly growing up and the appeal of the regular visit to 'Woolies' was waning. Len summed it up when they stood in the High Street thinking of what to do next.

"It's boring in there now, Eddie. It's just for little kids. Fenton-on-Sea doesn't really have any decent shops for boys of our age or older, not since…."

Eddie finished his friend's sentence.

"Not since George Canter sold his junk shop, eh?"

"Yes."

"We could try Watson's Electrical – he's got a toy and model section. Got some extras for my train set from there. He might have a sale on."

"What'ya looking for? Not another tunnel I hope?"

Watson's had one or two new things for Eddie to drool over including a nice dining car that he thought wouldn't look out of place with his three other carriages.

"One more to go missing," joked Len when Eddie saw it.

"Can you lend me eleven shillings, Len?"

"Haven't got eleven bob, mate," replied Len.

"Yes you have. I saw how much you've got when we were in Woolworth's."

"I meant that I haven't got eleven shillings to lend, mate. Could let you have eight as long as you pay me back when we get home."

Eddie thought for a moment. The price of the carriage was one pound, seventeen shillings and sixpence. Eddie had one pound, six shillings and a few coppers left from his Christmas money. Even with Len's loan he would still be over three shillings short.

Mr Watson's youngest son was serving behind the counter and seeing the boys, called out,

"What can I do for you two boys?"

"How much is the Hornby dining car, please?" asked Eddie even though the price ticket clearly showed 37/6.

"Can't you read?"

Jed Watson, rather like Gary Jones, had sworn that he would never work for his dad and this lack of commitment often showed itself in his attitude to customers, particularly ones younger than himself. Jed was only just eighteen.

"Oh, yes," said Eddie rather timidly.

Len was bolder and being originally from the East End of London had had the haggler's mentality bred into him almost from birth.

"Is that the best price you can do it for?"

"That's the price, best or not. Now, make up your minds. Do you want it or not?"

"Yes, I do," said Eddie forlornly.

"Then, that's thirty-seven and six, boy."

"Haven't quite got that much."

A different voice entered the conversation and with a much more pleasant tone.

"How much have you got, young man?"

Mr Paul Watson senior had come through from the back of the shop and now stood behind the counter. Eddie did a quick calculation. Jed Watson gave his dad an angry look and disappeared out back.

"One pound, fourteen shillings and five pence, sir."

"Well, what are we to do? You're Fred Compton's son aren't you?" Eddie looked a little embarrassed. He always forgot that his shock of red hair stood him out from nearly all of his contemporaries in Fenton-on-Sea. Also his dad was well known in the town for his clever ways of getting passengers across the country by rail.

"Yes, Mr Watson."

"Well I'll do you a deal, young man. You can have the carriage for the money you've got with you. I'll need your dad's help next month when I have to go to Birmingham on business, so one good turn deserves another, O.K?"

Eddie agreed, and hoped his dad would give freely of his help. Len gave his friend four florins and within a couple of minutes Eddie was the proud owner of a prized addition to his train set. Outside the shop Len said,

"I need that eight shillings when we get home, Eddie."

"No problem, mate. I'll ask Mum for my next three week's pocket money."

Eddie would worry about persuading his mum to give him an advance when he got home – he had, after all, got nearly ten per cent off. Len had an observation.

"I hope the engine with *four* carriages will negotiate the tunnel and the curve in the track when it comes out, boy."

Eddie didn't appreciate his friend's mimicry of the unfriendly Jed Watson and responded with,

"Of course it will, old man!"

Both friends' were excited by the prospect of seeing the elongated train negotiating the tunnel. What new adventure would it cause?

Wendy Carter had met Gary Jones when he'd been under her father, Dr Steven Carter, at Fenton Cottage Hospital. She often visited the hospital to see her dad as she was hoping to study medicine at university when she left Fenton Grammar at the end of the year. Eddie had seen her occasionally at school – she was regarded by all but the very youngest males as the most attractive looking girl at the school. Though Eddie and Len had still not developed the natural instinct to stare at every young female they saw, they still recognised her as the best of her species that they knew!

Gary Jones had the Monday afternoon off and had seen Eddie's sister for a coffee at lunchtime; such rendezvous' were still unknown to Jenny's parents. Len was the first to spot Gary as they came out of Mill Road and entered the High Street.

"Isn't that your sister's ex-boyfriend?"

Eddie, unlike his mum and dad, was aware of his sister's recent reunion with Gary Jones and said cautiously,

"Keep it under your hat, Len, but she's seeing him again, I think. Mum and Dad don't know. Dad has never forgiven him for the accident."

"Well he's not with your sister now. Look over there."

Eddie stopped walking and glanced to where Len was indicating on the other side of the High Street. Eddie smiled. He'd never liked Gary Jones and not just for the mickey-taking that he used to have to suffer at his hands. Like his dad, he blamed Gary entirely for the pain and anguish that he had put his sister through. Eddie would never forget that awful day when he had cradled his sister on the pavement of Fir Tree Close, not knowing whether she was dead or alive.

"You know who that is, don't you?" continued Len. "The beautiful Wendy Carter, Eddie, my son."

Eddie's smile grew broader as he watched Gary Jones continue to stroll towards the station with WC; the name he'd heard some of the sixth form boys use for her. Eddie willed Gary to show some public affection to WC; holding hands, arm round the shoulders, the faintest of touches, but no, the two young people just walked innocently side by side.

"Will you tell your sister, Eddie?"

"What can I tell? They're just walking together."

"You can tell her that you saw Gary with the voluptuous Wendy Carter and let her draw her own conclusions. You wouldn't be lying."

"Might be worth a try – I hate him, Len, you know."

"A lot of people do. They think he got off lightly; just a year's ban and a fine which I bet his dad paid – he's loaded."

Eddie stored the piece of information away in his mind to be used at the appropriate moment; innocent though it was. He and Len followed the couple (private eye-style) up the High Street but observed nothing the bit least romantic as Gary and WC said goodbye and parted company at the junction with South Road.

137

Len and Eddie returned to Eddie's house with the intention of trying out the new carriage. Eddie's mum was not best pleased, however, when her son told her of his latest acquisition.

"I haven't got your next three week's pocket money."

"But Len lent it to me and he needs it back, Mum."

"I'm sorry, Len, but Eddie had no right to impose on you."

"It's alright, Mrs Compton, he can pay me back when he has it."

"He'll pay you back tomorrow, Len and no later, I promise. His dad'll have to lend it to him when he comes home tonight. Eddie can ask him himself."

Eddie grimaced. He would face that confrontation later. For now he was keen do to something else.

"Can we try my new carriage out, Mum?"

"You have half an hour, Eddie and no more."

Eddie realised it was a little stupid to ask if his mum was going out with such a short time allotment and when they had the train set laid out with *Flying Scotsman* pulling four carriages, Len asked,

"Are we really going to start it up? Your mum is still in the house. What happens if we disappear?"

"You said you wanted a little danger, Len."

"Yes, but…."

Eddie flapped his arms and squawked chicken-style.

"Give me the controller," said Len gruffly.

Without waiting for Eddie's say-so, Len pushed the switch and the train moved smoothly off. Both boys held their breath when it entered the tunnel and waited for it to emerge.

"It's back to normal," said Eddie almost with disappointment. Len released the switch and the train came to a halt, complete and intact.

"I agree that it didn't disappear," said Len, "but only one carriage was visible for a while."

"That's what I meant. There was always some compression, right from when we first played with it."

"Shall I start it again, Eddie?"

"Why not."

Again the train did not misbehave and even when Eddie was brave enough to peer into the tunnel he saw nothing unusual. The boys soon realised that, without the train's fantastic antics, it was actually quite boring 'entertainment'. Len had discovered the same with his own set, culminating in its dismantlement as a way of alleviating the boredom. There were only a few minutes left before Eddie had to pack away for tea.

"That's enough, I think, Len. It's not going to do anything exciting and you know what; I think I know why."

"Oh yeah, Einstein. Pray tell me why."

"It's obvious really. My mum's still in the house. Before she was out when things happened and both times we only just got back to reality by the time she returned."

"Like it knows, you mean?"

"Something or somebody knows, Len. There's got to be a power in overall control. It's not ready to expose us to the danger of going missing."

"Just yet, you mean," said Len with a wink.

Eddie's dad arrived home at six precisely; as precise as the instructions and details he gave passengers. The first part of tea was dominated by Eddie's request for his dad to lend him the eight shillings he owed his friend.

"You shouldn't borrow money, son. I've told you many times."

"Yes, Dad, but Mr Watson gave me ten per cent off and, anyway…."

"Anyway, what?"

"Anyway you'll get enjoyment from playing with it. You always do."

'Fifteen-love', thought Eddie as his dad smiled.

"*If* I lend it to you it'll cost you four week's pocket money."

"But that's twenty-five per cent interest, Dad."

"Beggars can't be choosers."

Eddie had to agree as he could see that his dad's mind was made up. It was 'take it or leave it'. Anyway, he had nothing much to spend his money on at that time of the year especially with Woolworth's now seeming less attractive.

"O.K., Dad."

"Good, I'll give it to you in the morning before I go to work."

Jenny had remained quiet throughout Eddie's mini-humiliation. Ever since the accident she had teased her brother much less. She had been told later how upset he'd been and she knew what he must have been through, having been so close to the crash. Though no one really knew how she had come to be lying on the pavement, *she* thought she had an idea. 'Did Eddie pull me from the car'? She'd never mentioned her thoughts to anyone, not even Gary with whom she shared everything. Eddie, however, was bent on making his report.

"Saw Gary today, Jen."

Jenny had a worried look on her face. She suspected that her brother knew that she and Gary were seeing each other again, though not actually dating. This current open secret between brother and sister was reciprocated by one or two things that she'd kept quiet about Eddie. Was her brother going to share the open secret in front of her parents? She acted calm and nonchalant.

"Oh yeah?"

"Yeah, he was walking in town with WC."

"WC?" asked Eddie's dad whose attention had been seized by the mention of Gary's name.

"Yes, Dad, WC is the sixth form boys' name for Fenton Grammar's Marilyn Monroe look-alike – Wendy Carter."

"What – Dr Carter's daughter?" asked Eddie's mum.

"The very same," replied Eddie.

"I'd heard he's a changed character and he seems to be if he's going out with Dr Carter's daughter."

"I didn't say he was dating her, Mum – just that I saw them walking together."

"Well at least it looks like he might be with someone else," replied Fred Compton. "I just hope he doesn't cause her any problems. You haven't seen anything of him, Jenny, have you?"

Jenny looked as if she was about to burst into tears but managed to respond.

"No, Dad."

"Good," said her dad.

"What's the matter, dear?" asked Jenny's mum.

Jenny thought quickly.

"Nothing, Mum. Just the mention of his name brought the accident back."

"Oh I'm sorry, love. How stupid of us to talk about Gary in front of you. Eddie, you really shouldn't have mentioned what you saw."

"Sorry, Mum."

Later, Eddie would feel guilty for what he had said. It would be many years before he would acquire the maturity to know when to keep silent. For the moment the seed had been sown and anyway he'd only reported what he'd seen. It wasn't his fault that Gary was walking with WC.

Jenny hadn't arranged to see Gary again until the following weekend, but the following day, New Year's Eve, she managed to phone him. She finished work early at one. On the way home she used the telephone box near to the station to call, hoping he would still be at the showroom and hadn't gone home early. She knew that one of Gary's jobs was to take all incoming calls and then put them through to either his dad or the service area; a task which he often got wrong.

"Richard Jones' Cars; Gary speaking."

"Gary, it's me."

"Jenny, what's up?"

There was an awkward silence.

"Are you still there, Jen?"

"Yes, I'm still here, but not for much longer, Gary."

"What do you mean?"

"You were seen yesterday."

"Seen? So what?"

"So, you were with a girl. My brother saw you."

The line went silent.

"Gary?"

"Yes?"

"Well?"

"Well, nothing, Jen. Dr Carter's daughter stopped me in town after I'd spent some time browsing. She just wanted to know how I was. She'd seen me when I was in hospital with my broken wrist and her dad treated me. We were walking in the same direction, that's all. When we got to

South Road she went one way and I went the other. Did your brother tell you that?"

Jenny was not convinced.

"I don't believe you, Gary."

"Well, it's true. Can't I even talk to another girl when she asks me something?"

"How many other girls do you talk to, then?"

"I don't know, Jen. What am I supposed to do – ignore anyone of the opposite sex who talks to me? Anyway, I've got to go. My dad's coming. See you next Saturday."

"No you won't, Gary."

Jenny put the phone down and walked the rest of the way home, sobbing and trying to see if she could believe what Gary had said. Was she too possessive? Was Gary telling the truth? She would investigate before she deigned to see him again.

12

Scotland

New Year's Eve passed quietly for the Wilbys and the Comptons. Len and Eddie didn't see each other, with relations visiting both families during the afternoon and early evening. Jenny Compton was very quiet when she got in from her phone call to Gary and spent the rest of the last day of the year mostly in her bedroom. Unlike the previous year she didn't go out and celebrate with friends and her parents made no point of asking why – they just assumed that their daughter wanted to move into 1964 without dwelling on what had happened in 1963.

For the rest of the week the two boys planned and waited for the next time when Eddie's mum would be out of the house for a reasonably long time. It wasn't until the Saturday before they were due back at school that the opportunity arose. Eddie's sister and dad would be at work as normal and neither were due back home until about six. Ann Compton was off to Hamsden by train at nine and wouldn't be back until well into the afternoon. The 4th of January looked like maintaining the cold but sunny weather of the last few days. Fenton-on-Sea hadn't yet experienced the deep snow of the previous January when tobogganing had been the highlight of one weekend for the two friends. As Eddie's mum was leaving she paused in the hall and called to Eddie,

"What are you going to do today? I may not be back until two or three. I've left you some sandwiches in the pantry."

Eddie smiled to himself and shouted back from his bedroom,

"Probably go out with Len, Mum – O.K?"

"Good idea. Have fun."

'What fun he and Len might have!' thought Eddie as he heard the front door close. At least, if his mum came back early and he and Len weren't in, she would assume they were still out somewhere. It looked to Eddie that they might have most of the day for any adventures that might arise. He dialled the Wilby's number.

"Hello, Fenton 3947, Mr Wilby speaking."

"Oh hello, Mr Wilby, it's Eddie. Is Len about?"

"Yes, Eddie, I'll get him," and then in the background Eddie heard,

"Len! It's Eddie, son."

When his friend answered Eddie said simply,

"Coast's clear. Come suitably clothed."

Eddie had made the last comment since, being winter, he wasn't sure where they might end up, whether or not they stayed in the same time zone. Eddie quickly got dressed for winter conditions; thick pullover, duffle coat, scarf and gloves. He'd remembered that he and Len had been lucky that it had been unseasonably warm when they had stopped at Fliston.

Len checked with his dad that it was alright to go to Eddie's house and as he left he said to his dad,

"I might be out till late afternoon, Dad."

"Just be back before it gets dark, son. What about lunch?"

"I'll get something down town."

Half an hour later and the two boys had already tried out several circuits with no extraordinary results, prompting Len to say eventually,

"Try it the other direction."

Eddie removed the train and reset the engine and four carriages so that they would now run clockwise. Neither boy had ever made a note of which sense they'd had the train in before when they'd left the room.

"Here we go, Eddie," and Len pushed the switch.

Both friends backed themselves to the walls and waited, fully dressed and ready for action. The engine entered the tunnel and for the first time since Eddie had had the extra carriage, the whole train disappeared. Eddie counted the seconds from his watch.

"One, two, three, f…."

Suddenly there was no noise from the train. The room went dark but not completely black. Other unusual noises echoed in the background and the dining room seemed hollow.

"*Platform six for the nine fifty-three to Brighton. All passengers for the express to Oxford should now go to Platform eight. Please have your tickets ready at the barriers. The time is now nine forty-five.*"

Len and Eddie got ready to sit down but this time as normal light returned to the room they found themselves still upright. Len was first to see where they were.

"We're in a station, Eddie and it's a big one."

It certainly wasn't the two-platform, open-air station they knew so well at Fenton-on-Sea. The one Eddie and Len were standing in had two huge domed and glass roofs rising to several stories height in their respective centres.

"King's Cross, Len," observed Eddie from a platform sign. "We're in London, my son."

Len stood in awe. He'd lived in Whitechapel until he was eight and had been to Liverpool Street as well as Waterloo the previous summer with Eddie, but never to King's Cross. Eddie, however, was already thinking of their next move.

"I bet the *Flying Scotsman* is here, Len. I'm sure Dad told me it used to go from King's Cross to Scotland before the war."

Len came out of his trance and said,

"Looks like you could be right about the time we're in, mate. Look at the uniforms and clothes."

Len strolled over to an old-fashioned newspaper stand ignoring the inevitable stares. He peered at the front page of *The Daily Telegraph.*

"Friday, January the 4th 1935, Eddie!"

"Should have brought your timetable, mate," said Eddie.

"*Last call for passengers for the ten o'clock service to Edinburgh Waverley, calling at York and Newcastle. Platform ten for the ten o'clock Flying Scotsman.*"

Eddie and Len both looked at their watches.

"Five to," said Len. "Shall we...?"

"You bet!" but then Eddie paused and pulled his friend back from making a dash for the required platform. "Wait! We've no tickets."

"I know a way."

Eddie followed his friend and they reached platform ten with two minutes to spare.

"Two platform tickets, please."

"Tuppence, please and you'll have to be quick if you're seeing someone off, boys," said an amiable collector at the barrier.

Len thrust two pennies into the collector's hand, hoping he wouldn't notice that the dates embossed on both of them were over twenty years in the future! Len grabbed the tickets and ran down the platform. When a guard was busy helping an elderly couple onto the train, Len pulled and pushed Eddie into a middle third class carriage and then jumped up behind his friend.

"Just seeing our uncle off!" shouted Len in case the guard had seen them, but when there was no response the boys relaxed and strolled down the corridor until they found an empty compartment. They collapsed onto the green leather seats.

"Oh Len, what have we done?" said Eddie.

"Who knows, but I guess we're off to Scotland if we can avoid any ticket collectors," replied Len with a grin.

Avoiding ticket collectors was easy until they reached York where they arrived at twenty to one – both according to their watches and the station clock.

"At least time is moving at the correct speed, then," said Eddie.

"Yeah, but that means we can't possibly be back before your mum gets in."

"Len, it's only a game."

The train remained at York for ten minutes to allow passengers to leave and join it. Len realised what might happen next as they pulled out of the station.

"Better hide in the toilet; they're bound to check the tickets of the new passengers."

They squeezed into the nearest toilet at the end of their carriage, choosing a moment when no one was looking to avoid any embarrassment. Eddie was about to slide the sign to *engaged* when Len pulled on his sleeve.

"Leave it on *vacant*. The ticket collector will think it's empty, then."

Len stood behind the door and held it to. They waited until the train was up to speed and had heard the ticket collector call: "Tickets please!" Then they waited another ten minutes for him to make his return journey. Len poked his head out into the corridor and whispered,

"All clear."

Eddie followed his friend out of the toilet and they made their way back to their compartment only to find it occupied by a family of four. Trying to look unconcerned Len beckoned to Eddie to continue walking past the compartment. Fortunately, the very next carriage had been vacated by its former occupants at York and the two boys fell into it with some relief.

"Phew! That was close," said Len.

Eddie had a puzzled look on his face. He'd been quiet all the time they had been in the toilet compartment.

"What's up, mate?"

"Nothing, Len. I just thought I recognised the ticket collector's voice. It sounded familiar somehow."

That ticket collector had not, however, completed his return tour of the carriages as Len and Eddie had thought. Suddenly the young guard was standing outside the boys' carriage, peering in with a frown on his face and to the boys' horror he was going to enter their carriage.

"Thought I'd done this carriage. Did you lads get on at York?"

Len was quick with his response. The man seemed familiar somehow.

"Oh no, sir, we've been on since King's Cross."

Len prayed that he was not going to ask for their tickets but he simply said,

"Are you enjoying the ride? We might do the 'ton' later. What are your names?"

Something about the guard made Eddie speak up and give their real names and in full.

"He's Leonard Wilby and I'm Edward Compton, sir."

The young man's eyes lit up in astonishment.

"Compton? Well there's a coincidence – my name's Compton too. Fred Compton. Where are you from Edward?"

"Whitechapel in London, sir. Do you know it?" lied Eddie boldly and with a glazed expression on his face.

"No, I don't. I live in Hamsden in East Anglia. I work this route occasionally from London."

Len smiled slyly at his friend as both boys struggled to hide their excitement. The coincidence in the surnames had ensured that Fred would forget to check the boys' tickets as he left them with a slightly dreamy look on his face.

"Compton, eh? What a coincidence! Enjoy the rest of the journey. Next stop Newcastle."

Len had to be the first one to break the ensuing silence as his friend was too far down the road of fantasy to be able to put two words together.

"That was your dad, Eddie. Why didn't you say something?"

Eddie at last saw the funny side of the ghostly meeting.

"Oh yeah! What could I have said?" and he paused. "By the way, Fred, I'm your twelve-year-old son and your wife's expecting you home in Fenton-on-Sea at six tonight. You've got a seventeen-year-old daughter who is probably only a few years younger than you as well."

"Did he look like your dad?" asked Len more seriously.

"His voice was more or less the same."

"How old would he have been?"

"Well, this is 1935 which is twenty-nine years ago and Dad was fifty the year before last. So…."

"So?"

"About twenty-two or three, I should say," replied Eddie after some mental gymnastics.

"About the right age, then. Did he look like your dad?" asked Len again.

"I think so. Twenty-nine years is a long time and I've never seen photographs of him when he was younger. He was the right height but Dad's hair is grey now."

"It was him, wasn't it, Eddie? You don't seem too sure."

"Yes, it was him. He told me he'd worked on the Flying Scotsman before I was born and I know Mum is from Hamsden originally – she still has relations who live there. I just think I'm still a bit in shock. What a privilege to go back and see your dad when he was young – absolutely incredible!"

Len had a grin on his face which Eddie couldn't miss.

"What, Len?"

"You know what we should do?"

"Go on, tell me."

"Give him something or tell him he's got to remember something for the rest of his life. Then you can ask him about it when we get back."

"Like what? He'll probably remember our names for a while. Maybe that's why I was called Edward."

"How do you mean?"

"Maybe when I was born he remembered he'd met a boy called Edward Compton back in 1935, or the name was just somewhere in the deep recesses of his mind."

"What about me? He clearly doesn't remember me, Eddie, or he would have said something. We are best friends, after all."

"I expect he was too wrapped up in the coincidence to have stored your name away in his mind. Why would he? He must ask passengers for their names all the time."

Len was quiet for a few moments until his face lit up.

"You could tell him that one day he would live at 38 Fir Tree Close in Fenton-on-Sea."

"He'd think I was nuts, Len. How could I make him remember something like that? I'm not a fortune-teller. I'm only a twelve-year-old kid in his eyes, making up stories of the future that couldn't possibly be true as far as he would be concerned."

"True," said a disappointed Len.

Neither boy could think of anything that Fred Compton, the young guard, would believe or be prepared to remember. They also decided that they didn't have anything that they could give him that wouldn't just be thrown away at the end of the journey. Eddie, for one, was also worried that tampering with the past could have grave consequences for either or both of them. He had one final comment.

"I would like to see him again."

"You will, you fool!"

"I don't mean twenty years down the line. I mean now."

"If you go after him he might suspect something, Eddie. He hasn't actually seen our tickets and with the name coincidence he might delve a bit more into who you are and why you're on this train. That could make life very difficult."

Eddie eventually took his friend's advice and decided not to go looking for his 'dad'. In any case, it wasn't long before the train slowed as it made its approach to Newcastle and the two boys had to make their visit to the toilet compartment again. Looking through the small window Len could just observe that no passengers seemed to get on the train. He also spotted Eddie's 'dad' clearly leaving the train with his leather bag. He whispered to Eddie,

"Your dad's left the train, Eddie and I don't think he's coming back."

Eddie seemed to be pleased and disappointed at the same time but had been thinking about something else.

"When we get back, Len...."

"Yes?"

"What's to stop me telling my dad that I knew he was on this train on precisely January the 4th in 1935 and that he met two boys, one of whom had the same name as me?"

"You wouldn't."

"Why not?"

"Because, he wouldn't remember, Eddie."

"He might."

Len didn't immediately answer but expressed another reason why his friend wouldn't tell or be able to tell his dad.

"Anyway, when we get back, we'll have forgotten everything that's happened. Whoever or whatever is in charge of this game is never going to allow such a thing. We could change world history."

"How?" asked Eddie.

"Oh come on, Eddie, just think for a moment. We could tell someone about the Second World War or make a fortune betting on sporting events that we know the results to. It ain't gonna happen, chief."

Eddie mumbled his agreement, but his mind was already into the possible incredible fantasy of their situation. He wouldn't say anything more for the moment, he decided. He didn't want to think of the possible consequences of his phantom meeting and Len was right – even if he remembered the meeting, his dad's memory might be wiped clean or had been already, depending on which time zone they were in.

It started to snow heavily well before they reached the Scottish border. Eddie and Len had had no ticket problems after leaving Newcastle at five past two. Len seemed more worried than his friend about the advancing time.

"Your mum said she might be back at two."

"She also said she might be as late as three," replied Eddie. "She's often later than she says."

Len looked outside through a heavily misted window.

"Boy, look at that snow, Eddie. I'm hungry. When do we reach Edinburgh?"

"Don't know, mate. We seem to be slowing down."

Unbeknown to the two illegal travellers they had just crossed over into the land of the kilt and the haggis. Suddenly the carriage was plunged into darkness.

"What's happening?" asked Len.

"Tunnel I think."

The carriage jolted sharply and ground to a halt. Very dim lights came on which were no better than candles. The father from the family of four went past their carriage in the direction of the front of the train. Nothing happened for a few minutes until he returned and poked his head into the boys' carriage. He smiled and in a broad Scottish accent, said,

"Tunnel exit is blocked by a snow drift. It may be an hour or more before it can be shifted. Do you want to join us in our carriage?"

"No, sir, we'll be fine," replied Len.

Eddie looked at his watch. It was ten past three.

13

Awkward Questions

Both boys had known for a long while that under normal circumstances they would not be back home that afternoon. But these were not normal circumstances as Eddie pointed out after they had been stationary for ten minutes.

"It's still only a game. There must be a way out."

Alright, Einstein, please explain to me how we're going to get home today or even tomorrow"

"I don't know; I'm thinking."

Just then a guard appeared at their door and said,

"Are you boys on your own?"

"No, sir, our parents are in the next carriage," said Len hastily.

"Which one?"

"The one behind this one."

"Can I see your tickets, please?"

"Dad's got them."

"Where have you come from?

"London."

"Wait here until I get back. What are your parents' names?

"Mr and Mrs Manders," replied Len. "I'm John and he's Michael."

The guard left to find the boys 'parents' and Eddie finally spoke,

"Len, what have you done? We're in trouble now."

"Not if we're not here when he gets back. Come on let's go up the front of the train. I have an idea."

Before heading forward Len went to the carriage containing the family of four. Eddie stayed outside their own carriage while Len appeared to be asking a question of the man they'd seen earlier. Len soon emerged with a smile on his face.

"This train has got ten carriages and we're in the seventh from the front."

"So?" said Eddie.

"I think we need to be in the first four carriages and hope that one of them is a dining car like your set."

Eddie guessed immediately what Len was suggesting.

"You mean, if we can get into the first four carriages we may be spirited home, like before at Fliston when we got into the missing carriage."

"Precisely, my dear Watson!"

They walked forward down the corridor and were relieved to find they could get into the next carriage through a sliding door.

"Keep count, Eddie. This must be number six."

They repeated the process and got into the fifth carriage. They had to squeeze past several people who were going forward to see what was happening. Their winter coats provided a good cover for their modern clothing underneath. Len was first to the end of the fifth carriage.

"No door, Len!"

"What now, then," said Len as though he should have an answer.

"Only one thing for it – are you game?"

"What for?"

"Outside!"

Len turned to the nearest outer door and slid the window down. He reached out and quickly released the handle. He pushed the door open and climbed to the lowest step, barely able to see in the dim light. His head disappeared from view. Eddie followed but hesitated at the door until Len whispered,

"It's O.K. – it's only a couple of feet to the track."

Eddie reached the bottom step and Len helped him down onto the track. The two boys could see lights up ahead at the exit to the tunnel and they knew they had to be quick if they were not to be spotted. The tunnel was eerily lit only by the inadequate lighting from the carriages and it took some time to negotiate debris on the track as they walked in the gap between the train and the tunnel side. The atmosphere was heavy with noxious smoke and steam. Finally they were level with the fourth carriage which happened to be the dining car.

"Not this one," said Len. "There are far too many people and it's too open."

The snow was clearly very deep at the exit up ahead now having drifted against the front of the train while they'd been stationary. Finally they were outside the rear door to what they hoped was the third carriage.

"In we go," said Len.

"Be careful, mate."

Len stood on the step and peered into the corridor.

"It's clear."

The boys jumped inside the carriage and, almost without thought and certainly discussion, headed straight for the adjacent toilet. There was no time to find an empty compartment. Eddie sat on the toilet seat and Len stood squashed beside him. This time Len slid the sign to *'engaged'*. The light was just bright enough for Eddie to read his watch.

"Twenty-five past three."

As soon as Eddie had finished reading out the time a blinding flash of light lit up their cramped compartment to be followed almost immediately by utter blackness and silence. Len's whisper echoed in the confined space,

"Here we go, Eddie. Hold tight."

"Eddie, where are you? Are you home?"

His mum's voice echoed out of the blackness which became daylight as soon as she had finished the question. The dining room door opened before the two boys to reveal Ann Compton standing in the doorway. Eddie tried to pre-empt her question.

"Just trying the wrestling hold again, Mum."

"Yes, but where were you just now when I looked in here? I've only been upstairs to check your bedroom since and why didn't you answer when I shouted you?"

Eddie tried to stammer something but nothing came out. Len was brave and quick with a response.

"We must have come through the front door when you were upstairs, Mrs Compton and we didn't hear you."

Eddie held his breath. His mother didn't seem convinced.

"I didn't see you behind me in the Close and why on earth are you still in your outside clothes? They're filthy – what *have* you been doing?"

Eddie didn't know how to begin to reply to his mother's barrage of awkward questions, but started with answering the least controversial one.

"We ran up the road and probably didn't come into view until after you had gone inside, Mum."

"Why were you running?"

"Because we knew we were late."

"But how did you get your coats so dirty? Smells like oil to me – I hope it isn't, Eddie. It won't come off."

The boys studied their winter coats for the first time since returning from their other world. They were streaked with grime and Len noticed a large tear in his brown duffle coat.

"We played football on the 'rec' and it was quite muddy. Maybe there was some oil from the mower on the pitch and like Len said, we've only just got back."

Eddie knew that the last part of his answer was the sole piece of truth in his fabrication of lies. They had escaped the ultimate problem by seconds. His mum's questions, though awkward, weren't proving impossible to answer, at the moment, he thought. His mum seemed to be calming down and her initial black look was mellowing.

"I just don't understand you, Eddie. You always hang your clothes up as soon as you get in."

Eddie invented another 'story'.

"Len was going straight home because he was a bit late and because he didn't take his clothes off, I didn't bother."

Eddie's mum seemed to be satisfied with the excuse but the questioning continued.

"Yes, but why did Len come back anyway and why did you both come in here? Couldn't you try your wrestling hold outside? It's a pretty stupid place to do it."

Eddie looked embarrassed and couldn't think of an obvious answer. Meanwhile, Len had been looking round at the train set still in place on the table. He thought he could help his friend out with the third-degree he was getting from his mother.

"The reason I had to come back briefly, Mrs Compton, was that I'd brought over a piece of my train set and I was going to take it back before I went home. I was just about to leave and we were having a final bit of fun when you came in."

'Good old Len', thought Eddie. 'That should be the final piece in the jigsaw of lies'. But his mother had one last arrow to fire.

"Alright, but why haven't you eaten your sandwiches? I made your special ham and cheese ones. Did you go and buy food down town?"

Len took over again.

"We had some chips earlier. It was my fault. I was hungry so I bought us both a bag when we were down town. Sorry, Mrs Compton."

"Well that's very kind of you, Len, but Eddie knew he'd got sandwiches for his lunch. I shan't make them again, Eddie."

"I'd better be going. I've got to be home before it gets dark," said Len finally and he casually picked up one of Eddie's engine sheds as he left for home.

14

Discussions and Repercussions

After Len had returned home Eddie spent some time clearing away the train set. His mum had taken his coat and had informed him that only dry-cleaning would do to get rid of the grime and stains. He was going to have to pay for it too. Neither he nor Len had had a chance to inspect the engine and carriages for loss or damage, but all seemed fine except for his 'borrowed' engine shed. The apple green engine was the last piece to be put back in the box and, on closer inspection, Eddie noticed some scratches to its front. Suddenly, the amazing rail journey came flooding back. Could the marks have been caused by the snow drift? What else did he remember? All the furore of his and Len's return combined with his mum's salvo of questions had put the adventure temporarily to the back of his mind. He could remember most of the day: King's Cross; avoiding ticket collectors; hiding in toilet compartments; Scotland and snow. Something, however, was nagging him at the back of his mind. It had something to do with a guard and his dad was somehow involved, but....

Eddie's mum was still not best pleased with her son and he felt it diplomatic to spend the time up until tea in his bedroom, reading and thinking. When his mother called him for tea he found himself fast asleep curled up on his bed. He awoke with a fright thinking a ticket collector was about to throw him off a train in the middle of a blizzard and deep snow drifts. It had been a tiring day. His mum was at the bottom of the stairs.

"For goodness sake, Eddie; for the third time: tea's ready!"

Eddie jumped off his bed and glanced in his wardrobe mirror. He looked a sight. How did he get his face so dirty? Then he remembered the smoke filled tunnel. His mum must have put it down to a muddy football field. He dashed to the bathroom to make himself presentable shouting at the same time,

"Just coming – having a wash!"

Back downstairs his mum seemed to have forgotten his misdemeanours of the day as she was too busy telling Eddie's dad about the things she'd bought for the house in the New Year sales. A new everyday cutlery set at less than half price and some bathroom towels were occupying her conversation and, surprisingly, Eddie's dad seemed interested. He usually complained whenever his wife spent money on things that he thought they didn't need, but in both cases the items bought were at the top of his priorities as well. He had been getting fed up with bent and stained knives or rough towelling after a bath.

"Well done, love – quite a bargain."

Things seemed to be getting back to normal between the two siblings as well. Both in their own way had missed the playful banter and teasing that had been a part of their everyday lives since Eddie had been about five.

"Mum says you stayed out all day without lunch and got yourself really dirty. You're nearly thirteen, Eddie. When are you going to grow up?"

"I'd rather stay young than grow up like you, sister dear!"

"At least I can look after myself. Mum has to tell you everything. Even when you go to the toilet she tells you…."

"Jenny, that's enough," said her mother.

"I was only going to say that you still have to tell him to wash his hands, which is true, Mum."

After Jenny had gone into the lounge to watch some television and Eddie's mum repaired to the kitchen to wash up, Eddie and his dad were left alone at the tea table. Fred Compton looked up from his paper and smiled at his son.

"You know, Eddie, you really must try and do what your mother says. I didn't think you were that keen on football, despite your heroics last term. If you want to get to university you need to spend more of your spare time on your school work. Haven't you got something to do before you go back on Monday?"

"A bit, Dad."

Fred Compton felt he had done his bit in the parenting skills department and his tone changed.

"Fancy setting your train set up after tea? We don't seem to have played with it together for ages."

Eddie paused. Nothing had ever happened when in the past he and his dad had played with the *Flying Scotsman*, but….

"O.K., Dad," he replied a little cautiously.

Then, like the blinding flash of light earlier, he suddenly remembered what had been lurking at the back of his mind. The name of his train had jolted it out into the reality of the present.

"Dad?"

"Yes, son."

"Before the war, Dad, when you worked on the *Flying Scotsman*, can you remember…?"

Fred Compton grinned and Eddie paused while he tried to phrase the right question. Eventually he blurted it out.

"Can you remember working on the *Flying Scotsman* on exactly this day in 1935?"

Eddie's dad smile grew broader and he responded with an answer that his son had been expecting least of all.

"I didn't work on her before the war, son. I didn't start until 1946 when I was thirty-three. Up till then I was based in Hamsden where I met your mother. Why on earth did you want to know that?"

"No particular reason, Dad. I just picked a date at random. You know what I'm like for coincidences."

His dad seemed satisfied with the response but Eddie's mind was in even more turmoil than it had been before he'd asked his strange question. He would have to tell Len on the way to school on the Monday, if not before. Then he thought, 'What if Len doesn't remember my phantom dad'?

Father and son spent an hour or so with Eddie's train set and a more mature bonding began to form between them. Eddie, for one, *felt* older after his day's experience. No more was said about his careless and forgetful day and peace eventually descended on the Compton household.

Len met Eddie at the junction with South Road on Monday morning for the return to school after the Christmas holidays. Eddie still had nervous moments whenever he passed close to the scarred road surface at the end of Fir Tree Close and this morning was no exception. He was thus quieter than usual while he listened to Len rehearse the inquisition that he had faced from both his mum and dad as to the state of his coat and grimy face.

"I told her the same things that we told your mum, Eddie, I think, or I hope," he said at the end of his tale.

"Bet she isn't going to make you pay for your coat to be dry-cleaned like my mum is."

"No, she washed it yesterday and it should be dry tonight. Meanwhile, I've got to wear this old mackintosh. It's too small and I'll get laughed at."

"Me too, mate. Mine smells of damp."

They were halfway to school and Eddie finally managed to broach the subject of the 'Scottish trip'.

"You'll never guess what, Len."

"No I won't. Go on, surprise me."

"My dad didn't start work on the *Flying Scotsman* until after the war. That couldn't have been him we saw, or, if it was, then he was a ghost from another time as well, like we were. It's almost as though we both had to go back to 1935 and meet in a place that neither of us had ever been before."

Len had stopped walking and stared curiously at his friend.

"What the blazes are you talking about, mate?"

And then Eddie knew. Len *didn't* remember.

"Your dad wasn't on the train, Eddie."

The two friends started walking again and Eddie continued to try to describe the debated incident but without success. Len was having none of it and, after a while, both boys agreed that each had been allowed selective memories of the previous Saturday by whomever or whatever was in control of the game. They would have to return to the discussion at a later time as the entrance to Fenton Grammar School and harsh reality suddenly stood before them. What else had Len not been allowed to remember and, indeed, what had he himself forgotten? It would be some time yet before the two boys would return to a discussion of Saturday's journey. In some ways each of them wanted to forget it for a while and let time determine how important it was to them and, indeed, if any of the events had really happened. They both knew that what had happened or would happen in the future was only a game. In their normal games they always quickly forgot what had taken place anyway. Maybe the same would be true for their games of fantasy.

Jenny hadn't seen or made contact with Gary for a week when she got a surprise visitor in the shop the day after her brother had gone back to school. It was lunchtime and several of Fenton Grammar's sixth form were in the bakers for something to replace or supplement the meagre offerings in the school's dining room. All were male bar one and they were enacting their regular naïve charade of 'chatting Jenny up'. They had obviously long ago given up trying to flirt with the lone female who was with them. Jenny deliberately ignored all the false and purposeless flattery and addressed the one sixth form girl.

"Hi, can I help you?"

"No, but I think I may be able to help you, Jenny."

Jenny was slow at the best of times but the penny dropped immediately and her suspicions were quickly confirmed.

"I'm Wendy Carter."

Her brother's description of WC had been a very accurate one. Wendy was buxom without being overweight. She was slightly taller than average and she had beautiful curly natural platinum blond hair and, unlike many pretty girls of her age, she *knew* she was beautiful. This scared off many of her male peers who preferred the timid type who they felt able to flirt with without the fear of being humiliated. Wendy Carter was a dab hand at humiliating her male admirers.

Jenny's friendly smile evaporated from her face and she asked her standard customer question without a trace of emotion.

"What can I get you?"

"Nothing. Is there somewhere we can talk?"

"Why would I want to talk to you?"

Sam Arleson must have heard Jenny's brusque tone and briefly left his own customer.

"Are you alright, young lady?"

"Oh yes, Mr Arleson – I just wanted to have a private word with Jenny."

"Well we're very busy at the moment, as you can see. Jenny goes to lunch in ten minutes. Perhaps you two girls can talk then."

WC looked at her watch and said.

"O.K., I'll wait outside, Jenny," and with that she turned on her beautifully sculpted heel and exited the shop. Jenny hadn't replied and was already on her way to joust with a group of three sixth form boys who seemed anxious to be served by her.

Jenny was reluctant to leave the shop ten minutes later – she was determined not to have a conversation with her possible rival. Gary had done nothing to correct the impression she'd gained from her brother's sighting of him with WC. She'd received no phone calls from Gary even though she knew it would be difficult for him not to alert her parents' suspicions, but there were other ways of getting messages through. After some dithering while she chatted to Danny in the bakery at the back of the shop, she decided to confront Wendy Carter and walked out into the High Street to face the 'blond bombshell'. She couldn't see Wendy at first until her heart missed a beat when she spotted her across the other side of the road, and with a tall fair haired boy of Gary's build and age. He had his back turned toward the bakers and appeared to be looking in a shop window.

'How could he'? she thought and she was just about to turn back into the shop when the handsome young man turned round to face her. It wasn't Gary.

"Wait, Jenny!" shouted WC from the other side of the High Street. "Please wait!"

Jenny waited where she was while Wendy and the young man came across the road to meet her. They were hand in hand.

"Jenny, I'd like you to meet my boyfriend, Matt Davis. Matt, this is Jenny Compton. Jenny is Eddie Compton's sister. Matt was a prefect at Fenton Grammar until last year and he knew your brother – from the junior Maths club he used to help run."

Jenny felt awful but managed a pleasant enough smile.

"Did Gary ask you to come and see me?" asked Jenny.

"Oh no, Jenny – your brother was the one who asked me to talk to you."

"My brother – you mean Eddie?"

"Why, have you got another one?"

When Jenny didn't reply to her flippancy, Wendy continued.

"Eddie came to see me in school yesterday as soon as we started back after Christmas. He was worried that he may have led you to believe that Gary and I were going out together. How long have we been going out, Matt?"

"Nearly a year."

"When Matt was still at school, Eddie often used to see us together, but he wouldn't be aware that the relationship continued after Matt left last July. He feels guilty that his report of my chance and innocent meeting with Gary Jones may have led you to put two and two together and make five. I think his reason for doing it says more about his dislike for Gary than anything else."

"If you see him in school this afternoon, Wendy, you better warn him that I'll kill him when he gets home!" replied Jenny angrily.

"Oh don't do that. I think it was very brave of Eddie to try to put right his childish prank, because that's all it was, Jenny. I think your brother is at last growing up. It was a very adult thing to do to come and see me. You should be proud of him."

Jenny wandered down to the sea front after parting from Wendy and Matt. She spent some quiet time thinking about WC's words. In the end she came to the same conclusion as Wendy – she wouldn't 'kill' her brother. She realised that her kid brother was indeed growing up despite her cruel remarks of a few days before. She loved her brother more than she realised – there was an invisible and unbreakable bond between them that probably only brothers and sisters ever experience.

Eddie had spent a good deal of Tuesday worrying about the consequences of his chat with WC. Would his sister find out that he'd got the lovely Wendy to take Matt Davis to see her? What would be her reaction if she did find out? He was somewhat surprised and embarrassed when the two of them were left to wash up after tea. The minute they were on their own, and with the kitchen door closed, she said quietly,

"Thank you, Eddie, for what you did. I do love you."

If that show of soppy sisterly love wasn't enough for him it was then cemented by the most embarrassing hug that his sister had ever given him, topped off with a kiss on the middle of his forehead.

"Yuk! Let me go, Jenny!"

Deep inside Eddie was pleased that his sister respected him for what he'd done despite his coldness towards Gary. Time would tell if Jenny had found the right boyfriend and also whether he was still interested in her anyway.

Gary knew nothing of the meeting between Wendy and Jenny. He had never met Matt Davis, each boy having gone to different schools. He had thought about Jenny often over the previous week or so and had several times toyed with the idea of just going into Arleson's to confront her, but he hadn't been brave enough. It was with some relief that on the Wednesday lunchtime the phone rang and in reply to his normal,

"Richard Jones' Cars – Gary speaking," he heard,

"Gary, it's me – Jenny."

"Jenny, is that really you?"

"Yes, Gary, and I'm sorry."

"Sorry? What for?"

"For doubting you."

"It's O.K.," replied Gary as he thought he heard Jenny start to cry.

"I-I know your meeting with Wendy was innocent. My brother was just trying to stir up trouble between us. I don't think he likes you."

"That's not surprising, Jen, love – he blames me entirely for the accident. I'll just have to live with that and deal with all the other people who can't forgive me, but that doesn't matter, Jenny, as long as…."

"As long as what?

"As long as you've forgiven me."

"I have, Gary – you know I have."

Just then Gary's dad called him from the showroom and Jenny was left with,

"Got to go, love. Speak to you soon."

Jenny spent the rest of Wednesday in a dream world; occasionally giving customers the wrong change and even in one case, the wrong order. One thought floated constantly in her mind: 'He called me *love*!'

15
Anywhere

January continued to be cold, and with the dark evenings, the boys saw little of each other outside school where Len was heavily involved with the rugby squad. Light snow started to fall on the morning of Saturday the 18th, but it had stopped by ten o'clock barely leaving a covering. The boys hadn't seen each other for a fortnight at the weekend; the previous Saturday had been wet and very windy. Very little had been exchanged between them about their rail journey to Scotland; this year they were in different classes for almost all subjects, which were set by ability. Len had arranged with Eddie to call round if the weather was reasonable and at ten-fifteen his typical rhythmic knocking could be heard on the Compton's front door. Eddie opened it and was greeted with,

"Whatcha, comrade Len!"

"What ho, sport!"

As Eddie emerged into the watery sunshine after the brief snow shower, he immediately noticed that Len was carrying something in a brown paper bag.

"What've you got, mate?"

"My train – just the engine. Dad fixed the wheels at school in the workshop. Can I leave it here till later?"

"Why?" said Eddie with a bemused look on his freckled face. They hadn't moved from the doorway.

"Well, I was wondering if we could try it out later with your track and the tunnel. My transformer no longer works."

Eddie thought for a moment.

"O.K., Len, I'll put it in the dining room."

The boys made their way down Fir Tree Close thinking about the day ahead, but Eddie had been thinking about his friend's repaired train.

"You know what, Len? When we try your engine out, we should see if anything strange happens with my carriages."

"I don't think it will, Eddie – after all, the magic comes from your train because Mr Canter gave it to you same as he gave me my football. Your football doesn't misbehave."

"Haven't got one. Anyway the magic only seems to happen when the train goes into the tunnel, so maybe it's the tunnel doing it."

Len was about to tell Eddie about the strange anticipation he'd experienced from the controller when they'd first played with the set and without the tunnel, but he thought better of it.

"Alright, but can we try it later?"

"Yes, mate, of course, but I don't think there's any need to worry."

"Why?"

"Mum's not going out."

"Where's your dad?"

"Which one? If you mean my real one, he's at work. If you mean the phantom one, I don't have any idea!"

Len didn't seem to be amused and, by chance, the boys had reached their elevated position on top of the footbridge – the perfect place to restart the discussion that had lain dormant for a fortnight.

"Still harping on about that, are you?"

"Yes, Len, because we did see my dad. Even though he wasn't on the train in 1935, I know it was him and, despite what you say, we actually had a conversation about him on the train which you clearly don't remember."

"Well actually, I have started to remember bits of the day that maybe I'd forgotten, but I can't work out whether they did really happen or I've dreamt them since. I just don't know, Eddie," replied Len thoughtfully.

"What do you mean?"

"You told me about your dad when we walked to school on the first day this term, remember?"

"Yes."

"Well, maybe my mind took that in and now I'm beginning to believe it *was* true. After all, whatever we saw and did could all have been a dream anyway."

"You know that's not true."

"I suppose so, but I think we should swap our experiences of that Saturday in some detail. We haven't really done that yet, have we?"

Leaning against the guard rail of the footbridge the two friends talked for nearly twenty minutes. They both experienced a sense of relief at the end of their discussion and Eddie was certainly glad that it appeared that the only possible discrepancy was the sighting of his phantom dad. He summed up their talk.

"At least you can't say we dreamed it, Len, because there's no way we could have had such detailed dreams that matched in almost every respect whether by place or time. The odds would be millions to one."

That ended the conversation and the two boys slid and slithered their way down the footbridge in the quickly melting wet film of snow. They'd already decided that Woolworth's was off the agenda and headed instead for a shop that neither of them had been in for a long time – Grant's Emporium at the top of Steep Hill overlooking the promenade. Len had been uncomfortable when Eddie had mentioned the possibility earlier. He thought 'old Granty', as he called him, to be rather effeminate and dealt in things for girls only. One of Eddie's other friends at school had told him that Aloyisious Grant was now stocking second-hand toys and models and for boys too.

The snow had cleared completely off the pavements by the time they had reached the top of Steep Hill; a more appropriate name you couldn't wish to find. Very few pensioners used it as a way to the promenade and, if they did, they returned by way of the gentler East Hill. Even looking in Grant's shop window was an ordeal – you had to balance yourself with one foot several inches higher than the other in order to maintain a steady view of its display.

"There's nothing I can see in the window," remarked a hopeful Len who was first to arrive.

"Probably inside," said Eddie who was already on his way into the shop. He stopped with the door ajar. He'd suddenly been reminded of the many occasions when he'd also hesitated before entering another similar shop in Fenton-on-Sea.

"Remind you of anything, Len?" he said as he turned back to face his friend.

"Shut up, Eddie! Talking to Granty's bad enough without you bringing up George's junk shop."

"In we go, then," said Eddie with a wink. Surely old man Grant wasn't a dealer in things magical and fantastic as well?

Aloyisious St John Grant was well into his seventies and had unusually long white hair; unusual not because of the colour but because of the length. His Old Testament prophet-like appearance put many people off visiting his shop, expecting him to start reciting proverbs or predictions for their lives. Eddie could just remember being taken into the shop once before, on his sister's ninth birthday, in order for his mum to buy her a doll she been asking for. He'd been only four then and the memory of the visit was hazy to say the least. However, as Mr Grant

174

emerged from between some faded curtains, he did have the feeling that it had not been an unpleasant experience. Len had been in the shop once or twice in the past but he hadn't found the occasions as much to his liking.

"Good morning, gentlemen and how are we today?" asked Granty in his dulcet tones that always reminded Len of one of his aunties who lived in Peckham. He said nothing and pushed his friend forward.

"Fine, Mr Grant," replied Eddie.

"And what are we looking for this beautiful sunny day?"

"Have you any second-hand toys, like extras for Hornby electric train sets?"

In the background Len was waiting for the typical George Canter reply: '*Of course, boys; I have just what you're looking for*', but no such anticipation was evident from Granty's reply.

"Not really, dear; I do have some toy soldiers, but nothing to do with train sets, I'm afraid."

"Thank you, but no, sir; we're a little too old to be playing with soldiers now."

"Just as you like, dear. Can I interest you in something else?"

Len wanted to shout out: '*Don't call my friend, dear, please*'! but kept quiet; he didn't want to engage in conversation with old Granty. Aloyisious Grant continued.

"I have a nice set of encyclopedias that have just come in; they're quite inexpensive. I also have a box of old magazines and what look like timetables of some sort; they've only just come in. You're welcome to sift through them, if you desire. I think the rest of the toys are a little trivial for two such sweet intelligent boys as you."

Len was fuming now. 'Sweet? I'll give him sweet', he thought.

The word 'timetables', however had registered with Eddie and he replied,

"I'd like to have a look through the magazines and timetables, Mr Grant."

"O.K., follow me."

Eddie obeyed but Len remained where he was; he clearly preferred the relative openness of the front of the shop.

"Here they are, young man," said Mr Grant once they were in the storeroom at the back of the Emporium, and what an emporium! Row upon row of floor-to-ceiling shelf units stacked with objects of every kind and description, some of which looked as though they had been there years, if not decades. There were so many things that removing one single item would have probably brought a hundred crashing down. It had needed a balancing act of circus proportions to maintain the equilibrium of the storeroom. Fortunately for Eddie, the box was on the floor by the first row of shelves.

"I'll leave you to browse," said Mr Grant and he returned to check on Len. The magazines were mostly for gardeners and home handymen; the timetables were for old bus services, mainly in and around London. He dropped them all back into the box and nearly missed the slim pocket-sized book wedged down one side. He pulled it out and read the cover.

Anywhere by Rail

by

David Glaistor

The title seemed to jog something in his memory and as soon as he looked inside he remembered what it was. The book had a dedication on the first page.

To the memory of the railway engineer Jacob Denham Manders

1815-1863

A pioneer of British railways

Eddie flicked through the rest of the book, his hands shaking visibly, if anyone had been there to see. It seemed to be on the history of the early railways and how one man had almost single-handedly plotted the complicated network of tracks that formed the modern spider's web across the whole country; modern in the sense of 1929 when the book was written by the author. He closed it up and went back to the front of the shop where his friend seemed to be an unwilling participant in a conversation about Fenton Grammar School. Len would tell Eddie later that old Granty claimed to have been a teacher there before the war. Eddie broke in with,

"How much is this, Mr Grant?"

"That? What is it?"

"Just an old book on railways."

"Let me see it."

Eddie passed the small book to Mr Grant and waited nervously.

"Interested in old railways, are we, dear?"

"Yes, sir."

"Well, you can have it for sixpence. Do you want me to wrap it?"

"No, I'll take it just as it is, thank you," replied Eddie as he handed over the money and the exact amount as well. Len had already left the shop having used the opportunity of the break in his conversation to depart. He was waiting on a more level part of the lower High Street when Eddie emerged.

"What've you bought, mate?" asked Len.

"A book on old railways," replied Eddie almost nonchalantly.

"How old?"

"Last century, when they first started laying down the track."

"Why?"

Eddie stopped walking up the High Street and said,

"Look at the cover and the first page."

"Oh no!" said Len.

"Oh yes, mate! I knew I'd seen something like the title before. Remember that plaque in the tunnel in Ludmouth. '*You can go anywhere by rail*'. That must have been Mr Mander's motto."

Len was deep in thought and then asked,

"What do you think it all means? It can't be a coincidence that you found this book over four months after we discovered that rock tunnel and that was a million to one chance anyway; the tunnel was only exposed by the storm."

"And we actually met Jacob Manders," said Eddie.

"You mean, we *think* we met him; he was a ghost, remember?"

Eddie's mum was still in, as he had predicted, when they got back to Fir Tree Close. It was nearly noon; there was no time for the boys to play with the train set or to study Eddie's new book and Len made his way home to return that afternoon for the important business of the day. Eddie's mum seemed pleased that her son had bought what appeared to be an educational book.

"You're beginning to show a lot of interest in railways. Hope you're not thinking of getting a job like your dad's," she said as she saw the cover of his purchase. He kept his hand tightly closed round it so that it shouldn't pop open and expose the dedication page.

"No, Mum, I want to go to university to study Maths."

Ann Compton smiled warmly and Eddie used the distraction to make his escape to go and bury his new book at the back of his wardrobe.

When Len got home he was surprised and also excited to hear that Eddie's mum was going to come round for afternoon tea with his own mum. Ann Compton was trying to get Martha Wilby involved with making some things for St Andrew's church jumble sale on the first Saturday in February. They were going to spend two or three hours doing some craft work and picking out knitting and needlework patterns.

"Will it still be alright if I go round to Eddie's, then?" asked Len at lunch.

"Of course. I think she's assuming you will keep Eddie company till she or his dad gets back. What plans do you have?"

"Oh, just some card games and to see if my train still works now that dad's fixed it. Where is Dad, by the way?"

"He's gone to put some shelves up for Great Aunt Gladys in Hamsden and I don't expect he'll be back till this evening; he's doing errands and some other chores as well."

"What time is Eddie's mum coming round?"

"About three, but you can go back over anytime you like."

'Things are dropping nicely into place', thought Len. 'Maybe three hours to experiment with both trains'.

"I'll go about two," was what he actually said.

At about the same time as Len and his mum were sorting out their respective afternoons, Gary was taking Jenny for a coffee at The Corner Café at the junction of Mill Road and the High Street. They were getting bolder in their public display of friendship, but no holding hands or other expressions of romance just yet. Though her dad was still totally unaware

179

of their reunion, her mum did have an inkling that something was making her daughter seem more cheerful than she had been for some time. Her mother's inkling might become more concrete after that Saturday's visit to The Corner Café.

"Hello, Jennifer; you're looking much better now, dear," said a voice from out of nowhere.

"Oh hello, Mrs Thompson; didn't see you there."

Gary looked sheepish.

"How are you, dear? Have you fully recovered from your nasty accident?"

"Yes, but I still have to have physiotherapy on my shoulder and it aches sometimes when it's damp."

"Well, look after yourself and do be careful, won't you?" said Mrs Thompson looking directly at Gary. Gary, for his part, tried to make himself inconspicuous and shrank metaphorically into the corner. Mrs Thompson nodded to Gary but said nothing to him leaving Jenny with,

"Remember me to your mother; I expect I'll see her on Sunday at church."

"Yes, Mrs Thompson, I will."

After Mrs Thompson had left the café, Gary asked,

"Will she be a problem? Will she tell your mum that she saw us together?"

"Probably, on Sunday morning, but I don't care anymore, Gary. We can't go on hiding how we feel about each other forever and anyway I think my mum might suspect already. It's my dad that I fear."

"Not if he loves you, Jenny."

Jenny smiled, but inside she hoped that her boyfriend's sentiment wasn't going to be tested just yet.

After his lunch Eddie had some time to himself before his friend would appear for their experimental session. He retrieved his new book from its place behind his science fiction comics and began to read. He found most of it fairly boring but was interested in several unusual facts about the early railway network and how it had grown by the late twenties. His head could hardly comprehend the fact that at its peak in 1913 there had been nearly 25,000 miles of track in Britain. Despite Mr Beeching's cuts of the previous year, of which Eddie knew much from his dad, the British railway network had been contracting slowly since the twenties. The real object of his attention was, however, Mr Jacob Manders, whose story formed the first couple of chapters of the book. Born right at the outset of the birth of railways as a means of transport, he had clearly been a visionary beyond his time. His motto: 'you can go anywhere by rail', fitted his glittering career to a tee. Eddie discovered that he had been the engineer in charge of several difficult projects to get a railway to many out-of-the-way places. 'Why go round when you can go through', was probably a better catchphrase for him. Brief mention was made of the proposed Ludmouth beach tunnel, but Eddie could find no mention of his mysterious death or whether the tunnel had ever been finished. His short biography outlined his career up to 1862, when, for most of the time, he seemed to have been based in the West Country. Eddie was still deep in thought about Mr Manders and what had happened to him when his mother shouted from downstairs,

"Len's here, Eddie!"

Whether or not the two boys needed an excuse to spend the afternoon inside was clearly irrelevant when Eddie got downstairs. Len gave his friend the weather report and just loud enough for Eddie's mum to hear.

"It's sleeting, mate – horrible outside."

Once in the dining room and with the door shut Eddie told his friend about his research into Jacob Manders. Len was suitably impressed.

"He sounds as if he was the top man in the nineteenth century with regard to building railways and he was determined to make it possible to go anywhere by rail in this country."

"Yes, but no details of his death, Len."

"Maybe he didn't die. I mean, we saw him last August, didn't we?"

"Ghosts don't die, mate. That's why they're ghosts; they just hang around to haunt people."

"So he's haunting us, eh?"

"Yes, but not for a bad reason; George said no harm would come to us."

"I just don't see what the connection is between Mr Manders and George Canter," said Len finally.

It was half past two and the two boys had decided to try Len's engine first, in case Eddie's mum took some time before she left. They had finished setting up the layout with Len's English Electric Type 4 D series diesel locomotive attached to Eddie's four carriages. Such engines had been in service in the Eastern region since as early as 1958, but it was only a model, as Eddie soon pointed out.

"Nothing's going to happen, Len. It can't be a magic engine."

"We'll soon see. Has your mum gone yet?"

Just then Eddie's mum poked her head into the dining room and said,

"I'm off then, Eddie; I should be back before your father. Is there anything you need?"

"No, we're fine, Mum. See you later."

The boys looked at each other.

"Why are we nervous, Eddie," said Len. "As you say, mate, it's your train that does the magic. Are we going to try it as well?"

"Probably, later. Give me the controller."

Eddie took the small black box and with the train on the opposite side to the tunnel, he pushed the switch and said,

"Watch carefully, Len."

The train move away smoothly and with a normal sound. It entered the tunnel and emerged without any apparent compression or loss of time.

"Nothing, Eddie," reported Len. "It's working just like it used to when I first got it two Christmases ago."

The train continued on its way, passed by the station platform opposite to the tunnel and re-entered the tunnel. Eddie allowed the train to perform three more laps, but without any alarm. He brought it to a precise halt beside his station platform.

Here, let me try," said Len at last and Eddie handed over the controls. Len pressed the switch and Eddie watched in anticipation – it was Len's train after all. Again, three circuits went by with nothing unusual occurring that the boys could see. After the fourth circuit the train pulled smoothly to a stop at the station platform.

"Keep it going, Len; just one more circuit."

Len's thumb was still glued to the switch.

"Must be broken, Eddie. I'm still working it."

"Take your finger off it and try again."

Len did as he was told and the train started moving again only to stop after just one circuit and precisely beside the platform again.

"Let me try," said Eddie, but when he took the controller the train carried on serenely, completing several circuits without stopping.

"Have another go," said Eddie handing Len the controls.

"Look," said Len. "It's still stopping and I'm not releasing any pressure, honestly Eddie."

They tried swapping again, but it soon became apparent that the train would only stop for Len and always exactly beside the station platform.

"Well, do you still say it's not a magic engine, then?" asked Len pointedly.

"It hasn't really done anything magical, Len. You might be releasing your thumb without realising it. How do I know that you're not just having a joke with me?"

"Don't be stupid, Eddie. You saw that I didn't take my thumb off."

"Well, let me try one more time," replied Eddie.

This time Eddie did become convinced that the train was being controlled by some other power, as it slowed smoothly to a halt at the platform on each of the three circuits he tried.

"Now do you believe me?"

"Yes, Len, I believe you."

Eddie thought for a moment and then continued,

"It hasn't taken us anywhere though, has it?"

"Not yet, but there's still time," replied Len, but no matter how many times the boys tried, nothing further sensational happened, even though the train continued to stop at the platform after a few circuits each time, no matter who operated the control. After a while the boys got bored, prompting Eddie to suggest that they replaced Len's diesel engine with the *Flying Scotsman*. Len was not happy to proceed as the time by his watch had reached four o'clock and he argued that his friend's mum might be back as early as an hour from then. For whatever reason, Eddie insisted.

"Come on, Len, it's only a game."

"No, Eddie. We might end up anywhere."

"Exactly, mate!"

"But the weather's awful and you know what happened last time."

"Maybe we'll move to a different time and it'll be summer as well."

Len eventually relented and they swapped engines. Eddie took the control first and Len glued his eyes to the tunnel as the train started. It completed two circuits and Eddie said,

"Absolutely nothing, mate."

"No," said Len, "*and* there was no compression or slowing down when it went through the tunnel. Let me try."

Len took the controller and after several circuits it was obvious to both boys that Eddie's train no longer had any magical properties. Even when Eddie peered into the tunnel, he was so unused to it coming through at normal speed that the engine hit him in the face before he could lift his head out of the way.

"You know what I think, Len?" said Eddie after he had recovered from his shock meeting.

"What?"

"I think that the magic is slowly moving to your engine, almost as if...."

"As if we're being allowed to share the magic like we're suppose to with the presents anyway," interjected Len.

"Yes."

"In which case, Eddie, maybe the station platform is going to become important, and not the tunnel," said Len.

"Possibly, but I don't think anything more is going to happen this afternoon. If we try it again, then we're going to need much longer, even maybe a whole day."

"When did you have in mind?" asked Len.

Eddie suddenly remembered what his mum had said about an upcoming event at the church.

"I think my mum will be involved with the St Andrew's church jumble sale on Saturday February the 1st and your mum may be as well."

"What about your dad?" asked Len.

"I don't know whether he'll be at work or not; he works most Saturdays but not all. I'll find out when I can and let you know."

"Where do you think my diesel engine will take us?"

"Anywhere, if our friendly ghost is to be believed!"

The following morning Eddie went with his parents to church as normal. Jenny was still in bed when they left by car at ten-thirty, it being too wet to walk. She had been dreading Sunday morning since the previous lunchtime and the awkward meeting with Mrs Brenda Thompson. Would Mrs Thompson be there? Would she talk to Jenny's mum? Would she say she'd seen her daughter? All these questions had been going through Jenny's head and continued to do so all morning while she waited for her parents to return. She would have to face up to the problem sooner or later and it would probably be better if it was the former.

Her dad said nothing to her when he arrived home and she knew immediately from his silence that Mrs Thompson had shared her gossip. Jenny's mum wasted no time in talking to her daughter.

"Mrs Thompson from church says she saw you and Gary in the Corner Café yesterday."

The time had come to face up to her parents.

"Yes, Mum. What of it? We we're only having a coffee. Can't I even have a coffee with Gary?"

Fred Compton came back into the kitchen from hanging up his coat and couldn't hold back any longer when he heard his daughter.

"Jenny, the boy could have killed you. He's no good; everyone says so."

Jenny was close to tears and in a shaky voice trembling with emotion, she said,

"Dad, he's changed. He's learnt his lesson and if I can forgive him why can't everyone else? Why can't you and mum?"

Jenny burst into tears and ran from the kitchen to the safety of her bedroom. She did not come down for lunch and would not reappear for the rest of the day despite her mum's cajoling and, apart from a cup of coffee, her tea was left untouched outside her door. Eddie did his best to stay out of the discussion-cum-argument that ensued between Ann and Fred Compton. Jenny's mum was secretly quite pleased that the two teenagers looked like they were getting back together. Her dad was adamant that Gary was 'a wrong'un'.

16

A Test

To Jenny's great relief her parents didn't mention her liaison with Gary Jones all the following week; in fact her dad hardly spoke a word to her on any matter. She and Gary had decided not to meet each other for a while until, as Gary said, 'things cooled down'. Jenny did manage to make a couple of extremely brief phone calls; on both occasions Gary had been tied up with customers. Even his dad had noticed a change in his son for the better and had given him the responsibility of being out front in the showroom. Some other people in the locality had also commented on Gary's change for the better. Time would tell as to whether Fred Compton would come round to the same way of thinking.

Len was finding his schoolwork more difficult than in his first year, while his friend seemed to be sailing through with top marks in most subjects. English was still Eddie's worst subject though and was, indeed, the only one in which he and Len were in the same set – the lowest. It was in one such lesson on the last Friday afternoon of January that Eddie whispered to his friend as they sat side by side on the back row of room 46,

"Alright for tomorrow, mate? Come round at nine-thirty."

"Shh!"

"And just what is the meaning of the word 'documented' in this context, Compton?"

"Sir?"

"Asleep are we, Compo?"

"No, sir."

"Then be good enough to give us the benefit of your brain in this matter. What does the author mean?"

Mr Green was now standing right beside Eddie's desk and staring right into his eyes. Eddie couldn't avoid being honest.

"Sorry, sir, I wasn't paying attention."

"*Ah! Ah! Compton, and what do we do with boys who don't pay attention, then?*"

"I don't know, sir."

"*You don't know, eh? Well let me tell you. You will provide a 500 word essay on why it is a good idea to pay attention in class – Monday morning, on my desk.*"

"Yes, sir."

"*So, Wilby, you can help your friend out here. Give us your opinion on the question.*"

"What was the question, sir?"

"*Oh dear, two essays for me to look at on Monday morning. Hope you two both have a good weekend.*"

The English lesson concluded without further trouble for Len and Eddie. After registration and the two reprobates had got outside the school gates into South Road, they exchanged views on how they had both got their first punishments of the term or, in Eddie's case, of the year. Len put on a frown and did his best mimicry of their English teacher.

"I do believe, Edward Compton, or should I call you Compo, that it is entirely your fault that my progress in English was hindered today. Please tell me what punishment you deserve."

"You should have kept quiet and let me know that old man Green was watching me."

"I did!"

Len grinned at his friend and, as always, he bore no grudge.

"When are you going to do your essay, mate?"

"Tonight, I reckon. We might be fully engaged tomorrow."

"Got much other homework?" asked Len.

"Just Science and Geography, neither of which is due in till Tuesday."

The boys went their separate ways at the entrance to Fir Tree Close and Eddie called out as Len left,

"See you tomorrow. Don't forget your engine!"

"Wilco, chief!"

Fred Compton *was* at work on Saturday February the 1st and left home at eight-fifteen. Jenny left ten minutes later and Eddie's mum duly obliged also at ten to nine with strict instructions to Eddie not to get his clothes dirty and to eat the lunch already prepared in the pantry. When asked what he was going to do for the day, he said,

"Maybe Len will come round and we'll go down town as usual. Maybe we'll play some games – depends on the weather, Mum. I've also got quite a bit of homework to do and there's Grandstand to watch on the television this afternoon."

Eddie lost count of the penalty points he'd earned with his maker, but they were only little white lies he reckoned; his 'maybe this, maybe that' covered many possibilities. As she went out the front door his mum called back,

"The jumble sale finishes at four so I should be home by five. Bye!"

As soon as he had the house to himself, Eddie went to the bookshelves in the lounge where his dad kept his railway timetables and selected the one for 1964 that covered the Eastern Region, a copy of which Fred Compton always kept at home for reference. If they did go on a journey, at least he and Len would have something to refer to when and if they needed to get back. Something was telling him they might need more than just a timetable and he prayed that his dad's bureau was unlocked. Fred Compton had, for the first time on account of his long service, received a railcard which allowed free family travel at most times and on most lines that didn't involve going via London. Eddie's luck was in as he carefully placed the so far unused card in his wallet.

Len was on time and the two boys got down to the business of the day. When the layout was complete with English Electric Type 4 D209 in charge, Eddie told his friend of his precautions.

"I've got our family railcard. It can get us more or less anywhere for free if you're prepared to be my brother again. I've got Dad's Eastern Region timetable as well"

"We'll need a duffle bag or something to carry everything," said Len. "My mum's made me a packed lunch."

"Me too."

"Why do you think we need the timetable and railcard? Do you think we're going to be dumped somewhere?" asked Len.

"Don't know mate. I suppose I'm just trying to cover all possibilities. What should we do about clothes? Go as we are with our winter coats?"

"Have too; it's quite cold out. Better to have them and not need them than to need them and not have them."

Eddie smiled. His friend was growing up. He just hoped that they wouldn't feel old beyond their years by the end of the day.

"I'll get my duffle coat and bag, Len and then we'll get ready."

Once they were both fully clothed for a winter's day, Eddie put everything they needed in his duffle bag and they stood together by the dining room table. Len took the controller and the game began.

"Here she goes," said Len and the train pulled away from the station. Seconds later and it entered the tunnel with neither boy expecting anything to happen until the train reached the station. Consequently they were both taken unawares when the room was pitched into darkness at the precise moment the first carriage entered the tunnel. This time they both backed away to the same wall of the dining room and slid down into a sitting position supported by something comfortable beneath them. Suddenly the blackness lifted and they found themselves sitting in a carriage, squeezed in with four other people with whom they'd obviously been for some time.

"You lads alright? Did the tunnel frighten you? You look like you both seen a ghost."

"We're O.K., sir," said Len automatically, not knowing to whom he was replying until his eyes focused on the young stranger sitting opposite them.

"Good. Everyone has to change here anyway."

The other three passengers had already made for the corridor and the young man followed.

"See you, then," he said as he left.

Eddie and Len remained where they were while they gathered their thoughts. The train they were on had come to a halt almost immediately after leaving the tunnel, just like their train set had previously with Len's engine.

"*Llanphroig Junction. All change. All change.*"

A platform guard looked in through the open door and said in a strong Welsh accent,

"Now then, boys, let's have you. End of the line."

Len pulled Eddie up and they exited the train onto a small platform in an area of the country that clearly neither of them had ever been to before.

"Wow! Look at those mountains," gasped Len.

"It's definitely winter, mate," replied Eddie.

192

Not only were the mountain tops covered with snow, but so were the lower slopes and fields within in close proximity of the station.

"Wales, then," continued Eddie, but Len had already rushed to the front of the train and was staring at the engine.

"It's my engine, Eddie!" he shouted back and both boys noticed quickly that they and the solitary guard were the only people still on the platform. Eddie joined his friend.

"There you are – Type 4 diesel D209, so we must be roughly in our time or, at least, later than 1958," Len continued.

"You boys live in the village, then?" said the guard who was now standing beside them.

"No, sir. When's the next train out of here?" asked Eddie politely.

"This one goes back to Caernarvon in half an hour, just as soon as they shunt the engine to the back. You boys aren't going back yet, are you?"

"We've got a railcard, so we're travelling all over today," said Len quickly.

"Well if you miss this one, there's not another till three-thirty this afternoon," and with that, the guard was gone. Eddie looked at his watch: ten to ten.

"Time of day hasn't moved," he said,

"How do we tell what day it is?" asked Len.

"Should have asked that guard," replied Eddie.

"Oh yeah: '*excuse me, sir, but what year are we in*'? I don't think so!"

"Might as well go and wait for this train to go back to Caernarvon," said Eddie.

"Where's Caernarvon, then, mate?"

"Wales?" suggested Eddie trying to hide his sarcasm.

The boys made their way to the tiny waiting room, where they found a well-established coal fire to warm them. They had already deduced that it was much colder in Wales, than in Fenton-on-Sea. After a few minutes the deserted platform and waiting room soon became busy with locals from the village. Mostly women and children, many were carrying shopping bags for the ten-fifteen service to Caernarvon and the boys decided to leave the claustrophobic atmosphere of the waiting room to stand more anonymously on the platform. Eddie made a guess at the day of the week.

"It's got to be a Saturday, judging by all the kids."

"Could be the Christmas holidays," replied Len as he started to stroll around trying to see if anyone was carrying a newspaper – a sure way of gauging the date in the past. He failed miserably in his task and quickly returned to where Eddie was still standing.

"No chance, mate, and they're all talking in Welsh."

The only English voice they'd heard so far had been the guard's and as Eddie remarked, he had to speak English as an employee of British Rail. Soon they heard his lilting tones again over the tannoy.

"The train at platform one is the ten-fifteen service to Caernarvon."

The announcement was then repeated several times in Welsh and the boys made their way onto the train, trying to choose the emptiest carriage. Though there had seemed to be a lot of people waiting on the platform, they were all soon swallowed up in the train. Len and Eddie chose the first carriage directly behind the diesel engine.

"Apart from being in Wales, Eddie, where is Caernarvon?" asked Len after they were comfortably seated by themselves.

"I suspect it's in North Wales. I think I read somewhere that the vast majority of people there speak Welsh as their first language."

"So how do we get home?"

"We'll have to ask at the booking office and hope there's someone like my dad working there this morning – he'd know instantly."

"Tickets please," said the guard who had suddenly arrived unnoticed in the boys' carriage. Eddie produced his railcard and smiled confidently. The guard studied it intently and just as Eddie was thinking that there was going to be a problem, he said,

"Thank you," and quickly left their carriage.

They soon realised that the village of Llanphroig was high up in the mountains, as the thirty-five minute trip to Caernarvon station seemed to be all down hill. The train stopped at three other villages on the way down and everywhere outside was cloaked in a white blanket of snow, which seemed thinner as the train approached the town.

"*Caernarvon, Caernarvon station. All change! All change!*"

This was again followed by its Welsh equivalent as the train pulled to a stop and the boys jumped down onto platform three.

"Right," said Eddie. "Let's find the booking office."

Though all of the station signs were written in Welsh, the majority had the English translation written underneath, albeit in much smaller lettering. Eddie did the questioning.

"Excuse me, can you tell us how to get to Fenton-on-Sea?"

The female booking clerk looked blank. It was clear from her reaction that she was rarely asked about any English sounding place, let alone one situated on the other extremity of Britain to Caernarvon. Eddie spotted a calendar on the wall behind her.

"Where's that, then?"

"England, er, East Anglia. It's by the seaside."

"I can get you to Chester; it's the nearest big city in England and you can certainly get to Birmingham from there. What do you want singles or returns?"

"Neither. We've got a railcard, thanks. When's the next train?"

"Every hour, on the hour from platform one, but hurry it's gone five to."

The boys just made it onto the eleven o'clock express to Chester after a frantic dash over the footbridge and they were whisked quickly away, barely having experienced beautiful Caernarvon and its historic castle, which they glimpsed briefly as they pulled away from the station. Once settled in a carriage with one elderly gentleman as the only other occupant, Eddie whispered to his friend,

"Saturday, February the 1st; same as when we left. Chances are it's still 1964 as well, since the day and date agree."

Eddie eventually explained his conclusion after the old man had fallen to sleep in the warm carriage. Bangor, Colwyn Bay and Rhyl were the only stops that the steam train made on its way to Chester. The whole journey lasted just over one hour and twenty minutes and they were in Chester at twelve-twenty-two.

Chester station was busy and the two boys had great difficulty in finding anyone they could ask about trains to Birmingham; the queue at the booking office was too long for them to wait. Eddie had in the back of his mind that they were still a long way from home with, at most, five hours left. In the end they consulted a large timetable noticeboard.

"Next one is ten past one," said Eddie.

It was one o'clock, so they had time to buy a bottle of drink, and ate half their packed lunches while they waited in an anonymous middle carriage. It wasn't until they reached Shrewsbury that they were joined by anyone, a young courting couple who spent the whole journey to Birmingham holding hands, and occasionally engaging in more romantic gestures, to Len's disgust in particular. They arrived at Birmingham New Street on time, at ten to three and Eddie knew that they would have to ask someone about the next leg of their journey. They were about fifty yards from the booking hall when Eddie stopped dead in his tracks and grabbed his friend's arm in panic.

"That's Mr Watson over there," he whispered. "I'm sure of it."

"What, from Watson's Electrical?" queried Len.

"Hide he's coming this way!"

The two friend's ducked behind a tall pile of suitcases on a handcart and watched as, indeed, the said resident and businessman from Fenton-on-Sea strolled by. They waited until he had disappeared into a train carriage. Eddie immediately had an idea.

"I bet he's been here on business; I'm sure I remember him saying he was coming to Birmingham when I bought the dining car. Remember?"

"Vaguely."

"Come on," said Eddie. "Let's get on the same train; I bet he's going home to Fenton."

Len wasn't too sure.

"Bit of a risk, mate, on two counts. One: he may not be going to Fenton and two: he might see us."

"Got to be worth it, Len. We wouldn't need to ask anyone else to find our way back, then. Mr Paul Watson will show us the way."

Len finally reluctantly agreed and the boys boarded the three o'clock service to Rugby and stations south to London. This time the train was crowded, almost beyond capacity, and they had to stand in the space between two adjoining carriages, which, as Eddie pointed out, was an ideal position from which to see when and if Mr Watson left the train.

The jumble sale at St Andrew's church had been well attended and by three-thirty there was very little left to sell. Martha and Ann were exhausted after being on their feet since before ten that morning. Brenda Thompson made a beeline for Jenny's mum.

"Hello, Ann and how's your daughter now? Is she still going out with that Gary Jones?"

Ann Compton didn't like the 'nosy' Mrs Thompson and tried to ignore her.

"I said, is Jenny still seeing that awful boy, Gary Jones?"

"I have no idea, Mrs Thompson, not that it should be any concern of yours, I'm sure."

"Oh, there's no need to take that tone, you know. I'm only concerned that Jenny doesn't get into any more trouble. Aren't you worried, dear?"

Ann Compton was about to say something derogatory about Brenda Thompson's eldest son, who'd already been in trouble with Sergeant Owen Hughes for pinching cigarettes from Johnson's the newsagents, but she held her peace.

"No, I'm not. I think both of them have learnt their lessons – more than some people seem to."

Jenny's mum turned her back on Mrs Brenda Thompson and continued to help tidy up after the jumble sale. Though the sale had been scheduled to finish at four, Martha and Ann were already walking up the lower High Street when the church clock struck the hour.

"Fancy some tea in the Corner Café?" said Len's mum, and, if he'd heard the question, a voice would have shouted from over a hundred and fifty miles away,

"Go on, Mum, you've plenty of time!"

"Better not, Martha. I'm very tired and I'd rather get back and see what Eddie's been up to; it's getting dark."

It was also getting dark as the three o'clock from Birmingham New Street pulled into Rugby at ten past four. Both boys peered out of the door window, one in each direction, though Eddie had been certain that they were to the rear of where Mr Watson was. Len spotted him at once.

"He's got off! Let's go."

They managed to jump down onto the platform a second or two before the train lurched forward on its way to London Euston. In their haste to alight from the train, both boys lost sight of their quarry.

"Where'd he go?" said Eddie.

The station platforms seemed to be devoid of any trains once the one to London had departed. A few passengers were waiting on the platform from which it had just left. Suddenly Mr Watson emerged from beneath a sign which read, *Gentlemen.* He joined the other waiting passengers. This time the boys found that they were in an exposed position less than thirty yards from their leader and they quickly secreted themselves behind a large advertising hoarding. They ate the rest of their packed lunches and waited.

Mr Paul Watson had had his name over a shop in Mill Road ever since his father had died seven years previously and he was probably the most respected shop owner in Fenton-on-Sea. Now with his electrical-cum-toy shop in addition to the longer established ironmongery opposite, he claimed in his adverts that, '*you can get anything for the home at Watson's*'. He was a tall and thin man, in his late forties, with swept-back black hair not unlike that sported by the former owner of the electrical side of his mini-empire. His six and half foot height was useful not only in reaching items at the top and back of out-of-the-way shelves, but also in seeing over obstacles with ease. The boys would have to hope that he did not approach the hoarding too closely, even though the light was fading quickly.

"I wonder when the next train is due?" asked Eddie from their position of safety.

"And where it's going?" replied Len.

Eddie was looking at his watch.

"We've absolutely no chance of making it before my mum or dad gets home."

Little did Eddie know that they were still a hundred and sixty miles from the East Anglian coast, and that it could be much later that evening before they saw Fenton again, if, indeed, they made it at all that Saturday. Len was, however, eternally optimistic.

"It's only a game, mate."

"Yeah, and we've lost it. It was a test and we failed," said Eddie dejectedly. "I think we should phone someone."

"Don't be daft; I'm not admitting defeat yet."

As if on cue, a six-carriage diesel train pulled up to their platform and they could see Mr Watson move forward. They waited until they saw him into the first carriage and they then selected an empty compartment in the rear, in order to put as much distance as possible between themselves and the businessman. It was getting quite dark; it was twenty to five. When the ticket collector had checked their railcard, Eddie asked him a question.

"Excuse me, when do we get to our destination?"

"Depends where you're going, son."

Oh, er, all the way," replied Len quickly.

"The train gets into Cambridge at six-thirty."

After the guard had moved to the next carriage, Eddie reached for his duffle bag from the parcel shelf. He knew Cambridge was in the Eastern Region and, after a few minutes studying, he announced,

"There's a train from Cambridge at seven which gets into Hamsden at ten to eight. We could be back in Fenton by ten to nine if we make the eight-fifteen. We don't need to worry about Mr Watson anymore. He might as well not be here."

"Nearly eleven hours to go from North Wales to Fenton-on-Sea. What a journey!" said an exhausted Len who promptly closed his eyes and went to sleep.

The rest of the journey to Cambridge was uneventful. Eddie drifted in and out of sleep and Len seemed to remain in that state the whole way. Only the jolt of the train pulling to a halt brought him into the land of the living. Eddie looked at his watch: ten to seven – they were late.

"Quick, Len, the Hamsden train goes in ten minutes."

In their haste they almost forgot their nemesis and found themselves only feet behind him on the platform. Len pulled Eddie back until they saw him cross to another platform. A railcar with only four carriages waited and was to be their next transport. This time they had no idea which car Mr Watson had got into, so they selected the last one as before. Their luck was in because even though the car was open-plan, there was no sign of him. They felt back on safe ground when, after another uneventful journey, they arrived at Hamsden station at exactly quarter past eight, by Eddie's watch. Once on the platform they could not see Mr Watson anywhere and for a few seconds they thought he might be behind them, but there appeared to be no sign of him. Little did they know that Mr Paul Watson was still standing on platform two at Birmingham's New Street station.

They made the Fenton train with minutes to spare and collapsed with relief in their familiar train and surroundings. The lights were very bright from the station platform, prompting Len to say,

"It's like daylight outside, Eddie."

Eddie glanced through the window.

"It *is* daylight!"

He looked at his watch: eight-sixteen. Just then a young mother and her two children sat opposite the two boys. Eddie asked,

"Can you tell me the time, please?"

"Yes, it's a quarter past three, dear."

Len collapsed into giggles and Eddie just about managed a polite 'thank you'. They had passed the test. They hadn't panicked and they had avoided all possible traps, human or otherwise. Both of them wore smiles on their faces all the way back to their seaside town, where they arrived at ten to four. No one they knew observed them alight from the train, least of all Eddie's dad who was hidden at the back of the booking office having a cup of tea. They walked in through the open front door of number 38 Fir Tree Close at four precisely and vaguely heard St Andrew's church clock strike the hour in the distance. Eddie had been praying that the house had not been burgled, but all was well and they quickly packed the train set away. Len's engine and the four carriages had still been in position beside the platform. Hardly a word was exchanged between the two friends and Len left Eddie at quarter past four. He turned round in the doorway clutching his diesel engine tightly.

"See you Monday. Don't do anything I wouldn't do!"

"Had a good day, Len?"

Len nearly collided with Eddie's mum as she came in through the front door.

"Oh, yes, Mrs Compton; best day ever!"

Eddie had already dashed to the dining room the minute he'd heard his mother's voice, leaving Len slightly bemused. Did he have time to get the railcard and timetable from his duffle bag which he'd dropped in the understairs hall cupboard and return them both to their rightful places in the lounge? He'd accomplished half the task when he collided with his mum in the hall.

"What *are* you doing, Eddie?"

"Oh, just putting my bag away, Mum."

Eddie had managed to secrete the railcard in his trouser pocket, but the slim timetable remained in one hand behind his back.

"What have you got there?"

There was no real way to carry on the pretence and Eddie said,

"Oh, just dad's railway timetable. Len and I were checking how easy it would be to go to London for a day out sometime."

"You're far too young to be thinking of going to London on your own. Maybe when your thirteen we'll think about it and, besides, your father will be cross if he finds out you've taken one of his books off the shelf. You'd better return it at once before he gets in from work."

"Yes, Mum."

Eddie disappeared into the lounge while his mother went to the kitchen to make a cup of tea. The Eastern Region timetable was duly replaced on the shelf and, with the lounge door nearly closed, he eased open the bureau front and deposited the railcard were it belonged.

"Do you want a cup of tea, Eddie?"

"Yes please, Mum, I'm really thirsty. It's been a long day."

Eddie joined his mum in the kitchen and faced the inevitable inquiries into his day.

"Well, what have you done all day?"

"This and that, Mum. Went down town; played with the train set; walked along the prom – you know, the usual."

"Aren't you getting a bit old to still be playing with that train set? I don't see how you and Len can waste so much time with it."

"I know, Mum, but time just seems to fly when we do!"

17

Teenager

Eddie and Len remained in their respective dream worlds until they met again on the way to school on Monday morning. They actually shook each other by the hand as the only non-verbal gesture they could think of to indicate the extra bond that had been created by Saturday's incredible journey.

"What happened, Eddie?" asked Len eventually. "What on earth happened?"

"Time stood still, mate – we lost about five hours."

"Or gained them, whichever way you look at it," said Len.

"Did your mum and dad suspect anything when you got back?" asked Eddie.

"No, I was very tired and went to bed early, which did seem to surprise them a bit, I suppose. What about you?"

"I had to tell my mum that I borrowed one of Dad's timetables, but I don't think she told him."

"Must do the same thing again sometime, eh?" said Len.

"Not likely, mate. I don't want to do any more ducking and diving. I have had enough of train sets for a while."

Eddie had summed up how his friend felt too, but he had not wanted to express it first. The two friends continued on their way to school talking about the reality of the day ahead, including comparing what they had written in their essays for Mr Green.

The rest of the spring term passed peacefully enough and by the time of the week of Eddie's thirteenth birthday, the weather had become quite warm. For the first time that he could remember, his birthday was due to fall at the weekend on the third Saturday of March. Term was due to finish on Wednesday the 18th of March and the two friends had arranged to meet at Len's house the following morning. Thursday morning was quite springlike with a hint of showers later. The visits to Woolworth's had become so isolated that it was with some surprise that Eddie mentioned the possibility as soon as they had left 7 Lime Tree Avenue.

"I want to go to 'Woolies' today, Len."

"Why?"

"Mum and Dad say I can have a transistor radio for my birthday on Saturday and I want to go and see what they've got. They're cheaper than Watson's."

"Oh, you lucky sod. How much can you spend?"

"Up to five pounds."

"My dad says you can make them – Watson's have all the parts."

The second mention of the name sparked some memories into life for Eddie.

"Do you often think of our trip across Wales and England, Len?"

Len stopped walking; they were in South Road directly opposite Fenton station. He turned to face his friend.

"What do you think? Of course I do. I also began to wonder that because you hadn't mentioned it, it couldn't have happened or that, maybe, you remembered it differently to me."

After five minutes of swapping memories, it was clear to both of them that they remembered it in exactly the same detail. One thing bothered Len, though.

"Do you think Mr Watson was really in Birmingham on Saturday, February the 1st?"

Eddie pondered the question.

"There's one way to find out."

"How?"

"Ask him."

"What, just go straight up to him and ask him if he was in Birmingham on that date?" said Len incredulously.

"Why not?"

"Because he'll think you mad. What possible reason could you give for asking him?"

"Don't know, but I'll think of something."

Len scoffed at Eddie's outrageous suggestion and by the time they had reached Woolworth's the idea had been forgotten, or so Len hoped.

Eddie spotted the radio he wanted almost immediately, priced at four pounds and ten shillings.

"Are you buying it today?" asked Len.

"No, Mum's going to come in today or tomorrow and get it. I've just got to make a note of which one I'd like."

Eddie scribbled the details on a piece of paper from his wallet and the boys soon left the store. Once outside they noticed that although it looked like rain, Len wanted to play football on the 'rec', but Eddie hadn't forgotten his idea.

"I am going to go to Watson's, you know, Len. You can wait outside if you like."

Two minutes later and Eddie asked his question, boldly, but with a subtle touch.

"Did my dad find you a clever way to get to Birmingham last time you went, Mr Watson?"

"Oh yes, Eddie. Fancy you remembering that."

"Which way did you go?"

"Why do you want to know?"

"I'm interested in railways like my dad."

Well, let me think. It was a Saturday and Fred told me to go via Hamsden, obviously, but then not to London. It went Cambridge, Rugby, Coventry and Birmingham, though, as I remember it, I didn't have to change at Coventry on the way back."

"Do you go every month?"

"Most months – normally on the first Saturday. I haven't been this month yet, though. Last time would have been February."

Eddie was satisfied and Mr Watson seemed pleased that he had been able to help him in his investigations, innocent as he thought they were. Eddie then asked,

"What's the cheapest transistor radio you have, Mr Watson?"

"The cheapest? That would be the new *Slendertone Mark 3*; it's four pounds, seventeen and six."

"Thank you, Mr Watson. I may be back."

"Alright, Eddie. Remember me to your dad."

"Will do, sir."

Len was waiting patiently outside.

"Well?"

"The last time Mr Watson went to Birmingham was the first Saturday in February!" Eddie announced triumphantly.

"Elementary, my dear Watson," said Len and he laughed at his double meaning.

The boys headed back up the High Street and Eddie agreed, perhaps a little reluctantly, to go and play some football. Twenty minutes later Len had collected his 'special' ball and they were at the recreation ground. Though they had played with it a few times since the famous cup final victory by the under-13 football team, nothing noticeably unusual had happened. Eddie took his customary position between the posts.

"Penalties first, I think. Let's see how many you save out of ten," said Len.

"None, I suspect."

Eddie was correct. Whichever way he dived the ball seemed to avoid him completely. Len then tried shooting from about thirty yards, but Eddie still displayed his normal and acceptable talent for the game. Even when they swapped roles, Eddie couldn't kick the ball straight more than about once in four or five shots.

"Magic's wearing thin, Len," remarked Eddie who had clearly had enough by then.

"Like my ball. Look."

Len's football was indeed looking worn and marked, even though it wasn't in as bad a state as a previous football purchased from a certain junk shop. The signatures were barely readable and the glossy leather surface was scuffed and dull. After a closer inspection, Eddie asked,

"Was it like that when we started?"

"Don't think so – it's not a year old yet."

Eddie guessed what was happening.

"I think the game maybe over, Len."

"How do you mean?"

"Well, both presents from George have provided us with experiences we'll never forget, right? Maybe we've had more fun with the train set, but at least you scored the winning goal in the cup final. I just think that the magic is exhausted and we've had our fun."

"Would you like to prove your point by trying the train set again, Einstein?"

"Yeah, alright. What about this afternoon, then?"

Len brought his diesel engine round to Eddie's house just after two o'clock and the two boys patiently constructed the layout. Inevitably, after their last experience, they were considerably nervous. It was starting to rain outside and Eddie's mum was probably going to delay her visit to Woolworth's to buy Eddie's birthday present.

"Are you sure you want to do this?" asked Len.

"Why not? Let's try your engine first. If it's still a game and something happens, we'll just have to play it and make sure we win."

They tried out Len's engine and all seemed normal until about the fourth circuit when suddenly Eddie said,

"The dining car has gone!"

There were only three carriages left. Len put the controller down and looked into tunnel whence the train had just emerged.

"Nothing there."

"Try it again, Len."

Len tried it again and after three more circuits only his engine emerged from the tunnel. All Eddie's carriages had disappeared. This time Len lifted the tunnel right out of the way and turned it upside down to inspect it closely.

"Whoops!" he said, but Eddie didn't seem upset.

"Not to worry, Len. I was getting a little bored with it anyway. I'm thirteen on Saturday – time to move on."

"Won't there be a problem when your dad asks you where your train set is or, worse, asks to play with it?" asked Len.

"Hadn't thought of that. I'll have to make something up."

"What?"

"No idea."

They tried Len's engine several more times to see if the carriages would reappear but without success. Eddie then proposed that they try the

Flying Scotsman. He waited nervously while Len swapped the engines and prepared to press the switch.

"Here we go."

Len pushed the lever over and Eddie's engine began from the platform. At first, when the engine disappeared into the tunnel, they both thought that it had gone too, when it didn't emerge for several seconds. Suddenly the *Flying Scotsman* came out, coupled to the four missing carriages and, without Len releasing any pressure from the switch, the reassembled train stopped smoothly beside the platform. Eddie looked relieved.

"Well that's it, Len; I'm not trying it anymore. It goes away in its box; I think something is trying to tell us something."

"You could be right, mate. Looks like if you play with it again you might lose it permanently. Wouldn't be a bad idea, would it?"

After they had packed the engine and the original three carriages away in their box, Eddie and Len took the box and the other miscellaneous extras up to Eddie's bedroom where they were dispatched to the back of his wardrobe along with his little book on early railways.

They went back downstairs and, as if in agreement with Eddie's decision, the earlier rain had stopped and a warm sun shone on Fenton-on-Sea – not a time to be playing inside with model train sets. They weren't real, after all!

The pier had opened early even though Easter wasn't for over another week. One-armed bandits beckoned, as well as the other seaside pursuits that had been the boys' pastimes for the last two or three years. They wasted a good hour losing slowly, a few pennies at a time, until they decided to wander onto the beach to search for amber and anything washed up by the winter seas. They headed in the direction of East Hill, hardly noticing when they passed by the very spot where a previous adventure had started. Thoughts of fantasy or magic seemed to be occupying less of both of their psyches. It wouldn't be long before the harsh reality of science and scientific rigour would occupy Eddie's mind. They found little of interest, just some shiny black stones which Cyril Wilby would later identify as jet, a semi-precious form of lignite. He would also tell them that it was rare to find such stones on a beach so far south. The boys would spend much of the summer months looking for more of the material and extra pocket money would be earned from a jeweller in Hamsden who made jet into brooches and the like. The boys parted company at five and, as Eddie strolled up Fir Tree Close, he was hit with the realisation that he was growing up – train sets and other toys no longer seemed to have the same appeal. He was to be thirteen in less than two days, and a transistor radio would soon be his. He was looking forward to listening to radio stations from faraway places.

Ann Compton left it until well after lunch on Friday to go to Woolworth's for her son's birthday present. Her husband had already bought two return tickets to London for Eddie and Len, which could be used anytime over the next six months, but the radio was to be Eddie's main present.

"Yes, madam, can I help you?" said the assistant on the electrical counter in Woolworth's.

"Yes, I'd like a Bentham's 102 Am/Fm transistor radio, please."

"I'll just see if we've got one left in the storeroom. I know we sold a couple yesterday. I won't be a moment."

Eddie's mum waited, and waited, and….

"I'm sorry, madam, we've none left."

"Oh, when will you have them in again?"

"Not until a week on Tuesday; that's the next delivery, I'm afraid. We have some other radios. Who's it for?"

"My son, he's twelve – I mean thirteen."

"Oh, what a shame, the only ones we've got left are really for girls; they're pink and really they're only toys."

"Oh well, it can't be helped. Thanks for looking."

'It has to be Watson's', thought Ann Compton as she came out of Woolworth's, and then she remembered that Watson's closed early on Fridays, at four. It was ten past. She cursed under her breath and headed home, hoping that a crisp five-pound note would suffice for her son. He would have to be patient and wait until the Tuesday after Easter, the very last day of the month.

Eddie was clearly a little down on the Saturday morning when an envelope containing five pounds was the substitute for his radio. Though he didn't complain, his dad could see his son was upset at breakfast and tried to console him.

"Never mind, son. Your mum did her best and as my mum always used to say: '*All good things come to those who wait*'."

Eddie barely raised a smile, but his dad continued,

"I have a surprise for you as well."

"What, Dad?"

"How would you and Len like to go to London for a day sometime this summer?"

"When? Do Len's parents know? Does Len know?

Eddie's dad could tell from his son's numerous questions that he had selected the right present and said,

"Whenever you like. I have two return tickets valid up to September and yes, Mr and Mrs Wilby know and are happy for Len to go, but no, Len doesn't know. I thought you'd like to tell him."

"Thanks, Dad."

Eddie grinned broadly. His dad's gift was a very good substitute and he would still get his radio, provided he didn't spend the five pounds beforehand. He gave the five pounds to his mum and said,

"You'd better keep this, Mum. I'll only spend it."

Saturday's post was late arriving and Eddie waited patiently all morning. Only his sister had gone to work at Arleson's; his mum was busy baking a birthday cake and his dad was using the opportunity provided by the warm, dry weather to do some gardening. He usually received several postal orders from various aunts and uncles. By noon he'd almost given up hope of the postman ever arriving, but was first to the front door when the knocker sounded at five past. Their cheery postman stood in the doorway.

"Good morning, son. Quite a bit of post for you today."

"Thanks!"

Eddie took the small bundle of letters and the rectangular parcel, wrapped in brown paper. It was addressed to him and was plastered with foreign writing and stamps.

"Who is it, Eddie?" shouted his mum from the kitchen.

"Just the postman, Mum. Only one for you and dad; the rest are all for me."

Eddie's mum came into the hall where her son seemed to be in a trance as he was still looking at the parcel in his hands.

"What have you got?"

"Five cards, Mum, and this," and Eddie presented the parcel to her. Eddie knew who it was from and so did Ann Compton the moment she saw the Polish stamps.

"It must be from Mr Canter, Eddie. Oh, how nice of him."

"Yes, but how did he know it was my birthday, Mum?"

"I don't know dear – he was still in Fenton this time last year, before he sold his junk shop. Maybe he found out then. You are a lucky boy, you know. Lots of his customers got little monetary surprises after he sold up. I think it was his way of saying thank you to them all. You and Len got such nice presents as well."

Eddie didn't know really what to do. Would it be something that would tell his mum about their secret journey?

"Well, aren't you going to open it?"

"Yes, Mum."

Eddie methodically removed the brown paper to reveal the manufacturer's box. Suddenly Eddie exclaimed,

"It's a radio, Mum, and it's a good one. It was made in England too and it says on the box that you can get stations from around the world. How on earth did he know?"

"I don't know, dear. Who did you tell?"

"Just Len and some other friends and, er, Mr Watson in his shop when we went to check what he'd got, but that was only two days ago."

Eddie's mum seemed less concerned than he himself did about how George Canter knew that he had wanted a radio. Eddie was worried. He had hoped that his days of unexplained happenings were over. His mum brought him back to reality.

"Anyway, Eddie, you'll soon learn in life that coincidences do happen. Just be grateful that sometimes they're good ones as well. The fact that it's an English radio probably means he had it in his shop before he moved back to Poland. I bet you talked about wanting a radio when you were in last year looking for a train set."

"Probably, Mum," he said, even though he knew full well that he hadn't even wanted a radio the previous year, but….

Later that evening, when he checked the details on the box, Eddie found that the radio, like his train set, had been bought in Harrod's. He didn't tell his parents – as far as they were concerned Mr Canter already had the radio when he was in England. He also didn't tell them about the short note which he discovered tucked away under the radio, so that only he would find it after taking the radio out completely.

Dear Eddie,

Hope you like your present. How did I know you wanted a radio? Well, that has to be my little secret. Let's just say that God still moves in a mysterious way and always will. Give my best wishes to Len; I suspect that he's the only one that you'll tell fully about this letter.
Good luck in whatever you do in your life.

Your friend,
George Canter

Eddie carefully folded the note and placed it in the back of his wallet. He would have to think carefully before deciding whether or not to show it to Len. He would have some time to make up his mind as the Wilbys were going away for over a week, starting the following day, to stay with relations in Yorkshire and wouldn't be back until late on Easter Monday.

Len might be jealous despite his gift from the phantom Mr Manders.
After all, George Canter was real.

18

Train Crash

Karl Thompson was fifteen and had been in trouble at Fenton Secondary Modern School almost from the day he'd set foot inside its gates. He had been a constant source of worry to his mother, Mrs Brenda Thompson, a stalwart member of St Andrew's church congregation. In the fourth year at school, he had the chance of a new start on an apprenticeship in plumbing at Hamsden Civic College where he could start in September. On the first Tuesday after Easter, the 31st of March, he was due for interview at ten past nine in the morning. His mother had just about got him to dress suitably for the occasion, though his tie and shirt seemed to be constantly in opposition to each other. If one was tidy, then the other would react wildly against it. Mrs Thompson had insisted on accompanying her wayward son by train, leaving Fenton at eight-fifteen – insisted, because in the past he had deliberately missed equally important events for no apparent reason than he didn't feel like it at the time. Brenda Thompson had almost lost count of the number of watches she had bought or borrowed – he could tell the time, but sometimes it's meaning in relation to events, people and places seemed to escape him completely! For the first ten minutes of the journey they sat together in the second of four carriages pulled by a diesel locomotive of the same series as Len's model.

"For goodness sake, Karl, tuck your shirt in," said a thoroughly frustrated Mrs Thompson.

"Will when I get there."

"Do it now or I'll do it for you."

"No you won't."

Karl got out of his seat.

"Where are you going? Sit down please, Karl."

Karl ignored his mother and sidled to the front of the carriage where he stood in the small compartment next to an exit door. He glared back at his mother.

Tom Ballantyne had had a lot to drink in Fenton's Red Lion the night before. It had been Easter Monday and consequently a bank holiday. He had been off duty all day from his job as the signalman at Linham Junction, situated almost exactly halfway between Fenton-on-Sea and Hamsden, where a branch line split for Canford and other stations north of the River Wenham. As soon as a light turned green down the line and the Canford train had gone through, he had a minute to pull the lever to change the points back to allow the eight-fifteen from Fenton to continue to Hamsden. The process had never been a problem before, even when he'd had a worse hangover than he had that morning. He knew that the Fenton train often passed at a speed in excess of sixty miles per hour. He dare not make a mistake. The Canford train came through at twenty-five to nine and Tom put his head out of the signal box window and looked for the green signal. It seemed a little later than usual, but suddenly there it was. He turned and made a dash for the other side of the box which always had to be kept clear of clutter for just such situations. Tom Ballantyne's heavy grey shoulder bag lay on the floor and one of his size elevens got entangled in a strap. He tripped and, if he'd had a clear head, he might have had a chance of correcting his balance. He pitched forward, head striking the solid metal edge of the railing that surrounded the paraffin heater. Dazed and bleeding from a nasty head wound, he still managed to crawl towards the large levers that operated the points, but again the alcohol still in his blood stream slowed the process considerably. He swore under his breath and then out loud he shouted,

"Oh God, no!"

From a crouching position his hand just gripped the cold brass lever when a rush of air shook the signal box. He sat back in disbelief.

"Oh my God – no! No! No!"

He passed out from shock and the sudden rush of blood to his head sustained in his fall and attempted recovery. Somewhere in the back of his mind he thought he heard screaming and the noise of a huge explosion, then blackness.

Brenda Thompson heard and felt the strange sound and judder from the rails and shouted to her son,

"What's that, Karl?"

Karl didn't get the chance to answer as he was first thrown one way and then the other and eventually did an impression of someone falling from a trapeze. He ended up in a curious and almost impossible position between two rows of seat where luggage was normally the only occupant. He screamed,

"Help, Mum!"

He went silent. His mother hadn't moved as the train twisted and turned trying to find rails that matched the orientation of its wheels. She lent forward and covered her head with her arms and waited for the inevitable. Not many people are ever able to describe what it's like to be in a crashing train at sixty miles per hour. Mrs Thompson would remember bits of it and they would haunt her for the rest of her days. The noise would always be impossible to describe, whether human or mechanical. Suddenly the mechanical sounds stopped and the human ones developed into two different tones: low groans from those people who were seriously injured or high pitched screams from those less seriously so. Karl was screaming again. His mother wasn't, but she was an exception to the rule. She was largely unhurt; inertia and shock were probably her worst traumas. The rest of the carriage was a horrible mixture of diesel fumes and bodies; some moving; some still and some that wanted to move, but couldn't.

Gary Jones had boarded the eight-fifteen from Fenton, as usual, to go to work in his dad's showroom in Hamsden. He was one of the lucky ones, being thrown clear of the wreckage in a million to one act of déjà vu. Dazed, but only cut and bruised, he could hear the screaming from the Thompson's carriage. There was an eerie silence outside the train, with him and only one or two others on the other side of the twisted wreckage apparently able to walk. Gary headed for the screaming. He clambered up the carriage's side, which was leaning over from the vertical, and wrenched at a partially open door. He could smell the fumes and knew what might happen. He pulled himself in and the sights he would see that morning did more to make a man of him than any other experience he would ever have to face. Several of the walking wounded were helping each other to move to the doors. Within the next thirty minutes or so Gary displayed super human strength and resolve as all but three passengers were helped out of the carriage; some were carried screaming in pain because of their injuries. Whether some of the injured should have been moved or not, was irrelevant in light of the possible inferno that might ensue. Of the passengers that were left, one, a very elderly gentleman, was clearly dead and another was a young boy who appeared trapped in the space between the backs of two rows of seats. A middle-aged woman was holding his hand. Mrs Brenda Thompson did not recognise Gary Jones.

"Oh please help him! Please! He's my son!"
Gary said calmly,

"Please, you must get out. It may explode."

"No, I won't leave him. I won't!"

When Gary looked between the seats there seemed no apparent reason why the boy could not be freed. It seemed he was more in shock than anything else and was frozen rigid. Gary said something to him in a calm voice and at the same time, by pulling and twisting, brought him out into the open. His head was cut badly, but he didn't seem to have any other external injuries except probably for serious bruising. The boy suddenly saw his mother standing over him and he attempted to get to his feet. Gary grabbed him.

"Steady, lad. Lean on me."

Gary and Mrs Thompson helped Karl up and out of the carriage via an improvised ladder made up of suitcases and loose pieces of seat. None of them knew how long it had been since the crash since time seemed to have stood still, particularly for Mrs Thompson. However, on emerging, it was clear that the emergency services were well into their recovery procedures for passengers in the other carriages. A firemen spotted the three walking wounded and ordered them, and as many other people as could walk, away from the carriage. Gary and the Thompsons were the last walking wounded. The more serious casualties, some of whom Gary had helped clear earlier, were being stretchered to ambulances, which were still arriving at the ghastly scene. Fire was already visible from the carriage that Gary had just helped vacate. A minute later there was an explosion and the carriage was engulfed in flames, providing a natural cremation for one old man. Once by another waiting ambulance for the least hurt, Brenda Thompson turned to her son's rescuer and said,

"Oh how can I ever repay you? You must tell me your name."

Gary smiled through his blackened and bloodied face.

"It's Gary, Mrs Thompson. Gary Jones."

Mrs Brenda Thompson was not embarrassed. She simply hugged Gary as if he was her own son and, with genuine emotion, said,

"Gary, I'm so sorry. Please forgive me. We owe our lives to you. Thank you from the bottom of my heart."

Gary would be off work for a week with some bad cuts and nasty bruising. He'd also sustained a dislocated thumb which had probably happened before he started to help passengers off the train. Mrs Thompson had a few minor bruises and her son's cut head left him with a scar above his right eye that he would become quite proud of. In all, two passengers died in the accident; twelve had fractured limbs, or worse and a further thirty-seven needed some hospital treatment. There had been over a hundred people on the train. Accident investigators would later report that, for such a crash, they would have expected more deaths and serious injuries. Four passengers, three men and one woman, were singled out for praise and later for an award for the calm way they dealt with the immediate aftermath of the crash. Two of them were off duty firemen and one an off duty nurse. The fourth was Gary Steven Jones, a nineteen-year-old used car salesman.

Tom Ballantyne would be found crying in his signal box, a physical and emotional wreck. Though he would be prosecuted for causing the crash, the charges were never made to stick as no one could prove that he'd still been under the influence of alcohol. He was severely reprimanded for leaving his bag in such a dangerous position, but the rules didn't make it a sacking case. He never dared to drink in the Red Lion again and without returning to work he resigned his job with British Rail within six months of the accident and soon afterwards he and his family moved to another part of the country.

19

Acceptance

News of the train crash had filtered into Fenton-on-Sea all that Tuesday morning. Eddie had met up with Len at a quarter to ten for the first time since just before his birthday. They knew something major had occurred as they heard sirens soon afterwards. By the time they had reached the High Street they couldn't help but notice several ambulances on their way to the Cottage Hospital.

"What's going on, Eddie?" said Len, but Eddie didn't reply as he was still trying to think of a way to tell his friend about Mr Canter's gift and letter.

"Eddie! That's the fourth ambulance to go past us in the last few minutes. What *is* happening?"

"Don't know, mate. Maybe a plane's crashed."

Suddenly a group of four or five people came running up the High Street and headed for the station as though late for a train. The boys walked back some way until they were directly opposite the station. More people came running from the other direction.

"A lot of people are late for their trains today," said Len, but Eddie had guessed what was happening.

"There must have been a train crash and people are checking on their friends and relatives. My dad'll know."

The two boys crossed over the High Street and into Fenton railway station, but they found it nigh on impossible to move very far, let alone get to the booking office. There were several policemen around, certainly more than Fenton's normal contingent and Len stopped to speak to one.

"Excuse me, officer, what's going on?"

"A train's come off the rails at Linham junction and crashed at seventy miles an hour; lots of casualties. You'll have to keep out of the station. There'll be no more trains running today, lads."

"Which train was it, constable," asked Eddie.

"The eight-fifteen from Fenton to Hamsden. Now, move along, please."

Something in the back of Eddie's mind said he had to tell Jenny, his sister, but he and Len had only got halfway back to Arleson's when Jenny almost collided with them running in the opposite direction.

"Stop, Jenny! There's been a train crash," shouted Eddie as he tried to catch hold of his sister, but she was gone in a flash.

"I know, Eddie," she called back. "Gary catches normally catches it!"

The two friends tried again to get into the station but found it impossible; the crowd had grown two or three-fold. Nothing was to be seen of Jenny, so they made their way quickly back to Eddie's house. Aunty Beth from next door was with Eddie's mum when they arrived. An out of breath Eddie blurted out the news.

"Mum, there's been a train crash and Jenny thinks that Gary was on it."

"I know, dear – Beth was down town when the news broke. It's a bad one. Where did you see Jenny?"

"She was going to the station to check on Gary."

Nobody could tell Jenny much when, at last, she finally made it past the first couple of policemen filtering the genuinely concerned from the lookers-on. She did manage to find her dad who told her that the walking wounded and those with minor injuries were being taken to Fenton Cottage Hospital, while the more seriously injured were going to

Hamsden General. She ran out of the station and headed along South Road for East Hill. Meanwhile, Fred Compton helped liaise with the emergency services and the friends and relations who continued to arrive to get news of their loved ones. It would be his role for much of the rest of the day as no trains would run in and out of Fenton during that time.

Jenny ran all the way from the station to the Cottage Hospital at the top of East Hill. Ambulances passed her on the way and one nearly ran her down when she didn't look as she entered the hospital forecourt. Rushing straight to casualty she was initially held back by hospital staff, and the lone policeman who was attempting to control the growing number of extra visitors. All nurses and other medical staff were occupied with the emergency and at first she couldn't find anyone to ask about her boyfriend. By now the clock in the casualty waiting area read five to eleven. Eventually she was able to give Gary's full name to a volunteer who was coordinating the arrival and registration of the injured. She was then taken to a small room where other friends and relatives were also waiting for news. By eleven-thirty she feared the worst. She decided to check one final time to see if Gary had arrived and to prepare to find some way of getting to Hamsden General if he had not. Her dad would take her surely. Her heart was throbbing and her voice a hoarse and quavering croak as she asked another volunteer.

"Has a Gary Jones come in yet?"

"Jones, you say. Let me see. Yes, my dear, he's just been taken into casualty."

Jenny felt her heart pump stronger."

"Can I see him?"

"In a minute, I expect. He was a walking wounded. He's been something of a hero, you know. An ambulance driver told me he probably saved at least three passenger's lives. Are you a relative?"

225

Jenny replied proudly,

"No, I'm his girlfriend."

As soon as she had finished speaking, Jenny appeared to wobble and almost fainted until the elderly lady grabbed her and said,

"Are you alright, dear? You'd better sit down and have a cup of tea."

"No, I'm alright; I'll just wait here until I can see him. Thanks."

Gary was quickly attended to, his thumb being the only injury that had taken some time to put back in place. He emerged from a side room with a few stitches to a cut in his top lip and a large bandage encircling his head. He was holding his left hand vertically upwards and his thumb was swathed in more bandages. Jenny rushed forward to hug him but he held his up good hand in protest.

"No, Jenny! Please don't touch me; I'm very sore."

"Oh Gary, I was so worried. I thought you were…."

"No, love, you can't get rid of me that easily."

By this time, Gary's dad, Richard, had arrived; he'd closed the showroom for the day. Mrs Jones was still somewhere forty miles away on a shopping trip to Newbridge, a largish town in the west of the county. She wouldn't find out about her son's heroics until later that afternoon. Richard gave Jenny a small hug and then gave her a lift in his Jaguar back to Fir Tree Close before taking his injured son back to their home on the north side of the town. As he dropped her off at the entrance to her cul-de-sac, Mr Jones told Jenny she was welcome to come round in the evening to see Gary if she liked. It was ten to one when Jenny walked in through her front door.

Her mum rushed into the hall and hugged her daughter.

"Are you alright?"

"Yes, Mum, I'm fine now and, thank God, Gary's O.K. Have you heard about the accident?"

"Yes, it has even been on the news on the radio. What about work?"

"Mr Arleson has given me the day off."

Jenny then related what she knew about Gary's injuries and his heroics while Eddie and his mum listened intently. Len had gone back home sometime previously.

Jenny rested in her bedroom for most of the rest of the afternoon until at six she went round to the Jones' house. Fred Compton didn't arrive home until well after seven that evening, thoroughly exhausted but able to give as full an account of the crash as anyone else in Fenton-on-Sea. He was full of genuine praise for Gary Jones.

"I'm afraid I've been wrong about that young man. It appears he risked his life and limb to save several passengers. A senior fireman I met later said he'd never seen such a young person act so calmly and maturely. He said he'd give him a job any day," and the he paused. "Anyone can make a mistake like Gary did."

Eddie came down to breakfast the next day and his dad seemed in a good mood. He and his daughter had had a long chat the previous evening when Jenny got back just after nine. Jenny had ended up sobbing uncontrollably in her dad's arms and Fred Compton too had fought back tears. A new bond had been established between father and daughter that had been sadly missing for many months. Eddie found that his dad had made him his breakfast, something he only did on Saturdays when he wasn't at work.

"Boiled eggs – your favourite, son."

"Thanks, Dad. Heard anymore about the crash? Has it been on the news? I haven't switched my radio on yet."

"Two dead, but they're still investigating the cause. I think it looks like points failure. British rail skimping on maintenance again, I shouldn't wonder."

"Was Jenny crying last night, Dad? I heard her from my bedroom. Is she alright?"

"Yes, Eddie, she's fine. You've got a brave sister there. I've rung Mr Arleson and he says she can take as much time off as she needs, but I expect she'll go in after lunch. She's having a good sleep at the moment."

Eddie used the back of his spoon to crack the top of his egg and his dad burst out laughing as the egg disintegrated into nothing but pieces of shell.

"April Fool!"

This was a new one on Eddie – an upturned eggshell, previously emptied by his father!

"Nice one, Dad!"

The town was full of the news of the accident when Eddie joined Len at their arranged meeting place at the junction of South road and the High Street. Eddie was able to fill his friend in on the official story related to him by his dad.

"Do they know who the dead are?" asked Len as they paused outside the station entrance which was thronging with people trying to see if their train was running. Several chalk filled sandwich boards displayed information regarding changes and new timings. From what they could see, trains would not be running again until Friday at least. Len remarked,

"Can't go anywhere today. Mr Manders will be turning in his grave, if he's got one, eh?"

"Not funny, Len. Show a bit of respect for the fatalities."

"Sorry."

They moved on down the High Street catching snatches of conversation between the early shoppers as they passed. Eddie suddenly made up his mind to tell his friend about Mr Canter's surprise birthday present and Len's surprise trip to London. Eddie had decided to start with the more difficult news first and he said,

"Len, I've got something to tell you."

"What, mate?" replied Len who could tell from his friend's tone that he was about to say something important.

"Mr Canter sent me a birthday present."

"Oh, is that all?"

"You don't mind?"

"No, mate. I mean, I got one from our friendly ghost and you didn't. What did you get?"

"A transistor radio."

"So you've got two now. Hard luck."

"No, Mum didn't get one in the end. Woolworth's had sold out when she went."

Len asked the obvious question.

"How did he know it was your birthday?"

"Don't know, but it's not surprising, is it? He seemed to know everything about me last year."

"Yep, I suppose you're right. Is it a good radio?"

"You bet – from Harrod's again. I'll show you later."

They had reached the top of Steep Hill and if Eddie had known the meaning of the word, he would have said that his friend had been very magnanimous in his reaction to the first part of his news. He was about to tell him the second part when Len stopped walking.

"Granty's closed, Eddie. He never closes, especially midweek."

"Strange," said Eddie. I hope he's not ill; I like old Granty."

"I don't – he gives me the creeps," replied Len.

The two boys skipped and slid their way down Steep Hill and at the bottom, Eddie relayed his other bit of news.

"Got a surprise for you, my friend."

"What?"

"We're going to London for a day."

"We?"

"You and me, old man!"

"How?"

"Dad bought me two day return tickets for my birthday. One for me and one for you or anyone else I should care to take!"

Eddie had a sly grin on his face.

"Of course, I can take someone else if you rather not go."

Eddie paused.

"Only joking!"

"Thanks, Eddie and thank your dad for me. When can we go?"

"Anytime we like up to the middle of September."

For the remainder of the morning the two boys searched for more jet on the beach, but without success and eventually they wandered back up the town which still seemed in sombre mood. Grant's Emporium was still closed.

Fenton-on-Sea more or less returned to normal by Friday morning, three days after the accident. Though the Fenton to Hamsden line was clear for trains to pass slowly through Linham Junction, debris still littered the fields either side while the accident investigators did their work. One of the dead had been identified on the Wednesday as a young nurse called Helen Stackpole who had worked at Hamsden General Hospital; the other's charred remains were still being linked to dental and medical records. A male in his seventies or eighties was the best that the pathologist in charge could come up with.

With all the overtime that Fred Compton had put in during the week he was given the Saturday off. He needed it anyway to recharge his batteries. He was very quiet at breakfast, totally unlike his cheerful mood of three days earlier. After breakfast and without anything more than a 'see you later' to his wife, he got the Morris Minor from the garage and drove out of Fir Tree Close.

"Where's Dad going?" said Eddie to his mum.

"Don't know, dear. Perhaps needs some time to himself. It must have been a very trying and tiring week for him."

Despite this bland statement, Eddie's mum *was* worried. He had mentioned nothing to her and for the last day he had seemed to have something on his mind. She had disturbed him the previous evening when he looked as if he was trying to write something at his bureau.

Mr Richard Jones was under staffed that Saturday morning. Gary would not return to work until the following week. Consequently he had to remain largely out front and when Fred Compton walked in at a little after ten he was immediately approached by said owner of the showroom. He knew Eddie's dad by sight.

"Hello, Mr Compton – going to change that old Morris Minor at last?"

"No, I'm here on another matter. Is your son, Gary, around?"

"Afraid not. Doc says he should rest until next week. He was pretty badly shaken you know."

"I know. I wanted to apologise to him."

"What for?"

Mr Jones seemed to be unaware of any previous ill feeling from Eddie's dad towards his son.

"I'm afraid it's a private matter. I wonder if you would give him this letter for me."

"Of course, Mr. Compton. I'll see that he gets it tonight. If you'd known, you could have taken it round to the house back in Fenton. Did Jenny not tell you he wouldn't be back at work until Monday or Tuesday?"

"She told me that he said he would be back yesterday."

"He thought he would be, but Dr Carter said no, so I said no too."

Gary read Mr Compton's letter later in his room.

Dear Gary,

I wanted to you know that I am truly sorry for the feelings I've harboured against you, which Jenny has probably told you about. I have been feeling guilty ever since I heard on Tuesday how you risked your life to help and save several passengers on the train. Working on the railways all my life means that I know the dangers you faced, even though you probably did not.

I now know that you never caused the car accident on purpose and that it was just the wildness of youth. We may not all have had the consequences you had, but that's probably more by luck than judgement.

When I had a heart-to-heart with Jenny earlier this week it became abundantly clear to me the love she feels for you and also that the feeling was mutual.

You will always be welcome to come to see Jenny at our home.

Kind regards,
Fred Compton

Gary Jones' eyes welled up with tears. He made up his mind to go and show the letter to Jenny immediately. Afterwards, both he and Jenny felt a huge weight had been lifted of their shoulders as they began to realise they could at last lead a normal life again, not only with Jenny's family, but also with the rest of the residents of Fenton-on-Sea.

It was the following Thursday that the identity of the other dead passenger was revealed, after a detailed search through national dental records. Eddie and Len suspected who it would be when Grant's Emporium had remained permanently closed after the crash.

20

Eddie's Reward

Within a couple of weeks or returning to Fenton Grammar School all second year pupils were due to face their year exams. Based on only two term's work, they were, however, the most important ones that the pupils had met so far. Sets and teachers for the third year largely depended on the results. Consequently, Eddie, by choice and Len, by coercion, spent the last few days of the Easter holidays revising and, in Len's case, borrowing note books to fill in many missing gaps in his own. School opened for business on Wednesday, April the 8th and, as if on cue, the weather turned for the worse. By Friday, Fenton-on-Sea had had nearly two inches of rain and, at four on Friday afternoon, the boys sloshed and splashed their way home through flooded roads and paths.

"What'ya doing tomorrow, Eddie?" asked Len as they reached the parting of the ways at the bottom of Fir Tree Close.

"Got to revise. Dad says he'll treat me with something if I do well. He's already planning another summer holiday this year – says he needs the break."

"What's he going to buy you, then?"

"Don't know. Probably be a set of dictionaries knowing him."

"I'm going to escape with my life if I manage to pass a few exams."

"You'll be alright; just do some revision, Len."

"Hate it. You know I'd rather be outside playing sport."

"Well, not much chance of that this weekend."

It was raining again and the two friends parted company and went their separate ways.

Gary took Jenny out to the pictures on Saturday night. The Regal cinema was showing a decent horror film and she spent most of the evening with her buried under Gary's coat. Several people smiled pleasantly at Gary, both before and after the performance, with the occasional 'Well done'. He hadn't been used to such friendliness and politeness for some time, or, indeed, ever.

Jenny and Gary kissed and embraced after he had walked her home from the cinema. Jenny tried to invite him in to see her parents, but Gary was clearly not quite ready for such a meeting and declined the invitation. He was still sore, he said.

The relationship would blossom that summer to the extent that Jenny was invited to join Gary and his parents' for a fortnight's holiday on the Mediterranean in August.

The dreaded exams started on Monday, April the 13th and ran through to Friday, April the 24th. Results would be given to individual parents at a specially arranged evening on Tuesday, May the 12th. In the last couple of days before the evening, Eddie got an inkling that he had done extremely well in most, if not all, subjects. The odd knowing wink or nod from staff often gave the game away. Len suspected the complete opposite. He was pleasantly surprised that, when his parents got home after the evening, his dad had a smile on his face. Unfortunately, poor old Len didn't recognise that the smile was one of resignation and not of joy. Martha Wilby made herself scarce in the kitchen

"Well done, son."

Still Len did not see the arrows coming.

"You really have excelled yourself this time."

The bow was pulled back to its full extent.

"Bottom in six out of ten subjects and in the lowest quarter for the others."

The first arrow hit home. Len's face dropped. He didn't say a word. Cyril Wilby continued. The bow was drawn back again.

"We had to see Mr Hempsall personally in his office. What has been going on, Len?"

"I don't know, Dad. I thought I'd done O.K."

"O.K? You failed nine of your ten subjects. Only Miss Grainger in Art said you warranted a pass for your drawings and section of a steam locomotive. I mean, I ask you, what good is that going to do you – a pass in Art?"

"Sorry, Dad."

"Sorry are we? Well, from the start of next week you are going to have to resit seven of your exams; only Music, Art and Woodwork escape. You start revising properly tomorrow when you get in from school and you will do at least two hours every night; more at the weekend. If you don't pass at least half of them, then you can join me at Fenton Secondary Modern School, where I can keep and eye on you. You must be living in some kind of fantasy world if you think you can get through Fenton Grammar School by doing no work. Now get off to bed and think on, son."

The quiver was empty and Len went to the kitchen in tears and said,

"Sorry, Mum. I will pass them next time. I promise."

Martha Wilby tried to comfort her son, without lessening the salutary lesson just provided by her husband and said simply,

"We only want you to work to your ability, Len. Now go upstairs and I'll bring you a nice warm drink in a while. It *was* embarrassing at school, you know."

Len repeated himself.

"Sorry, Mum."

Later, in his bedroom, his dad's words came back to haunt and remind him of the past year: '*You must be living in some kind of fantasy world....*'

If the scene in the Wilby household felt like something out of a horror film for Len, the complete opposite was true at the Compton's. Eddie had come top in Maths, Science, Geography and Latin. He had come second in French and History. His teachers in Music, Art and Woodwork all agreed that there had been a marked improvement and he was in the top quarter in all three subjects. Only in English did he have some problems, with Mr Green commenting on some inattentiveness in class. Nevertheless, he had finished only just below halfway in the set, a marked improvement from the first year. Like Cyril Wilby, Eddie's dad made the same remark when he got in from the parents' evening.

"Well done, son."

"Well, how did I do?"

"Oh, not bad," replied his dad rather disinterestedly. Then he smiled and gave Eddie all his results.

"Like I said, not bad!"

"Good enough to get that surprise, Dad?"

"We'll see."

"Oh, Dad!"

Eddie's mum then joined in the conversation.

"When you see Len tomorrow, you don't gloat. I don't think he's done very well – I saw his parents waiting outside the Head's office.

"I tried to tell him, Mum, but you know Len."

"Yes, I do and I think over the next couple of weeks you and he don't see each other in the evenings or the weekends, just to give him the chance to catch up on his work undisturbed – alright?"

"Yes, Mum."

So there it was, thought Eddie later, Len will be 'confined to barracks', probably till half-term. Not much serious work was done in the last few weeks of term, however.

Len was in quiet and sombre mood the following morning on the way to school.

"Got a rocket off my dad last night, mate. Threatened me with moving me to his school. Can he do that, Eddie?"

"I don't know. I expect it's mainly up to our school to decide, but you didn't do that badly, did you?"

"You don't know the half, mate. Bottom in six subjects and resits in seven next week. I'm going to work like stink till then. I'll show him."

Eddie wondered whether his friend knew how to 'work like stink', but he wished him luck and said,

"Soon be half-term."

In his terms, Len worked as hard as he thought he could and, to his and his dad's great relief, he passed in five of his resits and improved his marks slightly in the other two – History and Latin. Cyril Wilby was genuinely pleased with his son, when a letter arrived in the post at breakfast on the last day before half-term: Friday, May the 29th.

"You can now enjoy half-term, son. I knew you could do it. What are you going to do?"

Len was suddenly reminded of the same break a year previously. Nothing could ever match what had happened that week!

"Haven't a clue, Dad, but I think Eddie gets his reward today for doing so well in his exams. We might play with that, whatever it is."

But there would be no way that Len could personally play with Eddie's reward. Eddie might let him borrow it, but only under his close supervision. If the two boys were to both get fun out of it, then Len would soon discover he needed a similar item.

At the precise moment that Len's dad was praising his son, Eddie was staring in awe at his reward.

"Wow, dad! Thanks!"

His brand new and first bicycle stood in front of him, proudly held by Fred Compton in the kitchen at 38 Fir Tree Close. It had been smuggled in from the shed before Eddie had got up that morning.

"It's got thirteen gears, son. Like the colour?

"Brilliant, Dad – red's my favourite."

"I didn't get a bike when I was his age," said Jenny who had just come into the kitchen.

"You didn't pass many exams, Jenny," said her dad.

"I did my best, though."

"If you call 'your best', going out each night before your CSE's, then, yes, you did your best!"

Jenny mumbled something about fairness, grabbed some toast and left for work, for which she was already late.

Cyril Wilby had an answer for his son's question when they both got in from school on the Friday evening.

"You can borrow mine."

"Really, Dad!"

"Yes, as long as you're careful with it and use the lock if you leave it anywhere."

Len had used his dad's Raleigh racing bike a couple of times in the past but had always found it difficult to ride. Now he was at least six inches taller and stronger to boot there should be no problem.

"Thanks, Dad. Have you got a new pump, then?"

"All ready to go – took it to school and serviced it myself."

The two boys cycled many miles over their half-term and, if they'd logged it, they would have found that their individual total was over a hundred by the Friday evening. They never strayed further than about eight miles from Fenton-on-Sea and discovered in the process quiet back roads that many of the locals did not even know existed. They were banned from cycling on the busy A132 from Fenton to Hamsden.

By the final Saturday of half-term, Len cycled round to Eddie's as usual and they set off down Fir Tree Close with no particular route in mind. At the junction with South Road, Eddie got off his bike and motioned for Len to do the same.

"I've had an idea, Len."

"What, mate?"

"Why don't we try to cycle to Hamsden?"

Len shook his head.

"We can't Eddie; we're not allowed – it's too dangerous."

"It is, on the A132, but I meant we try the back roads. I know we can get to Linham; I saw a sign the other day. Linham's got to be over halfway there."

"Can you remember how to get to the sign, though?" asked Len.

"Dad's lent me his AA handbook; the one we used before to find that place."

"I'm game, then, *Monsieur Anquetil!*"

They set off along South Road, past the two secondary schools and took the first exit at the roundabout from which the A132 started. There then followed a series of narrow windy roads combined with several crossroad intersections where the map was invaluable. After about forty minutes they reached the tiny village of Linham, so tiny that it didn't possess a church nor warrant a public house, consisting entirely of a farm and a hundred yards of cottages sprawling back on either side of the road. They stopped at the end of the buildings.

"Which way now, *Jacques*?" asked Len, using the first name of the three-time winner of the Tour de France.

"Straight on, I think. No, wait a minute. There's a sign over there," said Eddie pointing about fifty yards ahead.

The sign read: *Linham Junction ½* and underneath, *Hamsden 5*.

"Isn't that where the train crash was?" asked Len.

"Yes. Shall we go and see where it happened?"

"Why not; if it's on the way to Hamsden."

Five minutes later and they arrived at a level crossing which seemed to be a hundred yards or so from the actual junction, identified by an isolated signal box. A wide track ran parallel to the railway line which they followed until they were opposite the signal box.

"So here's where it happened," said Eddie. "Not much sign of it now."

The field on the opposite side of the line to the boys had clearly been recently ploughed, presumably to eradicate any remaining physical blemishes on the landscape. Signs that the track had been repaired were also evident from the several new sleepers and sections of shiny track. The boys leant their bikes against the fence and surveyed the scene in silence.

"They've put a small memorial up over there facing the line," observed Len after a while.

A simple stone plinth, with what looked to be a brass plaque attached, stood in a corner of the ploughed field surrounded by a circle of freshly planted shrubs. After a few more minutes of contemplation the boys rode back along the track to the level crossing. They immediately spotted a walker coming up along the road from the village. He appeared from a distance to be a young man dressed in khaki shorts and a white open-necked shirt. He had an old rucksack on his back.

"We could ask him if there's a back way to Hamsden. I bet he'd know," said Eddie.

The young man was close now and they could make out his features. He was tall, slim and sported a thin moustache. He looked to be in his early twenties. He came right up to them.

"Good morning, my lads and where are we off to this fine day?"

Something about the young man's speech seemed familiar to Eddie.

"We want to get to Hamsden but not on the main road. Should we carry on over the level crossing?"

"No, you mustn't, my dears. The best way is to follow the track you've just come down all the way till it meets a narrow road. Turn right and cross the railway line there, using the swing gate." The young man paused and looked wistful. "You must be careful when you cross the line; the trains come past there sometimes at over sixty. After about a mile fork left and that will bring you in to Hamsden near the railway station."

"Thank you, sir," said Eddie.

"Call me Ally; everyone does. It's short for Aloyisious – I hate the name. Got to go now. Isn't it a beautiful day, my boys?"

With that he quickly negotiated the pedestrian crossing over the railway line and walked on down the road. He was almost out of earshot when he turned round and shouted,

"Remember, Eddie, be careful when you cross the line – very careful!"

The boys were stunned into silence. Their fantasy world had returned. Len managed to break the silence.

"That was…."

"Old Granty or, should I say young Granty?" said Eddie. "Did you see his clothes – they were ancient. He's a…."

"Ghost," finished Len.

"But he's only been dead a couple of months. I thought ghosts had to be people that had died years ago, like Mr Manders," said Eddie.

"So you're an expert on ghosts, eh, my dear?"

"Don't, Len. It's not funny."

"Sorry. How old do you think he was?"

"Twenty-two or so, I should say," said Eddie. "He would have been that age around the time just before the First World War if my Maths is correct."

"What, you mean in the Edwardian era?"

Eddie eyes widened in amazement.

"Some History revision must have stuck, mate," said Len quickly and then he had another thought.

"We should follow him, Eddie. We're bound to catch him up on our bikes."

Eddie looked doubtful. Mr Canter's words came back to him: 'nothing bad will ever happen….' but then he remembered that George had been referring to the train set and football.

"I'm not sure, Len – we'd be chasing after a ghost and who knows what might happen. They're best left well alone and anyway, we're not playing with the train set now. I just don't feel confident. I don't think that this is just a game."

Len had already made his decision and was busy negotiating the transporting of his bike across the railway line via the two gates. Eddie waited while his friend reached the continuing road on the other side. Whether he looked away for a split second or not, he would never be able to say, but when he next looked Len and his bicycle had gone!

"Len! Come back!" but Len did not come back. He had completely disappeared into thin air. Eddie stood in panic for a few moments. What should he do? Wait until his friend came back? Follow? He decided to follow.

He checked up and down the line: '*be careful when you cross the line….*'. It was clear. He reached the other side and stood on the road, but it wasn't a road, just a dirt track. He looked down at himself. Yes, he was in one piece and visible. He hadn't disappeared. He looked around. The scenery had changed – the fields on either side looked less well-defined and regular in appearance. It felt colder and the trees were bare. He, and hopefully Len, had moved time. He walked with his bike a few yards forward and peered down the track. He could just make out the white-shirted Mr Grant in the distance, but where was Len? He looked back at the level crossing, but like the road, it wasn't there – the track just continued in that direction with nothing to break its passage. This was bad. He heard Ally's final words: '*very careful*'! Suddenly, as if from nowhere, Len was beside him and he was out of breath.

"Where were you?" asked Eddie in panic. Len looked more relaxed and panted,

"I just cycled after old Granty, but he seemed to get farther away the more I cycled."

"We've got to go back, Len. This is not right. I told you it's not a game."

"I guess you're right, but how? The crossing has gone."

The two friends stood in silence, until Len said,

"Watch me; keep your eyes fixed on me," and without another word, he climbed back onto his bike and rode back the way they had come. When he reached the position where Eddie thought the level crossing had been, he disappeared. Eddie followed and a few seconds later the two boys were back on a tarmac road laid down in the second half of the twentieth century. Relief was etched all over their faces. They looked back over the railway line, but all seemed normal.

"Well we're not going to Hamsden that way," exclaimed Eddie.

"We could follow old Granty's direction and cross the line further up," said Len.

Eddie's answer was short.

"No!"

Len grinned cheekily.

"Only joking, mate! I've had enough of ghosts and time travel. We must have gone back to before the First World War and what we saw was how the countryside must have been then."

"No railway line between Fenton and Hamsden back then," observed Eddie.

"So why did Granty say to be careful of the trains?"

"Oh, come on, Len, that's obvious. As a ghost he can move from the present to any other time. When he met us he was in the present, like us. As soon as he crossed over the line he went into the early nineteen hundreds."

Len was deep in thought again.

"How many more ghosts are we going to meet, Eddie? It's scary and also, for a brief time back there as we crossed the line, we were nowhere, you realise that don't you? Nowhere; stuck between two time zones!"

"You've hit the nail right on the head, Len. Space-time travel is just like that, mate. You can go anywhere at any time but still end up going nowhere. Unless…."

"Unless what?"

"Unless you don't come back!" said Eddie finally.

21

Now You See Him, Now You Don't

Whenever Len or Eddie went by train from Fenton to Hamsden that summer, both of them would glance nervously out of the window to see if Ally was walking the lanes near Linham Junction. On their rare journeys by the number 201 bus, they had a better view when they sat on the top deck, but, by whatever mode of transport they went, they never saw him again. Len joked to Eddie, on one such trip,

"Maybe he's aged and he's back in our time."

They rode their bikes again around Fenton-on-Sea but they never went within several miles of the area where the road had disappeared. June passed into July and Len became heavily involved in his summer sports; cricket and athletics and Eddie continued in his role as the Under 13's scorer. He was so good at it with his insistency on accuracy and neatness that he scored on one occasion for the first eleven. Eddie wasn't that keen on school at that time of the year – academic work was slowing down just when he wanted it to go faster. He was longing for the summer holidays when his dad had promised to reveal his second reward, a surprise week away somewhere.

The last day of term arrived on Friday, July the 24th and at tea that evening Eddie's dad had just finished his customary second cup of tea.

"Well I suppose you want to know when and where were going on holiday this summer, Eddie."

"Er, yes, Dad!"

"How does the *Summer Breeze* at Ludmouth sound to you?"

"Really, Dad?"

"All booked. In fact it was booked last year at the end of our stay; we had to choose which week earlier this month."

"When?"

"BB's expecting us late Monday afternoon."

"Brilliant!"

Despite his obvious excitement at the news he frowned a little and said,

"Oh, that's a shame. Len and I were going cycling to Canford to do a spot of fishing on the Wenham. His mum and dad have just bought him a complete fishing kit for the improvement he made at school. He will be disappointed, Dad."

"You'll be able to go with him in the weeks after you get back," said Eddie's mum.

"Suppose so; I wish he could come with us like last year – we had a fantastic time."

Eddie's dad put his April Fool's Day grin on and immediately his son guessed what was coming next.

"He is coming with us!"

"Oh, yes!" exclaimed Eddie. "Does he know yet?"

"Of course he does," said Eddie's mum. "His mum and dad told him at the beginning of the week. They had agreed as soon as he passed most of his resits, but they knew there was a possibility of him coming with us some time ago. BB only needed to know a week ago whether the booking was going to be for three or four."

"But, if he knew, why did he arrange to go fishing on Monday?"

"Len's cleverer than sometimes you give him credit for, Eddie," replied his mum. "He was told to keep it under wraps until you got home today. Did he do a good job?"

"Not bad. There were a couple of times when he winked at me about Monday, but I thought that was for another reason. The old fox!"

If the boys thought that the previous year's starting time had been early, then they got a shock when they discovered they were catching the 5.49 train from Fenton station on the Monday morning. Eddie made sure he packed his little book on the early railway system as well as his transistor radio with spare batteries. Len could not take his fishing rod and tackle owing to its awkward size, but his dad told him he would probably be able to hire a rod in Ludmouth. Monday morning turned out to be a much better day for travelling than the hot and sticky experience of the previous summer – it was cool and cloudy. The route was to be more or less the same as previously, but with one important alteration. The soon-to-be elevated Mr Beeching had closed the final two mile section of track from Ludmouth Junction to the seaside town proper, thus isolating Ludmouth even more from day trippers and chance visitors.

The 'family' of four arrived at Ludmouth Junction at two-twenty, fifteen minutes later than the previous summer. The boys easily found BB, recognising his battered Vauxhall Cresta before they spotted him. He was being accosted by an old tramp who seemed to want to engage him in conversation and was probably begging for a lift into Ludmouth. Within twenty minutes they were unloading their cases outside *Summer Breeze* having had to suffer BB's peculiar humour on the ride from Ludmouth Junction. Their summer holiday had begun.

The boys spent the first few days repeating their pastimes of the previous year together with some crab fishing off a small jetty, but it wasn't until the Thursday that they decided to see if they could find the rock tunnel again. They had both avoided discussing anything paranormal thus far on the holiday, even when they had already been fossil hunting and passed right by where they thought they remembered the tunnel to be. The tide was going out when they approached the large pile of rocks in front of the tunnel entrance.

"Can't see it, mate," said Len. "Everything looks different somehow."

"It's gone," said Eddie.

Len had climbed up onto a large rock and was staring at the cliff face.

"It's blocked. You can see where it was from here; it's covered with rocks and mud."

"Can you squeeze in?"

"You'd need to be as thin as a pencil, Eddie."

"Could we move some of the rocks and stuff?"

"Why do you want to? You seem awfully keen all of a sudden to rake up all that ghost nonsense again. Anyway you know it's too dangerous – it could all fall in and we'd be buried."

"I'm just a bit bored, Len and I thought Mr Manders might reappear or we'd hear the train again."

"Let's leave it, mate. Why don't we look for some jet? I'm sure there's a jeweller in Ludmouth who'd buy some."

Reluctantly, Eddie agreed. He knew Len was right, but something at the back of his mind was telling him that their experiences with the paranormal weren't quite over just yet.

They were out of luck with their search for any jet and at dinner that evening, BB explained that it could only normally be found on the north-east coast of England; Ludmouth was too far south and west.

"You can find amber and, of course, there are always the fossils," said BB after Eddie had asked him what else there was to do in and around Ludmouth. He thought for a couple of moments and then continued.

"You could always go on a treasure hunt, if your parents would let you."

"A treasure hunt? Where?" asked Eddie with some interest.

"Well, after they closed the line from Ludmouth to the Junction, walkers can now use the track as a way inland. They then take another footpath that swings back to the top of the cliffs west of here. They come back along the cliff path. It's about a seven mile hike in all."

Len was not impressed.

"I'm not doing a seven mile walk, BB!"

"You don't have to. It's about a mile to the station from here and you can walk as much or as little of the track as you like."

Len was still not impressed.

"Where's the treasure, then?"

"You'd be amazed at how much stuff falls off trains. Some people, I'm afraid, don't always take all their rubbish home at the end of their holiday. You get the smokers who stand at the open windows and drop lighters, or jewellery falls off their fingers or wrists. There are no tunnels between here and Ludmouth Junction so people stand with their heads right out of the window to cool their faces. All kinds of stuff can get blown off, from hats to mouth organs. Last week we had a walker staying here who found two lighters and a gold bracelet *and* he wasn't even looking for anything."

Len looked a little pale and Eddie remembered his friend's incomplete description of a ghastly scene involving his own model tunnel.

"Is it safe? Will we trip over the track?" asked Eddie.

"Not if you take it slowly and pick your feet up. In a lot of places you can walk beside the track on a grass verge."

Eddie's parents had overheard much of the boy's conversation with BB from their neighbouring table and his dad joined in.

"Sounds a good idea. At least you wouldn't be on a narrow country lane and get run over by a car. You could go tomorrow morning while your mum and I do some shopping and play a little bowls. I want ten per cent of all valuable items you sell! Oh, and by the way, I've found a place that hires out fishing rods for the weekend. The man in the shop said that the River Lud has got trout this year."

At breakfast the following morning, the last day of July, the boys were anxious to get started on their walk to find any treasure. Eddie was not that hopeful.

"Knowing our luck, we'll probably only find an old toilet roll."

"Or some tickets; might be quite interesting if their old."

By ten past nine they were already heading north from The Esplanade through the maze of back streets consisting almost entirely of guest house and small hotels. They couldn't believe that the town planners and/or the original railway company had allowed the station to be built so far from the town centre and seafront.

"It's not as though it's that steep a climb," said Eddie when they were about halfway to the old station.

"Stop moaning, Eddie. You seem to want to put a dampener on the day."

"Not a dampener, Len. I just think we're going to be unlucky. The weather already looks a bit dodgy."

They finished the first part of their journey by reaching Ludmouth's now deserted station at a little after nine-thirty; deserted apart from three or four freight wagons and a few seagulls. The closure notice and what the boys assumed were cancellation notices were posted in several places. There didn't seem to be any other walkers or treasure hunters in attendance.

"How do we get onto the track? We forgot to ask BB," said Eddie as they stood in front of the main entrance.

"There's a gate over there where people used to cross the line, I think," replied Len.

They found it relatively easy to find their way down onto the track, with no safety precautions needed since the station had closed three months previously. The sun was trying to peep through the clouds. At first, while they were close to the station, the going was arduous as the single track was penned in by the brick platform and then by embankments on either side and they had step carefully over the sleepers. Len was first to find anything of note, an enamelled British Rail lapel badge with *Guard* stamped on it. He immediately pinned it to his shirt and announced,

"Tickets, please!"

Soon the embankments gave way to decently wide grass verges on both sides and the boys took one each. After an hour of searching they had found two nice lighters – one of which looked as though it might be silver – a cloth cap and three small denomination coins. They could have picked up numerous bottles, empty and half-full cigarette packets and various useless pieces of clothing, like a sock and two left shoes. They ignored the various items of food in different stages of decay. Without realising it they were in sight of Ludmouth Junction and Eddie said,

"We'll have to turn back now – the other line is up ahead."

"About turn, driver!" said Len.

"Thank you, guard!"

They walked quicker on their return, only occasionally looking for things on the track. They had covered more than half of their journey and had just finished walking round a fairly sharp bend when they spotted a figure in the distance walking towards them.

"Another treasure hunter," said Len.

"Well, he's too late. We've got all the good stuff," replied Eddie.

The figure was so far away they couldn't tell whether it was male, female, young or old. Suddenly Eddie stopped walking.

"Listen, hear that?"

"What?"

"I can hear the noise of a train, like when we were in the rock tunnel, and it's getting louder."

Len heard it too and laughed.

"Oh no, it's started again. What's happening?"

Eddie looked blank as the noise seemed to be vibrating the rails.

"It'll pass; it's another test."

The noise got louder and they could at last identify the figure coming towards them.

"It's the tramp," said Len. "The one BB was talking to when we arrived."

The boys had given up worrying when the train noise would stop, but it was reaching a crescendo. The tramp was almost level with them and fear was written all over his face. The boys could feel the rails vibrating. A loud deep whistle followed by a deafening screeching noise sounded in the boys' heads. The tramp was right by them. Suddenly he grabbed both boys by the shoulders in a vice-like grip and in one movement hurled them both onto the grass verge to their left. A split second later the 'real' train screamed past them. Brakes screeched and the engine slid to a halt a hundred yards down the track. Back up the track Eddie rolled over and sat up, bruised but unhurt. Len moaned in pain.

"What happened, Eddie?"

"The train was real, Len. It was real!"

Earlier, Derek Thomas had left Ludmouth Junction in his Hunslet diesel shunting engine to bring three freight wagons back from Ludmouth's old station where they had been left after its closure. He had just got round Firbeck Curve when he was presented with his worse nightmare. At any other part of the track he would always have enough vision ahead and time to sound his whistle should there be people on the track. There, not twenty yards in front of him, stood two boys who seemed to be listening to something. He sounded his whistle and pulled hard on the brake lever. He momentarily closed his eyes and he would report later that he thought he had felt something hit the cab. His shunting engine came to a stop. He jumped down out of his cab and started running back up the track. He didn't look in front or under his engine. If he had he would have found nothing. The two boys were sitting up on the grass verge and he breathed a '*Thank God*!'

"Don't move, lads! Stay where you are! I'm coming." he bellowed up the track.

Eddie managed to stand up and tottered over to his injured friend.

"Where's it hurt, Len?

"I think my ankle's broken. Where's the tramp?

A third voice interrupted the boys.

"Are you O.K., boys? Stay still."

"I'm alright," replied Eddie. "My friend's hurt his ankle. What happened?"

"You were in the middle of the track and I thought I'd hit you. I just didn't have time to stop. Didn't you hear me coming? I sounded the whistle loudly. You must have jumped out of the way at the last second."

Eddie didn't reply except to ask a question of his own.

"Where's the tramp?"

"What tramp? There was no one else, thank God!"

While Derek Thomas attended to Len's ankle, Eddie was distraught. They had let their experiences with fantasy and the paranormal cloud their thinking to such an extent that they hadn't been able to distinguish it from reality. The train *had* been real, but they had ignored it as they had ignored noises and events in the past, because they had only been in a game. They had been lucky this time. It had been their worst nightmare, but it had been their own fault. Where was the tramp?

The engine driver carried Len to his cab with a homemade splint to his ankle and after a little while, he drove his shunter down the line to Ludmouth station where the emergency services were alerted and an ambulance took the boys to the local hospital. The police contacted BB and Eddie's mum and dad joined Len and their son within the hour. Derek Thomas would make his report to the authorities in due course and he would describe how lucky the two boys had been. British Rail would not lay any blame at his door. Larger notices would be posted in prominent positions at both stations. The inquiry would conclude a tragic accident had been averted, but more by luck than judgement. For whatever reason, Mr Thomas would not mention a tramp at any stage in the inquiry. If he had been asked about such a person, he would have said that one of the boys was probably delirious with shock.

After X-ray, Len found that he hadn't broken his ankle; it was just badly sprained and, with his and Eddie's minor cuts and abrasions attended to, they were back at *Summer Breeze* by late afternoon with Len proudly using crutches. Eddie's mood had lifted when they found that they were not in trouble with his mum and dad, except for ignoring the notices warning of possible shunting work. BB was apologetic, but Eddie's dad apportioned no blame – the boys had to learn to read properly. Nobody had at any time mentioned a tramp and the two boys had kept quiet.

22

The Tramp

It wasn't until later that Friday evening, when the boys were in their own room, that they were able to rewind their incredible experiences. Len started first.

"There was a tramp, wasn't there, Eddie?"

"Well, we saw him, Len, and he was the same one as BB was talking to when we first arrived. Like you, I'm certain of it."

"What would have happened if he hadn't been there?" said Len.

"God only knows. He saved our lives."

"How could a ghost do that? It's impossible."

Eddie was still bothered by his earlier thoughts immediately after their escape.

"Len?"

"What?"

"We were stupid, you know. We thought the train noises weren't real and they were."

"I know."

"That means in future though, Len, we have to take all events as being real."

Len smiled.

"But that's what everyone does anyway. It's only because we've experienced fantastic things that we now don't trust reality."

'Trust reality', thought Eddie. That's all they had to do, 'trust reality'.

Both boys were a little stiff and sore on the Saturday morning. Some of the their time was occupied by interviews with a local reporter from the Ludmouth Chronicle and a community police officer who spent time stressing the dangers of being near railway lines. Len, for one, found some of the advice slightly amusing given their otherworldly and more frightening experiences. Eddie listened intently thinking about the harsh reality of their narrow escape. A headline in the following week's Chronicle would read:

'Boys' lucky escape – local train driver's story',

By the afternoon the boys felt able and interested enough to do some fishing on the River Lud. Still feeling slightly guilty, BB offered to drive the boys and Eddie's dad to the tackle shop to collect the rods and thence to part of the riverbank where his local knowledge told him there would be trout. BB would return between five and six to bring them back to the guest house. Eddie's mum, meanwhile, would do some reading and a little more shopping. Len insisted on walking everywhere with his crutches when in fact he could hop reasonably well without them. His ankle, though still swollen, was vastly improved from the day before. He felt like a local celebrity, even though the reasons behind his elevation were not to be encouraged.

After a luckless afternoon's fishing, both Len and Eddie seemed to be overly quiet and not just because of the disappointment at not landing a trout. In BB's car on the way back Eddie shared their concerns with his dad.

"Dad?"

"Yes, Eddie."

"Dad, can we go home tomorrow?"

"Tomorrow? Why?"

"Me and Len don't feel that happy here now after our lucky escape."

Fred Compton didn't answer for a while and BB said,

"It's quite understandable, Mr Compton, you know. They must still be in shock. Sometimes it doesn't show itself fully for a couple of days afterwards."

Eddie's dad wasn't too happy at receiving BB's advice but didn't respond. Instead he turned round to the boys and said,

"Let's talk to your mum when we get back – O.K?"

"Yes, Dad," said Eddie and both boys felt better; the suggestion had been aired and had not received an instant negative answer.

By seven o'clock the arrangements had been altered. BB would drive the 'family' to Exeter in the morning, Sunday, since there was only a skeleton service from Ludmouth Junction. Thence they would be able to catch the London train and even though the journey would take nearly two hours longer, they should still be back in Fenton-on-Sea by six in the evening. The boys cheered up considerably on hearing the news over dinner that evening.

"Thanks, Dad, and Mum."

Eddie's mum smiled warmly.

"No problem, Eddie. Your father and I were ready to go home as well. It was quite a shock for us as well, you know."

Eddie was quiet and Len spoke for them both.

"We are really sorry, Mrs Compton – we just didn't read the warning notices and thanks for changing your plans for us."

Sunday's breakfast was the last meal they would have at the guest house and BB seemed to want to make it one to remember, giving them extra portions of nearly everything. Eddie and Len had spent some more time in their rooms the previous night discussing the near accident and Eddie had a question for BB after his parents had left to go and finish packing.

"BB?"

"Yes, Eddie."

"Are there any tramps in Ludmouth?"

"Tramps? Well, yes, we have one."

"What's his name?" asked Len.

"Oh, nobody knows his name, son. He's been here years."

"Years? How long?"

"Well Pat and I came here fifteen years ago and the previous owner mentioned that he'd been here all the time while they were owners, so I should say he's been Ludmouth's resident tramp since before the War."

"What's he look like?" asked Len casually.

"What does any tramp look like? Scruffy, old and dirty clothes, you know. But, now you come to mention it, there was one thing strange."

"What?" asked Eddie nervously.

"I saw him once or twice in the town and he was quite well dressed in smart clothes, but they looked like they were from another age. Maybe similar to what the Victorians used to wear. I thought he was in fancy dress."

"Is there anything else you know about him?" continued Eddie.

BB looked a little oddly at the two boys.

"What makes you ask all these questions about our tramp? Have you met him or something?"

Eddie could have said, '*Something*', but responded with,

"Oh, we saw him talking to you when we first arrived and we thought he was trying to cadge a lift from you," and Len added quickly,

"We've seen him a couple of times since and once he tried to say something to us. Eddie thought he was going to grab him or something. We we're a bit scared, that's all."

"Oh, he's harmless. He might have been trying to get some money off you. He would know you weren't local."

"But, is there anything else strange about him?" Eddie repeated his question.

"Only his catchphrase. I first heard him say it when I was collecting some guests from the station. He came up to me, and like you, I thought he wanted a lift. Instead he simply asked me where the train had come from"

"What did you tell him?" asked Eddie quietly.

"That it had probably just come from Exeter, and then, now let me get this right. Ah, yes, that was it – he said, *'That's not very far. You can go anywhere by rail, you know'*. He'd say the same thing every time he saw me at the station – *'you can go anywhere by rail'*."

23

Trusting Reality

For the rest of those summer holidays in 1964, Len and Eddie occupied
their time with all the real things that thirteen-year-old boys were
accustomed to. It was a warm and fine August and swimming, cycling
and the seaside amusements were their priorities. Eddie's train set was
banished to the back of his wardrobe and Len's football got swept out to
sea one day when Len kicked it too far in the wrong direction. Eddie
suspected that the action had been deliberate.

The boys had their day in London at the end of August and, though
the train journey provided a few memories of other more extraordinary
events, they thoroughly enjoyed what would turn out to be their last trip
together.

Jenny returned from her holiday with the Jones' family at the end of
August, with a suntan which she would try to maintain throughout the
winter, by what ever artificial means she could find. Gary received his
bravery award in late September and by the New Year would be taken on
and trained by the local fire brigade.

The autumn term was a period of change and rapid development for the
two boys. They each began to acquire a wider and different circle of
friends; Len with the more athletic and sporty type and Eddie with the
academia at Fenton Grammar. Consequently their own friendship started
to become more of an acquaintance. They chatted occasionally in school,
but rarely outside of it or about the fantastic experiences of the previous
two years. They were growing up and the reality of such a process took
over, physically and mentally. It would be some time until either of them
would be able to look back at that period and be able to admit to

themselves that what had happened had been a kind of reality, but it would be a hazy recollection at best. On the other hand, they would both continue for a while to appear nervous when certain sounds and events impinged on their everyday lives; the odd look over the shoulder; the occasional double take when someone said or did something that triggered memories. It would take time for them both to trust reality again.

THE HAUNTING OF EDDIE COMPTON

For the real Jennifer

It's not just what we inherit from our mothers and fathers that haunts us. It's all kinds of old defunct theories, all sorts of old defunct beliefs, and things like that. It's not that they actually live on in us; they are simply lodged there, and we cannot get rid of them. I've only to pick up a newspaper and I seem to see ghosts gliding between the lines. There must be ghosts all the country over, as thick as the sand of the sea .... We are, one and all, so pitifully afraid of the light.

(Ghosts, Henrik Ibsen, 1828-1906)

CONTENTS

1

Back on Track

Cyril Wilby had been Head of Woodwork and Metalwork at Fenton-on-Sea Secondary Modern School for six years. He had tried hard to ignore the rumours that had been circulating for some time, but it seemed certain that secondary education in the area was soon going to be reorganised, resulting in a huge comprehensive school. Fenton Grammar School was likely to become the upper school and Cyril's school would cater only for pupils aged 11 to 14. He had been reluctant to talk to his wife, Martha, about such a possible merger, as it might also have a bearing on his son's education, let alone the significant change in his own duties and responsibilities that would occur. Cyril's son, Leonard, was halfway through his third year at Fenton Grammar and, though he was far from being an academic star, he had made an enormous number of friends through his sporting ability – he was captain of both the Under 14's football and rugby teams. With all of these considerations beginning to nag him, Cyril eventually decided to broach the subject at teatime one Friday in late February that year, 1965. He was straight to the point.

"We may have to move, Martha."

At first his wife seemed not to have heard Cyril's bold statement and carried on munching on a sandwich.

"I said: we may have to move from Fenton, dear."

The mention of the name of their sleepy seaside town caused Martha Wilby to swallow hard and look directly at her husband.

"Move? Move where?"

"I don't know, but away from Fenton-on-Sea."

"Why? Have we got money problems? Can't we afford the mortgage?

"No, dear. I may have to get a new job."

Silence descended on the Wilby's dining room and Len Wilby was first to break it.

"Why, Dad? Are they giving you the sack?"

"No, son, not exactly, but…."

Martha Wilby went pale.

"So why have we got to move, then, Dad?"

"Have you not heard anything at school, Len?"

"About what?"

"About the two schools merging into one big comprehensive."

"Yeah, a bit. Hempsall said we probably wouldn't be taking any first years next September, but why should that affect you, Dad?"

Len's mum seemed relieved and interjected,

"So will you take them, then, Cyril?"

"Yes, and eventually we'll only have pupils aged eleven to fourteen, while Len's school will teach the older ones."

Len frowned.

"But why do you have to move, Dad?"

"Because I won't be teaching O-levels or CSEs anymore, just the young ones – I would hate it and, besides, I would have to apply for my own job in the reorganisation."

Martha seemed to understand, but Len was not convinced.

"But you'd get it, Dad; you're one of the best teachers they've got. Everyone says so."

"That's not really the issue. I just don't agree with comprehensive education. Bright kids like you, or your friend, Eddie, would initially be in the same classes as the weakest ones. It just won't work. We've always been the best place for the real strugglers."

Len's mum was still deep in thought until her husband smiled and added,

"You know what I mean, don't you, love? You know I would be miserable."

"Yes, I suppose so, but what will you do?"

"Look for another job where they're not likely to go comprehensive until after I retire in just over ten years."

Len didn't seem as worried as much as his dad thought he would be at his suggestion and he asked excitedly,

"Where?"

"I don't know yet, but maybe somewhere near London."

"What, where we used to live?" asked Len.

"No way," said Len's mum. "I'm not going back to the East End."

"No, dear, but I think places like Kent and Sussex have no plans to change for a while yet."

Martha Wilby seemed cheered by that but still had worries.

"What about my job?"

"Shouldn't be a problem – schools are always short of good chief cooks like you and…."

Cyril Wilby paused.

"And what, dear?" asked Martha.

"And you might not have to work at all if I get a better job. I've been thinking of getting into senior management. How does Deputy Head sound to you?"

"Really, Dad?" asked Len.

"Yes, I do most of the discipline now at school. Old Tommy Firth is hopeless at it, and that's another reason why it's not a bad idea to move – Fenton Secondary Modern has been going downhill for a while now."

Martha was smiling genuinely by now and said,

"So I could do more voluntary work?"

"Yes, love," replied her husband and turning to his son, he said,

"And what about you, Len – are you O.K. with the idea?"

"Definitely, Dad. Fenton is such a boring place; being nearer to London would be fantastic, especially if I can get to see Tottenham play at White Hart Lane on a regular basis."

"What about Eddie, son? Would you miss him?"

"I don't think so, Dad. We haven't done much together since last summer and the Devon holiday – he's so much cleverer than me that he seems to have got a lot of new friends in the third year at school."

Len's dad metaphorically breathed a huge sigh of relief as his family became attuned to the idea of the possible move from Fenton-on-Sea and tea concluded calmly with all three of the Wilbys thinking their own thoughts about what the future would hold for them. In his bedroom later, Len would be reminded of his dwindling friendship with his one-time best friend, Edward Compton, with whom he had shared some incredible and fantastic adventures over the previous three years.

'Will I miss him?' he thought. 'Why *had* their friendship diminished? Was it that they didn't want to be reminded of the fantasy world they had both been a part of? Did he himself still believe in phantoms and ghosts? Did his friend, Eddie, still have the same memories? What were those memories?'

All these thoughts aroused themselves in Len's mind that Friday evening – thoughts that had been buried in the deep recesses of his mind ever since his and Eddie's near fatal accident the previous summer. Little had been said between them after they had returned to the reality and normality of Fenton Grammar school in the autumn. He made up his mind that, like times of old, he would pay Eddie a visit the following morning which, being Saturday, would mean that they could spend some time together away from their own separate friends and individual pursuits at school.

Saturday, February the 27th arrived with a hint of an early Spring in the air and Leonard Wilby had a jaunt in his step as he left his house, 7 Lime Tree Avenue, to walk the few hundred yards to 38 Fir Tree Close, the home of his erstwhile friend, Eddie Compton. He hesitated for a moment or two as he stood in front of Eddie's front door. He then gave his familiar rhythmic knock and waited. A few months ago his friend would have opened the door almost instantly, but this time it was Eddie's mum, Ann Compton, who appeared in the threshold.

"Oh hello, Len; haven't seen you for ages. How are you?"

"Fine, Mrs. Compton. Is Eddie around?"

"Yes, come on in."

Eddie had just come downstairs and stood behind his mother in the hall. He looked a little nervous.

"Hello, Len. What's up?"

"Not much, mate. I wondered whether you were doing anything this morning."

"Nothing special. Why?"

"Well, it's such a nice day, I wondered if you'd like to go down town...." Len paused and then continued. "Like we used to."

Eddie didn't look too keen – he and Len hadn't really seen each other outside school since the previous October. What did Len want? He usually spent Saturdays playing football or rugby for the school, so Eddie was curious.

"If you like, Len. I'm not doing anything else."

Ten minutes later and the two boys were heading out of Fir Tree Close. Soon they reached the top of the footbridge over the railway line by Fenton station. By this time normal pleasantries had already been exchanged between the two boys, so when Len stopped walking, Eddie suspected his old friend had something important to discuss.

"I called round today because I wanted to talk to you, Eddie," Len said. "We are still friends, aren't we, mate?"

"Of course we are," replied Eddie. "I suppose it was inevitable we wouldn't see as much of each other after last summer, what with all the different things we do at school."

"I suppose so, but I think it might also be because of what we both went through on those fantastic adventures. I, for one, didn't want to be reminded sometimes of the near misses we had."

"What do you mean?" asked Eddie.

Len smiled and said,

"Well, we've been back in reality for about six months now and I've had no nightmares; nothing strange has happened to me and I like it, so I suppose I've subconsciously tried to avoid you where possible in case it should start again. Deep down, you're still my best friend."

Eddie's eyes looked watery and he said,

"You've always been my best friend too, and you always will be, mate. What happens in school is different."

Len grabbed his friend roughly and gave him a self-conscious hug, before stepping backwards and grinning. The two boys then spent several minutes chatting about the fantastic adventures of the previous two summers. Both were relieved to discover that they each remembered them in exactly the same way, culminating with their narrow escape from being run down by a train while on holiday together with Eddie's mum and dad in Ludmouth in Devon the previous August. Len had one final question before he would give his friend his own news.

"Have you seen any of our friendly ghosts since, or has anything happened to you out of the ordinary?"

"No, mate, to both questions. What about you?"

"Nothing also, apart from the occasional dream of magic carpets and railway tunnels. I still get a bit nervous when I'm at Fenton station and hear the noise from train engines. Thought I glimpsed old Granty wandering the country lanes once when I looked out of the train window on the way back from Hamsden."

Aloyisious St. John Grant had been the elderly owner of Grant's Emporium at the top of Steep Hill. He had tragically died in a train crash the previous year and had made a ghostly reappearance when the boys had been out cycling the country lanes not far from Fenton. His bric-a-brac shop had since been turned into small tearooms with lovely views over the promenade and sea from a small courtyard at the rear. Eddie had only made the twelve mile journey to Hamsden by bus since they had experienced their phantom train journeys the previous summer.

"We seem to have made a good start at trusting reality again, mate," concluded Eddie eventually.

"Yes, but I still wonder if anything like it will ever happen again, you know," said Len. "Do you think it will, Eddie? Do you want it to?"

"That's a 'no' to both, old son. A definite 'NO'."

"I agree. I'll just stick with my dreams like everyone else. Reality is much safer!" said Len finally.

The sun was shining brightly as Len gazed wistfully out to sea from their vantage point on top of the footbridge. He stared into the distance as he thought of his own possible new and bright horizon. Eddie was about to start walking again but Len put his hand on his shoulder and said,

"Eddie, I've got some news."

"What, mate?"

"We're probably going to be leaving Fenton."

"Leaving? Where to?"

"Don't know yet exactly, but my dad wants to leave Fenton Secondary because it will probably go comprehensive. We may go back to somewhere near London, if he can get a job. He wants to be a Deputy Head."

"Oh," said Eddie quietly. "When will you go?"

"Probably July or August if Dad gets a job for September."

"Do *you* want to go, Len?" asked Eddie.

"I think so. I mean, I haven't exactly done very well academically at Fenton Grammar, have I? It would be a fresh start for my O-levels. Dad says it's probably the best time this year."

Eddie was very quiet for the next few minutes as the two boys made their way down the footbridge and into the High Street. They had reached Arleson's the bakers where Eddie's sister, Jenny, worked full-time. Jennifer Compton was nearly nineteen and was going to start a hairdressing and beauty course at Hamsden Civic College the following September. Eddie peered into the baker's window and gave his sister a cheery wave. Suddenly, he turned back to Len and said,

"I shall miss you, mate."

"I shall miss you too, Captain," replied Len with a smile. "It's not the end of the world though, mate. You can come and stay with us after we move. I'll take you to White Hart Lane to watch some real football."

"No thanks, mate!" said Eddie. "That's one thing I shall definitely not miss."

"What's that?" queried Len.

"You going on about Spurs every time football is mentioned. There are other teams, you know."

"Are there? I hadn't noticed," said Len.

By the time the two boys parted company just before lunch that Saturday morning, the old friendship was back on track. What had kept them together as friends from the time when they had been eight-year-olds, seemed stronger than ever: the same humour; the shared experiences of some fantastic adventures and the knowledge that no one else knew what they had been through.

2

A New Job

After only two applications for a Deputy Headship, Cyril Wilby received his first letter requesting him to attend for interview just before Easter on Tuesday, April the 13th. The Banham School was a Secondary Modern School similar in size to Fenton Secondary and was situated in the small seaside town of Petersgate on the north Kent coast about sixty miles from London. The area seemed affluent enough to Cyril when he alighted from the train at Petersgate station that Tuesday morning. It was no more than a five minute walk along a respectable tree-lined avenue leading to the school which was set in a residential area not unlike that surrounding Fenton's two secondary schools. Cyril felt comfortable and relaxed on his walk to the school – he had a good feeling about the job being offered.

He arrived at Banham School's reception at eleven o'clock precisely for his interview scheduled at a quarter past. He quickly discovered that he was the only candidate that day. After a brief tour of the school followed by lunch, the main interviews began at two and ran for exactly two hours. In the final one he faced a panel of five; two female governors, a local authority official, the present Deputy Head and the Headteacher, Mr Peter Boulter. Cyril Wilby emerged from the Head's study at ten past four, exhausted but confident that he had given it his best shot. He was escorted to a waiting room to await the decision. Half and hour later and the Deputy Head came to take him back into the interview room. The panel was still in place. It looked ominous. Mr Boulter motioned to Cyril to sit down and said,

"Mr Wilby, I have one more question for you."

"Yes, Headmaster?" replied Cyril nervously. 'What now?' he thought.

"What would you say if we were to offer you the post of Deputy Head in charge of Pastoral Care, Mr Wilby?"

Cyril Wilby was lost for words.

"Come now, Mr Wilby," interjected the Chair of Governors. "What would you say?"

"What would I say?" stammered Cyril. He hadn't been expecting this. What should he say? He tried to cover himself in case he was still under interview and he was being tested.

"Well, Headmaster. If you were to offer me the post you've just described, then I would say, yes. *Are* you offering me the post?"

Peter Boulter smiled and the rest of the panel seemed to relax at the same time. The Chair of Governors winked at Cyril.

"Of course we're offering you the job, Cyril and I presume by your reply that you accept."

"Yes, Headmaster."

"Peter, please, and congratulations, Deputy Head."

Cyril Wilby retraced his steps along Station Avenue to catch the 5.10 train back to London Victoria. His mind was in a whirl. Had he really said yes? Was he really going to be a Deputy Head from September? How would Martha react? It would be a big change for Len, but he felt that both his wife and son were behind him; this was a family decision. He was in a much more positive mood when he reached the station, so positive that he began planning a mild celebration when he got home. Adjacent to the station was a row of shops and, spotting an off-licence, he hastily purchased a bottle of his wife's favourite wine – a 1963 sparkling Vouvray. It was five past five and he had to run to catch his train, choosing an empty carriage at the front so that he could think undisturbed about his momentous decision.

First stop was the small market town of Faversham where several new travellers joined the train. An elderly man entered Cyril's carriage. He smiled and nodded to the new Deputy Head and sat down directly opposite. Cyril Wilby looked at the old man with some curiosity; he was very smartly dressed, but his clothes were from another era. A deep red cravat, a wide brimmed felt hat, and what looked like riding boots, stood him apart from the usual commuters who frequented the train. Cyril put him down immediately as an actor from a small-town repertory theatre, probably off to an evening performance somewhere. The stranger seemed to be about to start up a conversation but Cyril Wilby closed his eyes as if he needed to snooze after a long day and the flamboyantly dressed old man leant back in his seat and stared out of the window.

The stress and emotion of the day eventually caught up with Cyril and, with the rhythmic vibration from the rails, he soon drifted off to sleep. He was jolted awake when the train pulled into Chatham. The old man had clearly also been asleep as he quickly looked out at the station and said,

"Where are we?"

"Chatham, I think, sir," replied Cyril.

"Oh, that's alright, I thought I'd missed my stop."

"Where do you want?" asked Cyril.

"I change at Bromley for Flixted Town."

The second name meant nothing to Cyril Wilby and he just nodded politely.

"My name's Jacob, by the way," said the stranger. "Jake for short."

Cyril declined the invitation to give his own name; he wanted to keep his own company and carry on with his thoughts of the future. The old man was persistent.

"Where've you come from, sir?"

"Petersgate."

"Ah, I see," said the man knowingly. "And where are you going to?"

"Fenton-on-Sea," replied Cyril Wilby, hoping the old man had never heard of such an out-of-the-way place and that the conversation would dry up. He was soon disappointed.

"Oh really. Now let me see; is the Beach station still open?"

"Beach station?"

"Yes, it was opened in '89 to cater for the new holiday trade."

"What, 1889?"

"Well, obviously. It could hardly have been there in 1789."

The old man smirked. Cyril Wilby said nothing. As far as he knew there hadn't been a second station in Fenton since well before the war.

"So is it still open, sir?"

"No."

The stranger at last sensed that his fellow passenger didn't want to talk and the two men settled back in their seats to concentrate on their own thoughts.

'Bromley, Bromley South'

The old man got up at the announcement from the station platform loudspeaker. He moved towards the door. He suddenly stopped and turned to face his fellow passenger.

"When you move to Petersgate, Cyril, make sure you look after your family carefully."

The old man left the carriage before Cyril had a chance to reply and, though he dashed out of the carriage to call him back, Cyril could not see him on the platform. He had disappeared. Cyril Wilby's heart was thumping. He fell back into his seat and tried to think clearly and logically.

'Even though I mentioned where I'd been, how did he know I was actually going to move to Petersgate? How did he know I had a family? How did he know my name?'

All these questions rushed through Cyril Wilby's brain. He found the last one easy to answer. **Cyril Wilby** was on a label fixed to his brief case. A copy of the day's interview schedule lay face up beside the case, but what about his family? A lucky guess? The bottle of wine? What was wrong with Petersgate to cause the old man to issue his warning?

By the time the train pulled into Victoria, he decided that he had probably been making a meal of an innocent remark. He had overreacted, probably as a consequence of the stress of the day and he might have misheard the old man in any case. Two hours later he arrived at Fenton station and memories of a quaintly dressed old man called Jacob had all but receded into the back of his mind.

Martha Wilby was waiting in the hall when her husband walked in through the front door at a quarter to ten that Tuesday evening. She rushed forward and hugged her husband.

"Well? How did you get on?"

Cyril Wilby put on as disappointed a look as he could and said,

"Bad news, I'm afraid."

Martha took a step backwards.

"Oh, I'm so sorry dear. Maybe it just wasn't meant to be."

Her husband smiled. He had his Christmas Day expression on his face – the expression he used every year to convey to his wife that he'd bought her something special. Martha knew at once.

"You got it?"

"Yes."

"Well done, Dad," called Len from behind his mum. "You're the best – I knew you would do it. When will we be moving? What school will I go to? Will…."

"Steady, son, I've only just got the job and it has to be confirmed in writing yet anyway. I'm exhausted and…."

"Give your dad some space, Len," said Martha Wilby. "He's only just got in. And what, dear?"

"And I need a drink – how about a nice bottle of fizzy Vouvray, love?"

"You remembered; it's my favourite. Let's get some glasses and go into the lounge and you can tell us about your day and the new school."

"Can I have some wine, Dad?"

Len's mum frowned.

"Just half a glass with some lemonade; you've got school in the morning."

"Last day before Easter though, so we won't be doing much," said Len with a grin.

Len didn't see his friend, Eddie, until they met up on the way home from school the following day. The last day of term, though hectic, always finished just after lunch and the two boys wandered up South Road in the early afternoon sunshine. As they passed Fenton Secondary Modern, Len stopped and stared for a moment at his Dad's present school. He turned back to his friend and said,

"My dad got a new job yesterday down in Kent, Eddie."

The two boys walked for a few paces while Eddie took in the news.

"So that's it, then; you'll be moving," said Eddie eventually.

"Yep. Dad says it'll probably be early August when we go, if we can get a house by then. We're going down next week after Easter to stay in a guest house while mum and dad look for property. They are going to put Lime Tree Avenue up for sale today or tomorrow."

"Whereabouts in Kent are you going? Is it by the seaside?"

"I think so – it's called Petersgate; nearer to London than Fenton-on-Sea."

"I've heard of that place, you know" said Eddie after a moment. "I'm sure Aunty Carol and Uncle Lionel live near there; I've heard them mention it."

"Where do they live, then?"

"I think it's called Hargate. I'll be able to stay with them if you don't have enough room."

"Excellent, chief."

'Quite like old times', thought Eddie.

"Did you tell your form master, Mr Collins, that you wouldn't be going into the fourth year?" asked Eddie as they reached the corner of Fir Tree Close.

"No, I'll tell him when I go back after Easter. I don't know which school I'll be going to yet. We're going to investigate that as well next week. Dad says that there's an all boys' Grammar School at Faversham and a mixed one in Petersgate itself. I rather like the idea of no girls! Faversham is only one stop on the train from where we're going to live."

The two friends parted company arranging to meet up again in three day's time on Easter Saturday – a trip to Hamsden on the train was the plan, taking in the football game at Freeman Street, the home of Third Division side Hamsden Town, in the afternoon.

Len's dad arrived home soon after his son – his news hadn't been received too well at Fenton Secondary. He would be missed. However,

Martha Wilby had good news for him when he gave her the customary peck on the cheek in their kitchen.

"Mr Donaldson at Walker's says he's already got a buyer for our house, and at the price we want."

"Really," said her husband. "When can they move?"

"Well – and this is the good bit – the husband is a teacher too. He's starting at Fenton Central Junior School in September. They're moving from Cambridge."

Cyril Wilby looked reasonably pleased but had a concern.

"It'll depend on how much property is down in Kent; we may need to extend the mortgage."

"Will that be a problem, then?"

"No, not with my new salary, I suppose. We'll find out next week, hopefully."

"When are we going, Dad? Is it still next Tuesday, like you said?" asked Len as he came in from the lounge.

"Yes, son. We catch the nine-fifteen train."

"You should buy a car, Dad, when we move. We may not be as near to your school as we are here."

"I know, Len. I'd already thought of that and I'm going to see if we can afford to buy one when we get back from Kent."

"Brilliant," said his son.

Len called round for his friend at nine-thirty on Saturday, April the 17th. Eddie was unusually quiet on the way to Fenton station. He and Len often paused at the junction of Fir Tree Close with South Road ever since Eddie's sister, Jenny, had been involved in a car crash there when her boyfriend, Gary Jones, had lost control of his Austin A40 eighteen months ago. Some people believed that Eddie may have saved his sister's life when he pulled her from the wreckage. Eddie had no recollection of the event except the poignant memory of cradling his injured sister on the very pavement where the two friends presently stood.

"Have you forgiven Gary for causing your sister's injuries?" asked Len quietly. He knew Eddie had hated Jenny's boyfriend in the past.

"Yeah, he's O.K. – he's training to be a fireman, you know. The fire brigade was impressed with the way he helped save people in the train crash at Linham Junction last year. Jenny's still besotted with him and he gets on well with my dad now."

Fred Compton had been equally antagonistic to Gary Jones after he had caused his daughter's broken ankle and dislocated shoulder, but following Gary's heroics in the aftermath of the train crash, he had warmed quickly to his daughter's suitor. Eddie's dad was the senior clerk in the booking office at Fenton railway station and had learned of Jenny's boyfriend's deeds first hand. Ann Compton, Eddie's mum, only wanted her daughter to be happy and she'd always known that, despite his faults, Gary Jones gave her daughter confidence and a spring in her step.

The two friends made their way into the High Street and were soon on Platform One and waiting for the ten past ten train to Hamsden. They had ten minutes in hand and Eddie was still quieter than normal. It was also clear to Len that it wasn't just memories of his sister's accident that were the cause.

"What's the matter, mate? You seem preoccupied."

"Oh nothing really. It's just that…."

"Come on, tell comrade Wilby. What's the problem?"

Eddie looked embarrassed, but after a moment he blurted out,

"I haven't been on a train since last year when we both went to London for the day. Since then, when I've been to Hamsden, I've always gone by bus or in my dad's Morris Minor."

"Why?"

Len knew it was a stupid question as soon as he'd asked it. The fantastic adventures they'd experienced when they had been on ghostly trains had clearly put Eddie off rail travel for life, especially after they had narrowly missed being run down by a goods engine when walking on a supposedly disused railway line in Devon the previous summer. He was quick to apologise and put his friend at his ease.

"Sorry. Stupid question, mate."

"That's alright, Len. I've got to put those unreal adventures out of my mind. Sometimes they do seem like a dream to me and that's the way I want to remember them."

"Me too. Just think, Eddie, nothing otherworldly has happened to either of us for at least eight months now, so I think we're back in reality now for good."

"Hope so, chief," said Eddie.

Just then, as if to cement that reality, the train for Hamsden pulled up at the platform and the two boys boarded it for their day out.

Meanwhile that morning, Cyril Wilby had some investigating to do. He hadn't forgotten the strange old man he'd met on the train back from Kent on Tuesday. His parting sentence had kept coming back and it bothered him. 'Look after your family very carefully'. Had it just been a natural thing to say if the man had guessed Cyril was a family man and about to move to Petersgate? Was he a psychic of some kind, rather than an actor – he had certainly been dressed like one? Cyril had racked his brains all week to try to remember the name of the old man's destination and it had eventually come to him as he lay in bed that Saturday morning.

Shortly after the two boys had boarded the train to Hamsden, Cyril Wilby entered the station forecourt and headed for the booking office. Fred Compton was surprised to see his friend.

"Hello, Cyril. You've just missed Len; he and Eddie have gone to Hamsden."

"Yes, I know, Fred; it's you I want to talk to."

"Oh, where are you off to, then?"

"Nowhere. I just need some information."

Fred Compton was curious – he liked to help people find the best and cheapest ways around England, but Cyril wasn't going anywhere, so what did he want? Cyril Wilby told a little white lie.

"Friend of mine at school is doing some research on railway stations and he needs some information about one down in Kent, Fred."

"Oh yes. Which one?"

"Flixted Town."

Fred Compton looked puzzled.

"Do you know which line it's on?"

"North Kent line; you change at Bromley for it."

"Ah, I think I remember. Just give me a moment."

Fred disappeared into what appeared to be a storeroom at the rear of the office. After a couple of minutes, he reappeared with a broad grin on his face.

"Found it, mate. Flixted Town was a station on the River Medway."

"Was?" queried Cyril.

"Yes, it closed before the war in about 1935 – something to do with a decrease in river trade. You alright, Cyril? You look very pale."

Cyril quickly regained his composure and said,

"One more question, Fred. You know we're moving down to Petersgate in the summer."

"Yes, Eddie told me."

"Well, what do you know about the place?"

Fred looked more curious.

"Nothing really; it's just the next station to Faversham where you can change for Canterbury and Dover, but it's not a significant junction in itself. I don't know anything about the town – why would I?"

"Oh well, my teacher friend will be pleased with the information about Flixted. I better get going."

Cyril Wilby turned to leave, but Fred stopped him.

"Wait a minute, Cyril. I've just remembered something about Petersgate. I'm almost sure I read somewhere in an old railway magazine or something that there used to be a mental asylum there in mid-Victorian times. It was used as an overspill from London. They used special trains to transport them from Victoria – couldn't have other passengers accompanying them, could they? I think it was closed down before the war when ordinary hospitals began to take some of the less serious cases. I did also read that some of them escaped once and that they didn't get all of them back. Apparently nobody knew what happened to them."

Cyril quickly said his goodbyes to Fred and made his way back home to Lime Tree Avenue. He needed to think. As he saw it, there were two possibilities. First, he could have misheard the name of the old man's destination or, second, he had met his first ghost! Being the down-to-earth man that he was, he soon decided that first option was the only possible explanation. He was less worried about the former mental asylum – after all, it had been closed for thirty years. By the time he had reached his front gate his mood had changed for the better. There were no such things as ghosts! As he walked up the path he suddenly remembered that he'd forgotten to ask Fred about the other 'station' – Fenton Beach. It took him a few short seconds to decide he didn't really want to know if and when there had been a station by the beach in Fenton-on-Sea. His family's future was too important and exciting to be worried about ghosts and railway stations from another time. He would make a conscious effort – he told himself – to avoid thinking about his chance meeting with the strange old man; his mind was only playing tricks. He had been very stressed and exhausted that Tuesday evening.

Len and Eddie had a good day together culminating in a 3–0 win for the Town over Seaton United. Both were in good moods on the train journey back to Fenton. The train had just slowed to pass through Linham junction – a speed limit of thirty had been enforced since the tragic crash of the previous year when the Hamsden train had come off the rails, resulting in two fatalities and tens of other casualties. Eddie seemed to be staring at something out of the window.

"Can you see him, mate," asked Len.

"What, Aloyisious, you mean?"

"Of course, who else?"

"Stop it, Len. I thought we'd agreed not to talk about ghosts and phantom trains. Aloyisious St. John Grant died in the train crash and that's that."

"We did see him afterwards, didn't we though?"

"Yes, we did, but it was a one-off – and it was probably all still part of the game we were allowed to play with my train set when we went on all those fantastic journeys. The game ended last summer."

"What about our friend and saviour, Mr Manders, then?" continued Len.

The two boys had narrowly missed being run down by a shunting engine the previous August in Devon. They had both been convinced that a tramp had pushed them out of the train's path at the very last moment, thus saving their lives. The engine driver swore later that there had been no tramp. The ghostly Mr Manders had appeared to them on a previous holiday to the same part of Devon and he seemed to have different guises, from well-dressed to a tramp. Eddie took some time to reply.

"All part of the game, mate. It was to teach us a lesson about believing in reality. We thought the train noise wasn't real because of what we'd been through before."

"But it was," said Len.

"Exactly. We have to live our lives in the real world as we grow up and, just like we eventually gave up believing in Father Christmas, it was a way of ensuring we would be able to. Presenting us with a situation where we faced ultimate danger, I think, was the best way of doing it. Staring death in the face is a great antidote against meddling in the world of ghosts and the paranormal."

Len smiled.

"You've spent a lot of time working that out, haven't you, O wise one!"

"We've had a lot of time since last summer," concluded Eddie finally.

There the matters of ghosts and paranormal experiences would rest until later that summer. In the meantime, it was to be hoped that Len's dad would not share his own experience of ghostly meetings with his son. Leonard Wilby would, perhaps, have been able to offer a solution to the identity of the exuberantly dressed old man from another age, whom his dad had met on the way back from successfully acquiring his new job.

3

First Impressions

The two boys didn't see each other again before the Wilbys were due to go on their exploratory trip to Kent. Both families spent a quiet Easter owing to the atrocious weather that hit the East Anglian coast, although Jenny had her boyfriend Gary's company for Sunday lunch – he was very much part of the family at last. The Wilbys spent some time organising the last minute arrangements for the Tuesday journey by rail. The sun appeared briefly late on Monday after nearly two days of incessant rain and strong winds. By that evening the wind had dropped to a mild breeze and the weather forecast looked good for the following day.

Len and his parents arrived at Petersgate station by mid-afternoon on the Tuesday and after a short taxi ride they checked into their small guest house for their four-night stay. The train journey had been uneventful for Cyril Wilby – no strangers had made themselves known to him. Both Len and his mum were impressed at how clean and well-cared for everywhere seemed to be. After some tea and a change of clothes the Wilbys left *Eastland Court*, their temporary accommodation, and headed for the town centre. Len noticed immediately that Petersgate was larger than Fenton-on-Sea and had a much better array of shops. The residents seemed more affluent as well. To his surprise Petersgate Grammar School was located right in the heart of the town, occupying about a hundred yards of frontage in the main thoroughfare, naively named Front Street. Though he'd previously warmed to the idea of attending the boys' grammar in neighbouring Faversham, he recognised at once the advantages of being at the heart of the town. He wondered if fourth years were allowed out at lunchtime. The school certainly seemed to be soaked in history and tradition as the sign outside main entrance suggested.

Petersgate County Grammar School
Headmaster Mr E.R. Crompton, M.A.(Cantab)
Established 1766
Usque conabor

"Two hundred years old next year," said Len's dad as they walked past the school gates.

"Looks it too," said Len who had spotted the similarity to his best friend's surname. 'This has to be a good sign', he thought. 'I wonder if the Headmaster's first name is Edward'. Len's mum interrupted her son's musings.

"Translate please, Len."

"Sorry, Mum – we haven't come across that."

Even if he had been taught the meaning of the Latin phrase it wouldn't have been much use as the subject was a complete mystery to Wilby Minor – he regularly came bottom in his class in both French and Latin, unlike his friend, Eddie, who always came first or second (a failure). Len's dad couldn't help.

"Didn't do Latin when I was at school."

After leaving the school, Len's mum and dad wanted to spend time visiting the several estate agents and knew that their son would only be a hindrance to their investigations. He was left to wander the town on his own under strict instructions that he rejoined them outside the school gates after exactly one hour. They synchronised watches and Len set off to explore the town.

Apart from buying a couple of postcards – one to be sent later to Eddie – Len didn't find too much else of immediate interest so he decided to make his way back up Front Street to have another look at his potential school. To his surprise one of the main gates was ajar and, plucking up courage, he entered the main grounds. If anyone stopped him he had the perfect excuse – he was hoping to start in September and he was new to the area. The school was much bigger than he imagined with further, and much more modern, buildings on the far side of three parallel rugby pitches. The reason for the gates being open suddenly became clear when a voice called to him from a large hut to his left.

"Hey, you there, what'ya doing?"

A burly, weather-beaten man was approaching. He had all the traditional looks of a school caretaker and a no-nonsense one at that. Len looked apologetic.

"Sorry, sir, the gate was open and…."

"May have been open, lad, but it's not open to you. What year are you in?"

"I don't go to this school yet, sir."

The caretaker seemed to mellow a little.

"You hoping to come here, then?"

"Yes, sir. My dad is going to be the new Deputy Head at Banham Secondary from September."

Bill Weaver was obviously impressed and Len realised for the first time what advantage he might have courtesy of his dad's new job.

"Have you seen Mr Crompton yet and it's Bill by the way?"

"Not yet. Dad only got the job a week ago and we're on holiday until May the 4th."

"We go back on the 3rd. You can tell your parents that. Just get them to ring Mrs Wilkinson in the office – she deals with all new applications. Where are you coming from?"

"Fenton-on-Sea."

"Never heard of it. Are you at a grammar school there, then?"

"Yes, a mixed one in Fenton."

"Shouldn't be a problem, then – I think there are plenty of places available in the fifth year. Had to get rid of a few, you know."

"I'm only fourteen, Bill, so I'll be starting in the fourth year."

"Hm, you look older, lad. What's your name?"

"Leonard Wilby, Len for short."

"Well, Len, I'll look forward to seeing you in September. Anything else you want to know now?"

"Do you play football?"

"Football, rugby and cricket; one term of each."

Len smiled; he felt at home. Bill Weaver began to show him the way out but Len had one more question which he wasn't sure he dared ask. However, he just came straight out with it. The caretaker had seemed friendly enough.

"What does the 'E' in Mr Crompton's name stand for?"

Len felt immediate relief when his question was clearly not perceived to be impertinent. Bill Weaver smiled.

"Never really been sure, but just between you and me, Len, we call him Teddy, but I don't know if it stands for Edward as usual or not. You'll see why it might just be a nickname when you meet him. It'll have to be our secret; I'm only allowed to address him as Mr Crompton."

That sealed it for Len; it was a good omen. He would constantly be reminded of his best friend. He had to go to this school.

Len emerged from the school grounds and found his parents waiting for him on the pavement outside. He was ten minutes late and they looked anxious.

"Where have you been?" asked his mother with some surprise.

"Oh, just talking to the caretaker, Mr Weaver."

"And is this the school you think you'll be going to, then?" said Cyril Wilby. "Have *you* made the decision?"

Len couldn't tell from his dad's tone whether he was genuinely cross or just being his sarcastic self.

"Looks a good school, Dad, and they've got places in the fourth year. Bill says so."

"Bill?"

"Sorry, Dad – Mr Weaver, the caretaker."

Len's dad's apparently stern face seemed to break into a pleasant enough smile.

"So you think you've made a good choice, do you, son? Did you go right to the other side of the school?"

"No, I just stayed by the main building while I talked to the caretaker."

"What did you see the other side of the playing fields?"

"How do you know there are playing fields, Dad?"

"Because, my son, the Banham School backs on to Petersgate Grammar; the sports pitches are often shared by the two schools."

Cyril Wilby put on his serious face again.

"Therefore, young man, I do not think it's a good idea for you to be so close to me; I have a reputation to create. Faversham Boys' Grammar would be a much better choice."

"But, Dad…."

"No buts, son."

This time Len was convinced that his dad was deadly serious and, trying not to show his disappointment, he walked behind his parents in silence down Front Street and into the town. He fought back the tears that demanded release. Martha Wilby could sense that her only son was upset

and just beyond the end of the main school buildings she turned round –
she couldn't keep up the pretence any longer.

"Your dad's only joking, Len. He wanted to be sure that you really
do want to go to Petersgate Grammar. Mr Dalby at the estate agents told
us that the school is respected by everyone in the town."

Meanwhile, Cyril Wilby had walked a few yards on in front and
now stood with a cheeky grin on his face staring at his son. He waited
while Len and his mother rejoined him and said,

"Almost an April Fool's joke, eh, son?"

Len was beaming. He punched his dad playfully in the ribs.

"Of course," his dad continued, "you'll have to come down again
for interview and trust that they accept your less-than-illustrious
academic record to date. You will have to hope that they will be
impressed by your captaincy of both the football and rugby teams."

Len's smile contracted a little. His mother had other news.

"We'll have no problem finding a house. There are plenty on the
market and at more or less the same price as back home. Your dad has
details of five we can see over the next two days. You will have an equal
say in what we choose."

'A bigger bedroom', thought Len. Everything seemed to be falling
into place and, when his parents announced that fish and chips were on
the agenda for later on, he was in seventh heaven.

The next two days were spent mostly visiting properties in and around
Petersgate, which Len found slightly boring despite his mum's assurance
that he would be able to give his opinion. By Friday morning it was
apparent that his parents had agreed between themselves that they would
make an offer on 23 The Park, a modest semi-detached situated less than
half a mile from the two secondary schools. It hadn't been Len's first

choice – his prospective bedroom was only marginally larger than his present one. It did, however, have an enormous garden, mostly laid to lawn – perfect for a small football pitch. His favourite had been on the outskirts of town and was detached. His dad said it was just too expensive and was on a busy main road. The Park was an area of town not unlike the avenues surrounding Fenton station where the Wilbys currently lived. It would be perfect for Martha Wilby as St Michael's Church was located halfway between The Park and the town. Two votes to one swayed it and, after a little negotiation, the Wilby's offer was accepted late that Friday afternoon. The elderly vendors would wait until August for completion – they were moving in with their son and daughter-in-law in Faversham. Cyril Wilby was relieved to discover that the increase needed in the mortgage would be much less than half that which he had been expecting. Solicitors, Edwards and Gilham in Fenton, would be informed the following Monday after the Wilby's return from Kent at the weekend. Contracts for sale and purchase would then be drawn up. The family would return to Kent at a later date to secure Len's place at Petersgate Grammar; the end of May being the most likely time.

Monday the 24th of May came round very quickly for Len. It was the day he and his mum would visit his prospective new school for interview while his dad spent some time at Banham Secondary. Len and Eddie had continued to associate with each other out of school, even though both of them continued to have their separate circle of school friends. Eddie's mathematical ability was again put to good use as scorer for the Under 14's cricket eleven where Len was one of the main batsmen. After the school game on the Saturday before the Wilby's trip to Kent, Eddie wished his best friend good luck.

"You'll get in, just concentrate on the sport, mate and anyway I've got some information for you."

"What?"

"I've translated the school motto for you."

"Where did you get that?"

"I had a peek at their magazine they sent you when I came round to your house last Saturday. I thought at least you ought to know what the motto means."

"And?"

"Well it's what you've got to do on Monday. It means '*I will do my best*'. Just get it into the interview with the Head somehow."

"Thanks, Edward, you're a real friend."

This false formality sparked a memory for Len of his last visit to Petersgate Grammar School and he continued,

"Do you know what the Headmaster's name is, Eddie?"

"Mr Wilby?"

"Close, mate. It's Mr Crompton and his first name might be Edward. Apparently those in the know call him Teddy."

"Dad calls me Ted sometimes, Len," said Eddie finally.

After the two boys parted that Saturday afternoon, Eddie became a little troubled by the strange similarity between his own name and that of his friend's prospective Headmaster. He quickly decided, however, that coincidences like that happened all the time. He was back in the real world now and for good.

'Teddy' Crompton welcomed Len and his mother into his study and Len could immediately see the reason for the moniker. Mr Edward Crompton was rotund and had a full head of curly brown hair; he was about fifty and he had a smile that made you want to cuddle him. Boys at Petersgate

Grammar School soon found that the aura was a perfect disguise for the strict disciplinarian that he actually was.

"So this is Leonard Wilby," he said to Martha Wilby.

"Yes, Mr Crompton," replied Len's mum nervously. She felt as apprehensive as her son. There was something about this Headmaster's eyes that seemed to look right inside you, she thought.

"And is your husband not with you, Mrs Wilby?"

"No, he's taken the opportunity to visit his new school – he's going to be Deputy Head there from September," she said proudly.

"Yes, I know – word soon gets round, you know, but it's a pity he's not here."

"He hopes to join us later," said Martha quickly.

Mr Crompton nodded and he turned his attention to her son.

"So young man, what talents can you bring to this school?"

Len stammered,

"I don't know, sir," and then after a moment's pause he said, "I'm captain of our Under 14's football and rugby teams."

"Really, and do you think that will help you pass your examinations and get you a good career?"

Len looked blank, but then remembered what Eddie had said to him two days earlier.

"The discipline and structure of sport helps me try to do my best at everything else including my studies, sir," and again he hesitated. "Like your school motto says: '*I will do my best*', and as captain I have to lead by example as well."

Martha Wilby's face widened in surprise. Was this her son talking? Her moment of maternal pride was soon curtailed when Mr Crompton said,

"Your academic record, however, doesn't suggest that you've been very successful at converting your prowess on the games field to your academic studies, does it, young man?"

Len was ready with his answer – he'd had plenty of time to think of it on the way down in the train that morning. Cyril Wilby was not due to pick up his new car until they got back to Fenton.

"No it doesn't, sir, but I always try my best; I can't do more."

"Ah, but that's the question isn't it? Is your best good enough for you to come here?"

Len's mum was visibly nervous but her son proved his worth again.

"I think so, sir – after all, I did pass the eleven-plus and I have made some improvements this year. There are at least half a dozen weaker than me at Fenton Grammar."

Although the Head's facial expression didn't change, inside he was impressed with Len's boldness and perception. There was something about this young man that said, Head Boy in three years time. He sat back in his swivel armchair and at last he smiled.

"Well, young man, we'll have to see, won't we? For the time being I think you should take a good look at us to see if Petersgate Grammar will suit you. I'll get Mr Simpson to take you both on a tour of the school. Mr Simpson is Head of P.E. and also the First Year – he'll be able to answer any of your questions."

Two hours later and with both his mum and dad in attendance, Len was back in the Head's study for the decision on his future school. 'Teddy' Crompton wasted no time in conveying it to the Wilbys.

"You'll be pleased to know that I can offer your son a place in our Fourth Year from September."

Len's mum and dad smiled and could hardly raise a 'thank you'. Len was straight to the point.

"Thank you, sir. I won't let you down."

"I hope not, Leonard," said Mr Crompton, sternly. "I hope not."

4

Another Garden

It was late June before Cyril Wilby finally decided on what car to buy. He had tried several garages in the area including Steve Paton's Autos on South Road, the closest to his home in Lime Tree Avenue. He hadn't been behind the wheel of a vehicle since his National Service days and he'd only driven army jeeps and trucks then anyway. If he was honest he didn't want to have a car – he'd always walked or cycled to his job at Fenton Secondary Modern and he'd never seen the need for one. However, he knew that with the move to Kent and his son growing up quickly, the family needed independent transport – a Deputy Head had to have a car, his wife insisted.

Jennifer Compton's boyfriend, Gary Jones, no longer worked for his dad, Richard, at the second-hand car showroom in Hamsden. Thus it was with some surprise that Cyril and Martha Wilby were greeted by the young trainee fireman at about ten-thirty on Saturday, June the 26th.

"Hello, Mr and Mrs Wilby – looking for a car?"

"Yes, Gary. What are you doing here?"

"Just helping my dad out. He's quite busy at this time of the year. I'm not on call this weekend."

The Wilbys walked further into the showroom and Gary followed attentively.

"What kind of car were you looking for, Mr Wilby?"

"Not really sure, Gary; something for a family with reasonable luggage space. Martha here says it has to be red. I'm not bothered about speed; I just want it to be economical and easy to drive. Though I passed my test when I was with the army doing my National Service, I haven't driven for some years."

"I see," said Gary. "We have a nice red two-year-old Vauxhall Victor. It has only done 17,000 miles."

Gary led them to a corner of the showroom where they found the nominated car. Martha's eyes lit up when she saw the gleaming and highly polished paintwork; the chrome wheel hubs shone brightly in the summer sunshine that cleverly illuminated Richard Jones' showroom. Cyril was not too sure.

"It's bigger than I wanted, Gary. How fast is it?"

"Oh it'll cruise comfortably at seventy – it's got a 1500 engine. She's beautiful, isn't she?"

"How much is it?" asked Cyril hoping it would be out of his price range. His wife seemed to be in a trance as she clung to his arm. He could feel her egging him on.

"Well, new, they're over eight hundred. It's the Victor Deluxe."

Cyril breathed a sigh of relief; he only had five hundred to spend. Martha relaxed her grip.

"But…."

Gary paused and pretended to do some mental calculations. He knew he would have to ask his dad for a price, but he wanted his potential customers to think that he knew exactly what he was doing.

"But?" queried Martha Wilby.

"But I'll just have to check one or two things with my father. I haven't got the latest second-hand guide out here in the showroom. Can you just wait a moment please?"

Gary's dad appeared from the office and took over the potential sale.

"Mr and Mrs Wilby? I don't think we've met; I'm Richard Jones. Gary, a coffee for our customers please."

Gary looked cross. They were *his* customers, but, as usual, his dad had taken over. He knew why he had joined the fire service and not followed his dad into the family business! He went to make the coffees.

The experienced salesman's technique was quickly put into practice. No mention of price. Richard Jones opened the passenger door for Martha.

"Take a seat, Mrs Wilby. Try her out for size and comfort."

Cyril Wilby climbed in beside his wife and sat in the supple leather seats. Martha looked like a little girl with her best ever birthday present. She gave her husband a kiss on the cheek. Cyril would have no choice.

"Start her up, sir," said Richard Jones.

Cyril turned the key and depressed the accelerator slightly. The engine purred into life. His last remaining hope was that it would still be out of his price range. He and Martha climbed out of the car and Cyril made a great pretence of inspecting the pristine bodywork for scratches and marks. He would find some fault with it, he hoped, but there was none. The tyres seemed to have little wear on them too. Cyril was all but defeated.

"How much is it, Mr Jones?"

Richard Jones grinned broadly. Another customer in the palm of his hand, he thought. He rarely displayed prices on his cars; it was essential that the customer fell in love with the car first. Then the price didn't matter. It worked every time.

"List price new is eight-two-five, Mr Wilby, but since it's the end of the month I can let you have it for, shall we say, six hundred."

Cyril Wilby shook his head and started to walk away. Martha didn't move and, instead, she took over the negotiations.

"Too much, Mr Jones – this car's two years old."

"Twenty-one months actually – it was first registered in September '63."

"We've only got five hundred, I'm afraid; such a shame."

To both men's surprise Martha Wilby rejoined her husband who had already moved towards the door. Just as she did so Gary called out,

"Coffee's ready."

Gary's dad strode after his lost customers and said,

"Please have some coffee before you go. Perhaps I can offer you a better deal too."

Martha Wilby released her grip on the door handle and turned back to face Mr Jones. She smiled knowingly. It had worked.

Once the Wilbys were seated in the back office, Richard Jones made great fuss of sifting through some papers, most of which were irrelevant to the matter in hand.

"The best I can do for you is five-sixty and that's my very best offer."

Cyril shook his head, but in his mind he had already admitted defeat. That had happened when Martha had planted a kiss on his cheek. She spoke for them both.

"We could go to five-twenty, couldn't we Cyril?"

"Yes, I suppose so," replied her husband with resignation.

Richard Jones sifted through a few more papers and said,

"I'll meet you halfway – five-forty and that's my final offer. Take it or leave it. You're robbing me at that too."

"We'll take it, won't we love?" said Martha.

"Yes, dear – provided you tax it for a year, Mr Jones," responded Cyril; his manhood eventually preventing him from allowing his wife to be able to boast afterwards that she had done all the negotiations.

"It's a deal. You have just bought a car, Mr Wilby. Well done!" said Mr Jones with some relief.

A week later, and with all the paperwork complete, Cyril and Martha Wilby drove off Richard Jones' forecourt in their shiny red car. Despite his lack of recent driving experience Cyril seemed to cope well with both the car's idiosyncrasies and Hamsden's Saturday morning traffic. They were soon on the A132 dual carriageway and heading back to Fenton-on-Sea. Reaching the straight stretch near Linham, Cyril applied more pressure to the accelerator and the Vauxhall cruised smoothly to seventy.

"Don't go so fast, dear. I thought you didn't like speed," said Martha.

"Sorry, love – didn't realise how fast I was going; it's so smooth."

Cyril Wilby eased his foot and the big car slowed to fifty-five and within ten minutes they had pulled onto the drive of number 7 Lime Tree Avenue to be greeted by their excited son.

"Wow, Dad!" exclaimed Len as the Wilbys got out of their new possession. "You'll have to clear the garage out more than you have done; it's bigger than I imagined."

Len was clearly dressed to go out somewhere and his mother said,

"You off to Eddie's, then?"

"Yes, Mum – I'll be out for most of the day. Eddie says he wants to do some things for old times' sake since we're moving in just over three weeks."

The Wilby's move was scheduled for the week after term was due to finish on July the 23rd. The removal firm had pencilled in the 29th and 30th for the two-day move. Len's dad didn't seem too pleased.

"We really need you to help with packing this weekend, you know. What does Eddie want to do that's going to take all day?"

"Don't know, Dad. He just said that there wouldn't be many more times to do all the old things we used to do on a Saturday – there's only three after today and I'm playing cricket on one of them."

"Well, you make sure you're back by five and then you can start sorting your wardrobe and bedroom out."

"Yes, Dad. See you later," and Len was already on his way out of the front gate.

On the way over to his friend's house he pondered the possibilities for the day. He didn't really know what Eddie wanted to do. It wasn't often that they had *all* of a Saturday together owing to his sporting commitments, but Eddie had insisted that they might need several hours. With his dad's curfew in place Len reckoned they had six or so. As he approached number 38 Fir Tree Close a distant memory came to the forefront of his mind. He suddenly had an idea what Eddie wanted to do and it made him very, very nervous. His worst fears were confirmed when Eddie's mum showed him through into the Compton's back garden where Eddie already had part of his plan in place.

"What'cha, comrade Len," said Eddie jumping to his feet. Ann Compton had already disappeared back through the French doors into the house. Len just stared at what was laid out on Fred Compton's neatly manicured lawn.

"Oh no, Eddie. We're not playing with your train set. No way!"

"Oh come on, Len – just one more time for old times' sake."

The two boys hadn't played with Eddie's *Flying Scotsman* train set for well over a year, not since the last fantastic train journey they'd been on just before Easter 1964. The magical train set, as Eddie called it, had been a present from the mysterious Mr George Canter who had owned the junk shop in Mill Road and had been the instigator of the boys' first fantastic journey two years previously.

"No, Eddie. We might end up anywhere and not get back this time. I have to be home by five."

"Len, it's only five past eleven now. We've loads of time and anyway, we're not in my dining room now; it's bright sunshine out here."

"But you know what might happen – we could be transported anywhere and to another time and be left to find our way back like last time," said an exasperated Len.

"Please, Len. Just for old times' sake."

Something in Eddie's tone made Len eventually relent. Was a greater power at work again?

"Oh alright, mate, but just once. It's too nice a day to be messing about with electric train sets."

Eddie grinned playfully. He picked up the controller which was plugged into his dad's extension lead powered by a socket just inside the French doors to the lounge. The wooden tunnel made by Len's dad was in place over one of the two straight sections of track that formed the sides of the large oval layout. Eddie pushed the switch and the engine and its four carriages moved smoothly away. A second or two later and it entered the tunnel for the first time in fifteen months. Both boys watched nervously. It emerged intact and without any apparent loss of time. Len seemed relieved; Eddie looked disappointed. Eddie kept the power on for three or four more circuits but nothing unusual happened causing Len to remark,

"The magic's gone, thank God."

"You try it, then," said Eddie.

Len shook his head, but his friend was insistent and he passed Len the controller. This time the train entered the tunnel and disappeared. Len dropped the small black box. Eddie gasped.

"It's gone! The magic still works!"

Suddenly, as if a total eclipse of the sun had taken place, the Compton's garden was pitched into utter blackness. Eddie screamed.

"Where are you, Len?"

There was no reply. Suddenly, as quickly as the pitch darkness had descended on the garden so it lifted in an instant to bright watery sunshine. Eddie was still kneeling on the grass but it wasn't his garden and Len was nowhere to be seen. He looked round nervously. He was in a very large garden, maybe three times the length of that at 38 Fir Tree Close, Fenton-on-Sea. It was lined on one side by a row of tall conifers with shrubs and flower beds dotted randomly on the other. He could hear voices from a small patio area at the far end of the lawned area. He approached tentatively. Where was Len? An elderly couple was drinking tea. It was late afternoon and summer seemed to be over.

"Excuse me," said Eddie. "Have you seen my friend?"

The two pensioners ignored Eddie's question. He thought the woman seemed familiar; the man did not. He repeated his question. They looked right through him. They were both blind. Suddenly the lady got up from her seat and turned to her husband.

"Finished with your cup, dear?" she said.

"Yes, my love."

The elderly man handed his wife his china cup and she turned back to face Eddie. He thought she was going to hug him but instead she seemed to pass right through him. She then walked back up the lawn to the large semi-detached house, defying Eddie's assumption of her disability. Her elderly husband sat back in his chair and closed his eyes. Despite his age, his clothes seemed fairly modern; it was at least 1965, thought Eddie as he sat down beside him. He stretched out his arm and carefully put his hand right through the old man's head. It confirmed what Eddie had been thinking. The elderly couple were ghosts from sometime in the future.

Eddie sat and waited for the lady of the house to reappear. After five minutes or so and with her husband snoring loudly, Eddie stood up. He would go and investigate where she was and, indeed, where he was. Instantly the blackness returned and he fell to his knees. A few seconds later and the summer sunshine returned. His friend was kneeling beside him with a comforting arm round his shoulder.

"What happened, Len? Where have I been?" cried Eddie.

"Nowhere, mate. You didn't move."

"But it went pitch black, Len."

Len gave his friend an odd look.

"No it didn't. It's been sunny all the time. You just seemed to go into a trance, but your eyes were open. When the train disappeared I dropped the controller and you screamed. A few seconds later and the train reappeared. You've been in suspended animation for about a minute in all I should say."

Eddie glanced down. The engine and four carriages were stationary on the track.

"But, Len...."

But Eddie didn't finish what he was going to say. He knew his down-to-earth friend wouldn't believe him. What could he say anyway? *'Oh I've just been to another garden sometime in the future and in a different place where I met two elderly ghosts'*. He thought not.

The two boys packed Eddie's train set away quickly and in silence. They both realised that their fantastic adventures might not be over despite the gap of almost a year. Len told his friend later that it had been a mild event at best (or worst) and could be explained by a trick of the light. Eddie, of course, thought otherwise but, as before on occasions, he kept his otherworldly experience to himself. Was he going mad? Was there something wrong with him that caused him to see things that weren't there? He would find out later the reason for the visit to the strange garden when he would see it again in tragic but all too real circumstances.

Len was home much earlier that day than expected – he and Eddie had spent a couple of hours in town and on the beach, but both found that they could not easily relax and do all those things that Eddie had planned. It was to be the last time that they would have a chance to skim pebbles on the sea, play the one-armed bandits on the pier or look for amber on the beach.

Eddie tried to put the ghostly time travel out of his mind that Saturday, but something kept nagging him about the identity of the elderly phantoms. He was sure he had recognised one of them – the woman's voice had been familiar, though she had been much older than when he'd last heard it. Len was fortunate that he was able to concentrate on the reality of his family's move to Kent by sifting through and filtering his possessions in his bedroom.

5

The Parting of the Ways

The following three weeks were very hectic for the Wilby family. What with farewell parties for both Cyril and Martha from their colleagues at Fenton Secondary Modern School and the inevitable packing and repacking at home, they hardly had a moment to consider or dwell on their move. Brown's Removals had finally decided that they could accomplish the 150 mile assignment in one day on Friday the 30th of July. The Comptons had arranged a small leaving party for Cyril, Martha and Len on the previous Saturday at Fir Tree Close, three days after the last day of the school term on the Wednesday. The two boys met as usual on the morning of the party – Len called on his friend at Fir Tree Close at nine-thirty. It would be the last Saturday that they would meet together. The Saturday routine had been in place for over six years from the time that Len had first moved to Fenton-on-Sea when the boys had both been eight. Eddie was waiting by his front gate. Len was riding his bike.

"Good morning, Comrade Len."

"Good morning to you, Captain Eddie," replied his friend as he dismounted from his new racing bicycle – a present from his parents for getting a place at Petersgate Grammar School.

The two friends hugged each other almost involuntarily. It was beginning to dawn on both of them how much they would both miss each other. Len clearly had a plan for the morning. The Wilbys were invited at three and Eddie had to be back by one at the latest.

"I thought we might cycle out to Linham Junction, mate," said Len when the embarrassment of the slightly unnatural clinch had worn off.

"Linham? Why?"

"I need to lay a few ghosts; one in particular."

"You mean old Granty."

"Yes, Aloyisious St John Grant, late of this parish."

"Why?" asked Eddie nervously.

"Because, like you when you had to play with your train set one last time, I want to see if his ghost is still walking the lanes near Linham."

Eddie knew that they could be playing with fire if Len's plan resulted in something similar to what he'd experienced when he had been transported to the other garden.

"I don't think that's a good idea, Len," he said.

"Why?"

"Because, I haven't forgotten the episode with my train set only three weeks ago. That's why."

"But nothing happened, mate. I'm not even sure that the train disappeared – you just panicked and hallucinated."

Eddie debated whether to tell his friend about his visit to the strange garden and the two elderly ghosts, but he knew Len wouldn't believe him. A cycle ride was only a cycle ride as well. Why shouldn't they do it? He had to trust reality otherwise he would go mad. He gave in.

"You're right, Len. What could possibly happen on a simple cycle ride?"

"Good man; get your bike and let's saddle up, Mr Merckx!"

The weather began to deteriorate slightly as the two boys cycled into South Road and headed for the roundabout leading to the A132. Linham Junction, the scene of the train crash in which Aloyisious St John Grant had died the previous April, was located between five and six miles from Fenton-on-Sea depending on which route was taken. Len and Eddie would take the back roads avoiding the main road to Hamsden. By the time they had turned left at the roundabout and were a mile or so into the maze of lanes that twisted and turned to their destination, it had become unseasonably chilly and quite dark for the time of year. They stopped briefly at a four-way crossroads and debated whether they should carry on. They were halfway there. Eddie was still not keen and he thought he had the perfect excuse to turn back.

"Come on, Len, it's going to tip it down in a minute. It looks like thunder too."

"Weather forecast was for warm sunshine all day – I checked before I set off this morning."

Eddie glanced in the direction of Linham and it appeared that his friend was accurate in his report. The black clouds directly above them seemed to be encircled by clear blue sky and their destination was in bright sunlight. It wasn't raining.

"O.K., mate. It'll probably be only a shower," concluded Eddie with some reluctance. They took the right-hand road and pedalled furiously towards Linham reaching the level crossing – near where the tragic accident had taken place – in just over ten minutes. As on the previous occasion, Len boldly wasted no time in negotiating the two pedestrian gates and crossed over the line. Eddie hesitated fully expecting his friend to disappear into thin air.

"Wait, Len!" he shouted. Immediately, Eddie was pitched into complete darkness. He couldn't see a hand in front of his face.

"Oh God, it's starting again," he murmured to himself. "Like before in the garden."

He knew he had no choice and he fumbled and stumbled his way across the line, listening intently for the sound of any approaching train. He reached the other side and stood with his bike on the continuing road. The blackness lifted. The dark clouds above him were nowhere to be seen. It was bright sunshine again. Len stood grinning a few yards in front of

317

him. Eddie breathed a sigh of relief as his eyes became accustomed to the bright light. He knew he had to ask his friend what he'd seen, but he sensed it had not been the same as his experience.

"Did it go pitch dark for you, Len?"

"No, mate. As soon as I crossed over the clouds just disappeared. You seemed to have great difficulty following me, like you were blinded by something; sun must have been in your eyes. It was pretty bright after the dark clouds."

Eddie smiled. He would not tell his friend what he'd experienced. There was no point in upsetting him before his imminent move to Kent. Keeping back such information, however, soon became pointless as Len said,

"Look over there. It's different from last time."

Further down the road behind Len, a huge complex of modern concrete and glass buildings glinted in the bright sunshine. They seemed to extend for several hundred yards in all directions. Eddie's jaw dropped. They were not in 1965. The road was much wider than when they'd arrived a few minutes earlier. The sun had clearly just risen above the horizon; it was early morning and no one else seemed to be about.

"Oh God!" he exclaimed. "We've gone into the future."

Len had already read the large signs posted on either side of the road about fifty yards further on.

Bexham Nuclear Power Station
Serving the community since 2010

Neither boy said a word. They were torn uncomfortably between exploring further and turning back to recross the railway line. Suddenly they spotted a tall man approaching from the direction of the power station. He looked to be about sixty and walked athletically. He shouted to them,

"Wait a minute, boys."

Eddie had a déjà vu moment when he thought he recognised the stranger's voice. Len seemed excited.

"What's up?" he asked.

"You can't come any further; you should not have crossed the railway line. There are signs. You cannot miss them. Now go back."

The voice echoed inside Eddie's head. He thought he'd guessed who the stranger was. Len was undisturbed but such thoughts and said simply,

"Sorry, sir. Come on Eddie let's go."

Len turned his back on the strange man and began wheeling his bicycle across the line. Eddie was still rooted to the spot as the man came to within a couple of feet. He had a white coat on with a lapel badge. Eddie read it. It immediately provided the catalyst that spurred him into action. He turned and fled, pushing his friend out of the way in order to escape the terror that was forming in his mind. He and his bike fell onto the road the other side of the line. He was joined quickly by a bemused Len, who shouted,

"Here, watch it, mate. What on earth's wrong?"

Eddie sat up and lied,

"I thought he was going to grab me or worse."

"He looked friendly enough to me, Eddie – a nice old boy."

The two friends stood up and, after dusting themselves down, Len said,

"The magic still works; another ghost, eh?"

Eddie's mind was in a whirl. What could he say?

"Not old Granty, though," he managed. "We must have moved fifty years into the future."

"Shall we go back?" asked Len.

"No way, mate. Not in a million years! We're tampering with the unknown. It's not right."

"I was only joking, Eddie."

The two boys wheeled their bikes away from the phantom scene. They were back in the mid-morning summer sunshine. There was not a cloud in the sky. Len was brave enough to turn round and stare across the railway line. It looked exactly like it had been when they had arrived about ten minutes previously. No nuclear power plant and no strange man. They had glimpsed into the future. Len shrugged his shoulders and mounted his bike. Eddie followed. The lapel badge flashed into his mind. It had read: '*Dr Leonard Wilby*'.

The two boys rode home in almost complete silence. Eddie tried to make sense of what he'd seen. What did it mean? Would his friend end up working at a nuclear power station? Where was Bexham? His brief glimpse at the countryside surrounding the phantom power station had suggested it wasn't in East Anglia. Final questions entered his head: Why had his friend appeared to him as a ghost? Did it mean that he was...?

Both boys continued to be rather subdued at the Compton's garden party later that afternoon prompting Eddie's mum to ask,

"Are you alright, Eddie? You seem rather quiet."

"I'm going to miss Len, Mum. That's all."

"Of course you are, but you'll see each other again. You both seem to think that this afternoon is a bit of a wake. Now come on, for goodness sake, cheer up."

Eddie forced a smile.

"Yes, Mum."

Eddie wandered to the bottom of the garden where his friend also seemed to be preoccupied. The ladies had repaired to the kitchen to prepare the party food. Fred and Cyril were talking cars on a bench near the house. The boys were reasonably out of earshot. Len gave his verdict on the morning's strange experience.

"We weren't near here, you know, after we crossed the railway line, Eddie."

"I know. The scenery was too hilly and it didn't feel as though it was close to the sea."

Len then asked the question that Eddie was dreading.

"Who was the old bloke – the one that stopped us going into the power station? I'm sure I've never seen him before. It wasn't Ally Grant, I'm certain."

"No," said Eddie quietly.

"What did it all mean, mate?" asked Len.

Again Eddie was short with his reply.

"Don't know."

Len continued.

"I reckon it's an omen or something – a pointer to something that's going to happen in the future. It was at least 2010, so I expect we'll have to wait a long time to find out, eh? It's another forty-five years, at least. We'll both be getting old, mate."

Eddie's heart was racing. He didn't reply and he turned away from his friend. Len wondered what was wrong.

"Did it upset you, Eddie?"

Eddie knew he had to change the subject. He couldn't share his secret with his friend. He thought about Len's move to Kent and said,

"It's not that, Len. It's just that this morning was the last time we would do things together. I suppose that strange countryside reminded me how far away you'll be in your new home. I don't know what it meant. I'm not sure it had to mean anything. Why do we see ghosts or dream weird things anyway? We've seen plenty of stranger and more frightening things over the last two or three years. I'm not going to worry about one more such experience," he lied. "I expect that after you move to Kent, we'll stop having paranormal visions, because that's all they are – just visions, Len. Nothing has ever hurt us."

"Yet," added Len.

Ann Compton had prepared a spread fit for a king – all the things that Len liked were there in the picnic party that, fortunately, quickly followed the two friend's discussion of otherworldly things. Reality returned to almost clear their minds of the morning's events, but Eddie would be haunted for some time by his special and personal meeting with the sixty-year-old version of his best friend. One final remark by Len's mum would also bring his other individual rendezvous with the elderly couple in the strange garden into added focus. It was just after six-thirty and Martha Wilby was helping Eddie's mum to clear away the aftermath of the picnic. Cyril Wilby was seated on the Compton's bench draining his third cup of tea – it had been a warm afternoon. Eddie had joined him for a chat about cars and Len's new school. Len had eaten too much and was visiting the toilet.

"What's Len's school like, Uncle Cyril?"

"It seems to be quite strict, Eddie. The Head is a strict disciplinarian."

"Len needs that, doesn't he?"

"Very observant of you, my boy. He won't get away with second best there. He'll have to work hard. You'll miss each other, won't you?"

"Yes. I hope he'll be alright."

"He'll be fine, Eddie."

'*Make sure you look after your family carefully*', echoed in Cyril Wilby's head. His wife broke his train of thought.

"Finished with your cup, dear?"

Eddie and Len didn't see each other again until the evening before the Wilbys were due to leave Fenton-on-Sea for good. Len had had too much to do during his last week and Eddie hadn't been able to face his friend again so soon after the doppelgänger at Linham Junction. He wanted to see Len desperately for one last time, particularly since he had bought him a small present as a token of their friendship. Fred Compton eventually persuaded his son to call round on Thursday the 29th.

"You must go and wish Len good luck, Eddie," he said just when it seemed that his son was going to disappear to his room to do some reading after his tea.

"Wish him well from us too," said Eddie's mum.

"Yes, Mum."

Eddie went upstairs to his bedroom and, pocketing Len's gift, he made his way to 7 Lime Tree Avenue for what would be the final time. Martha Wilby spotted Eddie before he had a chance to knock on the door. She was standing in the doorway as he walked up the front path.

"Hello, Eddie. I'm glad you've come. I've been trying to persuade Len all day to come and see you but he wouldn't."

Eddie smiled nervously as Len's mum ushered him into the bare hall. The house sounded hollow and echoey when Martha Wilby called upstairs,

"Eddie's here, Len. Come down."

A door opened and Len's voice echoed throughout the house.

"Tell him to come up, Mum."

Eddie climbed the stairs and went into his friend's bedroom. Len was sitting on his bed surrounded by boxes and other paraphernalia necessary for the following day's move. It all seemed so wrong to Eddie. Why did his best friend have to go? He was, after all, the friend that had been with him through all their incredible adventures – adventures that would have shocked the world if anyone knew. He was the friend that had looked after him since their junior school days and the friend that had kept the bullies away from him – those boys who were jealous or scared of his academic ability. He sat down beside his special friend and said chokingly,

"I've bought you a little present."

Eddie pulled the matchbox sized present from his pocket and placed it on the bed beside Len.

"Go on, open it," he said when his friend just stared at it.

"I didn't buy you anything, Eddie. I haven't had time, mate."

"Doesn't matter, Len. I'm not going anywhere – it's just something to send you on your way."

"Thanks, mate."

Len fumbled with the 'bon voyage' wrapping paper to reveal a small black box. He lifted the lid and gasped,

"Oh wow! It must have cost you a small fortune."

"Only a few weeks' pocket money. Put it on," said Eddie. "It will look after you wherever you go in the future."

Len's hands trembled as he lifted the solid silver St Christopher and chain. Eddie took the clasp and fastened it behind his friend's neck.

"He's the patron saint of travellers," said Eddie.

"I know. I've always wanted one."

He paused and then said,

"I'll never take it off; not even in the bath."

Eddie looked oddly at his friend's neck. The question that had bothered him all week still remained. Had the other 'Len' been wearing a chain? The white coat and close fitting tunic had hidden anything from view. Several times since the previous Saturday, Eddie had been on the point of taking the St Christopher back to the jeweller, but something stopped him on each occasion. He seemed to be caught up in some master plan for the future and it had frightened him. He couldn't tamper with the inevitable.

Eddie didn't stay long that evening. After a quick manly hug and a demand from Eddie that Len must write at least once a month, which he would reciprocate, the two boys parted. Familiar words were shouted and exchanged as Eddie walked down the Wilby's front path.

"See you, Captain Compton."

"Not if I see you first, comrade Len."

Both boys cried unashamedly as they went to sleep that night and both of them slept soundly undisturbed by dreams of phantoms and time travel.

6
Jenny Gets Some Advice

The weather matched Eddie's mood the following morning; it was grey, cool and damp. He wandered down the town at ten trying to avoid looking in the direction of Lime Tree Avenue. He also turned his head away from any red car or large lorry that passed him on South Road. Even the High Street seemed in sombre mood; few shoppers had so far braved the dank morning and most holidaymakers were still at their guest houses and B and Bs. Eddie ignored the shops and headed for the seafront. Len had told him previously that there was only sea between Fenton-on-Sea and the North Kent coast and that you could sail directly there. Standing on the promenade, Eddie stared out to sea at roughly forty-five degrees to his right and he immediately recalled a day in late May two years earlier. He and Len had 'flown' over that sea on their magic carpet at the beginning of their first fantastic adventure. Other thoughts came to him concerning Len and his family, especially after the previous day's party in his garden. He quickly gave a nervous shrug as if by so doing, he could banish them from his mind. It started to drizzle and Eddie walked back up the town, head down to avoid seeing removal lorries.

Unbeknown to Eddie, the Wilby's removal lorry didn't leave Fenton until just after eleven-thirty with the red Vauxhall Victor following. Cyril eventually overtook the lorry on the dualled part of the A132, arriving in Petersgate at three o'clock. Surprisingly, the lorry arrived only fifteen minutes later. By the time of the lorry's departure from Fenton, Eddie was already ensconced in his bedroom and reading a science fiction novel to cheer himself up with an escape into a fantasy world. He spent much of the remainder of the Friday in like manner – the weather did not improve.

Jenny Compton had the last day of July off from her job at Arleson's the bakers. She would normally work there on every other Saturday in the month. Her trainee fireman boyfriend, Gary, was spending the morning helping his dad at his second-hand car showroom in Hamsden. Jenny would take the eleven o'clock bus from South Road in order to meet him for lunch and shopping in the town afterwards. At breakfast Eddie announced that he wanted to go with her.

"But I've nothing to do now that Len's gone to Kent," he moaned at breakfast.

Jenny laughed.

"You are *not* going to play gooseberry. Go and find yourself a girlfriend or someone you can play trains with."

Jenny loved her brother dearly, but she still could not resist any opportunity to tease him mercilessly. She would probably do it for the rest of his life. Once an elder sister; always an elder sister – it went with the role.

"I don't play with trains anymore, sister dear."

"Yes, you do. Mum says you played with your toy train set only a few weeks ago outside on the lawn."

"That was different; *Len* wanted to do it one last time before he moved," lied Eddie. "I didn't enjoy it though."

'If only she knew', he thought. 'If only'.

"Well, Len's gone now, so get on with the rest of your life," said Jenny rather cruelly. Her mum interrupted the bickering.

"Stop it, Jennifer. Eddie is going to miss Len; they've been friends for such a long time. Just think what it would be like if Gary suddenly said he was going to pack up and leave you."

Eddie grinned at his sister. Jenny went quiet – she knew that it would be her worst nightmare.

"Sorry, Mum," and after an embarrassing pause she said, "Sorry, Eddie. I'll bring you something nice back from Hamsden."

The number 201 bus was fairly full when Jenny boarded it at the first stop in South Road. She managed to find an empty double seat on the top deck, so she wasn't squashed against any other passenger. Many people, holidaymakers included, had taken the opportunity provided by the wet weather to go shopping in the nearest large town. The beaches would be deserted for a change. Nobody else got on the bus right until it stopped unusually at the halt near the small village of Linham. Jenny's heart beat faster when she glanced at the field where the train crash had happened, and where her boyfriend had performed his heroics. She wanted to shout out and tell her fellow passengers of his deeds in saving some of the many injured from the burning wreck. Instead, she smiled with pride. He was *her* boyfriend and now he was going to be a fireman and a handsome one at that. The one extra passenger had climbed to the top deck and he stood nervously looking for a seat. Jenny spread herself across the two seats and looked nonchalantly out of the window, avoiding having to look at the new passenger. The passenger came down the aisle checking for empty seats. He stood by Jenny's seats.

"Excuse me, can I sit here?"

Jenny turned to face the voice and her mouth opened involuntarily. Standing over her was the most handsome young man she had ever seen. He was dressed in the most perfectly creased sailor's uniform. He was tall, muscular and had fair tousled hair. He looked to be about her age. She stammered,

"Yes, of-of course."

"Thanks."

Jenny quickly recovered her poise and, in her mind, she wondered why on earth a serving sailor would need to catch a bus at such an out-of-the-way place as Linham. She was too nervous to ask. He took out a cigarette case.

"Fancy a smoke?"

"No thanks. I don't."

"O.K. Mind if I do?"

"No, not at all."

"Thanks. It's been a long night."

Still Jenny daren't say anything. The sailor leant back in his seat and puffed smoke rings into the air. A couple of passengers opened some windows. Only one other person was smoking a pipe. The sailor closed his eyes. He seemed to be in a trance but was still able to tap the ash from his cigarette end at regular intervals until he finally stubbed it out as the bus approached the outskirts of Hamsden.

Ten minutes later the bus began to pull into the town's small bus station. The young sailor was the first to get up, clearly used to the jerky movement provided by the moving bus. He was about to walk up the aisle when he turned back and leant over Jenny. She could smell a mixture of after shave and tobacco smoke. It was not an unpleasant combination. He smiled and said,

"Take care, Jenny, and look after your brother over the next few weeks – he'll need your love."

Jenny froze in her seat and before she could say anything, the sailor had descended the stairs and had jumped from the still moving bus. She had a fleeting impression of something glinting around his neck.

Jenny was understandably subdued when she met up with her boyfriend. She had spent a few minutes searching the streets surrounding the bus station but the strange sailor had completely vanished. She decided against mentioning anything to Gary as he would only probably get the wrong idea. She would have found it difficult, in any case, to explain her total innocence in talking to the handsome young sailor. Gary was inordinately jealous of any of Jenny's casual admirers – and she had a few! Her mood, however, soon lightened after Gary had bought her lunch and treated her to a new leather handbag. It wouldn't be until much later that day that she would be reminded of her strange meeting on the bus.

Though Gary's driving ban – sustained as a result of his previous car crash – had been lifted, he had not yet bought another car and the young couple waited until Gary's father, Richard, had closed the showroom for the weekend. He gave them a lift back to Fenton in his Jaguar at a little after five-thirty. Jenny was in a good mood when she got back to Fir Tree Close. Eddie had just come downstairs from finishing his latest science fiction book when his sister came in through the front door.

"Look what Gary's bought me," she said triumphantly.

Eddie sneered.

"What do you want another bag for; you've got too many already."

"Three, if you must know, but this one is real leather," responded Jenny while she held the bag to her face and inhaled deeply. "Smell that," she continued, holding the bag out for Eddie to check.

"No thanks – I'd rather smell cigarette smoke. At least an animal hasn't been killed to make it."

Something that Eddie said – perhaps the mention of the word *cigarette* – caused Jenny to be reminded of the handsome young sailor. She ushered her brother upstairs before their parents were aware she was home.

"I've something to talk to you about, Eddie."

"What do you want?" he asked as she pushed and shoved him towards his bedroom.

"In private, brother."

Eddie sat on his bed while his sister remained standing by the window. This is important, he thought. What *could* she want?

"Eddie, I met someone today – on the bus to Hamsden this morning."

"So. Who?"

"A sailor."

"What's so special about that?"

"He knew me; he knew my name, Eddie."

"So. Plenty of people know you in Fenton-on-Sea; probably every boy or unattached man over the age of sixteen knows you, Jennifer Compton. You have a reputation. He probably used to go to Fenton Secondary Modern when you were there. How old was he?"

"About my age, nineteen or so – and, anyway, he wasn't from Fenton; I'm certain of that. He had his ship's name on his cap – HMS Connaught, I think."

"What did he want?" asked Eddie.

"He didn't want anything. He got on at Linham Junction and the only vacant seat was next to me. After he had sat down, he offered me a cigarette. But there's something else, Eddie."

The place name had sounded warning bells in Eddie's head before he asked,

"What?"

"He knew I had a brother."

"What did he look like?"

"He was tall, athletic and had fair hair."

Jenny omitted any description of his sexual appeal.

"How did he know me?" asked Eddie.

"He didn't say. He just told me...."

"Told you what?"

"That you would need looking after over the next few weeks and that you'd need my love."

Eddie grimaced.

"Did he remind you of anyone?"

"No, not really, but I think I may have heard his voice before. I just can't think where. His face may have been familiar, but...."

"But?"

"But his body wasn't. I'm sure I would have remembered seeing that before! Don't tell Mum about him, please, Eddie. She'll only worry or get the wrong idea. Promise?"

"I won't, I promise, Jenny."

"Good – I still can't think how he could know me or that I had a brother that might need looking after. I honestly think he has confused me with someone else."

"You mean there's another Jenny Compton in the area?" said Eddie with a smile. "I hope not, sister dear!"

"Well, I just don't know what to think; it's so weird that I'm beginning to think I must have dreamt the whole episode."

'If only you'd had the experiences that I'd had', thought Eddie, 'you'd think you were in a permanent dream!'

Jenny left her brother to his own thoughts. She didn't know that her 'weird' story had had more of an effect on him than she'd realised. For his part, Eddie hadn't dared question his sister about any silver jewellery that the young sailor might have been wearing. He didn't want Jenny to be aware that he might know his identity, if, indeed, it was the same person that he'd encountered on the strange road near the phantom nuclear power station. He wasn't about to share that piece of information with anyone, no matter how close they were. Even his best friend hadn't been told.

7

Letters

Exactly a week after Len had moved Eddie received a letter from his friend. He thought he recognised the handwriting on the envelope, and the Canterbury postmark confirmed his suspicions. He took it up to his bedroom to read; it seemed to contain several pages. He opened the envelope carefully and settled down to read. Len must have had help with the layout and spelling, he thought, but not, perhaps, with the punctuation.

> *23 The Park,*
> *Petersgate,*
> *Kent.*
> *August 4th 1965*

Dear Eddie,

> *Well here I am in sunny Kent. My bedroom is a bit bigger than the one I had in Fenton-on-Sea but at the moment I'm surrounded by boxes and piles of clothes. I don't have a wardrobe yet because the old one fell apart when we moved! The drive down last Friday was a bit scary as Dad doesn't really know the rule for overtaking on dual carriageways nor when to indicate when he turns corners. We hit eighty on the A2 and Mum screamed at him to slow down we stopped at a service area just after the Dartford Tunnel and after we returned from getting something to eat Dad couldn't get the car into reverse so we had to push until we could go forward which took ages.*

Eddie giggled as he reread the sentence, thinking what Len's previous English teacher, Mr Green, would have said. He read on, fearing more punctuation howlers.

Petersgate is a bit bigger than Fenton but I don't think the beach is as nice because it always smells of rotting seaweed and boy does it stink. Dad says its good for the garden as a fertiliser. Have'nt made any friends yet there arnt any families with children in our road. Probably make some when I start school next month.

Again Eddie cringed at the several punctuation errors, but, at least he could understand what his friend had written. The letter continued.

What have you been doing? Are you going away on holiday anywhere? We're not, I think. Dad says we've got too much to do before we go back to school. Mum's got a part-time job at a paper shop in town – not quite like her old one as chief cook at Dad's old school but it's good money, she says. Dad nearly pranged the car when he picked her up yesterday. I think he should take his test again, but he doesn't listen to me. We get free newspapers as long as we wait until Mum comes home with them – she brought three yesterday. The local paper is called the Petersgate and Hargate Advertiser and it is full of adverts, much more than the Fenton Times.

Eddie guessed that someone had started to help him punctuate – the improvement was obvious for all to see.

Dad's trying to get tickets for Spurs first home game on August the 28th – they're playing local rivals Arsenal. Hope I can go and Eddie, you'll never guess what…

Eddie paused to say out loud,

"No I won't, Len. Go on surprise me."

… Tottenham are coming to Freeman Street for a pre-season friendly on the 17th. You must go – you'll see some real football when they thrash Hamsden Town seven or eight nil! I think it's an evening kick-off at 7.30. I wish I could go but Dad says it's just too far and we wouldn't get back until the early hours. Hope you can go and send me a report. Please get me a programme if they print any for the match. They may not as it's only a friendly.

Have you had anything strange happen to you since I left? I haven't. Well, Eddie, I can't think of anything else to write so I'll sign off now. Dad helped with some of this letter – you know I can't write for toffee. Anyway I've got to go and help him plant some conifers down one side of the back garden which is huge, Eddie; you should see it. Next door's fence doesn't give us enough privacy, Mum says. Goodbye, mate.

Best wishes,

Len

Eddie straightened out the three-page letter carefully and found an old book to keep it in. Before he did, however, he reread the final paragraph several more times. He himself had been in a long garden with conifers down one side, but they had been tall, he recalled – well over head height. The paranormal trip from his own garden had been brief, but Eddie was sure that the conifers had been in place for several years and that the garden's occupants had been old as well. A story was beginning to form his mind, but it was jumbled and consisted of seemingly unrelated events. However, which ever way he looked at it, they all led back to his best friend, Len. What did they signify? Were the events just random or was there a purpose too them? He felt certain that someone or something was trying to give him a message.

He decided he would buy a folder to store his friend's cards and letters in; he would try to keep them forever. He would write his reply later when he had decided what to put in it and, more importantly, what to leave out of it!

Jenny hadn't had any more strange liaisons that week and she had continued not to mention the one that she'd had to anyone else, especially her parents, who would only worry. Nevertheless, when she arrived home from work that Friday she was determined to ask them how Eddie was, particularly as it was only a week since his best friend had moved. She had an opportunity when he was slow in coming down from his bedroom for tea. Her mum didn't seem to be overly worried though.

"He's alright, I think, dear; he just spends a lot of time by himself, but that's to be expected – Len's not here," she said somewhat obviously. "He was cheered up when he received a nice long letter from him this morning."

"I just wondered if he was O.K. physically, Mum. I know he's always been mentally disturbed!"

Fred Compton looked over the top of his newspaper.

"Physically? What on earth do you mean, Jenny? He's a healthy fourteen-year-old lad with all that entails. He's at the crossroads before he reaches manhood proper. Give him time and he'll turn out fine."

"I just thought he looked a little odd the other day, but I suppose you're right, Mum – he's missing Len."

"What do you mean – odd?" asked Jenny's mum.

"Kind of vague; as though he was somewhere else in his own little world."

Fred Compton grinned.

"Well you know your brother as well as anybody, Jenny. He's always seemed to be in his own world. He reads too many science fiction books, if you ask me."

"Better than reading railway timetables, Dad," said Jenny.

Eddie was standing in the doorway. Jenny looked sheepish. How long had her brother been there? She threw out a feeler.

"Hello, brother dear. We were just talking about you."

"Were you, sister dear? What's better than reading railway timetables?"

Jenny was visibly relieved. Her brother had only caught the very tail end of the conversation. Ann Compton said,

"Reading science fiction, dear. Your dad thinks you read too much of it."

"Does he? Well at least I *can* read, Mum – unlike my sister here who only buys magazines to look at the pictures."

'Well, thanks', thought Jenny. 'So much for sticking up for you and being concerned for your well-being. Thanks a lot, brother'.

Len was first to the post the following day; he had hoped that there would be a return letter from Eddie, even though he had only posted his own on the Wednesday. He wanted to hear his friend's news – he had a feeling that Eddie was missing him more than he'd realised. There was one letter for his dad; only a few people had their new address yet. He was clearly disappointed when he handed over the letter from South Eastern Gas.

"What's up, son?"

"Nothing much, Dad – I was just hoping that Eddie would have sent me a letter. I've sent him one."

"When did you send it?"

"Wednesday morning."

"Well that would be a bit quick to get one back in three days. This letter is postmarked Thursday and it's taken two days from Canterbury, seven miles away. I expect you'll get a reply by Monday or Tuesday."

"I suppose so," said Len finally.

On the surface, Len would never admit to having many emotional feelings. He had been very brave in accepting his parents' move but deep down, like Eddie, he was missing his best friend. He just didn't show it. His dad interrupted his thoughts.

"What are you going to do today? Your mum and I are going to do some more unpacking, but you don't need to stay in and help. It looks like a nice day outside. Why don't you do some exploring; go to Canterbury on the bus or something."

Len began to cheer up. His dad's suggestion sounded like a good idea and he had some saved money to spend too. The Wilbys weren't taking a holiday that summer and extra pocket money had been provided by way of consolation.

It turned out to be quite a long walk to the nearest bus stop from the leafy avenues of Petersgate where The Park was located. It was three-quarters of a mile to the Canterbury road where Len had a choice of stops which were a few hundred yards in either direction – left into town or right to the outskirts. He chose right and only just made the stop as a red and blue double-decker of the East Kent Roadcar Company lumbered up behind him. Climbing aboard, he made his way to the upper deck. The bus was full with Saturday morning shoppers and there was just one seat available next to an elderly and rather scruffily dressed man. The man clearly had hygiene problems and Len felt uncomfortable in the warm and stuffy atmosphere. He tried to breathe shallowly. The man seemed to be asleep.

Part of the journey took Len down the A2 in the direction of the East Kent coast which was jammed with holidaymakers heading for the beaches at Margate and Ramsgate. The bus slowed to a crawl. Sensing the change in the sound of the big diesel engine, the old man woke up. Len leant away to the aisle. The bus suddenly turned right, throwing Len back against the old man.

"Sorry, sir," he said politely.

The old man grunted. Len looked into the man's face for the first time. Len recognised the stranger immediately – it was the tramp who had saved him and Eddie the previous summer in Devon. It was Jacob Manders! Len was bold.

"Hello, Mr Manders. It's Len – Len Wilby."

The old man seemed not to have heard Len's greeting. A woman passenger directly behind Len must have heard what he'd said.

"He's deaf, dear. He can't hear you."

Len turned round to address the lady who had spoken.

"But I know him."

"Everybody knows old Bill. He used to be a policeman in Dover until he lost his hearing. That's why we call him 'Old Bill'. The name fits, doesn't it?"

'Bill' had gone back to sleep and Len turned back to look more closely at his face. He couldn't believe how he had made such a stupid mistake. The man looked nothing like the ghostly Mr Manders. His mind was playing tricks or….

The number 4A pulled into Canterbury bus station at ten-thirty and Len made to leave his seat, squeezing into the line of passengers all eagerly trying to get to the lower deck. A voice whispered from behind him.

"Be careful, Len. Be very careful."

Len turned round. 'Old Bill' still seemed sound asleep. All the other passengers were busily chatting to each other. Before he had time to investigate further, he was jostled forward and almost fell down the stairs and out into the warm morning sunshine. Len waited. A few minutes later and the conductor escorted 'Old Bill' down from the top deck and saw him safely on his way. The deaf old man shuffled across the road and was soon lost in the Saturday morning crowds. Len didn't follow. He didn't need to. The voice surely hadn't belonged to the old man or, indeed, Jacob Manders. It had been his best friend's voice.

One hundred and fifty miles north of Canterbury, the weather in Fenton-on-Sea had turned wet and windy. As Len was gazing in awe at the splendour of England's finest cathedral, Eddie made the decision to write a reply to his friend's letter. There was not much else he could do that morning. He sat at the makeshift desk in his bedroom and tried to think of what to say. It took him ten minutes and three wasted pieces of his mum's good writing paper before he found a way of starting the letter.

> *38 Fir Tree Close,*
> *Fenton-on-Sea,*
> *Suffolk,*
> *Saturday a. m.*

Dear Len,

> *Thank you very much for your letter and all your news. It's pouring down outside so I'm stuck inside. Jenny and Dad are both at work while Mum has just popped next door to see Aunty Beth.*

> *Not much has happened since you left except that my sister says she met a young sailor on the bus to Hamsden. I think she fancied him. She says that the sailor knew her name and also that she had a brother.*

I've never met any sailors in Fenton, have you? I'm convinced she made
the whole thing up, but it did worry me for a while as she said he got on
the bus at Linham Junction. Maybe my sister's seeing ghosts now. Maybe
it was a friend of old Granty or the bloke in the white coat at the phantom
power station, Len!

Eddie sat back in his chair and put his best fountain pen down. He had got through the worst bit – he didn't need to say who he'd thought the young sailor was, let alone the scientist in the white coat. He also didn't need to suggest that they might have been the same person. He got down to more mundane issues.

I've read two new science fiction books since you left and I now
have a library ticket which means I can take out up to four books at a
time. I was going to Hamsden on the train today but I'll have to go next
week as it's still raining hard, just ready for the football season which
starts in two weeks. Mum and Dad say I can go to see the Town whenever
I want and on my own, now I'm fourteen, except if it's midweek and in
term time. I will definitely go Tuesday week and watch Tottenham play.
Dad says that Town are a good bet for promotion to the Second Division
this year – we've just signed the Irish international, Johnny McBride for
£40,000, our most expensive ever purchase. But still nothing like how
much Tottenham spend on a player. I hope you won't be too upset when
Hamsden beat you on the 17th!
    It's carnival week coming up and the shops are taking part in the
'Window Competition' as usual. This year you have to find an object that
doesn't belong in the shop; something they wouldn't sell. There are fifty-
three altogether, so it'll keep me busy until I get bored. Does Petersgate

have a carnival? Do they have a football team? Dad says they might be in the Southern League.

My sister finishes at Arleson's in two weeks. She's been there since she was sixteen. She's off to Hamsden Civic College in September to start a Beauty Therapy and Hairdressing course – hope there's not a written exam. Dad had to help her fill out the application form, but I suppose Gary loves her.

One last thing, Len – Dad's going to buy a new car. Our Morris Minor is falling to pieces; we've had it for ten years. I want him to get a Jaguar, but Dad says they're too expensive. I think he might go for something like your dad's – I know he was a bit jealous when you got it. Hope your dad's driving is improving! Can your mum drive? My mum is going to take lessons soon. Dad had refused to teach her! Says she's too nervous to drive.

Well, no more for now. I will send you a programme from the match on the 17th. Take care of yourself. You never know I may see you soon.

Your best friend

Eddie

PS   Send me some photos of your new house and Petersgate.

Eddie carefully folded the four small sheets of blue Basildon Bond writing paper and inserted them into the matching envelope. He stuck the fourpenny stamp in the top right hand corner and addressed the front of the envelope. Condensing all his thoughts and worries into the letter had been quite emotional and, at times, he had found it difficult to know what to say. He thought he had done a pretty good job, omitting, of course, the possible sighting of his best friend's ghost.

343

He decided to finish the task there and then by taking the letter directly to the main post office in the High Street. The rain had eased slightly when he left the house and it wasn't an unpleasant experience to walk in the steady refreshing drizzle. It helped him to clear away any worrying and ghostly thoughts from his mind.

8

The Spurs Come to Town

Len got lost a couple of times as he wandered round the maze of back
streets in Canterbury. He occasionally caught glimpses of the deaf man,
but he didn't approach him. Eddie's voice had seemed to come out of thin
air – it hadn't come from 'Old Bill's' mouth, he thought; he had been fast
asleep when Len had turned round. Len was troubled but eventually put
the experience down to the oppressive atmosphere on the bus making him
feel giddy and sleepy. The familiar voice had been entirely within his
head, he decided.

He spent an hour or two browsing in the city's many bookshops,
both modern and antiquarian in nature, but found nothing to interest him.
A large bag of chips and a bottle of orangeade sated his hunger and thirst
and by two o'clock he found himself back at the entrance to the cathedral.
He hadn't gone inside when he'd first arrived that morning but the day
was now becoming unbearably hot, so he sought sanctuary in the shade
and the coolness within. He found a seat near the altar to rest and take in
the atmosphere. The cathedral was crowded with visitors of many
different nationalities. He sensed a presence behind him. It was enhanced
by a familiar smell. He turned round. It was 'Old Bill'. He nodded at Len
who stared back in silence. Despite the old man's advancing years, his
face looked somehow strangely familiar. He began to speak quietly.

"Spare a few coppers for an old soldier, comrade."

His voice echoed in Len's head.

"Ye-yes, sir," said Len.

'Old Bill' quickly pocketed the bright new sixpence that Len gave
him. He got to his feet and shuffled away down the main aisle. Len was

too stunned to follow. Only one other person had ever called him 'comrade'.

Eventually, Len managed to shake himself together and he made for the main entrance as quick as he dared without causing a scene. He was too late – Eddie's 'ghost' was nowhere to be seen. He sat down on some stone steps and put his head in his hands. He had to think. Unlike before, this time he was convinced that the old man had spoken with his best friend's voice. Could two people, who differed in age by over fifty years, have the same sounding voice? Was he just hearing things because he was missing Eddie and he wanted to hear his voice? Was it the heat of the day? Was 'Old Bill' how his friend would be in fifty or more years time? If this was true, then why, on the bus, did he warn Len to '*be careful, very careful*'? Was he in some sort of danger? All these questions kept stabbing at his brain like arrows.

He was lost in his own world for many minutes as he sat in the warm afternoon sunshine. He ignored the several passers-by who brushed past him in his position in the middle of the small square in front of the cathedral gates. He looked at his watch. It was ten to four. Where had the time gone? He'd been at the cathedral for nearly two hours. He stood up on stiff legs and began to make his way back to the bus station. Though he was troubled by the meetings with the old man, he wasn't as scared as he would have been had he known that his best friend's sister had had a similar meeting with a young sailor who'd also conveyed a message to her. He caught the number 4 bus for the return journey to Petersgate and fortunately, by the time he walked into 23 The Park, he had put the stranger events of the day to the back of his mind. He'd had enough of trying to work out what it all might mean.

The Fenton-on-Sea carnival turned out to be a virtual wash-out as the rain poured down all day on Saturday the 14th. Eddie didn't go and watch; neither did he win the 'Window Competition'. Neither boy experienced anything else exceptional and by the morning of the day of the pre-season friendly with Spurs, Eddie's mind was only focused on that evening's game. Because the evenings were still light until after nine, he had been allowed to take the train to Hamsden; it was the best way because Freeman Street was less than half a mile from the railway station.

Catching the ten past six train from Fenton, Eddie arrived at the ground at five to seven and was surprised how few people there seemed to be about. Had he got the wrong day? He had checked the local paper carefully, he thought. Town's usual Saturday gates were about 8,000, but when he had paid his three shillings and was stood in the North stand, he calculated that there were less than a few hundred inside the ground. He was able to get right down to the front – just a few feet from the touchline. By twenty past seven the crowd had only swelled to a thousand or so; the stadium looked empty and sounded hollow when any chanting started from the terraces. Eddie spotted a fellow grammar school pupil standing a few yards away. He was in the year above Eddie and Eddie only knew him vaguely. Eddie approached him tentatively and said,

"There are not many people here, are there?"

The older boy knew Eddie and surprised him when he addressed him by name.

"No, Mr Compton, there aren't. Apparently Tottenham are only sending their reserve team – it was on the radio earlier."

"Oh," said Eddie. "That's a shame. I was hoping to see Greavesy play."

"There won't be anybody we've heard of," said the older boy who then introduced himself as one Danny Chambers. Eddie mumbled

347

something in reply as Danny moved away to be some friends who'd just arrived. Eddie was cross. It was typical of the big London club not to send their first team. Hamsden Town F.C. of the Third Division was obviously not good enough to warrant a visit from their superstars. 'Still', Eddie thought, 'if we win, it will still be a victory against the mighty Spurs'. He opened his sixpenny programme and looked at the team sheets in the centre. At the top it read:

Hamsden Town F.C. v Tottenham Hotspur Reserves

It wasn't the mighty Spurs, just their second team. It didn't count. He didn't study their list of players. Town seemed to be at full strength with Johnny McBride at centre forward. Five minutes later and the visitors, mostly consisting of players in their teens or early twenties, took the field to a mixture of jeers and polite applause. A chorus of '*Come on the Town*' echoed round the nearly empty ground to greet the home side a minute later. Eddie moved to a position behind the north end goal; a lone cameraman sat on the grass in front of him.

Hamsden Town kicked off with their goalkeeper, Bob Dean, occupying the goal at Eddie's end. The first twenty minutes were interrupted continually by the over zealous referee until Tottenham scored a lucky deflected goal. Minutes later and the Spurs' fair-haired inside right headed just wide. The ball bounced on the retaining wall in front of Eddie and straight into his waiting arms. He caught it cleanly and was just about to throw it back when the momentum of the young reserve forward sent him almost crashing into the wall in front of Eddie.

"Give us the ball, mate," said the young footballer.

Eddie lobbed the ball into the young player's arms. He smiled knowingly and said,

"Thanks, Captain."

The tall fair-haired footballer winked and trotted back up the field.

Though his neck was bare, Eddie thought he'd guessed the identity of the inside right without the extra confirmation provided by a quick glance at the Tottenham team sheet. With eyes that struggled to focus, he read who Tottenham's number eight was. He *saw* L. Wilby. He closed the programme quickly. It was impossible, just impossible. This was unreal. This was a totally new twist in ghostly liaisons. Previously, the ghosts, whether of his friend or not, had not been real and they had disappeared afterwards. This one was his best friend, Len, aged about nineteen and his name was written down for all to see! It just couldn't be. He couldn't concentrate on the game for the rest of the first half and avoided looking at the opposition's number eight in particular. The half-time whistle blew. The players left the field with the score still 1–0 to the visiting team. Eddie looked at the programme again. He couldn't believe how stupid he'd been. He was beginning to see his best friend everywhere. Anyone tall and fair-haired seemed to fit the bill. The name on the opposition's team sheet actually read L. Wilton – a simple mistake? Eddie wasn't sure. Had his mind played a trick on him by letter or word association, especially when the young footballer had called him 'Captain'? He had to get to grips with himself or he might start seeing ghosts at every turn. He had been convinced that he had seen Len at the power station but the incident with the young footballer began to sow the seeds of doubt in his mind. If he could misread a team sheet he could misread a lapel badge. It had happened in a flash. However, it would not be long before Eddie would realise that he *hadn't* made a mistake at Linham Junction and also that a greater power was deliberately setting reminders in his path. His mind was not his own.

The second half proved to be disastrous for Hamsden Town. They eventually conceded three more goals with only a last minute penalty as a consolation. 4−1 wasn't a true reflection of the game and Town's defence would need to tighten up before the start of the season proper on the coming Saturday. Eddie didn't see the Leonard look-a-like up close again; he stayed permanently in or around Town's penalty area at the opposite end to where Eddie continued to stand. From a distance he couldn't understand how he had mistaken the young player for an older version of his friend.

On the train home Eddie sat behind Danny Chambers and his friends and he listened while Danny spouted off about how weak Town's defence had been.

"Old Fred Phillips was awful; he let that young inside forward run rings round him."

Danny turned round to Eddie and said,

"You did well to catch his header, Compton. I remember you saving a penalty in the Under 13's cup final. Are you in the Under 15's next year?"

"No, I was only a late replacement when the first choice keeper went down with flu in the epidemic. I haven't played football for the school since."

"Pity – you still seem to have the same anticipation. I'll never know how you guessed which way to go when you saved the penalty."

Eddie smiled as he remembered Len's 'magic' football. Just another episode from the fantasy world he and Len had occupied at times. Danny returned to his conversation with his friends while Eddie gazed out of the train window at the darkening sky. It had been an interesting evening.

The following evening, Eddie's dad brought a copy of the Hamsden Daily Star home from work for his son to read the report of the match. He presented it to Eddie with great ceremony at teatime.

"You'd better look at the back page, son. There's something that might interest you."

The back page had a photograph of a young fair-headed Tottenham footballer heading narrowly past a goal post. In the bottom right-hand corner stood a startled teenage boy catching the ball in both arms. Eddie remembered the cameraman; he must have moved quickly to one side when he saw L. Wilton leap skywards. Eddie's mum was full of pride for her son.

"I must get the original photograph, Fred. We'll have it framed. You never know but the young Spurs player might become famous one day – even an international. You just never know. He's certainly handsome."

Ann Compton continued to stare proudly at the photograph and her next words started Eddie worrying again.

"He looks a lot like Len, Eddie – or, at least, how Len could look in a few years time."

'So', thought Eddie, 'anyone can make the same mistake. He did look like Len'.

Later in his room, he would look at his programme again, double and treble-checking the name of the Tottenham reserve number eight. Each time it would still read L. Wilton. Nevertheless, it would continue to bother and nag Eddie for some time – the name was just too close to his friend's for it to be a coincidence. His mum thought he had looked like Len too. As he lay in bed that night, a question came to add another twist to his thoughts. 'Could ghosts come back as different people? Were L. Wilton and L. Wilby one and the same person? But that would mean that

Len was already....' Eddie dismissed the thought that was forming in his mind and went to sleep. That was stupid!

9

A Reunion on the Beach

On the Saturday following Eddie's first visit to Freeman Street, Hamsden Town provided the large holiday crowd of nearly 11,000 with a superb victory over Bestcott Rovers from England's second city, Birmingham. Two goals from Johnny McBride and two penalties struck home by their captain 'Woody' Bates saw Town to a comfortable 4–0 scoreline. Eddie was ecstatic after he had returned home on the train. At teatime he couldn't stop talking about the new Irish striker.

"He's brilliant, Dad. You should have seen his second goal. He must have hit it from forty yards. I wish Len could have been with me," he said wistfully.

"I expect he's gone to White Hart Lane, son," said Eddie's dad.

"I don't think so, Dad. Len said in his letter that Spurs' first home game was on the 28th; that's next Saturday. His dad was trying to get tickets."

"You'll have to write and tell him about the game," said Ann Compton.

"I will, Mum, but it's Len's turn to write. I wrote yesterday to tell him about Tuesday's game and I sent him the programme as well. We're going to send letters once a month, if we can. I'm keeping his letters in a folder."

"Did you tell him about your photograph being in the paper and that the Spurs striker looked a bit like him? That would cheer him up."

"I just told him about the photo, Mum."

Eddie's mum smiled and said,

"Wouldn't it be good if Len becomes a star footballer one day? You would be able to say that you played with him when you were boys."

"I don't think he's that good, Mum – he never made the county team when he was at Fenton Grammar."

Sunday turned out to be a scorching hot day with temperatures already in the eighties by the time Eddie's mum and dad left as usual for morning service at St Andrew's overlooking the seafront. It had been some years since Eddie's sister had accompanied them but just a few short weeks since her brother had joined her in protesting the point of such regular and monotonous attendance. Eddie's burgeoning interest in science and its opinion as to the origin of the universe had dampened his belief in God. That belief, however, had not been eradicated completely. Indeed, recent events had halted its slow deterioration. Eddie did believe there was a greater power at work in the world, or, at least, *his* world. He wasn't as yet aware, however, how much it was also impinging on his best friend's world.

After his parents had left to attend church and with Jenny still in bed, Eddie decided to take a good long walk along the Fenton's two-mile promenade. He would start in the middle at the foot of Steep Hill, go north to the end at Mason's Point and then retrace his steps to walk the promenade's full length to its other extremity, South End, before returning to his starting point. In all it would be a distance of at least five miles. It would give him time to think and, hopefully, put things into context and reality. He would let his scientific mind dominate and sort his worries out.

The promenade seemed strangely quiet as Eddie turned left and headed towards Mason's Point. Above, clouds had swept in off the sea and it had turned noticeably cooler. Eddie found it more comfortable than the walk down the High Street. He strode out with some vigour and determination. Looking up ahead, Eddie couldn't see another person between himself and the Point. 'Where is everybody?' he thought. There had been a fair few families heading for the beach when he had walked down the High Street. It was much cooler now and it seemed to Eddie that it was much earlier than he had thought. But he hadn't left home until after ten-thirty, he was sure of that. Mum and Dad had already gone to church by then. He looked east and out to sea. The clouds parted to reveal the sun lower in the sky than when it had last been exposed. 'Oh no', he thought. 'It's happening again'. He'd moved time. There were signs, however, that it was still summer: a deckchair attendant removing a tarpaulin; remains of ice creams and drink bottles on the beach. It was early morning. Eddie approached the attendant.

"Have you got the time, please?"

"Yes, lad – it's just gone half past eight."

Eddie thanked the man and moved on. The sea was right out; it had been high tide when he'd arrived on the promenade. He decided to walk on the damp sand by the water's edge. It gave him a better view of the seafront. All seemed normal. One or two beach huts and guest houses had had a fresh lick of paint, but there was nothing much else to tell Eddie that he had moved very far into the future or the past. He thought he knew the deckchair man by sight but he hadn't appeared greatly older or younger. Eddie walked on. After another fifty yards or so he spotted someone else coming towards him in the distance. Eddie strained his eyes and could just make out that the figure was a boy of about his own age but, perhaps, slightly taller. The boy approached. He had fair hair. Eddie nodded knowingly to himself. It had to be Len. The boy got to within ten feet. It was Len but, yet, it wasn't Len. This boy was taller, slightly broader and seemed older, about fifteen or sixteen. 'Len' spoke.

"What'cha, Eddie."

Eddie stammered his reply – he hadn't got used to talking to ghosts.

"Oh hello, Len – what on earth are you doing here, mate?"

"We've just come back for a few days. How've you been?"

"You didn't say in your letter that you were coming back."

Len smiled but didn't reply. He turned to walk in the same direction as Eddie whose head was spinning in disbelief. Here was a marginally older version of his best friend and this time it was definitely him, no question. Should he give him a hug or shake his hand? He decided against it for fear of there being nothing there to hug or shake. Should he tell him that he was a ghost come back to haunt him? Len sensed his friend's dilemma and changed the conversation to his own world.

"Did you see the final yesterday? What a fantastic result for our boys!"

Now Eddie was really lost and confused, but he had to ask the obvious question from his world.

"What final?"

"The World Cup Final, you idiot! We won 4–2; Geoff Hurst scored a hat-trick. You must have seen it."

It was Eddie's turn to remain silent. What could he say? However, he thought he knew which year he'd moved to. Len was definitely older and the next World Cup was scheduled for the following year so it had to be 1966 (Len didn't look five years older, that would make him twenty).

The two boys walked on in silence. All sorts of questions were going through Eddie's mind. Did Len know he was a ghost? On the other hand, if Len was real and in his own world of 1966, then did he think that Eddie was a ghost from the past? Had he glimpsed the future? Would Len and his family come back to Fenton-on-Sea next summer? One frightening question eventually cleared the other more philosophical ones away. Could he get back to August the 22nd, 1965 or was he stuck with his friend about a year in the future?

They reached the line of boulders that formed the sea defences at Mason's Point. The two boys had walked a quarter of a mile in absolute silence with Eddie, for one, longing to reach out and touch his best friend; longing to tell him that it was 1965 and that he'd only just moved from Fenton and, above all, longing to talk to him about what it all meant, like they always used to. Len, however, broke the silence first.

"Got to go, mate – our guest house is over there. May see you later."

Before Eddie had a chance to reply, 'Len' bounded up the beach towards the promenade. Eddie's last sight of his best friend was his bobbing head as he reached the road on the far side. He ran up the beach as quickly as the soft sand would allow but there was no sign of Len's ghost when Eddie reached the road. He somehow knew there wouldn't be – there were no guest houses within half a mile of that stretch of the seafront.

It had turned suddenly hotter again and, as Eddie turned round to look at the beach, the sun was once again high in the sky. The prom was filling up with holidaymakers out for a lunchtime stroll. Eddie breathed a sigh of relief. He had returned to 1965.

Eddie was too excited and on edge to complete his intended walk and he made his way back to Steep Hill via the Undercliff. He tried hard to remember what Len had said in their short and ghostly conversation but nothing would come back apart from the year – 1966. Bookmakers up and down the land would breathe a sigh of relief that some greater power had wiped Edward Compton's memory clear of any facts about future World Cup Final results!

Though Len had been slightly older, there had been something else different about him that Eddie couldn't quite put his finger on until he reached the top of Steep Hill and entered the High Street. He was deep in thought as he wandered past Neville's the jeweller, the shop where he'd bought…. All sorts of rings and necklaces glinted at him in the bright sunshine and instantly he remembered. Len hadn't been wearing his St Christopher. Eddie stared at his own reflection in the shop window. Len's neck had been bare; his simple white T-shirt hadn't hidden a thing. He'd promised Eddie he would never take it off. A few moments passed and eventually Eddie shrugged his shoulders and continued on his walk home. Len had been a ghost and ghosts could wear what they liked. Len's other ghost, the scientist at the nuclear power station, *might* have been wearing the medallion anyway. Jenny hadn't told her brother that the young sailor *had* been wearing a necklace of some kind and Eddie continued to think about the St Christopher for the rest of the walk home. He was late as a glance at the station clock revealed. It was gone half past one and Sunday lunch would be on the table.

Sunday lunch wasn't on the table when Eddie arrived home. In fact the Comptons wouldn't eat the wasted meal that day. Eddie's mum was waiting in the doorway to 38 Fir Tree Close when her son reached the front gate. She wasn't smiling. Eddie called up the front path,

"Sorry I'm late, Mum – forgot the time."

Ann Compton didn't reply and her strained facial expression didn't change. She walked forward and held her son in her arms. Eddie protested.

"Mum, stop it!"

Eddie's mum started to cry and Eddie could feel her body trembling. He knew something serious was wrong. He extricated himself from her hug and stood back to face her. They were now standing just inside the front door.

"What's the matter, Mum? What's happened?"

Eddie's dad was standing almost helplessly behind his wife in the hall and said,

"Get him into the lounge, love."

Eddie looked at his dad's face and said,

"Please tell me what's happened, Dad?"

Fred Compton ushered and cajoled his son into the lounge and pointed to a chair.

"Sit down, son. We've got some bad news to tell you."

Eddie looked round the lounge. His mum had remained in the hall.

"Where's Jenny, Dad?" croaked Eddie. "It's Jen, isn't it? Something's happened to Jenny."

"No, son – it's not Jenny. She's in her bedroom."

"Then, who…?"

"It's Len, Eddie."

Eddie heard his mum sob in the background.

"Len?"

"Look, son, there's no easy way for us to tell you this, I'm afraid."

What Eddie's dad said next didn't immediately seem to register in Eddie's head and he said,

"But I've just…."

As soon as he'd uttered these words, few though they were, he realised how, at the same time, they were both pointed and pointless.

10

Tragedy

Len and his dad had decided to get up very early on Sunday, August the 22nd – fishing off the pier at Deal was the order of the day. They set off just after eight on a beautiful sunny morning with a fresh, autumnal feel to the air. The journey via the A2 to Ramsgate would take about forty-five minutes. Cyril Wilby had checked the local tables and high tide was scheduled to be at nine-fifteen – the best time for mackerel and bass, he told his son.

Len's dad pulled the red Vauxhall Victor onto the A2 at the Queen's roundabout intersection and he opened the throttle as they headed east. He soon had the big car up to its cruising speed of seventy miles per hour. They crested the brow of a small hill and saw the East Kent coast spread out before them. The car's engine was purring and it seemed to Cyril that it deserved to be put to the test. He depressed the accelerator further and said,

"Let's see what she'll do, son."

"Oh yes, Dad. Give her all she's got. We can see for miles."

The road in front pointed like an arrow into the distance. There was nothing else on the road. The car sped on towards the horizon.

"What are we doing now, Dad," said Len excitedly.

His dad began counting out loud.

"Eighty-five, eighty-six, eighty-seven…."

The engine whined but was not protesting. They touched ninety. Three ravens and a magpie scattered into a field to the left of the car's speeding progress; a pigeon ignored the red tornado and was nearly crushed by the front wheels. Len looked back.

"Missed it, Dad – would have been twenty points!"

Len's dad grunted.

"I'll get him on the way back."

But he wouldn't be going back that way later that day. A roundabout signified the eastern end of the A2. It was still six hundred yards ahead. Cyril Wilby kept his foot down. He had never driven a vehicle at this speed; he had never had to judge when and how fast to brake. Army vehicles rarely went faster than fifty and the red Vauxhall was doing more than ninety. A large sign to the left gave the first warning to slow down and another followed almost instantly. Len shouted the obvious.

"Slow down, Dad. There's a roundabout!"

Len's dad hit the brake and the big car shuddered and weaved first left and then right as its driver fought to keep it in a straight line. They were less than a hundred yards from the walled roundabout. Len shouted again and braced himself.

"We're not going to make it!"

Beads of perspiration exuded from his dad's forehead as he gripped the wheel like a madman. If anyone had been following they would have seen a huge cloud of smoke pour from the screaming back wheels. Neither of them had a chance to say or even think anything more. The car hit the four foot concrete banking that surrounded the roundabout. If measured, the impact speed would have been recorded in excess of fifty-five. The engine compartment was crushed to a fraction of its size. The steering column buried itself in Cyril Wilby's chest. He felt no pain as he died instantly. Len was knocked unconscious as his head hit the windscreen. Thankfully, he too felt no pain as his mangled lifeless body was launched over the walled surround and almost to the other side of the roundabout. His bright silver St Christopher was torn off in the crash and landed a few feet away to his left. It would be found on the Monday by accident investigators who would eventually return it to Cyril Wilby's widow. Martha would just have time to replace it round her dead son's neck before his coffin was closed for the last time just before the funeral. It was just after eight-thirty. After a couple of minutes, the first of several cars stopped and the driver would be able to tell the police later the approximate time of the tragic accident. On a beach a hundred and fifty miles away, another fourteen-year-old boy had just asked a deckchair attendant for the time.

Before Eddie had received his tragic news that Sunday afternoon, Ann and Fred Compton had been home from church for just over an hour. The Reverend Henry Weaver had delivered his usual thought provoking sermon; friendship and earthly love had been his themes. As a consequence, Eddie's mum had decided to phone her friend Martha in Kent; Fred Compton was happy that the weekend call would be at the cheapest rate. He knew how long his wife could talk to her best friend. It was ten to one. A strange voice answered.

"Hello, can I help you?"

"Oh yes, can I speak to Martha, please?"

Silence. Ann thought she detected someone talking in the background. The pause seemed to last for ages. The voice came back.

"I'm sorry; she's unable to come to the phone right now."

"Oh," said Ann Compton, "will you tell her it's Ann from Fenton-on-Sea; I'm her best friend."

More discussion off-phone. Ann thought she could hear crying. What was wrong? She heard the telephone change hands to be followed by someone sobbing into it.

"Martha? Is that you? What ever is the matter?" asked Eddie's mum quietly.

"Ann, oh Ann," said Martha Wilby between sobs.

"What? What is it?"

Ann knew something serious had happened, despite her friend's tendency to exaggerate crises at times. The emotions she was hearing suggested a real tragedy of some kind. The line went silent for a few moments.

"Martha? Are you still there, dear?"

"I'm here," came the quavering reply. It was clear Martha couldn't go on.

She said simply,

"I can't talk now."

The phone was passed back to the voice.

"I'm sorry but Ann's had some bad news. I'm her neighbour, Sue Rogers. She wants me to tell you."

"What? What's happened?"

It's her husband and son; they've been tragically killed in a road accident. I'm so sorry. It happened earlier this morning at just after half past eight."

Ann Compton couldn't say anything and Sue Rogers continued.

"She's in good hands; some relations are on their way from Cambridge and a couple of us neighbours are staying with her till then. I believe it's her sister and husband who are coming down."

Martha had never talked to Ann about her family. She knew that her parents were both dead. Ann always felt like family – the two women were like sisters. She plucked up courage and said,

"We'll come down as soon as we can. Would you give Martha our sincere condolences and tell her we're thinking of her and that we love her dearly."

"I will; of course I will."

Ann couldn't manage the pleasantries of some parting words and put the phone down. She stood in the hall and cried uncontrollably.

There was, of course, nothing that the emergency services could do in the aftermath of the accident other than dampen down the smouldering wreck of Cyril's prized Vauxhall Victor. Identification would take place at a suitable and appropriate time. For the time being the next of kin had to be informed, details of whom were found from a diary that Cyril Wilby always carried. Two police officers and a young woman bereavement counsellor, provided by the service, broke the tragic news to Martha at about eleven o'clock at her new home in The Park at Petersgate. Martha didn't cry immediately and the counsellor knew that the shock often delayed any public outpouring of grief till later. Martha spent half an hour in complete silence. She alternated from sitting in a chair staring at a picture of her late husband and standing gazing out of the lounge window at her newly planted and rearranged garden. By the time her new neighbour, Mrs Sue Rogers, had arrived at the request of the police counsellor, she was ready to let her emotions take over and she cried freely into the arms of a virtual stranger. Sue held Martha for a good ten minutes until the first of many such natural and essential outpourings subsided, brought about only by the telephone ringing in the hall. It was ten to one and it was nearly two hours since Martha had received her tragic news.

Eddie's mum wanted to jump straight into the car and head for Kent, but her husband knew that too many visitors for Martha too soon would not be a good thing and Ann was persuaded to wait until at least the following day. On hearing the news, Eddie had disappeared immediately to his bedroom. He had not said another word to his parents after the initial attempt to tell them that he had just seen his best friend on Fenton beach. He spent most of the afternoon reading and rereading Len's first and only letter, recalling, at the same time, all the pointers there had been in the ghostly meetings with his friend which had culminated in the very last one at just after eight-thirty that morning. Eventually, he knew he had to ask his parents a vital question. He steeled himself and went downstairs. His mum had been listening for him all afternoon, not daring to enter his bedroom. She was already at the foot of the stairs to meet him. She held out her arms and said,

"How are you feeling, Eddie? Are you O.K?"

Eddie avoided his mother's clutches and said quickly,

"Do you know when Len died, Mum?"

Ann Compton could see at once that her son didn't want any motherly display of affection and, standing aside to let him pass, she replied,

"The neighbour said that it was probably just after half past eight."

Eddie smiled. The last piece of the jigsaw of ghostly clues dropped into place. His best friend's spirit had been fresh from his earthly body when Eddie had had the privilege to meet him on the beach. The fact that it had actually been after eleven that morning didn't matter. Len's ghost had arranged it to be at the same time as his death albeit nearly a year in the future. 'Clever touch, comrade', thought Eddie. 'But why hadn't he been wearing his St Christopher'?

The Comptons didn't head south until Tuesday morning. Ann finally spoke at length to Martha on Monday afternoon and, though it seemed on the surface that she was bearing up remarkably well, Ann could sense that her friend was in need of some familiar company, surrounded as she was by strangers and family she hadn't seen for years. Fred Compton still hadn't invested in a new car and the journey took the best part of six hours with only one stop for petrol in Essex. They eventually arrived at their pre-booked guest house in Petersgate at just before four in the afternoon. After a quick wash and change they were outside 23 The Park at five-thirty. Martha was clearly pleased to see them and her friend Ann in particular. Martha's sister and husband were the only family actually staying at the house. They were using the spare bedroom. The door to Len's room was closed; the room itself being still in the state it was when he had left it on the Sunday morning. Even his mother had not been in. Martha hugged her best friend on arrival.

"Thank you so much for coming. You don't know what it means to me."

There was a tear in her son's eye as Eddie replied for his mum who was crying unashamedly.

"We just had to, Aunty Martha. Len was, is and always will be my best friend as Uncle Cyril is yours."

Martha Wilby stood back from hugging her friend and, though she didn't reply to Eddie's remarkably mature eulogy, it had clearly provided her with a huge fillip as she smiled warmly at him. They both understood the other's loss.

Arrangements for the joint funerals were not to be overly delayed despite the necessary investigations that had to be concluded. The service would be held at St Michael's church on Friday, August the 27th at two-thirty. Eddie spent a lot of time until then by himself sitting in Martha's back garden. He was absolutely convinced in his own mind that he had been there before on a ghostly trip prior to the Wilby's move. Though the newly planted row of conifers was only about three feet high, they seemed to Eddie to be in exactly the same places. Even the patio area was just beyond the bottom of the lawn. Aunty Martha had been there too, of that he was certain, though she had been much older. He was equally convinced that Uncle Cyril had not. Recent events made that seem obvious. Who had been Martha's new companion?

Considering the Wilbys were so new to the area, the funeral service was very well attended on the Friday. Several of Martha's new church congregation were there despite many of them never having spoken to her – they came out of the extreme sadness that had enveloped the local community at such a tragic loss for people who had just joined their society. Though Martha didn't seem to have stayed in contact with many of her family, Cyril's side was very well represented, including both his aging parents who had travelled down by train from Scotland. The Deputy Head at Fenton Grammar School was also there accompanied by two of Eddie and Len's year group. To Martha's great surprise, 'Teddy' Crompton, Headmaster of what would have been Len's new school was also in attendance. The Banham School also sent a senior member of staff; the Head, Mr Boulter, was away on a touring holiday in France. No one came from Cyril's previous school.

Fred and Eddie had agreed to give individual eulogies for Cyril and Len and, while his son seemed strangely calm given his age and the circumstances, Fred was clearly very nervous when the vicar called him forward. Fred was brief, bland and almost clinical in his address which he read word for word from prepared notes, almost as if he was rehearsing the details of a long train journey cross country. Cyril's family didn't seem to mind; he didn't have any brothers and sisters and with the several moves needed in his profession he had few other long term friends. Martha nodded and mimed a 'thank you' when, after two minutes, Eddie's dad returned to his seat.

One of Martha's favourite hymns was followed by Eddie's eulogy. He walked confidently up to the pulpit without notes of any kind and a smile on his face which immediately lifted the sombre mood of the congregation. He looked briefly at his parents and began.

"Leonard Wilby was my best friend and he will always be so. He protected me at school when other boys tried to bully me and he gave me confidence to do those things that I often thought I couldn't do or achieve. If I had a problem, no matter how small, I could always go to Len and he would have an answer – often it wasn't the correct one but that didn't matter, even when he or I ended up in worse trouble and with a bigger headache. In Len's case, 'a problem shared was a problem doubled'."

Mild laughter relaxed the mourners. Eddie paused and continued.

"Len was not afraid to make mistakes. He was a superb sportsman, captaining both our school's football and rugby teams. He would, no doubt, have proved his prowess at his new school, Petersgate Grammar."

Mr Crompton smiled and nodded his agreement as several mourners turned to look at the well-known and respected Headmaster. Martha Wilby began to cry silently. Eddie's mum put her arm round her shoulders.

"He and I shared secrets that nobody else will ever unravel. We did things and went places that only we knew about, like all teenage boys growing up these days. Len was always the one for an adventure even when neither of us knew what the consequences would be. Len was brave and courageous and he lifted the spirits of all around him. Nobody disliked him and opposing players always respected him and shook his hand at the end of a football or rugby match. He said and did daft things at times but you couldn't wish for a better mate in a crisis. Maybe not blessed with the brain to think his way around a problem, he would often solve it with native wit and sheer strength of character. He made others

see the funny side of their predicaments. He laughed equally at himself as
he did at others and...."

Eddie paused.

"And I loved the rascal – I always will. No one could wish for a
better friend and he'll be mine till I join him again in more adventures
that we can now only dream about. God bless you, Len. You're a great
mate, comrade."

Eddie's sister stood up. She put her hands together and clapped
loudly. Seconds later everyone followed Jenny, not only to give thanks
for Eddie's eloquence, but also as a release of pent up emotion and to
express their tribute to Len when their own words couldn't possibly
match the ones spoken by Eddie himself. Martha Wilby came over to
Eddie and, holding his hand warmly, she whispered her own 'thank you'.
She kissed his forehead lightly and returned to her seat.

The Comptons seemed to be the only non-family members to return to
The Park for some sandwiches and tea after the funeral. Eddie noticed,
however, that there was one man who seemed to be unattached to anyone
from either side of the Wilby's families. During the wake in the garden,
Martha attended to his needs more carefully than she did any of the
family members – he was clearly a special friend from Martha's past. It
turned out that his name was Michael Conners and he lived in London.
He had been a teacher at the school that the Wilbys had once worked at in
the East End; Cyril in the woodwork department and Martha as a cook.
It was amazing what a fourteen-year-old boy could discover by simply
standing or sitting in the most apposite position whenever Martha and
Michael were talking.

Just before it was time for the Comptons to leave to return for their
last night at their guest house on Petersgate's seafront, Eddie had a déjà

vu experience that would provide him, and him alone, with an insight into Martha Wilby's future. Martha and Michael Conners were sitting on the patio area at the end of the garden. They were drinking tea while they discussed old times together. 'So that's who Aunty Martha's new companion had been on his earlier trip to the garden', he thought. He was glad that Martha would apparently find happiness again at some time in the future. Eddie's mother would remark later, on the drive back to Fenton-on-Sea, how happier her friend had seemed to be when talking to the tall stranger; happier than when with her own family, she would also observe.

11

The Beginning

Eddie 'saw' nothing more of his friend, Len, for the rest of the school holidays. He had gained great comfort in the knowledge that death didn't mean the end of things. Despite his love of science and the value of reasoned and logical argument, he knew he had been privileged to glimpse another world where the normal rules of such principles just didn't apply. He alone, he thought, had seen and experienced signs that told him his friendship with Len was not over. Indeed, it might only be just beginning. Surely the peeks into the future, whether real or not, had meant more than just a warning of his best friend's demise. So it was that Eddie approached the fourth year at Fenton-on-Sea Grammar School with more excitement and contentment than his family had scarcely believed would be possible. His belief that he was the only person living who had been witness to ghostly sightings was, of course, a fallacious one; his sister for one, however, had not yet realised that she had been talking to a ghost when meeting the handsome young sailor. What she had done was to keep a very careful eye on her brother in the days after his friend's death. It would be a long time before experiences would be shared between the two siblings.

The autumn term began on Monday, September the 6th and Eddie, for almost the first time ever – apart from on the rare occasion when Len had been sick – walked to school on his own. Both his teachers and fellow fourth years were instantly watchful of and sympathetic to his needs, as they were, also, to Len's many other school friends. Eddie found quickly that he was part of a fairly large clan of boys (and girls) who gained comfort in shared experiences concerning their popular schoolmate. A special assembly was held at eleven o'clock as the

371

school's token memorial to its former pupil. It was a moving service led by Mr Smithson, the Head of Boys' P.E. and Games and while nearly every other student bowed their head's with sad expressions covering their faces, Eddie sat with a proud smile on his. In the succeeding days a memorial plaque would be put in the main corridor just before the entrance to the school gymnasium. Leonard Wilby would not be forgotten.

As usual, the term didn't really get into full swing until the following week; timetables had to be properly checked for the O-level pupils and the normal issuing and – in some cases – return of text books had to be accomplished. To his great delight, Eddie found that he had double Maths first on Monday mornings and he had his favourite teacher, Miss Ware, too. Double French and double Physics would complete what would turn out to be his favourite morning of the week. He would learn to suffer the double dose of English Language in the afternoon. It was not his favourite subject and, to make matters worse, he discovered he had 'old man' Green again, as in the previous year. His only ever detention had been provided by the irritable Head of English. Maynard Green was two years from retirement and it had begun to show; he did not suffer fools gladly and young Edward Compton fitted into such a category to a tee, he had decided. So it was that Eddie was pleasantly surprised when, at the first lesson that Monday afternoon, Mr Green seemed unusually forgiving of his incorrect and wayward answers. Eddie did not know that all his teachers had been told of his special friendship with Leonard Wilby and that they were to be careful in their dealings with him. In the previous year he and Len had always sat next to each other in English – it was the only subject for which they had been in the same set. No one had so far sat next to him in the fourth year; the adjacent seat and desk to his left had remained empty out of respect.

Towards the end of the lesson, Eddie had given a particularly errant reply to a question; so much off beam that several of his classmates giggled audibly. Mr Green looked at them sternly and said,

"Well, you lot, at least young Compton here made a stab at the answer, which is more than can be said for any of you."

"Who'd have thought old man Green would have said that, Eddie."

Eddie looked to his right to see who had spoken but it was immediately obvious that no one had – nobody would dare. The voice spoke again and it was coming from Eddie's left.

"It's me, mate."

Eddie went rigid and hardly dared look back at the empty desk beside him. He instantly knew it wouldn't be empty when eventually he did turn his head. There sat his best friend, dressed so casually that he was clearly invisible to the rest of the class. Mr Green glanced at Eddie and was about to say something before he realised that Eddie seemed to be looking wistfully at the empty seat. Maynard Green ignored Eddie's apparent inattention and carried on the debate of the prologue to Henry the Fifth.

"It's O.K., Eddie – I've just come to see how you're getting on without me this year. You don't need to say anything, mate. We mustn't get you into trouble with old 'Greeny', eh?"

Eddie kept silent. Mr Green was getting more and more anxious as Eddie continued to stare at the seat beside him.

"Meet me after school, mate. I'll see you on the way home. Go home the normal way."

Eddie nodded his head very slightly and he turned to look at his English teacher. He sensed Mr Green was staring at him.

"Are you alright, Compton?"

"Oh yes, sir. I'm absolutely fine."

He had been about to add the word 'now', but had thought better of it at the last moment. Mr Green smiled and carried on with the conclusion of the lesson. Eddie knew what he'd find when he looked back at his adjacent seat – nothing.

Eddie was understandably both nervous and excited as he walked through the school gates that afternoon. He walked up South Road as usual trying to keep to the same side of the road as he and Len had normally done. Within ten minutes he was less than fifty yards from the turning into Fir Tree Close and still his friend had not put in a ghostly appearance. Eddie began to worry that Len would leave it until he was in sight of number 38 which might cause awkward questions if anyone, especially his mum, observed him chatting to a tree! He slowed to a dawdle and started to glance over his shoulder. What would Len look like? Though in casual clothes earlier that afternoon, Eddie thought that he had looked, more or less, about the same age as when he had last seen him for real. He had reached the turn into his road. Suddenly he heard a voice call out.

"Over here, Eddie!"

Eddie looked right. There on the opposite side of South Road stood Len. He looked as though he had just come from the High Street. Eddie paused to let a cyclist pass and then crossed over the road to meet his friend. He could at last speak to him.

"Hi, Len – it's really good to see you, mate."

"You too, Captain."

Eddie wanted to hug his friend but knew it was pointless. In addition, the sight of a fourteen-year-old boy hugging thin air would have got him some very strange looks. As it was Len beckoned to Eddie to keep moving as they walked side by side towards the High Street.

"Let's find somewhere where you can talk without making people think you've gone mad," said Len soon after they'd set off together. Len seemed to want to take the lead as they walked down the High Street and headed for the beach via Steep Hill. Disconcertingly, Len clearly wanted to walk right through people thus causing Eddie to gasp in astonishment which in turn produced stares from the people that were passing. He eventually stopped his 'trick' and weaved his way onwards like a normal human being.

The tide was out when they reached the promenade and Len 'led' his friend to the water's edge not far from the spot where their first great adventure had started. Len placed himself deliberately in such a way that it would appear that Eddie was merely gazing out to sea rather than conversing with a ghost! Eddie had a question that had worried him since he had first learned of his friend's passing.

"Did it hurt, Len? I mean in the accident."

"No, mate; not a bit. I don't really remember much. Dad and I were going fishing at a place called Deal. I remember being in the car and that I thought Dad was driving too fast, but nothing else."

Eddie thought for a moment or two. He had other questions but they seemed so stupid he barely dared to ask. He asked the obvious.

"What have you been doing since you…?"

Len seemed to know the difficulty that Eddie was having in understanding what was happening and he replied,

"It's not like living on earth in the real world, mate. It's totally different. Time has no relevance; you don't measure it by days or hours but just by a series of events that happen to you. As far as I can remember I've had three so far. I remember hovering over my coffin in a strange church and hearing bits of what you said. Thanks by the way, mate. Next thing I seem to recall is sitting next to you at school in old man Green's

375

class and setting up this meeting. Then I found myself near the station and something or someone made me arrive in South Road just as you were about to turn into Fir Tree Close. There was just nothing in between the events. I don't think I'm making them happen or making the decision to go where I go. Someone must have wanted us to meet. I'm glad they did, mate. It's really weird, you know – being a ghost."

Eddie relaxed and laughed.

"I suppose, Len, it must be a bit like when we went on our first fantastic journey when nobody could see either of us and we could move time and place quickly at speeds that were impossible for normal people."

Len also seemed to laugh.

"A bit, mate – except I don't get hungry; I don't sleep; I don't have to fulfil any other bodily functions and I can wear what I want and go where I like."

"But just now you said you haven't been in control of where you've been. Now you say you can go where you want."

"What I meant was that when I find myself in a new situation, then I can wander off where I like. I walked from the middle of the High Street to meet you, didn't I? I'm kind of just learning what I can do by myself and what is done for me. I think in time I'll be able to think myself to different places, times and events, just like…."

"Just like what, Len?"

"Just like you were able to think us to all those different places we went to on our magic carpet. Do you understand?"

"I think so. Which of the three things that have happened to you did you plan?"

"I'm not sure, Eddie. Probably I wanted to see you again and some other force engineered it for me, and you. I didn't plan to be at my own funeral – that just happened. I didn't actually plan to sit next to you at school – that just happened too, but I suspect whoever is looking after me made it possible. I was as shocked as you when I found myself next to you. We ghosts are obviously better at hiding our emotions though!"

Eddie was beginning to understand. Just then he heard a noise behind him and turned to find a dog making serious growling noises at his back. He moved a few feet to one side and immediately realised that he was not the object of the animal's displeasure. It was growling at a spot behind Eddie by the water's edge. Eddie turned back to tell his friend. There was no one to be seen. The dog stopped growling and trotted happily back up the beach to its master who shouted,

"She's alright, son. She won't bite!"

On his way back home Eddie realised that he hadn't had the chance to ask his friendly ghost some other questions concerning his other meetings with him. One bugged him all that evening. Why hadn't Len mentioned the meeting on Fenton beach that had occurred just a few minutes after his death? The other sighting of Len's ghost had been in the future, but the most recent had not, or had it? In the end, Eddie decided that, perhaps, Len hadn't mentioned anything else because, for him, the events hadn't yet happened including the one in 1966. Whatever the reason, Eddie also began to think that Len was not the only one with special powers. He himself might be able to see into the future and be aware of what Len's ghost might do before it happened.

Because of his ghostly rendezvous, Eddie eventually arrived home after five-thirty that Monday and, naturally, faced some awkward questions from his mother.

"Where have you been?" she asked as he came in through the front door.

"We had Maths club until five and I helped tidy up afterwards," he lied.

"But I thought the Maths club was on a Wednesday."

"It was last year, Mum, but that was the junior one; I'm with the fifth and sixth form now."

Eddie didn't immediately realise that he would have to invent an excuse for being home late on a Wednesday as well when the Maths club was really scheduled. He would have to face that problem later. His mother had some news for him.

"Aunty Martha phoned this afternoon; she'd been going through some of Len's things at last. There was a couple of things she thought you might like."

"Oh, Mum – like what?"

"An old railway timetable from the thirties that she said someone had given Len once for his birthday and…."

Eddie interrupted quickly.

"Did she say who had given it to him?"

"No, dear, she didn't."

Eddie breathed a sigh of relief. He would have had difficulty in explaining to his mother who Mr Jacob Manders was.

"What else did she say I might want?" said Eddie.

"Just his football that Mr Canter sent him; apparently you can still see some of the signatures on it. If you want both things she'll put them in a parcel and send them through the post."

"Tell her yes, Mum."

"O.K., Eddie."

Eddie's mum paused and then continued.

"What do you think Len was doing getting an old railway timetable? It wasn't the kind of thing he was interested in, was it? I expect your dad will want to have a look at it when it arrives."

Eddie knew immediately that he had made a mistake. His dad was bound to read the inscription inside the timetable and there was no way he could explain who Mr Manders was especially when Eddie's parents thought he was someone that the two boys had made up to get them out of a difficult situation. He thought quickly and said,

"On second thoughts, Mum, I don't think I'd like to have the timetable or football. It wouldn't feel right to have some of his things. I'd rather Aunty Martha kept them or gave them to charity."

Ann Compton looked oddly ay her son.

"Are you sure? I think Len's mum wants you to have them and she might be upset if you refuse."

'This was proving to be difficult', thought Eddie. He relented.

"Oh, O.K., Mum, I'll have them."

"That's good – I'll phone her back tomorrow."

After tea that evening, Eddie spent a good deal of time thinking about how he could prevent his dad from seeing the railway timetable. There didn't seem to be an obvious solution except one that would involve his friendly ghost. He needed to talk to Len urgently and how was he to engineer that? He had two or three days at the most and he might not see him for weeks. The opportunity would present itself the very next day.

Len was waiting in the same position on South Road when Eddie returned home from school. Eddie saw his friend immediately and quickly crossed over the road to meet him.

"Good afternoon, Captain," said Len. "I gather we have a problem."

"Yes, but how did you…?"

"How did I know? Well, we ghosts can find out lots of things without anyone knowing. I saw my mum going through my things and I was there when she phoned your mum about the timetable and football."

"Thank God," said Eddie.

"No, mate – thank *me*."

"So how can you help?"

"Already fixed, Eddie. I just haunted Mum for a few minutes so I think you'll find she's changed her mind and now she wants to keep them. I have real power, mate."

"Thanks, Len."

"No problem. I'm sorry I can't stop and talk for longer but I've things to do and places to go to. Bye!"

As before, Len immediately disappeared from sight but, this time, Eddie wasn't sure if he'd looked away from his friend for a split second or not. This was getting interesting, he thought, as he made his way home. Could he just call up his friend at will whenever he needed help? That would be good!

After school the following day, Eddie's mum told him that Martha had changed her decision to let him have the timetable and football – she was going to keep all his things as they had been in his room the day he had died. Eddie was relieved. Len was a star! With the senior Maths club being changed from a Wednesday to a Monday evening as well, Eddie began to believe that his guardian angel could also help with problems when he hadn't even asked for such assistance.

While Eddie was adjusting to his new life at school without his earthly friend, the other change in the routine of the Compton household also began the following day, the 16th of September. Jenny started her beauty therapy course at Hamsden Civic College. Sam Arleson still wanted her to work at his baker's shop on Saturdays and in the holidays. Equipment for her course had already cost her and, indeed, her parents, well over a hundred pounds. She was a bit nervous when she boarded the bus – the cheaper of the two forms of transport – on the Thursday morning. This apprehension was not only because it was her first day at college but also because it was the first time she had travelled to Hamsden by bus since her meeting with the young sailor. Apart from her brother, she had still not mentioned that meeting to anyone.

12

A Ghostly Day Out

Though Eddie tried hard over the next few weeks to urge his friend to put in another appearance, he had no success. By the middle of October he was beginning to think that he would never reappear, even when he might desperately need him for some crisis or other. However, when Friday, October the 15th dawned unusually warm and sunny, Eddie's hopes of another liaison were strangely lifted. Whether it was the summery weather, reminding him of the last such meeting, or the fact that, like Monday, his school day would conclude with English, he wouldn't be able to decide. He just knew something would happen that day. He couldn't wait for his English lesson with Mr Green to start. But he knew there could be a problem. Sally Barber had taken to sitting next to him in Len's old place – she had only started at Fenton Grammar that term and thus had no qualms about sitting in the seat next to Eddie. Eddie had a plan to prevent her doing so, but he knew he had to get to room 46 before anyone else, including Mr Green, if he was to carry it out.

As usual, everyone in Mr Green's fourth year English class was silent on entry to room 46, until Sally Barber's voice echoed round the room.

"Sir? Sir?"

"Yes, Miss Barber and what is the problem?"

"Sir, someone's spilt ink all over my seat and desk."

"Well go and sit somewhere else."

"Yes, sir."

Mr Green came over to the back row to inspect the desk and chair. He stood right beside Eddie.

"Are you responsible for this, Compton?"

"No, sir. I don't use black ink as you know, sir. It was like it when I got here. It probably happened over lunchtime."

Eddie sat nervously hoping that Mr Green wouldn't ask to look in his bag where lurked an empty bottle of black fountain pen ink specially bought at lunchtime for the purpose. Maynard Green just grunted. It was Friday afternoon and he couldn't be bothered to investigate further. He would inform the caretaker later. He walked back to his normal position at the front of the room.

"*So, set four, we return to Act Four, Scene Two.*"

Eddie didn't really hear anything that was said over the next ten minutes or so. His mind was elsewhere as his eyes glanced constantly to his left. He was fortunate that Mr Green didn't ask him any questions and that he didn't notice his fidgety behaviour. Copious amounts of blotting paper lay in place soaking up most of the black liquid. Would Len get it on his clothes? As Eddie was posing the question in his mind, he looked briefly to the front. When he turned back, there was Len sitting in the ink-covered chair. He was smiling broadly.

"*Good trick, mate,*" he said loudly – indeed, so loudly that Eddie thought everyone would hear. The class carried on as normal. Eddie was about to whisper something when Len continued.

"*Don't say a word. Just listen.*"

Eddie gave the barest of nods.

"*Fancy a day out tomorrow, Eddie. Put your left hand on the desk for yes.*"

Eddie's left hand appeared on his desk.

"*Are you doing anything special?*"

Eddie replaced his left hand with his right. The code worked!

"*Meet me outside the station at nine. I have plans.*"

Left hand changed to right. Mr Green had spotted Eddie's inattention.

"Concentrate please, Mr Compton. You have homework on this scene over the weekend."

"Yes, sir – sorry, sir."

"Is that ink bothering you? You seem to be more interested in that than Shakespeare."

"It's just a bit smelly, sir."

"Well, please pay attention, Compo. I won't tell you again."

"Yes, sir."

Eddie looked down at his copy of Henry the Fifth. Out of the corner of his left eye he could see that the chair next to him was empty.

Saturday was as pleasantly warm as the previous day; an Indian summer had arrived in Fenton-on-Sea. Eddie prepared his parents by informing them he would likely be out for most of the day. As Fred Compton was leaving for work at the station, he inquired,

"Where are you off to today, then, son?"

"Thought I might go to Hamsden for the day. Town are at home this afternoon."

"You may have to come back on the bus. Engineering work starts on the track near Linham Junction this evening. What train are you going to catch this morning?"

"The ten past nine, I expect. Depends on...."

"Depends on what?" said Eddie's mum.

Eddie thought quickly. He'd nearly said the wrong thing.

"Depends on whether I want to go that early, Mum."

It seemed a lame qualification to his statement and his mother looked a little oddly at him, but instead she asked,

"What about your lunch? Do you want me to make you some sandwiches?"

"No, I'll get something in Hamsden."

Eddie's mother seemed satisfied but, nevertheless, she still smiled knowingly. She thought she knew what Eddie had been originally planning to say. Her son must have his first girlfriend.

"Well have a good day. You'll have to get a move on – it's quarter to already."

Eddie managed to get to the station forecourt just as St Andrew's church clock sounded the hour. Len didn't seem to be in sight. The clock finished striking and Eddie wandered towards the station entrance. A strange sight suddenly greeted him. His dad was walking side by side with his best friend. Fred Compton spotted his son and came up to him accompanied by Len at his side. Eddie's friend grinned cheekily but it was Eddie's dad who spoke.

"Just off for my paper while there's a lull – I'm showing young Dave the ropes this morning."

"*Come on, mate, I want to catch the ten past train.*"

Eddie wasn't sure who to reply to first, but managed,

"Have to go, Dad; it's five past."

"See you later, son."

"*See you later, Mr Compton.*"

Eddie turned and waited until his dad was out of earshot.

"That was not nice," he said to Len.

"Sorry, mate – it was just a bit of fun. I'd been to check the train times and saw your dad on the way out."

Eddie bought a day return to Hamsden from Dave Barton and just managed to catch the ten past nine train from platform one. Hamsden was

385

where Eddie's ghostly friend wanted to go as well. The train was packed with Saturday morning shoppers and Eddie couldn't find two seats until Len whispered,

"I don't need a seat, mate!"

Eddie found one vacant seat in the front carriage next to a young blond girl of about his own age. Len promptly sat on her lap! Eddie looked totally shocked. Len leant over and whispered in his ear.

"Bet you wish you could do this, eh?"

The blond girl couldn't see or feel anything. Eddie sat in silence and waited. He didn't have to wait long for Len's 'plan' to begin. The ten pat nine train was one of the few trains that stopped at Linmouth Junction and as it began to slow down, Len got up and headed for the door. Eddie followed. No one noticed that the door appeared to open of its own accord a split second before Eddie turned the handle. Eddie jumped off the train and followed his friend to the end of the single platform.

"What are you doing, Len?"

"Want to go for a walk, mate. I want to see if we can see Ally Grant or that other bloke we met – the one in the white coat. Something about him bothered me."

There was no point not telling his friend now, thought Eddie but he started cautiously.

"You mean you don't know who he was?"

"No. Should I?"

"I saw the lapel badge he was wearing."

"So what did it say?"

"It read *Dr Leonard Wilby.* I mean, Doctor! You would never have become a doctor, mate."

Len's ghost didn't reply. Eddie offered an explanation.

"You know what I think, Len?"

Len shook his head. He was clearly disturbed.

"I think we met your ghost many years in the future and it was in a guise of someone that you always wanted to be – a nuclear scientist."

"I never wanted to be a scientist. I only ever wanted to be a professional sportsman and, anyway, you might have wanted to see my name on the lapel badge. It might have just been mind association. I was with you at the time, remember?"

"Yes, but maybe ghosts age and you somehow 'became' the scientist or you can change into someone else just by thinking about it."

"Maybe. I haven't tried it yet."

"Are you sure, Len?"

"I think so. Why?"

"Because I met you on Fenton beach on the day you died except it wasn't 1965 it was 1966, I think."

Eddie still could not remember what Len's ghost had talked about and it was also soon obvious to him that Len had no recollection of the event either.

"No way, Eddie. The first time I saw you in the flesh was at my funeral."

Eddie shrugged his shoulders.

"As I said, it was in the future, like when I saw the old scientist and, anyway, even though you seem to be in control of your actions as a ghost, you are still a ghost."

"What do you mean?"

"I just mean that how we see ghosts is probably different from how you want to be seen. The sightings that you don't remember were meant for me alone and they may never actually happen to you. And…."

"And?"

"And there maybe more than one of you; at least three I should say!"

Eddie's sister would have shouted, 'Four!' very loudly if she had been able. Len smiled.

"That would be good, but surely I'd know what my other ghosts were doing."

"Not necessarily, mate. Your separate apparitions could live in their own worlds, independent of each other."

"Pretty good this dying lark, eh? I can be as many people as I like now. I could even play football for Tottenham one day."

"You're not in control, Len. It's not your choice, I hope. God is in charge."

Eddie debated inwardly whether to tell his friend about the young fair-haired Tottenham reserve footballer, called L Wilton, or about his sister's possible sighting, but decided against it on both counts.

Without realising it, Eddie and his ghostly friend had been walking for a few minutes and had reached the level crossing through which they had seen the other world of the nuclear power station. Even Len didn't seem confident about crossing the railway line.

"I'd better go first, Eddie. Any real person won't be able to see me, but there might be a problem if there's another one of my species over the other side. Wait for about a minute before you come."

Eddie waited until Len had reached the other side of the railway line and he was relieved when he didn't seem to have disappeared from view. Eddie timed a minute on his watch and then ventured across too. Immediately he reached the other side the weather and time of day changed completely. It was twilight and icy cold; the ground was frost-covered. Eddie's watch still read five past ten. Len was nowhere to be seen. A man in a white coat was approaching and Eddie feared who it would be. Dr Leonard Wilby looked the same as he had the last time Eddie had seen him. He said more or less the same thing too.

"I'm sorry but you can't come any further. This area is restricted."

This time Eddie did not turn and run.

"Hello, Len."

"Do I know you, young man?"

"It's Eddie – Eddie Compton. We both lived in Fenton-on-Sea when we were boys."

Dr Wilby frowned.

"Eddie Compton, you say? Why yes, I do remember you before we moved to Kent and I…."

Eddie was excited. This was a new twist.

"Really? What do you remember?"

"Well, let me see. I remember you were clever at school and I also seem to remember something very strange happened to us, but I just can't…."

Dr Wilby again didn't finish. Suddenly he shook violently and looked to be about to shout or scream something but a flash of bright light hid his body from Eddie for a fleeting moment. Almost at once the normal twilight returned. Dr Wilby had gone and Len was standing in front of Eddie.

"Hi, Eddie. Where've you been?"

"I followed you straightaway but you'd disappeared."

"I only went about a hundred yards up the road. When I turned round, you seemed to be talking to thin air, so I came back to see what you were doing. Who *were* you talking to?"

"You!"

"Me?"

"Yes – Dr Leonard Wilby. It was like before at the nuclear power station and it was winter."

Eddie looked round as he was speaking. It was a beautiful autumn morning.

"I think you're beginning to see ghosts, Eddie!" said Len's ghost.

"I have three words for you, comrade Len."

"What?"

"Pot, kettle and black."

Len grinned widely.

"You mean the old scientist was me?"

"Yes, I suppose he must have been another of your ghosts, but in forty or fifty years time. Both times I've seen him, he spoke with your voice, only older."

"Why don't I know anything about it?"

"Because it hasn't happened yet. I was just given a glimpse into the future, like we looked into the past when we saw old Granty and it was about 1910. Obviously at some point in the future you will decide that you fancy being a nuclear scientist."

Len seemed to be satisfied with Eddie's explanation.

"I'd rather be a footballer!"

Eddie smiled.

"Anyway," Len continued. "I came here to see if we could find Mr Aloyisious Grant."

"Why, in particular?"

"He's the only other ghost that I might be able to talk to in this locality. He didn't die much before I did; it would only be about eighteen months ago. The only other ghost is Mr Manders and he must have been dead for a hundred years."

"Have you not seen your dad yet, then?" asked Eddie.

"No. I don't want him to be a ghost. I don't fancy him haunting me."

Eddie didn't know whether to laugh or cry. He thought he might have touched a nerve with Len. He tried to look on the funny side.

"How can one ghost haunt another ghost? I thought you were all supposed to belong to the same union."

Len's reaction told Eddie immediately that ghosts didn't have the same emotions as their human counterparts.

"I'm just a beginner at this game, mate, so I don't have the same feelings as you. I don't feel sad that my dad's dead and he doesn't haunt me. I only have good memories of him."

After their discussion on the behaviour and characteristics of ghosts, Eddie and Len decided to recross the railway line; there was no sign of anyone else in sight on their side of the crossing – whether human or not. As they walked back to the platform at Linham Junction, Len had some bad news.

"We have a problem that I forgot to mention to you, Eddie."

"Oh yeah?"

"Yes – when I checked the times of the trains that actually stop here on a Saturday, I found that there isn't another one until three-thirty this afternoon and that still goes to Hamsden."

"So have we got to wait until then to get to Hamsden?" asked Eddie.

"We? I don't have to wait to get anywhere, mate!"

Eddie thought for a moment.

"Do you reckon you could get us both to Hamsden, Len?"

"How?"

"What about you trying to think us there?"

Len stopped walking. They had reached the isolated station at Linham Junction.

"I suppose so, but I'm not sure what I can do though."

"Just think of Hamsden."

"Unfortunately, Eddie, I don't think like real people. I can't plan things in my mind. I can only concentrate on things that are right in front of me. Everything else is a bit of a haze."

"Do you remember Hamsden?"

"Vaguely. What did we do there?"

"Went shopping when we couldn't get what we wanted in Fenton."

Len screwed up his ghostly face trying to remember. Eddie thought of something.

"Your dad bought his new car from Richard Jones' Cars in Hamsden."

Though Len hadn't been with his parents when they had purchased the doomed vehicle, it did seem to jog something in Len's ghostly brain.

"I remember a big shop, Eddie. I think it was called Osborne's. I bought some toys from there once when I was small. Is there a shop called that in Hamsden?"

Eddie smiled and said,

"Yes. It's the biggest department store there. All you've got to do is th…."

But Len had already been thinking of it and suddenly they were pitched into darkness. Eddie would remember later that he'd had the distinct feeling that someone or something had touched his arm. A second later and light returned, albeit of a subtly different kind. It was man-made. Eddie looked round; he was inside a department store.

Once his eyes had adjusted to the shop lighting, Eddie focused properly on his new surroundings. Len didn't seem to be with him. Had

392

he made the trip? He walked a few paces towards a shop counter; it was the toy department. Suddenly he heard a familiar voice.

"Hello, Eddie. It is you, isn't it?"

Eddie didn't at first look in the direction of the voice; it wasn't the kind of thing that Len would have said given they had only just been together a minute or two earlier.

"Thought it was. How are you, mate?"

Eddie turned and looked to his left. It was Len, but this version seemed to be two or three years older.

"Len?"

"Yes – who did you think it was?"

"I don't know. It's just that you look much older than when I last saw you."

"I'm seventeen now."

Eddie relaxed when he heard the word 'now'. It was another of his friend's ghostly guises come back to haunt him.

"Where did you just come from?" asked Eddie cautiously.

"I don't know. My mind's a blank, mate."

Another voice entered the conversation.

"Who *are* you talking to, Eddie?"

Eddie turned to his right. It was the familiar version of his best friend. There stood Len's younger ghost dressed as he had been when they had been at Linham Junction. Len's older ghost then said,

"What did you say, Eddie?"

Eddie didn't turn back and answered the first question.

"You're not going to believe this but I've just been talking to another version of you, but he's older. Look behind me, Len."

Len peered past his friend's shoulder and said,

"There's no one there, Captain – at least no one that could be me. Not a nice one anyway."

Eddie turned round. The older Len was still standing in the same position. He was waiting for an answer to *his* question and then it dawned on Eddie. Neither ghost could see the other! Eddie turned back to the younger Len.

"Just a moment, Len."

Eddie turned away from his friend.

"Go away, please, I'm busy."

"Oh, don't be like that, Eddie; I'm your friend."

"No you're not, you're a bad ghost."

"You think so, eh? I'll show you how bad I can be; just wait and see."

The 'evil' ghost vanished instantly. Eddie knew he had guessed right. You couldn't have two 'good' ghosts – evil always opposed good.

"What was that all about, mate?" queried Len.

"Although you couldn't see him, there was another ghost, but I knew he wasn't you. He just looked how you might have looked if you were about seventeen."

By now, quite a few people had witnessed Eddie's odd behaviour as he constantly turned left and right and talked to empty air. The young lady assistant behind the counter said,

"Are you alright?"

"Oh yes, just talking to myself. Sorry! Couldn't make up my mind which way to go."

Eddie didn't know it but he had been fortunate that the shop assistant had been too far away to hear exactly what he'd said. She, of course, had not seen nor heard anyone else.

The 'real' Len had already moved some distance away from Eddie and he beckoned to him to join him. Once Eddie was out of earshot of anyone else who might have heard his weird and one-sided conversation, Len said,

"I think that bloke over there heard some of what you said and he's talking to one of the shop security staff."

"It wouldn't have made much sense to him," said Eddie.

"Exactly! All the more reason for him to get you certified insane! Let's get out of here."

Once they were outside and hidden in the anonymity of the Saturday shoppers, Eddie spoke in some detail about his conversation with Len's 'bad' ghost. Len had a theory to explain its existence.

"We're all made up of a good side and a bad side, mate. I'm the ghost of my good side, but somewhere out there there's a ghost who represents my bad side. Stick we me, Captain."

"Don't worry, comrade; I will. I sent the other one packing."

Len looked tired as though the morning's events had taken a lot out of him.

"Good show, Eddie. I'll have to go now; I'm tired, but I'll see you again soon."

Before Eddie had a chance to say anything, Len became a blur in the crowd of shoppers. He had gone. Eddie looked at his watch and he couldn't really believe his eyes. It was ten past two.

Eddie still saw the game at Freeman Street after he had grabbed a bite to eat consisting of a pie and chips ate at a café next to the ground. Town lost 2-1, but Eddie's spirits were not dampened after his earlier excitement. However, in the train on the way home, a couple of thoughts came to him which were not altogether pleasant. Firstly, what *could* the

395

'evil' ghost do to him when he'd promised to show him how bad he could be? Though this was frightening and disconcerting enough, the second thought hardly bore thinking about. What if Len's younger ghost was actually the bad ghost and the seventeen-year-old version was the good one?

13

Return to Petersgate

Over the next few days, Eddie began to realise the enormity of what Len had been able to do with his instant space travel, even though it had only been about six miles. Of course, such a thing was not new to Eddie, or Len, but when it had happened before both of them had been alive. Now, Len didn't exist and he himself, who did, had accompanied him!

The autumn half-term arrived on Friday, October the 29th and Eddie had been looking forward to it with some anticipation. Would his friend pay him another visit? What had he been doing in the time since the Hamsden trip? Nothing had happened at school – no ghostly classmates sitting beside him or meeting him on the way home. By the Saturday morning, Eddie began to put his own plans into operation, starting with some homework up until lunch, because of the weather and because his sister was out with her boyfriend, Gary, so the house would not be blaring with loud music. That would be followed, in the afternoon, by a trip to Hamsden with his dad to buy a new car. Fred Compton's green Morris Minor 1000 had finally all but given up the ghost. It had hardly been used since late August when Eddie's dad had first made the decision to get rid of the rust bucket. Fred Compton didn't like spending money, especially large amounts, and his slowness in making the decision mirrored this reluctance.

So it was that, at a little after two, Eddie and his dad climbed into VAP 205 and headed for Richard Jones' showroom in Hamsden.

"What are we going to get, Dad," asked Eddie as they crawled onto the A132 at all of thirty-five miles an hour.

"Don't know, son. Let's see what he's got first. I'm not buying today."

Eddie knew he had to persuade his dad to change that decision before they reached Hamsden – he was sure that his mum had been keen for him to accompany his dad for the very reason that she knew that her husband would be reluctant to come to a decision. Eddie had to push his dad into a deal that day and no later.

"We'll be lucky to get this old girl to the showroom, Dad."

"It'll get there – it's never let me down yet."

Eddie stared to put the pressure on. Emotional blackmail could be the key.

"We don't want to have an accident though, like…."

Eddie's dad didn't reply at first. He knew what his son had been about to say. Eventually he said,

"That happened because they were going too fast. This thing struggles to get to fifty now."

"Precisely, Dad. Sometimes you need a bit of speed to get out of situations that have been caused by someone else's bad driving."

"Maybe, Eddie. You seem to know a lot about driving a car given you don't drive one."

Eddie thought he had done enough. He didn't want to antagonise his dad further. He said nothing more until his dad pulled the car onto the forecourt of Richard Jones' Cars. He made up a little white lie.

"He had some nice cars in the other Saturday when I came with…."

Eddie suddenly felt himself sweating.

"Who did you come with last time, Eddie?"

"Oh, I just met Tom Dunn on the way to the match and we stopped to look in the window."

Eddie's dad seemed satisfied and they got out of the old Morris. Eddie breathed an inward sigh of relief. Mr Richard Jones seemed surprised to see Fred and his son.

"Good morning, Fred. Jenny's gone out with Gary for the day, I'm afraid, if you were looking for her. She didn't say you'd be coming."

"No, Richard – She'd probably forgotten. We've come to look for a car."

"Well, it's the end of the month so you've come at the right time if you want a good deal. It's about time you got rid of that old banger of yours. It'll soon be a vintage motor. What are you looking for?"

"Oh, I don't know. What have you got? I don't want anything similar to what you sold Cyril Wilby."

"No, I quite understand, but the tragic accident was nothing to do with the car. It was mechanically sound and tested. I had the Kent police round, you know. They told me that the brakes had worked as well as they could, given the speed the car had been doing. They can tell that from the skid marks."

"Yes, I know, Richard. You cannot possibly hold yourself to blame in any way, but I would prefer something not quite as fast or sporty."

"O.K., Fred. Let me see what I can show you."

Richard Jones walked over to the back of the showroom.

"Here we are – this might suit you. It's a two-tone Hillman Minx; 1600 hundred engine; top speed about seventy-eight and it's only just a year old with less than 10,000 on the clock. Nice ember-red and cream."

Since Eddie had been walking directly behind his dad and Mr Jones, he saw the car last, but it wasn't the car that caught his eye first. Sitting on the bonnet was Len's good ghost. He smiled when he saw Eddie and put a finger to his lips. Eddie wandered to look at another car while Len followed. Out of earshot Len said quickly,

"I'll see you tonight in your bedroom, about nine."

Immediately he had finished this instruction, he disappeared and Eddie strolled nonchalantly back to the two men.

"Seen something else, young Eddie?" asked Mr Jones.

"No, I think the Hillman looks nice."

An hour later and Comptons senior and minor were on their way back to Fenton-on-Sea; all the paperwork had been completed and Eddie's dad would take delivery of his new Hillman in about a week. He had spent more than he had wanted to but not more than he had budgeted for at worst. His son seemed preoccupied on the return journey.

"You're quiet, Eddie. Didn't you like the car?"

"Sorry, Dad. What did you say?"

"I said: did you not like the car?"

"Oh yes, Dad. I was just thinking of something else."

Eddie's dad did not pursue his questioning. He had learned over the previous weeks not to disturb his son's 'quiet moments' since the loss of his best friend.

It was eight-thirty and Eddie had made the excuse that he wanted to do some reading in his bedroom. Both his parents fully understood his need to have his own space and not only because he still missed Len, but also because it was a natural phase of growing up. In future, he would very rarely spend Saturday evenings watching television with his mum and dad.

At ten to the hour, he locked his door and sat on his bed. Which Len would appear? He needn't have worried as Len's younger version arrived dead (?) on cue at nine o'clock. Eddie had been standing looking out of his window at the night sky and, when he turned back, there was his friend sitting on his bed, grinning like a Cheshire cat.

"Very punctual, comrade," said Eddie.

"I don't have a watch, mate. It would appear that my good half can dictate precisely when I should become visible. I've told you before that nothing happens to me between such visitations. I just move from one to the next. It's an easy life."

"So what do you want, Len?"

"I've come to ask a favour of you."

"How on earth can I help you?"

"I want you to come on another trip with me – only a slightly longer one this time."

"Where?"

"Petersgate. I want to go and see my mum."

Eddie looked a little puzzled.

"I thought you said you didn't have feelings."

"I don't, at least not in the same way as you, but I just want to see how she's getting on. She lost her husband and her only son after all."

"Why do you need me to come, Len?"

"There are two reasons. Firstly, you're my best friend and secondly, I'd like you to see my new house and garden."

Eddie nearly said, 'I've seen the garden', but instead replied,

"Alright, I'll come. When did you have in mind?"

"How about next Saturday, whatever date that will be?"

"It'll be the 6th of November."

"November? And here's me thinking it was still summer."

"You mean you don't know what month it is?"

"No, as I said, I move from event to event. Time has no relevance. It just stands still and I can't get older unless my good side needs me to

401

for some purpose or other. Right now I'm the still the same age as you, but maybe I'll be older in the future."

"I've already seen a couple of older versions of you, one of which still worries me."

"Which one?"

"The seventeen-year-old evil version I met in Osborne's."

"Don't worry about him; I can deal with him. I'll show him how bad I can be too."

Something jogged Eddie's memory but before he had time to remember, Len said,

"Got to go; I'm tired. See you next Saturday. Be ready at nine outside the station."

Len's image vanished in a blur. Eddie sat down on the bed. It felt cold. He was trembling. Eddie cast his mind back to the Saturday that he and 'Len' had been at Osborne's in Hamsden. The other ghost had said more or less the same thing as his friend had just said: '*I'll show you how bad I can be*'. Worse than that, thought Eddie, the good Len had added the word 'too', which meant that Len's good ghost had at least heard the bad one and probably must have seen him too, despite his denial. The good Len had lied which meant that he might not be….

Eddie was understandably cautious when he met Len on the following Saturday and, during the week before, he'd already made the decision that he would not go anywhere with Len until he had asked him about his apparent lie. Len seemed to know that something was on Eddie's mind.

"Good morning, Eddie. You look a bit worried."

They stood together on the station forecourt and Eddie said,

"I don't think you were quite truthful about not seeing your evil ghost in Osborne's."

Len smiled guiltily.

"I know I wasn't mate."

"Why not?"

"Because, at the time, I didn't know what *you'd* seen and heard. I didn't want you being scared so I hoped you would just think it was a trick or something."

Eddie wasn't convinced.

"But why didn't you say something afterwards, instead of pretending you hadn't seen him?"

"I did, Eddie. I tried to explain who the other ghost might have been. Remember, I'm as new to this game as you are. It was as much of a shock to me to see an older me standing behind you! I'm sorry I didn't say I'd seen him; I was scared too, you know. I just wanted to get away and think, like, I expect, you did this week."

Eddie began to relax; his friendly ghost's explanation seemed to be plausible. It was a difficult thing to know if a ghost was lying when they didn't exist in the first place!

Len had already turned away but not towards the station as Eddie imagined he would do. Instead, he seemed to float out of the forecourt and back up the High Street. Eddie followed but had difficulty in keeping up. Where was his friend going? He just about managed to keep him in sight until, at last, he realised where the ghost was bound. Eddie slowed to a walk and caught up with Len outside his old house in Lime Tree Avenue.

"What have you come here for?" asked Eddie as he reached his friend who was leaning against number 7. "You didn't live here when you died, you know."

Eddie thought for a moment that his friend had had a memory lapse, but Len soon corrected him.

"I know, stupid, but I thought I'd like to see my old house first. It's been painted, you know."

"I didn't – I haven't been up here since you left. What are we going to do now? It's getting a bit awkward for me just loitering outside your old house."

"I need to try and focus on my mum and being here helps. Strangely enough, I can't really remember what she looks like. I just have a sense of her – a warm feeling inside."

Len looked wistfully up to the window of what had been his parents' bedroom and suddenly Eddie was blinded by a flash of bright white light. A second later and normal daylight returned. He found himself standing in the familiar garden in Petersgate. It took a few seconds for his eyes to adjust back to the light which was provided by the weak autumn sunshine. The garden looked a little unkempt since the last time he had seen it after the funerals. Eddie began walking towards the house where he presumed Len had gone after he had arrived. He got to within ten yards of the lounge window when he spotted the back door begin to open. Not knowing who it would be, he dived for cover behind a holly bush to his left. It was Martha Wilby and she was heading for what looked like a small shed at the side of the garden behind him. He knew that he would never be able to explain his sudden appearance in her garden so as she passed him, he dived the other way and made for the open door. He prayed that he could find the front door and that it would open quickly and easily. Fortunately the back door led into the kitchen whose other door opened onto the hall. A couple of seconds later and he flung himself at the front door and into the small front garden beyond. There was still no sign of Len and he was getting nervous. He completed his escape by walking nonchalantly down the front path and out into the road. Nobody seemed to be about in The Park. He crossed over the road and waited outside number 24 where, to his relief, he could stand beside a telephone box without drawing attention to himself. Where was Len? Had he gone into the house? Another possibility was forming in Eddie's mind. Had Len reached Petersgate at all?

After five minutes, a female resident from number 26 came to use the phone. Eddie strolled away until he was about fifty yards from the box but still able to see number 23. At first, he didn't see Len emerge from Martha's house. He just seemed to appear in the front garden as though he'd been spirited there from somewhere else. Eddie tried to attract his attention without causing a disturbance of any kind. Len saw him and started to walk across the road. He looked happy. He got half-way and a passing cyclist rode straight through him. Len didn't deviate from his original course and reached Eddie completely unscathed.

"A man on a cycle rode right through you, Len," said Eddie once they had been reunited.

"Didn't feel a thing, mate."

"Where've you been?" asked a relieved Eddie.

"Well, when I arrived here I found myself in mum's lounge and she was sitting on the sofa. She must have sensed something. I think she may have felt I was there, you know, Eddie. She kept looking nervously round the room and eventually she went out the back door and into the garden. When she came back she was carrying an old piece of wood and she proceeded to search the room as though she was looking for a ...."

"Looking for what?"

"A mouse or something, I suppose. A couple of times she seemed to pass right through me and, Eddie, I could smell her perfume. I'm sure of it."

"I expect she mistook your presence for the type of noise a small animal would make. You could be right, mate," agreed Eddie. "What did you do then?"

"After she had decided that there was no mouse, she sat back on the sofa and carried on with her knitting. It was just like old times, Eddie, and she looked happy and content. The house looks tidy and well-cared for. She's going to be alright, Eddie. I'm so pleased."

"Did you go anywhere else in the house?"

"I went into my bedroom and she's changed it. It's just a spare room now and she's got her sewing machine in there too."

"Doesn't that make you sad, Len?"

"No it doesn't. It means Mum is beginning to get over her losses and is starting a new life. That makes me happy."

Eddie looked sad and uneasy.

"Come on, cheer up, Eddie. Death's not the end of the world! Let me show you a bit of Petersgate before I spirit us back to Fenton-on-Sea. How long have you got today?"

"I'd like to be back by lunchtime; Dad's collecting his new car this afternoon and I'm supposed to be going with him and Mum."

"No problem. What's the time now?"

Eddie looked at his watch.

"Five past ten."

"Excellent – we should have plenty of time to see the sights."

As usual, Len took the lead out of The Park and he headed initially for the beach via a series of side streets that ran off the Canterbury road. He seemed to float over the ground and Eddie again had some difficulty in keeping up. Petersgate didn't have a promenade as such, Eddie discovered; the road was bordered by a low sea wall with a pebbly beach on the other side. Eddie soon noticed something else too – the smell.

"What's that horrible smell?" he asked as he peered over the sea wall. Len replied,

"The seaweed. Dad said it would be good as a fertiliser for the garden. They clear it in the summer months, but it's left to just rot this time of the year, unless a storm or high tide washes it away."

Eddie looked out to sea and then said,

"Fenton-on-Sea is over there; nothing but sea between here and there."

Half an hour later and Len had led Eddie to Petersgate Grammar School in Front Street. Eddie was obviously impressed with the old buildings.

"Looks posh, Len."

"Maybe from the outside; it was alright inside. At least the Head, Mr Crompton seemed to be nicer than old 'Hempers'.

Eddie looked at the Head's name on the board outside the main gate; so similar to his own. Was it just a coincidence? Len broke his thoughts.

"Well there we are, I never actually got to go here, mate, but Mr Crompton came to my funeral. That was good of him, wasn't it?"

"Yes, it was," said Eddie. "We ought to be getting on if you're going to show me anything else."

"Just the town and the cemetery at St Michael's where Dad and I are buried. I can show you my grave. Won't that be spooky?"

"No," said Eddie with a grimace.

They walked quickly down into the town which, though more compact than Fenton, seemed to Eddie to have more and a greater variety of shops. Just for fun, Eddie bought a souvenir postcard of Petersgate to take home with him. Len wasn't happy with his friend's purchase.

"You shouldn't do that, you know."

"Why not?"

"Because you don't seem to realise that today's trip with me can't be real in your earthly sense. You were spirited here with a ghost, mate!"

"I just want to see if the postcard stays with me when I get home or whether it disappears."

"It'll vanish. Don't you worry about that."

"We'll see," said Eddie with a smile.

The visit to St Michaels' church cemetery seemed to be more poignant and sad to Eddie than to his friendly ghost, who, on arrival, said nonchalantly,

"That's where I am, Captain. Dad's next to me."

Simple named and dated gravestones had been erected above the grassed mounds. Eddie felt a cold shiver go up his back as he glanced at his friend. Len seemed to be struggling to stay upright. Suddenly, he toppled forward and became a blur that hovered horizontally above the grave and then vanished completely. Eddie shouted involuntarily,

"Come back! Len, come back!"

Eddie looked round anxiously. The small church cemetery was empty of anybody else, human or otherwise. He wandered frantically round and round Len's grave murmuring,

"Oh God, he's gone back into his coffin. Oh God!"

He stopped his manic movement. He tried to calm down and think about the situation logically. Immediately he remembered his own words that he'd spoken to his friend on a previous occasion when they had been discussing the philosophical side of the behaviour of ghosts. In his mind he repeated some of what he'd said.

'You're not in control, Len ... God is in charge'.

Eddie felt both reassured and totally distraught. How was he to get back home? What could he say about where he'd been? God had taken Len back to his grave and he alone knew when he would release him again. They had tampered with things beyond their comprehension and this was the result – his worst nightmare. What could he do? Then a thought came to him. He had to pray to God, even though he'd never really believed in him, apart from the times, often before Christmas, when he'd wished in his mind for the present he really wanted. Was that prayer? He could remember vaguely the Reverend Weaver saying something about having faith and belief in God if you prayed. You had to truly believe that God, and only God, could answer your prayers. Eddie fell to his knees. He had always really known that it had been God that had shown him and Len all the fantastic things they had seen. He *did* believe even though he would find it difficult to admit it to anyone else, but he did, there and then, admit it to himself.

"Oh God, I do believe that you can bring Len back and help me to get home. Please help me. I know you're the only one I can turn to. I put my trust in you. Amen."

"What *are* you doing, mate?"

Len's voice echoed in Eddie's head. He opened his eyes and looked to his right. There, towering over him, was Len.

"Oh, thank God! I thought you'd gone back into your grave."

Len looked bemused.

"I don't know what happened. It just went black for a moment as if I was moving to my next appearance like before. Then I found myself standing on Fenton beach and you were kneeling beside me."

Having had his eyes closed while he had made his supplication, Eddie hadn't really been conscious of his environment. He put his hand down by his knees and felt wet sand. He stood up and looked all around him. Len was right. It was Fenton-on-Sea beach and they were right by the pier. He looked at his watch. It was twelve-thirty. 'Thank God', he thought. 'Len had come back'.

"Oh that was really scary, Len," he said.

Len did not reply. He was nowhere in sight.

14

A Shared Secret

Eddie just managed to get home by one o'clock and after a quick lunch he joined his mum and dad for the ride to Hamsden to change their car. Once again his dad commented on his quietness.

"Are you alright, son? What did you get up to this morning?"

"Not much, just a long walk on the promenade and a bit of shopping in Hamsden."

"What did you buy?" asked his mum.

"Nothing much, but I did find an old postcard shop and they had one of Petersgate which I bought for two shillings – a bit expensive but it'll remind me of Len."

"Have you got it with you?"

"Yes, it's in my pocket."

Eddie knew he was pushing his luck as he hadn't bothered to see whether the postcard he'd bought in Kent was still there, but he could always say he'd lost it or left it at home. He reached in his back pocket and handed the card to his mum.

"And this cost you two shillings? It's got three pence written in pencil on the back."

"The man in the shop said it was more because it wasn't a local scene."

"Why didn't you let me ask Aunty Martha? She would have got you eight for the price you paid for this. Such a waste, Eddie."

"Yes, Mum; I just bought it on the spur of the moment, I suppose."

Eddie was even quieter on the rest of the journey to Hamsden. This was incredible – something tangible from his paranormal visit to Kent. It was scientifically impossible, but the proof was in his hands. He studied the back more closely as his dad drove onto the showroom forecourt. He was relieved that his mum had not also seen the shop's name printed in tiny lettering in the top left hand corner:

M.K.Johnson Stationers
25 Lower Front Street
Petersgate
Kent

"Come on, Eddie, you can't stay in the car. You'll end up at the scrapyard."

Mr Richard Johnson was holding the passenger door open. Eddie had been in a trance-like state for a minute or more and his parents were already on their way to the office.

"Sorry, Mr Jones. I'm just coming."

Eddie seemed to be more cheerful on the way back to Fenton in the Hillman Minx; it had been a new twist to find the postcard still in his pocket and it was exciting. He couldn't wait to tell Len. Reality and fantasy had, once again, become intertwined. However, his active mind was telling him that there could also be a serious and frightening problem with that concept. There might be a possibility that fantasy could take over completely and he would end up in the same world as his dead friend, with no way back. It had nearly done that in Kent. His wanderings were broken by his dad, who said,

"Do you like the car, Eddie?"

"Yes, it's very comfortable in the back – much more room than the old one."

"Good. It'll have to last us a good few years."

"Are you going to let Jenny learn to drive in it, Dad?"

"I don't know yet. Has she said to you that she wants to drive? She never seems to be interested in cars, not since the accident anyway. Now that Gary's got his licence back, there probably isn't the need and not many girls of her age do drive in any case."

"Would you teach her, Dad?"

Fred Compton didn't answer. Eddie's mum did.

"I don't think your dad would be very good with her. She'll have to save for lessons if she wants to learn."

A few minutes later and Fred Compton drove his new car, almost proudly, onto the drive at number 38. It was just after four. While his dad pottered about checking out his new possession in more detail, Eddie spent the rest of the afternoon watching Grandstand on television. After tea, he repaired to his bedroom to do some reading and more thinking about the momentous events of that morning. His quiet cogitation was disturbed at a little after six by a knock on his door. After a brief pause while he hid the postcard under the bed covers, he shouted,

"Come in!"

Expecting his mum, who had taken to checking on his welfare at regular intervals since Len's death, he was surprised to see his sister standing timidly in the doorway.

"Can I come in, Eddie?"

"Ye-yes," he stammered. "What's up?"

"I want to talk to you."

Eddie looked nervous and slightly embarrassed at the same time.

"What about, Jenny?"

"About you."

"Me? I'm alright. If Mum's sent you to see how I am coping without Len, I'm fine."

Jenny had already sat on the bed next to her brother.

413

"Mum doesn't know I've come to talk to you. She and Dad have gone for a ride in the car."

Eddie's embarrassment changed totally to nervousness. His sister only ever talked to him if she either had a favour to ask or she wanted to tease him.

"I've got something to tell you that's been bothering me for ages."

Eddie got more nervous. Jenny continued.

"You remember when I told you about meeting the young sailor on the bus to Hamsden?"

Eddie knew what was coming. He had spent many moments thinking about what his sister had said before when she'd met the sailor. He'd guessed at the time that the sailor had been Len's ghost but had put the incident to the back of his mind and there it had stayed until a little while after his friend's death. He still hadn't mentioned it to Len's ghost. He knew that Jenny had been forewarned of something that would make him sad and in need of her care and love. He'd even thought that he should have told Len about it before he had died, but what could he have said? The sailor hadn't mentioned Len; it could have been anything that would mean the Eddie would need looking after. Jenny was getting impatient while her brother seemed to be in a dream.

"Well, do you remember?"

"Yes, of course I do. What about it?"

"I think the sailor knew that something tragic was going to happen to you, Eddie, and he was warning me about it. Do you think he knew that …?"

"Knew what?"

"Knew that Len was going to die."

Eddie said nothing.

"Well, do you?"

414

"How on earth could he know? He was just a sailor, wasn't he?"

It was Jenny's turn to be silent before she said,

"I think he was more than just a sailor. I think I know who he was, Eddie."

Eddie tried to look surprised.

"Who?"

"Len."

Eddie said nothing. What could he say? He wasn't about to 'spill the beans' on the whole story. He was cautious.

"What makes you think that?"

"Because I think I remembered his voice. It sounded like an older version of your friend. Could it have been a ...?"

"What?"

"A ghost?"

"Do you believe in ghosts, then, Jenny?"

"I'm not sure, but what other explanation could there be? He knew me; he knew I had a brother and he knew that soon you'd need my love and care. If it was Len's ghost, could he have known that he was going to die?"

"You're making several assumptions, Jenny."

"Maybe, but I'm convinced it was Len."

Eddie couldn't hold back any longer.

"I've seen him since his death, you know."

"*Seen* him!?"

Eddie hesitated. Had he said too much? He qualified his statement.

"In my dreams, I suppose. I can sense also him during the day sometimes. I talk to him."

"Does he talk to you?"

"I'm not sure. Maybe I pretend that he does. Have you seen him or the sailor since?"

"No, I don't think so. I just feel …."

"Feel what?"

"I just feel maybe I could have done something or told someone, other than you – Mum, perhaps."

"When did you think or know that it was Len? Before or after he died?"

"Oh, well after. Maybe only in the last week or so."

"So, what could you have done? You didn't even have a connection to Len before he died. No one knew what was going to happen – only God."

Eddie tried to forget that he had more or less guessed that Jenny's sailor had been Len's ghost, almost from the moment she had first told him, but nothing had ever suggested itself to him that Len was going to die soon afterwards. The ghost had only made reference to Eddie himself. Jenny went on.

"Do you believe in God, then, Eddie?"

"Yes, I do. Do you?

"I'm not sure, Eddie. If there was a God, how can he let all the sufferings in the world go on?"

Eddie said nothing. He didn't feel like debating such issues with his sister.

"I don't know. Have you told anyone else about your thoughts, Jenny?"

"No. Do you think I should?"

"No. We ought to keep it a secret just between ourselves. Nothing can be changed."

"I suppose you're right. Thanks for listening; at least I don't feel guilty anymore. Nobody could have foreseen Len's tragic death, could they?"

Eddie was about to say, 'God could', but he thought better of it.

Jenny leant across the bed and planted a light kiss on his forehead. He breathed an inward sigh of relief. It was their secret.

15

An Old Friend

The following day, Sunday, Eddie was persuaded to attend morning
service at St Andrew's; his discussion with Jenny had provided the
motivation and impetus to return to thoughts of God and religion. He'd
known for a long time that despite his interest in scientific rigour, other
powers existed which were beyond man's understanding. Recent events
had only served to confirm this belief – ghosts could not be man-made.

   The Reverend Henry Weaver was his usual thought-provoking self
and Eddie found himself in his element when he discovered that the
sermon for the day was concerned with the afterlife. Eddie had been
acquainted with the Christian message for years, without really taking
much interest in what it meant for him. He really could not understand
that there had to be only one way to salvation and heaven, whatever and
wherever that was. Just because someone was born in a non-Christian
country should not mean that they were doomed to hell and damnation. It
wasn't their fault that they would never be taught or discover about
Christianity. What had happened recently had convinced Eddie that the
important thing was to have a belief in God and to trust that his greater
power could solve any problem, as long as you put your trust in him.
Admitting this to oneself, Eddie believed, was the universal solution to
personal contentment and salvation. The Reverend Weaver seemed to
have elements of this in his sermon that Sunday morning and Eddie felt
comfortable in the knowledge that a learned minister of the cloth
concurred with his own beliefs. Though he'd never spoken personally to
St Andrew's respected vicar before, Eddie decided to ask him a question
as the Comptons left church. His parents had gone on ahead as he paused
to shake the Reverend Weaver's hand.

"Can I ask you something, Reverend Weaver?"

"Of course you can, Eddie. What's on your mind?"

Eddie was straight to the point with the innocence of youth.

"Are there such things as ghosts?"

"Ghosts?"

"Yes."

"Well now, that's an interesting question, my boy. Why do you ask?"

"No particular reason; I just wondered."

Henry Weaver smiled. He thought he knew why Eddie had asked the question.

"It couldn't have something to do with your recently departed friend, could it?"

Eddie looked a little embarrassed.

"Maybe – it would be nice to see him again."

"Yes, it would and you will one day, Eddie, when we return to our maker."

"I know, but is it possible to see people who have died before then, while we're still alive?"

The Reverend Weaver paused before he answered.

"I don't know, Eddie. What do you think?"

Eddie was mature enough not to reply with, 'You're the one who should know, vicar', and said instead,

"I suppose God can do anything and if he wants us to see people who are already dead, then, yes, I believe it's possible."

"I think you've answered your question. With God, all things are possible as long as we believe."

It was clear to Henry Weaver that Eddie had another question and he asked,

"Something else troubling you?"

After a few seconds, Eddie responded with,

"Can ghosts appear only to some people and not to others?"

"Anything is possible with God, Eddie."

Eddie smiled. 'If only you knew, vicar', he thought.

Fred and Ann Compton had already reached the Red Lion by the time Eddie had finished his extended conversation with Reverend Weaver. The Comptons always called in for a quick drink before Sunday lunch while their son often wandered slowly through town window-shopping. Eddie, for once, decided to take a detour down Mill Road instead of going straight back up the High Street; something he hadn't done for many months, indeed, not since Mr George Canter had owned the junk shop there. Watson's Electrical had replaced it and so it was with some surprise that Eddie discovered the shop open. Paul Watson never opened on a Sunday – he wasn't allowed to by law and he certainly wasn't supposed to trade. Eddie peered in through the window; no lights were on and there didn't seem to be anyone in the shop. Eddie pushed on the open door and went in.

"Come in, my boy. What can I do for you?"

Eddie froze. He hadn't heard that voice in over two years but he had recognised it immediately. He looked around nervously but there was no one to be seen. It was his mind playing tricks again and now he was hearing voices in his head.

"How have you been, Eddie?"

George Canter's voice was coming from behind the counter. Eddie stared at the spot straining his eyes to see if he could make out the source of the phantom sound. The shop had gone suddenly dark.

"Wait a minute, Eddie."

Eddie waited. The shop was now pitch black, making the daylight outside seem unreal. A minute passed with Eddie in complete darkness and silence, broken only by his own shallow breathing and loud heartbeat. A bright light suddenly flashed in front of him causing him to blink and jerk his head back violently. The temporary blindness took a few seconds to wear off and afterwards Eddie knew what he would see. There in front of him, less than four feet away, stood a smiling George Canter.

"Hello, Eddie."

Eddie opened his mouth but no words came out, just an incomprehensible groan.

"Yes, Eddie, it *is* me. I've been waiting for you. I just knew you would come today," said George.

"But what are you doing here? Are you…?"

"Dead?"

"Ye-ye-yes."

"Of course I am, Eddie."

"But how did you get here?"

"Oh Eddie, have you not seen some of my friends already?"

"Your friends?"

"My fellow ghosts. I thought you'd be ready to see me by now and wouldn't be too frightened or dismiss my visit as all in your mind."

Eddie was stunned again into silence. George continued.

"I've seen Len, Eddie, and Mr Grant who owned the shop at the top of Steep Hill – he likes to stay out near Linham where he passed away."

"Where did you see Len?" asked Eddie excitedly.

"He was wandering along the beach earlier this morning."

"Did he see you?"

"No, he seemed to vanish when I got close. I already knew he was dead, but God obviously didn't want us to meet just yet."

Eddie was longing to ask George how he himself had died but couldn't seem to phrase the right question. He managed instead,

"How did you know Len had died?"

"God told me about the car crash, Eddie. You didn't see me but I was at the funeral."

"I miss Len, George."

"I know you do, Eddie, but he will still come and see you whenever he's allowed, you know."

"I suppose so, it's just that…."

"What?"

"It's just that I wish sometimes I could join him."

"What, on a permanent basis?"

Eddie managed a weak grin.

"No, but just whenever I wanted to, like we always used to. I wish I could go to him for advice or just be able to talk to him."

"You will one day," said George with a soft smile. "But you can't go just yet, my boy; you've got your whole life ahead of you."

"So had Len."

"Tragic accidents happen, I'm afraid and there's nothing anyone can do about them. Only God can protect us if we believe, Eddie, and even then he allows chance to play its part in the tapestry of life."

"Do you think that Len was meant to die, then?"

"I don't know, Eddie. Was Aloyisious St John Grant meant to die in the train crash? That was just another tragic and, perhaps, unavoidable accident."

"Have you spoken to Ally – I mean, Mr Grant?"

"Just once this summer when I was allowed to come to Fenton-on-Sea for the first time since I'd left. He told me he liked to walk in the country lanes near Linham and that's what did whenever it was possible."

"Len and I saw him, George – not long after the train crash in the summer of that year. He was dressed in clothes from the early part of the century."

"You and Len were being prepared, I suspect, for you both to be able to cope with Len's tragic death."

Eddie paused. The time had come to ask the difficult question.

"George?"

"Yes? You want to know how I died, I suppose."

"Only if you want to tell me."

George spent a few minutes telling Eddie of the new life he made for himself in the Polish city of Bialystok where he had been born. He had become an antique dealer and had nearly completed his first year of training to become a part-time Rabbi at the new synagogue in the city. Then tragedy had struck. Many years of heavy drinking had caused irreparable damage to his liver and the end had been mercifully quick; just a matter of months culminating in his demise just over a year previously. Eddie listened with sadness until, when George had finished, his melancholy was relieved by his ghost saying,

"Don't be sad, Eddie; I've never felt better or more content. I've seen my parents and my sister and I have made my peace with them and with many of my Jewish friends who died in the holocaust and the burning of The Great Synagogue in Bialystok."

Eddie was about to recount some of the adventures that he and Len had been on since George had left England to go back to Poland, but it was clear that his old friend was becoming tired.

"I'll have to go now, Eddie, but I'll see you again. I will look out for you and try to make sure you don't come to any harm. Goodbye."

"Goodbye, George," replied Eddie but he found himself talking to thin air. George Canter had gone, but another voice echoed in Eddie's head.

"What do you think you are doing, Eddie Compton?"

Eddie spun round to find Mr Paul Watson, owner of Watson's Electrical standing in front of him. He was not best pleased.

"Oh, oh, the door was open, Mr Watson so I thought you ...."

"Was it, young man? That still does not give you the right just to walk in, and you know I don't sell anything on a Sunday."

"No, I'm sorry, sir. I was only looking. I thought I could see someone through the window but it must have been a trick of the light."

"Trick of the light, eh? Are you sure you weren't trying to pinch something."

Eddie looked nervous.

"Oh no, Mr Watson – I would never steal anything. I've just come from church with my mum and dad. Honestly."

Mr Watson seemed satisfied and he said,

"I only came to do some stocktaking and then for a pint. I must have forgotten to lock up behind me. It was lucky I came back for something or the shop would have been open until tomorrow morning. Actually, Eddie, I've just left your mum and dad in the Red Lion, so that checks out part of your story but you shouldn't go into private premises, open or not. Now get off home before I change my mind."

"Yes, Mr Watson."

With that, Eddie made his way out of the shop while Mr Watson disappeared into the stockroom at the back.

Eddie's mum and dad were understandably curious when he arrived home almost at the same time as they did, given that they had been in the Red Lion for over forty minutes.

"How come it's taken you until now to get home?" asked Fred Compton as Eddie joined his parents at the front gate.

"Went for a walk along the beach and then looked in a few shops."

Eddie's mum and dad seemed to accept their son's answer. They knew he often wandered off to be by himself and after a knowing look from Eddie's mum, they made their way up the front path and into the house. Once inside, it was clear that Jenny was not at home, even though her mother had left her in charge of the roast dinner. Ann Compton found a scribbled note on the kitchen table.

'*Had to go out. Won't be long. I've done all the vegetables and turned the oven off.*

Love Jenny'.

Eddie's mum was clearly puzzled.

"I wonder what's happened. Why would she go out on a Sunday morning? Gary's away for the weekend on a fire training exercise."

"That *is* odd," said Eddie's dad, "but I'm hungry and want my dinner. I hope it's not burnt."

The three Comptons had just sat down to their roast lamb dinner when the front door was heard opening and Jenny rushed into the dining room.

"Sorry I'm late. I had to do some emergency babysitting for a friend."

"What friend, dear?" asked Jenny's mum.

"Carole Wilson was looking after her brother Tommy until her mum got back from Hamsden and she had to go out. She phoned me to see if I would babysit Tommy for an hour while she went to see her boyfriend."

Eddie's mum seemed satisfied but Eddie himself knew his sister was lying. He would ask Jenny later where she had been. There was something about her demeanour, and the vague wink she'd given him when giving her explanation, which suggested her absence might have something to do with their discussion of the previous day.

This time it was Eddie who knocked on his sister's bedroom door later that afternoon. He rarely, if ever, went into Jenny's 'boudoir', as he called it. At first, his sister didn't acknowledge Eddie's quiet tapping until his persistence paid off.

"Yes, who is it?"

"Me, you dumb blond. Who did you think it was – Elvis?"

Jenny opened her door about a quarter.

"What do you want?"

"To talk."

The door opened to its full extent and Eddie walked in and sat on his sister's dressing table chair. Jenny had returned to her position propped up on her bed. Magazines lay scattered beside her and she looked as though she had been expecting her brother. Eddie was straight to the point.

"Where did you really go this morning, Jenny? Carole Wilson doesn't have a brother and you know it."

"So why didn't you give me away at lunchtime?"

"Because you winked."

Jenny leant forward on the bed and fixed her gaze on Eddie.

"I think I've seen another ghost."

"Where?"

"Here – he came to the house this morning just before twelve."

"Why did you think it was a ghost?" asked Eddie with disbelief echoing in his question.

"I'll tell you in a minute."

"Did you recognise him?"

"I think so. It looked like…."

"Who, Jenny?"

"That man who used to own the junk shop in Mill Road – Mr Canter, I think he was called. Mum said he'd gone to Poland a couple of years ago, so that's why I started thinking that he might be a ghost."

"What did he want?"

"You."

"Me?"

"Yes, he asked me where you were and I told him you'd gone to St Andrew's with Mum and Dad."

"What did he say then?"

"He just thanked me and put his hand on my arm, but …."

Eddie guessed what Jenny would say next and he helped her out.

"But you couldn't feel his touch and his hand went right through your arm."

"Yes. It was really spooky, Eddie. I was touched by a ghost."

"What did he do then?"

"He just turned round and walked down the front path. I lost sight of him when he'd gone out of the front gate. What does it all mean, Eddie?"

"I don't know."

Jenny looked close to tears and after a pause she said,

"He said something else, Eddie."

"What?"

"He said that I should keep a close eye on you and to try to make sure that you didn't get into any trouble. It felt like when Len's ghost warned me that you would need my care."

"Maybe your imagination ran away with you when you thought you were talking to a ghost," said Eddie. "Maybe you were just reminded of what Len had said because Mr Canter appeared to be that ghost. Remember, Jenny, ghosts aren't real."

"He seemed real enough to me, Eddie. Am I going mad?"

"No, you're not going mad but it still doesn't answer my question as to why you went out."

"I tried to follow him."

"And?"

"When I got to the gate I thought I could still see him in the distance and he appeared to be waiting near the end of the road. It had taken me a few minutes to write the note and get some clothes on so he must have been there a while. By the time I got to South Road he had moved again and I assumed he'd gone down the High Street. I eventually spotted him near the turning to Mill Road but when I got there he had disappeared. I wandered about for a while looking for him by which time it was getting late and I returned here."

Eddie looked pensive. He had another question.

"What time did the man you thought was Mr Canter, disappear?"

"About twenty past twelve."

'Just about the time that I left church', thought Eddie. His sister's story began to make sense. He debated whether to tell his sister of his own ghostly meeting, but decided against it. Jenny had had enough of phantom strangers for one day. Fear was etched all over her face. Their shared secret was becoming more difficult to keep too.

Later that evening Eddie began to feel sad for his old friend, George Canter. Why did have to die when he was such a nice and generous man? Eddie consoled himself in the knowledge that George had appeared to be content and had found peace in death. With Len's passing as well, death did not seem such a bad thing after all. At least two people had an air of happiness that they had not possessed when they had been alive.

16

Nightmares

Eddie spent much of that Sunday evening in his room, reading and thinking about the conversation with his sister. He realised that she had experienced as startling an encounter as he had done, and though nothing really extraordinary had happened to Jenny, she seemed fairly convinced that it hadn't been just a figment of her imagination. He knew that his sister wouldn't say anything to anyone else, for fear of being ridiculed and, perhaps with time, she would forget the whole thing. What had George meant by his warning though? In the end Eddie decided that it had probably been a natural thing for him to say because Len had died and George was concerned for Eddie's well-being in the future. He was comforted, however, by the fact that George had seen Len that morning, but disappointed that his best friend hadn't come to see him as well. By the time Eddie went to sleep, he had reconciled this omission with the knowledge that Len was not in control of his visits to the real world.

It was a gloriously sunny late autumn day and Eddie was gazing wistfully out of the window of Room 46 where he was listening to Mr Green drone on about a particularly difficult scene from the end of Henry the Fifth.

"And what does the phrase, '*stops the mouth of all find-faults*', mean, Mr Compton?"

"Sorry, sir?"

"*Stops the mouth of all find-faults.* What does Shakespeare mean, please?"

"I don't know, sir."

"Well hazard a guess, please."

Eddie tried to locate the phrase in his copy of the play but only a nudge from Sally Barber, indicating the turn of a page, helped him find the right place. Mr Green was getting angry.

"Well?"

Suddenly Eddie's world was plunged into darkness and somewhere in the distance he heard,

"I'm waiting."

Eddie's mouth wouldn't open; he was terrified, and then, in the gloom, he could just make out Mr Green bearing down on him with an ugly-looking cane in his hand. The cane was raised above his head and descended quickly in an arc with a frightening swish. Eddie ducked and fell off his seat onto the floor. Normal light returned. He heard raucous laughter from all around his prostrate position. Mr Green was still standing, arms folded, at the front of the classroom.

"You will see me at the end of the lesson, boy. Now return to your seat and sit on it properly. I'll show you later what I do with boys who don't pay attention and fall of their chairs for no apparent reason."

After the lesson had finished, Mr Green told Eddie to go and wait for him in the assembly hall where his punishment would be meted out. English, being the last class of the day meant the main hall would be empty. It was with some apprehension that Eddie walked across the upper quadrangle and into the barely-lit hall. What punishment had Mr Green in mind that entailed the use of the assembly hall? Was Eddie about to be made to read out the whole of the last act of Henry the Fifth from the stage? He opened a side door and walked into the auditorium. It was empty; not even a cleaner in sight. Eddie climbed up the three steps onto the main stage. He'd rarely been in such an elevated position during his time thus far at Fenton Grammar School. He walked to the lectern and pretended to be making a speech as if he were the Headmaster, Mr D J Hempsall. A familiar voice sounded out from somewhere behind him.

"Now we will see how we make boys like you learn to pay attention, Compton."

Eddie looked round. There was no one there. The voice continued.

"Go to the lectern, place your arms on it and make a straight back with your legs apart. You're going to feel a little pain in your backside in a minute."

Eddie had never been caned before and he was scared. Could Mr Green do this? Wasn't Mr Hempsall the only one allowed to issue such punishment? How hard would he be hit? He put himself in the position as directed by his English teacher.

"Good, now wait while I fetch my special thin cane with the metal end."

Eddie waited and he began to tremble with real fear. This sounded as if he was going to suffer some serious pain. Surely a teacher could not do this. He would show his parents the weals. It was getting darker outside and his back and sides were beginning to ache. Where was Mr Green? He glanced at his watch – it was twenty to five. How long had he been standing in this awkward position? Twenty, thirty minutes? Suddenly, he heard footsteps echo on the wooden floor behind him, to be followed by the sound of a cane being swished through the air. He began to cry. He'd never ever been this scared before. He could feel Mr Green's hot breath on his neck. His English master put his face against Eddie's ear and said,

"Now it won't hurt too much provided you keep absolutely still and don't turn round. Prepare yourself. One, two, three ...."

Eddie braced himself for the first blow. He heard the cane make its arc through the air. He screamed.

"No, oh please, no!"

The cane must have missed because Eddie felt no pain. He waited for a second attempt but now there was silence apart from his own heavy breathing and intermittent sobbing. He tried to turn round but his body was rigid with fear and seemed to be locked in position. Eventually, he prised himself upright and turned his head. Mr Green was nowhere to be seen. The voice echoed throughout the hall.

"Hope that scared you, Mr Compton. Please pay attention in my lessons in future. Now, go home."

After a few moments while he regained his composure, Eddie made to leave the stage to go home. He decided there and then that he wouldn't mention Mr Green's sick idea of a school punishment to his parents. His dad would only have said that he deserved it and what were a few tears to complain about anyway? Eddie knew that what Mr Green had done was not ethical, but he had learned his lesson – he would pay attention from then on. He jumped down off the stage and made for the door. It was locked. He walked to the back of the hall and attempted to open both of the only other two exit doors. They were securely locked. The school assembly hall had windows but they were high up and all looked tightly closed. He looked at his watch – it was ten past five, but it seemed later judging by the darkness of the sky which was visible through the windows above him. He shouted,

"Help! Help! I'm locked in!"

Surely not everyone had gone home. He began to panic as he ran to the first door again and shook it violently. Then the horrible thought took hold – he could be locked in until morning when the cleaners would be the first to open up the hall. His parents would be worried by now. Would they think to come and find him? How would they know where he was anyway? Would they know who to contact? Eddie sat down on a chair and cried out loud,

"Please, someone help me! Help my mum and dad find me."

Minutes passed and it had become almost pitch black in the hall. His panic got worse as he put his head in his hands. He tried shouting again.

"Oh God, please help me! Please, please help me!"

"It's alright, Eddie, just wake up."

Light beamed into his face as he opened his eyes. He was in bed and his mum, in her nightdress, was standing over him. It had been a nightmare. He sat up with a jerk and wiped the cold sweat from his brow. His mum sat down on his bed and said soothingly.

"You've had a bad dream, Eddie, that's all. You've been shouting for a few minutes and woke us all up."

"What did I say, Mum?"

"Couldn't hear or understand most of it, but you were obviously in some sort of trouble. What was the nightmare all about?"

Eddie tried to recall his dream but nothing would come back – just a vague impression that it had been something to do with school. By morning he would discover that even that fleeting memory would have gone from his head. He would remember later, however, that he had had a bad nightmare that seemed to have drained the very life out of him. He hoped he would not have another one very quickly. His mother left the landing light on for the rest of that night and his bedroom door ajar. The emotional exhaustion eventually forced him into a dreamless sleep until morning.

All was not well for Eddie at school the next day. He felt lethargic and he was troubled by the restless night he'd had – he still had no memory of the bad dream. He couldn't concentrate on his favourite subjects, Maths and Science, in the morning and, by the afternoon English lesson with Mr Green, all he really wanted to do was to go home and sleep. Something about his English master's demeanour told him that he was not pleased with his latest essay on Henry the Fifth that was due back that afternoon. Mr Green took great pleasure in handing individual pieces of work back to his pupils with the inevitable cutting remark even if the recipient had produced a superb essay. Eddie didn't have to wait long; his essay was the fourth to be discussed.

"Well, Compo, I'm afraid you have excelled yourself this time. It certainly isn't your usual rubbish."

Eddie gave a relieved smile.

"No, Mr Compton, it's better than that. This time it's utter and complete rubbish. Well done! You'd better see me at the end of the lesson."

Mr Green flung Eddie's exercise book onto his desk but he hardly noticed it. His memory had been jogged as unrelated pieces of his nightmare began to come back to him. He had been in Mr Green's lesson then, he was sure of it. But what had happened? He knew it hadn't been pleasant but he just couldn't remember the detail. He had an hour to wait for his punishment for the terrible essay. He was tired and wanted to get home to sleep. Fortunately, Mr Green left him well alone for the rest of the lesson, a good part of which was spent on the other twenty-three recipients of his English teacher's caustic remarks. His own essay appeared to have been by far the worst.

At four o'clock by his watch, Eddie found himself once again standing on the assembly hall stage; though this time it had to be for real. Mr Green had told him to go straight to the hall after the end of his lesson. He had remembered most of his nightmare from the moment he had entered the poorly-lit building. The situation presented to him, however, was far worse than his dream. Not only did he know what was coming, but he also knew that this time there would be no rescue by his mum out of the nightmare. He had remembered from the previous night that he had been locked in the hall and, though the memory was vague, he recalled being in a blind panic and shouting for help. Panic began to set in again as he sat forlornly on the sole chair on the stage. Frightening thoughts entered his brain. Was his current situation real or had he been plunged into another nightmare? How could he tell reality from fantasy?

Half an hour passed by his watch and Mr Green did not appear. Was this to be his punishment – a silent detention? After another five minutes, he decided that he had enough; this wasn't fair. Half expecting the door to be locked he made for the exit. To his relief it opened easily and he emerged into the twilight. Immediately his feet sank into something soft and cold. It had been snowing and heavily. But it was only early November and, though it had been a cold day, snow was definitely not forecast. Eddie trudged forward and, once his eyes had adjusted to the pure-white surroundings, he looked around himself. Terror and panic set in simultaneously. He wasn't in the upper quadrangle or anything like it. He looked back over his shoulder. The assembly hall had disappeared! Whichever way he looked, the landscape was an unbroken panorama of white. He was in an enormous flat snowfield that stretched to the horizon in all directions. No landmarks were visible and it was unbearably cold; he had on only his normal school uniform with an extra pullover for the chill autumn day. The frightening thoughts returned. This wasn't a dream; he had been at school, hadn't he? He'd been plunged into a fantasy world and there was no Len to help him. This was not good. Nightmares when sleeping were bad enough, and to be expected occasionally, but this was different. How could you have a nightmare during the day? What should he do? He tried to pinch himself on his cheek to see if he himself was real, but he couldn't make his fingers close; they were already too cold. He looked at his watch – it was a quarter past three. He looked again. That could not be right; it had already been at least half past four when he had left the hall. He edged forward in the snow; it was getting very deep, deeper than any snow he'd ever known. It was above his knees and soon he could hardly lift his legs to move. He was stranded and seemed to be sinking, sinking, sinking ….

"Wake up, Eddie. Time to go home."

A familiar girl's voice sounded in the icy air around his head. He felt a light touch on his left arm. A deeper voice spoke.

"What is it, Sally?"

"It's Eddie Compton, Mr Green; he's fallen asleep."

Footsteps on a wooden floor. Chairs being moved loudly. Chattering voices.

"Asleep, eh? I'll give him, asleep!"

"I don't think he's well, sir. He looked very pale when he came into the lesson."

A gentle shake of his right shoulder. He felt warmer and safe.

"What's happened?" asked Eddie as his head jolted upright from its position lying on the desk.

"You fell asleep," said Sally Barber.

"Are you alright, Compton?" asked Mr Green with surprising sympathy in his voice. Eddie looked around him. He was back in Room 46 and his classmates had all left to go home. Only Sally and Mr Green remained and both had anxious looks on their faces.

"I'm O.K., sir. Must have fallen asleep. I'm sorry, sir."

"That's alright, young man. I bet you've got a touch of flu or something. Better get your mum to take you to the doctors. Will you be alright to get home on your own?"

"Yes, sir, I'll be fine. I didn't sleep well last night, that's all."

Sally Barber walked part of the way home with Eddie and, after she had left him at the entrance to Fir Tree Close, he dawdled while he pondered the afternoon's event. One horrible thought kept coming back to him: 'How could he ever feel safe in going to sleep again, whether at home in his bed or anywhere else, especially when the nightmares had seemed as real as reality itself'?

17

Déjà Vu

Eddie got very little sleep that Monday night and by the morning he was looking almost as pale as his clean white shirt. He had tried desperately to keep his eyes closed but even with the light on, it was well after two before he entered the dubious sanctuary of oblivion. His mother showed her concern at breakfast.

"You look awful, Eddie. Do you feel ill?"

"No, Mum, I'm just very tired. I didn't get much sleep again."

"Why? Is something troubling you?"

"I don't know, Mum," he lied. "Bad dreams I suppose."

"Well you're in no fit state to go to school. I'll ring and say you're sick."

"No, Mum, I'll be fine. I've nothing to do at home."

"Precisely, that's just what you need – a day of complete rest. I'll make an appointment at the doctors for some sleeping tablets or something. It's probably just a growing phase. You're not still fretting about Len, are you? I know you miss him, but you've got to move on, Eddie. Haven't you got other friends at school?"

"A few, Mum, and I'm not really missing Len now. I'd rather go to school; I'd be so bored at home. It's only tiredness."

"Well alright, then, but I will make an appointment for you to see Dr Rees and we'll see what he says."

"O.K., but only as long as I can go on my own; I'm fifteen next year and make the appointment for after school, Mum."

"Just as you like, but you might have to wait a few days."

"No problem, I'll have got some sleep by then."

Eddie thought afterwards that that intention might prove difficult unless he could talk to Len or even another friendly ghost, like George Canter. They were bound to know what was happening to him. Len, for one, had always solved his non-academic problems in the past and he couldn't discuss his fears within anyone else, least of all his parents.

All the fourth year at Fenton Grammar had an afternoon of House football on the Tuesday afternoon, but Eddie had been excused; his mother had insisted on writing a note because of his lack of sleep. Along with three others he had been despatched to the library to do private study. Together with a few sixth-formers, who hadn't got permission to go home early, there were only about a dozen students occupying the school's second largest room. Its beamed and sloping ceiling together with some internal buttresses allowed some occupants to be hidden from view of anyone else in the library. Eddie found one such space at the far end and settled down to write up some science experiments. He had a science fiction novel in reserve should he finish the school work. The library was uncomfortably warm and despite his previous fears, Eddie felt safe and was soon fast asleep with his head resting on a pile of books, strategically placed on the table in front of him.

Len had had a feeling for some time that his best friend was in need of his company and counsel. He had been provided with a brief visit to the beach at Fenton-on-Sea just two days previously and had walked for about half a mile wondering why he was there and what he was supposed to do. Memories of George Canter had come back to him for a while that Sunday morning, but then all at once he had gone into his normal ghostly sleep and oblivion. He now found himself outside the familiar library at his old school. The clock outside read twenty past three. In his ghostly disguise, Len had quickly learnt that he didn't need to do mundane things like open doors and he glided quietly and unnoticed 'through' the library wall.

Eddie had slept soundly for about fifty minutes when he first began to dream. He could hear a familiar voice which sounded as though it was coming from a long way off.

"*Wake up, old son.*"

'I'm not asleep', thought Eddie as a cool waft of air blew on his neck. He tried to form the words with his mouth but his lips were glued together.

"*Your old friend Len is here. Now open your eyes.*"

This time an icy draught blew directly into Eddie's face causing his eyelids to flutter.

"*That's it, Captain. Time to come back to the land of the living.*"

Eddie's head dislodged itself from his pile of books and only his body's natural instinct to protect itself saved his face from dropping onto the table. He sat up with a jerk.

"Wha-what!" he muttered blindly.

A chorus of '*Shut ups*' broke out from several sixth-formers as Eddie groaned some more.

"It's me, Eddie."

Eddie's eyes at last opened fully and he focused on his best friend.

"Len? How …?"

"Shh! I'll do the talking. Only you will be able to hear. Just nod whenever you need to."

Eddie nodded. Aaron Johnson of 6Sc2 smirked at the fourth-former's strange behaviour but put it down to the natural emergence from

441

his deep sleep. Len continued to address Eddie from his position standing directly in front of the table.

"I want to talk to you again, Eddie. I've things to tell you and I suspect you have things to tell me, eh?"

Eddie nodded.

"I have one or two surprises for you and an explanation of some things you and I have seen in the past – O.K?

Eddie nodded. Len leant forward and looked directly into his friend's eyes holding his gaze.

"Go to Freeman Street next Saturday."

Eddie hesitated slightly while he took in this simple but direct instruction. He nodded. Len disappeared immediately in a blur. Len's voice, however, continued with a qualification of his order.

"Go and watch the game from behind the goal in the North Stand."

Eddie nodded involuntarily at the empty space in front of him. The bell for end of afternoon school rang loudly.

It wasn't until the following evening that Eddie's dad brought home the Wednesday edition of the Hamsden Daily Star, which always featured Saturday's forthcoming game. Fred Compton took his usual leisurely time in perusing the paper and Eddie had to wait patiently for him to finish. Having finished his second cup of tea after his dinner, Eddie's dad put the Daily Star down on the table beside him.

"Can I have a look, Dad?" asked Eddie politely.

"Of course you can, son, but there's nothing much in it; just more and more adverts."

Eddie took the paper up to his bedroom trying not to arouse his parents' suspicion. They seemed to be discussing plans for that Christmas including a possible invite to Martha Wilby for whom it would be the first such occasion without her son and husband. As he climbed the stairs he could just hear his father saying,

"Well, she might want to be on her own, love."

From a previous visit to the garden at number 23 The Park, Eddie had his suspicions that Aunty Martha would not be on her own.

Details of Saturday's game were always contained on the inside back page and Eddie turned there immediately. He looked at the headline:

'TOWN TAKE ON NEW BOYS BRADFIELD ORIENT'.

Eddie started reading. Bradfield Orient had been promoted from the Fourth Division at the start of the current season after a runaway success as champions. Eddie knew little about them except that they were based in south-east London not far from first division Crystal Palace who often supplied them with young players. The game was to be played at Freeman Street as Len had indicated – kick-off, three o'clock. Eddie had in the back of his mind how and in what form he would meet Len ever since his friend's instruction in the library. He couldn't wait for Saturday to come round. For each of the three nights until the big day, Eddie enjoyed a dreamless and reinvigorating sleep; his colour improved to such an extent that his mother cancelled the doctor's appointment arranged for the following Monday.

By Saturday, the 13th of November, the weather had turned cold with early morning frosts. Though the morning was dull and overcast, by the time Eddie caught the half past one train to Hamsden, it had brightened considerably with a late autumn sun trying to peep through the clouds. Eddie had to stand for most of the way; the four-carriage diesel railcar was packed with both football fans and early Christmas shoppers. No one of any significance, human or otherwise, got on at Linham Junction and the train arrived safely at Hamsden station at four minutes past two. Eddie spotted several of his fellow fourth years as he walked along the platform to the station exit that opened onto the broad thoroughfare that led down to Freeman Street.

"Going to the game, Compton?" shouted Bob Felton from about five yards behind him. "Want to come with us?"

Robert Felton was an inferior version of his best friend, Len – blond-haired, sporty and the new captain of the Under 15's football team. He was, however, arrogant and had a reputation as a bully, particularly of those either younger or smaller than himself. Bob Felton was the last person Eddie wanted to be seen with especially as he had private business to attend to as well. Eddie turned bravely to face his questioner.

"No thanks, I'm meeting someone in the North Stand."

Bob threw back his blond head and laughed. The North Stand was for cissies and families and definitely not for the budding hooligans that he and his friends were destined to become.

"Suit yourself, but don't talk to any strange men, Compton!"

The bully and his loyal following of three associates hurried past Eddie, each giving him a not so friendly push against his shoulder. One whispered in Eddie's ear,

"Take care, Edwina and beware of the bogeyman."

Eddie laughed inwardly at his moronic peers and he walked slowly so that the gang of four would be as far away as possible before he reached the ground. Leonard Wilby would have made mincemeat of young Robert Felton, thought Eddie, as he strolled down Station Road. Len had always despised the bully when he had been at Fenton Grammar. It took Eddie nearly twenty minutes to dawdle the half mile and he arrived at the North Stand entrance at just before half past two. The North

Stand was pricier to get into than most other parts of Freeman Street but, at least, he would be unlikely to meet any other grammar school pupils there. Len had chosen well.

It was clear to Eddie, as soon as he got inside the ground that the crowd was going to be well short of full capacity and he was able to acquire a good position behind the goal with ease. Christmas shopping was obviously the main priority for many of Town's normal fans. It was not surprising given their lowly league position; a serious leg injury to their star forward, Johnny McBride, had not helped in their quest for goals and their leaky defence meant they were haunted by fears of relegation to the fourth tier of the football league. For their part, Bradfield Orient had brought a sizeable contingent of travelling fans who, to Eddie's dismay, had been allocated a large section of the North Stand directly behind him. The Orient had continued the success of the previous campaign and was currently lying in third position. It was going to be a hard game for the lowly Town.

Eddie had bought a match programme for sixpence but it wasn't until he had established his position a few rows back from the concrete retaining wall that he decided to open it and look at the teams. He already knew what he would find. There on the opposition team sheet, playing at inside right, was one L.Wilton.

At five to the hour precisely, the visitors took the field first and Eddie strained his eyes to pick out their number eight. He looked younger than when Eddie had last seen him playing for Spurs in the pre-season friendly. He appeared to be barely out of school and this was soon confirmed by an overheard conversation between two of the visiting supporters.

"That boy Wilton is playing again today."

"He looks a good prospect for a seventeen-year-old."

"Yeah, he came from Palace's youth team that reached the youth semi-final last year."

It wasn't until the second half that the visitors were kicking towards the North Stand goal after establishing a two-goal lead, courtesy of two assists from the young Wilton. The déjà vu moment happened in the sixty-third minute with one subtle difference. This time the young inside forward picked up the ball on the half-way line and strode purposefully forward delicately avoiding desperate tackles. Reaching the edge of the penalty area, he drove a low rasping shot which skimmed the left-hand goalpost and straight into Eddie's waiting arms. Several of the crowd in his vicinity shouted,

"Well caught, son!"

"Give us the ball, Captain," said young Wilton.

Eddie moved to the concrete wall and handed the ball back and got just close enough to hear a whispered,

"Go to the players' entrance after the game."

A silver St Christopher glinted in the low afternoon sun.

For the rest of the game Eddie's mind was in turmoil. This could not be possible despite all the other ghostly encounters. The young Orient footballer was *real* and yet he looked and spoke like Len. He wasn't a ghost. It just did not make sense.

At the end of the game, Eddie made his way round to the other side of the ground, joining several other fans seeking autographs from their favourite players. He was filled with apprehension as to whom or what he would find. He didn't have to wait long as the visiting team seemed to be anxious to get back to London where they could celebrate their resounding 4–0 victory. The jubilant Orient side filed onto their waiting coach and Eddie counted each member of the team one by one. Wilton was the last to board, but board he did, without any acknowledgement of Eddie. He thought he overheard the young number eight talking to a fellow player and his voice did not seem so familiar as before. Something about his walk also was different from his best friend's gait. As with the pre-season friendly, he had been confused by the similarity between both players in name and physique. A voice spoke from behind him.

"Good trick, eh, Eddie?"

Eddie turned round and there stood Len grinning from ear to ear. He appeared to be same age as earlier in the week in the school library. Immediately Eddie tried to put his hand on Len's arm and felt just empty space. For the first time ever he was pleased that Len was a ghost!

"How did you do that, Len?"

"It takes a little practice but I've learnt that we ghosts can take on other forms, you know. We can get inside other people's heads and become that person for a short while. Mr Larry Wilton had absolutely no idea that, for a few moments in the second half, he spoke a couple of sentences to a young fourteen-year-old boy. In addition I was able to make you think that it was me. He has gone back to London blissfully unaware of anything unusual."

"But he had a St Christopher round his neck."

Len smiled.

"Are you sure he did? Did you touch it?"

"Well, no, but I saw it."

"No, Eddie – you saw and heard what you were allowed to see and hear. There's a big difference, you know"

Eddie was deep in thought.

"So it was you back in August before you died. You were playing for Spurs' reserves."

Len looked puzzled.

447

"What do you mean?"

Eddie then described the incident with the Spurs' player called Wilton at the pre-season friendly. It was news to Len and he could only offer one explanation.

"I must have gone back in time and given you a taste of what is possible when you are a ghost."

"Maybe it was a warning that you were going to die. I just assumed that, because you had recently moved, I was missing you and I kept seeing you everywhere I looked. I *wanted* you to be the young Spurs' player."

"Probably so, Eddie. I just know as a ghost I can probably be anyone or anything I want to be and I can go anywhere I choose. Today I was a lower-league footballer. Next time I might be a first division superstar or a brain surgeon or a …."

"A nuclear scientist?"

18

Invisible and Alone

Len didn't stay much longer with Eddie at Freeman Street; once again his exertions seemed to have exhausted him. He left Eddie with a whispered cryptic comment.

"Green will change to blue. Wait for the sunshine."

Apart from the possible reference to his English teacher, Eddie couldn't really find a satisfactory interpretation for the strange words. It would be another fortnight until an explanation would become apparent.

The days following his visit to Freeman Street were void of any significant dreams at night for Eddie and with proper rest; he did not drift off into sleep during the day either. The weather was typical for November – dull and misty with thick fog at times. The sun was notable by its absence. His English lessons were uneventful and he reached the afternoon of Friday the 26th in relaxed mood as he went to his last class of the week with Mr Green. His academic nemesis was in a good mood for a change, even complimenting Eddie on his recent essay on a poem of Robert Frost.

"A good attempt by you, Mr Compton; quite out of character. Did someone help you with it?"

"No, sir. I like poetry, especially his *Ghost House* poem."

Eddie had found the poem fascinating. Some lines in particular stood out for him:

'*I know not who these mute folk are …*'
'*… And yet, in view of how many things,*
As sweet companions as might be had'.

When he read the first line, it had worried Eddie to begin with. Ghosts were supposed to be silent according to Frost, but then he realised that they *were* silent to all but those they wished to communicate with. The final two lines of the poem gave him great solace – Len was much nicer dead!

Eddie beamed with pride for most of the rest of that English lesson. He couldn't remember a time when an English teacher had given him any praise. The day felt better all round and, even outside through the window of Room 46, he could see a deep yellow sun peeping from behind the clouds against a sky of rich blue. Len's final words at the game came back to Eddie with real meaning. *'Green will change to blue. Wait for the sunshine'*. Something was going to happen very soon.

Eddie was filled with anticipation when he got up on Saturday morning. Fenton-on-Sea awoke to a beautiful day with a golden sun and a clear blue sky; all the ingredients contained in Len's cryptic remark. Something was telling Eddie at breakfast that he needed to be prepared for a complete day out and he organised himself accordingly when his mother asked him about his plans for the day.

"What are you going to do today? You need some fresh air after your recent problems."

"Yes, Mum. I think I'll go to Hamsden for the day. Town are at home this afternoon as well."

Eddie guessed that Len might meet him near the station as he had done before and his plan would cater for that possibility. Len hadn't mentioned any specific meeting place in his strange words. His mum looked pleased that her son was going to spend his Saturday in the way that any normal boy of his age would.

"Good idea, Eddie. Have you got enough money?"

"I will have if Dad gives me this and last week's pocket money," replied Eddie glancing in the direction of his dad who was about to get up from the table to go to work at the station. Fred Compton paused and made great play of digging deep into his trouser pocket as if he had to scrape together his last few pennies to make the required sum. He opened his hand to reveal no more than a few pence and shook his head in resignation. Eddie's head went down in mock sadness to match his dad's pretence of poverty.

"I only get four shillings a week, Dad. Can't you spare it for your favourite son?"

Eddie pretended to sob. His dad reached inside his British Rail jacket and produced his old brown leather wallet from which he extracted a crisp pound note.

"Get me a match programme and it's yours."

Eddie raised his head in a pretence of excitement and said,

"Done. Thanks, Dad."

"That's alright, son. Have a good day and enjoy yourself. It won't be many more months before you will have to work on a Saturday to get your own pocket money."

Eddie didn't tarry outside Fenton station when he went to catch the ten past nine train. He had decided that if Len was to appear he would do so in his own time. Despite his plea of poverty, Eddie had over three pounds in his wallet and pocket; he seemed to spend less without anyone to help him do it on a Saturday. He had enough money to get him a long way by train if need be.

The train was not as packed as that on the Saturday a fortnight previous. It was too early for the football fans and even for all but the most enthusiastic Christmas shoppers. Eddie found a seat in the front carriage with an empty one beside him, just in case …. He settled back and tried to enjoy the ride to Hamsden.

Linham Junction was the first place where he thought his friend might put in an appearance, but no one got on or off and the train progressed as normal towards its destination, reaching Hamsden station at just after a quarter to ten. As he alighted from the train, Eddie pondered his situation. What should he do? He had fully expected that Len would have shown himself by then. It was nearly five hours to the match at Freeman Street and he didn't really have any shopping that he wanted to do. Ten minutes later and he found himself wandering aimlessly among the early morning shoppers in the High Street. He began murmuring to himself.

"Where are you, old boy? Where are you?"

He half expected that his quiet plea would do the trick, but apart from an odd look from a passing shopper, nothing happened. Then he remembered that, on another occasion, he and Len had been transported to Osborne's department store. He headed further up the High Street towards Hamsden's largest shop and, once inside, he made for the same counter in the toy department where the previous rendezvous had taken place. Without trying to look conspicuous he studied the glass-fronted cabinets containing a variety of toys for sale. A familiar voice whispered from behind him.

"You're here again, then, Captain. It's been a while."

Eddie turned to meet his friend who was standing with his usual cheeky grin.

"What have you been up to?" continued Len.

Len looked a little older than when issuing his riddle outside the players' entrance at Freeman Street, but Eddie had begun to realise that he was seeing him so infrequently that he was bound to appear to age

452

between visits. Eddie whispered so no one else should hear, although, fortunately, the only other person in the vicinity was the shop assistant and she was a good twenty feet away.

"Not much since I saw you after the match."

Len seemed to ignore Eddie's reply and, coming right up to him, he asked in a low voice,

"What do you fancy doing?"

"I don't know – I thought you had plans after your riddle about green turning to blue."

Len said nothing. He looked puzzled. Suddenly, in a reversal of roles, another voice entered Eddie's head.

"*Keep away from him, Eddie. Leave him to me.*"

Len continued to stand with a frown on his face. Eddie turned round to face the source of the new voice. Another Len stood less than six feet away and he had a silver St Christopher around his neck. He walked past his open-mouthed friend and said something incomprehensible to the evil ghost who promptly vanished from sight. The real Len returned to Eddie's side and said,

"Let's go somewhere we can talk," and, as if to prove his identity, he continued, "A dull Green day has become a blue day full of sunshine, eh?"

Five minutes late and Eddie had led his friendly ghost to where the High Street began to merge with the more residential area of town. A few hundred yards further on and they were outside the entrance to the War Memorial Gardens. Once inside, they found a wooden bench, conveniently hidden from view of most of the rest of the almost deserted haven of small lawns and shrubberies. Eddie sat down while Len stood in front of him. No one but Eddie would hear what Len was about to say.

"You have to be careful, Eddie. My evil ghost seems to frequent Osborne's on a regular basis. Always ask him only something I would know to check if it's me or not."

"I was just about to, Len. He obviously was unaware of your riddle or even meeting me after the match at Freeman Street."

"Good, but there's another way of knowing."

"How?"

Len pulled his St Christopher forward from his neck.

"Look for this. I'll always wear it from now on, but still be careful because he may get one for himself."

Eddie thought for a moment.

"We need a coded signal, just in case."

"What do you suggest?" asked Len.

"Something from my past that I haven't even told you, in case …."

"In case?"

"In case, as your ghost, he can remember everything that he experienced when he was alive as your evil half."

"What about something that has happened to you after I died?" said Len.

"I think he'd know that as one of your ghosts. He seems to know where I am at times so he's probably been stalking and haunting me without me being aware."

Len appeared to nod his agreement.

"Can you think of something? You used to tell me everything."

"There is something, I think, that I haven't told another living soul."

Len grinned.

"Have you told a dead one, then?"

"Not yet; you'll be the first!"

Len's grin got broader.

"Go on, then, tell comrade Len. I promise never to tell anyone, living or dead!"

"I stole something once."

"What?"

"Well, it was before you and your family came to Fenton-on-Sea from London."

Eddie looked guilty as he continued,

"I was about seven and Mum and I were in Woolworth's on a Saturday morning. While she was paying for some sweets and with nobody looking I pinched an extra sweet from the tray on the counter."

"And you're sure no one saw you?"

"Absolutely certain, Len."

"Well? What's the big secret?"

"I'll tell you what kind of sweet it was."

"And?"

"It was a chocolate éclair."

"So that's the signal – chocolate éclair?

"Yes."

Len wasn't totally convinced.

"Only one problem, Captain."

"What's that?"

"My evil ghost is probably listening or can read my mind."

"Got to be worth trying though."

"O.K., Captain," said Len finally.

Eddie stood up from the bench as an elderly couple with a dog appeared to want to sit down. The dog barked loudly at the empty space in front of Eddie and then began to growl menacingly. The pensioners reined it back with suitably corrective words. Eddie made quickly for the exit to the gardens with Len's ghost in tow.

"Animals can sense you," said Eddie as they reached the road.

"They have stronger senses, I suppose," responded Len.

Eddie stopped walking back towards the town centre and, with no one in earshot or sight, said,

"Why have you come back today, Len?"

"Aren't you pleased to see me?"

"Oh yes, and I've had some bad nightmares that I wanted to tell you about anyway."

"I know, Eddie. I sensed you had a rough time with old man Green."

"He's been O.K. with me recently and the nightmares have stopped."

"Good. I did try to haunt the old duffer and give him a taste of his own medicine."

"Wow! You can do that?"

"Sometimes, but only if the power is used for good and not to just gain an advantage over somebody or some thing."

Eddie began walking again and before they reached the busy town centre itself, he began to tell Len about George Canter's death and the meeting with his ghost. As he talked he kept his head down as if looking at the pavement. Len didn't seem to be aware of either event even though George had been only a few yards from him on the morning in question. Len, also, wasn't as sad as Eddie thought he should have been on learning of their special friend's demise.

"Death is only a beginning, Eddie. George is more content now and he has his whole death in front of him," he joked. "Maybe I'll get to see him in the non-flesh."

Eddie smiled at his friend's relaxed attitude to the most difficult and frightening subject the human race had to face. He made death seem fun and to be looked forward to!

Len stopped his ghostly walk in a conveniently quiet spot and said, "I'll tell you why I've really come today."

"Why?"

"I thought you might like a day out. You can choose where you would like to go and I'll see if I can engineer it."

"What – anywhere?"

"Anywhere you like."

"Will you be coming with me?"

"How would you get back without me?"

"True."

Eddie had already been thinking of a possible destination, ever since he knew that Len could transport them across distances.

"I really would like to go back to Devon where we had our two holidays together with my mum and dad," said Eddie after a short pause.

"You mean Ludmouth."

"The very place."

"There won't be much to do there this time of the year, you know."

"I know but it would be fun anyway especially if old Mr Manders' ghost is still about in the shape of the local tramp."

"That always worried me, Eddie, you know."

"Why?"

"Because, if you remember, he grabbed us and pushed us out of the way of the train and saved our lives. How could a ghost do that, old son?"

"I don't know," said Eddie, "but I'm glad he did."

"Well, I don't think I can push people," said Len. "Let me try."

Len came right up to Eddie and put out his hands as if to push him.

"Can you feel anything?" asked Len.

"No, it just feels cold and odd."

"Odd?"

"Yes, it makes me want to take a step backwards but there was no physical sensation."

Len looked surprised.

"Maybe I can do it, then. With practice, I suppose I could probably push you backwards without you feeling anything. It's mind over matter, mate."

One or two people were beginning to pause and stare at Eddie as he was talking at the empty space in front of him. Some even asked him some obvious natural questions.

"*Are you alright, son?*"

"*Did you say something?*"

"*Pardon – were you speaking to me?*"

Ignoring the awkward queries, Eddie crossed over the road and headed down a narrow alleyway. Len followed, and when he had caught his friend up, they continued their conversation with Eddie leaning against a tall brick wall. He pretended to be looking through his wallet in case the occasional person passed by.

"So you want to go to Ludmouth, Eddie?"

"Do you remember much about it, Len?"

"Of course. Let me just concentrate and think."

Len wandered a few yards further down the alleyway with his ghostly head bowed to the ground. Eddie waited and expected a sudden and extreme change of light but, instead, Len's image got fainter and fainter until about twenty yards away it disappeared completely. Eddie followed cautiously until he reached the spot where his friendly ghost had vanished. Some invisible force seemed to prevent any further progress and, try as he might, he could not get any further down the alley. Even attempting to stay as close to either wall proved fruitless – there was no way through. A couple of young children walked towards him from the other side of the invisible barrier and giggled at his strange and frantic behaviour. Eddie began to concentrate his mind on Ludmouth and anything associated with the south Devon seaside resort – fossils, black sandy beach, their bed and breakfast and the rock tunnel. Nothing seemed to work. He needed the right code to pass through to the other side. Then it hit him – the code!

"Chocolate éclairs," he murmured and he tried immediately to walk through the invisible barrier. Suddenly, there was no longer any resistance and in flash of bright light, he passed through. Eddie was used to allowing his eyes adjust to the light and he kept them closed for a few seconds until, when he opened them again, he was astonished to find himself in almost total darkness. He reached out his hands to the front but felt nothing. He edged to his left until his shoulder touched something cold and hard – it was solid rock. He edged back to the right until again he felt solid rock. He was in a tunnel. It had to be the old abandoned railway tunnel that he and Len had explored when they had been on holiday in Ludmouth for the first time, now over two years ago. Eddie's voice echoed loudly even though he spoke quietly.

"Len? Where are you, Len?"

Apart from the faint noise of the sea from behind him, silence reigned in the tunnel. Len was not there. Eddie moved carefully forward until within a few yards he met the inner end of the tunnel, marked by an impenetrable pile of rocks and large boulders. Using one wall as a guide, he turned back and made for a possible outer exit to the tunnel in the direction from which the sound of the sea was coming. It had been blocked on the last occasion that he and Len had visited Ludmouth but it seemed to Eddie that it was his only possible means of escape. The darkness began to lighten as he approached the front of the tunnel. He could see daylight coming from a ragged hole at about head height in front of him. It looked small in diameter but Eddie knew he had to try it. One of his worst nightmares had always been crawling through underground tunnels only to find he reached a position where he could neither go forward or back, unable to move until the flesh dropped from his bones, by which time it would be too late! By moving a large rock into position to stand on, Eddie was able to haul his head and shoulders into the cavity; he hoped the rest of his torso would follow. His slimness, for once, was an advantage as he pulled himself through the hole. As his head emerged into bright sunlight, he started to recall all the derogatory name-calling he had received from fellow pupils during his life: 'Beanpole', 'Skinny boy' and, worst of all, 'Dipstick'. By using both arms, he eased the rest of his body out onto the welcoming pile of rocks that rested against the cliff face. He slid and slithered in his prone position until he rolled onto the wet sand about five feet below. Apart from a few scrapes to his knees and elbows, he was unhurt. He turned over onto his back and breathed a huge sigh of relief. After a few moments, he raised himself into a sitting position and studied his surroundings. It was just as he remembered it – the red cliffs at Ludmouth on Devon's Jurassic Coast. It felt chilly and just like the sunny late autumn day that he'd left in Fenton-on-Sea, but was it Saturday, November the 27th 1965? His watch read ten forty-five.

Eddie brushed the wet sand and loose pieces of rock from his clothes and turned to walk the half mile to Ludmouth's Esplanade, the road that fronted the sandy beach and contained many of the better guest houses and small hotels. He felt in a more relaxed mood knowing that he had probably conquered one of the worst situations that he was likely to be faced with that day. Now all he had to do was find Len's ghost and, at least, he would have a passport back to the reality of Fenton-on-Sea.

Despite the uncomfortable realisation that he was totally alone in a place that was a day's journey from home, Eddie kept telling himself that Len was bound to put in an appearance sooner or later. Judging by how much it normally cost him to travel by train to Hamsden, he also thought that, if the worst came to the worst, he would have enough money to get a fair way home.

Ten minutes after emerging from the rock tunnel, he found himself standing opposite *Summer Breeze*, the guest house where his mum and dad had taken him and Len on two interesting summer holidays. He was still not totally convinced that he was in real time, but crossing over The Esplanade and peering through the window into the reception area, he could make out by the clock there that it was eleven o'clock exactly. Boldly, and without a thought for what he would say to the owner, affectionately known as BB, Eddie walked calmly inside.

Bob Brewin was standing behind the small counter in the reception area when Eddie made his entry. He didn't look up as Eddie approached and said,

"Surprise, BB!"

Bob Brewin still did not move or acknowledge Eddie's remark.

"It's me, BB – Eddie Compton. I've stayed with you a couple of times in the summer."

Still no response. Eddie began to raise his voice.

"I'm from Fenton-on-Sea. You must remember me."

While Eddie had been trying to communicate with BB, a guest had come down to reception. She was now standing uncomfortably close to Eddie and waiting to be attended to. BB looked up immediately and said,

461

"Good morning, Miss Taverner – going out?"

"Yes, BB, and I shan't be in for lunch."

"Well, have a good day. The weather looks set fair."

The elderly lady said goodbye and headed for the door. It began to dawn on Eddie – somehow between the tunnel and the guest house, he had become invisible! To double-check, he waved his arms frantically in front of BB's face but Bob Brewin eyes just followed Miss Taverner's exit from his guest house. He decided there was no point in remaining where he was and Eddie followed Miss Taverner out into the weak mid-morning sunshine. He recrossed The Esplanade and found a familiar seat on the promenade. He needed to think. Surely Len would come.

Eddie could see both the good side and bad side of his position. On the one hand, he could go unnoticed wherever he wanted, including boarding any relevant train that would get him home, but on the other, would he return to his normal physical state before he got there? The second question also raised another worrying problem in his mind. Had he been turned into a ghost and, if so, did that mean he was already …? Had something irreversible happened to him when he had followed Len through the invisible barrier in the alleyway back in Hamsden? If it had, did it also signify that Len's ghost had experienced a similar transformation which meant he had become invisible even to him? Without Len, he quickly realised that there was only going to be one solution to his problem. He had to make his way back to Hamsden by train and return to the alleyway. It was half past eleven by his watch and previous experience told him that it was at least a six hour journey, if all the connections were quick and smooth. Unfortunately, Ludmouth's nearest station was now at Ludmouth Junction and that was nearly three miles from where he sat. He calculated that he wouldn't get back to Hamsden until at least half past six that evening and so probably wouldn't make it home to Fenton until an hour later, given the probable detour to the invisible barrier. Shrugging his shoulders at the unavoidable decision, he got up from the seat to start the walk to the distant station. He crossed The Esplanade and quickly made his way up into the main town.

While he walked, Eddie thought about the excuse he could give his parents if he did actually arrive back late that evening. Normally, after the game on a Saturday, and even if he missed a train or dawdled, he would still be home no later than six-thirty. He had a couple of school friends that lived in Hamsden and he would say that he met one at the match and had gone home for tea with them. All that was necessary was a preliminary phone call which he would make from some convenient telephone box on his journey. Almost after he had sorted his plan, he realised that there was a huge problem with it. In addition to his invisibility, no one seemed to be able to hear him either. BB certainly hadn't heard him even when he had spoken loudly at the guest house. He broke into a trot as he entered the northern end of Ludmouth's residential area. He would just have to make every connection as quickly as he could. The 'tea-with-a-friend' excuse would have to suffice and without any prior warning to or permission from his parents.

Eddie found he couldn't make very quick progress along the disused track from the old Ludmouth station to the one still open at Ludmouth Junction. It had become overgrown and a dumping ground for rubbish of all kinds. Frightening memories of his and Len's narrow escape from the shunting engine came back to haunt him as he passed the spot of the near-tragic accident. It spurred him on to run and jump even more recklessly as he avoided broken sleepers and thick clumps of grass. He didn't reach the initial destination until nearly one o'clock and then discovered that the next train to Exeter wasn't until a quarter to two. He was fairly sure that direct trains ran to London at regular and frequent intervals from there. Some rough calculations from previous journeys home from Ludmouth suggested to Eddie that his original estimate of a six-thirty arrival at Hamsden would have to be revised. It was likely to be after eight o'clock with another hour or more needed to make it home finally. However, sitting on a platform seat in the bright and presumed November sunshine, hunger and thirst became his immediate concerns. He would have to procure something to eat and drink – it should be easy, given he was invisible. He dismissed any guilty thoughts about what he was going to do next as he headed for the small station buffet.

A meat pie and a bottle of cold milk satisfied Eddie's main physical needs. He left one traveller slightly bewildered when, having gone to the counter to get a knife and fork, he returned to discover his plate contained only vegetables. The milk had caused less consternation when it disappeared from a newly arrived crate on the platform. Without realising it, Eddie was fortunate that anything he touched, or indeed ate, became likewise invisible. He also managed to satisfy his curiosity as to the date when he spotted an overhead electric calendar which read:

November 27.

All connections were reasonably smooth and on time and Eddie found himself at London's Liverpool Street station at half past five. The various journeys had been interesting to say the least. Avoiding passengers sitting unknowingly on his lap was the worst difficulty and, in the end, he spent most of the way to London standing in the corridor. One young woman got a shock when she discovered a toilet was engaged only for the door to open mysteriously by itself as she waited for the non-existent person to vacate it! On several other occasions Eddie had to squeeze himself against the corridor side as people walked past him, sometimes discovering afterwards that part of their clothes had become disorganised or dislodged.

Eddie did, in the end, decide to make a phone call from a call box on platform seven; no one would notice the receiver raise itself upwards unaided. He would then argue later that he had tried to call his parents but he would tell them that he hadn't been able to make the connection. After his day wandering as a lost soul, it was cheering to hear the reality and comfort of his mum's voice when she answered his silent call.

"Hello, Fenton 3566."

"Hello? Who's speaking please?"

Eddie was also relieved to hear her third and final sentence.

"Hello, is that you, Eddie?"

After he had replaced the receiver, Eddie smiled, knowing that if he had been phoning from Hamsden on the way to a friend's house, he had chosen about the right time to make the call. His fictitious friend's parents, of course, were not on the phone.

The six o'clock train to Norwich and all intervening stations departed on time and Eddie reached Hamsden at twenty-five to eight. As soon as a young couple tried to walk straight through him as he walked along the platform, he knew that he had to head for the alleyway just off the town centre where he would try to restore himself to his natural visible form. It was a moonless night as Eddie threaded his way into town avoiding people off to the pubs or other places of entertainment on a Saturday evening. At first, he turned down the wrong alleyway and had to backtrack until he found the right one. For a few moments he was even panicked into thinking that the alleyway no longer existed and had disappeared along with Len's ghost. Reaching the spot where he had been transported to Devon that morning, he suddenly realised his mistake when the invisible barrier again stopped his progress. Despite his use of the special code, he could still not pass. He knew at once that he had to approach it from the other side. Peering through the gloom, illuminated only by a single weak neon street lamp, he tried to work out how he could get there. He retraced his steps to the first alleyway he'd tried and was relieved when it exited on a road parallel to the one at its entrance. He walked in the direction of where he thought that the correct alleyway ought also to exit but, to his horror, a six foot wooden fence blocked any possible way through. Eddie managed to find a knot hole to look through and, despite the gloom, could just make out that the real alleyway led into a builder's yard directly behind the fence. He looked round him – the quiet back street was deserted apart from a couple of squabbling cats. He reached up and grabbed the top of the fence with his bare hands. By using all his strength, he managed to haul himself into a position astride the fence and thence natural momentum and gravity provided the impetus for him to fall to the ground on the other side. He lay on his side for a few moments listening for noises but no one was about. Apart from a graze to one elbow which would not become visible until later, he was unhurt. He dusted himself down as best he could in the darkness and headed for the single street lamp which marked the alleyway he needed.

"Chocolate éclairs," he whispered as he stood where he thought the barrier to be. Suddenly, as before, the darkness was lifted in a bright flash of white light and Eddie walked casually through.

"*Just in time for the game, Captain.*"

Eddie rubbed his eyes and looked at his watch. It was a quarter past two. Len stood grinning in the alleyway.

"Well done, Eddie. I knew you had the resources to accomplish the little mission I set you."

"Little? It was a nightmare at times, Len. I thought you were coming with me."

"I never said I was, you know. I just asked how you would get back without me. It appears that you still have some of your old powers."

"I didn't do anything special."

"But it helped that you were invisible, eh?"

"You knew that would happen?"

I guessed it might when I set up my plan for you. After all if you can see me when I'm a ghost why can't you develop other powers too? I somehow knew it had happened when you came through the barrier."

"Where did you go to?"

"Nowhere – I sensed you had reached the rock tunnel and then I went into one of my suspended periods. The next thing I knew was when you said the special code for the second time and I returned here. I have no knowledge of what you did after you reached Ludmouth. You'll have to tell me sometime. Now go and enjoy the rest of your day. All this scheming and thinking has exhausted me. I'll be in touch very soon. You're turning into a trainee ghost, Captain."

Len vanished before Eddie had a chance to reply. It had been an extraordinary day so far. It took on a stranger twist when Eddie looked down at his dusty duffle coat and the slight tear in the right elbow.

19

I Could Have Been Anything

As far as it was possible for Eddie, he enjoyed the rest of his extended day out. Town gained a creditable 1–1 draw against a side ten places above them in the league, but when he arrived home at five to six that evening, his mother was the first to spoil his euphoria.

"What on earth have you been doing, Eddie? Your coat is in such a mess."

"It's nothing, Mum. I was pushed to the ground at the game and grazed my elbow, I think."

Eddie's dad entered the questioning.

"Did you get me my programme?"

"Oh sorry, Dad, I forgot. You can have mine – I don't need it."

Eddie was made to go and have a hot bath before his tea and, afterwards, his mother applied loving care and a plaster to his elbow. He went to bed very early that night having been out of the house for nearly fifteen hours, whether real or imagined. He slept fairly well, despite his mind trying to get to grips with the new twist in his relationship with ghosts. Ought he to be worried that he had become one for a few hours?

The weeks up to Christmas seemed to pass slowly for Eddie and he wasn't sure that he was content with his ordinary life as it became in those days. No more nightmares, strange events or visits from ghosts, whether Len's or not, impinged on his waking or sleeping moments. The school term finished on Friday, December the 17th and thoughts turned to Christmas shopping. The previous two Saturdays since the 'trip' to Devon had been spent for Eddie mostly inside owing to the inclement weather. When he awoke on the morning following the end of term, blue sky coupled with a crisp and cold atmosphere led him to recalling that extraordinary day. Though much colder, the day had a similar feel to it and at breakfast he announced to his mother,

"Town are home today, so I think I'll spend the morning in Hamsden doing some Christmas shopping and then go to the game."

"Well, if you do, don't go and get into any trouble like last time. I don't want to have to repair your coat again."

Eddie mumbled something about it having not been his fault but knew he couldn't guarantee that some kind of 'trouble' might not come his way if Len put in an appearance.

Eddie was not as anxious to leave so early as the last time – he didn't want another unnaturally long day if his friend should have plans for him. He caught the ten-forty train from the station and was in Hamsden at ten past the hour. The journey had been an uncomfortable one with the train packed with Christmas shoppers and a few early football fans. Eddie stood all the way watching continually for any ghostly appearances. There were none and he was somewhat relieved when he was able to stretch his legs down Station Road on his way into town. He had one initial destination in mind.

The alleyway looked the same as it had done before, infrequently used except by the residents of the few houses on each side. The vehicle entry to the builder's yard was located in a neighbouring street that bordered it. Pedestrians only used the alleyway on weekdays to gain entry to the yard. Eddie approached the invisible line with caution, both hands out in front of him feeling for the obstruction. He felt nothing as he passed the street lamp that had marked the barrier previously. He walked to the end of the alleyway and retraced his steps several times but without anything impeding his progress. He'd already decided in his mind the next destination if the alleyway proved fruitless in his search for Len and the excitement he might bring.

Osborne's was as busy as anyone could ever remember and the toy section was probably the busiest of all the departments. Eddie was jostled and pushed in all directions until an alcove in a wall provided a safe haven for a few minutes where he could also observe his surroundings. He didn't have to wait long until his friend put in an appearance. A tall burly security guard was making his rounds in the toy department and quickly spotted Eddie apparently loitering in the quiet corner he had found.

"Now then, Captain, we can't have you just hanging around here – not unless you're going to buy something. How have you been, Eddie?"

The speaker was a tall, fair-haired man in his middle to late thirties and, though handsome, he had clearly seen better days. Some tattoos on his wrists and hands indicated that he had been a boxer at some time in the past and he had the air of someone who had been used to mixing with the more criminal element of society. Eddie could see a silver chain around his neck, though not what hung at its lowest point which was hidden underneath a smart shirt and tie. He continued to speak when Eddie seemed reluctant to reply to his original question.

"Don't be scared. I can be anything I want now, Eddie, just like you were able to go anywhere you wanted to last time, so I can choose to be all the people I never got a chance to be. I always fancied a security guard's job – plenty of perks, eh? Easier than being a footballer as well."

Edie began to relax. This was another new twist – his friend could now change form at will. 'Len' ushered Eddie away from his safe haven and said,

"Come on, you'll have to move from there. I'll get the sack if I don't move you on. I'll see you in about half an hour when I take my break for a smoke. I'll be waiting for you out the back at the goods entrance. I may be in another form. I always fancied being a policeman!"

Eddie nodded as 'Len' moved to let him pass. He continued to say nothing as he made his way quickly through the crowds and out of the toy department. Once out of the shop, he had a chance to ponder the brief meeting. Had it been the real Len? How otherwise could he have known about the trip to Devon? Eddie cursed his stupidity for not asking for the code word. He would have to satisfy his curiosity in a few minutes time, but he was beginning to guess what conclusion he would reach – Len had hated people who smoked and boxing had always been about his least favourite sport.

Eddie waited at the back entrance to Osborne's for at least twenty minutes past the supposed time for 'Len's' break. It soon occurred to him that the evil ghost had only ever appeared in Osborne's toy department, thus almost confirming his growing suspicions. He was also not that surprised when, after another few minutes, a young policeman approached him to ask him why he was hanging around in such an unusual place.

"Come along me lad. Move along. Move along."

Even the policeman's language seemed contrived and stereotyped and when Eddie stood his ground and grinned cheekily, it got worse.

"On your way, sunshine or I'll book you for loitering with intent. Move along now."

Eddie at last made his coded reply.

"I'll go, officer, if you give me a chocolate éclair."

The policeman was clearly not amused.

"Right that's enough cheek from you, my lad. You are coming with me to the station."

Although his suspicions were now totally confirmed, Eddie realised also that he had pushed his luck almost too far as the policeman made a grab for him. Another voice shouted from over his shoulder.

"*Run, Eddie. Run as fast as you can, mate.*"

Eddie turned and ran as the voice had commanded him. He felt a cold and clammy grip on his left wrist but his momentum quickly broke it and within seconds he was out of sight of the evil ghost. Pausing for breath at the junction with the High Street, he was relieved to see Len's good ghost standing waiting for him. Eddie positioned himself so that no one passing would see him speaking. Len then said,

"Well done, my boy. That was a close one."

"You're not kidding. I should have checked straightaway with the code word."

"We may have to use a different one from now on, now that he's heard it," said Len. "Have you got any ideas for something that I wouldn't already know and is particularly unusual?"

Eddie thought for a moment and then said,

"My mum's middle name."

"Which is?"

"Blythe"

"That *is* unusual. Let's just hope that my evil ghost isn't listening."

"He didn't seem to recognise the first code. He was too busy showing off as a policeman."

Len seemed satisfied but he was also curious as to how Eddie's suspicions had first been raised.

"What initially made you think the ghost wasn't me?"

"Because he smoked and had obviously been a boxer and when he said he always wanted to be a policeman, I knew for sure."

"How so?"

"Well, you would never smoke; you hated boxing and policeman even more! They would be the kind of things that …."

Len interrupted to finish Eddie's sentence.

"Only my evil side would like, eh?"

"Yes, precisely, and that's how I knew he was evil."

Len smiled at his friend's astute reading of the situation but had a warning for his living friend.

"Just be careful if he plays a double bluff and appears to you in one of my favourite occupations, like a footballer."

Eddie raised his eyebrows in agreement. He had had a lucky escape but he had to ask Len one more question concerning it.

"How did he know I'd been somewhere I wanted to last time we met, Len?"

"Simple, mate. I still have a small part of me that is evil and devious and that part was able to convey the information to my evil ghost. I've told you before that we are all made up of good and bad. The ghost you saw was how I could have become if I'd lived and allowed my evil side to dominate. Some people, like murderers and rapists, let their evil sides take over completely and even rid themselves of any vestige of conscience that they might have left."

Eddie liked it when Len made it seem so simple and he smiled inwardly at the irony that in death, Len appeared to be the more intelligent and thoughtful person. By the time Eddie had absorbed all that the good ghost had said, Len's image had already begun to fade and just before it vanished completely, he heard Len say,

"Have a good day, Eddie. I may see you later, and this time, use the new code immediately."

Eddie could hardly believe the time by his watch after Len had left him. It was already past two o'clock. Whereas two weeks earlier, he had gained several hours, this time he was convinced that he had lost about an hour. He quickly grabbed a sandwich and a drink from Pritchard's Coffee House and headed for Freeman Street. It looked like there was going to be a large crowd at the game; many husbands and their sons had had enough of Christmas shopping for one day.

Local rivals, Borchester United were to be Town's opponents and they had brought a large contingent of fans from the small market town thirty miles to the north of Hamsden. As soon as Eddie had got into the North Stand, it was clear to him that there was going to be a capacity gate of over 12,000. Try as he might, he found he was far too late to get a position behind the goal and eventually he ended up no more than a few feet from where he had come into the stand. During the game he adopted a relaxed posture that allowed him to sway with the crowd around him; it being impossible to resist the movement, at times, which mirrored an undulating wave of the sea.

Hamsden Town won the game 2−1 with both the home goals being scored by Eddie's favourite centre forward, Johnny McBride. Getting out of the ground proved a struggle for Eddie's slimly built frame and by the time he had reached Station Road he was exhausted. After the sunny December day, a thick damp fog had begun to descend on the crocodile of fans that made its way up to the station. By the time Eddie had reached it, his coat and ginger hair were wet with drops of water. Many more fans seemed to have opted for the trains in preference to the buses – rumours had already started that some had been cancelled due to the denseness of the fog. Eddie found he was too late to catch the first train back to Fenton; it was packed almost beyond safety. Since the next one was not until ten to six, he decided to get a cup of tea in the station café. It was surprisingly empty and he was able to sit by himself at an isolated table near the door. The sound of laughter could be heard from the bar next to the café where many fans had repaired for a post-match drink. The warmth of the café had a soporific effect on Eddie and despite his cup of tea, he struggled to keep his eyes open.

"Is this chair taken?"

Eddie tried to focus his heavy-lidded eyes on the owner of the voice. It belonged to a tall elderly man with distinguished silky grey hair.

"N-no, sir," stammered Eddie in a whispered voice.

"Thank you, young man. Have you been to the game, Captain?"

The old man sat down and Eddie smiled.

"Len?"

"Of course, Eddie."

Eddie looked thoughtful.

'*This has to be the good ghost. He's such a friendly and nice looking man, but* ….'

"Such a Blythe game," he said.

"Would that be spelt with a 'y' like your mum's middle name, Eddie?"

"It really is you Len!"

"Yes, and well done. I thought you'd failed the test."

Now he had been shaken wide awake, Eddie found he could recognise his friend's voice, although it came from the mouth of a man who appeared to be well into his sixties.

"Who are you supposed to be, Len?"

"How about a retired doctor?"

Eddie was silent while some people made their way out of the café. One lingered by the door as if he had forgotten something. Eddie frowned

– had he heard him talking to the empty chair in front of him? When the man had gone, Eddie asked,

"Is that what you always wanted to be, then – a doctor?"

"I've always admired them for what they do, but I never wanted to be one. I just wasn't clever enough. Now I can pretend. Isn't it fun?"

Eddie was not so sure.

"It's not that good when people can't see you."

"You can, mate, and that's important to me. Could I pass for a retired doctor?"

"Yes, I suppose so. Do you feel like one?"

"Stupid question, Eddie. I've told you before that I don't feel things. I just imagined what I thought a retired doctor would look like and here I am. Another good trick, eh?"

"It's your good side doing it, then?"

"Yes. Good attracts good, I suppose, like my evil ghost associated himself with bad people."

"The police aren't bad."

"I think the one who tried to grab you was, mate. He had all the hallmarks of a bent copper."

Eddie nodded. Len looked tired and he added,

"You'll have to catch you train soon. I just wanted you to know that we ghosts can appear in many different forms. I could have been anything, you know. Evil should not be allowed to have all the fun."

In the time it took Eddie to look out the door to see the next Fenton train arriving, Len had disappeared.

In the train on the way home that foggy December night, Eddie amused himself by considering the idea of Len as a doctor in real life: issuing wrong prescriptions; recommending the wrong leg for amputation;

diagnosing an incurable disease instead of flu – the list was endless.
'Stick to being a footballer, Len', he thought.

20

A Shady Deal from the Past

Ann Blythe Compton seemed more cheerful than Eddie expected when he got home just after twenty to seven; the train's progress had been slow owing to the dense fog but, surprisingly, his mother didn't seem as though she had been unduly worried. She met him the hall and handed him a towel to dry his wet face and hair.

"Sorry I'm late, Mum. I couldn't get on the first train and then we travelled at less than thirty all the way home."

"That's alright, dear. I expected as much," she replied with a smile. "I have some news, Eddie."

"What, Mum?"

"Aunty Martha's coming for Christmas."

"What? On her own?"

"Yes, love. What a silly question."

Eddie realised that he'd almost said too much with regards to Martha Wilby's possible new companion. That was for the future.

"Good show," said Eddie as quickly as he could. "When she's coming?"

"Christmas Eve. Your dad'll pick her up from the station."

Later, in his room, Eddie decided it would be nice to have Len's mum to stay. Apart from the certainty of a Christmas present from her, it would also provide a link to his best friend. It would be interesting to hear his auntie's news since she had lost her husband and son. Had she received ghostly visits from Len that she'd been aware of? Maybe, also, Len would use the opportunity to put in an appearance.

Eddie's dad duly picked Martha Wilby up from the station at five-thirty on the afternoon of Christmas Eve – he had finished work at four and had been able to get home to fetch his car for the purpose. She looked attractively dressed as she walked down platform one to meet Fred. After a quick peck on the cheek, Eddie's dad carried her small suitcase to the waiting Hillman Minx. Fred had expected his wife's best friend to look sad and dowdy but the woman who sat beside him in his new car was far from that. Her hair had been permed in an ultra-modern style and her pale green suit looked like one of the latest London fashions. Extra make-up and red lipstick combined to make her look ten years younger. She was clearly at one with the world and enjoying life. Eddie's dad swung the Hillman off the station forecourt and into the High Street.

"New car, Fred?" asked Martha.

"Not brand new, Martha. The Morris Minor had just about had it, I'm afraid."

"I'm going to get a car," said Martha. "I'm learning to drive."

"Good," said Fred as they turned into South Road. "It'll get you out and about again after …."

"Don't be afraid to say it, Fred. You mean after Cyril and Len died. Life has to go on you know."

As he pulled the car onto the drive of number 38 Fir Tree Close, Fred Compton wondered if all the make-up and new clothes were a normal part of Martha's daily image and, if so, was there someone special that they were for?

The two women hugged each other for an almost abnormally long time with Eddie's mum in tears and barely able to speak. Her friend seemed to be much more in control of the emotional situation.

"Now, now, Ann. Please don't cry. It's so good to see you and Fred."

Martha gently pushed Ann into a position where she could look into her wet eyes.

"I'm alright, Ann, you know. Really I am. Now where's Eddie?"

Eddie emerged from behind his mum and gave his 'aunty' a hug. She smelt of exotic perfume; quite unlike his best friend's mum that he'd known when Len had been alive.

"You've grown taller, Eddie and filled out a little. You're making a nice young man."

Martha paused and for the first time since arriving, she looked sad.

"Len would have been fifteen just over a week ago, you know."

Eddie wondered how his aunty would have reacted if he had told her that he had recently seen her son in the café on Hamsden station and that he had looked at least twenty years older than her!

Christmas Day arrived with a significant change in the weather. As if by celestial command, the day dawned free of fog with a deep golden sun in a clear blue sky. Eddie awoke in the somewhat pleasurable knowledge that it would be the first Christmas that his sister would not be at home. She was spending the long weekend with her boyfriend's parents, Mr and Mrs Jones. She would go straight from there to do some holiday work at Arleson's the bakers on the Tuesday. She needed whatever money she could get while she was at college.

When presents were exchanged under the tree, Eddie appeared to be a little nervous as he started to open his from Len's mum. Surely it couldn't be Len's railway timetable, could it? He was relieved when he discovered a book on mathematical tricks and puzzles together with a five-pound note tucked inside – more money than he had received from all his other real aunties and uncles combined. He was understandably ecstatic.

"Wow! Thanks, Aunty Martha."

"That's alright, Eddie. I don't have Len to buy for this year."

Eddie replied in like vein.

"Neither do I. I got him a card though – it's upstairs. You can have it if you like."

"That would be nice, Eddie. Thank you."

Eddie thoroughly enjoyed the main two days of Christmas with Len's mum and his own parents. With the Monday a public holiday as well, the normal festivities were extended into a third day. It was clear from a chat that he had on the evening of the 27th that Len's mum had not had any supernatural encounters with her dead son. She and Eddie had been delegated to do the washing-up after another enormous meal while Eddie's parents took a well-earned rest in the lounge. Eddie was bold enough to start what he knew might be a difficult conversation.

"Do you talk to Len, Aunty Martha?"

Martha Wilby looked a little oddly at Eddie.

"No, dear, I don't – at least not for some time. We have to move on and not dwell in the past. I know he's gone to a much better place and talking to empty space would only be self-indulgent, you know."

'If only you knew', thought Eddie as Len's mum continued.

"I used to talk to both of them and I'd get so annoyed with Len's dad in particular, for driving so fast that day, but I soon decided that it was pointless apportioning blame. He didn't do it on purpose and what's done is done."

"You do believe in God though, don't you?" asked Eddie.

"Yes, I suppose so – most of the time anyway. What about you, Eddie?"

"Oh yes, I believe in God."

"Do you also believe that you'll see Len again one day?"

Eddie knew he would never be able to say what he ought to say and managed instead,

"Maybe, but not in the same form as he was when he was alive."

If Len had been watching, Eddie hoped he would be 'patting him on the back' with a ghostly hand. After Martha gave Eddie a comforting hug, the conversation moved on to less ethereal and less difficult topics and the washing-up concluded in harmony.

Martha Wilby returned to Petersgate by train on the morning of Tuesday the 28th with some sadness for Eddie. He had warmed to Len's mum's new approach to life over her short stay. In addition, he was disappointed that her son had not deigned to put in an appearance over the festive period. Surely he could have made the effort.

The sales had already begun in earnest when Eddie wandered into town the following day. The unusually sunny and dry weather was continuing as he headed for Fenton-on-Sea's limited range of shops with money to spend. As he entered the High Street, he had an uncomfortable felling of déjà vu. As if on cue, a familiar voice called from behind him as he passed the station forecourt and it immediately brought back memories of a Saturday morning almost exactly to the day three years previously.

"*What ho, sport!*"

Eddie stopped to usher Len's ghost behind the high station wall, where he could speak out of sight and earshot. This time, he knew he had to confirm the speaker's identity before he started any conversation.

"Whatcha blithe comrade."

"Is that with a 'Y' or an 'I'?"

"You tell me," replied Eddie now facing the ghost full on.

"Depends how your mum spells it, mate."

"It's you at last, Len. Where have you been?"

"Nowhere, mate. The last thing I remember was pretending to be a retired and respected doctor of medicine who was taking time out of his busy schedule to talk to you on a foggy December night on Hamsden station. Christmas has obviously come and gone."

"Yes and we've had your mum to stay for a few days. She went home yesterday."

"How ironic that I should miss her when she came back to Fenton-on-Sea. How did she seem?"

"She's well, Len, and seems to be getting on with life – new clothes and hair-do. She looked happy."

"Did she mention me and Dad?"

"Only briefly, mate. She doesn't blame your dad for the accident and she still loves you. She bought me a Maths book and gave me five pounds for Christmas."

"Lucky sod. She never spent that much on me when I was alive."

Eddie's position was becoming exposed as more people started to filter into the forecourt for the trains to Hamsden. Len followed the high wall until he found a large oak tree which would hide his friend from view completely. Eddie stood with his back to the wall as if studying the trunk of the old tree.

"You know what my dad thinks, Len?"

"What?"

"He told me he thinks she might have a new man in her life."

Len smiled and Eddie thought he seemed pleased, but he decided against telling him about Michael Conners, the teacher who had been at the funeral. He didn't think that Len needed to know just yet about the future long-lasting relationship between Mr Conners and his mum which had probably had its inception at his and his dad's wake! Eddie changed the subject.

"Why have you come today?" he asked with some excitement in his voice.

"Just to try something out, Eddie."

"What?"

"You'll see – just follow me."

Eddie watched as Len's good ghost began walking quickly for the station exit. He seemed to glide over the ground and was almost lost to Eddie's sight before he knew it. He had to run quickly in order to catch him up fifty yards or so down the High Street. The town was too busy for words to be exchanged without causing curiosity and Len held a finger to his lips when Eddie was about to say something. Five minutes later and Len had led his friend to the turning into Mill Road. It suddenly dawned on Eddie where Len was going. It had become cloudy overhead and by the time he had reached Watson's Electrical it was strangely dark. Within seconds the light had vanished completely and Eddie struggled to find the shopfront. Something was happening again and he just hoped his friendly ghost was in sole charge. After a few seconds, the darkness started to lift gradually. Eddie immediately felt different, somehow smaller and not quite himself and when he caught sight of his own reflection in the shop window, all was revealed. He looked to be about twelve and was wearing clothes that he hadn't seen for several years. Len was nowhere to be seen. A voice came from the shop doorway.

"Well, are you coming in or not, Eddie?"

Len had already entered the shop and had poked his head out to see where his friend had got to. He looked much younger too and when Eddie raised his eyes to read the sign over the shop, he knew finally what had happened. In place of what should have been a sign advertising Watson's Electrical, Eddie read,

'*Canter's Junk Shop*'.

Eddie knew what it signified. He had gone back in time to a similar day just after Christmas in 1962 when he and Len had once before gone into the junk shop with money to spend. Before he followed Len's ghost into the shop, memories of several fantastic adventures flashed through his mind. He had the mind of a fourteen-year-old but it was trapped inside an eleven-year-old body. This was going to be interesting to say the least!

Len was standing in a corner away from the shop counter when Eddie entered. He could see from the expression on his face that he also was aware of what had happened. Eddie turned back to the counter to face the smiling and apparently friendly face of Mr George Counter. He too looked exactly as he had done on that Saturday three years ago.

"Well what do you want, my boy?"

Even the words seemed to be familiar to Eddie and when he replied he didn't seem to be in control of the situation.

"I just wondered if you had any science fiction books in, Mr Canter, sir."

'This was not right', thought Eddie. 'Why had he been so formal?' Len was still watching from the corner of the shop. George didn't seem to have noticed him.

"Of course I have. Just let me fetch them – you can have them for next to nothing, Eddie."

After George had disappeared into the back of his shop, Len came over to Eddie and whispered in his ear.

"Be careful, Eddie. Be very careful. Watch out for his tricks."

Eddie knew what 'tricks' Len was referring to and he nodded in silence.

Almost immediately, George emerged from his back rooms carrying a pile of magazines which he placed ceremoniously on the counter.

"Here you are, Eddie my boy. There must be twenty or more."

Again Eddie found himself replying as though from memory. He was not in control of his thoughts or his voice.

"What do you want for them, sir?"

"Well to you, Eddie, I charge one shilling only."

Eddie was beginning to see where the deal was going but, once again, he played his part unwittingly.

"I'll take them please, Mr Canter."

Eddie produced his wallet from his pocket and extracted the crisp new five-pound note that his aunty Martha had given him. He handed it swiftly to George Canter and, without waiting for any change, took the pile of magazines from the counter and turned to make his way out of the shop. As he did so, George turned back to his till, opened it and was just about to deposit the note there when Eddie caught a glimpse of Len moving quickly towards the counter. He thought he heard his friendly ghost shout,

"Run, Eddie! Run!"

In a flash and with seemingly impossibly long arms, Len reached over and grabbed the note from George's hands. George, for his part, looked both shocked and relieved – almost as if he knew what he had been about to do was wrong. By this time, Eddie had dropped the pile of magazines and was running out of the shop. If he had glanced back, he would have seen the sight of George Canter scrabbling frantically on the floor behind the counter but, of course, he wouldn't find the note that he thought had been blown out of his hand by a sudden draught.

The weather and light had returned to normal when Eddie reached the pavement outside the shop. Len was waiting for him across the other side of Mill Road where he was watching some customers enter the shop Eddie had just vacated. Once again, the sign above it advertised Watson's Electrical. Eddie crossed over to meet his friend. Len smiled and pointed to the pavement beside his foot and Eddie immediately bent down to pick up his five-pound note.

"That was a close one, Captain," said Len.

Eddie positioned himself with his back to a lamp post and pretended to be looking in a shop window. Len came and stood beside him.

"Too close for comfort, Len," replied Eddie. "What was that all about? Why did you let that happen?"

"I arranged my little demonstration just to show you that everyone has an evil side, including our sadly departed friend George."

"So that was his evil ghost?"

"Got it in one, mate. That's how he used to be before he went back to Poland. Of course, he did repay everyone he'd robbed by his former shady dealings and even though he didn't know why he was doing it, he was aware that it was wrong."

"So he has two ghosts; one evil and one good?"

"Everyone has, Eddie, I think."

A couple of people had, by this time, joined Eddie in browsing in *Needles and Pins*, Fenton's dress-making shop. Eddie began to walk back up Mill Road to the High Street. Len went on ahead and began to show off to Eddie by dodging the cars and bicycles in the road. Five minutes later, and with Eddie out of breath from his run through town, Len had led him to the deserted beach at the bottom of Steep Hill. Eddie followed his friendly ghost right to the water's edge. Facing the sea and in a breathless voice, Eddie said,

"What's the hurry, Len?"

"No hurry, Captain – just trying to keep you fit."

After a pause, he continued.

"Now you are beginning to understand the difference between good and evil, I hope. Evil must never be allowed to triumph but it is always there even …."

"Even?"

"Even after death, Eddie. You already know that I can still be bad – you've met my evil ghost and, you never know, there maybe more than one of them."

Eddie thought about it for a moment, but in the end decided against asking Len if there could be more than one of his good ghosts as well. It could prove the start of a long and difficult discussion and Len looked tired again. The morning's demonstration seemed to have taken a lot out of him.

"I'm going now, Eddie. Look after yourself and be careful when you talk to ghosts. Even close and respected friends can be bad."

After he had spoken these last words, Len seemed to walk a few paces into the shallow water. Without a splash or even a ripple of any kind, he vanished into the sea.

21
Evil Returns

Eddie didn't remain down town for very much longer after his encounter with Mr Canter's evil ghost. He too was at least mentally tired and, unless he made the trip to Hamsden, Fenton-on-Sea's shops really didn't have much to offer a fourteen-year-old boy, especially one of Eddie's intelligence. Indeed, the excitement and wonder of the previous few months had begun to make any normal earthly pursuits seem trivial at best. Life was good, yes, but death seemed to provide more interesting and unusual avenues.

Eddie did make a trip to Hamsden but not until 1966 had started. He was due back at school for the spring term on Wednesday, January the 5th and he decided to take the train early on the Tuesday morning. He had found the previous six days a little mundane and had spent them mostly working through his new mathematical puzzle book and some forgotten school work. Town were not at home; they had a third round F.A. Cup tie against a side a division above them so Eddie hoped the crowds would not be too large despite the New Year sales still being in full swing. He caught the ten past nine train as usual with every intention of being back well before lunchtime. He was in a good mood when he reached Hamsden after no alarms or ghostly visitations and having been able to sit all the way. The weather, though damp, was unseasonably mild and Eddie felt a little warm in his school duffle coat.

Before he got to the town centre proper, Eddie had already made a tentative decision not to visit Osborne's, concentrating, instead, on the few but well-stocked bookshops. He met Sally Barber from school for a brief chat outside Pritchard's Coffee House but, despite some perceived gentle encouragement, he didn't invite her to go inside with the standard,

'Fancy a coffee?' routine. After five minutes, they parted without Eddie really realising that the young lady in question had more than a soft spot for her intelligent fellow fourth year.

By eleven o'clock, Eddie had exhausted all the possibilities of things to do or buy in Hamsden and with some inevitability about the decision he made his way towards Osborne's department store. One small paperback on famous Mathematicians in British history was his sole purchase of the morning. Within ten minutes he had reached the toy department on the top floor. It was far less busy than the Saturday before Christmas when he had had the confrontation with the security guard but no such person seemed to be around this time. 'Action Man' was the latest craze on sale in Osborne's and though more entertaining than the normal run-of-the-mill toys, it didn't appeal to Eddie's inquiring mind despite its fantasy overtones. An eager sales assistant approached him and the young man asked politely,

"Is there anything I can help you with?"

"No thanks, I'm just looking," replied Eddie with equal politeness.

The young assistant smiled while Eddie studied his features carefully. With some disappointment, he quickly decided that, however good a disguise the assistant might be sporting, he definitely wasn't Len. The young man moved on to speak to someone else.

"You're beginning to see me everywhere, Captain."

At first, Eddie thought the voice was coming from entirely within his own head but a quick glance to his left revealed Len grinning from ear to ear. Because he had been taken off guard, Eddie had forgotten the essential identification routine and replied,

"I knew you would come, mate."

Len shook his head with resignation and said,

"Haven't you forgotten something?"

Eddie realised his mistake and without trying to make any sense, said,

"Sorry, you caught me at a blithe moment."

"Is that spelt with an 'I' or a 'Y'?"

"Same way as the woman's name."

Len paused and then said,

"So that's with a 'Y', then, like your mum?"

"Yes, comrade Len. It's good to see you."

"Who are you talking to, Eddie?"

This time, the second familiar voice came from his right and Eddie turned sharply round. A second and identically dressed Len stood less than six feet away. The new ghost continued.

"I told you last time to be very careful when you spoke to anyone, Captain. I presume you're talking to one of my ghosts."

"Yes, and the real one as well," replied Eddie sarcastically.

"The real one? How do you know he's the real one?"

"Because he knew the code."

"And what is the code, then, Eddie?"

Eddie grinned at the pathetic attempt to draw the special signal out of him. This bad ghost wasn't very clever!

"Nice try," he said.

"Well, let me see now. I wonder if it could be your mother's middle name."

Eddie's grin receded slightly. He couldn't possibly know, could he?

The 'good' ghost entered the conversation from Eddie's left.

"He doesn't know, Eddie. Ask him what it is."

He called the evil ghost's bluff.

"Which is?"

"How about Blythe?"

"Is that with an 'I' or a 'Y'?"

"A 'Y' of course."

Though they clearly couldn't see each other, the new ghost moved past Eddie and stood unknowingly side by side with the first one. Eddie could now see them both together for the first time and he realised that he had a problem. Little did he know, but in a moment it would get worse. In the meantime, he studied each ghost carefully. He had been totally convinced that the first had been the real one but now he was not so sure. They had both sounded like Len's good ghost and they were identical in every other respect. They had both passed the security check with ease too. The second ghost had a slight advantage in that he knew he had warned Eddie to be careful on a previous occasion but that proved nothing really. Both ghosts came from the same person anyway. Matters then took an awkward twist. As if they were being orchestrated by another power, both ghosts swapped position and then, to Eddie's horror, they did it again and again, until after a dozen or more swaps, he was totally confused as to which ghost was which. His eyes had become fogged in the process of trying to keep track of either or both of them in their macabre dance. To make matters worse, the young shop assistant returned and said to Eddie,

"Are you alright, young man? You look like you've seen a ghost."

Eddie mumbled that he was fine and waited where he was until the assistant was out of sight. Eddie knew that the sensible thing to do was to get out of the store as quickly as possible particularly if both ghosts were evil ones! Curiosity, however, got the better of him.

"You've got to choose one of us," said one ghost.

"You've got to choose one of us," said the other.

Whether this was mimicry or not, Eddie wasn't sure. If they couldn't see each other they probably couldn't hear each other either, he thought. Two voices then echoed in his head:

"Choose good or evil."

"Choose evil or good."

"Good or evil."

"Evil or good."

"Good or evil."

"Evil or ...."

The voices were incessant. Some shoppers stopped to look at Eddie who was now transfixed and staring into space. He had to choose and quickly too. He couldn't understand why but it felt like his life depended on it – almost as if he made the wrong choice he would be damned forever. The odds were even. It was the worst possible choice to have to make even though millions of gamblers did it everyday but only for money. This seemed to Eddie to be a matter of life or death. He closed his eyes and prayed.

'O God, help me choose right. I want to choose good, not evil.'

Eddie opened his eyes. He didn't have to make the choice. Only one ghost remained in front of him. After a few seconds, Eddie regained his composure. He had faced his most frightening choice ever and had survived. Len indicated to Eddie to follow him and a few minutes later they were both in a quiet side street just off the town centre. Len was first to break the tension.

"Good always triumphs over evil."

Len could tell that Eddie was still nervous when he said,

"How do I know that you *are* the good ghost, Len?"

"You don't, I suppose. It's a matter of faith. Do you want me to be the real ghost?"

493

"That would be a difficult question if you're not."

"Have faith, Eddie. I am the good ghost. Take a look behind you."

Eddie turned to look back up the street to the shops. He could just make out the other ghost, smoking a cigarette and clearly up to no good. He appeared to be arguing with a young woman and had hold of her handbag which he was trying to steal. Moments later and two men had freed the bag from his grip but then they themselves suffered abuse, both verbal and physical, as Len's evil ghost threw wild punches in all directions. Eddie was convinced and he turned back to Len to apologise for doubting him. The good ghost had vanished.

22

Snow

After Len's abrupt disappearance, Eddie returned home quickly that morning without further alarm or hindrance. It had been an interesting excursion to say the least though he was not altogether sure that he should read too much into it. It had been a lively demonstration of the battle between good and evil, it was true, but as to it having any significance for his future he had his doubts. Indeed, his immediate future was definitely concerned with harsh reality and the return to school the following day. Len was lucky in the fact that he could continually amuse himself and others with the fight against the darker forces at work within the human psyche and in the universe at large. Eddie definitely did not have the time or inclination to continue to dwell on such issues – final preparations were needed ahead of the spring term.

Eddie had not spoken to his sister for some time about George Canter's warning to her so it was with some surprise that she came to see him in his room just before he was going to bed. She stood nervously in the doorway until Eddie invited her to come in.

"What's up, sister dear?"

"I just wanted to wish you luck for the new term, Eddie."

Eddie looked up in disbelief. It was not the kind of thing that Jenny would even think about let alone say! There had to be a reason.

"Why? Do you know something I don't?"

"No, I just remembered what that man or ghost said to me about you having to be careful."

"What, Mr Canter?"

"Yes, him."

"Have you seen him again, then?"

"No, not really."

"Come on, Jenny. You either have or you haven't. Which is it?"

"I had a dream last night and in it he came to the door as before and said more or less the same thing to me again."

"Dreams are just dreams, Jenny," said Eddie.

"I know and I don't usually remember them but this one I did."

"What else do you remember?" asked Eddie trying not to show too much interest.

"Not much more than that which happened for real back in November. This time I ran after him straightaway but he was always just out of reach. He went out of our road again and followed South Road into the High Street and down Mill Road where he seemed to disappear into what must have been his old shop. I seemed to follow him in and …."

"And?"

"And there was nothing there – nothing but a big black hole and I couldn't stop myself from falling and falling until I woke up in a cold sweat. When I woke up this morning I didn't really remember much about the dream and it's only been this evening that I've managed to piece it altogether."

Eddie thought for a moment. He decided that there could be a simple explanation.

"I expect it was just your mind remembering what happened in November, that's all, Jenny. There's no significance in the black hole. That was probably your body getting ready to wake up. We've all fallen down holes in our dreams."

Jenny seemed comforted by Eddie's interpretation and when he gave her a reassuring hug she left in a reasonably happy mood with Eddie saying finally,

"I will be careful, Jenny. Who would you be able to talk to about complicated and philosophical issues if I wasn't around?"

Jenny didn't know what the second adjective meant but she had got the gist of what her brother was saying.

The school term began in earnest the following day and by the weekend thoughts of ghosts and the forces of good and evil had receded to the back of Eddie's mind. When he had discovered that Sally Barber was not at school on the Friday owing to sickness, he did think that the empty seat beside him in English that afternoon might be filled by his friendly ghost, but Len did not put in an appearance. By the Saturday morning the weather had taken off its mild face and replaced it with a cold and frosty glare. Snow was promised before the weekend was out with forecasters predicting the worst snowfall for three years. Distant memories of a day spent with Len, tobogganing down East Hill, came back to Eddie as he wandered into town that morning with no particular purpose in mind. Though Town had a home league game that afternoon, he had decided to avoid Hamsden and its largest department store in particular. He wasn't ready to face any more encounters with the clashes between good and evil. The previous one had been bad enough and he was scared that, if there was another one, it would be far more difficult to handle.

By the time Eddie reached the junction with Mill Road, a light snow had begun to fall. There was little wind to speak of and the cloud cover above suggested that it was probably going to snow for a very long time. He had read somewhere that, at its worst, snow could pile up at the rate of somewhere between half and a full inch per hour. He pulled the hood of his duffle coat over his head and continued down the High Street towards the sea. It felt good to be walking in the ever-increasing snow and Eddie began to experience an inner peace that he hadn't had for some time. He felt light-headed and almost euphoric as he crossed over the promenade and onto the beach which by then was covered by a good inch of snow. The sea was as calm as a mill pond; it looked oily and strangely inviting. 'Wouldn't it be nice to just walk into it and …?' he thought as he stood right at the sea's edge. Other thoughts of the life that his best friend appeared to enjoy came to Eddie at that melancholic moment. The air was thick with falling snow and visibility out to sea had diminished to less than fifty yards. An eerie silence had descended all around him and as he turned away from the water in an effort to shrug off any more morbid feelings, Eddie was presented with a sight that matched the eeriness he felt both inside his head and in the air that surrounded him. He rubbed his eyes in disbelief. He knew he hadn't drifted off to sleep so this was no nightmare like the last time in the school assembly hall. This had to be real. He knew he had woken up that morning. Suddenly he could hear a voice which was coming from somewhere above him.

"Go home, Eddie. Go home now or you may never get home again."

Eddie looked up into blackness; it had stopped snowing and the sky was dark and brooding. His eyes lowered to the strange sight before him; a sight that he had seen before but had forgotten until then. Fenton-on-Sea had vanished completely and had been replaced by a snowfield of Arctic proportions. It stretched away to the horizon in every direction and was bare of anything, natural or man-made. He turned back to the sea and discovered that the pure white panorama was all-encompassing. His nightmare came back to him fully with one important difference – last time he had woken up out of it in his bed at home.

After Eddie had walked round in a complete circle searching in vain in every direction for landmarks, he suddenly realised that he had completely lost his bearings. Which way was now home – which was the sea? It was pitch black overhead and it was a starless and moonless night. The voice had said for him to make for home straightaway, but where was home? Unlike with the ghosts in Osborne's, this was not a just a choice of two directions – one good, one bad – it was a choice of an infinite number of them. And that was assuming both that the snow would allow him to walk back safely and, more importantly, his home still existed! He walked around for a few moments thinking of what to do. Should he just wait for the scenery to change back? Was this another test of good against evil? Was he the only one who could save himself? Trying to rein in the panic that was forming inside him, he did the only thing possible that he could think of – he fell to his knees and bowed his head to pray.

"O God, please help me get back home. I know that you are the only one who can choose the right direction. Please, please help me!"

After his supplication, Eddie stood up and feigned confidence within himself.

"Show me!" he shouted. "Show me a sign. Make the choice for me."

He waited expectantly. He looked left, then right, then behind him and finally turned to face his original direction. Was that a pinpoint of light on the horizon? He walked forward; the snow was up to his knees. He trudged fifty yards and stopped. The light was brighter and seemed nearer. He tried to run and promptly fell flat on his face in the snow. He crawled forward on all fours and looked again at the source of his possible salvation. He could suddenly make out shapes. He jumped up and ran blindly forward into a fresh blizzard but this time, underfoot, the snow seemed less deep; only up to his ankles. Fortunately within a few yards, he stopped again to try to take in the view ahead. He couldn't believe his eyes. Not more than a hundred yards ahead stood a familiar tall building – St Andrew's Church! He approached with caution. The snow had stopped and now there was barely a covering on the ground. Eddie read the sign outside the main door:

'*PRAISE AND THANK THE LORD ALL WHO ENTER HERE*'

By the time he reached home, Eddie had discovered that time had moved on considerably that Saturday. Though the church clock seemed to indicate that it was nine-thirty, he also knew that it had not been working properly for some time, as, when he reached it, the more reliable one on the station façade indicated ten past three. A quick calculation told Eddie that he had been out for over six hours. At the same time, however, he also realised that he could only really account for about one of them. He was both mentally and physically exhausted. Despite this, he was, at the same time, filled with euphoria and excitement at his remarkable escape from a seemingly impossible situation. He appeared able to call on God at will to save him when in perilous situations. However, this mood was tempered by his mother when he opened the front door of number 38 Fir Tree Close – she had clearly been worried.

"I thought you said you were only going to be an hour or so. Where on earth have you been?"

Eddie hadn't prepared a reason for his lateness; his mind had been on other things on the way home and any invented excuse would have probably not been believed anyway so he said absolutely nothing. He put on his best guilty smile and hoped his mother would draw her own possible romantic conclusion. She did.

"You've been out with a girl, haven't you?"

Again Eddie was silent as he moved past his mum, intending to go straight to his bedroom. His mother persisted gently with her questioning. She actually seemed quite pleased.

"Was it Sally? She's such a nice girl, Eddie."

Eddie halted his progress and turned.

"Yes, Mum."

His mother clearly took the affirmative reply to confirm her suspicions. Eddie, for his part, felt he hadn't actually lied, as his answer could have been interpreted as merely being an agreement with his mum's simple assessment of the suitability of Sally Barber. He completed the escape to his bedroom unaware that his mother would probably never again question his movements too closely. As far as she was concerned, her only son was in love.

Eddie didn't eat much for the rest of Saturday. His lack of an appetite fitted perfectly with his mother's conclusions and so she didn't disturb him. For his part, he spent much of the time until he went to bed, thinking about the morning's events. He found it, at the same time, both worrying and exciting that Len had not been party to his escape from an impossible situation. As on a previous occasion, Eddie was beginning to sense that he had been privileged to 'look behind the curtain' and gain a glimpse and knowledge of a world where God was truly in charge as good and evil fought each other on a daily basis. The question that kept coming back to him, however, was: 'Why?' He would have to debate this with Len the next time he appeared.

23
Wrong Choice

It was to be another couple of weeks before Len would pay Eddie another visit and it was under unfamiliar circumstances when he did. Sally Barber's illness had been a short-lived stomach bug and she had quickly returned to school on the Monday after Eddie's adventure in the snow. Eddie's mother continued to smile knowingly at him whenever he was late from school or elsewhere. Eddie was happy to go along with the charade whenever it suited his purpose and he needed a silent excuse to cover it. By Friday, January the 21st, he had almost given up hope of Len appearing again, especially when the adjacent seat in English was always occupied by Miss Barber.

The afternoon English lesson became a very trying experience for Eddie. On three separate occasions he had given wrong answers to Mr Green's questions despite some helpful prompting from Sally beside him. In the end, Mr Green decided to leave him alone for the last ten minutes of the lesson, concentrating instead on the brighter pupils at the front of the class. At the end of the lesson, Eddie found that Sally appeared to want to accompany him on part of his walk home. Though such a thing had happened occasionally in the past, it had always been by chance and not by design as he thought on that afternoon.

Once they were walking in South Road and had exchanged and exhausted their views on the afternoon's lesson, Sally changed subject abruptly taking Eddie completely by surprise.

"Are you doing anything tomorrow?"

He was awkward and diffident with his reply.

"Er, I don't know. Er, I don't think so. I suppose I might be going out sometime."

"*Make up your mind, mate. She's about to ask you out.*"

Eddie glanced to his right to see Len walking boldly in step with the two teenagers. Sally continued unaware of the invisible interloper.

"Well, if you're not, I was wondering if you'd like to go to Hamsden to do some shopping and so on."

"*Ask her what she means by 'so on', Eddie?*"

Eddie ignored Len's facetious question and said,

"Maybe. I'll have to check with my mum first, Sally. I'll give you a ring later, if that's O.K."

Sally looked disappointed at Eddie's non-committal response but she smiled sweetly enough and replied,

"Fine – you've got my number, haven't you?"

"Yes," he lied and then, to his great embarrassment, she came right up to him and planted a kiss on his cheek. She then skipped and ran her way down South Road towards the High Street. Len burst out laughing.

"Well, you *are* a dark horse and no mistake, mate. She fancies you, old boy. Not a bad looker as well."

Eddie moved to a low wall where he sat down as though watching the traffic pass by. Len sat beside him.

"Stop it, Len," said Eddie. "It's bad enough having to deal with a lovesick girl without you playing gooseberry as well."

"Sorry, Captain. I thought you'd be alone on your walk home. I was going to take you on a day out tomorrow but I can see you're going to be otherwise engaged."

In the distance Eddie thought he could just make out Sally turning and waving back at him. He was beginning to feel pressurised and pulled two different ways at once with equally attractive choices. However, he made an instant decision. He could see Sally anytime and he hadn't made a commitment to her anyway whilst Len might not be able to come back for some time.

"No problem, Len. I'll come with you. Anyway, who wants to go shopping …?"

He didn't finish the sentence with 'with a girl' as somewhere deep inside he was actually incredibly flattered by Sally's invitation but his love life could wait, couldn't it?

"Are you sure, mate?"

"Yes, certain. I see Sally everyday at school. What did you have in mind for tomorrow, Len?"

"You'll have to wait until the morning for the destination. Let's just say it's somewhere that neither of us has ever been before."

"Really? That sounds exotic."

Len grinned and said finally,

"Be outside the station no later than eight-thirty in the morning."

"Are we going by train, then?" asked Eddie excitedly but as soon as he had phrased the question, Len vanished before his eyes.

Eddie couldn't find the Barbers' telephone number when he looked later that evening; they were ex-directory. He decided he would apologise to Sally when he saw her at school on Monday. She would understand.

Eddie slept fitfully that night as a mixture of guilt and excitement fought for his attention. In the end, visions of fabulous cities and island paradises won the day and the sleep that eventually came extended until just after eight o'clock. He had to wash and dress quickly when he realised he had overslept so badly. Grabbing some toast and a coffee, he was barely able to respond to his mum's question.

"Where are you off to in such a hurry, Eddie? Got a date?"

Ann Compton could tell by the look on her son's face that she was correct in her assumption. As Eddie bolted for the front door and, between mouthfuls of toast and marmite, he managed to say,

"See you later, Mum. I don't know when we'll be back."

Whether it was a Freudian slip or not, his mum didn't get the chance to say, 'I knew it, Eddie. I just knew it'; her son was already halfway down the front path.

Despite his late awakening, Eddie was only seven minutes late arriving at the station, but he cursed himself when he realised that, in his haste, he had not brought any money with him. To make matters worse, Len was nowhere to be seen. When the station clock displayed a quarter to nine, he decided to check inside the station to see if he could find his friend's ghost. He knew he had until at least ten past if Len was proposing to go by train to Hamsden. He avoided passing the ticket office where his dad would be at work and checked as much of the two platforms as he could. With very few people about, it was easy for Eddie to decide that Len was not in the station or at least, if he was, he wasn't showing himself. Eddie wandered disconsolately, head down, out of the station.

"Oh good, you have decided to come, Eddie. I bet you didn't have my phone number after all."

Eddie looked up to see an impossible nightmare standing before him. Sally Barber was accompanied by another girl who Eddie thought he recognised as another pupil from Fenton Grammar. Eddie thought hurriedly.

"Can't stop, Sally, I've got to go back home; I've forgotten something. I'll catch the later train and see you in Pritchard's for coffee at about eleven, O.K?"

505

"Ye-yes, O.K.," stammered Sally. Her friend looked amused. Eddie ran out into the station forecourt and didn't stop until he had made the High Street out of the sight of either girl. He paused for breath and realised that he had been fortunate. He was also glad for Sally that he hadn't ruined her day and that she had still been able to go to Hamsden with someone. He would worry on Monday about a reason for not being able to join her for coffee though.

When Eddie heard the familiar noise of the ten past nine train making its way out of Fenton station, he made his way back to the forecourt still hoping to find Len waiting for him. When he discovered that there was no sign of him, he began to think that he had made the wrong choice for his day out. The next train to Hamsden was at twenty to the hour and it didn't take him long to resolve to take it if Len's ghost hadn't shown by then. Being entertained by two girls didn't seem too bad a substitute for a ghostly trip, no matter how exotic.

The next train duly arrived and Eddie boarded it as planned. He was cross both with himself for being late, but also with Len for not waiting just a few short minutes longer. The train went straight through to Hamsden; Linham junction had raised Eddie's hopes but the nine-forty did not stop there on a Saturday. Walking into town, Eddie became a little nervous at the thought of meeting up with Sally and her friend; he knew he wasn't experienced with girls. He silently wished that Len's ghost would still appear and to that end, he toyed with the idea of going to Osborne's. However, he quickly dismissed the thought from his mind; he didn't want to be faced with more impossible choices.

He had just reached the town centre proper when some glossy posters caught his eye in a shop window. East Shires Travel was advertising all their summer holidays to places far and wide. Gorgeous technicolour views of Paris, New York and Rome shouted at the more well-heeled passers-by. To pass the time and delay a visit to Pritchard's Coffee House, Eddie began to imagine himself going to any of the three destinations. He tried to decide which one he would like to visit first. Rome won the day; he and Len had been to Paris and the Big Apple looked too brash and busy for his taste. Architecture like that of the Colliseum appealed to Eddie much more than skyscrapers and the like. He could also recall some phrases that he'd learned in Geography or History at school: 'Rome wasn't built in a day'; 'When in Rome, do as the Romans do' and, most appropriate for him 'All roads lead to Rome'. There was a fourth one but it escaped him at that moment; it couldn't be important, he decided. Yes, he thought, it would be nice to go to the Eternal City. Even the very name fitted in with his recent experience of the everlasting fight between good and evil.

"And that's precisely where I was going to take us until you didn't turn up on time like I asked."

Eddie didn't know how long his friendly ghost had been standing beside him or that he could read his thoughts too. He quickly did his security check of the ghost's identity and when all was well, he said,

"I was only a few minutes late, Len."

"I know, mate, but it was fun watching you agonise over what you should do. It'll teach you to be late in future, eh?"

"You mean you were just playing with me?"

"A bit – I did wonder what you would do if I didn't show up."

"You've been following me as well?"

"Yes, but you would never have seen me; I was too well hidden. When you reached the travel agents, I could sense what you were thinking and you actually started talking to yourself, believe it or not."

Eddie raised his eyebrows.

"What did I say?"

"Something about all roads leading to Rome."

Eddie said nothing further as it seemed that his friendly ghost had already started preparing *his* 'road' to the Eternal City. Len's face was a mask of concentration and within a few seconds, Eddie was plunged into the familiar darkness and absolute silence.

It was a beautiful spring morning when normal light returned. The Italian capital was at its finest with the pink almond blossom in full bloom. Flower sellers pushed their handcarts full of mimosa and violets and the air was heady with scent. As Eddie looked around him, he marvelled at the splendour of one of the most beautiful cities in the world. He and Len were sitting in one of the many parks in the city and it was mid-morning judging by the position of the sun overhead. No one would take any notice of the lone young boy talking to himself in a foreign language after Len began the conversation.

"What do you think, then? I thought I'd choose May; it's such a nice month and …."

"And?"

"And three years ago this month we thought we were going there on our first fantastic journey. Do you remember?"

"Vaguely – you must have a good memory."

"Certain things come back to me more clearly now that I'm dead."

Eddie looked puzzled.

"Did you say three years ago?"

"Yes, it was late May 1963, I believe."

"But when I left Hamsden it was only January the 22nd."

"Yes," said Len. "We've moved forward in time but only by about four months. You've done that before, Eddie."

"Not with you as a ghost though. That's a bit scarier, Len."

"Not as long as I'm with you, but …."

"I knew there would be a 'but'."

"But I have an extra surprise for you."

"What?"

"While you're in the future you're invisible to everyone except for me. You're my trainee ghost. You have an advantage over me as well."

"Oh yeah. What?"

"You still have your real body. If you didn't have it you'd be a full ghost and you know what that would mean."

Eddie looked down at himself.

"Go on," said Len. "Feel yourself."

Eddie pinched his own left arm and then slapped both thighs. He laughed out loud.

"I'm real and invisible. It's magic, Len – absolute ruddy magic."

"Yes it is, but be careful. Because you have a real body you can still get hurt or even drown, so don't go falling off any bridges or the like. No one would be able to help you because they wouldn't be able to see you."

Edoardo Giordano drove a *camion rifiuti* for his living; he was a good and honest garbage disposal expert – a dustman. His job was to visit some of Rome's central parks to collect the tons of rubbish from the hundreds of bins located there. He lived about eight miles out of the city not far from the recycling and waste disposal plant where he took his truck at the end of each day. Though his cargo was often smelly as well as dirty, he was proud that he kept the paintwork of his truck in pristine condition. It was thus with some surprise and disappointment that, when he checked it at the end of that late spring day, he found the front bumper and grill had sustained some damage. There were several small dents and scratches on the surface of the metal. He was certain he hadn't come into contact with anything that day and thus it was a complete mystery to him how they had got there. There was no trace of animal hair or bird feathers; it was not uncommon to have fatal arguments with the wildlife on the country roads near the disposal plant. He also decided that it would have had to have been a fairly large animal to have caused such damage. In the end he thought it could only have been caused by another vehicle reversing into his truck while he had left it unattended.

24

Another Eden

Eddie made two tragic but human mistakes in his eagerness to see Italy's capital; one before he set off and one during his all too brief visit there. He forgot that Italian drivers use the right side of the road and not the left, which, combined with the broadness of some thoroughfares, meant that he should have exercised extra care when crossing one to rush to see one of the city's sights. He never saw his namesake and his big red truck and, just before the fatal moment, he was reminded of his other mistake in not recalling the fourth clichéd phrase concerning the Eternal City. 'See Rome and die' might just have swayed his choice of day out back to the safety of Pritchard's Coffee House and the promise of his first relationship with a member of the opposite sex. These two mistakes, however, actually disguised a more fundamental reason for his wrong choice for a day out. On occasions before, when faced with much more difficult and frightening choices, Eddie had sought help from the God in whom he put his trust. On the more mundane matter he had neglected to do so, choosing to take his own judgement over divine counsel.

For Eddie's part, however, he had found contentment and his friendship with Len had been restored to completeness for eternity. From then on he would be able to see and communicate with him whenever he wanted to. As Len had told him in the past, he wouldn't grow old, or tired, or hungry. He wouldn't need money or clothes or somewhere to live. He wouldn't need to get angry or jealous or sad. He would never be scared again and he wouldn't need to sleep. He would exist forever as a happy fourteen-year-old in a world that was peaceful and ordered. Above all, he would never have to worry about man's biggest fear ever again.

When he didn't return to his home in Fenton-on-Sea that cold January day, the emergency services would make their statutory searches but sadly, of course, without success. Sally Barber would report later that she had seen Eddie running away from Fenton station and that he was going to meet her later in Hamsden. It would turn out that she had been the last person to see him as nobody else reported a sighting of him afterwards. A few months later and the powers that be would declare that Edward James Compton was posted as officially missing, presumed dead. That assumed verdict would not be finalised for another seven years. Some people, Eddie's mum and sister included, formed the opinion that he had never really been the same since his best friend had been tragically killed in a car accident. They consoled themselves and others with the hope that the two boys' special friendship had been rekindled for eternity.

HEAVEN ON EARTH

For Rachel, who has already started the journey

'He whom I wished to see,
Wished for to hear;
Where's all the joy and mirth,
Made life a heaven on earth?'

Lady Caroline Keppel (1735-?)

CONTENTS

1

Awakening

Edward Compton had been 'asleep' for just over two months, but it hadn't been a real sleep; it hadn't been caused by tiredness nor had it been a natural sleep. You see, Eddie was dead. Like his best friend Len, who had been tragically killed in a car crash a few months previously, shortly after moving with his family to Kent, Eddie too had met an untimely end but in rather more strange and unearthly circumstances. His sad demise had occurred in of all places, the Eternal City – a very appropriate appellation for the departure lounge for his escape from this world because, indeed, now Eddie had all eternity to look forward to. On the face of it, as far as their parents and families had been concerned and up to the time that he moved away, Leonard Wilby and Eddie had spent their early teenage years like any other boys growing up in the early sixties in a typical seaside town on the East Anglian coast. As far as the two best friends were concerned, nothing could have been further from the truth, given all the fantastic adventures they had been on involving time and space travel. Indeed, after Len's sad passing, Eddie, while still 'alive and kicking', had gained great comfort in also miraculously being part of the ghostly world which his late-departed friend had started to inhabit. Unfortunately, one such ghostly adventure had led Eddie to pass for 'real' into that ghostly world where he had previously only been a temporary observer.

"*C'mon, Captain, it's time to wake up!*"

A familiar voice echoed in Eddie's head, but all around him was still an all-enveloping blackness. The voice continued.

"*It's me, Eddie.*"

Eddie suddenly felt a warm glow within and the darkness seemed to lift as bright sunshine began to filter into his new world. He tried to speak.

"L-Len?"

Laughter.

"Got it in one, mate. Welcome to my world!"

Eddie's eyes flickered open and he began to take in his new surroundings. '*This isn't Rome*', he thought as he tried desperately to recall his last living moments in the real world. Fortunately, any memory of his tragic end had been wiped from his mind 'forever'.

"Where am I?"

"Fenton-on-Sea, mate. Good old, boring Fenton."

Eddie looked around him. Now wide awake, he found himself sitting on a familiar bench on the promenade with the beautiful blue sea in front of him. Other sights registered themselves with him; the pier to his right, the lightship on the horizon and Len himself, standing smiling directly in front of him – all familiar reminders of his home town.

"How …?"

Len finished Eddie's attempted question.

"How did you get here?"

"Y-yes."

Len looked sad and with a tinge of guilt etched lightly on his face, he said,

"I tried to stop you but you just didn't see it and …."

Eddie held up his hand – he didn't need to hear anymore. His response was brief.

"Don't, Len. Stop it!"

Len sat down bedside his best friend and put his arm round his fellow ghost; in so doing, neither of them felt anything physical.

"It's alright, Captain," said Len. "Look on the bright side. We can now see each other whenever we want and think of the other advantages."

"Such as?" asked Eddie.

"Well, for one, no one can see either of us now."

Eddie's mood seemed to lighten a little and Len continued.

"And we can go anywhere we want and when we want to as well."

The warm glow returned and Eddie began to feel an inner contentment beyond anything he had ever experienced in his real life. He felt safe and happy to be with his best friend again. What did he have to worry about? He wasn't going back to school; he wasn't going to have to take any more exams; he wasn't going to have to go to university or get a job and, above all, he wasn't going to die! He was going to 'live' forever, a contented fourteen-year-old, except ….

"What's up, Eddie?" asked Len seeing his friend apparently in deep thought.

"How old are we, Len?"

"Well, we *would* have both been fifteen now, mate."

"Fifteen?" asked a bemused Eddie. "But I was only fourteen when I …."

"Yes, but that was in January. Look around you, old son. It's high summer now and, anyway, we'd already moved forward to May when you had your unfortunate accident, so you could say that you were already fifteen then, although since our last time travel all happened on the same day, you could also say that you stayed as fourteen."

Eddie went quiet while he appeared to do some calculations.

"So really I've been dead for about six months in real time and it's the summer of 1966?"

"Yes, Captain, July 30th to be precise, but there's one thing you're forgetting."

"What's that?"

Len smiled warmly at his ghostly friend.

"We actually don't age, unless that is …."

"Unless?"

"Unless we want to, of course."

"We have that in our power, Len?"

"Who knows, old boy? Anything maybe possible in time. Just enjoy the ride, my friend – at the moment, you're fourteen and I'm fifteen. How long we've been dead is irrelevant; six months, a hundred years; it's all the same to us now, Ed."

Eddie ignored the shortened appellation of his name, even though Len never called him by it when they had been alive because, apart from the date seeming to jog something else in Eddie's memory, he was still frowning over the apparent conundrum – there was a problem with his calculations. He shared the puzzle with his friend.

"I left Fenton-on-Sea on January the 22nd, right?"

"Yes, if you say so," replied Len with a twinkle in his eye.

"But we had moved forward in time to late May when we went to Rome and so …."

"So you've only been dead for two months or so," said Len. "What does it matter?"

Eddie seemed satisfied with his friend's explanation but his mathematical and ordered mind would remain unhappy for some time with the apparent paradox – it appeared to him that he had 'lost' four months of time whether it was regarded as real or not. Of course, if Len was right, it really didn't matter as they weren't going to age anymore in the future, whatever that meant. Future, past, present – all might be mixed up in his new world.

While he was thinking on the matter, still sitting with head bowed, other voices abruptly entered Eddie's head.

"Come on, dear, let's sit down; my feet are killing me."

"Good idea, love; it's a bit too hot for a walk."

Eddie looked up to see not only Len with a cheeky smile on his face, but also an elderly man and woman looming over the promenade seat. The lady was just in the act of depositing her ample rear end directly on Eddie's lap, when he came to his senses with a start, even though he would never have felt any contact. Force of human habit caused him to jump upright and straight into Len's friendly but ghostly embrace and he then knew something was wrong. It wasn't just the lack of physical contact when he seemed to pass right through his friend's ethereal body and into the bright sunlight behind him. That sunlight should have been reflecting on a silver St Christopher round Len's neck; the St Christopher that his best friend had promised he would always wear, in life and death. Len's open-neck shirt could not disguise any such jewellery. Something was wrong. Turning back to face his friend's ghost, he asked quietly,

"Where's your St Christopher, Len?"

"What did you say, my love?"

"Nothing, dear. I never said a word."

Len ushered Eddie a few yards down the promenade and out of earshot of the elderly couple who had obviously and strangely heard his friend's question. They walked side by side down onto the pebbly beach and on reaching the water's edge, Eddie repeated his query.

"I said: Where's your silver chain?"

"What sil …?"

Len didn't finish as he guessed that he'd been caught out. Eddie knew what he had to do next. After Len had died, they had developed a secret code to make sure of each other's identities when Len reappeared to Eddie in ghostly form. This exchange of codes had been vital in Len's case as his ghost could appear in different forms, both good and evil.

Eddie smiled and began to take control of the situation. He tried out the code.

"What a *blithe* day, comrade!"

Len looked nervous but tried to bluff his way through.

"Have you swallowed a dictionary, Captain?"

"Just like your mum's middle name, mate, but spelt with a 'Y'. Am I right?"

Eddie turned to look behind him. Immediately his eye was caught by a stab of bright white light as the strong sunshine glinted off a silver St Christopher hung round the neck of a second and similarly dressed Len. Len's 'good' ghost had given the correct response to the secret code. His 'evil' ghost continued to stare embarrassingly at Eddie, apparently unaware of, and blind to the new ghost.

"What are you looking at?" asked the evil ghost.

Eddie did not turn back or reply. With the good ghost already running back up the beach, Eddie quickly did likewise with the good Len shouting,

"Run, Eddie – as fast as you can, mate!"

Eddie didn't stop until they had both reached the pier, further down the promenade. Predictably, given their phantom guises, neither boy was out of breath. Eddie looked back, but the evil ghost had disappeared. Len was first to comment.

"Oh, Eddie! What have I told you? You must remember the code when we meet. I have a good side and an evil side and he was my bad ghost."

Eddie looked a little sheepish and embarrassed by his simple error.

"Sorry, mate; I just forgot."

"We'd better change the code again," said Len.

"What do you suggest?" asked Eddie.

"It can be anything – we'll just make something up now."

Eddie looked doubtful.

"Won't your evil ghost be listening? After all, he is part of you."

"Not now I'm dead, I think. I don't seem to have evil thoughts anymore. He's a totally separate entity."

"You think? You mean, you hope, comrade," said Eddie.

"Well, he didn't know about your mother's middle name, did he?"

"You heard him speak, then?" asked Eddie.

"Yes."

Eddie was clearly still not convinced because he then said,

"The evil ghost knew about our trip to Rome; the timings and my accident, you know. He was with you then."

Though Len went quiet, the news didn't seem to bother him too much.

"I told you he's a separate entity. I have no control over where he goes. We'll just have to hope that he's elsewhere right now. He didn't know the last code."

"I suppose you're right," said Eddie as he thought for a moment. His mathematical mind soon provided an idea for the code.

"What is the twentieth prime number, Len?"

Len looked totally bemused.

"You are joking, aren't you? How on earth would I know that?"

"It's seventy-one, mate."

"Seventy-one? I suppose that'll do – after all there's no way I would have been able to work that out while I was still alive!"

"True!" agreed Eddie and Len smiled back at his friend.

"You know it works both ways, don't you, Eddie?"

"What do you mean?"

"I mean that you have an evil side as well so that there's probably a bad 'Eddie' ghost wandering around out there."

Eddie looked a bit nervous for a moment until Len said,

"We'll just have to ask each other the question."

"No need, Len – as long as the correct question and answer are exchanged, it doesn't matter who asks it. Only we know the precise question and the answer."

Len looked knowingly at his friend.

"You're right again, maestro! You were always the genius at school."

"And you were the brilliant athlete and sportsman, Len. I feel safe again knowing you're with me again on equal terms, you know."

"We'll make a great team as ghosts, eh?" said Len.

Within ten minutes the boys found themselves, whether by design or not, in the High Street of Fenton-on-Sea on the busy Saturday morning at the end of July. Passing by or through the shoppers, Eddie began to sense a certain excitement in their faces and demeanour. Suddenly, as the two friends paused outside Woolworth's, Eddie understood the reason for the many smiling faces. A previous meeting with Len's ghost, almost at the moment of Len's tragic passing, had occurred in the future the day after this date – July the 30th, 1966. Len seemed to realise what Eddie was thinking.

"You know what today is, don't you?" he said.

"I think so," replied Eddie. "I remember this date from back in January – it's the World Cup Final this afternoon at Wembley."

"Spot on, and England are in it against West Germany."

Somewhere in the deep and dark recesses of Eddie's mind lurked something that was struggling to surface into a concrete fact, but nothing immediately presented itself to him. Strangely, he just felt he ought to know the score even before the game had been played. For his part, it was clear that Len did not possess such prior knowledge also.

"Hope we win," he said. "I think Germany are favourites, though."

Eddie suddenly felt exhausted; he remembered how easily his friend seemed to tire when he too had first taken on his ghostly role. He tried hard to fight the vagueness that threatened to take control of his new and delicate psyche. He had earlier been thinking about and looking forward to exploring his old haunts in his home town, not least of which was number 38 Fir Tree Close which he had left for the final time on a Saturday morning in late January earlier that year. He had a longing, of sorts, to see his family again; his sister, Jennifer – Jenny; his mother, Mrs Ann Compton and his father, Mr Fred Compton. Though he did not now possess the delicate and transitory emotions of a living and breathing person, he, nevertheless, thought it would be nice to see how his closest relations were doing. Jenny would be twenty now. Had she managed to keep her place at Hamsden Civic College on the hairdressing and beauty course? Was she still going out with Gary Jones? Was the relationship heading for permanence? All these thoughts rushed almost instantly through Eddie's ghostly mind. He seemed to have developed the ability to sift and process several different ideas simultaneously and even his friend's next few words hardly disturbed those thought patterns.

"You look tired, Captain," said Len, almost reading his friend's blank but slightly wistful face. Eddie emerged from his trance with a ghostly shudder, his brain and mouth appearing to work independently of his current thought process.

"Yeah, mate – almost enough excitement for one day."

"Pity," said Len. "I was going to suggest a trip down to London this afternoon; it's only about eleven now."

Eddie seemed to perk up.

"You mean you can take us to the game?"

"Why not? At least I can try to spirit us there. My ghostly powers have developed somewhat since we last met, and I managed to get us to Rome, didn't I?"

By now the two boys were 'resting' their ghostly forms against the glass frontage of Woolworth's window, unbeknown to the many passers-by. Eddie seemed to be drifting into sleep and invisibility, and within seconds he began to vanish from his best friend's ghostly view. Len whispered softly, though no one could now hear either of the two young ghosts,

"Come back, Eddie; stick with me – I need to be able to see you. You'll feel refreshed after our invisible journey. Please come back."

Eddie's ghostly form reappeared briefly and instantly Len began to contort his face while he concentrated on spiriting them through space and, maybe, time. Eddie saw and felt nothing apart from that now almost familiar warm glow inside him. His 'world' went dark as he drifted into oblivion. His initial awakening had lasted less than an hour.

2

Wembley

The next time Eddie came back to the land of the 'living dead', he felt somewhat refreshed and more relaxed than his first awakening into the bright sunshine of Fenton-on-Sea. Before his eyes began to open involuntarily, the first contact with his new world was via the medium of sound. A staccato chant pervaded Eddie's head.

"England! England! England!"

The next contact should have been physical had he been clothed in physical flesh. He would have found it hard to stand up as the crowds thronged and jostled along Wembley Way; a cacophony of sound emanating from a rolling ocean of red and white. For Eddie it was different. He seemed to be able to stand still without fear of being crushed by or pushed along on the crimson tide. He could, if he had wished, outrun the excited crowd and dodge, weave or just go straight through the unseeing bodies making their slow but relentless progress towards the twin towers. Where to go? That was the question.

"England! England!"

The chants were incessant. Eddie veered left as Wembley Way opened up into a large plaza before the stadium. He put himself into the largest open space he could find away from the eager and expectant crowds. All he could do was watch and wait. The clock high on the stadium read ten to three. The crowds began to thin out. Where was Len? Was he going to come and meet him or was it up to Eddie to find his friend? Five minutes passed. Eddie heard a roar from inside the stadium. The teams had obviously taken the field. No one came.

A loud whistle blew; the crowd observed a respectful silence; '*God Save the Queen*' rose to the heavens. Eddie walked nonchalantly to the nearest turnstile. No one challenged him as he glided smoothly into the ground.

The teams were lined up facing each other when Eddie at last found a suitable vantage point high up in the stand and almost opposite the half-way line. England were to attack the goal to Eddie's left. Len had still not put in an appearance. Had he been capable of human emotions, Eddie would have found the experience rather scary as he stood alone among the thousands of unknown fans. As it was, he felt relaxed and excited by the prospect of being able to watch the game, almost like a god, from his superb position above the field of play. Unlike all the other fans, Eddie found he could stand at the top of one of the wide gangways while stewards ushered the latecomers past, or occasionally, through him. He could also, if he wished, move freely around the ground and even venture onto the pitch if he could build up the confidence to do so. No one would see him, would they? He was a ghost after all. But did he have the faith to believe he would remain invisible and silent to everyone? Would God allow him to accomplish such an outrageous exploit? It would be a good way of making Len aware that he was in the ground. Surely he would then be spotted by his best friend from whatever position he himself had found? He would still be visible to Len, wouldn't he?

After a few minutes, the crowd were suddenly hushed. A ball crossed into England's penalty area was misheaded by the full back, Ray Wilson and Helmut Haller burst through to beat the diving Gordon Banks; 1–0 to West Germany. Only twelve minutes had passed. While the teams made their way back to the centre-circle, Eddie continued to look at his forlorn hero, Banksy, as he stood in the goalmouth in frustration at the ease with which the opposition had scored. Then Eddie saw him – standing nonchalantly leaning against the left-hand post, arms folded and shaking his head at the England goalkeeper. It had to be Len! Even at a hundred yards away, Eddie could make out his friend's distinctive blond hair and that bold, god-like pose. Eddie quickly made his decision and wandered silently and unnoticed down the gangway to the low retaining wall which he straddled with ease. Jumping onto the touchline and past the St John's Ambulance men, the linesman and some other important onlookers, Eddie headed for the right-hand goal, still not yet having the courage to walk directly across the pitch to his friend. Another German attack was imminent and Gordon Banks rushed into the centre of his penalty area. Eddie was now behind the goal and Len had moved away from the goalpost. Eddie whispered as loud as he dared,

"Len, I'm here, behind you!"

There was no response from his friend who was concentrating earnestly on the failed German attack as the ball now headed upfield and away from danger. Gordon Banks returned to his position on his goal line. Eddie crept closer, pretending to hold onto the goal netting for presumed security. He stood inches behind his friend and said quietly,

"I'm here, comrade."

Still no reaction. England had been awarded a free kick midway in the German half. Len seemed to tense. Eddie could hear Gordon Banks shout,

"*Go on, Bobby, swing it in for Geoff!*"

Bobby Moore lined up the kick. The crowd looked on excitedly. Eddie moved in front of Len, possibly blocking his view. Instantly Len moved to his right and shouted,

"Get out of the way, you idiot! I can't see!"

The free kick swung into the area. Geoff Hurst leapt unmarked and glanced his header beyond the astonished keeper; England had equalised and the crowd erupted in a sea of red and white. Len jumped high in the air and then spun round to face his friend.

"You made it, then, Captain."

"Yes, and you knew I was behind you, didn't you?" replied a slightly cross Eddie.

"Just my bit of fun, Eddie – I actually saw you outside in Wembley Way and followed you into the ground. We must have landed outside within feet of each other. Once inside I kept my eye on you until the game started and then I made my way here. I knew you would eventually see me if I stood by the goal, but I didn't expect them to score so easily or so early. Wilson made a real howler with his header to let that blond-haired bloke score."

Len paused and looked quizzically at his friend and when there was no immediate response to his facial promptings, he said,

"Well, what have you got to tell me, old son?"

"Not much – my arrival here was pretty much as you described."

Len grinned wryly. The game had restarted and the play had shifted back to the German penalty area. Len persevered with his questioning.

"And you're sure there's nothing else you want to *ask* me?"

And then Eddie realised his mistake and his ghostly face reddened to match his ginger hair.

"Whoops, Len! I'm sorry, mate."

"No need to say sorry to me, Eddie. Anyone could make such a *prime* mistake."

"So what is the twentieth prime, comrade?" asked the embarrassed Eddie.

"I believe that would be the number seventy-one, Captain, sir," replied Len.

The secret codes having been exchanged correctly, the two ghosts stood side by side to concentrate on the game as it entered a crucial stage.

"Next team to score wins it," said Len.

"Let's hope it's us, then," replied Eddie who was unaware that, in his embarrassment and excitement, he had encroached a few yards onto the pitch. Len quickly joined him as they both struggled to see the action in the distance at the other end. Eddie had almost read his friend's mind before Len eventually said,

"You know there's nothing to stop us just wandering right into the middle of the pitch and getting right up close to the players and the ball."

Eddie moved nervously back to the touchline. Len could not be serious, could he?

"No way, Len," he whispered from his new position of relative security, but as soon as he'd said it, he knew what Len would do. Despite his nervousness, Eddie also knew that they had been invisible and silent to everyone so far. If they did become visible they were, after all, just ghosts. They had no physical form. No one could catch them and who would believe anyone who said they'd seen a ghost in the middle of the pitch at Wembley! How ridiculous would that be? Eddie made a quick decision and followed his friend onto the pitch.

Back in April, Eddie's dad, Fred Compton, had reached a milestone in his working career with British Rail – he had, either side of the war, completed twenty-five years as ticket collector, guard and finally, senior clerk in the booking office at Fenton-on-Sea railway station. The management and his colleagues had bought him and his wife, Ann, a couple of special gifts, one permanent and one to be used on Saturday, July the 30th that year. Because of the tragedy that the respected couple had suffered in January, the gifts were rather more extravagant than was normal for such an occasion. Losing a son and not being able to bury him was more than most people could bear but Fred and Ann had been stoical in their grief and recovery, helped in no small way by the knowledge that their son had joined his best friend, Leonard Wilby, for an eternity of boyish fun and adventures.

The first gift was a beautiful silver pocket watch, appropriately inscribed and perfect for a man who had always been fastidious with his information on the timings of trains and in the day to day running of his private life, too. The second was to be shared with his wife or anyone else that Fred should choose to accompany him – two front row tickets for the World Cup Final at Wembley on the last Saturday in July. With England on home soil and one of the likely favourites, Fred had hoped all spring and early summer that Ramsey's boys would make it to the pinnacle of footballing success and reach the final. His prayers had been answered as he and Ann took up their seats just feet from the touchline and almost on half-way, giving them a perfect close-up view of the players and the game.

It was just a few minutes before half-time and the score still remained 1–1. Ann Compton was fidgety and in need of some natural relief, judging by some of the strange and awkward poses she was displaying in her seat.

"What is the matter, dear?" asked Fred, even though he knew the weakness of his wife's bladder.

"I need a wee," she whispered. "I'll have to go now, Fred."

"Can you go on your own? I don't want to miss any of the match."

"I think so. We passed some signs at the top of our gangway – you know I always keep a lookout when we go anywhere new."

"Don't be long, then. I'll look after your seat."

With her husband's blessing, Eddie's mum made her way quickly to the top of the stand. There were less than five minutes left before half-time. England were on the attack, but it was quickly broken up by a tall, young and handsome German player who in later years would become to be known as 'The Kaiser' and a thorn in England's side in many future games between the two countries; not only as a player either.

Meanwhile, Eddie and Len had 'ghosted' their ways past several England defenders, each of the phantom boys possessing a slippery and stealthy movement that not even the great Martin Peters would ever be able to emulate. They took up their positions in the middle of the centre-circle, from where they had just about the best view of anyone; player, referee or crowd alike. While Eddie remained more or less in a static position with his ghostly mouth wide open in sheer astonishment at their audacity and good fortune, Len did his best impression of a little dog as he pursued the ball everywhere round the pitch, even once standing inches in front of a German free-kick and pulling all kinds of faces at the player about to take it. He didn't even flinch when the ball seemed to shoot straight through his stomach and chest area without deflection or loss of speed. After a couple of minutes, Eddie began to relax when he eventually became absolutely certain that neither of them could be seen or heard by anyone. He ventured towards the touchline on the half-way line to watch an England throw-in to be taken by the captain Bobby Moore. Len joined him and began shouting at his blond hero,

""Throw it to Bally, Bob!"

As if by magic – although Len would swear later that it was *his* instruction that had penetrated Bobby Moore's mind – the ball was thrown directly to little Alan Ball who waltzed round two German players and set off for the opposition penalty area. Eddie stayed on the touchline while his friend skipped alongside the England number seven until Ball took on one too many defenders and the ball was cleared back up into the England half. Just before Eddie was about to set off to rejoin his fellow ghost back in the centre-circle, he suddenly heard a voice inside his head.

"Turn round, Eddie; your dad's come to see you."

The words had hardly registered with Eddie before his body seemed to turn round of its own accord to face the crowd. He immediately got the shock of his life (?). There, not ten feet away in the front row, sat his dad. Eddie moved right to the retaining wall and in an almost nonchalant voice, said quietly,

"Hello, Dad. How have you been?"

No sooner had the words left his lips than Eddie realised how stupid he'd been in expecting to get an answer – ghosts couldn't be heard by ordinary people! He smiled to himself as he walked away, thinking how lucky his dad had been to get a ticket for the final. Once back on the pitch, Eddie turned back once more and gave a cheery wave to his dad. He hadn't felt much emotion at the strange meeting. He hadn't really felt much of anything. He was reminded of Len's words, when he had been alive, about ghosts not having the same feelings as living people. It seemed true – he felt neither happy nor sad at having seen his dad once again. It was just another event to be catalogued in his new life/death. However, he was reassured that his dad had looked well and happy which seemed to please him, but where was his mum? Was she still at home or had she come with his dad? Eddie rejoined his friend just as the referee blew his whistle for half-time and Len motioned to Eddie that they should follow the England team to their dressing room. At first Eddie looked reluctant, but as soon as Len began to disappear from the pitch he quickly followed suit, not wishing to be left alone on the pitch surrounded by one hundred thousand real living people!

Fred Compton was still rubbing his eyes in disbelief and muttering to himself.

"It couldn't have been him; it just couldn't have been. Eddie's dead – dead and gone."

"What did you say, dear?"

Ann Compton had returned carrying two ice-cream cornets.

"Wha …? Oh, nothing, love. I thought I saw someone I knew in the crowd," he lied.

"Who?"

"Oh nobody you would know. Just someone from work."

Fred's wife looked at him oddly. She was fairly certain that no one else from Fenton station had got tickets for the final. She sat down beside her husband and handed him his ice-cream which he promptly dropped onto the ground, his hands shaking uncontrollably. Ann Compton knew immediately that something was wrong. Her husband was clumsy at times but he would never drop an ice-cream. Never!

"Whatever is the matter, dear? You look like you've seen a ghost."

And then Fred Compton knew he would have to tell his wife. He began to stammer.

"I know you won't believe me but I-I think I've seen Eddie."

Ann Compton went silent and her face went deathly white. The two of them had hardly spoken about their departed son after the first few days of mental anguish. Because no body had ever been found, both of them, in their own ways, still harboured hopes that he would be found alive, even after over six months. Fred's wife, however, was made of sterner stuff and quickly gained her composure, dismissing any impossible thoughts back to the deep recesses of her mind where they belonged. She and Fred had to continue with their lives and not dwell in the imaginings of the past.

"Oh don't be daft, Fred. You know he's gone. Was it just another of your visions? I still see Eddie in my mind, you know, but that's all it is – just in my mind."

Ann tried to bring her husband back to reality by licking her ice-cream tantalisingly in front on his face. Fred seemed to brighten up a little.

"I don't know dear. I just can't believe what I saw. He was standing right in front of me, just by the wall and, Ann …."

"What?" gurgled Ann Compton through her ice-cream.

"He was on the pitch, right by Bobby Moore and he came over and said hello to me."

"Oh now you're talking absolute nonsense, love. No one else could have seen him or else there would have been a real commotion. Shall I ask that chap next to you if he saw a strange boy walking on the pitch? I will if you like."

"No, of course not. I suppose you're right – it *was* all in my mind. Perhaps I just wanted to see him on today of all days. You know how much he would have loved to have been here to watch the final."

"I know, dear and he is in spirit, I'm sure. Now, shall I go and get you another ice-cream?"

"No, I'm alright now – just my mind playing tricks on me. I mean, how could a fourteen-year-old boy get onto the pitch unnoticed?"

"Precisely," said Ann Compton.

Fred sat back in his seat and tried to relax while he waited for the players to return for the second-half. Despite the couple's agreed explanation for what he thought he had seen, Fred Compton would remain convinced of what he had actually seen and heard for some time to come. One thing prevented him from pursuing the matter further and possibly with the authorities too. After his son had turned and waved to him from the pitch, Eddie had vanished into thin air, spirited away in as quick a flash as he had appeared. Fred Compton was fairly certain that he had had an encounter with his son's ghost. The question that was nagging him, while he stared blankly at the empty pitch, was: 'Would he have more encounters with his son?' In some strange way, Fred Compton rather hoped he would.

The England dressing room was steamy as tired bodies exuded moisture after forty-five minutes of toil; shirts were soaking wet both from sweat and the effects of a couple of unseasonable rain showers. Thunder had been heard in the distance but the dressing room was oddly quiet as Alf Ramsey stood, besuited like a bank manager, and talked without emotion about what he wanted his players to do in the second-half. It really was like he was merely telling his team that they only had to do such and such and they would win. His ordered and unflappable approach seemed to breathe confidence into the players beyond that which their abilities warranted. Eddie and Len sat side by side at one end of the changing room and watched in awe as the great man explained carefully his tactics for the second-half. A simple *'Now go and win it'* echoed in the eleven gladiator's ears as they eventually strode back onto the turf at the end of the interval. The two boys followed them out in silence realising they had witnessed a master at work. All the team had to do, led by the colossus that was Bobby Moore, was follow the maestro's instructions as spelt out and in another forty-five minutes England would be World Champions.

Neither boy had said anything to each other while they had been sat in the dressing room; they had been too much in awe of the close proximity of all the fabulous footballers who, up until that day, had been nothing more than names that they had read about or seen occasionally on television. In the pause while the players lined up again for the second-half, Eddie told Len about seeing his dad in the stands. Len seemed more interested in the event than Eddie thought he would have been, given the fact that his own dad had died with him in the tragic car crash. As they stood in the centre-circle waiting for the referee's whistle, Len said,

"Show me where you saw him, mate."

Ignoring the play that had started, Eddie led his friend to the far touchline where his dad had been sitting. Len became quite excited when they found Eddie's mum and dad sitting next to each other and, like Eddie earlier, shouted a greeting from the touchline. Eddie hung back a little and even though he didn't show it, he did feel some comfort at seeing his mother again. Both his parents seemed well and happy, judging by their smiling faces and linked arms. It had pleased Eddie to see them, albeit in an unemotional sort of way, like a box that had been ticked in his progress as a ghost. He called to Len,

"Come on, mate; they can't see or hear you. Let's get on with the game – I don't want to miss a goal."

Len turned away from Eddie's parents; he too seemed able to quickly put his unusual meeting behind him and he ran past his friend and into the opposition half where another England free-kick was about to be taken by Captain Moore. This time, Len appeared to sit on the ball while Moore lifted it into the penalty area causing Len to jump into the air in a show of mock pain and surprise. Eddie arrived at his friend's side just as Len was making more drama over climbing painfully to his feet. Out of the corner of his eye, Eddie saw Roger Hunt head Bobby Moore's free-kick narrowly wide. The stadium clock read ten past four and in their seats, Eddie's parents were once again enjoying the match, both unaware of their son's best friend's attempt to make contact – they had neither seen nor heard anything untoward.

After a while, Eddie and Len began to get a little bored with chasing the ball and pulling faces at the German players, or the referee, occasionally shouting comments at both parties in an attempt to sway the progress of the game, but, of course, to no avail – as ghosts their powers did not yet extend to the miraculous. They were being allowed to keep just a watching brief. The match was nearly entering the last ten minutes when England were awarded a corner. While Eddie remained by the centre-circle, Len trotted forward and turned to shout to him from his advanced position on the edge of the German penalty area,

"I hope Bally takes it and swings it in for big Geoff!"

From his own position nearly thirty yards away, Eddie couldn't hear his friend's pointless remark, but Alan Ball duly obliged as requested and Geoff Hurst seemed to complete Len's pleading only for the big number ten's shot to be deflected. Fortunately it rebounded to England's footballing ghost, Martin Peters, who strode forward and slotted the ball home. The crowd, who had been quiet for some time, erupted in a deafening crescendo. Len turned to his fellow ghost and smiled with a look of, '*I told you so*!' Eddie merely punched his fist in the air and shouted,

"Two – one! Two – one! Come on the boys in red!"

The two boys followed the England players back to the centre-circle for the restart; there were just over ten minutes left. Surely England could hold on and they almost did until, in the very last minute, the Germans were awarded a free-kick a few yards outside the penalty area on the left-hand side of the field. Lothar Emmerich, the opposition number eleven and winger was delegated to take it. It had been given for a highly innocuous, albeit slightly clumsy challenge, by the tall and gangly Jack Charlton; Len had understandably shouted to the referee,

"That was never a foul, ref – the clown just fell over! Big Jack never touched him!"

The boys watched nervously from the edge of the area as the young German forward swung the ball in low and menacingly. Full-back George Cohen could do nothing more the block the kick as he attempted to clear it, but the ball skewed to Wolfgang Weber who rushed through to score. Gordon Banks ran to the referee patting one of his palms to indicate that there had been a handball by one of the Germans as the ball had crossed into the six-yard box, but the referee waved him away and the goal stood. Karl-Heinz Schnellinger, the likely handball culprit, made his way back to his own half, hiding his guilt brilliantly. The boys stalked him on his nonchalant walk, Len even trying to trip him up in his frustration and disappointment. On the way back to the centre-circle, Len mumbled to Eddie,

"That should never have been allowed. It wasn't a foul in the first place and then that bloke handled it. That Swiss referee needs to see an optician."

"He might need to see a doctor after the game, if he gets out of the ground alive," said Eddie with equal annoyance at the obvious injustice.

The game restarted, but in no time at all, the referee blew the whistle for full-time and the England players trudged to the touchline to join their manager for a pep talk before the statutory period of extra time. The Germans were smiling and those of them that were not totally exhausted had a spring in their step after their 'lucky' escape. Len and Eddie stood audaciously right next to Alf Ramsey, one on each side of him, nodding sagely to the players at every word he uttered. The 'bank manager' was again calm and collected; no panic, or even frustration, seemed to be etched on his face. No shouting, no histrionics, just a calm delivery of his message that they, the players, would have to go and win the game all over again. He told them that they were the better side and deserved to win, so that's all there was to it. He then left the players to their own thoughts and preparation with just one final word to his rock, Bobby Moore, who nodded his agreement to whatever instruction had been given. Meanwhile, the German manager, Helmut Schön, was talking non-stop with an animated expression on his face while the German players seemed to be far away in worlds of their own. The England team had listened to their manager in silence and with as much concentration as their tired bodies would allow in the circumstances. Time would tell as to which had been the more effective team talk.

The first ten minutes of added time were a tense and careful affair with neither side being too adventurous. With only a few minutes left of the first period, the ever-industrious Alan Ball put in a cross for Geoff Hurst to turn, swivel and shoot from close range. The ball hit the underside of the bar with both boys having taken up positions next to the England number ten. They watched excitedly as the ball dropped, almost in slow motion to the ground, both of them willing the ball to fall down behind the goal line. Len even shouted the hoped-for result while the ball was still feet off the ground.

"Goal! It's a goal – we've scored!"

Geoff Hurst turned to the Swiss referee with arm aloft, claiming the goal. German heads shook in denial. Referee Mr Dienst looked uncertain. Ninety thousand of the crowd bayed,

"Goal! Goal!"

To the right, the linesman had his flag raised. What did it mean? Eddie and Len ran over to him quicker than any of the players and almost before Mr Dienst had spotted him. Eddie was shouting,

"It wasn't off-side, mate. The ball was over the line!" and then he added inanely, "I saw it; I was only feet away. It was a goal."

Mr Dienst trotted over and Swiss/Russian sign language ensued. Mr Bakhramov nodded vehemently. German players wagged fingers and shook their heads. Mr Dienst made his decision, correct or not and, as if to make sure that there would be no argument, the linesman seemed to agree and pointed his flag to the centre-circle. Had Mr Bakharov been trying to signal off-side, but had 'chickened out' at the last moment? A jury vote of nine to one might have been a powerful catalyst in the final decision. This time, it would be Eddie that would say later that his own shouting and gesticulation in front of the linesman had persuaded him to award the goal. Whatever the real reason, which would perplex fans and pundits alike for years, the goal stood; England led 3−2 and Eddie and Len trotted merrily back to the centre, heaping their praises on big Geoff Hurst as they ran beside him.

The rest of the first period and most of the second continued to be a tense affair with neither side giving an inch. Alf Ramsey had been once again calm and confident at the interval, saying very little except the odd quiet word to one or two players. As far as he was concerned, England were justly in front and would go on to win the game.

The last minute beckoned and a reckless German attack broke down. Many of their defenders had gone forward in a desperate attempt to score a last-minute goal. Booby Moore spotted the defensive gaps and kicked the ball deep downfield to the unmarked Geoff Hurst who raced forward and blasted an unstoppable shot into the top left-hand corner of the net. Some people had run onto the pitch to join the two boy-ghosts in premature celebrations. The score was 4−2 and England were going to win the World Cup. Though commentator Kenneth Wolstenholme's words, 'Some people are on the pitch. They think it's all over …,' would become a fitting epitaph for the nation's victory for years to come, their true meaning would only ever be fully understood by two beings who had actually preceded the pitch invasion by nearly two hours. If either of the two boys had managed to hear the famous words, they would have both laughed inwardly at all the fuss and attention concentrated on the few living souls who had dared to run onto the pitch during play. It had almost been commonplace for the two ghostly teenagers!

3

Visitations

A few seconds after the referee blew his whistle for the end of extra time, and therefore of the whole match, Eddie's presence on Wembley's hallowed turf ended abruptly with a return to blackness and oblivion. His second awakening had lasted less than three hours. He would sadly miss his friend's antics as Bobby Moore lifted the Jules Rimet trophy high above his head; the grinning Leonard Wilby doing a 'Nobby Stiles' type jig at his side. He also would miss seeing Len trying to 'fly' from the presentation balcony as a quick way of getting back to the pitch. If the daring young ghost had been a living and breathing person, he would have surely ended up with several broken bones or worse. As it was, his aerial trick was cut short when he too returned to the sleeping state of oblivion. As would become the norm on such occasions, the two ghosts would not necessarily depart their earthly visitations at the same time. Unlike in life, they really had become 'free spirits' although under strict but random control from on high. God was their master now and he would determine when they next met. Until that time they would 'sleep' without form or any kind of restriction on time. Len had been accustomed for some time to being on his own when making earthly visits; Eddie had not. He still had much to learn on his new journey.

Ann and Fred Compton managed to get back to their ember-red and cream Hillman Minx by half past six, a remarkable achievement given the huge and excited crowd that left Wembley that afternoon. Fred had decided to park a good half a mile away from the ground. He was pleased to see his car had survived its visit to the huge open car park unscathed;

no scratches or bumps that he could see. Within fifteen minutes they were back on the A406 North Circular Road and heading for the A12 that would eventually take them back to Hamsden and thence by the A132 the final twelve miles to their East Anglian seaside home in Fenton-on-Sea. Fred Compton still seemed rather tense on the return journey. Ann did not question him and remained quiet until he had negotiated the unfamiliar roads back beyond Romford. It was to her relief that, as soon as he spoke, she realised that the tenseness had been due to the unfamiliarity of the road system rather than any aftermath of what he had told her earlier that afternoon.

"*Now* I know where I am," he said. "I've been guessing for the last hour, you know."

"You must have had a guardian angel guiding you, love," replied his wife with a knowing smile.

"What – you mean Eddie?"

"Well, you never know. I often think he's watching us."

They were on the A12 now and Fred flicked the switch to turn the lights on. It was well over a month past mid-summer and with the cloudy evening, at eight o'clock it was starting to get dark. Ann Compton sat back in her seat and her eyes began to feel heavy as she drifted off to sleep, aided by the Hillman's encouraging engine noise. For the first time for a while that day, Fred began to relax also and, with his wife asleep, he thought about the earlier visitation from his son. He remained convinced that he had seen Eddie's ghost that afternoon and that his son had seen him in return. His wife's words suddenly came back to him: '*I often think he's watching us*'. He steeled himself to look in his rear-view mirror, but when he did he saw only the reflection of dull headlights and grey/black tarmac. '*Don't be daft, Fred*', he told himself. A cold shudder went up his spine and he focused his mind and eyes on the road ahead, trying to read the number plates of the cars in front of him and the mileposts as they flashed by: '*Colchester 12, Hamsden 31*'.

The Comptons made it safely home to 38 Fir Tree Close that evening, without alarms or delays. Ann Compton didn't wake up until they had already passed Linham a few miles from journey's end. The next few weeks remained uneventful for them both as the school holidays passed into September. It had been a busy time for Fred in the station booking office; the weather had been good for travelling by rail and the whole country was still bathing in the excitement of England's victory in the World Cup. People were relaxed and enjoying the warm weather by taking days out; the train suited many for the comfort and worry-free journeys it provided.

September moved into October and Fred's duties became easier as passengers were mainly restricted to commuters and local people bound for Hamsden's reasonable shopping centre. Thus it was that Fred had had a quiet morning on Wednesday, October the 19th and by ten o'clock, the station was more or less empty of passengers needing guidance or tickets. Taking the opportunity afforded by the lull in business, Fred made his way to the back of the booking office to do some general tidying up and filing. He hadn't left the front counter for much more than a minute when the push-bell sounded. It rang twice more before he returned to the glass window. This customer was clearly impatient for a ticket or, possibly, just directions. Fred was almost speechless when he heard the client's question.

"I need a ticket to Ludmouth in Devon, please."

The stranger was a man of about six feet with greying swept-back hair and a pleasant smile. His accent, though faint, wasn't local and Fred was pretty certain that he hadn't seen the well-dressed man before. But there was something about his manner and his speech that seemed familiar to Fred Compton. Apart from his own family holidays taken by rail to the south Devon seaside town in a couple of previous summers, no one had ever requested a ticket to the quiet Devon backwater. On both of the family holidays, Eddie's friend, Leonard Wilby, had accompanied them with almost fatal consequences when, on the second occasion, the two boys, having wandered onto a disused railway line, had nearly been run down by a shunting engine. Many memories flashed through Fred Compton's head as he tried to regain his composure to reply to the stranger's unusual request.

"Will that be a single or a return, sir?"

"Oh, a single will do."

"Do you know the route, sir?" asked Fred politely and with more confidence.

"I think so – Hamsden, Liverpool Street and then a train west from Waterloo. Am I right?"

Fred looked a little surprised at the stranger's knowledge.

"Yes, that's correct, sir. Just remember to change at Exeter."

"Of course, and I guess the train from there only goes to Ludmouth Junction, right?"

"Yes, sir," said Fred.

"How much will that be, please?"

Fred made great play of looking through timetables and price lists, even though he knew the fare off by heart.

"That's four pounds, seventeen shillings and sixpence, sir," he said eventually. "The next Hamsden train is at twenty to eleven."

The stranger nodded politely and placed what looked like a brand new five-pound note in the revolving tray and said,

"Thanks, Fred – keep the change."

With that, he picked up the ticket, Fred having already turned the tray so that it was on the customer side. The man then turned to walk away, leaving Fred with astonishment written all over his face. After a few paces, the man turned back and over his shoulder, said,

"Eddie's doing fine, Mr Compton – he's happy now. Remember me to your lovely wife. Tell her that George sends his regards."

Fred Compton's eyes seemed to glaze over and thus he hardly noticed that the strange man had vanished instantly from view. Almost on auto-pilot and certainly by force of habit, Fred turned the revolving tray round and his nightmare suddenly got worse. The tray was completely empty! He was torn between two possible courses of action. One: go after the man or, two: try and find the missing five-pound note. He went for the former and ran out of his booth, his mind racing and his heart pumping, but it didn't take him more than a few minutes to search Fenton's small and compact railway station. The man was nowhere to be seen. Fortunately, no one else had turned up at the ticket office when he returned, breathless and shaking with fear. The crisp new note was nowhere to be seen either; it hadn't slipped out of the tray and onto the floor, and there had been nobody else in the vicinity who might have picked it up. Eventually, Fred found himself slumping into his old leather armchair at the back of the office. He had put a sign in the booth window: 'Back in ten minutes'. He needed time to think.

The voice, and then the words that the man had spoken, had confirmed the identity of the strange man in Fred's mind. George Canter had been, up until about three years previously, owner of the junk shop in Mill Road. He had gone back to his native Poland after much criticism of, and doubts about, his selling methods for which, thankfully, he made amends before he left. But Fred had since learnt that Mr George Canter, or Georgi Kantechuk, to give him his birth name, had died of liver disease in his home town of Bialystok in eastern Poland. Fred knew what it meant – he had just had his second encounter with a ghost, but a much older version of the Polish Jew. The man's comment regarding his wife had merely served to rubber-stamp his conclusions – Fred had suspected that George Canter had been 'sweet' on her while he had lived in Fenton, even giving Fred cause to speak to him about it and to warn him off. Fred also remembered how George had taken an interest in his son, Eddie; although the incident with the mysterious object, which Eddie had purchased in Mr Canter's junk shop, had made Fred doubt the sincerity of that interest. The missing fiver fitted with Fred's ghostly conclusion also. But where was the ticket? A vanishing ghost who had no physical form couldn't take a small but solid object away, could he? Fred leapt up and rushed out to the forecourt in front of the ticket booth. A middle-aged lady was approaching. She came right up to Fred and said,

"I found this over by platform one. I think somebody must have dropped it and it's still valid for today."

Fred took the ticket and said robotically,

"Thank you, madam. I'll keep it until someone comes to claim it. I think I know who bought it. What a careless thing to do."

The lady made her way back to catch the Hamsden train which had just pulled into platform one. Fred Compton returned to his booth. Strangely, he felt better about the whole incident. It tied up a loose end over the ghostly meeting – the five-pound note hadn't been real but the ticket had, and ghosts couldn't take real things away. It made sense to Fred. Reality and fantasy (?) had just collided on Fenton-on-Sea railway station and Fred Compton had survived the extraordinary encounter. By the time his next customer arrived at the ticket office, his fear and uncertainty had been replaced by an inner calm when he recalled the ghost's words:

"Eddie's doing fine – he's happy now."

In some strange way, Fred Compton had just started a journey like his son before him. He would not be so afraid nor off guard if another such visitation should take place in the future. In the meantime, he thought it wise to keep his own counsel over the matter; his wife needn't be told – it would only cause her grief, or worse, if she formed the opinion that her son was still alive.

Gary Jones had been dating Eddie's sister, Jenny Compton, for well over three years and, though there had been some problems at the beginning of the relationship, the path of true love had been level and even for quite some time. Gary was twenty-two and, after spending three years of his life in various temporary jobs, including working rather reluctantly for his father at Richard Jones' Cars in Hamsden, he had, at nineteen, found a worthwhile career. He had recently completed his two-year probationary training programme in the fire brigade and had become a fully retained-firefighter. Jenny was in her second of two years at Hamsden Civic College. A month following her father's strange encounter with Mr Canter, the young couple were to be found taking coffee in the Steep Hill Tearooms overlooking the promenade gardens at Fenton-on-Sea. It was just after eleven on the morning of Saturday, November the 19th. Jenny was trying to discuss a matter that seemed to be making her boyfriend a little nervous and awkward.

"Well are we going to get married, then?"

Gary attempted a 'dead-bat' reply.

"We're far too young to think about things like that, Jen. I've only just started with the fire service proper a couple of weeks ago. We don't have any money saved yet and, anyway, where would we live?"

Jenny frowned at her boyfriend's dismissive answer and said,

"Getting married isn't just any *thing like that*. It's the most important thing that most people do in their lives, Gary, and besides …"

Gary was silent – he knew what was coming. Jenny was predictable when she continued.

"And besides, your parents are loaded. Surely they would help us out. You're mum idolises you since you became a fireman and got away from your dad."

Gary sighed and took a sip of coffee. Best let Jenny run out of steam before he replied. She poured on the heat.

"Don't you want to marry me, Gary? Don't you want to be with me every day *and* every night? Don't you want to have …?"

Gary couldn't remain silent any longer.

"Of course I do, love. It's not that and I suppose it's not the money either. It's just that …"

"Just what? If you love me and the money isn't an issue, what else is there?"

Gary looked embarrassed and said,

"I just don't feel ready for such an important step in my life. It's a huge responsibility to have a wife to look after and children to raise. It will tie us down for years. Now I'm earning some good money in a stable job, I want us to have some fun out of life. God knows you deserve it after losing your brother, and besides, you don't finish college until next summer. Then you'll have to get a job."

"Will I, Gary? queried Jenny coyly. "Can't I just be a lady of leisure and stay at home with my three children?"

"Now you're being silly," said Gary. "If we're to buy a house, we'll both need to work for a few years – you're still only twenty, Jen love."

Gary's cautious logic began to have the effect he'd planned. Jenny pouted and replied,

"Oh, I know you're right, Gary. You always are and that's why ..."

"That's why?" said Gary raising his eyebrows.

"That's why I L-O-V-E you," said Jenny spelling out every letter so that no one else in the tearoom should hear. As Gary leant across the table to kiss her, she glimpsed an old man at the adjoining table smiling at the young couple's public intimacy. Jenny looked slightly embarrassed before the young fireman sat back in his chair and said,

"I'll make you a promise, Jenny. I promise you that if you get a job next July when you finish college, then I'll marry you before the autumn of the following year. That should give us two years to plan the wedding and to save for the deposit on a house and so on. Deal?"

Jenny stuck out her bottom lip in a feigned sulk and replied,

"I suppose that will have to do, but aren't you forgetting something, Gary?"

Gary thought for a moment.

"No, I don't think so. Getting you a job, the wedding and buying a house are the only things we need to worry about."

Jenny pouted even more pointedly. How slow could her boyfriend be? She gave up her promptings and came straight to the point.

"I haven't said I'll marry you yet, you know."

Gary smiled.

"But you will, won't you."

"I might if you actually ask me, Gary!"

Gary looked really embarrassed now and after a brief pause while he scanned the tearoom to see if anyone was listening to their intimate conversation, he said quietly,

"Will you, Miss Jennifer Compton, at some time in the not too distant future, give me the greatest pleasure any man could ever have and do me the honour of becoming my wife?"

Jenny's mouth dropped in awe at Gary's beautiful and thoughtful words. She would realise later that Gary had probably been preparing himself for some time for such a moment as that grey November day. She was quick with her reply.

"Yes, Gary, I will."

Further kisses were exchanged and Jenny broke the tension with,

"Now go and buy me the most expensive engagement ring you can find."

In her highly charged emotional state, Jennifer Compton hadn't noticed that the old man had moved his chair much closer to their table and had probably heard much of what the two of them had said to each other. When he spoke, however, his words indicated a greater knowledge of Jenny's personal life than the couple's conversation might have suggested. He leant across and whispered in Jenny's ear. She instinctively lowered her head and looked down at the table.

"It's a pity that Eddie won't be present to see you get married, Jennifer. He still loves you, you know and you will see him soon, I have no doubt. Remember, you still share a secret."

Jenny froze and lifted her head to look at her boyfriend who seemed to be concentrating on the view out of the window to his side.

"Gary!" she started, but sensing movement at her side, she glanced in the old man's direction. She couldn't believe her eyes. In the brief second it had taken her to lift her head, look at Gary and then turn back to the old man, he had vanished.

"What, love? Whatever's up? You look like you've just seen a ghost."

To begin with, Jenny said nothing. It was clear from Gary's reaction that he hadn't seen the old man whisper to her. She tried to remain calm and find out what he had seen.

"I hope that old man didn't hear us talking, Gary."

"What old man?"

"The one who was sitting there at the next table."

Gary pulled an odd face at his girlfriend.

"No one's been sitting there all the time we've been here. That's why I chose this table. Those things I said were meant for your ears and your ears only, my love."

4

Eddie Awakes Alone

Jenny didn't immediately pursue her somewhat strange remark with her boyfriend and Gary, himself, didn't put it down to anything more than her nervousness caused by the emotion of the occasion. He was, however, concerned for her welfare and state of mind.

"Are you sure you're alright?"

Jenny pushed back her hair and tried to pretend that nothing untoward had happened.

"Must have been imagining things, I suppose."

Gary relaxed and, continuing to try to reassure Jenny, said,

"There was an old man in the tearooms earlier but he sat over there by the door. Maybe you caught a glimpse of him out of your eye and because of your excitement you thought he was a lot closer."

Jenny looked thoughtful. Was Gary just making it up to appease her or had there really been a man by the door? Jenny decided to seek confirmation one way or the other; she was careful with her choice of words.

"Oh him – you mean the really ancient old boy with long flowing white hair?"

"Yes, he looked like a biblical prophet; probably in his eighties."

So that was it, thought Jenny and she began to relax inwardly. Gary had described perfectly the man who had spoken to her. But she also knew that she was convinced that he had been sitting right by them on the closest table for some time. Gary must have seen him if he was …. The thought remained hanging in Jenny's mind. It had been a while, indeed, not since her brother had been alive, but she realised that she had just had another ghostly visitation.

Jenny decided to 'put the matter to bed' and said finally,

"Well at least I'm not going mad, then. I expect you're absolutely right. I do remember catching sight of an old man when we first came in. He looked so unusual he must have made such an impression on me that he was in my mind's eye when you asked me the vital question."

Gary smiled pleasantly.

"He looked a nice old boy – almost from another age."

Gary looked at his watch.

"God look at the time. It's gone twelve and the train goes at twenty past. We're going to have to run if we're going to make the afternoon performance at the Embassy cinema in Hamsden – the film starts at one-fifteen."

Jenny busied herself checking her make-up in her hand mirror while Gary paid the bill at the counter. They joined each other at the door where Jenny asked,

"And what are we going to see?"

"It's called *Blow-Up*," replied Gary. "It's supposed to be good."

"What's it about?"

"No idea, love, but what else can we do on a miserably grey day like today."

They were walking up the High Street by now and Jenny replied,

"Well, if we were married we could go home and make …."

Gary didn't allow his girlfriend to finish her suggestive remark.

"Jenny! Don't be naughty."

They eventually made the film with five minutes to spare, and Jenny's previous involvement with the slim dividing line between reality and illusion continued. Parts of the film were a perfect reminder to her of the illusory event earlier that morning in the tearooms at the top of Steep Hill.

In the weeks leading up to Christmas, Jenny often thought back to that cold, grey morning in mid-November. She tried to convince herself that nothing really had happened but without much success. Though its memory started to wane, particularly with the excitement of Christmas approaching, she couldn't find any other explanation than her original and inevitable ghostly conclusion. The old man's words were both strange and comforting. What had he said? At first she couldn't quite remember them exactly until she decided to write her best recollection down in her diary. One day in early December she wrote,

'Eddie loves you and is coming to see you soon. It's a shame he won't see you married. He still shares your secret.'

Without really knowing it, Jenny had recorded the old man's remarks correctly, albeit, not in the same order nor with precisely the same words. The first part excited her to think she might see her brother again and the second reminded her that they had both had ghostly experiences before while Eddie had still been alive. She, at least, had told no one else of such happenings. Those events had served to convince her that the old man in November had been a ghost.

Eddie couldn't feel cold or heat or any other physical sensation and when he next awoke, it was only the absence of leaves on the trees and a white frost on the ground that told him it was winter. As before, he found himself on the seafront at Fenton-on-Sea, though not this time in a sitting position. Clothes, of course, were irrelevant to his situation but at least he had some on. Remarkably, when he looked down at himself, he discovered he was appropriately dressed for a winter's day, sporting his old duffle coat over some clothes that seemed familiar to him. He wasn't aware that all of the clothes he was wearing had been given away or destroyed some time ago. As he walked to the foot of Steep Hill, he chuckled to himself at the simplicity of his new existence – he didn't even have to dress himself, let alone wash or perform other necessary and natural human functions. He felt no tiredness or lessening of his walking speed as he negotiated the aptly named incline up to the High Street. Len had not yet appeared and though Eddie kept glancing around in the hope of seeing him, he wasn't unduly bothered that he hadn't shown his face. It would be fun to try out his new abilities on his own and he quickly made the decision that there was only one place that he wanted to go to that morning, for morning it seemed to be by the position of the winter sun. The town was virtually deserted and Eddie immediately deduced that it was a Sunday which, with the bells of St Andrew's Church sounding a coherent tune, narrowed the actual time down to just before eleven as the morning congregation was summoned to worship. Christmas decorations and gifts in the shop windows further narrowed the date to mid-December. Eddie's mental guess was pretty accurate given that it was actually Sunday, December the 18th, exactly one week before Christmas Day. The fact that it was still also 1966 was not yet apparent to Eddie as he reached South Road and the entrance to Fir Tree Close. Who would be at home at number 38? Should he have gone straight to St Andrew's where his parents were almost certain to be at that time on a Sunday morning? Would just his sister be at home? That would be quite nice, he thought as he glided up the front path of his old house, grinning to himself when he walked straight through the solid wooden front gate.

Jennifer Compton *was* at home that morning, but she wasn't well, having gone down with a bad cold at college on the Friday which, coupled with a nasty sore throat, had left her feeling very sorry for herself. This was made all the worse by the fact that her beloved Gary was on duty all weekend in Hamsden. She had taken up almost permanent residence in her bedroom that weekend, propped up by several pillows and surrounded by various pills, throat lozenges and tissues.

By eleven-thirty Jenny began to feel the effects of her second *Beecham's Powder* that morning and her eyes began to close as she gave in to a welcoming and healing sleep. Dreams came to her quickly, but nothing meaningful nor connected, just snippets of memories and emotions. Soon, however, they became more coherent and Gary began to figure in most of the random scenes, including several wedding visions, culminating inevitably in Jenny trying to form the words, '*I do,*' but without success. Her final dream became an impossible mixture of questions and strange interruptions. The important bit in church was not going to plan and Jenny was becoming distraught.

"*Will you take this man …?*"

"You lazy girl; always asleep."

"*… to have and to hold ….*"

"I come all this way and all you can do …."

"*… in sickness and in health ….*"

"For goodness sake, wake up!"

"*… as long as you both shall live ….*"

"Wake up, Jenny! Please wake up!"

If Eddie could have mustered up some kind of physical force, he would have sat on the bed and shaken his sister by the shoulders. He had to make do with his phantom urgings in the hope that they would permeate her sleep. He knew he wasn't making any human sounds or, at least, nothing that any living person could hear. Jenny began to stir and, with a moaning that seemed to say,

561

"Shut up and go away – I'm getting ma …," she woke with a start. Her head jerked backwards from its drooping position and glazed eyes stared into space from beneath her fevered and moist brow.

"Well, at last, Elizabeth Taylor awakes."

It was true that Jenny was awake at last but, as far as she was concerned, her dream was still continuing, for there, at the end of her bed, stood her recently departed brother, looking exactly the same as the last time she had seen him apart, that was, from his clothes – the clothes that she herself had helped get rid of.

"Eddie?"

As soon as she heard her own question she knew that she was finally awake and her dream was over. The old man had been right. Eddie had come to see her. She rubbed her eyes and looked again.

"I knew you'd come, Eddie. I just knew it," she said quietly.

Eddie's ghostly face seemed to frown.

"Oh yeah? How did you know? Even I had no idea I was coming here until about forty minutes ago."

"Someone told me I'd see you soon."

"Who? Someone I know?" asked Eddie, thinking that his best friend had been up to his tricks and had paid Jenny a visit without telling him.

"I don't know who he was, but I know he was a ghost. I saw him last month in the Steep Hill Tearooms when Gary and I had a coffee there."

"How did you know he was a ghost?"

"Because Gary didn't see him and yet the old man came and sat right beside me and whispered in my ear. Gary said there hadn't been anyone sitting next to us all the time we were there, so I just knew."

"Did you tell Gary you'd seen a ghost, then?"

"No – he wouldn't have believed me so what would have been the point?"

Jenny got up from the bed and moved to be beside her brother who was still standing at the foot of the bed. She tried to reach out and touch him and Eddie began to laugh.

"What *are* you doing? You can't feel me, you know."

Jenny gave a little squeal of surprise mixed with excitement as her hand passed through her brother's chest.

"Are you sure you can't feel that?" she asked.

"Of course not."

"Not even a tickle?"

"Jenny, I'm a ghost. Anyway what did this man look like? You said he was an old man."

Jenny returned to her bed where she curled her legs under her and continued to look in awe at her brother. *She* had questions to ask too.

"Yeah, really old – long flowing white hair and quite well-spoken with a posh voice and a bit effeminate – quite tall for an old man."

The description fitted only one man that Eddie had ever known and it confirmed his sister's story, for that man was indeed dead and able to walk a ghostly path. Aloyisious St John Grant had been the owner of Grants' Emporium for years before his untimely death in the Fenton train crash two years previously. Grant's Emporium had been turned into Steep Hill Tearooms after his death. How appropriate, thought Eddie, that the old man should put in an appearance in his old shop. Again, all these thoughts were processed much more quickly by Eddie's ghostly brain than any human one could have done and there was no apparent delay before Jenny asked,

"Do you know him, then? I mean, did you know him?"

Jenny seemed to be joining in quite naturally with the spirit of the conversation.

"I think so, and so did you. It sounds like it was Mr St John Grant, who used to own the Emporium on Steep Hill, where you and Gary …."

"Where we had coffee?"

"Precisely."

"He died in the train crash, didn't he," said Jenny.

"Yes, he did."

Jenny started to fidget a little. She had many questions to ask her brother including the obvious one of how and when he had passed into his new 'state', but she also knew that her parents were due back at any time. Her bedroom alarm clock read twelve-thirty.

"Mum and Dad will be back soon, Eddie. You'll have to make yourself scarce."

Eddie did his best to laugh and Jenny realised at once that her statement had been a stupid one.

"I'll hang around and see them," said Eddie, "but, no, I won't make myself visible to them, Jenny."

"You mean you can disappear from view at will?"

"I hope so. I was invisible until I came into your bedroom. Beside, I thinking haunting people is an individual thing. No two people ever see the same things."

"You hope," said Jenny.

"Well if they do see me it will be a nice family reunion, eh?"

Jenny glanced at the clock. She knew she had to ask the question. She started nervously.

"Can I ask you a question, Eddie?"

"No need, I'm not going to give you an answer."

"You don't know what I'm going to ask."

"Don't be stupid, Jen, of course I do. You want to know what happened to me on that Saturday last January."

"Well?"

"I can't give you an answer, Jenny, because I don't know. All I can remember is catching the train to Hamsden and then my mind is a blank."

"Sally Barber said you told her you were going home when she and Liz Roberts met you at the station. Where did you go, Eddie?"

Eddie's ghostly face looked flustered and he feigned anger.

"I tell you, I just don't know – now change the subject."

Jenny went quiet for a few moments and Eddie turned to look out of the window. He couldn't tell his sister what had really happened that day – it would lead to all manner of discussions about his and Len's adventures over the previous three or four years. He couldn't recall the last and vital piece of the jigsaw anyway. He had been in Rome with Len's ghost, and then oblivion had subsumed him until he had returned as a ghost at the end of July. Though Jenny was sympathetic to and open-minded about the ghost world, she wasn't yet ready for his life story, oh no, not just yet! Just as he sensed that Jenny was about to ask another question, Eddie spotted his mum and dad coming up Fir Tree Close and the warm inner glow returned as he noticed them arm in arm, something that he had never seen them do when he had been alive. If he had had a working heart it would have been warmed with contentment. Instead, he turned back to Jenny and said,

"I'm awfully tired now, sis. I can feel myself going. It's been nice seeing you. I'll come again"

Eddie's image began to fade in front of Jenny and she just had time to say one last thing. She hoped it would register with her brother.

"Gary has asked me to marry him and I've said yes. We're getting married the year after next and …."

Eddie had all but vanished as Jenny finished in a rush of words.

... we're getting engaged at Christmas."

Eddie had gone. Jenny hoped that he had absorbed at least the first part of her final words. She curled up on her bed. She was so pleased that her brother seemed happy and that death appeared not to have the finality and terror that had always scared her from being a little girl, listening to all the doom and gloom about heaven and hell on a Sunday morning at St Andrew's Church. A minute or so later her mum poked her head round the door and said,

"How are you feeling, Jenny love? Not at death's door, are we?"

Jenny nearly replied that she actually had just been through it and had just got back but, instead, she said,

"No, Mum, but I am feeling a little better. Had a nice sleep with some pleasant dreams."

5

Some Harmless Fun

The 'Summer of Love' was in full swing when Eddie next broke the
shackles of death, and when he became aware of his surroundings, it was
obvious to him that he hadn't landed back in Fenton-on-Sea. His first
contact with the earthly world was through the medium of music.

> *'If you're going to San Francisco,*
> *be sure to wear some flowers in your hair ....'*

As he listened to the words of the song and while his eyes tried to
focus on the world around him, he thought initially that he had arrived in
the land of the free, but the accents of the people around him were
definitely Anglo-Saxon, even vaguely familiar – Len spoke with a similar
brogue. Finally, his ghostly eyes opened fully. He discovered he was
surrounded by a crowd of mostly young men and women, though with
their long flowing hair styles, it was difficult to tell the difference in some
cases, the final distinction often being the growth of facial hair on some
of the throng. Eddie noticed that some were carrying placards and,
straining his neck above the crowd, he could read some of the slogans.
'America out of Vietnam' and *'Ban the Bomb'* were among the
commonest. It was a mass protest of some kind and Eddie had found
himself right in the middle of it. As he kept pace with the massed crowds,
he tried to work out his location. Being still a fourteen-year-old boy who
was less than five feet in height made it difficult for him to see over the
people around him, tightly packed as they were as they rolled along. He
hadn't yet developed any ghostly skills which would have enabled him to
levitate above the crowd, and just passing through them seemed pointless
as the crowd stretched as far as a human eye could see in all directions.
The day was hot and, though Eddie had no feeling in that respect, he was

at least dressed for the occasion. Had he been visible – and who knows if he was – he would have drawn odd looks only because of his age and not because of his clothes which were an old summer shirt and jeans. The Almighty had got him ready for the day with suitable attire. A voice called to him from behind.

"You're a bit young for this, aren't you, sonny?"

Eddie stopped and turned round, allowing the crowd to pass by and through him. He stood still for a few seconds. The voice came again and from very nearby.

"Just keep walking, Captain; I'll catch you up in a minute."

And then Eddie knew who it was and within a few seconds Len was at his side, grinning like a Cheshire cat as he thrust his face into his own.

"Good morning, Eddie. Welcome to London."

So that was it, thought Eddie – a summer's day in England's capital and his best friend's birthplace. But he wasn't going to be caught out this time by the excitement of the situation. He had already been thinking of what he would and should say if Len had put in an appearance. Remaining in their standing positions while the last few stragglers of the crowd passed on, Eddie asked,

"Good morning to you too, comrade, and pray tell me, what is the twentieth prime number?"

For an awful moment Eddie thought Len was going to reply by questioning his sanity at receiving such a ridiculous request but he got the answer he had hoped for.

"Why that would be seventy-one, old sport. Am I right?"

"Spot on, Len. Good to see you."

The two boy-ghosts now found themselves virtually alone in a fairly large open space; alone apart from a few foreign tourists who clearly had no part in the receding demonstration. Eddie leant on his friend's superior knowledge of London.

"Where are we, mate?"

"Look over there," replied Len.

Eddie glanced up at the imposing sight of Nelson's Column.

"Well?" asked his friend and Eddie paused for thought.

"Erm – Trafalgar Square, I suppose."

"Well done, Captain."

They wandered over to a low stone wall where they sat down, or at least, pretended to. Their actual position in space and time had become less and less important to them but, just in case someone could see them, they took on normal human actions as best they could.

"What was that all about?" asked Eddie.

"Vietnam war protest, I think. Judging from what I could make out their all off to the American Embassy in Grosvenor Square."

"Did you also gauge what year we're in?" continued Eddie.

"Not sure really, but possibly 1967. It's definitely not 1966; there are no signs of World Cup fever. People's minds seem to be on other things."

"Hair styles have changed, Len. What's that all about? I thought Beatlemania was dead."

"They're called hippies, I think. They seem to protest against anything and everything," replied Len. "Especially anything to do with capitalism and America – hence the anti-Vietnam war demonstration."

Eddie smiled at his friend's trivialisation of life and anything controversial concerned with it. Len kept things simple. And, at that moment, his mind was on their more immediate prospects.

"So what do you fancy doing in the big metropolis?"

"Don't know. What is there to see?" asked Eddie.

Eddie had only once before been to London and that had been with Len too on a day-out by train from Fenton-on-Sea when they had both still been in the land of the living. On that occasion they had spent most of the day in the shopping areas of Oxford and Regent Street.

"London Zoo in Regent's Park is worth a visit and Covent Garden is good – they have lots of entertainment there. It's a bit pointless going shopping or looking for somewhere to eat, isn't it?"

"We could look," said Eddie. "I don't intend trying to buy or eat anything."

Len burst into a ghostly laugh.

"I'd like to see you try! If it's like everything else, your hands wouldn't be able to pick anything up. Think about it – you're a ghost! And as for trying to swallow something, well, the mind just boggles at the thought!"

"Yeah, but there are such things as poltergeists, you know. They can make things move and jump about. That would be fun to try in a big department store. We could scare people witless. I bet I could do it."

Len thought for a moment, searching the remnants of his human mind. After a brief pause, he said,

"Well, we could head north for Regent's Park where I can show you the zoo and on the way we can go down Oxford Street where you can visit Selfridge's or John Lewis for your little games."

Len's fairly accurate knowledge of London suggested to Eddie that Len had done some homework before they had met up a few minutes earlier. After all, Len had only been eight when he had left Whitechapel in the East End. What Eddie wasn't aware of at that moment was that his friend wanted to try an unusual and outrageous experiment when he got to London Zoo.

"Let's go, then," said Eddie.

"Right you are, Captain. Follow me."

The boys headed away from the midday sun and, at the north end of the square, Len took them left past the National Gallery. A poster advertising the latest exhibition confirmed to them that the year was indeed 1967 and also that the month was probably August, judging by the dates printed thereon. Up the Haymarket they glided, Eddie soon learning that, like Len, he could move more quickly and smoothly with a little practice. Within five minutes, they had reached the bustling and colourful Picadilly Circus and, continuing north, they were soon at the lower end of Regents Street where Len paused to let Eddie catch up.

"Hamley's toy shop is up ahead on the right. Want to look in there, mate?" asked Len.

"No, Len. You are forgetting that we would have both been sixteen by now, given its August 1967. We may look like fourteen-year-olds, if, indeed, anyone could see us, but I, for one, feel that my mind has aged if not my body. I'm not really interested in toys and things like train sets anymore."

"O.K., Captain. Thanks for the lecture. Straight up to Oxford Circus, then."

The two boys weaved their way through the shoppers; it was still difficult to decide whether it was a weekday or a weekend, though the likelihood of the mass protest being held mid-week seemed unlikely. On reaching Oxford Circus, Len managed to find a newspaper vendor and right under his nose he perused the day's news. He quickly found what he wanted and turned back to Eddie and announced,

"Saturday, August the 19th, 1967, mate."

"Good, it's so nice to know what day it is," said Eddie sarcastically.

Soon they were gliding down the middle of Oxford Street, heading west and letting taxis and buses run through them as they did so. Eddie was less adventurous than his friend who would try to throw his arms round any of the passengers and, in one case, round the driver himself. Eddie had still not really got used to his newly acquired freedom and steered a more modest course, even flinching if a vehicle of any shape or size came near him. He did, however, let a vicar on a bicycle ride over him; surely a man of the cloth would be the most likely person to see him if he needed to take evasive action, he thought. Suddenly, Len stopped and, pointing right, exclaimed,

"There it is – Selfridge's. One of the best shops in London and expensive, too."

"In we go, then," said Eddie.

Without fear of being seen, the two boys stayed initially on the ground floor, pretending they could smell all the sweet vapours that the perfume counters were emitting. After a few minutes of investigation, Eddie decided on his first trick. Selecting what appeared to be the most expensive display counter, he positioned himself next to a glamorous middle-aged lady who was, with her false platinum hair, clearly dressed and painted well beyond her actual class in society. In short, she looked like a barmaid trying to be a princess. She was spraying her neck and forearms liberally with *L'Amour* and as she put the perfume bottle down, Eddie made a grab for it with his invisible hands. Just as Len had said earlier, his hand closed right round and through the bottle; it didn't diverge from its path back to the counter. Len grinned and said,

"Told you so – you're not a poltergeist yet, old boy."

Eddie wasn't about to give up, though. The lady reached for another 'tester' and just before her hand closed round the bottle, Eddie screwed up his face in concentration and stared at it without a even a hint of a ghostly blink. 'Madame Pompidour' let out a faint shriek of surprise as the bottle slid about six inches away from her. Len's jaw dropped in equal surprise. The lady reached for the bottle a second time and Eddie repeated his trick as the bottle returned to its original position. When she tried to pick it up for a third time, only for it to slide towards her and onto the floor, shattering into tiny pieces, she gave up and walked quickly away from the counter with an air of: '*It wasn't me; I never touched it*'. Later that day she would drink several more gin and tonics and eventually put the whole bizarre event down to the two or three she had had before she had entered the famous department store. While an assistant cleared away the broken glass and attempted to clean the floor of expensive perfume, Eddie was gloating and already thinking of demonstrating his new found skill elsewhere.

"There you are, Len, I *can* do it. Maybe you can, too."

Len shook his head.

"I've tried it."

"When?"

"Just then, when you did your trick. I concentrated hard to see if I could stop the bottle but I couldn't. Looks like you've got the power and I haven't. What next, then?"

"The clothing floors, I think."

"Not ladies' fashions, I hope."

Len already had visions of his friend disrobing a young lady in one of the changing rooms. If he could move a perfume bottle, he could probably (re)move someone's clothes also!

"No, don't worry – I'll stick to gents' clothing. Confuse a few old men, eh?"

Len still didn't look too happy but his friend was already heading to the escalator for the third floor where said department was located.

"Wait for me," he shouted and he just managed to catch Eddie up as he put his foot on the lowest step. Len jumped in front and said,

573

"I'll show you a trick, Captain. Watch this!"

Without using the handrails for support, he took two giant strides, touching the moving stairs just once on his way to the top and unaided by the motion of the escalator. In so doing, he probably broke the world long jump record, and twice at that!

Despite it being the weekend, the gents' clothing department was surprisingly quiet. The hot weather had, no doubt, a lot to do with it with traditional smart clothing not being a priority except for the more mature gentleman. Indeed, there seemed to be only two customers in view and Eddie made his mind up straightaway which one he wanted to surprise. A tall, elegant and smartly dressed man of about seventy was trying on straw hats, which judging by his lack of hair, seemed to be an absolute and immediate necessity for him, given the present weather conditions. Eddie strode up to him and from less than a yard away proceeded to stare intently at his head, now covered by the latest offering from the young male sales assistant. In no time at all, the hat dislodged itself from the old man's scalp and took off into the air as if blown there by a strong wind. The old gentleman jerked his right hand upwards in a vain attempt to stop its progress and said to the assistant,

"You must have a window open, young man. Go and close it and fetch me that hat."

The young assistant retrieved the hat and said nothing in reply about a window; he knew that there wasn't one open in his section. The old man tried the hat again. Looking in the mirror held by the sales assistant, he gave a satisfied smile at its comfortable fit and stylish looks.

"Yes, I'll take this one. How much is it, young man?"

The assistant reached up to look at the tag hanging from the brim of the hat and, just as he did so, it flew off the man's head in the opposite direction to its first journey. The customer assumed that the young assistant had been the cause when looking for the price tag and said in an angry and frustrated tone,

"What are you doing, boy? Be careful, you'll ruin it."

"But, sir, I didn't touch it. You must have jerked your head suddenly."

The man had nearly had enough.

"Don't be impertinent young man. I did no such thing. Now fetch it and tell me the price."

"Yes, sir. Sorry, sir."

The hat was safely retrieved for the second time. Cash and receipt were exchanged with the old man saying,

"Thank you, young man. There's no need to wrap it – I'll wear it straightaway."

"Yes, sir," replied the bemused assistant, and the old man walked proudly away from him with his new hat firmly on his head, or so he thought. Eddie had other ideas. The man hadn't gone more than three or four paces when the hat again took off into the air but this time vertically upwards, landing neatly on an uncovered light fitting which was several feet above head height. The lightly coloured straw hat had found a new role as a makeshift light shade. Neither boy could contain himself any longer and Len croaked,

"How did you do that, mate? That was brilliant!"

"And enough fun for the time being, I think," replied Eddie. "Let's get out of here."

As the two boys turned to go they caught sight of a bewildered and extremely angry old man berating the young assistant who, with a colleague, was vainly trying to get the hat down with a long window pole, before the straw got so hot it started to smoulder.

575

Len still seemed to know where he was going as the two young ghosts headed out of Selfridges and back up Oxford Street, where, reaching Oxford Circus, he turned left. He was setting a furious pace as he led Eddie into Portland Place almost at a run. Crossing the Marylebone Road, he turned and said to his friend,

"That's Regent's Park ahead; I'm sure I went there with Mum and Dad when I was about six. The zoo is somewhere over to the left."

Len slowed to a normal human walking pace as they entered the Park, and Eddie could tell immediately from the high fences and other safety measures that the zoo was indeed just on their left. They made their way into the Park where Eddie began to dawdle while his eyes were taken by all the sunbathing young ladies who were sporting themselves on the grass in the sun.

"Come on, Eddie, there's no need for that," said Len. "Remember, you're only fourteen and not supposed to be interested in members of the opposite sex; you turned down Sally Barber's invitation on the day before you departed your previous life."

Eddie looked wistful, trying to hard to recall what his friend was talking about, but his memory was hazy and disjointed. Sally had been a new girl to Fenton Grammar's fourth year and had taken to supporting him in his worse subject, English, by sitting next to him in most of the lessons. He shook his ghostly body and joined Len in looking for their planned destination. Some strange and somewhat frightening animal noises could now be heard from behind the boundary fence to their left. Eddie stopped walking for a moment.

"What's that?"

"Only the lions or tigers, mate."

Eddie looked around nervously, as if said animals might actually be roaming free within Regent's Park. Len reassured him.

"Don't worry, Captain, they're kept securely locked in pens and cages."

Eddie relaxed a bit; animals were not among his favourite things after a nasty experience with a dog when he had been seven.

"Thank God for that," he said.

They followed the boundary fence right round to the main entrance at the north side of the zoo. Eddie gasped at the entry prices but Len remarked at once,

"What's the problem, mate? We ain't gonna pay."

Len led the way straight through one of the turnstiles and into the main concourse. The zoo was packed with tourists eager to see what strange and exotic creatures lay within her tall fences.

"Where to first, comrade?" asked Eddie.

"Lions and tigers, I think. Kill or cure your fear of animals, eh?"

Following the signs past the gorillas and the picnic areas, they came across the tigers near the southern end of the zoo. A magnificent male lay basking in the early afternoon sun; the head of his female counterpart could just be seen poking out of a wooden cage at the rear of the pen.

"Wow!" whispered Eddie. "They're huge."

"And kill you in seconds if they got out," replied his friend.

Eddie failed to see the funny side of Len's ridiculous words and backed away from the pen until Len then said,

"Oh come on, Eddie, get real – I think you're safe, aren't you? You can't die twice and, anyway, you're invisible."

Invisible they might have been but something was happening inside the tiger's pen. A small crowd had gathered as the lioness joined her mate and then both animals came over to stand inches from the boys on the other side of the metal fence. Simultaneously, they leapt at the fence, each with a tremendous roar and mouth wide open to show their massive and incredible teeth. Several people, who had been standing a good distance away, jumped in terror at the tiger's unusual behaviour and the frightening sound of the metal fence being shook with almost unearthly force. From out of the shade a keeper came running. The roar and the fence rattling were repeated. Some of the crowd gasped. The keeper seemed angry and, as he stood right between the two mesmerised ghosts, he said,

"Who did it? Who's upset Solomon and Sheba?"

No one moved or said a word. No one had been within ten yards of the pen before the animals went into their rage, only …. The keeper made strange, but obviously comforting noises, and the two lions returned quietly to their former peaceful states. Eddie and Len had backed away behind the gathering crowd and the younger ghost was first to speak.

"They sensed us, didn't they, Len?"

"I don't know, mate. I mean, how could they?"

"Because they have different senses to us – same way that some cats apparently know when their owners are about to be ill, I suppose."

Eddie paused and then said,

"Is that why you wanted to bring me here? To show me that?"

"No, I wanted to do something much more dangerous, or, at least, unusual."

"What?"

"I'll show you at a different pen."

"Where?"

"I don't know yet. Let's just have a look round at the other animals. There are loads to see."

"Something a little less scary, please," begged Eddie.

"How about the monkey house?"

"I suppose so. As long as they're small and timid."

The monkey house appeared to be only a bit further on at the very southernmost extremity of the zoo and the two boys reached it at a slow walk in a couple of minutes, with Eddie steering a course down the middle of the pathways. They approached with caution, but the several different types of apes and monkeys carried on with their normal business, seeming not to notice the two ghost's presence outside their cages.

"All seems fine," said Len. "Looks like they can't sense us."

Eddie moved closer to Len who was standing right next to the cage.

"Ugh! Look at that one's red bum," said Eddie, "and that one has got his thing out!"

While Eddie continued to stare at the monkey's strange anatomy and behaviour, Len moved a few feet away from his friend. Eddie immediately sensed that Len was going to do the 'something' he had been promising to do since they entered the zoo. It also seemed that he didn't want Eddie to try and dissuade him from so doing, though what Eddie could have done, short of remonstrating and shouting some silent and ghostly words, was a complete mystery to him. Suddenly Len moved forwards and passed right into the monkey's cage. Still the animals carried on with their 'monkey business'. To Eddie's horror, Len walked right up to a male and female orang-utan who were picking insects out of each other's coarse hair and plonked himself down in front them. Eddie tried to mouth some words but his throat had gone dry; a meaningless gasp was all he could muster. A few seconds went by and Eddie became a bit more relaxed about the situation. Len, of course, was right, what could the apes to do to them? But the sight of his best friend sitting between two sizeable orang-utans was, nevertheless, still not easy to come to terms with. Both weighed over ten stone and were prone to avoid human contact – Eddie had already read the sign fixed to their cage. Len grinned cheekily at his friend and called out,

"This is was what I was going to try with the tigers, mate!"

Eddie gave a nervous wave but did not reply. Suddenly, the male orang-utan looked fidgety, rocking from side to side on its haunches and uttering a high-pitched screeching noise. Len turned round and looked up into the ape's reddish-brown and heavily-set face. As he did so, the orang-utan *appeared* to place its right hand squarely on Len's head and began to gently stroke and lift his blond hair. A few seconds later the female did likewise with her left hand. Eddie couldn't stand it any longer.

"Please come out, Len!"

Len seemed to agree with his friend's request. He got to his feet and walked calmly through the wire cage front and back onto the pathway. He immediately called to Eddie.

"That was fun, Captain. You see, we can do things now that living people are not allowed to do."

"Or want to do," called back Eddie.

Len wandered the few yards back to stand beside his friend and immediately Eddie's face went a shade whiter than his normal ghostly colour.

"Len! Your hair! Look at your hair!"

Len moved to a glass-fronted cage a short distance away and looked at his reflection. He could hardly believe his eyes when he discovered his hair had taken on a 'Ken Dodd' appearance, and after an electric shock at that. Though no one could see him, his ghostly mind still possessed some vanity and he hurriedly tried to hand brush it back into something resembling his usual appearance. He returned to Eddie with a quizzical look upon his face.

"Well, explain that, will you?"

Eddie shook his head in disbelief.

"Impossible, Len – just impossible. How could a living, breathing animal ruffle your hair like that when you're a ghost? It's just not possible, mate."

For the first time for a while that Eddie could remember, his friend seemed at a loss for words; he was genuinely puzzled and disconcerted.

After a short walk back to a picnic area situated roughly in the middle of the zoo complex, the two boys sat down on the grass next to a family with two young children. Even Len now seemed to prefer the predictability of humans. They hadn't spoken much on the way there.

"They must have touched you," said Eddie at last. "Didn't you feel anything? Your hair couldn't have got into that state without you feeling something, surely."

Len shook his head.

"No, not as much as to make it such a mess. I did think there was a light breeze, but that's all."

Eddie had obviously been thinking deeply about the significance of the event when he then said,

"I wonder if it means that we can do the same to people or animals."

"We haven't tried anything yet, have we?" replied Len. "The trick in Selfridge's was done without contact."

"Yeah but that was an inanimate object."

Len shook his head again.

"But we've walked straight through living people and them through us and neither of us felt anything or disturbed anyone."

"Maybe we have to concentrate, like when I concentrated on the perfume bottle."

Len moved himself a few feet away from Eddie as the two young children began to pick daisies right next to him. Eddie followed, and they spent some time in silence just watching the two little girls, one blond and aged about seven and one aged a year or two younger with curly ginger hair that matched his own. Eddie recalled the times when he had been about the younger girl's age, and all the teasing or even name-calling he used to suffer because his hair colour stood him out from the crowd – he had been the only one in his class of thirty at Fenton Central Junior School. He wondered if the little girl had already faced similar teasing and how she would cope with it. While Eddie was thinking wistfully about his own childhood, the children's parents began to pack their picnic away, the mother calling to her offspring,

"Maggie, Hilary, time to go. Come and help tidy up, please."

The older girl was quick to her feet and went over to her mother and proudly presented her with the daisy chain she had just made. The younger one seemed content to lie on the grass in the sunshine. Eddie smiled as he could see how she was trying to avoid having to help her big sister. Eddie's sister had often got out of the washing up after a Sunday lunch with a similar tactic – retiring to her bedroom and pretending to be asleep with a headache had worked on several occasions in the Compton household. Mother called again,

"Maggie, will you please come and help otherwise there will be no ice-cream for you, my girl!"

Maggie got slowly and reluctantly to her feet and sulked her way over to her sister where she then made minimal effort to assist. Her dad patted her on her head and she clung to him for protection as her big sister began shouting at her.

"She always gets away with it, Mum and I ...."

Eddie didn't really concentrate on the rest of the argument that was starting as he had glanced at his friend who seemed to be drifting off to sleep. Len looked tired after his 'brush' with the orang-utans. In no time at all, his image started to fade and then he was suddenly gone. Eddie's friend had gone back to 'sleep' and he was alone again.

That day had provided a quick learning experience for Eddie and Len as trainee ghosts and, as he made his way back out of the zoo with no particular purpose in mind, Eddie pondered his progress. Several questions came to him in the afternoon sunshine. Did everyone end up as a ghost or was the experience only given to a chosen few? If everyone who died did become a ghost, why hadn't he and Len seen any others yet, apart, that was, from a few familiar faces? There would have to be billions, if not trillions, of ghosts wandering the earth from the beginning of time, if everybody became one. His poltergeist trick hadn't been that difficult to perform, he thought and yet it had always seemed to him that it would have been an extremely rare 'event' in real life, if such things ever happened at all. That, on the other hand, meant that ghosts like him and his friend might be extremely rare. However, as he left London Zoo that afternoon, he didn't reach a satisfactory conclusion, torn as he was between thinking that he was in elite company, or that he was merely one of an unimaginable host who remained unaware of one another, until something or someone forced their paths to cross.

Although Eddie made it safely out of the zoo and some way back towards the city's West End shopping area, he, like his friend, soon became tired and this time his visit to the real world finished abruptly while he was still walking. He felt warm inside (?) as he disappeared back into oblivion.

6

Wedding Day

Plans for Jenny's and Gary's wedding had gone well so far during the first half of 1968 and the all-important day was fast approaching as the final pieces of the jigsaw were being put in place. The stag and hen nights had been arranged for Thursday, September the 12th, with the big day arranged for the Saturday that week. Both young people had the following week off; Jenny from her job at 'Curls and Twirls', the hairdressing salon in Hamsden and Gary from the local fire service. In her year at the salon since leaving college, Jenny had worked hard and had already risen to the manager's number two. The honeymoon was to be taken in London. Gary, courtesy of his parent's generosity, had booked a reasonably expensive hotel in the West End for four nights, while the remainder of the week was scheduled for more cleaning and decorating at their newly acquired flat in Hamsden. It overlooked one of the main squares in the centre of town and was perfect, Gary had decided, for going on nights out, with cinemas, restaurants and pubs within a stone's throw of the front door of their ground floor apartment.

In the intervening months since the ghostly encounter with her brother, Jenny had not experienced any further such events. Yes, she had had strange dreams, but nothing remotely similar to something where she had actually been awake and talking to him. Indeed, even memories of that single event had begun to recede and, at times, she had come to question what had really taken place. Her father, too, had not had any other visions since the one at Wembley Stadium over two years previously. He and his daughter had had the occasional conversation about Eddie and, though nothing has ever been said between them, there did seem to be a tacit understanding that they each knew more than they were prepared to let on. Father's knew their daughters and daughters their fathers more deeply than most people might imagine. One such conversation actually occurred on the very morning of September the 14th, just as Jenny and her mother were going to start the preparations for the day. The two of them were alone in the lounge with Fred Compton going through the arrangements for the day with his daughter. His fastidious approach with timings and events often spilled over into his private life, too.

"What time is the car coming?"

Jenny sighed. She knew her dad of old.

"You know what time, Dad – quarter to eleven."

"Are you sure that gives us enough time, Jenny?"

"The driver says so and he should know; I mean he must have done hundreds of weddings at St Andrew's and it's only a five or ten minute drive from here – you should know that. You and Mum have done it enough times."

"But the wedding is at eleven – we may have less than five minutes when we get there; the bridesmaids have got to be organised and your dress straightened for the procession into the church and down the aisle."

"Oh, for goodness sake, stop fussing! What does it matter if I'm late? It's the bride's prerogative."

But Fred Compton wouldn't let up – he had to let his nervousness out somehow, and his daughter was bearing the brunt of his anxiousness.

"The Reverend Weaver said that there's another wedding scheduled for twelve."

Jenny had had enough.

"Dad! Shut up!"

She got up from her chair and went over to her father and kissed him lightly on his forehead and said,

"Just calm down, Dad. Everything will be fine. I want you and Mum to relax and just enjoy the day – you deserve it after all the help you've given me and Gary, especially with the deposit on the flat. It's going to be a perfect day; perfect in every way except for …."

Jenny paused and looked wistfully out of the window. Her dad seemed to understand.

"I know, love, but Eddie will be looking down on you in spirit. Maybe he'll be there."

Jenny was about to burst into tears but her father's words had struck a different chord at that moment of charged emotions.

"What do you mean, Dad?"

Fred Compton realised he had chosen the wrong time to discuss his deeper thoughts and said hurriedly,

"I didn't mean literally, love – just in our hearts and minds."

Jenny then let her emotions go and, hugging her dad, the tears rolled down her cheeks. Fred Compton, too, had wet eyes when his daughter eventually stood up.

"Now go and get ready and make me the proudest father alive," he said, gently patting her hand.

"Thanks, Dad. I will try."

As she joined her mum for all her necessary facial preparations, Jenny was left thinking that the tacit understanding had started to become a little more concrete between father and daughter.

St Andrew's was pretty full for the wedding of Jennifer Olivia Compton and Gary Steven Jones; Mr Richard Jones was well-known in the area, despite his dubious occupation as a second-hand car dealer. It was mostly unwarranted – Fred Compton had himself bought his latest car from Gary's father and had had absolutely no problems with it over the three years he had owned it. Fred Compton, too, was well-liked in Fenton-on-Sea and the Comptons as a family had often been in people's thoughts since their son had gone missing over two and half years ago. Many people had thought that the Compton's fate had been worse than if their son had been confirmed dead and they had buried his body. They were still in limbo and his disappearance was still listed as: '*Missing, presumed dead*'.

Jenny looked absolutely stunning as she walked up the aisle with her father. Her long white flowing dress had been selected from the best bridal shop in the area and it fitted and suited her to a tee. She had allowed her blond hair to grow to a length that required careful pinning to get her headdress to fit properly and securely. Even unromantic Gary gave an inward gasp when he glanced over his shoulder and saw her for the first time in all her wedding-day beauty. Halfway down the aisle, her father whispered,

"You look absolutely beautiful, Jenny. I'm so proud of you, love."

"*So am I, big sister.*"

"Thanks, Dad."

"*Yeah, well done, Dad.*"

Fred Compton felt his daughter stiffen, but he immediately put it down to Jenny's nervousness as she approached the altar and the love of her life. That wasn't the reason, however, as Jenny had glimpsed something out of her right eye – someone else was walking beside her up the aisle! Unnoticed to begin with, Eddie, dressed in his Sunday best, had accompanied his sister on her right side all the way from the time she and her father had entered the church. Jenny's body and dress had hid him from her father's view, if, indeed, he had been given the privilege to see or hear his son. He hadn't.

Understandably, Jenny was considerably apprehensive when she eventually stood side by side with Gary and the age-old ceremony began. When it came to her turn to express her vows, she had to concentrate doubly hard on her carefully rehearsed words.

"I, Jennifer Olivia Compton ...."

"*I Jennifer Olivia Compton,*" mimicked Eddie from his position still at her side, his interruption sounding like an echo in his sister's head.

".... take you, Gary Steven Jones, to be my lawful wedded husband, to have and to hold from this day forward ...."

"*Are you really sure, Jen. You can still change your mind.*"

".... for better or for worse, for richer, for poorer ...."

"*Take his money, sis.*"

".... in sickness and in health, to love and to cherish ...."

"*Well, O.K., if you're really sure.*"

".... from this day forward until death do us part."

"*Well I guess that's that, then.*"

Then the young couple's day took a real turn for the worse. For her part, Jenny had managed her vows superbly, notwithstanding the ghostly comments from her dear departed brother. However, when it came for the best man to provide the ring, Eddie exercised his role as a poltergeist by projecting it from his open palm straight into a vase full of water and assorted flowers. Gary murmured something to his best school friend about trying not to be so nervous, having naturally assumed that the ring's flight had been due to sweaty and trembling hands, or even the three stiff whiskies earlier. It then took a few minutes for the ring to be retrieved; the vase had to be emptied into another and the flowers similarly redistributed. Eddie made himself scarce among the congregation, in case his sister should have put two and two together. His next trick could take place from a distance, he thought.

All was well until the couple came to make their walk back down the aisle. With all eyes now fixed firmly on the happy pair, Eddie performed his caper. He had noticed one of his little cousins standing right at the end of a row of pews next to the side of the aisle down which Gary was about to walk. Just as the proud new husband passed the smiling blond-haired boy, Eddie 'persuaded' him to stick out a leg and trip him up. Gary catapulted forward, catching his foot in Jenny's dress which ripped with a loud noise. He ended up in an undignified prostrate position on the floor. He got to his feet as quickly and in as dignified way as possible and, fortunately, found himself to be unscathed. The only real damage was to his pride and his wife's dress. Fortunately, the ripped garment had seemed to be the least of Jenny's worries when she helped him to his feet. There was, of course, some inevitable laughter and comment, particularly from some of Gary's fire service colleagues.

"Call yourself a fireman!"

"How many have you had, Jonesey?"

"Under the wife's thumb already, mate?"

Eddie was also laughing, in his ghostly way and, unnoticed by anyone, he was already climbing into the back seat of his dad's Hillman Minx. He wasn't going to miss the reception at the Marine Hotel set in the beautiful cliff gardens at the top of East Hill.

The Marine Hotel was the plushest such establishment in Fenton-on-Sea, and its booking had only been enabled with a substantial contribution from Gary's parents. Richard Jones had also provided the bride's car without charge, a vintage white Rolls Royce which was part of his normal hire fleet. It was a modest gathering – about sixty guests had been invited, and the reception lunch was to be held in the East Room, a superb open-plan area decorated and furnished in the art deco style of the twenties.

The addition of large potted palms gave the room a definite continental feel. By the time all the introductions and handshaking had taken place, Eddie was already in his place behind one such palm. He still possessed doubts at times that he would remain invisible, particularly as his sister had been able to see him, but he had no immediate plans to disturb the gathering that afternoon. He just wanted to watch the proceedings out of general interest and to be able to discuss them with his sister should he want to at some time in the future. Len would have called it a 'watching brief'.

The meal was quite an opulent affair with five courses, smoked salmon, prime rib of beef and Black Forest gateau being three of the most popular choices. Jenny had begun to relax as soon as she and Gary had climbed into their white Rolls outside the church; memories of the mishaps there seemed to have been forgotten. Though she knew that her brother had been with her up to and including the time when she had said her vows, she was still totally unaware of his involvement in the two 'pranks' afterwards. She had put the accidents down to nervousness on both the best man's and her new husband's part. She was strangely both relieved and disappointed that Eddie hadn't seemed to have followed her to the hotel, and she heard no phantom interruptions to any of the speeches that followed the meal. She knew that both her dad and Gary had been very nervous about delivering their contributions in front of an audience that contained many strangers to each of them. In her mind and known only to her, Jenny's day had been made all the more perfect by her brother's ghostly visit, albeit in somewhat awkward circumstances. Despite his continual and comical interruptions, she had felt a warmness and contentment that he had given his blessing to their union. Gary Jones hadn't always been accepted by her brother as she still remembered quite well.

By three-thirty, the photographer had begun to take some rather more informal shots than those of the wedding party and guests that he'd taken earlier outside the church. The warm late summer sunshine showed the cliff top gardens off to perfection, with the deep blue sea in the background. Mr Ralph Hollister was at liberty to show off his artistic skills. He started with the newly-wed couple, before they went off to change into something less formal for the evening disco and party, scheduled to start at seven. A taxi had been booked to take them to their London hotel at eight-thirty. He appeared satisfied with the first three shots he took with the North Sea in the background, but suddenly became annoyed when he asked the couple to face out to sea. The art deco architecture of the Marine Hotel, lit by the brilliant afternoon sun, provided a romantic background which he didn't want to miss.

"Please get out of the shot, young man," shouted Ralph Hollister with some irritation. A look of confusion spread across Gary's face when he looked about and saw no one fitting the photographer's description within twenty yards of the scene. Jenny looked more apprehensive than confused as she, too, glanced round. No, Eddie didn't seem to be there, she thought. Mr Hollister refocused his camera and took two quick shots of the happy couple. After a few minutes, the photographer left Gary and Jenny to themselves and she pre-empted Gary's inevitable question by saying,

"It must have been one of my young cousins messing about. He probably ran behind us just as Mr Hollister was going to take the picture."

The incident clearly hadn't concerned Gary as much as Jenny thought it might have done when he replied,

"What, love? Yes, you're probably right – these budding David Baileys can be very sensitive."

Jenny suspected that there *had* been a young man attempting to join in their photo session and, of course, she knew it hadn't been one of her cousins.

A few days later, when Mr Hollister developed his photographs from the Compton-Jones wedding, he would discover to his annoyance that three of his shots had been ruined by the addition of a grinning teenage boy dressed in a smart suit. In one – taken with the hotel in the background – he was standing right between the happy couple, with arms folded over his chest which was stuck out like a soldier on parade. Needless to say, Mr Hollister destroyed the offending photographs and accompanying negatives, so that Eddie's final little trick was thwarted at the last moment. It would have to remain an unanswered question as to what Jenny or Gary or the rest of their families would have done if the photographs had reached public circulation. If Mr Ralph Hollister had possessed an inquiring mind, bordering on the scientific or detective, he might have searched through the other hundred or so photographs to see if he could identify the object of his annoyance, but, being of the more artistic temperament, Eddie's concrete images were lost forever.

7

Moon Dance

Eddie had thoroughly enjoyed the day at his sister's wedding. Whoever or whatever was now in charge of his 'life' – whether the God he had begun to trust, or some other natural phenomenon – his silent prayers had been answered. He had seen Jenny get married and had had some fun at her and Gary's expense, too. Annoying the photographer had suggested, however, that it was not only friends and family that might be allowed to see him; he had sensed that neither Jenny nor Gary had been aware of his presence at that time. As he wandered alone, and once more invisible in the cliff top gardens, he amused himself thinking about the prospect of his family getting the photographs back with his cheeky face staring at them from some of them. He knew it shouldn't be possible, but, given everything else that had happened, you just never knew ….

It was getting quite late when Eddie began to feel the inevitable tiredness creep up on him. The last thing he would see that day would be a beautiful harvest moon rising over the sea and his last thought would be about how huge and close it seemed to be.

The new Mr and Mrs Jones made their taxi to London and spent a gloriously happy honeymoon there. It would not be long before the seeds of the next generation would be sown and by the following July, Jenny announced to Gary that she was pregnant. Fortunately, number 4A Beaumont Square, Hamsden was a two-bedroom flat and they would spend the next few months getting it ready for the new arrival(s) due at the end of the year, 1969.

It was to be after his sister's news had been made public that Eddie would be awakened again; this time, also, he would soon be joined by his best friend. Loud and raucous noises greeted him before he was allowed the power of sight. Unfamiliar noises – car horns, people shouting in English but with a strange twang – greeted his ears.

"*Watch it, bud!*"

"*Can't you learn to drive, lady?*"

"*The sidewalks are for walking on, fella!*"

Eddie's eyes opened slowly. It appeared to be fairly early in the morning, judging by the long shadows being cast by the sun. He found himself in a wide thoroughfare, lined on each side with expensive looking shops. Strange cars were rushing by him, big and futuristic looking, many being coloured a bright and garish shade of yellow with black letters printed on their sides. He was in the middle of the road and he began to panic momentarily until he remembered what powers he possessed. At first he thought he was viewing the scene in a mirror as things seemed to be the wrong way round. Then he realised that it was the cars that were causing the illusion – each line of traffic was being driven on the wrong side of the road! He moved carefully to the pavement and from his position further back from the cars, he was able to read the lettering on one of the yellow cars:

'New York Cab Co.'

So that was it, he thought – the good ol' U S of A and the capital at that, the Big Apple. This was exciting. As a ghost it seemed he could cross boundaries, oceans and time zones. The question was: Why? Why New York? As he dawdled along the pavement (sidewalk), he also wondered if Len was going to join him on what was clearly a new and different adventure. That it was morning was quickly confirmed by looking at the faces of the businessmen hurrying to their offices. They did not have the relaxed looks of men who had just completed a good and tiring days' work. Neon signs off all colours flashed all around him and looking up, he realised the main reason for the long shadows, which, in some cases darkened the entire road. Skyscrapers reached into the sky, blocking the sun from casting its warming rays on the scene below. One of the neon signs confirmed the exact date and time to Eddie: July 16th, 08:52. The year was a little bit more difficult to ascertain. Eddie's ghostly mind, though not as good as a human one at remembering things, did allow him, in this case, to recall that it had been September 1968 the last time he had been awake. A newspaper stand quickly provided the answer: 1969 and, apart from gleaning the date, Eddie was astonished to read the headline of one of the papers.

'MAN TAKES OFF FOR THE MOON TODAY
Apollo 11 all set for launch this morning'

Eddie took a ghostly step backwards – surely it couldn't be possible? He did remember back when he'd been alive that there had been talk of putting a man on the moon by the end of the decade, but he had hardly believed it – something to do with a speech by the late President John Kennedy. And here he was in the very country that was going to attempt such an incredible feat. Eddie was excited. His visit surely had to have something to do with it. Where was the launch to take place? New York? No, that couldn't be right – it was Cape Canaveral in Florida where all the other space rockets had lifted off. His immediate thoughts, however, were disturbed by a familiar voice which spoke in a fake American accent.

"Hi there, buddy! Welcome to the land of the free."

Unlike the previous time in Fenton-on-Sea, Eddie was caught off guard and forgot to check the identity of the person to whom the voice belonged. His excitement at waking up in New York on such a momentous day had led his mind elsewhere. When he turned round to see his possible friend, he even failed to notice that 'Len' did not ask the relevant question either.

"Hi ya, Len. What's up?"

"Not much, Compo, just doing some jaywalking. It's good fun to do it here because it's actually an offence, you know. I've been having quite a blithe time."

And then it hit Eddie like an arrow right between the eyes which pierced his head with the cold, hard realisation of his mistake. This 'Len' had used the old code which he must have picked up on a previous occasion. Eddie said nothing and carried on walking for a few moments in order to see what the ghost would do. Predictably, he repeated the question.

"I said: I've had a *blithe* time."

"Have you really? So what?"

"So, aren't you going to check something out with me, Ed?"

"Don't call me Ed, please."

"Don't call me Ed, please," mimicked the evil ghost. "Ooh, aren't we the touchy one?"

Eddie got more confident.

"Go away! Just, go away and leave me alone."

"Go away? I'm not going anywhere, sunshine. I'm going to be bad, oh, so bad."

Another familiar voice entered the conversation from somewhere to Eddie's left.

"Run, Eddie! Run!"

Without stopping to check where the new voice had come from, Eddie propelled himself forward in a straight line and ran as fast as he could, straight through several pedestrians until he reached a wider stretch of sidewalk where there were fewer people about. He looked nervously behind him and was partially relieved to see only one familiar person who was strolling nonchalantly in his direction. Coming up close, 'Len' said,

"He nearly got you, mate."

Eddie folded his arms and stared back at the ghost.

"Ask me the question, Len, please?"

"What question?"

"You tell me, comrade."

The ghost looked thoughtful.

"Well, let me see. How about, what's the capital of France? No – not that one? Well, what about, the capital of England? No, that's wrong, too. Oh, I don't know. What do you want me to ask you?"

Eddie turned to run again but then the ghost said,

"Only kidding, Captain. What *is* the twentieth prime number?

Eddie was still not sure and said,

"Well, that would be seventy-three, I do believe."

"Oh, very clever, Eddie. Now give me the correct answer."

Eddie smiled.

"No, *you* give the real answer."

"O.K., if you wish, but I have to say that you're being just a teeny bit pedantic, mate. The correct answer, as you well know, is seventy-one."

"Thank God; it is you, Len."

"Indeed, my friend. I'd have thought you would have realised that when I knew the right question to ask, but you can't be …."

Eddie finished Len's sentence.

"Too careful? You're damn right I am, comrade Len."

By now the two boys had reached what seemed to be a major intersection of roads and Len pointed to a sign high up on an adjacent building.

"Look, we're at Fifth Avenue and Times Square."

Eddie didn't seem to be that interested in their location and replied, "You know what's happening today, don't you."

Len expressed his ignorance of the moon shot.

"No – should I?"

Then Eddie told him, in as calm a manner as possible, about the headline he had read earlier and his passive excitement suddenly became much more animated when passed to his friend, who said,

"Wow! Where? We've got to go and see it."

Even when his friend informed him that the launch was scheduled to be at least a thousand miles further south in Florida, Len's excitement did not abate.

"So? We can get there – hopping on trains and planes is not a problem for us. Won't cost us anything and when we get close we'll just follow the crowds. There must be thousands going."

Len's normal down-to-earth approach had made the problem seem so easy until Eddie really brought him *down to earth*.

"Yeah, but the paper said that the Saturn Five rocket is due to take off at about nine-thirty this morning and the time has already got to be past nine o'clock."

"Ten past, to be precise, Captain," replied Len, looking at a huge clock hanging above Times Square. He was not to be beaten as he then said,

"Still no problem – we'll just think our way there. After all, someone must have landed us here on today of all days for a reason, don't you think?"

Eddie had been thinking more or less the same thing just before he met his friend and replied,

"I'm game if you are. Who's going to do the thinking?"

"We both will. On the count of three we both start concentrating on …."

Len paused and said,

"Where is it?"

"Kennedy Space Centre at Cape Canaveral in Florida," said Eddie.

"On three, then. Ready? One – two – three – go!"

Eddie didn't have time to do anything but blindly follow Len's command and as soon as he said 'three', he screwed up his face and concentrated on their proposed destination, hoping that God would take control of their improbable mission.

"This is Apollo Saturn launch control. We've passed the six-minute mark in our countdown for Apollo 11, now five minutes, 52 seconds and counting. We're on time at the present time for our planned lift-off at 32 minutes past the hour. Spacecraft test conductor Skip Chauvin now has completed the status check of his personnel in the control room ….'

The monotone voice of the Launch Control Announcer droned on to the world-wide television audience as the two boy-ghosts found themselves in a location where no one on earth could ever have imagined another normal human could be at that particular time. There were already, of course, three people in the location where Eddie's and Len's ghosts found themselves – Neil Armstrong, Michael Collins and Edwin 'Buzz' Aldrin.

"T minus five minutes and counting …."

The two ghosts had no trouble fitting into the space capsule as their invisibility allowed them to roam free and, though they could see and hear each other, none of the three astronauts had the same privilege.

"*T minus four minutes and counting ....*"

"Can you believe this, Eddie?" asked Len, after both boys had regained some sort of ghostly composure.

"Yep, we're going to the moon, mate," replied Eddie grinning from ear to ear. "We can float where we want."

Eddie and Len had taken up positions with their backs to the instrument panels and seemed to be able to hover there unaided. The astronaut's view would not be blocked – ghosts didn't need space to occupy!

"I may try going outside later on," said Len, boldly.

Eddie pulled a face. His friend could not be serious, surely!

"*T minus one minute 54 seconds and counting .... Our status board indicates that the oxidiser tanks of the second and third stages have pressurised ....*"

"Well, what could go wrong, Eddie?" queried Len.

"Not much, I suppose. You might just float away into space and have to wander the infinite universe forever. Apart from that it should be plain sailing!"

"I'll just keep in contact with the capsule."

Eddie burst out laughing.

"How, sunshine? What will you use to cling on with? Your hands won't work, you idiot."

"Well, whatever or whoever has got us here and keeps us in the capsule will keep me fixed to it if I'm outside. I mean, I won't need oxygen, will I?"

"Who's to say that God will allow you to stay in contact if you try something daft like that?"

"So he's in charge, then, is he?" asked Len.

"Someone is."

"*T minus 50 seconds and counting …. Neil Armstrong just reported back it's been a real smooth countdown ….*"

"Yeah, I suppose you're right," said Len reluctantly. "Don't worry, I'll behave, mate."

"Good, now get ready," replied Eddie.

"*T minus 15 seconds …. Guidance is internal, twelve … eleven … ten ….*"

"See you in space," said Len.

"*… nine … eight … seven … ignition sequence starts, six … five … four … three … two … one … zero, all engines running. Lift-off, we have a lift-off, thirty-two minutes past the hour, lift-off on Apollo eleven.*"

Though Eddie and Len might have been subjected to some incredible noises and vibrations in the next few minutes, their ghostly ears and bodies were able to withstand them in comfort. Of course, no oxygen or similar protections were necessary as they floated around the cabin, watching in awe at the culmination of man's ingenuity and technological progress.

One minute into take-off, the three crew members were experiencing forces in excess of 3g and the Saturn Five rocket began to disappear from view beyond any cloud cover, leaving a trail of exhaust gases and a sound like rolling thunder. In less than four minutes, the Command and Service Module completed its final separation from the top of the massive Saturn rocket and the three-plus-two astronauts were left isolated in the CSM, on course for the moon. By the time the CSM had stabilised and the three genuine astronauts had started to carry out all the necessary checks and monitoring tasks, the two ghosts had both become drowsy. Eddie was the first to return to ghostly oblivion, followed within a few seconds by his friend. If either of them had known that they would lose 'consciousness', they would have panicked beyond belief in the realisation that they were leaving earth, maybe forever.

When they next 'awoke', Eddie and Len found themselves in a much smaller environment and accompanied by one less astronaut. Neither of them questioned how they had got to their new position, presumably unaided by human intervention – it was another reminder of their over-arching and divine guide. Unbeknown to the boys, 'Buzz' Aldrin and Neil Armstrong were already focusing on the necessary tasks to land the Lunar Module on the moon's surface. The LM, *Eagle*, was small and compact inside and the two ghosts were forced to merge into one entity, even though it was probably unnecessary given their ethereal nature. Like Siamese twins, they could not see each other and, in addition, talking gave them each the impression that the other's voice was coming from inside their own head.

"What's happening, Eddie?" asked Len, assuming his friend's superior scientific knowledge would provide an immediate answer.

"Not sure, mate – we're probably in the capsule that's going to do the landing on the moon."

"Oh, wow!" was all Len could think of to reply.

Somewhere 240,000 miles away, Mission Control was issuing continual updates to about one third of the world's population.

"This is Apollo control at 100 hours and 14 minutes. We are now less than two minutes from re-acquiring the spacecraft on the 13th

revolution .... We're presently 25 minutes from the separation burn that will be preformed by Mike Collins in the command module to give the lem and the CSM a separation of about two miles ...."

"We're going down," said Eddie.

"Wow!" repeated his dumbstruck friend.

After a couple of real-time minutes, the boys sensed that *Eagle* had separated from the CSM. The announcer was trying to maintain his dignified monotone. More seconds passed.

"We are now in the approach phase ... everything looking good. Altitude 5,200 feet .... Altitude forty-two hundred feet ...."

Then one of the astronauts spoke.

"... 400 feet, down at 9 ... 8 forward ... You're pegged on horizontal velocity ...."

Seconds later, 'Buzz' Aldrin continued,

"Altitude velocity light, three and a half down, 220 feet ... 100 feet three and a half down, nine forward ... 5 per cent fuel remaining ... things looking good ... forty feet, down ... picking up some dust ...."

Then Neil Armstrong called out the words that would become some of the most quoted ever with regard to space travel.

"Houston, Tranquillity base here. The Eagle had landed."

Eruptions of spontaneous applause and cheering from Mission Control could be heard all around the world as Armstrong's words were received.

"Roger Tranquillity, we copy you on the ground. You've got a bunch of guys about to turn blue; we're breathing again, thanks a lot."

Though neither ghost could see the other, each of their faces was rigid with excitement and anticipation and Eddie managed at last to speak with a note of caution in case his friend started to take things into his own hands.

"Wait, Len. Please don't try and walk through the sides of the module. Just follow the astronauts out when they are ready."

It appeared, from the movement within the module, that Armstrong and Aldrin had been on the moon for some time. The boys noticed that both men had donned extra equipment, including what appeared to be tightly fitting suits that consisted of several layers of an aluminium coloured reflective material.

"They won't get far in those," remarked Len.

"You're forgetting that there's very little gravity on the moon, mate. They'll be almost weightless like they were earlier," said Eddie.

"Will we be, too?" asked Len.

"That remains to be seen, but I think that would be possible, don't you?" laughed Eddie. "We're weightless already!"

"Hm, could be interesting," said Len.

Just then, the two men moved towards the hatch door and, after decompressing the LM, they pried the hatch open. Neil Armstrong was the first to back out of the module and onto the top of the lander's ladder. He quickly deployed a TV camera which was focused on the ladder and the first black and white pictures of the moon were transmitted back to earth. Armstrong started a running commentary as he descended the ladder.

"I'm at the foot of the ladder ... the surface appears to be very, very fine grained ... it's almost like powder. I'm going to step off the lem now ...."

Although Mission Commander Neil A Armstrong would be the first human being to set foot on the moon, he wasn't the second 'being' to follow him. One Leonard Wilby preceded the Lunar Module Pilot, Edwin 'Buzz' Eugene Aldrin Jr., by a couple of seconds as, ignoring Eddie's earlier request, he leapt/floated down to the moon's surface to stand proudly by Commander Armstrong as he uttered the historic words:

"That's one small step for man ... one giant leap for mankind."

"That was one very easy step for us ghosts ... one tiny jump for ghostkind," mimicked Len. In Fenton-on-Sea, England, it was 2.56 in the early hours of the morning of Monday the 21st of July, 1969.

After a few minutes of solitary exploration by Neil Armstrong, 'Buzz' Aldrin was guided out of the module by his co-astronaut. Eddie had not appeared, much to Len's impatience, while he had stalked Neil Armstrong around the moon's surface on the first few tasks of the mission. As soon as the second astronaut reached the foot of the ladder, however, Eddie came out of the module and, like his friend almost twenty minutes earlier, he jumped and floated to the dusty surface. The dust was not disturbed in the process. Len was quick to point out how different it was for the ghosts to move around.

"Just like being on earth, Captain. We can just walk and run normally."

It was true; Eddie found that they didn't bounce over the moon's surface like the astronauts, and their movement was unencumbered by heavy moon suits and oxygen tanks. Despite his misgivings, everything seemed to be fine to Eddie and he did a little jig, causing Len to observe,

"That's quite a moon dance for you, mate."

Eddie barely heard his friend's comment as he had quickly stopped dancing to go over and read the plaque that the astronauts had just uncovered. Len joined him with two giant strides. They stood and read,

'Here Men from the Planet Earth First set Foot Upon the Moon
July 1969, AD
We Came in Peace for All Mankind'

"We came, too," said Len after a few moments.

"Yeah, along with thousands or even millions of others of our kind, eh?" remarked Eddie.

"Don't be daft," said Len. "You couldn't have got anyone else in the lunar module."

Eddie looked deprecatingly at his friend.

"I thought you were supposed to be the experienced ghost, comrade. We ghosts have other ways of moving around – we didn't have to come by rocket."

"Mm, I suppose so. Haven't seen anyone or thing that shouldn't be here, though."

Eddie's face contorted in fear.

"Well, what's that over there, then?"

Len spun round with terror etched on his face, too.

"What? Where? I don't see anything."

"Got you!" shouted Eddie, triumphantly and his friend then made a mock attempt to push him to the ground. Eddie, needlessly, backed away to avoid Len's outstretched hands. After recovering themselves, Len said,

"We could go and do some exploring – the astronauts are presumably not going back yet. They don't seem to have been here long."

Eddie glanced at the two men who were busy trying to unfurl the Stars and Stripes to leave as a permanent fixture to commemorate their visit to the moon.

"I'm not sure, Len. We should only do it if we can keep the lunar module in sight."

"O.K., but like you said, there must be other ways of getting back to earth, if, indeed, we have to go back."

"What do you mean?"

"I mean that we could stay here."

Eddie looked strangely at his friend.

"And just what would be the point of that, pray tell? There's nothing much to do up here."

Len had to agree that the lunar landscape was pretty flat and barren with few, if any, points of interest. With an unspoken agreement that they would not go out of sight of their transport, the two boys set off to explore. The light seemed to be good and they glided their way in what they thought to be the most interesting direction, dotted with small hills as it was. Not having any landmarks to judge their speed by, they covered a good distance in no time at all and without really knowing it. Eddie kept glancing over his shoulder at the lunar module, but being distracted by an interesting rock formation, he neglected to continue to do so for a couple of minutes. Eventually, Len turned round to check on their relative position and instantly exclaimed,

"It's gone – the lunar module's gone!"

Eddie turned round and gave a gasp, but then he guessed the reason.

"I forgot that the horizon is much nearer on the moon, because its diameter is only about a fifth of that of the earth, so it can be reached more quickly."

"Now you tell me!" yelled Len.

"No problem," said Eddie, reassuringly. "We'll go back now by just retracing our steps. There's obviously not much to see – it's deader than Fenton beach in winter!"

The two ghosts turned back and set off in the direction they thought the lunar module lay. Within a few hundred yards, however, it was clear to them both that they must have missed it. The 'moonlight' was fading fast, much faster than sunlight on earth and they began to panic.

This time Len seemed less concerned than his friend.

"We need some ghost tactics," he said. "We'll have to think our way there."

While Len screwed up his face in a mask of concentration, Eddie scoured the horizon for any familiar landmarks that they'd passed on their outward journey. He couldn't recognise anything and, after about five seconds, turned back to see how Len was getting on. When he did, he discovered to his horror that Len had vanished completely from off the 'face of the moon'.

"Len! Len!" he shouted.

It was getting quite dark and Eddie began to experience real panic, even though the cognitive part of his ghostly mind was telling him not to be so stupid. He began to wander blindly around, calling Len's name. Minutes passed and he was just about to give up and try to think of his next move when he thought he could just make out an object on the horizon. Running and gliding over the moon's rough surface, he reached the lunar module in less than a minute. His excitement at being back at the spacecraft was short-lived however, as the astronauts appeared to be safely locked away in their module and Len was nowhere to be seen. He felt tired and his mind didn't seem to be able process his thoughts. He called out as loudly as he could, but knew that no one could possibly hear him. He fell to his knees and prayed. He blacked out and passed once more into the safety of oblivion with his mind in turmoil as to what was going to happen to him. He hadn't thought for one moment that his friend had already preceded him by several minutes.

8

What Might Have Been

If Eddie could have felt extremes of temperature he would have been extremely hot and uncomfortable the next time he woke. Again, unusual sounds were the first signs that he had exited his slumber. Waves lapping on a beach, the rustle of trees in a gentle breeze and unfamiliar music playing from a radio in the background, formed a pleasant image in his mind's eye before his real ones opened. When they did and focused in the bright sunshine, he found himself prostrate on a sloping sandy beach of pure white and very fine sand. Shadows flicked across his eyes as he looked skywards to see the fronds of overhanging palm trees. He was somewhere exotic. He rolled over onto his side and took in the scenery. He was not quite alone, as to his right he glimpsed a heavily oiled young white-skinned couple who were sunbathing about fifty yards away. To his left, and within twenty yards, lay a single black man whose radio was blasting out reggae music which was not altogether unpleasant to Eddie's untrained ears. Eddie looked down at himself and discovered that the powers that be had dressed him suitably for the occasion. His old white tennis shorts and t-shirt felt familiar and comfortable. He would not look out of place if he became visible. Though he knew that the chances were very slim, if not infinitesimal, he still glanced about nervously when he got to his feet.

The young couple seemed to be asleep when Eddie wandered over. He was extremely curious as to see who they were and if he might recognise either of them. There had to be a reason for his arrival on what appeared to be such a lonely and isolated beach, he thought. Apart from the coloured man, there wasn't another soul in sight, although there did seem to be movement and noises coming from an old tin shack-cum-beach bar at the top of the long sandy beach.

The man and woman appeared to be in their early twenties and each had acquired a deep tan, their well-oiled bodies glistening in the strong sunshine. Both had wedding rings on the third finger of their left hands. They were married. As Eddie circled the young people, there wasn't much else his inquiring mind could determine about the strangers. The man had about a week-long growth of beard on his face which, perhaps, gave an indication of how long they had been on holiday, for holidaying sun-seekers they clearly were. Despite the vague disguise, Eddie was absolutely convinced that he had never seen the man before. At first, when he had approached the young couple, he had thought or hoped that they would be familiar, possibly even being close family, but if, as he suspected, it was later than 1969, then Jenny and Gary would have appeared slightly older. Close inspection of the recumbent couple had revealed them to be only just out of their teens. He wasn't, however, so sure of the girl and he began to study her more carefully, even dropping to his knees for a closer view.

"Are you doing anything tomorrow? … I was wondering if you'd like to go to Hamsden to do some shopping and …."

Eddie jerked his head upright and looked around himself. It was instantly clear that the voice had come from inside his head and it was familiar.

"… you've got my number, haven't you?"

The voice was more than just familiar now. Identical words to the ones he had just 'heard' had once been spoken to him on a Friday afternoon in late January of 1966. That day, he had been accompanied on his walk home by one Sally Barber, a fellow pupil in Fenton Grammar School's fourth year. Other snippets of a hurried conversation resurfaced.

"Oh good, you have decided to come, Eddie ...."

Then he heard his own voice reply.

"Can't stop, Sally, I've got to go back home; I've forgotten
something."

The girl began to stir and opened her eyes. Eddie jumped away and
out of her eye line though there was no need as she had been immediately
blinded by the sun. She rolled over onto her stomach, laid her head down
once more and closed her eyes. A familiar movement, the shape of the
eyes or just wishful thinking – whatever the reminder had been, Eddie
knew that he was looking down at Sally Barber and, for the first time
since his passing, his ghostly soul felt real emotion. He was looking at
someone who could have become his first girlfriend when he had been
fourteen. He had, however, made other plans for that late January
Saturday with disastrous and fatal consequences. If only he had taken
Sally's offer up of a trip to Hamsden for shopping and 'so on' – to use her
words uttered on the walk home the previous day – *he* might have been
the young man who was currently lying beside her on this faraway beach.

After a couple more minutes spent thinking about what might have
been, Eddie wandered away with no particular plan in mind. Out of
nothing more than idle curiosity, he made his way slowly over to the only
other person in sight on the small secluded beach. For the first time he
studied his surroundings. The beach was small; no more than three
hundred yards wide and fifty deep and hemmed in by groves of palm
trees that flowed right to the water's edge. Behind the beach was a narrow
dirt track that wound its way up into densely forested hills. The small
beach bar seemed to have no more than two or three customers and their
only means of transport in and out seemed to be a couple of open-topped
jeeps. At least one of the vehicles had markings on the side to indicate it
belonged to some small boarding house further inland. There was no

other sigh of human life or habitation – the little cove was clearly a closely guarded secret. From his scant knowledge of the music blaring from the tinny radio that lay next to the muscular coloured man, Eddie made a mental guess that the beach's location was somewhere in the Caribbean. The West Indian reached over and turned up the volume.

'*After she walks away*
Then sadness comes
And without your love
Then you'll find out how
Hard it is to be alone'

Eddie caught this verse in its entirety as he stood beside the young man who, by then, was sitting up and singing along to the words, greatly helping Eddie with the translation from the West Indian dialect into something approaching English. The young man looked sad as if the lyrics of the song had some personal significance. In the background and behind him, Eddie could hear an argument start up between Sally and her husband.

"*… I didn't go to her room last night, Sal, honestly.*"

"*So where were you until two-thirty? Solomon said he closed the bar at one.*"

"*A walk, I told you, just a walk.*"

"*Where?*"

"*Anywhere – what does ….?*"

Eddie wandered back as the argument was getting more and more heated. Sally's husband obviously could not account for about an hour the previous night and Sally suspected the worse. By the time Eddie reached the couple, Sally had got up and, flouncing her way back up to the small shack, she managed to persuade another young white man to drive one of the jeeps. They sped away up the hillside in a cloud of dust; presumably back to wherever she and her husband were staying. Meanwhile, Sally's husband had assumed a sitting position with hands clasped round his knees, staring blindly out to sea.

'Then sadness comes …

… to be alone.'

Eddie felt sad for Sally. *He* would never have done anything like her husband was being accused of – Sally was too nice. Suddenly, he felt alone, too. Oh, how life can be so cruel, he thought. He wandered up the beach hoping that Sally would be happy for the rest of her life and would find true companionship.

The *Pineapple Cove Beach Bar* beckoned Eddie as he thought of his own loneliness at that moment. Being a ghost was fun most of the time, when there were things to do or people to annoy, but here on this isolated beach, at least two other people had cast a shadow over his visit back to the living world. Eddie felt the need for the sound of happy voices as he climbed, unnoticed, onto one of the cane bar stools. There were three other such seats, only one of which was occupied by a small Asian looking man of about thirty. The owner, Carlos by name, and clearly Latin by descent, sat opposite him behind the low bar. Both men were drinking what looked to be some kind of coconut punch, laced, no doubt, with rum. Dried pineapples hung on strings from the bar's wooden ceiling – giving any tourists a feeling of authenticity to the place. One minute after Eddie had taken up his position at the bar, the only other tourist, apart from Eddie himself, came and sat between him and the Asian man. Sally's husband was in need of a drink.

"A cold beer, Carlos, please."

"Yes, sir, Mr John. Comin' right up."

Carlos had a strange accent, a combination of Spanish and native Jamaican. Cards for taxis and restaurants, which lay scattered on the bar top, indicated that Eddie had indeed landed in the 'yard'. John nodded to his fellow drinker.

"Alright, Mo? How's business?"

"Not bad, John. When are you and the missus going back home?"

"Got another four days yet, but to tell you the truth, I'm ready to go now. I'd rather be back fighting fires than fighting Sal."

"You been up to no good again, then?"

"No, Mo – just because she saw me talking to another girl back at the hotel last night, she thinks I must have slept with her or something."

Carlos brought John his drink and interrupted the conversation.

"And did you, Mr John?"

John took a long swig of beer straight from the bottle and replied,

"Did I what?"

"Sleep with her."

"Oh, not you and all – of course I didn't. We just had some innocent fun; kissing and snogging, you know."

Carlos winked and said,

"I say nothing, Mr John."

"Well," continued Sally's husband. "You've got to have a bit of fun now and again, especially on holiday. She'll come round, she always does – loves being married to a fireman."

John finished his beer and ordered another. Eddie was simultaneously appalled and curious. How could anyone treat his wife like that, particularly one as nice as Sally? John seemed a thoroughly nasty piece of work. Eddie's curiosity stemmed from the mention of John's occupation. Did he work with Gary in Hamsden or had Sally moved away from the area before she had met him? Eddie had also been thinking about what time zone he had moved to after his and Len's journey to the moon which had been July 1969. Was he still in 1969? He tried to do some mental calculations. Sally had been about fifteen in early 1966 and she'd looked about twenty or twenty-one on the beach although, with her skimpy bikini, it was difficult to tell exactly. It was therefore, he decided, probably at least 1970.

While these questions had been going through Eddie's head, Mo, which turned out to be short for Mohammed, was trying his best to reprimand his fellow drinker.

"You shouldn't do naughty things, John. Your wife seems to be a lovely person. Don't mistreat her. You'll lose her, you hear?"

Mo's accent was pure Jamaican, despite his Asian ancestry. Eddie's ears pricked up at John's reply.

"I know, Mo. My mate Gary in the fire brigade back home lost his wife. Upped and took their two-month-old baby and went back to her parents."

"Why?"

"She caught him with some lipstick on his shirt collar. He'd been calling in on an old girlfriend on his way home some nights and word got around the station. Someone told his wife and, bingo, that was that."

By this time Eddie was getting quite upset within himself; the bar on having emotions as a ghost was being lifted for the second time that day. The timings all seemed to fit. Jenny and Gary got married in September 1968. It was quite possible, therefore, for them to have at least a baby of that age. If only he could ask John for the full story. John's third beer loosened his tongue still further.

"Yeah and he regrets his mistake – lovely girl she was. Lost her brother when he was fourteen, so she's had a bit of a rough life one way or another, you could say."

"Accident?" asked Carlos, joining in the conversation again after providing John with his fourth bottle.

"What?" said John.

"I said, did her brother die in an accident?"

"Oh, no – he just went missing one day. Never found a body. He maybe still alive somewhere, I suppose, but not very likely since it's been over four years now."

So that was it, thought Eddie, 1966 plus four years and a bit would make it the summer of the first year of the new decade, 1970. Also, he had been brought to the isolated beach just to find out, by chance, that Gary and his sister had split up after having a child and that he was an uncle. For one brief moment he wished he'd stayed in the oblivion of death. Real life was so cruel and hard, full of pain and regrets. Real life could be hell on earth. Why couldn't things just be good and straightforward for everyone? There were a lot of bad people about in real life, he concluded. It was much better to be dead where, at least, you couldn't get hurt, or into trouble, or lose your husband, and you certainly couldn't get ill or die. He and Len had already crossed man's biggest hurdle. Poor old Jenny – she didn't deserve this.

After a few more minutes, Eddie had had enough of listening to John, Mo and Carlos exchange views about the female race. 'Mr John' was getting fairly drunk, with his temporary companions doing their best to restrain him, but Carlos' profits were down and he'd quickly got him on to more exotic and expensive drinks. Just as Eddie jumped lightly off his stool, the driver of the jeep returned – he seemed to be employed by John and Sally's small hotel whose name was emblazoned on the jeep's sides. *Bay View Hotel* must be some way up into the hills, thought Eddie, judging by how long it had taken the driver to get there and back. Leaving the driver to join the other two men, Eddie set off up the dirt track to investigate. He thought he might be able to see how Sally was before the hotel jeep was once again employed to bring her husband back up to their accommodation. His own feeling of loneliness had receded – the day seemed to be designed for him and him alone and he was not missing Len much at all.

The walk-cum-climb would have been difficult for even the fittest of people, but Eddie, as usual, found it easy to glide along, sometimes taking giant strides on his journey up into the wooded hills. In less time than it had taken the jeep driver to get to the hotel and back, Eddie came in sight of the low, white-painted, two-storey building whose veranda seemed to enclose all four sides of the modest looking brick and wood structure. It seemed to be out of place in its grounds that had obviously been reclaimed from the natural forest that enclosed it. Once through the final trees, Eddie could see that the Bay View Hotel had seen better days but, on entering the foyer, he also noticed how clean and tidy everywhere was. It looked to be simply but adequately furnished for its guests who would, in any case, spend very little time there during the hours of daylight. To the right of the main foyer, the long bar looked inviting to thirsty and hot customers, but only the occasional rainstorm would probably attract most people to be there during the day. It was empty when Eddie looked in. He returned to the foyer and wandered over to the long low table that constituted reception. It was unattended, which mattered not to Eddie as he didn't possess the power of human speech in order to inquire which room Sally was in. He did, however, notice a calendar hung at an angle on the wall behind the table. The year, 1970, agreed with his earlier surmise but the date did not. It was, according to the page displayed, Friday, February the 13th. The scary associations of the date were bad enough for Eddie but to find also it was winter seemed even odder. Not being able to feel the difference between heat and cold, Eddie had assumed by the dress of the people on the beach, that it was summer. Little did he realise that day temperatures in Jamaica in February averaged out at 82 degrees and night ones at 72, with little or no rain all month. Winter in Jamaica was really a continuation of summer, just a little drier.

Eddie was at a loss as to what to do next – there didn't appear to be a key rack behind the table and, though it contained several drawers, Eddie had no physical way of opening them and his mind power, such as it was, failed to reveal their secrets as well. After a while he decided to investigate the hotel without directions. He soon discovered that the long front of the building was not reciprocated by its depth as he soon found himself in a large inner rectangular courtyard which was surrounded on all sides by about forty cabins. The second floor was galleried in an old colonial style but with less cabins leading off it, seeming to consist only of larger and more luxurious rooms and suites. The gallery was fit for purpose, as getting cool breezes to flow through the rooms had been essential in the hotel's construction. Eddie estimated that, in total, there were more than fifty rooms and suites to check if he was to find Sally. Glancing back down and around him, Eddie could quickly see that the courtyard was empty, except for a solitary gardener tending to various potted plants and shrubs which looked in dire need of water.

In room 33, on the north side of the ground floor, Sally Barber was alternating between sobbing and muttering oaths, both under her breath and out loud. In the end she only had one thought on her mind.

"Oh, I want to go home!" she cried to the ceiling. "I hate him, I hate him. Oh how I hate him!"

She then cursed her husband vehemently with words that she hardly was aware were part of her vocabulary and, with one final scream

618

of frustration, she threw herself back onto the bed and buried her face in the covers.

Outside, Eddie heard her final shouting as he passed the first room on the north side, number 31. He skipped the last few yards and was soon outside number 33. If Len had been with him he would have boldly walked straight through the door, open or not. Eddie paused outside for a moment while he listened again. The shouting and screaming had been reduced to low sobs which soon subsided completely. Eddie made ready for the pass through the door of number 33. Somewhat to his surprise his progress was halted the moment his body reached the door and, try as he might, his newly acquired skill seemed to be no use. He took a pace backwards and tried the secondary method of concentrating his mind on the door. To begin with nothing happened; the door was proving difficult to crack. He tried again and this time the door creaked open a couple of inches but not wide enough to squeeze through if it was to continue to thwart his progress.

Inside room 33, Sally was just drifting off to sleep when the noise of her bedroom door opening caused her to wake with a start.

"John? Is that you? Go away and leave me alone."

When John didn't enter the room, she got up and pushed the door shut and locked it with the key – she was sure that she had done that when she'd first got back. She returned to the bed with a sigh. He wouldn't be able to get in now, she thought.

Eddie watched as the door closed and then he heard the bolt slide home. He tried again and this time he imagined himself inside the room, even though he'd never been inside it. Fortunately, he had a rough idea of the layout of the room – a cleaner had been working in room 17 when he'd walked by and he'd stolen a peep inside. He heard the bolt slide back and this time the door opened almost halfway. Before Sally had a chance even to get up off her bed, Eddie slid easily into room 33. He turned round as soon as he got inside to see Sally putting her weight against the door and cursing it under her breath. She turned the key in the lock, took an upright chair from a corner of the room and wedged the top of its back under the door handle. With that, she fell back onto the bed. Almost as many curses had been directed at the door as had been directed at her absent husband earlier. Exhausted, she rolled over onto her side and closed her eyes.

Fortunately for Eddie's tender years, she had put on shorts and a top to cover her tiny bikini. Had she not done so, thoughts of what might have laid in store for him, if he'd lived, would have troubled him again. He seemed to have made up his mind what he was going to say to Sally, whether or not she was asleep.

"Sally, I don't know if you can hear me, but I hope some of what I say sinks in."

Eddie paused and seemed to gather himself.

"I'm really sorry that I didn't come to Hamsden with you that day. I realise now that I made a big mistake. All I can say is that I am happy where I am now and I'm having fun with my old friend Len, who, no doubt, you remember. I'm so sorry that you and your husband have had an argument, but I have to tell you that I don't think he's a very nice man and, even though he says he didn't go to her room last night, he did kiss and cuddle that girl. If you don't believe me just ask Carlos or Mo down at Pineapple Cove – he was bragging to them earlier."

Sally turned over onto her other side and gave a sleepy sigh. Eddie paused to see if she would wake and, when she didn't, he continued with his last message.

"And Sally, if I'd lived you would have been exactly the kind of girl I would have loved to have fallen in love with and married. I think you're gorgeous now and far too good for the likes of John. Don't stay with him, Sally – he'll only do it again. He doesn't respect you even though he thinks and says he loves you."

Sally moaned. Eddie blew her a kiss and this time, with his mission accomplished, the door did not provide a barrier to his exit and he was soon outside and crossing the courtyard. As he wandered back to the beach, waiting for his next return to darkness, Sally Barber left the Bay View Hotel in a taxi, with her suitcase aboard and bound for Kingston airport en route back to her mother in Fenton-on-Sea. She had tears in her eyes – tears that were not only because she knew her short marriage was at an end, but also for the memory of a fourteen-year-old boy she had once asked to go shopping in Hamsden with her on a Saturday in late January 1966. Her dreams had provided the catalyst for her decision to leave her husband.

John Richardson was very drunk. Already he had fallen off his stool on two occasions to be helped back onto it by Mo and Carlos. He was getting more and more voluble and angry.

"I'll show 'er when I get back. I'll show her who's boss, I will!"

"Of course you will, Mr John," said Carlos.

"You've had enough, my friend," added Mo.

"I'll let you know when I've 'ad enough. I can take my drink and anyone who says I can't is a …."

John's befuddled brain prevented him from thinking of an end to his sentence. The jeep driver, Wesley by name, came over and put his arm round the young Englishman.

"Come on, sir, I'll run you back up to the Bay View – sleep it off, eh? I expect young Miss Sally will be worried about you. I'm sure she didn't mean those things she said."

John threw back his shoulders to shake off Wesley's grip and promptly fell to the floor for the third time.

"Help him up, Wes," said the barman. "We'll get him in the jeep."

Carlos came round the bar and helped the driver with the drunken man. Fortunately, he did not put up a fight as the copious amounts of alcohol had at last deadened his senses and numbed his body beyond the point of physical resistance. By dragging and half carrying him, Carlos and Wesley, directed by Mo, eventually dumped Sally's husband unceremoniously in the back of the jeep. It would not be until the early hours of the following morning that he would wake up to find he was alone in room 33 where Mo and Wesley had left him.

Eddie barely noticed the jeep as it roared past him scattering dust and stones in all directions – he was too deep in thought to be bothered with his earthly surroundings. His visit to Sally's room had shown him another use for his new role and 'gifts' – they could be used to do good deeds and not just to have fun. He somehow knew that his advice had been received and understood by Sally – advice which, if given by a real fourteen-year-old, would certainly have been ignored. People might listen to ghostly guidance when all other earthly counsel had failed. The idea that God might use him to right wrongs or change things for the good filled him with some pride and anticipation for his next visit. He would have to tell Len when they next met, even though he might not be as receptive as himself. Just like in life, Len wanted to have fun. Philosophy was for other people far cleverer than him.

When Eddie got back to the beach bar, it seemed to be totally deserted; stools were stacked on the bar and glasses and bottles tidied away. The beach was empty, too, though in the distance Eddie could see a small dinghy about fifty yards off shore. Carlos was fishing for his dinner.

Eddie strolled down the beach to take a closer look. The barman seemed to be fishing with a simple bamboo cane and line which, judging by his excitement, meant that dinner was going to be lavish. For no apparent reason, other than for something to do, Eddie waved at the fisherman. To his shock and utter surprise, Carlos stood up in the small boat and waved back. Eddie nervously waved again and Carlos then shouted,

"Plenty of snappers for supper, Mo! How's our friend?"

"Sleeping it off, but Wes said that there was no sign of Sally."

Eddie's ghostly heart started 'beating' again as Mo walked past him from behind. Eddie breathed a sigh of relief – he'd had enough for one day without being visible to people as well. That was his last thought as night descended on his world again and he disappeared into oblivion.

9

Little Ed

By the end of the first year of the new decade, Jennifer Compton and her baby boy had been living back at number 38 Fir Tree Close for nearly a year. Even thought the Comptons had plenty of room for mother and son in their three-bedroom semi, tensions at times ran a little high. Eddie's sister had walked out on her husband, Gary, back in early January that year. Her husband's philandering had been the last straw in a year or so where Gary had not, by any stretch of the imagination, started married life in a sober and responsible fashion. As soon as their first child had been born, within fourteen months of the wedding, he had taken on a whole different attitude to Jenny and his new charge. He had already started to drink a lot almost immediately after returning from honeymoon, calling in at pubs on his way home from work. He seemed to regard the wedding as some kind of final piece in his relationship with Jenny and not as a confirmation of his love and care for her and the start of a new life, where give and take had to become a reality for them both. It certainly wasn't like that as far as Gary was to be concerned. He seemed to be the embodiment of male chauvinism in his total lack of responsibility with regard to his fatherly duties, when it came to nappy changing and feeding etc., or, indeed, even with day to day household chores. Jenny was often the recipient of remarks such as: '*I'm working and bringing the money in, so why should I do the ...?*'

At first, Fred, and particularly, Ann Compton had welcomed their daughter and their grandson back with open arms. Jenny's dad had originally had some misgivings about Jenny's choice for a boyfriend when she had only been sixteen, but as he had come to know Gary, over time he had come to like and respect him. He was thus disappointed when the split became permanent. For her part, Ann Compton gained great enjoyment from having her daughter back and her grandson to play with and care for, too. But after nearly a year without Jenny working and able to contribute to household expenses, things had become a little tight financially and, not for the first time, Jenny's dad raised the issue at teatime on Wednesday, December the 30th. Fred Compton had returned to work after his short Christmas break only the day before.

"Here am I the only one working and you two sit at home all day, and little Eddie here has two mothers to look after him."

"Call him Ed or Edward, Fred. You know how I don't like Eddie," said his wife.

She then went on to say something about how much effort was required to look after a baby in the early months, but it seemed to have little effect on what her husband seemed determined to say.

"Surely, Jenny, you can at least go back part-time at Curls and Twirls. You said Mrs Winter said you could when you were ready. Isn't it about time now, given that Ed isn't waking you up much during the night and you won't be as tired as you have been?"

Fred seemed to mellow a little as her patted his daughter's hand.

"I know it's hard, love – I remember how your mum was with you and Eddie during the first year."

Jenny's mum suddenly seemed to be in agreement with her husband.

"I can look after little Ed during the day, love – your dad is right, we do need the money."

Jenny had said nothing while listening carefully to her parents and balancing Ed on her lap to feed him.

"Well?" said her dad. "What do you say, Jenny love?"

Jenny carefully lifted her son into his highchair and eventually replied,

"I just think that Gary should be paying you both to look after his son, Dad. Ed is his responsibility before he's yours."

Fred Compton sighed.

"And he will, believe you me, when you decide to get divorced. At the moment, unfortunately, you have taken custody of Ed and will have to look after him."

"He did send him some nice Christmas presents," said Jenny's mum in a conciliatory tone.

"Big deal, Mum!"

"Anyway," continued her dad. "Don't you think you need to get back to doing the things you like and are good at? You're a talented hair stylist now – everyone I know says so."

Her dad's persuasiveness and flattery began to make an impression.

"Well, if I did, I'd only want to do afternoons, Mum. Could you look after Ed then?"

Fred Compton smiled as his wife replied,

"Of course I could – it would be an absolute pleasure to spend some quality time with my grandson and, anyway, he sleeps a lot in the afternoons, Jenny."

"I know," said Jenny. "I just need to be here in the mornings."

And then she smiled and turned to her dad and said,

"Actually, Dad, I have been thinking about going back to work, but I didn't want you to think I was just going to dump Ed on you and Mum during the day."

"You silly girl," said her mum. "You wouldn't be dumping little Ed on me, love, and your dad is at work all day."

"Good, that's settled, then," said Jenny's dad.

Len and Eddie had not seen each other for nearly two 'years' when next their paths were to cross. The 21st of March 1971 was to be an unremarkable day for the human race; a day like any other day with no momentous achievements or events. It would have been, however, Eddie's twentieth birthday. It didn't seem like the first day of spring in Fenton-on-Sea when Eddie awoke from his year-long slumber. It had been a cold and frosty morning which, by his early afternoon arrival, had turned dank and drizzly. Again, his ears were the first to provide some indication of his exact location. This time, the almost complete absence of sound was to be more of a clue to those days of the week it couldn't be than those that it could. When his eyes eventually focused on his surroundings they confirmed quickly that it wasn't a weekday. Having found himself standing in the High Street and facing Woolworth's, Eddie could see by its unlit windows and absence of customers that it had to be a Sunday. Glancing up and down Fenton's main street completed his evaluation. He noticed he had been provided with his old duffle coat which covered some familiar warm clothes underneath.

"We've picked a good day to come back, haven't we, Captain?"

Almost unobserved, Len had appeared at Eddie's side and he didn't give his friend a chance to make a mistake this time as he continued with,

"Please tell me what the twentieth prime is?"

Eddie didn't bother to try any clever extra security checks and replied simply,

"Seventy-one, mate."

"Seventy-one it is, Eddie *old* boy," replied Len with added emphasis to 'old'.

"Less of the old, comrade!"

"Ah! Ah! And you don't know what the date is yet, then? Or do you?"

Eddie knew he was being challenged. He gave it his best shot.

"Judging by the shop displays across the road and the absence of shoppers, I would say it's a Sunday sometime around Easter and therefore in late March or Early April."

Len looked suitably impressed.

"Not bad, not bad. And the year?"

"Well," said Eddie as he cast his mind back to the date of his Caribbean interlude. "At least 1970, but probably 1971."

"Even better," said Len. "Now, what about the date? All I'll tell you is that it's a Sunday in March 1971."

Eddie walked around in a circle while he pondered Len's question. This was fun to have a puzzle over which to exercise his considerable mental ability. However, even his mathematical brain wouldn't allow him to do the necessary calculations to work out which days in March 1971 would be Sundays, even if he could remember any reference point to start from. Len expected him to get the answer so there had to be another clue. Len hadn't said much else since arriving except for implying he was old ....

"Got it, Len," said Eddie with a start.

"Well?"

"March the 21st – my birthday!"

"Well done, Captain! I knew you wouldn't let me down."

"How did *you* find out the date, Len?" asked Eddie.

"Usual trick. The newsagents on Steep Hill still had some of yesterday's papers in the window and, like you, I knew it had to be a Sunday."

By this time, and without discussion, the two boys had already started walking up the High Street. Eddie was curious as to what his friend had been doing since their incredible trip to the moon.

"So what happened to you on the moon, Len?"

"Don't know, mate. I can't remember much. Suddenly I was with you heading back to the lunar module and then it just went blank."

"What have you been up to since?"

"Nothing. After I disappeared into oblivion, the next thing I knew was finding myself at the bottom of Steep Hill about ten minutes ago. Anything in between is a complete blank. What happened to you after I left?"

"Not much more on the moon. I ran round in a panic looking for you, got back to the lunar module to find it locked and then, like you, I must have passed out. But I have been back to earth since – just over a year ago on February the 13th."

Eddie then spent the time it took the two ghosts to walk up to the entrance to Fir Tree Close to report back on his Caribbean adventure. Len was impressed but also added,

"I told you that you should have gone to Hamsden with Sally that day."

"Yeah, thanks for that. Hindsight is a wonderful thing, Len."

Len made no comment on Jenny and Gary's reported separation and he remained silent until they had reached number 38. It had been obvious to him from Eddie's story that his friend wanted to see how his sister was as soon as possible. The two boys paused for a moment outside the Compton's front gate.

"You didn't like Gary from the start, did you Eddie."

"No, I suppose not, but I had grown to like him and so had Mum and Dad. Like Sally and her husband, you just never know what's going to happen when a relationship is formalised by marriage."

"That's pretty deep, mate. You're only supposed to be fourteen, you know."

"You and I may still look fourteen but I'm beginning to discover that our minds and souls age with our natural years."

Len mumbled something about still feeling he was fourteen and didn't want to be twenty, to which his friend said,

"And I'm an uncle, Len."

"Uncle Eddie, eh? It has a nice ring to it," said Len. "Can you be an uncle at twenty?"

Eddie ignored a possible debate over his age and asked, rhetorically,

"I wonder if I've got a niece or a nephew"

"Only one way you're going to find out," replied Len. "That is, if your sister is still living here and we can get in."

Eddie nodded and walked through the closed gate. He would have to share his other thoughts with his friend at a later time. He would choose his moment to discuss the idea of using their extraordinary powers for good and not just for their own amusement.

Sunday lunch with the three generations of Comptons had been a longer affair than usual that Sunday. A lavish turkey roast had been followed by a dessert to die for and all accompanied with a bottle of good champagne, provided courtesy of Jenny's new wages. Fred and Ann always tried to celebrate on their late son's birthday in style and without tears. Eddie's mum said every year that the day had to be enjoyed by all and was not to be a time for sadness. Of course, on the previous five occasions someone had always disobeyed Ann Compton's rule and had eventually dissolved into a state of 'self-indulgent grief', as she would call it. By three o'clock, Fred Compton was on his second glass of whisky – he'd also managed two large glasses of bubbly with his lunch. Given that he'd also downed a couple of pints in the Red Lion after Sunday morning service at St Andrew's, he had just about reached his 'emotional' state that afternoon. It would be his turn to exhibit the self-indulgency. His wife, suspecting he had gone well beyond his normal limit for alcohol, had quietly repaired to the kitchen to wash the dishes and leave her daughter to cope with her husband's inevitable outpourings. Little Ed had toddled after his grandmother on chubby and still somewhat unsteady legs.

"He would have been in his second year at University now, you know, Jen."

"Yes I know, Dad. Do you think it would have been one of those posh ones?"

"What? Like Oxford or Cambridge? I don't know, love. Maybe we wouldn't have been able to afford it."

Jenny's dad drained his glass and reached for the bottle containing the 'water of life'.

"Dad, don't have anymore. You know Mum doesn't like you drinking too much."

"s'only once a year."

"No more after this one, then? Promise?"

"Y'p. I promis'."

"Dad, you're already slurring your words."

"No, I'm no'."

Jenny reached over the dining room table and picked up the bottle of good malt, screwed the top firmly back on and took it into the kitchen. She smiled at her mother and said,

"Get the bed ready; he's had too much, Mum."

By the time Jenny got back to the dining room, it appeared that her dad had been carrying on the conversation without her.

"… was the brightest boy at Fen'on Grammar. I said, he was the brightest boy at school, you know."

"Yes, Dad, I heard you," said Jenny as she sat down at the table.

The next five minutes were taken up with Jenny listening patiently while her dad lauded all his son's achievements, including some that hadn't even belonged to him. In the end, however, Fred Compton didn't cry, and when he saw his wife and grandson return from the kitchen, his normal sensible, serious and responsible nature took over and he agreed with his better half that he needed a couple of hours sleep. It had been a tiring week at work, he said!

After her father had gone upstairs, Jenny laid little Ed down for his afternoon nap in his cot in 'Uncle Eddie's' bedroom, as she called it. She then went back downstairs and joined her mum to watch a film on television.

Len kept himself a few feet behind his friend as they walked up the Compton's front path, more out of respect for Eddie than anything else – it was Eddie's family and not his own, which now consisted only of his mother, Mrs Martha Wilby in Kent. Len watched as his friend passed smoothly through the freshly painted front door. He waited a few seconds and then walked forward to follow Eddie but, as soon as his body got within a few inches of the door, some invisible barrier prevented him from doing so. He tried again several times but without success and, even when he tried to think his way in, nothing happened. In the end he realised that this visit was for Eddie and Eddie alone, and he wandered back down the path and out into the road. For the next ten minutes or so, he paced up and down to the end of Fir Tree Close, occasionally coming back to check on any happenings at number 38.

Meanwhile, his friend had found the house very quiet and, at first, Eddie thought that no one was at home. He looked in the kitchen, which seemed to indicate nothing; it was clean and tidy as usual. Approaching the far end of the hall, he at last heard the familiar sound of a television. It was just after four o'clock. Eddie hesitated nervously before trying to enter the lounge – he had heard no sounds of a baby crying and, so far, he had seen no other signs of one either. Although he hadn't observed the Sunday afternoon ritual in the Compton household for over five years, he did remember that his parents would never usually have been watching television at that time. He walked forward and listened. He thought he could hear other sounds above those emanating from the television – two female voices above the background noise. He metaphorically drew breath – he hadn't been in his old lounge for a very long time.

"*Have you seen much of Gary, Jenny?*"

"*No, not much, Mum – last time was before Christmas in Hamsden when I went for my lunch with Jean one day at Pritchard's.*"

Eddie entered the room and the very first thing he noticed was a large framed photograph of himself, hanging in obvious pride of place over the mantelpiece. It looked like one taken at Fenton Grammar when he had been in the third year. The next thing was the two women, both of whom were sitting side by side on the settee. Jenny was reading a fashion magazine and his mother was knitting – nothing much different here, then, thought Eddie. He glided over to his old armchair and sat down. The rest of the room seemed much as he remembered it, except for a fresh lick of paint and a few extra photographs of mother and baby. Closer inspection could not reveal whether the baby was a boy or girl. There were no wedding snaps to be seen anywhere. Eddie listened to the conversation, with one nagging thought in his mind. Where was his dad?

"He was with a girl, Mum."

"Did that upset you?"

"No. It would have done a year ago, but it only confirms that I made the right decision."

Eddie's mum stopped knitting.

"You did love him though, didn't you, Jenny?"

"Yes, I loved him with all my heart and soul, but sometimes I think I loved him too much, Mum."

"Too much?"

"Yes, Mum, no one can be that perfect. I'd put him on a pedestal from the day I first went out with him when I was sixteen. I saw in him what I wanted to see – I loved the Gary of my dreams. I ignored some warning signs early on – I was looking through rose-tinted spectacles."

It was obvious to Eddie that this was probably the first time that mother and daughter had actually shared their thoughts on what had led up to Jenny's separation from Gary. Both seemed to have tears in their eyes and Jenny's mum relieved the tension by saying,

"Let's have a nice cup of tea and try to put the past behind us."

"I have, Mum, and I'll have a coffee, please."

Jenny's mum left the room and it gave Eddie a chance to study his sister more closely. Though she looked older – she had to be twenty-four by then, he thought – motherhood had enhanced her beauty. She'd let her blond hair grow below shoulder length and though her eyes bore some emotional scars, overall she had grown into a lovely young woman. Eddie also noticed that she had let her natural cheek and eye colours come through; much less 'paint' was evident. Hearing the lounge door open, he moved away from his sister as his mother returned from the kitchen carrying the drinks.

"Here we are, love, just as you like it with cream."

She then put her own cup of tea down and said,

"I'll just go and check on your father – he had far too much to drink lunchtime."

"O.K., Mum. Will you look in on little Ed for me. He might be waking soon."

"Yes, love."

Eddie's face formed into a proud grin. His little nephew was called Ed, then. Also, and almost more importantly, his dad *was* here and not ....

"Jenny named him after me," he said out loud.

Soon, Ann Compton returned to the lounge to be with her daughter.

"They're both fine, Jenny," she said as she sat down beside her.

Eddie had spent the few minutes while his mum had been upstairs with a warm glow inside him and it was about to get warmer. Since it was clear to Eddie that mother and daughter were going to spend the rest of the afternoon in a comforting and sleepy silence, he made his way out of the lounge to explore upstairs. His dad had obviously overdone it earlier but his main and immediate desire was to see his baby namesake.

Eddie guessed where little Ed would be and, with the door half open, he was able to squeeze into his old bedroom without any ghostly trickery. Baby Ed was awake and standing up with his hands on the top of the cot side. He was smiling. Apart from the nice surprise that his nephew had suddenly woken, the first thing Eddie noticed was the baby's colouring. Though it was still very short, his hair had a gorgeous ginger tint and his face possessed that freckly quality similar to his own. He really was a little Eddie. His older namesake couldn't prevent himself from saying something in his silent world.

"Hello, little Ed. I'm your Uncle Eddie."

What happened next would haunt Eddie for some time to come, even though he knew that such a haunting was ridiculous. Spontaneously, as Eddie spoke his words of introduction, little Ed reached out both his arms to his uncle and gave an excited smile which said: '*Pick me up, Uncle Eddie*'. Uncle Eddie took a step backwards but little Ed's face took on an even more beseeching look and his chubby little fingers opened and closed in a gesture of desperate pleading. 'This can not be happening', thought Eddie. 'I must be dreaming it'. He quickly moved his position, but the little boy's eyes seemed to follow him round the room until, when Eddie had squeezed himself into a corner of the room, little Ed climbed round the sides of his cot in order to be as near as he could to his uncle. Whatever emotions Eddie experienced at that moment, given that his ghostly body didn't usually exhibit any, the strongest one that enveloped him was fear – he was downright scared. He backed himself along the bedroom wall until once again he squeezed himself through the half open door and out onto the landing. Immediately, little Ed gave a screech of frustration and burst into tears. Eddie didn't wait to see if matters got even worse and the little boy suddenly said something. At that precise moment, his mind would have interpreted any incomprehensible baby groan or gurgle as sounding exactly like his name.

Downstairs, mother and daughter heard the baby crying.

"He's awake, Mum. I'll go up," said Jenny.

Her mother offered no response – the exhaustions of the day had taken her to the land of sleep and upstairs, her husband had, at that precise moment, exited the same place with the comforting words,

"Now then, little fellow, don't cry."

Fred Compton was awake and heading for the baby's bedroom. His son was halfway down stairs when Jenny 'brushed' past him.

"I'll get him, Dad. You go and have a wash and tidy yourself up. You'll scare little Ed looking like that"

Jenny's dad looked awful – hair all over the place, sweaty face and reddish eyes. After Jenny had eventually brought little Ed downstairs, it would be several minutes before she would be able to pacify him. Her mother would blame Jenny's father for looking in on him in such a 'wild man' state, as she would say.

Eddie didn't stop until he had made the passage through his parent's front door and down the path to the road. Len was on one of his many walks back from the end of the Close. Spotting Eddie from a distance, he ran down the middle of the road to greet his friend.

"Well, is it a boy or a girl?"

"A boy," said Eddie curtly and without further comment.

"What's up, mate? You look awful. You should see your face – it's ghostly white."

Len laughed at his own joke, but Eddie didn't smile. He had started to walk quickly again as though he was trying to put as much distance between himself and his nephew. Len caught up with him as he turned into South Road.

"Slow down, mate. What's happened? Has someone …?"

Eddie eased his walk to an amble and said,

"No, no one's died, if that's what you thought."

"I don't know what to think, Eddie. You'll have to tell me. What is it? What on earth's wrong?"

Eddie stopped walking altogether.

"You won't believe me, I just know you won't."

"Believe what? You're annoying and frightening me now."

And then Eddie told him. After his slightly garbled story, Len asked,

"You mean he could see you?"

"Well, I am a ghost, Len."

"But you think he knew who you were, as well?"

"I don't know, but he wasn't afraid of me – he wanted me to pick him up and hold him. He wouldn't have done that if I was a complete stranger, would he?"

"But you are a complete stranger, Captain. He's never seen you before."

"He might have done."

"Oh yeah. How?"

"There was a large framed photo of me, taken when I was about thirteen, hanging on the wall above the fireplace."

"And you mean he recognised you from that? Sounds a bit far-fetched to me."

"Well how else could he know me?"

"I don't know. Maybe you just saw what you wanted to see. You wanted him to like you, I mean. Perhaps he's just a very friendly little boy who puts on a cute performance for anyone, if he wants to get his own way. You know what some kids are like."

"I suppose so, but whatever the reason, Len, he could definitely see me. I suppose I shouldn't be that surprised as, like I said, I am a ghost."

"We both are," said Len. "Little Ed's first encounter with the paranormal, eh? Hope he hasn't been scarred for life by your visit."

At last Eddie seemed to cheer up and he said,

"My sister looked beautiful, Len, and she seemed happy without Gary. She's back at work at 'Curls and Twirls', I think."

"What about your mum and dad?"

"Their fine, except Dad must have had too much to drink at lunchtime and had been packed off to bed. When I was there, I suspected that they'd had a mild celebration, it being my birthday today."

"That's nice, Eddie – better than being sad and miserable."

Len paused and then said, almost with wistfully,

"I wonder what Mum does on my birthday? In fact, I wonder what she does on any day during the year."

"Haven't you been back, then?"

"Not since the time just after I died and when you were still alive, Eddie. Remember, we don't come back very often, do we?"

"True. You would like to see her again, wouldn't you, though?"

"I think so – I'd like to sometime. The only problem is that Kent's a long way from the places I keep ending up. Here or America, for example."

"Maybe you've got to want to go back and see her. As soon as I found out about Jenny's marriage break-up, I wanted to go and see her, and here I am. It just happened for me."

"Would you come with me?"

"Yes, of course, but I'm not in charge. Perhaps a little prayer to the powers that be might help, no?"

"I'm not sure I would know how to pray. Never really been keen on things like that, Eddie."

Eddie grinned sarcastically at his friend.

"Really, and you a ghost, as well. You do believe in an afterlife, don't you?"

"I-I don't know," stammered Len.

"For goodness sake, Len. What do you think you're doing now?"

At last, Len grasped Eddie's point. He went into an awkward silence as, suddenly, Eddie's view of the world around him started to get blurred. Len watched as his view of Eddie also became hazy. It had been a long and mentally tiring experience for his friend. Within seconds, Eddie had vanished to return to a period of inanimate rest. After a few more minutes while he thought about his own mother down in Kent, Len followed likewise.

10

A Familiar Jaunt

Eddie was to emerge again from his restful void much sooner than on previous occasions – less than three weeks had passed, measured in earth terms, when he awoke to bright sunlight. He found himself in a standing position and facing a familiar view. With the Cork Lightship to his left, the pier to his right and a bright blue sea in between, he was nowhere else but in his hometown of Fenton-on-Sea. Eddie shook himself down and looked uncertainly behind him. It plainly wasn't a weekday this time, judging by the number of people promenading in the sunshine and it probably wasn't God's day of rest either – the pier's amusements were clearly open for business. It had to be a Saturday, and the height of the sun, coupled with the abundance of early spring flowers in the tubs on the promenade, pointed to April as the most likely month. Eddie began to wander back up the beach to see if he could determine anything more about his new arrival.

Len was waiting for him on the promenade, squeezed tightly and incongruously between two elderly ladies on a wooden bench. Eddie didn't forget the security check and was pleasantly surprised when Len responded promptly with the correct answer. Walking up the beach, he had been half-expecting Len's bad ghost to appear as it had been some time since it had presented itself on any new arrival.

"Good morning, comrade Len," said Eddie cheerfully.

"Good morning, Captain Compton, and a beautiful spring morning it is, too."

"I guessed it was spring and a Saturday as well, I should think."

"Is it? You have me at a disadvantage this time, mate. I've literally just arrived. Saw you down on the beach and found myself between these old dears. Recognise either of them?"

Eddie studied the two ladies, both patently beyond their God-given allotted time span.

"No, mate. Should I?"

Len stood up and, turning to face the old women, he said,

"Look at the one on the left. Some years ago you used to sit in a room with her for four or five hours everyday."

Eddie walked closer and looked into the lady's face.

"Well?"

"Oh yeah, it's my old teacher at Fenton Central Junior School, Miss Wise," exclaimed Eddie. "She liked me – thought I was good at arithmetic. I finished all the books she gave me. In the end she had to make up worksheets just for me."

"Correct," said Len. "Don't know the other one, though. Do you?"

Eddie shook his head and said,

"No, but she might be her sister. They look alike."

The two Miss Wises' got uneasily to their feet, and arm in arm, they walked slowly away down the promenade. The boys replaced them on the seat.

"Well?" queried Eddie. "Why do you think we're here and when is it?"

Len had been counting as St Andrew's Church clock had been sounding the hour.

"Eleven o'clock, mate," he said. "Looks like spring but apart from that, I couldn't be more specific. No doubt, you'll tell me. As to the why, I have no idea."

Eddie gave his opinion.

"I think it's a Saturday in April and maybe still 1971. It doesn't feel much different to last time. We'll go up town in a minute and find out some way or other."

Eddie paused and gazed at his friend as he suddenly recalled their conversation on the last occasion they'd been in the living world.

"Don't you want to go and see your mum, Len?"

"I did try praying, but if God wanted me to go there, I think, I would have landed there instead of here. Besides, I don't think I'm ready yet."

"O.K., so what are we here for?" asked Eddie.

"Maybe for just for a bit of fun. Our lives shouldn't only be tied up with the past or trying to help people. We don't have responsibilities, do we?"

"True," agreed Eddie. "Perhaps God will have a mission for us on a later visit."

"You and your missions. Let's just enjoy ourselves, mate."

"Right," said Eddie. "That's enough waffling and discussion; so, where do we go? What do you fancy doing?"

"Another ghosts' day out," replied Len.

"Where?"

"Let's wander up the town and first of all determine what the date is – then we can decide."

"O.K., but on one condition," said Eddie.

"What?"

"We don't use any of our powers to get where we're going to go – no thinking our way there. I don't want to risk being separated from you. We both go together and by normal human means as well. It will be much more fun – no tickets to buy and we can get on any form of public transport without being seen or heard.

"Agreed," replied Len. "And we could slip into the odd Rolls Royce as well. I've always fancied being driven in a Rolls."

Eddie grinned. This day was going to be fun, he thought.

Inevitably, there seemed to be only one obvious place for the boys to head for initially that morning as a starting point for their day out. Fenton-on-Sea railway station was still, despite Dr Beeching's axe that had been wielded a few years previously, the quickest and most efficient way to exit the quiet seaside backwater. Eddie had also always been reminded by his father that the railways were the safest means of transport, public or private. On the way up the High Street, it didn't take them long to realise that it was Easter Saturday – the shop window displays, and the many people carrying Easter eggs, confirmed the date. In addition, the year was indeed 1971 as Len was able to verify from newspapers on a stand outside the main station entrance, above which the clock read eleven thirty-five on their arrival. Inside the station forecourt, they paused to debate their ultimate destination.

"Your choice, Len," said Eddie.

"Yeah, but we must both want to go there, right?"

"O.K., but we have to go to Hamsden first – we can't get anywhere else until we do."

"Obviously."

Len's knowledge of the geography of the United Kingdom was not as wide or as detailed as his friend's and he spent some time in deep thought.

"Come on, Len, make a suggestion," urged Eddie.

"Well, not London – we've been there for some fun," replied his friend. Then Len's face lit up.

"I know, Eddie. What about somewhere we've both been before on holiday?"

Eddie was pleased that Len was about to suggest the one place in England that he also wanted to go to, but had been reluctant to mention it first in case Len didn't agree.

"Where?" said Eddie, coyly.

"Devon."

Eddie milked the moment.

"Devon? Why Devon?"

"Because that's where we ...."

Len stopped speaking as he spotted Eddie's ironic grin get even wider. When the penny dropped, he said,

"You knew where I meant all along, you clown!"

"Yes, and, remarkably, that's where I would like to go to, too."

Ludmouth, a small seaside town on the south Devon coast, was the place where Eddie's parents had taken him and his friend on two consecutive summer holidays when they had been twelve and thirteen. It had been in Ludmouth, too, where they had first had encounters with a friendly ghost, culminating in a near-death experience with a diesel shunting engine. Both boys had clearly realised that they could now go back in their new ghostly roles, and not just as ordinary living tourists. As he would remind Len later, Eddie had also been on an additional and solo excursion to Ludmouth, in mysterious and fantastic circumstances during the year before he died.

The boys made for Platform One to wait for the Hamsden train which ran every half an hour on a Saturday. Len confirmed the day's precise date on the sign hanging above the platform.

"April the 10th, Captain, sir."

"So that makes it a quick return visit to the land of the living, comrade. That's less than three weeks since we were last here," replied Eddie.

"Who's counting?" said Len with a shrug of his shoulders. "We're still fourteen by the look of it, though I'm beginning to think we need some new clothes. It won't be long before we'll look out of place."

For the first time that morning, Eddie studied his clothes in detail. Again he found he had been dressed in a familiar, but definitely ageing, pullover and pair of trousers whilst his friend, though similarly attired, had a light cotton jacket for extra warmth – England in April could still be chilly.

"I could do with one of those," observed Eddie.

"I think you could arrange that for yourself," replied Len slyly. "We just need to find you a nice trendy clothes shop and all you have to do is somehow persuade a jacket to land on your shoulders. A quick demonstration of your powers as a poltergeist should do the trick, literally!"

Len's suggestion didn't seem to sit too well with Eddie's ultra honest nature, but he had to agree it would be good fun to try the stunt. The vision of a jacket lifting itself of a rack and then moving smoothly out of the shop, apparently unsupported by anything tangible underneath, appealed to his scientific mind. That is, of course, if the jacket didn't become invisible, as he would be, when it joined its wearer. That would be a big disappointment, thought Eddie.

Though the 11.50 train was busy for the last shopping day before the Easter break, the two silent entities found seats in a middle carriage. But, as Len would continually observe: '*Who needs room when we can fit in anywhere?*' At least, in their present positions, facing each other across a carriage, they could see each other talking. Having passed Linham Junction, Len wanted to check the route that they were going to take beyond Hamsden.

"Do you remember how to get there, Captain?"

"More or less. We catch the London train from Platform Two, I think, and then get across London by underground to Waterloo for the train to Exeter, possibly changing at Salisbury. Once we get to Exeter, we change for the train down to Ludmouth Junction and walk the rest of the way."

"Or jump in BB's free hotel taxi."

"We probably won't be there in time and I bet it'll be long after dark when we get there, unless …."

"Unless? Unless what?"

"Unless we can get a faster train from London to Exeter. If you remember the route we went on with my mum and dad from Waterloo seemed to take ages. I seem to remember Dad saying that there was an express service from Paddington direct to Exeter."

"So, we go for that, then," said Len. "How long will it take altogether?"

Eddie muttered some mental calculations out loud and then said,

"It's still got to be at least five hours just to get to Exeter from the time we leave Hamsden, assuming there's a train that leaves around half past twelve and we can get across to Paddington in forty minutes, *and* there's a train leaving for Exeter within twenty when we get there."

"Half past five, then," said Len.

"Yes, plus the time from Exeter to Ludmouth Junction plus however long it takes from there to Ludmouth town."

"Worse possible case scenario?"

Eddie thought briefly and replied,

"Seven-thirty."

"Best case scenario?"

Eddie did some more calculations.

"Well, if we can cut the time to cross London to twenty minutes, and we're able to jump from one train to another each time within ten, and BB is there with his taxi, we could make it by just after six."

"We can do it, Eddie. Remember, on the underground we won't have any tickets to buy; we can glide quickly through queues and if we have to, we can hurl ourselves down escalators. And if a train is just about to leave when we arrive at a station, we can jump through the door of the one we're on; run and leap to another platform and jump into the next train, even if it's already started to move."

Eddie had to agree that they did have the powers to increase the speed of their journey, but he wasn't quite so sure that they should use all the ones his friend had described. However, with their train already pulling into Hamsden, they had no more time to discuss the problem or, indeed, what they were going to do when they got to Ludmouth if twilight was fading fast into night.

Exiting the train, Eddie shouted after his friend, who had leapt off first,

"Platform One! Platform One! There's a train there. Run!"

Less than a minute later both boys were sitting in an empty carriage waiting for the 12.25 express service to London Liverpool Street to leave. They were already ahead of Eddie's schedule by five minutes.

Apart from a worrying moment when Len seemed to dose off, causing Eddie to think for one moment that he was going to disappear, the journey to Liverpool Street was otherwise uneventful. The train arrived only two minutes late at four minutes past two. Following Len's earlier suggestions for crossing London quickly by tube, the two boys reached Paddington at twenty-one minutes past the hour – their time cushion had risen to six minutes. Unfortunately that was soon wiped out when they discovered that the next train to Exeter and Devon would not be until ten to three. With some time to kill, they headed for a row of station shops, one of which turned out to be selling, rather conveniently, a range of designer denim jackets and jeans. Eddie perused such labels as he could see until, after a few minutes, he thought he'd found a jacket that might fit him. He called his friend over to discuss the next step.

"So how do you reckon I can do this, Len?"

There were four or five other customers in the open-fronted shop and Len replied,

"You need to concentrate hard and try to imagine the jacket on your shoulders."

"What if the jacket starts to move and someone puts it back because they think they've knocked it off the rack?"

"We need a distraction, Eddie, I think. Let me see what I can do. You get ready for my signal and if it works, run like hell – O.K?"

Eddie nodded, fearful of what his friend might have in mind. Len sidled over to the other people in the shop. Once he had engineered a position that was roughly in the middle of them, he started his 'distraction'. A split second later all the lights in and just outside the shop went out, plunging the immediate area into semi-darkness. Simultaneously, a shelf of men's shirts deposited its wares amongst one or two of the customers. Despite the gloom, Eddie saw his friend raise his thumb at him. He closed his eyes and concentrated. Pandemonium had broken out at the back of the shop as the assistant tried the light switches and customers stumbled about, bumping into more racks of clothes and thus causing even more chaos. Len heard Eddie shout,

"Got it! Let's go!"

Len joined his fellow ghost outside the shop and grinned cheekily.

"Very nice, Captain, it goes with your role."

Eddie looked down at the grey denim RAF-style bomber jacket. He really did now feel like Captain Compton.

"Alright, Mr Navigator, get us to our transport, please."

Len led the way to Platform Six where the express to Exeter was waiting. Being Easter, it was heavily packed with families making a late getaway for the weekend. Eddie and Len found it more convenient to park themselves in the space near an exit door in the very front carriage. To begin with, Len placed himself on top of a pile of suitcases while Eddie stood opposite him surrounded by further luggage. Len was perched so high that, had he been composed of living flesh, his head would have almost touched the ceiling. His precarious position on top of a pile of four large cases would also not have been a stable one. An even stranger thing happened when they had just left Reading after about thirty minutes of their journey. Eddie was first to notice that a smartly dressed man of about thirty had suddenly appeared between them. Though there was no need, Eddie backed himself in a corner and then, realising what the man was going to do, said,

"Look out, Len, he wants his case."

The man reached up with both arms and pulled the top suitcase off the pile. Instinctively, Eddie reached out to stop his friend falling forward. Instead, as the man took his case away to find a more convenient position for it, Eddie was astonished to observe his friend remain stationary, suspended in his sitting position in mid-air! Len glanced down below himself.

"Oh, wow! That's a new trick, Captain – I can fly!"

"Be careful, Len," said Eddie with natural but unwarranted concern.

"I will, old boy."

Len folded his arms and struck the regal pose of a king on his throne. Eddie was still concerned for his friend's welfare.

"Can you move? Can you get down?"

"Don't know, mate. It doesn't feel any different from before and why should it? I wasn't actually sitting on the cases to begin with, was I?"

"Well, try."

Len tried to relax and he reached down with his hands, but with no physical leverage possible, he stayed exactly where he was.

"Whoops!" said Eddie. "You'll have to stay there now."

He then appeared to burst out laughing.

"Shall I pull the communication cord and get someone to come and help you?"

Even Len was getting anxious by now.

"Don't be funny, Eddie. Get me down. I don't feel right."

"Well, you got up there in the first place. You must be able to get down again. Try thinking your way down."

Len screwed up his face and concentrated. He looked to be in some kind of discomfort. Then his position got much worse.

"Nothing's happening, Eddie, and ... I-I can't move at all now."

"What do you mean?"

Len seemed to have gone completely motionless. His words seemed to have to force themselves through his pursed lips.

"I can't even move my arms or legs now and my eyes ...."

Eddie looked at his friend's face. Cold blue eyes stared back at him. Len tried to finish his sentence.

"My mouth won't ...."

Eddie took a pace backwards. This is serious, he thought. His friend appeared to be in a state of suspended animation and was locked into a waking oblivion. Had he gone back to his 'resting' state, only while he was still visible to him? He tried to climb onto the cases but only seemed to pass through them and his friend. Soon, even Len's image began to fade and, within a matter of seconds, he vanished from Eddie's view.

Eddie began to pace up and down his cramped space between the piles of cases. What was he to do? Had Len really gone back to sleep? It could be days, weeks, or even years before he reappeared. Though there were some advantages for him if he were a free agent again, Eddie was worried that things had taken a new twist.

As Eddie was deep in thought, the well-dressed man suddenly returned with his case and Eddie watched as he returned it to the top of the pile. For no apparent reason, he set off to follow him as he made his way back to his seat. He hadn't gone more than a couple of paces when he heard a voice behind him.

"*Good day, Captain. How've you been?*"

Eddie's face lit up and he turned round to see his friend once again perched on top of the pile of luggage.

"What happened, Len? Did you feel anything?"

"Been asleep, son."

There seemed to be something different about his friend that Eddie couldn't quite put his finger on to begin with. Something *had* happened to him, though, and then, while Len sat grinning, almost insolently at him, he realised that his friend was wearing a different pullover and no jacket.

"You've changed, Len."

"Have I? Can't say I've noticed."

Len's replies had been curt and detached. Eddie knew what he had to ask next.

"Tell me, Len, what's the twentieth prime?"

"How the hell should I know, Ed?"

Eddie repeated his security question.

"The twentieth prime – what is it?"

"I've told you – I don't know, why should I?"

"Because, if you were Len's good ghost, you would know the answer straightaway. That's why."

The ghost gave a mocking smile.

"But I'm not, young Ed. I'm bad, really bad and I can do bad things, too. Just wait and see."

Eddie walked forward and confronted the evil ghost face to face. He then screamed as loud as his ghostly lungs would allow him to.

"Go away! Go away! Get thee behind me Satan!"

The ghost gave a derisory grin and said,

"Alright, I'll leave you for now, but I'll be back sometime. You can't get rid of me yet. Oh, no – not just yet."

The evil phantom vanished from sight. Eddie smiled and, 'patting himself on the back', said quietly,

"I beat him – I beat the devil."

Instantly, Len's ghost reappeared on the cases. He was dressed as he had been when they started their journey that morning. He seemed to have at least heard some of Eddie's conversation with his alter ego.

"And it's seventy-one, before you ask, Captain."

"Thank God for that," replied Eddie. "What on earth was that all about? I had to deal with your evil ghost, you know."

"Yes, I know and I think I know what happened too, Eddie, or, at least I can hazard a guess."

653

"What?"

"*I* think it was something to do with the fact that I was attached to the cases when I was sitting on them, and when that man removed the top one, I somehow lost contact, not only with my seat, but also with this world as well."

Eddie frowned and looked doubtful.

"But that would mean that every time we sat on something and someone took it away, we would be taken too."

"It's a possibility, isn't it? We might also disappear if we were leaning against something and our support was suddenly removed. We haven't been in a place where that's happened yet, have we? So, who knows?"

Eddie tried hard to remember any other occasion when either of their supports, whether they had been sitting or standing, had been removed suddenly. He had to admit he couldn't recall one such event.

"We'll just have to be careful from now on," he said at last.

"Yeah, but it's not likely to happen very often. As long as we sit or lean against immovable objects, no one can pull them away from us, can they?"

"Hope you're right, Len. That was quite scary when you went, to have you replaced by the very embodiment of evil – pure evil. He didn't even flinch when I called him Satan."

"Me too, Eddie, but to be on the safe side we should change the code. He presumably knows the question now," said Len.

The Exeter express thundered into a tunnel as Eddie nodded and said,

"He might go and learn all the first few prime numbers as well. It has to be a totally different question and answer."

Len suddenly had a brainwave as light flooded back into the carriage as well.

"I remember that we heard 'Buzz' Aldrin say something strange immediately after he followed Armstrong onto the moon's surface. Only we and the two astronauts could have heard it. Do you remember what he said to Neil Armstrong?"

Eddie did remember because it had been a whispered remark that Mission Control in Houston almost certainly didn't hear or, if they had, it surely would have been made public – it was so trivial given the historic nature of that moment.

"As I recall, he said, '*Monterey Jack or New Jersey Blue, then?*'"

"Well done! What a memory," said Len.

"I suppose it stuck because it was such a light-hearted thing for Aldrin to say after the seriously dangerous feat they'd just achieved. So, what will the question and answer be?"

"Easy," replied Len. "One of us asks what 'Buzz' Aldrin's first words were when he stepped onto the moon in 1969"

"Monterey Jack or New Jersey Blue, then?"

"Precisely."

11

Good Ghost, Bad Ghost

Bob Brewin had had a long day, driving guests from the station at Ludmouth Junction to his and his wife's bed and breakfast on The Esplanade in Ludmouth itself. Families often chose the Saturday of the Easter weekend to start a week-long holiday in the quiet seaside town on the South Devon coast. The station at Ludmouth had closed a few years previously, and visiting holidaymakers who arrived by rail found that it then became about a three mile trek from the station at Ludmouth Junction to the town proper. Bob and his wife, Pat, ran a modest guest house, *Summer Breeze*, on the seafront and BB's courtesy taxi service was, short of walking, the only means of transport for new guests to get from the Junction to their accommodation.

The last train from Exeter, that had passengers booked into *Summer Breeze* that day, was due to arrive at Ludmouth Junction at six twenty-five p.m. It would be BB's tenth pick-up since the first arrivals at eleven that morning. He was tired but also pleased that he and Pat had a full guest house for the forthcoming week. They'd even had to close bookings at the end of February; such was the attraction of the quiet Edwardian backwater where time seemed to have stood still since that era of grace and gentility. Elderly couples loved the seaside town for the nostalgia it generated for them, and, despite its lack of amusements, Ludmouth was good for children of a certain age and temperament, playing on the sandy beach and fossil-hunting being two of the more traditional pastimes.

The Exeter train was late arriving – by over ten minutes in fact. The only visible passengers to alight at the terminus were a middle-aged couple by the name of Grayson. It clearly wasn't their first visit to BB's

B and B, as Bob Brewin seemed to recognise them immediately they emerged onto the station forecourt. He leapt from his old and battered twelve-seat mini-bus and hailed the new arrivals.

"Bert, Edie! Over here!"

"Hi Bob, good to see you," called back Bert Grayson. "Weather looks set fair."

BB took the couple's two suitcases and deposited them in the back of the mini-bus via the rear doors. Bert and Edie Grayson climbed in through the sliding door at the side. The two additional passengers had already followed the Grayson's luggage in through the back. Climbing over the cases, they took the two rearmost seats. It was twenty to seven and there was about an hour of daylight left. BB started the engine and steered the mini-bus out of the station for the ten minute drive to *Summer Breeze*.

"I've put you in the same room as last year; at the front on the first floor, just as you requested," said BB.

"Great," said Bert Grayson. "I bet you've been busy bees this weekend, haven't you?"

BB smiled tiredly at his guest's pun. He'd had to get used to them, given his own abbreviated nickname – he gave out enough of them himself as well.

"Pat does all the real work – I'm just her bumble, I mean, humble helper."

Eddie and Len cringed.

"Same old BB," whispered Len.

"He's a gem," replied Eddie and then he asked, "What are we going to do when we get to Ludmouth?"

657

"No idea, Captain – it'll be dark soon. I suppose we could do some real haunting; scare a few guests and make Summer Breeze into a tourist attraction, being haunted and all. Make BB and Pat loads of money."

The mini-bus and its four passengers had reached the outskirts of the main town by now as Eddie replied,

"What – all night?"

"Well, what do you suggest, then? We can't do much in the dark."

"Something will turn up, Len. It's bound to. We could always go to sleep."

"Where?"

"Anywhere – on a floor, in a chair, anywhere."

"Can we sleep and still remain conscious?" asked Len after some thought. "Whenever I've felt tired in the past, I've just disappeared back to oblivion and nothingness. We might not reappear for months or even years and then not together either. Bit of wasted journey, then, don't you agree?"

"Like I said, something will present itself. Let's not worry till we get there. We can go to the bar, legally, and listen to the conversations. Have a few laughs with the guests – maybe break a few glasses or spill a few drinks."

"Now you're talking," said Len, as BB pulled the mini-bus onto The Esplanade.

After an hour of twilight, in which they wandered along the promenade and up into the town, identifying old haunts and familiarising themselves again with what Ludmouth had to offer, Eddie and Len returned to *Summer Breeze* at eight o'clock. Pausing outside the guest house, Eddie glanced to his right at the shadowy shape of the Red Cliffs in the distance.

"I wonder if the rock tunnel is accessible again; it was blocked by rocks and boulders the last time we both came, but there was a narrow entrance from the beach when I came on my own just over five years ago."

"When you became invisible, eh?"

"Yes, Len, and I don't recall it to be a very pleasant experience either, given I was still alive then."

"Better now you've got no physical form, Captain," replied Len as they glided through the half-open door to the guest house. As they did so, Eddie's mind continued to dwell on his previous visit. He had always wondered, since his physical death, whether his invisibility that day had been an omen of his impending demise. He had been given half the attributes of a ghost while still a living and breathing being. Within a few short weeks, he had passed over to full membership of the exclusive club.

Len was clearly heading for the bar when Eddie caught up with him in the small foyer of *Summer Breeze*.

"Wait up, Len. Don't start any of your tricks without me."

"Tricks? What tricks, mate? I'm just going to relax and study our fellow guests. Sort a few likely candidates out."

"For what?"

"Don't know, yet."

The guest house private bar was relatively quiet – the small dining room on the other side of the foyer still seemed to be full and only one or two people had wandered in for an after-dinner drink. Len made for the empty window seat which was likely to be shunned by most of the guests; it had a hard wooden surface and was more for decoration than for comfort.

"This should be a good place to sit, Eddie. No one else will want to use it and try and sit on us."

The boys had a good view of the bar and the door leading to the foyer. A young couple, obviously in the early stages of a relationship, was perched on stools at the bar and the only other occupant, an elderly lady, reading a copy of The Times, was sitting in one of the few available easy chairs situated next to the window seat. Eddie could read the headlines on the front page of the lady's newspaper with ease, and it was clear to him that April the 10th 1971 didn't seem to be a particularly momentous day in the history of the world. The old lady muttered something under her breath as the middle sheets of the large and unmanageable newspaper suddenly released themselves from her grip and fell to the floor. She bent down to pick them up and, in so doing, knocked her gin and tonic off a side table. Again she cursed quietly, picking up her empty glass with one hand and her missing pages with the other. To add to her frustration, the rest of her newspaper slid off the arm of her chair to lay soaking in the remnants of her spilt drink. She really had had enough by now and, using the worst language her gentile nature would allow, she muttered loudly,

"Oh, botheration. What a wretched nuisance."

"Got her!" said Len unexpectedly.

Eddie turned to his friend and said,

"You've started already, haven't you?"

"Yes, I thought she needed livening up. She looked a bit too stuck-up for my liking."

By this time, BB had emerged from behind the bar and, with much fussing and flapping about, he managed to calm the lady down.

"I'll get you another drink, Miss Taverner – on the house and here, let me take your paper and sort it out for you."

"You can throw it away; it's ruined and, anyway, I've read most of it. You might just save me the crossword, though. I'm going up to my room, before it gets too crowded."

BB rescued the newspaper and the lady's empty glass and called after Miss Taverner,

"Don't you want another G and T?"

"You may bring it up to room number fourteen at once, please, Mr Brewin."

BB seemed to baulk at Miss Taverner's formality and self-important command.

"BB won't like being treated like that. He hates being called anything but BB," said Eddie. "It's a wonder he puts up with her – I think she must be a regular visitor. I'm sure there was a Miss Taverner staying here the last time I came."

"Well, we'll perhaps we'll pay her a visit later on given that she was kind enough to let us know which room she's in. A little trip to room fourteen at about two tomorrow morning might be a fun idea. No white sheets or anything, just one or two tricks with her curtains or the light switch, eh?"

"You really didn't like her, did you?" said Eddie. "We could give her a heart attack or something."

"I suppose you're right; maybe we should select another guest for a haunting – someone who is likely to be of a less nervous disposition."

For the next two hours or so, the two ghosts listened in on several conversations as the bar filled up with guests relaxing after their dinners or returning from walks on the seafront. They occasionally shifted their position to stand near couples or families and, just before eleven with the bar empty of families with children, Eddie suddenly became uneasy about one particular gentleman who was sitting by himself in the chair Miss Taverener had vacated earlier.

"I'm sure that old bloke over there seems to be watching us when we move, Len."

"What – that funny looking chap who came in about ten minutes ago?"

"Yes, the one who looks like a painter or one of those arty types."

Len turned to stare at the old man who, to his surprise, stared back at Len, instantly giving him a sharp nod of his head.

"I think you're right, Eddie – he *can* see us, and I think I know who he is."

Eddie looked blank.

"Who?"

"Oh, come on, Eddie – think. Who sat next to us at dinner the first time we came here?"

"You mean, Mr Manders."

"Yes, Mr Jacob Denham Manders, our friendly ghost and saviour when we nearly got run down by the shunting engine," said Len.

"That means only we can see him, then."

"Yes, unless there are some other ghosts in the bar."

The boys suspicions were quickly confirmed when a middle-aged man, who seemed to be the worse for drink, wandered over from the bar and plumped himself down on the old man's lap. Mr Manders raised himself gracefully into an upright position, his body passing through that of the seat's new occupant. Before either boy could move, he had glided out of the bar, his image fading quickly before he had reached the door. Though Len then ran right out onto The Esplanade to look for him, he found no trace of their friendly ghost who could take on disguises from an elegantly and flamboyantly dressed Victorian gentleman to a common unkempt tramp. It was a few minutes while Len completed his search before he returned to the bar, where he remarked to Eddie,

"No sign of him – looks like we have competition, mate."

"Maybe, but I somehow don't think Jacob Manders is the kind of ghost to just indulge in scaring people or having fun at their expense. If he does do anything, I would say it would be to help people who are in trouble. He saved our lives, remember?"

"True," replied Len, thoughtfully.

By this time all the remaining residents had left the bar to retire to their rooms for the night and, though he looked a little edgy, Len seemed anxious to have some more fun.

"Upstairs, I think," he said.

"Are you sure?" asked Eddie. "It seems a bit mean to me – upsetting people, especially if they're of a nervous disposition."

"Oh, what the heck – what harm can we do?" Len said with some insistence. It was quite clear to Eddie that Len was going to get his own way. He followed his friend out of the bar and upstairs. It was fast approaching midnight.

BB had taken a double gin and tonic to room fourteen a few hours earlier, and its effect had put Miss Taverner to sleep well before eleven. At precisely two minutes past bewitching hour, according to her small bedside alarm clock, the ceiling light came on. A few seconds later it went out and over the next minute or so the light flickered on and off repeatedly until eventually it disturbed Miss Taverner who awoke reluctantly. The light remained on for the time it took her to get out of bed to turn it off. It was extinguished a split second before her finger touched the switch, causing the light to come back on instantly. She pushed the switch again and the light flicked on and off. Miss Taverner was cross now, and she was just going to go and find BB, when the light went out for a final time. The room stayed dark for the next few minutes while the elderly lady settled back to return to sleep. Hardly had she closed her eyes, before her alarm clock fell with a clang to the floor. Pulling the light cord above her head, Miss Taverener cursed and reached down to return it to the bedside table. Immediately there was a rush of air as the heavy bedroom curtains were flung wide open, knocking a couple of ornaments on the window sill to the floor. Miss Taverner's anger had given way to fear bordering on terror by now, particularly when her bedroom was then plunged into darkness. She screamed and headed for the door only to find that, when she tried the handle, it was locked. She screamed again and, this time, loud enough to wake the dead. Less than a minute later, a dishevelled and barely-dressed BB arrived and, after a warning tap on Miss Taverner's door, he turned the handle and walked in to find his elderly guest sitting huddled on the floor in the middle of the room. Both lights were on and the curtains were fully closed with nothing else out of place.

Miss Taverner did not finish her night's sleep in room fourteen. Though all the guest's rooms were fully occupied, she slept the remainder of the night on a Put-u-up in a box room on the top floor. She checked out at eight in the morning without paying her bill. She would never return to *Summer Breeze* for any future breaks.

Eddie had not waited in room fourteen while Len had finished his cruel and thoughtless party tricks. He had left the room to return to the bar the moment Miss Taverner had screamed for the first time, remarking as he did so,

"I've had enough of this, Len. I'll see you in the bar when you've grown up. Be it on your conscience if she has a heart attack, or worse."

As Eddie sat in an easy chair in the bar, dimly lit only by some security lights, he pondered his friend's rejoinder to his final remark: *'Conscience? What conscience? We ghosts don't have consciences'*.

His thoughts were suddenly broken both by a piercing and glass-shattering scream from upstairs and a whispered but commanding voice from close by.

"Get out, Eddie! Get out now and run as fast as you can. I'll see you on the promenade."

The voice sounded familiar and certainly friendly. Immediately, Eddie realised his mistake. He leapt out of his chair and ran out of the guest house, gliding unchecked through the locked front door. He didn't stop until he had reached a bench on the promenade a good way from *Summer Breeze*.

"You didn't check his identity, did you? When Len came back from outside, you just assumed it was still his good ghost. His good one came to find me and when he couldn't, he disappeared like me. I can only presume he has gone back to his resting state."

Mr Jacob Manders had joined Eddie on the promenade bench and had a comforting smile on his aged face. Eddie said nothing. Was this Mr Mander's good ghost? Was the whole episode a double-bluff? Who could he trust? As if Jacob Manders could read Eddie's mind, he said,

"Trust me, Eddie; I am on your side. My evil side disappeared years ago. I'm much further down the road than you. I always wanted to be good like you. Eventually, my good side won the day and, hopefully, on a permanent basis, too. As for Len, I'm not so sure. He can be good, but he also seems to enjoy his evil side. He's got to control that, you know, if ...."

"If?"

"If he is to progress as a ghost."

Eddie had the distinct impression that Jacob wanted to say more but didn't think his young ghost was ready for what he had been about to say. Whatever it was, Eddie felt safe and confident that Jacob was a good ghost and he began to relax a little. This was getting to be interesting; he would have to be extra careful from then on. If ever his friend's good ghost went out of sight, for no matter how short a time, he would always have to repeat the security check when he came back. If only he could trust Len, he thought, it would be so much easier. But, as Jacob had just said, his friend had a lot to learn. Somehow sensing it was not going to be possible, Eddie turned to thank his friendly tramp, but Mr Jacob Manders had vanished from the bench next to him. Eddie followed suit in a few more seconds.

12

Free-Fall?

Len had no recollection of his final few minutes in Ludmouth. For his part, one moment he was chasing ghostly shadows on the seafront and the next, everything went dark and blank. The two boys had found themselves back on familiar ground – the forecourt of Hamsden railway station. It appeared to be autumn, judging by the falling leaves on the road outside. It was clear and sunny with a crisp feel to the air. The station was busy with commuters exiting the trains and making their way into town. The station clock read 09.05 hours.

"Did you not even sense something was wrong, or that your bad side had taken over?" was Eddie's opening question after the new security checks had been done and he had related to Len the events at BB's guest house after he had gone walk-about.

"No, not a thing," said Len, who had been clearly disturbed by Eddie's story of the events that had taken place after he had departed the land of the living. The two ghosts had taken up positions leaning against a high wall and well away from any passengers.

"I wouldn't have done those things, Eddie, you know I wouldn't. I might have thought about it, but only in fun. I hope Miss Taverner was alright."

"So do I," said Eddie. "So do I."

Eddie hadn't yet told his friend of Mr Mander's warning and Len seemed to sense there was something else.

"Did Mr Manders say anything more?"

"Yes, and it concerns you."

"Me? How?"

"He said that he thought you could be good, but that also you enjoyed being bad sometimes. He said ...."

"Enjoyed being bad?"

"Yes, and that you had to try and control the urge to do evil things."

Len looked very unhappy at his friend's remarks.

"It wasn't the real me when my bad ghost did those things you said I did in Miss Taverner's bedroom. You know me better than anybody – you don't think I'm evil, do you?"

"No, of course I don't and Mr Manders didn't say you were – just that to progress as a ghost, you should concentrate on doing good things and, I suppose, limit, or eliminate entirely, those times when having fun might cause grief for other people. Remember, Len, you had already earlier thought about annoying Miss Taverner in her room when she was asleep. Where there's the thought to do something evil, you're not far short of doing it for real, because in our new state we have to be careful even when we just think about things in case we make them happen. You can have as much fun as you like as long as you don't hurt anyone else physically, or mentally. I think that's what he meant. I need to be able to trust you as well and not have to continually check that it really is you."

"Same thing works the other way round, too, Eddie."

"How do you mean?"

"I mean that your bad side could take over one day and I meet your evil ghost."

"Yes, I know, and it's all down to trust and faith. We have to trust each other, Len. O.K?"

"Of course. I want to be good and I'm not a bad person. I just don't think sometimes, I know, but there's no malicious intent. I'm not like that, you know?"

"I know, comrade, but since we have more freedom now to do much as we please, I suppose we have to be careful that we don't go over the top and take innocent pleasure to unhealthy excess."

"What a mind! And you're only fourteen. You could have become Prime Minister if you'd lived."

"I doubt it – I'd have settled for a Maths teacher or a scientist, pushing back the frontiers of knowledge," replied Eddie. "That would have been even better."

Almost unconsciously, the two boys had begun to make their way down Station Road and into town. Neither was interested in the time of year or, indeed, if it was still 1971. Their weighty discussion had made mundane things seem trivial. Fortunately, by the time they had reached the shopping area proper, Len had started to relax – it had clearly taken him some time to absorb all Eddie's friendly advice and to rid his mind of feelings of guilt and embarrassment. He cheered up quickly when he saw a poster in the East Shires Travel Agency.

"That would be fun, Captain, and we can't upset or harm anybody."

"What are you looking at?" asked Eddie as he peered over his shoulder.

"Parachute jumps at Beacon Hill Airbase; Saturday and Sunday afternoons at two – beginners welcome," said Len.

Eddie guessed where his friend's mind was going.

"You mean …?"

"Why not? We don't need a parachute."

"Need one? We wouldn't have one, you idiot!"

"Well, you should be O.K. – you've already done something similar a few years ago. Remember Paris and the Eiffel Tower?"

Eddie smiled as he did indeed recall a day in May 1963 when the two twelve-year-olds had taken their fantastic trip across Europe via France's capital. Eddie's special powers that day had allowed him to jump off the top of one of the world's tallest man-made structures and free-fall to the ground unharmed. Len's present suggestion would pale that into insignificance.

"Where is Beacon Hill, then?" asked Eddie at last. "I'll only go on two conditions, Len."

"Which are?"

"One: you behave and don't try anything funny and two: we try to get there by normal means; no spiriting us there again."

"Agreed, and the instructions for getting there are on the poster, if you look."

"But there is another problem, Len, my son."

"What?"

"Is today a Saturday or a Sunday? It didn't seem very likely with all the people getting off trains. They looked like they were off to work."

Len looked deflated, until another thought occurred to him.

"We don't actually need an aeroplane that's carrying parachutists. We could just hop aboard any aircraft that happens to be taking off."

"What kind of airbase is Beacon Hill, then?" queried Eddie.

"I think it's run jointly by the RAF and the US Air Force; the Yanks have jets and bombers that fly in and out. Fancy flying at Mach One, Biggles?"

"Now that sounds like fun," said Eddie, warming to the idea. Surely Len wouldn't try to interfere with the controls or anything else concerned with flying an aircraft. Then a worrying thought occurred to him. He couldn't think how he had missed the problem.

"You realise we have no mass or weight, Len, and remember the problem you had when that bloke removed his suitcase on the train."

"So what? We won't be sitting on suitcases," said Len.

"You're not thinking straight, Len. If we're standing or even sitting in the plane and then we somehow get out of the aircraft, we might just remain suspended in space like you were before. To all intents and purposes, the plane would be acting like the pile of suitcases as our contact is removed. And besides, you haven't explained to me how we would get out of the plane yet."

While Len frowned again, and despite his own misgivings, Eddie began to think that it would be fun to investigate the problem, in any case. Probably the worst that could happen was that they would disappear temporarily back to oblivion as Len had done on the train. They weren't doing anything bad after all; just trying an experiment. Then, Len had an answer to Eddie's question.

"We try thinking our way through the fuselage."

"And if that doesn't work?"

"And if that doesn't work, we forget the whole idea and stay in the plane until it lands."

"You promise you won't try anything else," said Eddie, sternly.

"Like what?"

"Like trying to make a door open. You could depressurise the cabin and kill people."

"I promise, Captain Biggles. I'm not that stupid."

"So how do we get there?"

Len pointed at the poster.

"Train from Hamsden to Seaton Market and a number 33 bus to Beacon village. The airbase is half a mile north of the village on the B1079."

"And what do we do when we find the airbase is surrounded by the inevitable ten foot high wire mesh fence and patrolled by American soldiers?" asked Eddie.

"So what's the problem? One of your conditions was that we should use ordinary methods of transport to get there. You didn't stipulate anything about what would happen when we got there, Captain. Why can't we just walk under or through the barrier or, failing that, walk through the fence?"

Eddie's earlier suggestion that it wasn't the weekend was quickly confirmed when they arrived back at Hamsden station. Wednesday, November the 15ᵗʰ 1972 promised to be a beautiful autumn day; crisp, sunny and with hardly a breeze to speak of. The rail and bus journey to the village of Beacon was smooth and uneventful with the two ghosts the only 'passengers' to alight at the terminus outside St Mary's Church. Within ten minutes they were standing outside the largely American airbase, having initially dared only to reach a position about one hundred yards from the main and closely-guarded entrance.

"It looks more like twelve feet than ten," said Eddie.

"So?" said Len, with no apparent concern. "Through here or up to the barrier and wander round it?"

Eddie looked hesitant and Len, failing to understand the reason, said,

"Are you still worried that we'll be seen, or something? We're invisible, for God's sake!"

"No, I'm just trying to keep our escapade as honest as I can – just to see how little or how much we need to use our special powers. It's like a real test, then, so that if we ever did have a problem we might be able to resolve it quickly and easily."

Hardly waiting for Eddie to finish stating his concerns, Len had already started walking boldly towards the barrier and guard boxes, one positioned on each side of the entrance. Eddie paused for a moment and then followed his friend. A big American car was just about to exit the base and, trying not to look at the guards, the boys strolled past while the barrier was still raised.

"Smooth as a nut," said Len. "There was never going to be a problem."

"*Hey, you guys, stop!*"

Eddie froze on the spot. Len looked back over his right shoulder.

"*Hey, bud, you forgot your ID.*"

"It's alright, Captain – he was talking to the driver."

Eddie didn't seem to be amused.

"Let's get out to the airfield quickly."

When the boys had covered the half mile or so needed to reach the runways, there didn't seem to be any flight activity going on. There appeared to be three landing strips, roughly forming a triangle with overlapping sides. One seemed to be under repair judging by the two or three JCBs and accompanying civilian workmen. The other two stood empty except for a huge military transport plane at one end.

"That looks a possibility," observed Len. "Plenty of room inside, if we needed any!"

"Can you make out what it is?" asked Eddie.

"Definitely one of theirs, judging by the markings. Let's get closer and I'll see if I can identify it – it's absolutely enormous."

Eddie knew that if anyone could tell what the plane was, it would be his friend, who had taken a keen interest in aircraft in his real life, provided that was, it hadn't been introduced after 1966.

"A Lockheed C-5 Galaxy, Captain!" exclaimed Len when they had got to within fifty yards of the enormous plane. Eddie's mouth dropped and remained open while he tried to gauge its actual dimensions.

"It's got to be at least the height of two houses and a hundred yards from wing tip to wing tip and about the same in length."

"You're right about the first bit – it's just over sixty feet high, but the wingspan and length from nose to tail are between seventy and eighty yards, if I remember correctly," replied Len, proudly. "And, it only needs just over a mile of runway to take off and land, which is not bad given it's about the largest plane in the world."

Suddenly, two of the four General Electric turbo engines roared and thundered into life. If Eddie and Len had been made of living flesh, they would have needed urgent surgery to their ears, but, instead, they watched in wonder, transfixed by the giant aircraft as it shuddered into life. The second two engines fired and Len brought them back to the reality of the moment.

"Quick, before they lift the cargo ramp."

The two ghosts bounded towards the gaping mouth at the front of the plane, jumping the last few feet to land safely on the ramp whose end was already three or feet off the ground. Once they had walked to the back of the aircraft, the two boys could easily see, by the empty cargo hold, that this was going to be no more than a training flight if, indeed, they weren't just testing the engines. Seconds after they had found sitting positions against some empty pallets, the huge nose configuration descended from its elevated position and the aircraft was sealed for flight.

"Shouldn't we be strapped in by some harnesses," queried Eddie.

"Don't be daft, mate, you should know we won't move – we didn't when we went to the moon."

And move they didn't, as minutes later the aerial monster lumbered down the runway and, defying gravity with extraordinarily consummate ease, lifted off the ground. Way up towards the front of the aircraft they could just hear the voice of the pilot communicating with the airbase, confirming their flight path and status.

"You do realise, Eddie, that if we do float down to earth, we'll have to get ourselves back to Hamsden by public transport if we're to stick to your rules," said Len.

This time, it was Eddie's turn to mock his friend's remark.

"Why? Is that where you live now? We don't have homes now, you numbskull. We can go anywhere we like until our batteries run dry and one or both of us go back to sleep. We may even just have to hang around for a while, and I mean that literally!"

After about twenty minutes of what seemed to be a fairly steep climb, the giant plane seemed to level out and Eddie listened carefully for an indication of their final cruising height.

"*It's a beautiful day up here, Beacon Two – our air speed is 417 knots and our altitude is 27,350 feet. Visibility is good. Please advise of any adverse weather on our height and heading.*"

"Roughly five miles up, Len, or nearly at the height of Everest."

Len gave his normal simple response.

"Wow!"

"It's highest I've been since we flew back from Poland in May 1963, Len."

"Me too, then, I suppose," replied Len. "Well, are we going to see what it's like outside?"

"Ye-es, if you're ready."

"I'm ready, Captain; just give the order."

"Roger, Navigator. Proceed to abandon the aircraft."

"Which way, Skip?"

Eddie pointed to the fuselage to their right.

"Let's try there."

The two ghosts stood up and moved slowly to the aircraft's side where they stopped when their faces were a few inches from the internal metal carcase. Eddie then said,

"We both walk forward together – on three, O.K?"

"Roger, Captain. Message received and understood."

Eddie started counting.

"One – two – three, go!"

Both ghosts closed their eyes and took a step forward. Len screamed with delight almost before the two boys found themselves suddenly in bright sunshine.

"I'm flying! I'm in the air!"

Eddie watched as the Galaxy shot forward at over four hundred miles an hour. They were suspended in space at nearly 30,000 feet and their transport had left them; it was already heading for the horizon. His friend's 'body' was about five yards in front if him and slightly to his left. He seemed frozen in his last act of movement, with legs astride and arms front and back. Though he couldn't seem to move his head, and felt also that his own body must be fixed in a similar position to his friend's, he was able to respond verbally.

"Well, not exactly flying, Mr Navigator – just floating, and I think therefore my guess was right. We can't fall."

Expecting both their bodies to 'freeze' completely and even the power of speech to disappear, Eddie was mildly surprised when Len seemed able to swivel his body in order to face him.

"How did you do that?"

Len moved gracefully over to Eddie, almost as though he was just swimming in the sea off Fenton beach.

"Easy – I cheated and concentrated my mind on turning round and coming over to you."

"So my experiment has worked," said Eddie. "We can't seem to defy the normal laws of science. Zero mass; zero weight; zero acceleration."

"Whatever you say, Einstein. More importantly right now, are we going to try to think our way to the ground?"

Ten minutes before the Lockheed C-5 Galaxy had left the ground at Beacon Hill airbase, British Midland Airways flight number BM201 had taken off from Manchester airport at 11.40 heading south for London Heathrow. The newly operational Boeing 707 was only half-full; the rest of its passengers would be boarding in the capital for the fully-booked three-hour flight to Majorca for some late autumn warmth. At 12.30 precisely, its complement of seventy-eight passengers and crew were increased by the addition of two invisible non-paying guests.

Eddie and Len had tried in vain for several minutes to get their bodies to move vertically downwards, but their only permissible motion proved to be in a horizontal direction. Whatever power was in overall control that morning, they were able to rendezvous with the 707 over the Cambridgeshire fens. As Eddie would admit later, the chances of them having been at precisely the same necessary height were millions to one. Fortunately their lateral speed proved to be sufficient to complete the rendezvous within a few seconds of Len spotting the Boeing from several hundred yards away. Their final entrance into the plane was as easy as had been their exit from the Galaxy a short time earlier.

At ten to one, flight BM201 commenced its approach into London Heathrow. Eddie and Len had found two rear seats with only one flight attendant for company.

"So, we're landing at Heathrow, Captain? That manoeuvre was out of this world, almost like we were meant to do it."

"Yes, Navigator; you did a good job, but I think you're right – we had a little help I suspect. God certainly does moves in a mysterious way and it's still only lunchtime. Pity we can't sample the airport food, eh?"

"It's sleep I need," said Len. "I'm bushed."

As his friend made his remark, Eddie watched as Len's body faded into nothingness. He had been granted his request. It had been a good day, thought Eddie. Len had behaved himself and an interesting experiment had been accomplished. What would happen to him when the plane landed at Heathrow and where would he go next? He closed his eyes to think of the possibilities.

13

Confirmation of Evil

By the time Christmas was approaching in 1973, little Ed had grown into a chubby, freckly and ginger-headed four-year-old, who loved nothing more than to accompany his grandma when she went shopping in Fenton-on-Sea. He hadn't inherited all of his late uncle's characteristics; he clearly wasn't going to be skinny or indeed, shy. Though Eddie's sister and her son had moved out from her parents' home earlier that year – when Jenny's divorce from Gary had finally come through – Ann Compton often helped her daughter by looking after her grandson while Jenny was at work. Christmas Eve was always a busy time at 'Curls and Twirls' and, with no pre-school playgroup to go to, Jenny's mum had little Ed until three that afternoon. During term-time, Jenny still only worked mornings so she could collect little Ed at lunchtime. During the holidays she had to manage as best she could, using a combination of her mum and a couple of local neighbours on her modern housing estate, conveniently situated just north of the avenues where Fir Tree Close was located. She was only renting – a compact two-bedroom semi, but its proximity to her parents' house meant that she could walk Ed down there before she caught the train to Hamsden. Gary had moved away from the area and saw his son only very occasionally. After the less than amicable divorce, he seemed to lose interest in the upbringing and welfare of little Ed, confirming the original disinterest when he had been born.

Ann Compton had some last minute shopping to do in Fenton that Christmas Eve morning and little Ed was clearly excited at the prospect, after Jenny had left him with his grandma at just after eight o'clock. Fred Compton had left for work early at seven-thirty because of the likely rush of last minute passengers. By nine, Jenny's mum was doing some dusting with little Ed as her number one helper. The cleaning team had reached the lounge where little Ed was always given the responsibility of cleaning his uncle's photograph and frame.

"Nanny?"

"Yes, Ed."

"Nanny, can we go to Woolworth's?"

"Probably, love."

"Will Father C'ismas be there?"

"I don't know; I expect so, but only if you've been good. He doesn't see naughty little boys."

Ed went silent and after a pause, he said,

"Mummy says it was only an accident."

"What was, dear?"

"I b'oke a plate, Grandma. I didn't mean to."

"Of course you didn't but don't break Uncle Eddie, alright?"

"No, Grandma."

Little Ed paused at he gazed at his uncle's image.

"Was Uncle Eddie always good, Grandma?"

"Yes, dear, most of the time."

"What was the baddest thing he ever, ever did?"

Ann Compton wanted to say something like: '*Running away from home and leaving me and Grandad*', but she said instead,

"Oh, I don't know; coming in late with his clothes dirty or not concentrating in English at school."

"That's not very bad, Grandma. I always get my things dirty."

"It was for him, my little love."

Little Ed gave Uncle Eddie back for his grandma to return him to his place on the wall and said,

"I wish Uncle Eddie would come back, Grandma."

"So do I, little Ed. So do I."

By ten-thirty, little Ed and his grandmother had started to make their way out of Fir Tree Close and into South Road. It was cold and frosty with ice still on the ground. Despite having recently had his fourth birthday, little Ed still helped take his pushchair on any trip into town. He rarely got in it anymore and it seemed now to be needed only as some form of comforter or pal for him. This morning it gave him added stability on his little chubby legs with some of the roads and paths still icy. Ann Compton found it invaluable for carrying her shopping and handbag. This particular morning, she had been looking forward, for some time, to a very rare visit to Russell Jones' in the High Street, conveniently located directly opposite her grandson's favourite destination. Russell Jones' was, for Fenton-on-Sea, a fairly chic and modern fashion shop and Ann had had her eye on a particular blouse and skirt for Christmas Day. Her grandson, of course, had other ideas when they reached the door to the dress shop.

"Woolworth's, Grandma. There's Woolworth's. San'a! San'a! San'a!" he gabbled, tugging at Ann Compton's sleeve."

"In a minute, Ed, love. Just wait until Grandma has done her shopping. Then we'll go and see Father Christmas."

It would be over half an hour before grandma and grandson would emerge from Russell Jones' and, when they did so, little Ed was understandably anxious and excited.

Little Ed's namesake had woken from his slumbers at almost precisely the same time as the two shoppers had entered Russell Jones'. Eddie was quite excited to find that it was Christmas time and the last day before the big day as well. That excitement was enhanced by the nostalgic surroundings he had found himself in – the very shop that was little Ed's favourite as it had also been his when he had been his nephew's age. Eddie found the next half an hour quite absorbing as he wandered round the shop, looking at all the modern toys and games for sale. Surely it would not be long until his friend joined him, given all the memories of those times when, on a Saturday, he and Len would spend their pocket money, or just wander round the shop looking at all the things they wanted but couldn't afford. When it became clear to Eddie that Len wasn't in Woolworth's, he headed for the door to the High Street where, to his great surprise and joy, he immediately spotted his mum and little nephew emerging from Russell Jones'. He desperately wanted to shout out a greeting, but instead, he had to watch in horror as little Ed wrested his hand from his grandma's grasp and ran into the road. It seemed to Eddie that his little nephew appeared very excited and was shouting something as he left the pavement. Though it was difficult to read the little boy's lips at that distance, Eddie had the distinct sense that he was saying something like,

'*Uncle Eddie! Santa, Uncle Eddie! Santa!*'

Had it not been so icy, little Ed would probably have got across the road safely that morning. As it was, with his grandma screaming for all she was worth, he slipped and fell to the ground right in the middle of the road. The nightmare immediately got worse as Eddie watched, in slow motion, as his nephew disappeared under the front wheels of a single-decker bus, whose driver had been trying desperately to pull up from fifty yards further up the High Street. The number 201 slewed sideways, its rear end colliding with Ann Compton and her pushchair, throwing them both into Russell Jones' window. Glass could be heard shattering as the bus then followed suit. The whole event had unfolded in less a matter of seconds. Thankfully, with the bus obscuring his view, Eddie could no longer see either his mother or his nephew, but he knew he faced the harsh reality that neither could have survived such a horrendous accident. People were rushing from all directions.

"*Get an ambulance!*"

"*Get out of the way – I'm a doctor!*"

"*Good trick, Ed, eh? Best one so far. I told you I'd be back and you couldn't get rid of me.*"

Eddie glanced to his right. Evil had returned. Len was grinning from ear to ear with his arms folded across his chest in a triumphant pose that said, '*I did that – I can do anything*'.

"You murdering devil!" screamed Eddie. "Murderer!"

"How do you know they're dead, Ed? It might be far worse; they might be maimed for life and wish that they had died. Shall I go and see and finish the job off? Dead Ed, eh? That even rhymes. Dead Ed, dead Ed dead …."

Pure evil was chanting and it had to be defeated. Eddie closed his eyes, fell to his knees and prayed.

"Oh God, please save Mum and little Ed. Please make them alright and send the devil away. Please, oh God, I beg you. Save my mum and nephew."

"*Hi ya, Eddie. What are you doing, Captain?*

"Go away, you murderer. Get thee me behind me, Satan!"

"*What are you talking about, mate? It's me, Len.*"

Still Eddie remained on his knees and repeated his supplication. The screams and noises had stopped, but there was no sound of an ambulance coming. '*Where, oh where is the ambulance?*' thought Eddie. He dared to raise his head and open his eyes. His mother and nephew were still standing on the opposite side of the High Street, waiting for a single-decker 201 bus to pass, as its driver steered it gingerly over the icy

683

surface. If Eddie could have cried at that moment, he would have shed an ocean of tears as the realisation of what had happened sunk home. Evil had returned to display its power, but Good had triumphed in the end. Len's good ghost was still standing at his side and said,

"What was that all about, mate? Looked to me like you were praying. Anyway, what did 'Buzz' Aldrin say when he first stepped on the moon in 1969, Captain?"

"Monterey Jack or New Jersey Blue, then?" mumbled Eddie. "Oh God, Len, you won't believe what's just happened."

"Hey, that's your mum, Eddie, isn't it? Just walked past us into Woolies. Is that your nephew, then?"

"Yes, Len, that's little Ed."

"Wow! He looks like you, old son."

14
More Confetti

It wasn't to be very much longer that cold Christmas Eve before Eddie began to feel tired after such an emotional and terrifying experience. He and Len had followed Eddie's mum and nephew back into Woolworth's, though Eddie hardly had the concentration to pay much attention to his friend's curiosity about his mum and nephew. Len was particularly taken with the family likeness that little Ed had acquired.

"He's got your hair, but your sister's face. He's going to be a bit fatter than you as well."

"Anyone would be fatter than me," replied Eddie. "I was always skinny until I ...."

"Your mum looks happy, too, mate," continued Len.

"Yeah, I think she must enjoy being a grandmother. Don't you want to see your mum again?"

"Not until just now when I saw yours, Eddie. I often wonder if she ever married again."

Eddie didn't reply immediately to his friend's rhetorical question – he recalled the wake after the funerals of Cyril Wilby and his son. Martha Wilby had been engaged in deep conversation with a strange man then, who had seemed to Eddie at the time to have been more than just a distant friend. Also, though he had just managed to hold a conversation with Len, his mind was still spinning from what he had just witnessed and the horrible trick that his friend's evil ghost had just performed – that friend who was cheerfully taking to him at his side.

"I think next time I come back I should definitely like to go and see her again. Find out how she is, you know," continued Len when his friend remained silent.

"What? Oh yes – good idea, mate. I'll come with you if I'm allowed."

"Allowed?" asked Len.

"Yeah, if God allows us to meet up again soon."

"You and your God, Len. Are you certain he's doing all this for us?"

And then, at last, Eddie at last managed to blurt out all about the extraordinary event that had taken place outside in the High Street a short time earlier.

"Oh, I'm sorry, mate. I didn't realise. You don't think I had anything to do with it, do you?"

"No, but …."

Len's head drooped, and when Eddie didn't continue, he said,

"You do, don't you? You do think I knew it was happening."

"I don't know, Len. I'm tired."

Len began to get angry.

"Eddie, I'm your best friend, mate, for goodness sake. What on earth are you saying? That I'm evil? That I know what my bad side is doing? We've all got a bad side – or don't you even believe that?"

"I told you, I don't know what I think. I know we can all be bad, but your evil ghost is still part of you and it seems to want to dominate you. You mustn't let it do that, Len."

Len looked genuinely upset now and said,

"And how do I do that? I'm not trying to be bad, if that's what you believe. Something outside of me must be trying to take me over and I can't feel it happening – honest, Eddie. You have to believe me and help me. I don't know what to do."

"Just trust and believe that God can beat him for you – that he can erase him from your soul or as much of him as to render him harmless. Put you faith in God. He won't let you down, Len."

Eddie wasn't sure whether Len had absorbed his friendly advice as he felt his body begin to shut down and return to temporary oblivion. Somewhere in the distance he thought and hoped that he heard Len say,

"I will put my trust in God, Eddie. From now on I will be good."

However good Len's intentions were in eventually deciding to go and see his mum, he would later discover that there was always going to be a potentially difficult problem in trying to achieve his somewhat belated wish. Martha Wilby had quickly decided after the tragic double loss of her husband, Cyril, and her son, that she would try to get on with the rest of her life with a positive attitude. The role of a grieving widow and mother was not going to be her métier for the rest of her days. Indeed, within the first few months of her double tragedy, she had become not only a woman of substance, but also one who was determined to make the best of her not unattractive looks. Cyril Wilby had left her well-provided for – enough for her to lead an independent life of leisure combined with church voluntary work. By Christmas of her annus horribilus, she had attracted one or two admirers in the small north Kent seaside town of Petersgate, where as a family the Wilbys had moved only a matter of weeks before they were to be reduced from three to one. Her one special admirer, however, did not live in Petersgate, nor was he a recent acquisition. Michael Conners had known Martha Wilby for more than fifteen years, ever since she and her husband had been colleagues at a secondary school in the London's East End. Cyril had been a woodwork teacher and Martha a cook in the school kitchen. Michael Conners had been the sole attendee from the Wilby's previous school at the double funeral in late August 1965 and afterwards, the two former colleagues began a telephone/letter-writing relationship. By the end of 1967 it had blossomed into something more tangible, and for the next five years, whilst still spending the majority of their lives as individuals in different locations, they spent an ever-increasing minority in each other's company, both in Petersgate and in Whitechapel. Several holidays at home and abroad were taken in tandem and by the summer of 1973, on one romantic trip to Paris, Michael Conners proposed to Martha Wilby. She hesitated only for a couple of seconds before responding in the affirmative. They were both fifty-three years old.

Decisions had to be taken over where they were to live after their marriage, planned for April the 6th the following year. Michael still had up to another seven years to go before his retirement from his post as Head of Humanities at Friar Lane Comprehensive. For her part, Martha didn't really want to sell her house in Petersgate which would be an excellent retirement area when her husband-to-be reached that time. In the end, the couple decided to live in Michael's bungalow in Whitechapel until his retirement, while 23 The Park would be rented out until the couple moved back when Michael retired. They chose to rent it to some students – a young married couple who would only use it in term time, leaving it available for their own use in the school holidays. If not perfect, it seemed to be the best compromise, given that Michael needed to be near his work for a few years. Martha and Michael moved in together in the London bungalow a few days before Christmas and 23 The Park was rented to two medical students from early January 1974. Martha had given in to Michael over the venue for the wedding and it was booked for one p.m. on Saturday, April the 6th at St Margaret's Parish Church just off Brick Lane. The reception was to be at the Garden Hotel in Sebastopol Square at two-thirty. It would be a small gathering – less then thirty guests, most of whom were Michael's friends and family. Martha's sister and her husband were her only relations to be invited. Apart from her old friends from Fenton-on-Sea, Fred and Ann Compton, Martha would only have a few other representatives, all from St Michael's Church in Petersgate, where she had worshipped before moving to Whitechapel.

Before he left for his welcome rest after his friend's bombardment of his conscience, Len had made up his mind that he really did want to visit his mother on the next occasion he was raised to 'life'. As consciousness left him that Christmas Eve, his mind offered up a silent prayer to extend his verbal testimony of a split second earlier. However, he would have to pass a difficult test if he was to accomplish his desire – a test that would, once and for all, establish the genuineness and sincerity of his aspiration to see his mother once more.

It was nine-thirty on a bright but chilly April morning when next he awoke to the land of the living. His surroundings were familiar to him, though that familiarity had not been long established before he had departed his natural life. Before his eyes were allowed to open, however, his ears were presented with unfamiliar voices – ones that his mind was certain it was not acquainted with.

"Are you going to work this morning, Phil?"

"No, I thought I'd leave that project on brain tumours until tomorrow. Prof Micklesen doesn't want to discuss it for at least another week. How about you, love?"

"No, I've just one experiment to write up and I can do that when you do your work. Let's go out for the day. I fancy doing some shopping in Canterbury with a spot of lunch at the Bishop's Finger."

Len could see by now and he found he was sitting in a pleasant and familiar room. His eyes immediately focused on a couple of framed photographs standing on a table to his side. One was familiar; one was not. The one he recognised was of himself and his dad, taken outside their old house in Fenton-on-Sea on the very morning of their move to Kent. The second photo was also of a man of similar age to Cyril Wilby, but unknown to Len. Then Len knew where he was. It had to be the lounge of his new house in Petersgate; the house that he and his dad had left that fateful day in August 1965 to go fishing off Deal pier; the house from which his mother had returned after burying her husband and son on the same day and the house that now seemed occupied by other people.

"Right, love, I'll just have a quick shower and we'll be off in ten minutes," said Phil.

"O.K. – that's great."

Len had quickly decided that the young couple must be students and very much in love as they made their way out of the lounge to get ready for their trip to Canterbury. Within a quarter of an hour, he had the house to himself. Despite his invisibility, he had remained in his position in the lounge until he had heard a car pull out of the drive of 23 The Park, Petersgate.

Though there were many familiar things belonging to his mother in the house, its general untidiness told Len that his mother was no longer living there. For several minutes Len couldn't work out what the apparent contradiction could mean. If she had moved, why had she left many of her possessions let alone most of her furniture? Although it had been nearly eight years since he had been inside the house, and the decor had changed, it still had his mother's stamp on it, but where was she? What had caused her to leave everything behind when she had left? But had she left? It would have made sense to Len at that moment if his mother had taken in the students for the added income the rent would provide her. He leapt up and ran upstairs to his mother's bedroom, passing piles of books and folders on the stairs – his mother just couldn't be renting to these students; not if she was still living here.

Not only was his mother's bedroom clearly being used by the two students, but also the other two rooms were not even fitted out as bedrooms. One, his former room, seemed to be an office and the second was piled high with boxes and general junk. 'No', thought Len as he returned downstairs, 'Mum is not living here anymore'. It was ten past ten and Len was beginning to get a strong feeling that he was in the wrong place and needed to be elsewhere that morning. He started to look for any clues as to where his mum might have gone. He began in the kitchen where he remembered his mother always kept a message board, on which she used to leave him notes or jot down important reminders. Though the cork board was still there, it contained nothing of relevance for Len. The calendar for 1974, hanging next to the board, also contained no clues to his mother's whereabouts except to answer one question that had concerned him. A note had been made in the space for April the 1st, which read, '*Rent due – send cheque to Mrs Wilby.*' So, his mother still owned the house and was indeed renting it to the two medical students. Nothing else in the kitchen gave any indication of a forwarding address for the rent or mail and Len returned to the lounge for any clues as to where his mother might be living. He found nothing of use, unable as he was to move or pick things up. With nothing else in mind, other than curiosity, he looked in more detail at the photograph of the strange man on the small table. To his surprise, and perhaps by a slice of preordained luck, he found a slim pocket-sized diary for 1974 lying open behind it. By walking round to the side of the table, he could just read what was written on the two open pages. At first, with '*University of Canterbury*' stamped at the top of each page, it didn't at first suggest it would be much use, but at least the owner seemed to be an avid recorder of anything and everything. The entry for April the 6th – the probable date that day, given the calendar in the kitchen – was plain enough even for him to read. What he read there gave him another reason to the question as to why his mother was not there. The entry read:

'*Mrs Wilby's wedding, St Margaret's, Whitechapel*'.

Underneath, and in a different hand, someone else had written:

'*And we're not invited*'.

Len took a step backwards. His mother was getting remarried and, no doubt, to the man in the photograph, and the wedding was that very day. He knew at once that, not only must he try to get there, he was also expected to get there. Everything pointed to it – his arrival at his mother's house on the precise date and the pure chance that the diary had given him the details. It all made sense. It was now half past ten and he had to get a move on. When *was* the ceremony and could he get there on time? He knew more or less where the church was, from the time he had lived with his mum and dad in the East End, but how was he to get to Whitechapel? He made for the locked front door and, to his relief, walked right through it and out into The Park. No time for niceties today, he thought, even though Eddie might not approve. His hazy memory of his three-week residency led him into the town and the railway station. By chance (?), the London train was due to leave at ten to the hour and Len slipped aboard behind two young ladies. The train was less than half-full and Len was able to find a seat with ease.

Nothing happened to concern Len until the train reached Chatham at twelve-fifteen, when it was swelled to capacity by the many shoppers bound for the city. He made himself scarce by occupying, as usual, the space next to an exit door. By the time the train pulled into Victoria, something was telling him that he was late and that the wedding was about to begin without him. Running down the platform at the station with the clock reading 12.57, he tried to consider his options. He knew roughly how to get to Whitechapel, but wasn't there an easier way? What would Eddie have done? He passed through the ticket barrier and suddenly remembered what his friend's last words to him had been:

'*Put your faith in God. He won't let you down*'.

Len stopped running and bowed his head. With no one other than the intended recipient to hear, he said out loud,

"Please God; get me to my mum's wedding. Please, oh please, get me there. I truly believe that you can do it."

The last sound that he heard as his special transport whisked him away from Victoria was a clock sounding the hour.

St Margaret's Church was barely a quarter full for the one o'clock ceremony; twenty-nine wedding guests, eleven regular parishioners, four church helpers, two churchwardens, a photographer, the organist, the bride, the groom , the best man, a lone photographer and the Reverend Bob Anderson made up the entire congregation – in all fifty-three living souls. In addition, one dead soul stood smiling invisibly directly behind the Reverend Anderson.

Like Eddie had been at his sister's wedding four and a half years previously, Len was both proud of and amazed by his mother's radiance and poise. If it had been possible, there would have been a tear in his eye when the wedding vows were exchanged. It warmed Len's ghostly heart to see his mother so obviously happy with her new man and he even hoped that his dad, Cyril, was looking down and giving his seal of approval to her new marriage. Len knew her dead husband would have wanted her to be happy.

"*And I am, son.*"

Almost without thinking, Len replied to the voice out loud,

"What? Are you here, Dad?"

"I'm right behind you, son."

Len turned round to see his dad. He looked exactly as had that fatal summer Sunday in 1965. Like his son, he hadn't aged a bit and he looked happy with his wife's decision to remarry.

"I'm glad your mum did this today. I knew Michael at Friar Lane; he was a History teacher when I was there. He was a nice man and I always suspected he had a soft spot for your mother."

By this time, Mendelssohn's Wedding March was accompanying the new Mr and Mrs Conners down the aisle and Len and his dad slipped cheekily in behind them.

"Where's the reception, Dad?" asked Len as they fitted in step with the happy couple.

"Don't know, Len. I only arrived a few minutes ago when you thought of me, I guess."

"Didn't you know you were coming, then, Dad?"

"No – this is my first visit back to the living world."

"Really?" queried Len. "Where have you been?"

"Nowhere, Len. In my grave, I suppose, if your mum had me buried."

"She did," said Len, as father and son emerged from the church into drizzle that had just started to fall. Neither of them seemed to be certain of what to do next, until Len said,

"We'll just have to jump into one of the cars, Dad."

"There won't be room, son. All the places will be taken."

And then Len burst out laughing. His dad was new to this game, he thought.

"Dad – we're ghosts! We don't occupy space. If we sit on someone's lap, they wouldn't feel a thing. Which lady do you fancy?"

"Len! Don't be rude."

Len smiled. His dad still thought he was fourteen, even though his mind had aged. He played along.

"Sorry, Dad. Here, be quick, there's room in that one."

Len led his dad to a red Datsun and, while the driver put a wedding present on the back seat, the two ghosts followed it in before the door closed behind them. The car moved off with a sudden jerk, causing the woman passenger to say,

"Careful, Fred, you'll break the vase in the back."

"Sorry, love, I'm still haven't got used to the clutch."

"*Dad! It's Eddie's mum and dad.*"

Fred glanced in his rear-view mirror and nearly floored the accelerator.

"Oh my God, it's ...."

"*It can't be, Len.*"

"What are you doing, Fred?"

"*It is, Dad – it's Uncle Fred and Aunty Ann and Uncle Fred's seen you.*"

The car came to an abrupt halt as Fred pulled the car to the kerb. He turned round and said,

"Oh, God, it's happening again, love."

"What is, love?"

"I thought I saw Cyril Wilby and Len in the back seat."

"*Told you, Dad.*"

Ann Compton looked round.

"There's no one there, Fred. It's your mind playing tricks again for the umpteenth time. You really should go and see someone."

"There's no one there now, but I'm sure there was."

"*I really am a ghost now, son.*"

"Yes, Dad – you are."

The car pulled away from the kerb.

"It was just your mind, love. It's been a while since we've seen Martha and memories of Cyril and Len would have come back to you, that's all. Made you see things that aren't there."

"You're right, love."

"No she's not Uncle Fred. Oh no, she's not."

Cyril Wilby and his son could easily have walked to the Garden Hotel – Sebastopol Square was less than half a mile from the church and Len's dad had clearly been there before.

"We used to have our staff end-of-term parties here, Len. Years ago now, but it hasn't changed much," he said as they stood outside the hotel.

The two ghosts had just jumped out of the car, using the opportunity provided by Ann Compton when she had opened a rear door to retrieve her wedding present. This normal type of exit from the car had been a close run thing, and Len knew that he could have shown his dad his extra powers and just emerged through the locked door. There would be time for a demonstration when his dad was more accustomed to his new role.

Fred and Ann Compton found that, apart from Martha, they really knew no one else at the reception. They had met Martha's sister at the funeral, but that had been nearly nine years ago. While the wedding lunch was comfortable enough for them, being a sit-down affair, the after-lunch party was less so. Never a couple to socialise easily with strangers, they ended up fairly isolated at a small table for four in one corner of the intimate hotel room – isolated, that was, apart from their two observers.

Fred had already had a pint and a glass and a half of champagne by the end of the meal and once he changed to fruit juice, he seemed to become fidgety and somewhat agitated. He had wanted to have a couple of stiff whiskies, but Ann Compton had put her foot down, given that he would be driving them back to Fenton-on-Sea at about six. Downing his third orange juice, he looked at his watch.

"Ten to five, love. We ought to be making a move – try to get home before dark."

"We can't go yet, Fred," said Ann. "Not before Martha and Michael leave for Paris at six. It wouldn't be right."

"*No, you can't Uncle Fred – you've got to see Aunty Martha off and throw some confetti.*"

Cyril Wilby and his son had spent most of the time since they'd been at the reception, watching and listening to the various conversations. Len's dad had found it particularly absorbing to move from group to group, comparing and contrasting opinions on all things from their fellow guests to the suitability of the happy couple. Len had hardly said a word in that time as he watched his dad become more accustomed to his role and, whenever he tried to tell his dad about all the adventures that he and Eddie had been on since the accident, he seemed either totally disinterested or downright sceptical, uttering dismissive comments to suggest that his son had simply dreamt the events. Soon, Len had given up, having decided that his dad probably wasn't going to be receptive to such adventures until he had experienced similar ones himself.

"Oh I need a real drink," said Fred.

"No, Fred," said his wife. "You've got to drive me home and you've already had enough. What is the matter? You don't usually drink at events like this. Still seeing things? Because if so, the drink will only make it worse."

"Not since the car. I just feel odd – need calming down, I suppose."

"Odd? What do you mean – odd?"

"Just not right, as though someone is watching me, love."

"Watching you?"

"Don't keep repeating what I say," replied Fred. "You sound like a parrot."

"Oh, sorry. I'm only trying to help, Fred," said Ann, irritably.

"Well, don't."

"Let's go, Dad, and leave them alone. I think Uncle Fred can sense us."

"O.K., son, let's go and listen to your mother."

For the next ten minutes, Fred and Ann Compton sat in silence, after which time, Fred seemed to have recovered his composure and got up to get himself another orange juice. When he had sat down again, he said,

"Sorry, love. I didn't mean to snap. I'm O.K. now – I'll be much better when we get back to Fenton."

Ann Compton patted her husband's hand and said,

"Just relax now, love, it's nearly half past five."

By the time Len and his dad went to look for Martha, she and her new husband seemed to have disappeared. Only by listening to Martha's sister did they realise that the happy couple had gone somewhere else in the hotel to change into their going-away clothes. Though his mother hadn't got married in a traditional white wedding dress, the outfit didn't look comfortable enough for travelling. They returned a few minutes before six to cheers and final goodbyes before they emerged from the hotel into the ever-persistent drizzle. Within a minute or so, their changes of clothes were wet and peppered with confetti which stuck to them like sequins. The taxi whisked them away to a chorus of friendly farewells.

"Don't do anything I wouldn't do!"

"*You'd better look after her, Michael, or you'll have Len and I to answer to.*"

"Have a great time in gay Paris!"

"*I love you, Mum. Please don't forget me.*"

"*Or me, love. I'll always love you, Martha.*"

Cyril Wilby had already turned away by the time Martha waved back at him and mouthed, '*I love you, too, Cyril*'. Len returned his mother's wave on his father's behalf and nodded his acknowledgement.

15
Viking

Eddie sensed a certain finality when he next paid a visit to the real world. Much that had happened to him over the previous nine years of earth time had begun to make him believe that all the good and bad adventures had only been a precursor to something more important. Living a 'Heaven on Earth' was a wonderful experience and was probably only given to a privileged few, but there was only so much you could enjoy. With some of the frightening encounters he had had with evil, he was beginning to look forward to a more permanent sleep each time he returned to the peace of oblivion. He had even begun to think that that peaceful oblivion was a kind of heaven, too.

Eddie had soon realised on this, his latest visit, that it had indeed been over nine years since his tragic, but legitimate, departure from the real world. It was the 20th of August, 1975, as he wandered aimlessly past the railway station in Fenton-on-Sea on the opposite side of the High Street. Two minutes earlier, he had confirmed the date by looking at the newspapers on the rack outside Johnson's the newsagents. Another headline in one of the papers had also attracted his eye and, though it had only warranted a small portion of a front page, it had registered itself in Eddie's mind for later consideration. It seemed to be late afternoon and, pausing outside the station, he observed from the clock that the time was five-thirty.

While ambling up the High Street he had gained the strange but distinct feeling that this was going to be the last visit to his home town. Almost as if to remind him what Fenton-on-Sea had meant to him, he spotted a familiar figure coming out of the station forecourt. Fred Compton was leaving work as usual on this Wednesday. Eddie crossed over the road and started to follow his dad. Whether his feelings of finality were imagined or not, at that particular moment, he felt he needed to say goodbye to his family for one last time.

When Eddie reached number 38 Fir Tree Close, it was soon obvious that his mum and dad had visitors for tea. He had kept a fair distance behind his dad all the way back from the station but he couldn't fail to see, or hear, his young nephew running down the front path to greet his Grandad.

"Grandad! Grandad! We've come for tea and Mum says we can play with the train set."

Little Ed rushed into Fred Compton's arms just as Eddie reached the front gate. Several thoughts rushed into his head. The first thing that struck Eddie was that Ed's hair had changed from ginger to a deep brown; the second was how much he had grown. He clearly wasn't going to be skinny like his uncle, and his earlier chubbiness had been replaced by an unusually athletic build for a boy of five. The third thought brought memories flooding back to him; memories of his own train set and all the adventures it had provided. Then, the final thought hit him: '*Was it his own set that Ed had mentioned*?'

Grandad and Grandson walked hand in hand up the path and into the house while Eddie paused to prepare himself for seeing his family. After a few moments he wandered up the path and through the closed door. It was obvious from the crying that was coming from the lounge that Ed's request had been temporarily refused until after tea. Smiling to himself, Eddie made for the kitchen where he found his mum making sandwiches. Suddenly, as he stood watching her, he began to feel that he was intruding on a different life and a different time. The feeling got stronger the longer he gazed at his mother. Her whole demeanour seemed frozen in time – a very different time. As if to confirm his earlier feelings, the realisation suddenly hit him that he didn't actually want to stay long in the house – a place where he didn't now belong with the people that had meant so much to him in the past. It had been a mistake to come back – he had moved on. On a sudden impulse, he walked straight through the adjoining wall to the lounge where he found Ed, Jenny and her dad. Ed had dried his tears and was sitting next to his Grandad on the settee. His sister was reading a magazine. Half-expecting his nephew to acknowledge his presence as he had once done before, Eddie slid into the spare armchair. As he listened to the normal family conversation, Eddie's feeling that he was intruding began to sharpen. He didn't want to stay where there were so many memories, and he definitely didn't want to watch his nephew playing 'trains' with his Grandad, particularly if it was his own old *Flying Scotsman* set. He just didn't feel comfortable – he felt awkward and unable, of course, to join in the conversation. When his mother called from the kitchen he'd had enough.

"Ed, tea's ready!"

Before anyone had a chance to get up in response to Ann Compton's announcement, Eddie mouthed an '*I love you*' in three different directions and strode purposefully out of the room. He made the same gesture in front of his mum as she carried a plate of sandwiches through into the dining room. When he got to the front door, he turned back and though nobody could hear, he shouted at the top of his voice,

"*Goodbye Mum, Dad, Jenny and Ed! I'll love you forever.*"

He then turned and walked through the door behind him, praying it wouldn't bar his progress. He didn't stop until he reached the road outside the house where he was hit with the final realisation that he would never see any of his family again. That was, until ….

As he sauntered his way back towards the town, it seemed to Eddie that he had reached a crossroads in his new life. His former earthly existence, highlighted by the meeting with his family, seemed to matter less to him now – it had to be time to move to the next level of his new one. Other questions came to him. What if he wasn't going to remain a ghost forever? What if he went back to oblivion and stayed there for eternity? Like a prisoner on death row, he wanted to do as much as he could before his present 'heavenly' existence changed. God's universe was vast and even infinite and he was still confined to a tiny corner of it. There had to be more that his special powers would allow him to do. What more fun was there to be had in his ghostly role before his powers diminished or even expired completely?

"*Good evening, Captain.*"

Eddie had reached the High Street and hadn't noticed Len suddenly walking beside him. He was quick with his check.

"Before you say anything else, Len; what was the first thing 'Buzz' Aldrin said after he walked on the moon in 1969?"

"Monterey Jack or New Jersey Blue, then? Yes, it is me, Eddie."

"Good; I've things to tell you."

Eddie then shared all his most recent thoughts on their present ghostly existence and, after his friend had listened in silence all the way down to the foot of Steep Hill, he was mildly surprised by his response.

"Yeah, I've been thinking the same thing, too."

"You mean you're ready to leave this earth even it meant that you might never come back?"

"Yep – like you say we have powers that ought to be able to take us anywhere in the universe, or beyond."

"Beyond?"

"Why not? Who knows what's out there? I mean, we got to the moon, didn't we?"

"What about you mum? Don't you want to go and see her?"

"Done it. Saw her get married last April the last time I awoke."

"Really?"

And then it was Len's turn to share the details of his visit the year before, concluding with,

"So, I told her that I loved her. I know she'll be happy, so there's nothing really to keep me here now. Tottenham are never going to win the league."

Len paused and then asked,

"Do you have anything in mind for our last meal, as you called it?"

Then the headline came back to him: '*Mars launch tonight*'. Suddenly, St Andrew's Church clock started striking the hour. Eddie counted.

"Well?" said Len. "Do you?"

"Six, seven – seven o'clock. Sorry, Len. Yes, I might have."

"Well, are you going to tell me, or are you just going to check the time?"

"I needed to know, Len – if we're to catch the rocket that's taking the orbiter and lander to Mars. It takes off from Cape Canaveral at about twenty past ten this evening our time."

"You are joking, aren't you?"

"No, I'm not joking, Len."

By ten past seven, the two boys had wandered down to the water's edge to prepare for the transglobal attempt. Eddie had insisted that they stand on the beach at more or less the same spot where they had left Fenton-on-Sea twelve years previously for the first of their fantastic adventures. It had taken some time for their thought messages to get through to their 'mission control' – Len's name for the ultimate power that was guiding them. In the end, with Eddie beseeching his own 'ultimate power', and his friend eventually concurring, the two ghosts vanished from their former seaside home. Eddie's last action was to turn and look at the reassuring image of St Andrew's Church, standing firm and proud atop the cliffs behind him. It provided him with a reminder of who *his* 'ultimate power' was. Len's last action was more secular, as he shouted,

"Cape Canaveral here we come! Get ready, you Martians, Captain Compton and Navigator Wilby are on their way."

It was eight-fifteen on a warm August evening with many holidaymakers still strolling on the promenade and children catching the sun's last rays on the beach.

The boys' transmigratory bodies hadn't travelled such a distance on earth before, and at first, when they next reformed, both ghosts were slightly bemused by their new location, both having assumed that they would be actually in or on an unmanned space capsule, no matter how small it might be.

"Where the heck are we?" asked Len.

Eddie looked around him and said, almost sarcastically,

"On a beach, mate."

"Where's Cape Canaveral, then?"

Eddie grinned at his friend.

"Haven't you opened your eyes or something, yet?"

Len raised his eyes from the beach and looked inland.

"Oh yeah! Quite big, isn't it?"

The Titan rocket towered into the air in front of them, despite Eddie's guess that it had to be about a mile inland. He tried also to guess the local time.

"I think Florida is five hours behind us, Len."

"So if our journey here was almost instantaneous," continued Len, "it's about half past three now and we have nearly two hours to get there."

"I'm not sure, Len," replied Eddie, cautiously. "It feels and looks later, if the sun sets in Florida at about the same time as in England."

"So what do we do?" said Len.

"Well, since we didn't go direct to the launch site, I suspect we have to make our own way there – another test, I guess."

"What – we walk?"

"Can you see another way? We can hardly thumb a lift and there certainly isn't any public transport out here – it looks barren and deserted."

"Everybody's gone to watch the launch, I suppose," said Len.

"Come on", said Eddie, "there looks like a road over there."

The two ghosts glided up the white sandy beach to a wide concrete road which seemed to run in a straight line in the direction of the rocket. Len read a small sign at its start.

"Washington Avenue."

Suddenly, in front of them, they saw billowing white smoke rise in an enormous cloud above the ground, to be followed a moment later by an almost deafening roar which even their ghostly ears couldn't miss.

"Whoops, she's taking off," said Len.

"No, probably just testing the engines. I don't think space rockets take off immediately the engines first fire, but we'd better run and fast, mate."

"Come on, then," said Len, "let's run."

If the two ghosts had possessed normal human frailties, their ears would have been given a severe testing by the time they had covered about half the distance to the rocket site. They crossed over a junction, ignoring the several policemen and military personnel who were preventing traffic getting too close to the launch and, following a smaller road, strangely called Church Lane, they soon reached the more aptly named Astronaut's Boulevard. They now found themselves less than 200 yards from the launch pad and on a very wide road that actually seemed to be more like a runway. Passing through security fences and up and down bunker-like embankments, they reached their initial goal in less than five minutes. It was clear to the two boys that take-off was imminent as the voice over the public loudspeaker indicated.

"T minus 3 minutes and counting. All systems are looking good."

"Now what?" asked Len as they stood on top of what appeared to be the last fire-safety embankment surrounding the launch pad. "We'll be incinerated if we go down there."

Below them was a massive concrete circle that was fifty-foot high in white noxious smoke. The flames that were shooting sideways from the rocket engines reached almost halfway to their vantage point.

"Oh don't be so dumb, Len – we can't get hurt, but that's not our real problem, mate."

"T minus 2 minutes and counting."

"And that is?"

Neither boy had really noticed that they were holding a perfectly normal conversation. They barely seemed to notice the noise from the rocket's engines.

"How we get to whatever's on top of the rocket," replied Eddie as he pointed skywards. "And then how we get in."

"We have to think our way there and hope it works," said Len. "We haven't been brought all this way just for the sideshow."

"*T minus 60 seconds and counting.*"

Eddie looked sternly at his fellow ghost and said,

"We don't hope, Len; we pray, and now. So for God's sake, pray!"

"*T minus 50 seconds and counting.*"

Eddie and Len bowed their heads and prayed, and each in their own way.

"*T minus 20 seconds and counting.*"

Len couldn't concentrate on his own supplication and said,

"Nothing's happening, Eddie – it's not working."

Eddie didn't respond as he continued with his prayer until the boys' world was suddenly plunged into darkness. The sound of the final countdown began to fade from their hearing.

"*... nine ... eight ... seven ... six ... all engines at maximum power ... three ... two ... one ... zero. We have lift-off. Viking One is go!*"

In earth time it was to be another ten months before the two ghosts became aware of anything new. On June the 19th 1976, Eddie and Len had their first 'close-up' view of the Red Planet, albeit from over 2000 kilometres above its surface. They had woken from their sleep to find themselves sitting on a very peculiar spacecraft. The orbiter had certainly not been designed to carry humans, and though its shape was immaterial for the transport of two ghosts, it was an odd experience for them as they sat, each on two wing-like structures that protruded from the main body of the instrument-carrying craft. This time, Len had pre-empted his friend by making the security check from his position a short distance away. In his excitement at the discovery of their new environment, Eddie had forgotten to do the usual verification of his friend's identity.

With small engines to correct the tilt of the spacecraft, the Mars orbiter also carried the lander that would eventually be ejected to the surface of the planet. Both ghosts spent some time after the identity checks studying which part of their spacecraft *was* the lander and, more importantly, how they would get in or on it. It didn't look obvious to them how they would land.

For the next month, the two ghosts watched each other from a distance of a few feet, fixed in a curious state of inertia, neither able to move nor speak. To make their existence even stranger, the powers of thought and sight were *not* denied them, and for the next thirty-three earth days they could do nothing more than study the planet's surface from distances varying between two and fifty thousand kilometres. Though they had been given a privilege that was beyond all but the characters from a science fiction novel, it was initially mentally and psychologically tiring and a kind of a living torture, even for their ghostly minds and souls.

On July the 20th, by earth time, things started to change for the two ghosts. Firstly, their ability to move and speak returned and secondly noises could suddenly be heard from the main body of the orbiter.

"Wh-what's that?" shouted Len. Eddie shrugged his shoulders as both boys stood upright and walked towards the middle of the weird looking craft. Unlike the probable reaction of normal beings, neither ghost felt much after-effect from their static ordeal. Indeed, their memories of it seem to fade quickly as they began to realise that something important was about to take place.

"I bet that's the orbiter beginning its separation, so that the lander can drop down to the surface," replied Eddie. "It sounds like some retrorockets have been fired to slow the whole thing down before separation. Look down, Len – we're much closer now."

Len glanced down and saw that Mars no longer had any curvature. They were so close that it appeared flat and covered by dust clouds, some of which they were passing through at that moment in their low orbit. They could only get brief glimpses of the surface below.

"I checked before and I think we'll have to get on that thing below us," said Eddie. "I think that must be the lander."

"And just how do you suggest we get down there? We can't jump – nothing would happen if we did, and we don't have the ability to hold on to anything, anyway," said Len. "Do we pray again?"

"No, I think there's a way that we can get onto the lander. Look, see down there – there are some footholds below us on the side of the orbiter. We just step down onto the first one and as long as we keep one foot in contact with something, we should be alright. It doesn't look more than three or four feet."

The rockets were sounding louder now and without waiting for his friend to reply, Eddie took a step onto the first foothold. Len watched as he then removed his other foot from the orbiter and second later, Eddie was on the lander. However, 'on the lander' was a poor description for his final position. With no flat surface to sit or stand on, he seemed to be hovering just above the complicated array of instruments which the lander mainly consisted of. Quickly, Len copied his friend's manoeuvre and joined him in a similar position and orientation.

"We're not in contact with it, Eddie," said a bewildered Len.

"No, I know, but we're going with it, I think."

Suddenly, the boys looked to their right to see the orbiter disappearing into the distance. Such was the separation speed; it was out of view in less than a second. Below them, more rockets fired as the lander prepared to come out of orbit and into the planet's atmosphere. For nearly three hours, the two ghosts chatted happily to each other as the lander was slowed in preparation for its landing. Soon, three huge parachutes were deployed and after a few more seconds, three legs were extended to form a tripod beneath the vital collection of instruments. Less than two minutes later the lander arrived on Mars with a relatively light jolt. The two ghosts felt nothing as they just seemed to slide off the lander and onto the Martian surface. Standing up, both boys dwarfed the lander and its bundle of instruments, cameras and scientific experiments by a couple of feet. Their eleven-month space ride was finally over, and they found once again that they were able to walk and even dance normally on the Martian surface, unhindered by the lack of any usual sustainer of human life. Len even shouted his own greeting.

"Martians, we come in peace as the first beings from earth to visit your planet. We come for all mankind."

They were soon to discover, however, that Len's claim to exclusivity was totally mistaken and unwarranted.

16

Universal Evil

Len's carefree attitude to his new environment seemed to know no bounds, as he jogged up and down for a hundred yards or so in every direction surveying the barren and eerie landscape. A Martian twilight had descended on a tundra-like and featureless plain of reddish-grey dirt and rocks. Overhead, a thin grey mist cloaked the Martian surface, forming a ceiling as low as twenty feet. Patches of white frost dotted the landscape indicating the temperature of the boys' hostile surroundings. Eddie did his best to ignore his fellow ghost's over-eagerness to explore what lay beyond their immediate horizon by remaining near to the lander and inspecting its apparatus that occasionally whirred into life. In the end a few chosen words brought Len back down to earth.

"Stop a minute, Len!" he shouted as his friend was passing the lander on another of his short scouting missions. "Just slow down, will you. I want to talk to you."

Len trotted back to the lander, his enthusiasm obviously still close to fever pitch.

"What's up, Captain? I want to go and find some Martians. You can't be tired, surely?"

"No, I don't feel tired, Len; I'm just a bit disorientated, I suppose." Eddie paused for a moment and then said,

"You do realise something, don't you?"

"What, mate?"

"You do know that, despite what we said about wanting to explore the universe, we have no apparent means of leaving this planet. I think you'll agree that, from what you've seen already, it looks pretty boring up here, and are you really sure you would never want to go back to earth, either?"

Len went quiet and the sudden silence seemed to have a hollow ring to it, making their new world even eerier than before. It wasn't long, however, before he tried to lighten the mood.

"We'll just have to go and find the Martian equivalent of Cape Canaveral and go on a mission."

Then Len paused and, after a moment, he said,

"But seriously though, we knew that before we set off. I'm not going to miss anything back on earth – are you?"

"I don't know, Len. I agree – back in Fenton it all seemed so boring – the excitement had started to wane, but this doesn't look much better, does it?"

"Death is what you make it, Captain."

The doubts that Eddie had articulated about the finality of their new situation had been actually nothing more than an expression of his own concerns and worries. There was no question that Len's characteristic bravado had helped him ease his anxieties, but as the two ghosts set off to investigate the Red Planet, Eddie was still unsure where their so-called 'last mission' was taking them and, indeed, what they would find when they had completed it.

Len was typically jovial as they walked away from the busy lander, remarking on the camera that was snapping photographs behind them.

"We'll be on the front pages in a few days; I wish I'd combed my hair."

With Eddie half-expecting the lander to start moving on its three legs and follow them, he broke into a trot with Len calling out,

"Hold on, Captain – what's the rush? We've got the rest of our deaths!"

Eddie glanced back as his friend caught up with him. He looked past Len at the lander, now some fifty yards distant, and he had the distinct impression that the camera was still trained on them, as if it was following their every move. His musing was quickly broken by his friend.

"Not so fast, mate – are you sure we're going in the right direction?"

"What right direction? Everywhere looks the same to me."

"Not over there, Eddie," replied Len, pointing at the horizon to their left. "Seems to be brighter there."

Eddie looked to where his friend was indicating, and at first, he struggled to make out any difference in the horizon. After his eyes had refocused on the distant line, however, he suddenly saw what Len meant. Rather than a general lifting of the Martian twilight across the whole horizon, the brightness seemed to be coming from a concentrated source.

"Someone's shining a torch," said Len.

"Don't be daft," replied Eddie.

"Well, it's not a fixed light. Look – it's moving from side to side."

Eddie said nothing. His eyes now were fixed rigidly on the light which was getting brighter and closer by the second. It got to a position about a hundred yards away before Len said excitedly,

"It's on the ground – it's rolling along the ground."

The two ghosts watched, mesmerised as a ball of light, the size of a football rolled towards them on the red dirt surface. It was powerful enough to brighten the surrounding area for a distance up to thirty yards in any direction. It came to within a few feet of the astonished ghosts and stopped. The light seemed to have a fluorescent quality, illuminating the ground with a blue-green radiance. Len seemed to be less fearful than his friend and, while Eddie watched open-mouthed, he walked calmly towards the ball of light, his foot getting to within a few inches of it before it suddenly backed away on its original path to stop again after about ten yards. The two ghosts waited. Then the ball of light moved forward again and this time it came to rest right in front of them. Len took aim to 'kick' it with his right foot and Eddie shouted,

"Stop it, Len! You don't what it might do."

Sensing Len's intention, the ball instantly moved to its left and back again, the oscillation taking less than a second. Like something out of a computer game, it then proceeded to dance and weave left and right, as if to say: '*Catch me if you can*!' Eddie relaxed and smiled. The light seemed friendly enough and wanted to have some fun. As soon as Len then withdrew his foot, the light ceased its crazy dance and backed away again.

"What's it doing?" asked Len.

The ball came forward once more and Eddie and Len watched as the process was repeated, the ball backing further away each time. Eddie then seemed to guess what it was doing.

"I think it wants us to follow it, Len."

To try and test out his theory, Eddie walked forward to within a couple of feet of the ball. After a pause, it backed away again and stopped. Len joined his friend.

"You seem to be correct," said Len. "But the question is: Why?"

"Don't know, mate – it obviously wants to take us somewhere or show us something. We might as well follow it and find out."

The ghosts walked forward together and all at once the light did a strange hop into the air before continuing on its backward path.

"It's happy now," said Len. "It's just nodded to us that we should follow it."

The light continued on its path towards the horizon for more than half an hour, if the boys had been able to measure it in earth time. If they got too far behind, it would wait until they were within twenty yards or so and continue – thus keeping them in its circle of illumination and guiding them safely forward.

With nothing to gauge time, it was impossible for the two ghosts to estimate how far they had walked when the light came to an abrupt halt in front of them. Eddie had picked a point on the original horizon when they had set off, but they had soon passed it and the process was repeated several times more before the ball of light stopped. Though tiredness was not an issue, boredom certainly was.

"What now?" asked Len. "I'm getting fed up with this."

"Maybe it has forgotten where it is," replied Eddie.

"Oh yeah? I somehow doubt it, mate."

Eddie didn't think so, either, as he had formed a strange feeling that the light was just checking on its followers' welfare. Suddenly, the ball started to move again, but this time, at right angles to its original path. The two boys turned to their right to follow it and within a few hundred yards, the scenery started to change. The Martian surface was now criss-crossed by a series of ravines, some shallow and some impossibly deep to the boys' ghostly eyes in the dim light. Without their guiding light, one or both of them might have walked into one of the gorges, even though their innate ability to float would have probably saved them from disappearing completely into the bowels of the planet. Soon, their tortuous trail led them on a slow descent into their own ravine, flanked on both sides by sheer rock faces of unknown height. As their route became narrower, tiny balls of light appeared to line each side of their path, where, even at Martian midday, very little natural light would ever reach. Their friendly ball suddenly had a double array of junior companions forming a guard of honour for the two ghosts' progress. Eddie was becoming nervous.

"I don't like this, Len. Looks like we're expected."

"Just laying out the red carpet for their earthly visitors, I think, mate," replied Len, almost casually. "They won't have seen the likes of us before – I'm game to see their leader."

"You think that's what's happening? We're being taken to their leader?"

"What else could it be?"

The light ahead of them had suddenly stopped again. It waited while the ghosts caught up after their brief conversation. As Eddie and Len approached, it seemed to grow brighter and the extra light was concentrated all in one direction at an angle to their path, illuminating what looked to be a deep hole or shaft. Reaching the very edge of the hole, they could see that a flight of rock steps led downwards in a spiral staircase that seemed to have no foot. The ball of light joined them at the top of the hole. Shrinking in size, it bounced its way down the first few steps and waited.

"It wants us to go down there?" queried a nervous Eddie.

"In for a penny, in for a pound," replied his friend. "Come on, let's go."

Len descended the first three steps. The light descended three more and stopped again. Reluctantly, Eddie followed, and a few steps at a time, the two ghosts slowly made their way down the rock staircase, turning through 360 degrees on so many occasions that Eddie lost count. Towards the bottom of their descent, the light in front of them began to fade as more permanent and static light from below filtered upwards. Reaching the last few steps, their 'friendly' guide disappeared completely and their path opened up into an enormous cavern on an Egyptian pyramid scale.

Len's reaction was predictable.

"Wow!"

The two ghosts walked forward into a roughly hemispherical chamber, whose diameter had to be at least the length of a football pitch. Stone staircases, similar to the one they had just descended, spiralled upwards from three other positions on the circumference of the cavern, which in turn was brilliantly lit by a huge ball of light, floating near the top of the chamber's ceiling. Smaller balls illuminated the staircases and marked the very edge of the arena. It was both a magnificent and frightening sight for the two human ghosts.

"So where are the Martians, then?" asked Len, looking round the massive chamber. There was no sign of any movement on the cavern floor, which was composed of flat, bare rock. Apart from some places where the rock was so shiny it reflected flashes of the unnatural fluorescent light, the floor was completely devoid of any defining features. The boys had by now reached the centre of the enormous chamber and, standing back-to-back, they gazed at its distant edges.

"There can't be anyone here, Len," replied Eddie after a while.

"Depends what you mean by, anyone."

"What do you mean?" asked Eddie.

"I mean, we have no idea what things look like on Mars. For all we know, those lights might be the inhabitants of this place – the one that brought us here seemed alive enough to me. It appeared to know what we were doing."

The two ghosts swapped positions and studied the cavern some more. The boys' conversation echoed off the sloping rock walls in their silent surroundings. Eddie seemed to be disturbed by the noise, but Len was getting impatient.

"I wonder what would happen if we just climbed back up the way we came. Would anyone or anything would try to stop us, do you think?"

Eddie, sensing danger, said,

"Don't try it, Len. I'm sure we haven't been brought all this way just to be sent back the way we've come."

"You mean we're prisoners here?"

"No, not exactly prisoners, but we are guests of whoever has brought us here. Remember, we're visitors to this planet."

"Well, they're not treating us like guests – keeping us waiting like this."

Rather than approach the staircase they had come in by, Len walked casually over to the one that was diametrically opposite to it. Eddie waited nervously in the middle of the chamber, issuing a note of caution as he did so.

"Be careful, Len."

Len reached the foot of the staircase and peered up into the black hole that enclosed it.

"Nothing here," he shouted. "It's just like the other one."

Len's voice caused such a disturbing echo that even he took a step backwards as it reverberated round the cavern. The echo bothered Eddie and he called to Len to return to the chamber's centre.

"Something's not quite right, Len," he said.

"What?"

"It's the echo."

"What about it?"

"I don't think we should be able to make an echo – we're ghosts after all."

"Why not?"

"Because our voices aren't real and we're imaginary beings, so how can we make sounds that echo off something that is real, like the rock walls. It doesn't make sense to me."

"So, perhaps we're the only things that can hear the echoes," said Len with some disinterest in his friend's apparent conundrum. "After all, we can hear each other's voices, so why not their echoes?"

"Because if our voices create sound waves that solid walls can reflect, then those same sound waves could be heard by living beings as well. No?"

"You may be right, Mr Compton, but you'll never know, will you, because there are no living beings down here, my dear – only us."

The new voice echoed around the underground chamber, but nothing was visible to either boy to suggest its source.

"What the …?" muttered Len.

"Stay still!" shouted Eddie as suddenly the overhead ball of light swung to its left lighting up one of the staircases. Slowly, figures came into view from the bottom of the stairs. First, one, then another and finally a third black-robed 'being' strode into the arena, like gladiators into a coliseum. The leader threw back his black hood and approached the quivering ghosts.

"Hello, my dears and how are we today? Surprised to see me, no doubt."

Eddie had recognised the sycophantic voice almost immediately he had heard it from the staircase as Len did now.

"Oh my God, it's old Granty!" he exclaimed.

"Yes, Leonard Wilby and Edward Compton, it is I, Aloyisious St John Grant, late of Fenton-on-Sea and former proprietor of The Emporium on Steep Hill that bore my name. I understand it's been turned into some tearooms now. What a shame. I do believe I met your sister there some time ago, young Eddie, and what's more – I saw her boyfriend propose to her."

"Yes, I know, Ally – she told me."

"Really?"

Though Len had always been uneasy with old Granty's effeminate ways, he was brave enough to say,

"What are you doing here, Mr Grant, then?"

"Oh, Leonard, my dear – please call me Ally like your nice young friend does. We don't stand on ceremony down here."

Len and Eddie cast glances behind Aloyisious Grant at his two companions, neither of whom had removed their black cowls. Eddie, for one, knew that all was definitely not well. The last time they had seen old Granty's ghost he had seemed normal with a pleasant and caring attitude. This version of him spoke in a creepy and sarcastic tone. Eddie knew what that meant and his friend had sensed it, too.

"Your Ally's evil ghost, aren't you," said Len. "And who are the people behind you?"

"Evil? I'm not evil, Leonard Wilby. Whatever gave you that impression? No, my dear boys, I'm here to help you two travellers – show you the ropes, you know. You've done well to get here and now you need some advice and assistance if you're to pass to the next level. You won't believe what I can do for you."

Len said nothing as Eddie noticed a faint smile begin to form on his friend's face. Ally Grant continued.

"Let me you show you my two friends. I know you're both dying to know who they are. I suspect they will be familiar to you. Step forward, friend!"

The first cloaked and hooded figure moved to stand on Ally's right.

"This is my first assistant, so to speak."

The black hood was thrown backwards in a show of pomp and ceremony. Eddie gasped.

"George? Is it really you, George?"

"Of course it is, Eddie, my friend – your old ally and fellow adventurer, George Canter."

"Mr Canter?" stammered Len in disbelief.

"Yes, Len, and please call me George."

"Sorry, George."

Ally smiled knowingly and turning to the final hooded figure, he said,

"Step forward, friend!"

As before, the figure move forward and flamboyantly threw back his hood.

"Mr Manders!" exclaimed Len.

"Hello, Len and Eddie. It's nice to see you both."

'So, here they all are', thought Eddie, 'three characters from his and Len's past, both real and imagined; three men of vastly different characters and backgrounds; three men, whose lives spanned a century and a half, but also three ghosts who were, each and every one, evil – pure evil'. But Len was not as sure and remarked,

"It's good to see you all again. We wondered why we'd been brought here."

"Shut up, Len! Don't get involved. Don't be deceived by them."

George Canter looked genuinely shocked at Eddie's reaction.

"I told you, Eddie, it is me. Why don't you believe me?"

"You don't quite look right to me."

"Look right? How should I look?"

"I don't know – just different."

Ally Grant interrupted the debate.

"Don't I look and sound the same, Eddie, my dear?"

"Or me?" echoed Jacob Manders and then even Len realised the truth of the matter as the three ghosts chanted in unison.

"How should we look? How should we look?"

"Who shall we be? Who shall we be?"

Suddenly, as if to make the point and demonstrate their power, the three ghosts covered their heads with their hoods. They remained motionless for a few seconds and then threw back their hood s again.

Both boys gasped in astonishment when they realised that all three ghosts had interchanged their heads. George's body was surmounted by Jacob's head; Jacob's body by Ally's head and Ally's body by George's head. A new chant started.

"Who are we now, boys? Who are we now, boys?"

As Eddie and Len watched in horror, the process was repeated again and again until Eddie shouted,

"You're all evil! Go to the devil! Get thee behind me, Satan!"

"Go to the devil! Go to the devil!"

Eddie's incantation wasn't working – the evil ghosts weren't going anywhere. Eddie tried again.

"Oh God, rid us of this evil before us, I pray thee."

"I pray thee. I pray thee," the ghosts chanted.

"It's not working, Eddie. Their power is too strong."

"Good can always defeat evil," shouted Eddie as the chanting got more rhythmic and louder.

"Well, it's not beating this evil," shouted Len above the incessant noise. "We'll have to make a run for it."

Len turned to run for their entry staircase, but he hadn't gone more than a few yards when his legs suddenly ceased moving and his body became frozen in space. The three black-robed figures advanced towards him. Eddie sank to his knees and prayed.

"Please save Len. Please save him."

Ally Grant got to within a couple of feet when Len's body broke its invisible shackles and Len fled to the bottom of the staircase. Eddie then lost sight of him as he disappeared into the blackness of the exit shaft. Muttering more prayers to himself, Eddie got off his knees and bolted after his friend. Behind him he heard more rhythmic chanting.

"Come and join us! Come and join us!"

"We will get you! We will get you!"

"Just you wait and see! Just you wait and see!"

Eddie didn't wait and he wasn't stopped like his friend. He made it to the staircase. It was black, pitch black and he could hear Len above him.

"I can't see, oh, I can't see. Where are you, Eddie?"

"I'm here, Len. Just stay where you are."

Eddie prayed again. Len shouted,

"It's getting lighter. I can see. Quick, Eddie!"

For the next few minutes and with just a few feet separating them, the two boys bounded up the spiral staircase, guided by the unknown light source above them. Len waited at the top of the shaft until Eddie emerged once again into the narrow ravine. The light source had moved a long way ahead of them by this time, providing only a dim target to make their escape complete. The gentle incline which led there was now in darkness – all the tiny lights had disappeared, no longer providing a guide to the chamber of evil.

17

Mind Talk

Not until the two ghosts had reached the top of the narrow ravine, following the dim and distant guiding light, were they ready to stop and discuss their experience of evil. With the latticework of deep gorges immediately in front of them, it was time also to consider their next move – neither wanted to face the possibility of sliding or falling into another ravine. The Martian night had taken over completely and even Eddie was unsure how long it would last.

"We could be in darkness for days if we stay here, you know."

"You mean day and night are not the same as back on earth?" asked Len, somewhat surprised.

"I don't honestly know what the difference is, but it's not going to be the same."

Both ghosts had seemed to want to talk about anything else but their recent experience until Eddie then suddenly said quietly,

"Were you nearly fooled by those three ghosts, Len?"

Len didn't respond straightaway and Eddie continued.

"Because, if you did think they were Ally's, George's and Jacob's good ghosts, just remember that evil attracts evil – good is an individual thing."

"No, I don't suppose I was really fooled. I just can't understand how three such nice men could have anything evil about them. I mean, apart from old Granty's effeminate and ingratiating manner, they were all thoughtful and caring men – at least one of them saved our lives. Even though old Granty was weird, he wouldn't hurt a fly in real life."

The light in the distance had all but disappeared by now and the two ghosts had difficulty seeing each other's faces. The mist overhead seemed to have thickened, too, as Eddie replied,

"Everyone has an evil side, mate. Look at you for example; I seemed to remember you pulling a nasty stunt in Fenton with my little nephew. What matters in the end is not giving in to it as a permanent choice."

"I never see your evil side very often, Eddie, except …."

"Except?"

"Except when you think you know it all and try to tell me how I should behave. Thinking you're always good and always right is evil too, isn't it?"

Eddie seemed reluctant to reply – he knew his friend had highlighted his biggest failing: pride.

"Yes, I know I'm evil, Len, but I am trying to do something about it."

"There you go again – showing off," said Len.

It was clear to both boys that an argument was about to ensue and sensing it, Eddie tried to be more humble, as he said,

"Sorry, Len – I don't mean to always sound smug and self-satisfied; I just want to make sure neither of us ends up in the wrong place where evil reigns supreme."

"You mean …?"

"Yes, you can say it, Len – hell."

It was pitch-black now and with the mist descending to ground level, the visibility was virtually down to zero. Len was anxious to be moving.

"I want to get out of here, Eddie."

"And how do you propose we do that? We can't even see to move an inch."

"Only one way, Captain," replied Len. "We have to think our way out again."

"So, where do you want to go?"

"Anywhere that's a long way from this evil place."

Eddie thought for a moment and said, almost jokingly,

"How about infinity, or just the edge of the universe, as we know it?"

"Edge of the known universe will do me, mate. I'm not so sure about infinity. I don't think such a place exists."

"O.K., Commander Armstrong – the edge it is. Maybe we'll discover extra-terrestrial life there."

"Good," said Len. "We can go and haunt some little green men who've got two heads."

"As long as you don't try and pull any evil stunts again – O.K?"

Eddie didn't see the evil grin that had appeared on his friend's face. It was to be an invisible pointer to some future sorrow.

"O.K.," replied Len after a split-second pause.

In the blackness, neither ghost dared move their position as they concentrated their minds on their next space journey. While Eddie's avid reading of science fiction books and magazines presented him with some relevant images to think about, his friend struggled to imagine anything other than scenes similar to the Martian landscape. After a short time, Eddie broke the silence with,

"We're going to have to try something different, Len. This isn't working."

"You try praying, then – I'm still not sure God listens to me."

Eddie resisted the temptation to tell his friend he had to really believe before his prayers would work, given their earlier conversation. He didn't want to appear arrogant and superior as Len had suggested. Though there would be no difference in his vision, Eddie shut his eyes and prayed. Suddenly, through closed eyelids, he sensed the blackness had lifted slightly. Len immediately whispered,

"The lights are back on again. What did you do?"

"I hadn't really started," said Eddie as he looked backwards to see the dual strip of tiny ball-lights was illuminating the narrow ravine leading back to the chamber of evil. Len was standing further away from him than he had imagined and Eddie shouted an immediate warning.

"For God's sake, don't step backwards, mate. Walk forward slowly."

Len realised from his friends' tone that he must be on the edge of one of the many deep slits in the ground and, without looking back, he walked forward gingerly.

"Without realising it, you must have started to walk when you said you wanted to leave this place," said Eddie.

The lights behind them seemed to be burning brighter now and it then hit Eddie what might be about to happen.

"We'd better get out of here, Len."

"That's what we were trying to do, I thought, Captain."

Suddenly, noises broke from the ravine behind them, and they were rhythmic again.

"*We're coming to get you! We're coming to get you!*"

"*You belong to us! You belong to us!*"

For some strange reason, Eddie and Len seemed to be rooted to the spot, unable to move a muscle. The chanting stopped abruptly. The three black figures came into view about fifty yards down the sloping ramp. George, Jacob and Ally hadn't given up their quest for the boys' souls. Though the chanting had stopped, Eddie could hear their muttered conversation as it echoed off the steep sides of the ravine. It was too indistinct to determine individual voices and, in any case, back in the chamber they had all begun to sound the same.

"That Eddie Compton thinks he's too good for us; it'll be hard to persuade him to join us."

"Yes, but Mr Leonard Wilby would like to be one of us, I think. His soul seems sometimes to be in tune with our beliefs. We may get him quite easily."

By the look on Len's face, now dimly lit by the tiny lights, it was clear to Eddie that his friend had heard little or any of the evil ghosts' threatening words. The chanting started up again with the three black-hooded figures less than ten yards away.

"We want you, Leonard Wilby! We want you, Leonard Wilby!"

"Come and join us! Come and join us!"

Suddenly, the evil troop stopped their advance – changing quickly from Indian file to a line of three abreast the narrow path. The middle figure took a step forward. He spoke softly with an intonation that was a curious mixture of all three of the ghosts' voices.

"Come, boys, we mean you no harm. We want you to have fun, and you can, if you join us. You like playing tricks, don't you, Leonard?"

"Sometimes."

"Well, we do tricks beyond your wildest imagination. We can make people do things. What do you say, young Wilby?"

"Say nothing," said Eddie quickly, before his friend could reply. He and Len were still transfixed and unable to move. The three black figures moved forward as one. Eddie fell to his knees and held two fingers up in the sign of the cross; the only thing he hadn't thought of trying until then. Suddenly, the lights in the ravine started going out one by one. Eddie held his finger cross firm and the first figure fell to the ground in a cloud of dust and white vapour; to be followed quickly by the second and third in similar manner. Mobility immediately returned to the boys' ethereal bodies and they found themselves able to walk forward to the fallen men. With very little light to show them the way, they reached the spot where the three evil ghosts had stood to find they had literally disappeared 'in a puff of smoke'. Len then turned to Eddie and said,

"Now, for God's sake, get us out of here!"

As Len, almost unwittingly, made his plea for divine intervention, the final light suddenly shone brighter, allowing each boy to see the other's face in eerie and gaunt detail. They were given this dubious privilege for no more than a few brief seconds before utter blackness returned to that part of the Martian surface. Little did either boy know, but that was to be the last time they would ever be able to see each other's face again.

To all intents and purposes, it was to be irrelevant how long the two ghosts would be in peaceful oblivion after their excursion to Mars. Whether it was a few minutes or several million years was of no consequence when they finally 'awoke'. In fact, neither boy could really tell if they were awake, or indeed, when such an event had happened. They each discovered quickly that they could hardly even call themselves ghosts, let alone boys, any longer. Once before they had been deprived of physical, albeit ghostly, movement, but their new situation paled that into insignificance. Now, neither boy possessed the power of hearing, speech or sight – they were deaf, dumb and blind. Though it was stating the obvious – without sight, they could not see each other; without hearing, they could not hear each other and without speech, they could even not tell each other about their first two handicaps. Even if they had been able to see, there would have been nothing of their bodies to be seen. In short, they were without shape or form, bereft of everything except for one small, but important faculty – they still possessed their minds. This was the one sense in which they could still call themselves 'beings' – they could think and, unlike that tragic part of the human race who were also lacking in the three most vital senses, they would soon find they could exchanges their thoughts between each other as well. Eddie would have argued that they had souls as well which, together with their powers of thought, still set them apart from animals of a lower class.

Given all of this, it was also clearly irrelevant where they were in space and time, or even whether they were both in the *same* place and in the *same* time. Indeed, since they couldn't occupy space anyway, the idea didn't even seem to warrant consideration. They had reached the ultimate level in their development, no longer even able to wander invisibly through the universe, or to impinge on any human being's psyche. Their existence was solely defined by and encapsulated in their own minds and their ability to think. Their desire to reach the distant parts of the cosmos had been thwarted at the last moment.

The 'conversation' took some time to get started as both boys' minds struggled to cope with their own internal machinations. It wasn't until 'Len' began thinking of his friend that the thought transference began. It was a stumbling beginning as both minds tussled with and sifted out snippets of extraneous suggestions. If either mind had been able to convert its thoughts into a verbal or written communication, the following would have been a good representation.

'*I wonder where Eddie is.*'

'*Nowhere – where are you?*'

'*The same.*'

'*Did you get to the edge of the universe?*'

'*Don't know – this might be it.*'

'*Are we awake?*'

'*Can't tell.*'

'*Can you feel or see anything?*'

'*No – can you?*'

'*No.*'

'*I think I must be dead.*'

'*You already were.*'

'*Is this real death, now?*'

'*Don't know.*'

'*What's the capital of England?*'

'*London. Why?*'

'*Just checking.*'

'*What's my name?*'

'*Edward Compton. What's mine?*'

'*Leonard Wilby. Are you being good, Leonard Wilby?*'

'*Can't do anything else.*'

'*What thoughts have you had?*'

'*I want to go to sleep.*'

'*Have you had any bad thoughts, Len?*'

'*Yes.*'

'*What were they?*'

'*Can't tell you – they're evil.*'

'*I just got them anyway while you were thinking of them.*'

'*Oh yeah – what were they?*'

'*You want to go and join the black ghosts.*'

'*How did you know that?*'

'*I told you – I read you.*'

'*I want to go. I want to go.*'

'*Well, go then.*'

'*Come with me.*'

'*No, Len.*'

'*We'd get our senses back.*'

'*How do you know that?*'

'*Ally told me.*'

'*When?*'

'*Just now.*'

'*How?*'

'*Same way you knew I wanted to go.*'

'*You're swapping thoughts?*'

'*Yes – you don't have exclusivity.*'

'*He's evil.*'

'*No, I'm not, Edward.*'

'*Don't go, Len.*'

'*Do go, Len.*'

'*I may do. What can you offer me, Ally?*'

'*Your invisible body back.*'

'*He's lying.*'

'*Am I?*'

'*Go away, Satan!*'

'*I'm bored with this, Eddie.*'

'*Just think of some nice things.*'

'*Like what?*'

'*Things you always wanted to do. Imagine playing football for England.*'

'*Mm – that's nice.*'

'*What else?*'

'*Think of your mum.*'

'*Mm – that's nice.*'

'*What else?*'

'*Imagine you're in heaven.*'

'*What does that mean?*'

'*You'll be happy and be able to see everyone again.*'

'*Are you in heaven, Eddie?*'

'*Don't know.*'

'*Do you want to go to heaven, Eddie?*'

'*Yes – do you?*'

'*Don't know.*'

'*Remember when we went on holiday to Ludmouth?*'

'*Mm – that's nice.*'

'*Remember when you scored the winning goal in the inter-school cup final?*'

'*Mm – that's nice.*'

'*Remember when we went to Poland on our fantastic journey?*'

'*Mm – that was exciting.*'

'*That's heaven, Len.*'

'*What? I do not understand.*'

'*Heaven is anything you want it to be – anything that makes you feel happy.*'

'*So, am I in heaven?*'

'*Don't know.*'

'*You don't want to go to heaven. Come with us.*'

'*Go away, Ally.*'

'*It's not Ally, Eddie – it's your old friend George.*'

'*Ugh!*'

'*Would I lead you into trouble, Eddie?*'

'*Yes – you're evil.*'

'*Am I?*'

'*Ye-es.*'

'*You don't sound sure, Eddie.*'

'*Come on, Captain, let's go and join George.*'

'*Come on, Eddie. Come on, Eddie. Come on, Eddie.*'

'*You only have to think of it and we'll make it happen for you.*'

'*I'm going, Eddie. I don't want to stay like this forever.*'

'*Come on, Eddie. Come on, Eddie. Come on, Eddie.*'

'*I don't want to go to …, Eddie. I want to go to ….*'

'*Please, God, save me!*'

18
Limbo

And then …?